THE GIFT OF THE GUARDIANS

Author's Revised Edition

THE GIFT OF THE GUARDIANS

Author's Revised Edition

Book I of The Bard's Heresy

Justin D. Bello

ISBN-13 (Digital): 979-8-9900597-2-6
ISBN-13 (Print): 979-8-9900597-3-3

The following work of fiction is set in a fantastic, but quasi-historical world, and contains graphic violence and sexual content that is intended for mature audiences. Readers should be advised that much of the mature content is based upon realistic situations that were part of an extremely violent period of human history. Potentially disturbing scenes include vivid descriptions of battle, blood and gore, murder, torture, implied sexual assault, attempted sexual assault, and violence involving animals.

To Dominique, George, Heidi, and Sebastian, with all of my love.

And to all those seeking their great adventure, may you realize that you already walk the path.

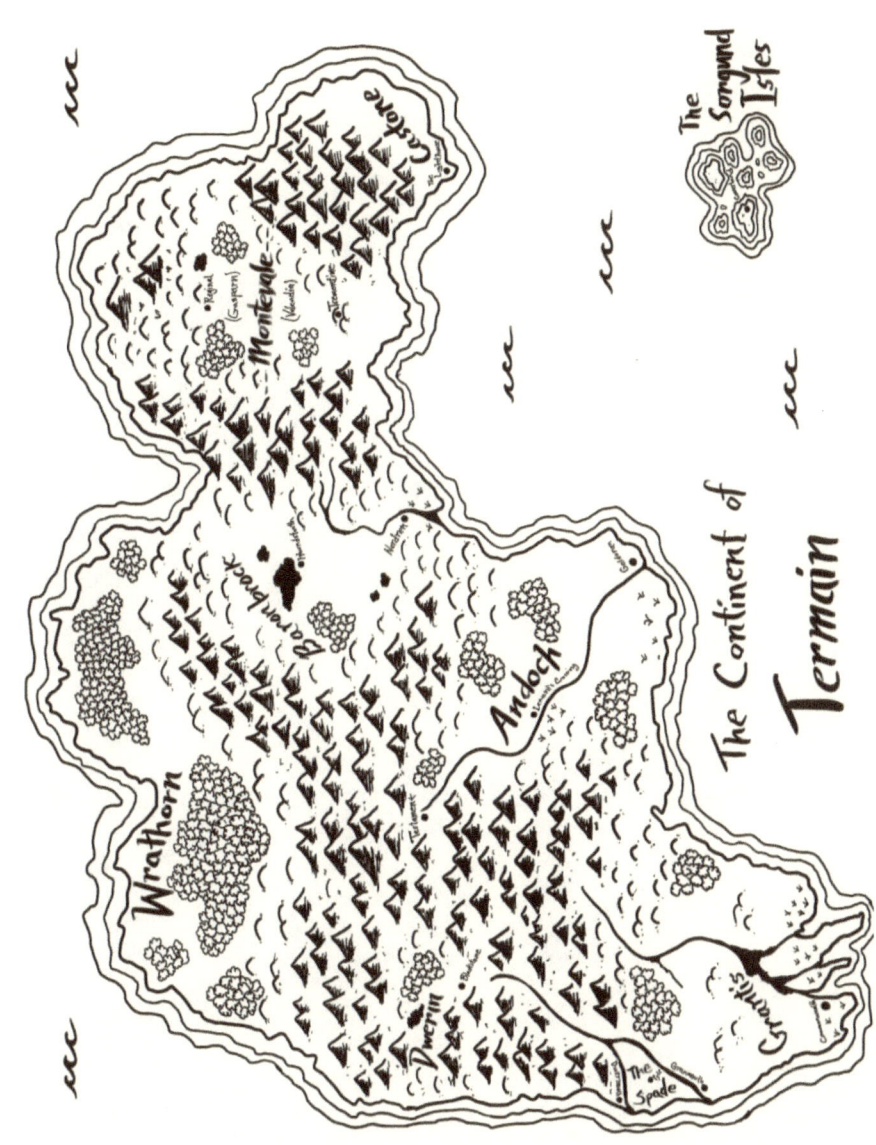

Table of Contents

xi

PROLOGUE

At the crossroads beneath the shadow of the broken watchtower, three figures stood together in silence, gazing up at the midsummer moon.

"This is where I turn aside," the first declared, resting his hands upon the hilt of his sword. Like his fellows, he was clad in dark colors to match the myriad shades of the wilds.

The second man, lithe and nimble, straightened like a reed and folded his arms across his chest. "You go to fetch the boy?" he asked.

"To take him home."

The third man, older than the first two and marked by a bushy gray beard, gave a grunt of assent. Across his shoulders, there hung a circular wooden shield, though its face had been covered with a strip of leather so as to hide its emblem.

"Make for the Crossing," he said. "If I know our friend, he will not risk safety for the sake of haste, and those he cares for, he will have taught the same."

The swordsman gave a nod. "Fergus and I will cross the mountains afoot, but we will return with the boy by river and sea."

"Beware the Hammer," the rogue said. "They say he haunts Galdoran these days."

The old man tugged at his beard. "The Hammer is the least of our worries if what Sigmund says is true."

The swordsman eyed the ground. "Do you believe him?" he asked. "Have the followers of the Dark Brother finally decided to act?"

The graybeard's face grew ashen. "I do not know," he said. "Though I have never known him to be wrong before, and it has been some time since anyone has received word from the Cup or the Shield."

"Then let's hope that this is the exception that proves the rule," the rogue said. "Their deaths would be a terrible blow."

"To say nothing of what it would mean to see the key in the hands of the Dibhorites," the swordsman added, "and if it's true that they have infiltrated the Order…"

"Then you had best get the boy away from there as soon as possible," the old man grunted. "Rest assured, when Prince Kredor becomes King, he *will* seek an empire, and the prophecy will be one step closer to completion. Already he courts Dwerin while the nobles ready for war against Grantis. I doubt Valder's body will be long cold ere the kingsmen muster as well."

"He will get little help from Dwerin." The rogue smirked. "The Beinn Brothers enjoy fighting among themselves even more than the Horses of Montevale. Leave it to me. By year's end, the Ironmen of Dwerin will all have gone to rust."

"I hope you're right," the old man said. "For it seems the Guardians have decided to end the War of the Horses themselves, no doubt in exchange for the victor's support of Kredor. If thus should come to pass, then the Brock will be all that remains."

"Kredor will not take the Brock," said the swordsman, "not while the Galadins still live."

"Aye, then you had best take care that you do not lose the last of them."

"I have sworn to guard him with my life," the swordsman whispered, "as you well know."

"I do," the old man said. "But if what Sigmund says is true and Kredor or the Dibhorites discover who he really is…then his death may be preferable to his capture."

The swordsman's eyes flashed. "It will not come to that."

"But if it does—"

"It will not!"

The old man breathed a sigh and, in a deep, resonant voice, intoned:

When all the lands of Calendral are bound by Callah's Key,
The Bard shall sing a doleful dirge for Wisdom's unheard plea,
For the Testament unto the Light will seek to snuff the Flame,
When the slumbering Beast of Dibhor wakes, who shall bear the blame?
The Armies of the Dead shall march whilst all the Children weep,
And the Scions of the Brother Dark shall rise from their long sleep,
If the last of Aiden's Blood is spilled to profane the Lady's Grace,
Will any man be left alive to rise up in his place?
So heed the words of Wisdom and mark well the strains of Song,
The Pariah whose heart remains still pure will be welcome erelong,
For all that Guard must take up arms to hold the night at bay,
Else who will rise to bring the Dawn and drive the Dark away?

"Such a fine singing voice." The rogue grinned.

The old man ignored him. "Kredor seeks an empire, the Keepers may have found the Key, and the bloodline of the Saint is dwindling," he told the swordsman. "All signs point to the Bard's prophecy, to the end times, to the return of the Beast."

"The Bard's Heresy, some call it," the swordsman muttered.

"Aye, but not you. Not us," the old man nodded. "We know better."

The men fell silent, brooding. At length, the rogue stretched his legs and breathed a heavy sigh.

"If the end is nigh," he said. "Then standing around here will do naught but speed it along." He turned to the old man. "We should go. The ship won't wait forever."

The swordsman gave a nod. "Take care of yourselves."

"And you," the rogue said.

"Weal or woe, we meet at Houndstooth come spring," the old man declared, "if we live that long."

CHAPTER 1:
CORONATION

The late summer sun shone brilliantly upon the stone walls of Castle Testament just as it had, it was said, on every Coronation Day since the first. Atop each of the castle's nine towers, bright red banners bearing the emblem of the white key danced like great flames in the morning breeze. From the elevated plaza that stood before the gates of the castle keep, the Keystone, the nobles sat resplendently arranged by title and rank in two large grandstands, whispering to one another in anticipation. Shading them from the sun billowed bright silk pavilions, vertically striped with the same red and white as the tabards of the kingsmen, soldiers of Andoch's standing army, who stood separating them from the masses below. With equal excitement, if significantly less restraint, the common folk from far and wide descended upon the city of Titanis to mingle with their urban brethren, filling the cobblestone streets surrounding the castle until not even a rider at full charge could find passage through the excited throngs. Truly this would be a day of great rejoicing, one that, by the good grace of the gods, would not see its equal for a long time. For it was not every day, every year, nor even every decade that a city crowned a new king.

At long last, a bevy of heralds processed from the main gate to assemble in formation at the base of the castle plaza. Noble and peasant alike grew silent as the men raised their trumpets to their lips and blew a hearty fanfare. From within the keep, two cherubim pages, garbed in red-and-white motley and bearing the standard of the King, led an honor guard of armored knights of the Order of the Guardians. Each man was clad in plate and chain polished to such a shine as to rival the sun.

After this glorious procession came their leaders, the Council of Five. The Loremaster, in burgundy robes and carrying his ancient leather tome, *The Book of Histories*, walked alongside the Grand Hierophant in his shimmering white gown and silver miter as he leaned heavily upon his oaken cane. Behind them followed the Warlord in his great suit of plate armor embellished with gold leaf. His heavy plumed helmet he carried in one arm while across his back hung his massive silver great sword, Duty. To his right walked the Chancellor in robes of bright scarlet. In his hands, he bore the Light of Justice, a silver lantern that symbolized the light of law and order guiding all civilized men.

Finally, at the end of the great procession came the final member of the council. His armor, crafted of red gold, outshone even the Warlord in splendor, and his tabard of purest white silk glimmered like the snow upon the mountaintops north of the city. In his hand, he carried the Key of Salvation, the scepter of the realm fashioned thirteen hundred years ago by the Lady of Light herself, and upon his brow rested the ancestral crown of the Drudish Kings. For he was none other than Kredor Drude II, Guardian-King of Andoch, and no one walked beside him.

As he crossed the threshold of the Keystone into the plaza, a great cheer rang out that seemed to shake Castle Testament to its very foundations, for Kredor II had been a well-loved prince, and to peasant, noble, and soldier alike, his assent to the throne was regarded with great hope for the future.

When the applause showed no sign of abating, the heralds raised their trumpets again and blew another fanfare. They had to repeat it twice more before the citizens finally fell silent and the new King could step forward to speak.

"Over thirteen hundred years ago," King Kredor began, "in the place where we all now stand, a great battle once took place that would decide the fates of all the people of all the realms across all the lands of Termain.

"On one side stood the forces of Kalius Wrogan, the Warlock, whose Army of the Dead sought to plunge all the lands into a darkness from which there would be no end. They poured forth like a terrible plague, razing farms, villages, and castles alike, ravaging the countryside, slaughtering men, women, and children without discretion, and finally attempting to call forth the unholy Beast of Dibhor created by the Lord of Darkness himself.

"On the other side stood only a small band of men. Simple men. Honest men. Farmers. Craftsman. Traders. They were heavily outnumbered, outmatched, with no formal training in either arms or armor. These were men fighting not for vane glory nor for the promise of some great reward, nor even fighting even for their own lives. Rather, they fought for their families, for their friends, for their children, and their children's children, and for the children of generations yet to come. They fought to oppose what they all knew was the greatest evil ever before faced by men, an evil the likes of which no man has faced since. But thankfully, by the grace of the Brethren, they were led by two of the greatest heroes ever to walk the lands of Termain, Aiden Galadin and Halford Drude.

"Now I do not need to remind you of the tale. Any child raised in the Church of the Kinship can recite the story of St. Aiden and the First King just as well as any of us—how they led their men in a final assault against Wrogan's fortress, where Aiden faced the Warlock in single combat, sacrificing his life so that the Lady of Light above could seal the Dark Brother's Beast away forever. How my ancestor, Halford Drude I, who alone stood at St. Aiden's side in those final moments, razed the evil fortress to the ground and fulfilled the Great Saint's vision by building in its place a kingdom of hope, a city free of fear that would stand against the forces of darkness then and now and forever!"

The masses cheered uproariously at the mention of their homeland's past glory. Shouts of "Andoch forever!" and "Gods bless, King Kredor!" echoed through the crowds. When they fell silent again, the King continued.

"And for over thirteen hundred years, this kingdom of Andoch, this city of Titanis, has done so, from King Halford's time through the time of my father, King Valder IV, and by my solemn oath, through my time as well." King Kredor raised the scepter aloft and all standing dropped to one knee. "This I swear," the King continued, "as I take up the crown of my father and my father's father and all the Kings before me, that under my reign, this kingdom, this city, will continue to shine like a beacon of light against any darkness threatening the lands of Termain."

When the King lowered the scepter, the gathered masses erupted in one tumultuous roar. The heralds blew their fanfare, bards throughout the crowds sounded pipes and drums, children rang little hand bells, and the enormous bronze bell atop the Tower of the Hierophant chimed in glorious celebration.

The revelry began at once as the King and his council, followed by the nobles, withdrew inside the Keystone, and the common folk in every public house and city square made merry to cries of "Long live the King!"

At the western end of the plaza, halfway up in the great library that was the Tower of the Loremaster, three boys in the burgundy robes of Loremaster's apprentices sat beside the window, gazing below at the excitement. The first—tall, lanky, and bird-chested with dark, unkempt hair—rose, shaking his head, and slumped down heavily in a chair beside one of the many massive bookcases lining the walls. "You know that scepter's actually a fake," Royne said, selecting a book at random. "Every new King gets another one made so they can bury the old one with his father." He blew the dust from the leather binding and began flipping idly through yellowed, crackling pages. "The real one's been lost for centuries, if it ever really existed in the first place, which I doubt."

The second boy—short and enormously plump with gingery hair sprouting in a great poofy mushroom from the center of his head—returned to the long table in the center of the room, where he had been doodling pictures of fabulous creatures with ink and quill. "Well, who cares about the stupid scepter anyway? We've got a new king, and I think it's rather exciting," said Thom, adding a set of horns to an already rather angry looking unicorn. "Hob said the Chancellor swore that the Coronation Feast would be even better than last year's Harvest Day Festival. I just hope we get to go."

Without turning, the third boy climbed up to sit on the windowsill. He seemed the waypoint between his friends' extremes: lean but not too skinny, tall but not towering, hardy but with the musculature of youth rather than fat. His hair was the color of burnished gold, and his eyes were gray as a summer storm.

"It'll be up to Rastis," Lughus said matter-of-factly. "Though from up here, he didn't look to be enjoying it much himself."

"Well, Rastis never cares much for feasts," Thom said. "He'd rather sit by the fireplace with a book for his dinner and a pipe for dessert."

"So would I," Royne chimed in.

"You don't smoke a pipe."

"I could, and I'd rather spend my time with a book than with that lot of nobles down there."

Thom smiled. "Even the girls?"

"Well, maybe not the girls." Royne snorted. "Though I doubt they'd have much to say to us anyway. 'So you're an apprentice to Loremaster Rastis, are you?'" he mocked.

"'Is it true that all you do all day is read?'" Thom joined in. "'And that none of the books even have any pictures?'"

"Aye, except for the secret one the Loremaster carries"—Royne smirked—"but it's filled with nothing but dirty ones. Of course, if you'd like, my dear, I can show you what they look like…"

"Ewww." Thom giggled. "You would say something like that."

Royne shrugged, turned a page, and held up a finger. "You can quote me. The only difference between a castle and a brothel is the price the ladies pay for their clothing. They all take it off just the same and just as easily."

Lughus sighed and shook his head, scanning the shelves for his next assignment. "Why do you have to be such a misanthrope?"

"Because it's better than blind idealism." Royne laughed. "The sooner you accept the reality of people and the fantasy of virtue, the happier you'll be, my friend. No man is truly noble and no woman truly chaste, least of all among the gentry."

"Not all of them are so bad, surely?" Thom asked.

"Well, maybe not your mum, Thom. Cattle don't wear clothing."

"Shut up!" Thom crumpled a piece of parchment and tossed it at Royne's head.

"Don't worry, Thom." Lughus smiled. "Even if she was a cow, I'm sure Royne would still fancy her."

Royne pursed his lips and shrugged. "Probably."

"Oh, shut up!" the chubby boy whined. "At least I knew my mother!"

"Aye, I knew her too," Royne said. "She was in the stew last week. I never ate a bit of beef so juicy!"

"Shut up!" Thom grunted, crumpling his remaining parchment. "We'll just see whose mother was a cow!"

"What? You're going to look into a mirror?"

Royne picked up the first wad and tossed it back at Thom just as the chubby boy let fly with a volley—and misfired, showering Lughus with snowballs of paper. Soon, the three boys were scrambling throughout the study, throwing paper, laughing, roughhousing as only good friends do, let alone friends who, for most of their sixteen years, had been raised as brothers. Finally, when all the paper had run out, Thom rushed Royne in a desperate charge and used his sheer bulk to tackle the lanky boy to the floor. As Lughus hurried over to separate the two, a burst of derisive laughter from the doorway checked him. Together, the trio of apprentices gazed up to see three more boys their age—tall, muscular, and smug. In place of the hooded habits of the Loremaster's apprentices, however, they wore the short ivory tunics of the Warlord's cadets.

"Well, well," said the foremost of them, "getting your hair ready for the feast? I see you already have your dresses."

"Pryce," Lughus said as Thom and Royne hurried to their feet, "what are you doing in our tower?"

"Oh, we go where we please," the cadet said smugly. "However, this time, we have permission."

Royne made a face.

"Who let you in?" Thom asked.

"Rastis's pet barbarian. That dirty savage Hob. Warlord Rood asked me to fetch a book." Pryce smirked, holding up a thin manuscript, *The Historie of the Blyndale Siege*. "I was supposed to get it yesterday, but it slipped my mind, what with all the drilling and the sparring and the real work that we do over at the Warlord's Tower."

"I'm just surprised you can read," Royne said.

"Aye," Pryce growled. "And I'm good with a sword too. You'd be wise to remember that."

"Not as good as Lughus, though." Royne smirked. "Didn't he beat you in the tourney on the Feast of Perindal last year? It'll be here again in only a few months. I hope you've been practicing."

"Shut up, Royne," Lughus muttered.

"I believe he knocked you out, didn't he? You charged, he parried, and somehow, you fell flat on your face. When you finally came to, weren't you crying?"

"Royne, shut up!" Lughus hissed.

"I'm just trying to remember what happened," Royne grinned, feigning innocence.

Pryce advanced on Lughus until his face was only inches away. "Is that what you think, boy?" he hissed. "That you're better than the Warlord's First Cadet?"

Lughus leveled his gaze to meet Pryce's glare. "You have your book, Pryce. Just leave."

"Maybe there's something else I came here for," Pryce said, "while the masters are all away at the keep, and there's no one to interfere."

"Wait, wait, wait!" Thom said, holding out his hands. "Really! There's no reason to fight. Like Royne said, it'll only be a few months until the tourney, and you can decide it all then, right? If we get in trouble now, we might not be allowed to go to the feast, and why ruin the day?"

"Shut up, Thom Fatty," Pryce said. He poked a thick finger into Lughus' chest. "I don't need a sword to beat you."

"Because you *can't*." Royne grinned.

All at once, Pryce pushed Lughus back against the table and threw a right cross to his eye. Lughus braced himself and bucked upward, punching Pryce hard in the stomach with his own right, followed with a hard left. The other two cadets, Lane and Deran, leaped to Pryce's aid, grabbing Lughus by the shoulders and pinning him back down on the table top. Pryce wound up to hit him again, taking advantage of the apprentice's helplessness.

Sweating profusely with fear, Thom rushed forward to pound a pudgy fist ineffectually into the center of Lane's back before collapsing into a ball on the floor. At once confused and amused, the cadet began to kick him; however, Thom's foolery in distracting Lane freed Lughus's left arm long enough to turn Pryce's sucker punch into a glancing blow, and a moment later, he felt his right arm slip free when Royne whacked Deran across the back of the skull with *The Complete Compendium of Wrathorn Herbs and Remedies*.

Not wanting to waste the chance, Lughus blocked Pryce's next attack and countered, driving his fist up hard into the cadet's nose. Enraged and bleeding, Pryce clutched at Lughus's hair, and, with a cry of madness, began pounding his skull again and again against the oaken tabletop.

"WHAT IN THE NAME OF THE BLOODY KINSHIP IS GOING ON IN HERE?"

Lughus, slipping out of consciousness, felt Pryce being ripped off of him and thrown to the far side of the room. Lane and Deran let go of Thom and Royne and stepped back in fear. Bearded, bristling and bursting with muscle,

Hobart Brindlebairne, scribe of the Order, Loremaster Rastis's personal steward, and perhaps the largest man in the city, stood in the center of the room, bringing an end to all hostility save perhaps his own.

"I will ask again," Hob growled. "What is this madness?"

Six sets of eyes examined the floor. Finally, Lughus shook his head to gather his wits and spoke. "Nothing."

"Nothing?" Hob repeated, shocked. "Nothing!"

Five other voices chattered suddenly in agreement.

Hob wiped a bead of sweat from his brow, and the veins on his forehead sank back into his skull. At length, he thrust a thick finger at Pryce. "You told me you were fetching a book for the Warlord. Do you have it?"

"Yes, sir," Pryce said, picking it up from where it had fallen on the floor during the scuffle. "Right here."

"Then get out."

"Yes, sir."

The three cadets scrambled out of the study into the central stair of the tower, their hurried footsteps clattering on the stone steps.

"Your master will hear of this!" Hob called after them, then turned to the three remaining apprentices. "As will yours."

"We're sorry, Hob," Thom choked.

"Sorry," Royne added.

"We're sorry," Lughus said quietly.

Hob breathed a heavy sigh and reached out to turn Lughus's ringing head around to get a better look at his already-blackening eye. Thom's cheeks were lined with tear streaks, and blood trickled slowly from Royne's hooked nose.

"Well, all I'll say is that I hope you gave those bastards as good as you got." He shook his head. "Now go clean up, lads. *Quickly.* Rastis is waiting downstairs in his chambers."

"Isn't he going to the feast?" Thom asked suddenly.

"He made his appearance." Hob grinned, his former anger melting away as suddenly as it had flared. "Now you lot get going so I can make mine."

The Loremaster's Tower was arranged in five levels, connected by a long, stone staircase that spiraled upward all the way to the conical roof at the spire top. The first floor housed the majority of the books, texts available to all readers, and was the only floor that was not generally restricted to any outside of the Loremaster's command. The second floor was divided into more

11

specified collections necessary for more esoteric study. It also housed many of the personal diaries and journals of past and departed Guardians held in wait for those later members of the Order to succeed them. The third floor held the archives and the reliquaries, which were generally kept locked, as well as a handful of study rooms such as the one from which the boys observed the King's coronation speech. On the fourth floor were the private quarters of the apprentices, scribes, scholars, and sages in service to the Loremaster, a place for them to take their meals, and a parlor for reading, studying, or quiet reflection. The fifth and final floor of the tower, though traditionally serving as the private quarters of the Loremaster himself, had not seen use under the current Loremaster Rastis Glendaro, who, as age began to claim him, relocated his chambers to a smaller, though more accessible location in the rear corner of the first floor, leaving the fifth floor a place in which owls, ravens, and other vagrant birds now called home.

Lughus led the way up the stairs to the boys' cells on the fourth floor. Quickly, he dabbed water on his eye and checked the back of his head where Pryce had pounded him against the table to discover that although there was a large, painful lump, he was not bleeding. The swelling around his eye socket was already considerable and no doubt turning color, but there was nothing he could do about it now. As he made his way back to the stairs, Royne caught up with him, pinching his nostrils together in a small piece of white cloth, followed shortly by Thom plodding along sullenly behind him, still sobbing.

"By the Brethren, would you stop blubbering, Thom?" Royne complained. "Lane didn't even hit you that hard."

"He kicked me!" Thom blubbered indignantly. "A lot!"

"You shouldn't have gotten involved." Lughus sighed. "Neither of you."

"There were three of them and three of us," Thom said. "One of them kicking me would have meant one less attacking you."

"And face it, Lugh," Royne added, "Thom's got a lot more in the way of padding to protect him than you or me."

"Shut up, Royne," Thom whined.

"Well, you didn't have to pick a fight with them like that," Lughus added, hurrying down the stairs, "and then throw me out in front of it."

"Don't fool yourself." Royne snorted, testing his nose to see if it was still bleeding. "They came here looking for a fight. All I did was get it over with."

"You don't know that."

"Shut up, Thom."

At the bottom of the stairs, Hob was waiting. At the sight of them, he shook his head in exasperation but said no more and led them through the tall maze of bookcases to the door of Rastis's private chambers.

"Rastis," Hob called, knocking as he burst in, "here they are, no worse for the wear."

"Thanks, Hob," they heard Rastis say. "Enjoy the feast."

"Aye, sir," Hob nodded for the boys to enter and then hurried on his way.

Rastis's chambers were really nothing more than two cells the size of the apprentices' connected by a small doorway that had once served as the private rooms of the tower's former door warden. The rear room held only a bed, a trunk of old clothes, and a small lectern for *The Book of Histories* while the front room had nothing more than a wooden writing desk, a small stove, and a table with a few chairs. The old Loremaster was seated there now, smoking his pipe and waiting for his teakettle to boil. He was a small man, scarcely over five feet tall, with lively eyes and a thick gray beard. As the three apprentices filed into the room, he glanced up briefly before returning to his pipe.

He sighed. "Should I even ask?"

The boys exchanged glances. "Do you really think you need to?" Royne replied.

The old man suppressed a smile, shook his head fondly, and sat back comfortably in his chair. "I suppose not," he said, "but come. Sit down."

The boys took the remaining seats around the table as Rastis produced four teacups and a clay pot of dried leaves from the top of the writing desk behind him. When the water finally boiled, he removed the pot from the fire, poured it into the teakettle, and let it steep. Some time passed without a word being spoken. However, the boys were used to this, for one of the earliest (and hardest) lessons they had learned was to be comfortable in moments of silence.

"How else can you hear the song of wisdom without first knowing how to listen?" Rastis would ask them.

At length, when the tea was ready, the old man poured. "So you watched from the window, I take it?" he said pleasantly, "and you heard the King's speech?"

"Yes, sir," the boys said together.

"The story of St. Aiden and King Halford who founded the Order."

"Yes, sir."

"Then let me ask you," Rastis said, "what do you think?"

The boys glanced at one another. "What do you mean?" Lughus asked.

"The King," Rastis said. "What do you think of him?"

Lughus and Thom exchanged a glance. Royne studied his teacup.

"The people love him," Thom said. "The ladies think he's handsome, and the men say he's a great warrior."

"When the Thorwick Clan crossed the mountains from Wrathorn two winters ago, it was Prince—King Kredor who mounted the defense," Lughus said. "He slew their war chief in single combat and mounted his head on a pike at the base of the mountains."

Thom shuddered. "Bloody."

"That's true," Rastis said, chewing his pipe stem. "What do you think, Royne?"

Royne shrugged. "About what?"

"The King," Rastis said. "What are your first impressions?"

Royne sighed, looking slightly uncomfortable. "Well, to be honest, I didn't really care much for his speech."

"Didn't care much for his speech?" Rastis repeated, appearing surprised. "Why is that?"

"Well," Royne began, "all he did was tell half of a story, and half of it wasn't even the truth."

Thom's eyes widened in alarm. Lughus stared at the table, sipping his tea. Rastis's bushy gray eyebrows furrowed. "Am I to understand, Royne," Rastis said, motioning toward the lanky boy with his pipe, "that you're calling the King a liar?"

Royne shifted awkwardly in his seat. "No, not exactly. I mean, he didn't lie," he said, "but the story he told them was only the legend that the common folk tell, and even then, he left out certain details."

Rastis raised an eyebrow. "Such as?"

"Well, for starters," Royne began, "he said that all of the men in St. Aiden's army were farmers and tradesmen, like Aiden himself. Common folk. But that's not entirely true. Most of them were, but some of them were younger sons of nobles or noblemen who had fallen out of favor. Halford Drude was the son of one of the oldest noble families in Old Calendral, but

14

the last emperor stripped them of their lands before Kalius Wrogan seized control of the empire."

Rastis nodded. "True."

"And this whole Army of the Dead business"—Royne sighed— "it's all nonsense. The men who followed Wrogan were men of flesh and blood like any other. They did wear the bones of their enemies as trophies and gave sacrifices to the Dark Brother, but they were still just men."

Again, Rastis nodded, and the boys could see the beginnings of a smile tugging at the corners of his lips. "Anything else?"

"Just one thing," Royne said. "He said that it was Aiden's 'great vision' to establish Andoch, but that's not true either. Aiden was not from Calendral. He was from Baronbrock, and after the war was over, he meant to go back to his wife and son there. It's the whole reason why when he died, his bones were sent back and they built the great cathedral over his tomb. They even changed the name of the barony to Galadin to honor him and his family. He never had any designs on becoming a king. It took nearly a century before his descendants would even agree to accept the leadership of the province named after them."

"Perhaps you're right, Royne," Rastis said, pausing to take a sip of his tea. "But if that's the case, why would King Kredor not explain all that in his speech?"

"Because the common folk are stupid," Royne blurted out, "and no one really cares about the truth. They'd rather hear a good story, cheer their heads off, and get on with the feasting."

Rastis sighed and returned to his pipe. "Simple, perhaps, Royne, but not stupid. You've been taught from childhood in the Tower of the Loremaster while most of the common folk have never even been taught to write their own names. Of course, since the three of you have had the benefits of formal education, so much so that you were able even to identify and dissect the factual anomalies in the words of the King"—he paused—"I expect that telling me the real story, the full history, of St. Aiden and the King, should be quite simple for the three of you?"

Thom shot Royne an angry glare. His hopes of attending the coronation feasts stalled even further. Lughus poured himself more tea.

"Thom," Rastis said, "why don't you begin?"

"Yes, sir," Thom said. "Where do I start? With the Warlock?"

"Don't call him that," Royne muttered.

Lughus winced as Thom's meaty foot kicked him under the table in its attempt to reach Royne.

"I think you'll need to start a little before that, Thom. Begin with Calendral and the emperor as they were at Kalius Wrogan's time."

Thom folded his hands on the tabletop to recite the story as he had heard it from the time he had first become an apprentice. "Thirteen hundred years ago, Andoch and all the other realms across the continent of Termain were part of the Imperial Kingdom of Calendral and ruled by Emperor Landus Veirne."

"People still believed in the Church of the Kinship, but since the Order didn't exist yet, it was led solely by the Grand Hierophant as opposed to the Council, sort of like it is today in the other realms. The lord-baron governs Baronbrock, the archduke rules Dwerin, and the elected senators lead Grantis, but the Order sends a provincial hierophant to run the church in each realm under orders from the Grand Hierophant and the Guardian King."

"In any case, thirteen hundred years ago, the Grand Hierophant in Calendral was a man named Kalius Wrogan, and unlike today where we only honor the Father, the Sister, and the Three Brothers, at that time, they still gave homage to the Fourth Brother, Dibhor. Wrogan was a devout Dibhorite."

"Good. Stop there for a moment, Thom," Rastis interrupted. "Lughus, explain to me 'The Creation of the Kinship' as it is told by the Hierophants."

"Yes, sir." Lughus nodded. He paused a minute, took a deep breath, and began to recite, "In the beginning, there was only the great darkness of the Void, ageless, timeless, and endless. When the Lord-Father, Alantir, awoke to find himself in the center of the emptiness, he felt lonely and determined to fill the Void with his creation. So from out of the ether, he called forth his children—four brothers, and a sister."

"And their names?"

"Tengale the Lord of the Skies, Perindal the Lord of the Lands, Galdorn the Lord of the Seas, Dibhor the Lord of Darkness, and Callah the Lady of Light."

"Good. Continue."

"With the help of his children, the Brethren, Alantir created the heavens, the seas, the land, the plants and animals, and finally men, who were said to be the Father's greatest creation and his grandchildren," Lughus said. "At last, when it was all completed, and the Father was content, he granted each of the brethren the power to create one great work of their own heart's design as a reward for their aid."

"The first three brothers used their gifts right away to serve their new kinsmen, man. Tengale, who loved the forests, designed the holy oak trees to shelter them. Holy oak is said to be hard as steel and light as a feather, which is why it's so rare now. Perindal thought that man should have a companion to walk alongside him through his life, so he created the spirit hounds, great golden war hounds that can track and hunt in any season or any weather and can bring down a bear as easily as a cat can take down a mouse. Galdorn believed that men should be able to ride across the lands as easily as a wave upon the seas so he created the searoans, horses with the dappled colors of the ocean and faster than any others. Dibhor and Callah saved their gifts, though, and did not use them until the time of St. Aiden"—Lughus shot Royne a quick glance—"at least according to legend."

"Very good, Lughus," Rastis said. "Back to you, Thom."

"Yes, sir," Thom said. "In Wrogan's time, the empire was beginning to come apart. Emperor Veirne was known as a reveler and in his first year on the imperial throne spent half of the treasury holding private feasts and festivals in his own honor. Before long, the generals did not have the coin to pay their soldiers at a time when the provinces seemed in a constant state of rebellion. Thieves' guilds took over control of most of the trade inside the cities while bandit troops seized the trade routes outside, usually aided by the guards that were supposed to arrest them. The capital city of Calendral, Floraine, was especially bad. Murder, rape, and looting became everyday occurrences, and the libraries and universities that made the empire famous were soon replaced by taverns, brothels, and fighting pits."

Thom paused to sip his tea, took a deep breath, and continued. "Midway through the second year of Emperor Veirne's reign, the treasury had been completely emptied. The barbarian clans in Wrathorn succeeded in driving the emperor's soldiers out of the north, and the sea folk in the Sorgund Isles set fire to the emperor's largest fleet."

"Right," Rastis said, "and what is the name they give to those two events, Royne?"

"Weylin's Rebellion and the Dawn of the Flaming Waves," Royne answered with a slight air of boredom. "Weylin was the chieftain of the most powerful of the Wrathorn Clans at that time, and although Thom said largest fleet, it was actually the second largest fleet. The largest fleet was sailing along the coast of Dwerin, rescuing the soldiers that the Wrathorn had trapped at the mouth of the Frostwyrm River."

"However, Royne." Rastis smiled mischievously through a wispy cloud of pipe smoke. "You're forgetting that on their journey to rescue the trapped men, the First Fleet suffered heavy losses in one of Dwerin's famous coastal squalls. So strictly speaking, Thom was right. The Sorgund fleet was largest at the time of the fires."

Lughus suppressed a laugh, and a satisfied smirk spread across Thom's freckled face. Royne ignored both of them, muttering, "I suppose. Strictly speaking."

"Continue, Thom."

Thom cleared his throat smugly.

"And don't look so sullen, Royne," Rastis added with a laugh. "You'll get your chance in a moment. Go ahead, Thom."

"All right," Thom said. "After all this, the emperor finally decided to act. Since the Wrathorn Clans were thought of as only savage barbarians and the Sorgunders considered nothing more than pirates and thieves, Emperor Veirne declared that any who took up arms against the authority of the empire was an enemy of civilization itself and more akin to a beast than man. Henceforth, he declared that they would be treated as such with yoke and harness and could be bought and sold at any market across Termain as long as a tax was paid to the imperial treasury. Some of the nobles, like the Drudes, disagreed with the emperor's decision to allow slavery, but rather than listen to them, Veirne simply stripped them of their lands and seized their fortunes. A few of them were even enslaved. By the end of the following year, the treasury was full, and the ranks of the armies were swollen as soldiers flocked to the emperor's banners, eager to take enemy captives as slaves. It was believed that Veirne even began planning to invade the other continents in hopes of increasing the size and influence of the empire. This is where Wrogan really comes into it."

"How?" Rastis asked. "Now, Royne."

"Like Thom said," Royne admitted humbly, "Wrogan was the Grand Hierophant of Calendral and a Dibhorite. The Dibhorites were different from the rest of the Church of the Kinship. Unlike the other members of the Brethren, people did not honor Dibhor out of love but rather out of fear and appeasement. When the Lord-Father created men, as the hierophants tell it, Dibhor was angry and full of envy at Alantir's love for them. He hated his 'cousins' and swore vengeance. It's believed that this was the reason why Callah, the Lady, saved the Father's Gift of Creation, for she knew Dibhor would use his to create something to harm mankind."

Royne paused. "I'm getting ahead of myself, though," he muttered, "In any case, as the Lord of Darkness, Dibhor was believed to be able to see into the darkness of men's souls and was the member of the Kinship responsible for punishing them accordingly. To Kalius Wrogan and the other Dibhorites at the time, the Empire of Calendral was an empire of sin and evil. And largely, it *was*, which is probably why so many of the poor folk later followed him."

"Now, other than the Dibhorites, there were few devout worshippers of the Kinship at that time, and the Grand Cathedral in Floraine was often empty with the exception of Wrogan and his few followers. According to legend, in the spring of the fifth year of Emperor Veirne's reign, Kalius Wrogan claimed that Dibhor himself appeared to him in a vision clad in black armor and readied for war. Apparently, the vision decreed that mankind had become rife with sin and evil and that, as punishment, Dibhor intended to wipe those who did not repent from the face of the Father's Creation. Wrogan himself would act as Dibhor's Prophet of Doom, and only those who devoted themselves, body and soul, to the Lord of Darkness would find salvation. To prove it, he told Wrogan that on the night of the summer solstice, the capital city would fall victim to a horrible plague and that the dead would soon outnumber the living. He commanded that any who died from the disease not be buried or burned but placed within the pews of the great cathedral. Since they were absent in life, they would be present in death. The plague would continue until the entire cathedral, nave, transepts, and all, was filled with the 'unfaithful.'"

"Throughout the spring, Wrogan and the other Dibhorites preached Dibhor's prophecy to the people throughout the city and surrounding lands in Calendral, but no one paid them any mind. On the night of the solstice, however, the plague hit. Since it mostly affected the poor and the slaves, few cared much beyond the loss of their property. In any case, Wrogan and his people did what they were instructed, collecting the bodies and placing them in the cathedral, and by the Feast of Harvestide, it was completely full."

Royne paused. "This is where the legend the King mentioned comes in."

"Go ahead," Rastis said.

"Supposedly"—Royne sighed—"at dawn on the following morning, while the people of Floraine recovered from the previous night's celebrations, the doors of the Grand Cathedral flew open, and the bodies of the plague-dead had returned to life. With Wrogan at their head, the undead ravaged the city, and by the end of the week, the emperor, the nobles, and any of the generals not in the field were all dead. Wrogan became known as the Warlock, and soon, the undead soldiers were replaced by living men eager to follow their new theocratic ruler. However"—he paused—"I don't believe in this whole Army of the Dead business."

"Why not?" Thom asked. "It's a very good story."

"Exactly," Royne said, shaking his head. "Thousands dead of plague, and the nobles don't notice? I don't believe it. Nobles may be ignorant, but they're not *that* stupid."

"Then what did happen?" Thom asked.

"Thom," Lughus said, "he's had to have made you listen to him over a hundred times before. You really don't remember?"

Royne ignored them. "I have no doubt that Kalius Wrogan was an evil man. However, if there is one good thing that can be said about him, it is that he hated slavery." Royne sat up straight in his chair to make his point. "I believe," he said, "that the plague never happened. Wrogan and the Dibhorites were preaching to the poor and sometimes to the slaves, surely not to the nobles. Some had also written that the Grand Cathedral had been closed and placed under guard when Wrogan displeased the emperor, forcing him to hide out in the underbelly of the city. Therefore, I believe that Kalius Wrogan, the so-called Warlock, did not lead an Army of the Dead but a rebellion of slaves and poor folk who saw serving Dibhor as more appealing to lives of misery and squalor while the emperor bathed in gold!"

Rastis nodded kindly. "A sound theory, Royne. Truly."

"Thank you, sir."

"Oh, don't encourage him," Lughus muttered.

Rastis turned to him. "Can you take it up from there?"

"Me?" Lughus asked.

"No, the bloody Warlord." Rastis smirked. "Yes, you, Lughus. Tell us the story of St. Aiden."

"Oh, right, of course," Lughus agreed readily. He sat up straighter in his chair. Thom's stomach groaned, and he glanced behind them, wondering if it was still daylight outside. Royne poured himself the last of the tea.

"After Wrogan took control of Floraine, it was only a short while until he controlled the entire empire. Fueled by religious fervor, he sent his armies out across Termain, slaughtering any who refused to swear allegiance to him in the name of Dibhor. Before long, he declared Dibhor to be the only true god and claimed that the rest of the Brethren were false idols. Any caught worshipping them were to be put to the sword as infidels. There are stories of entire towns and cities worth of men, women, and children being tortured, slaughtered, or burned alive. Driven by fear, Wrogan's armies marched across all of Termain, retaking Wrathorn and the Sorgund Isles, and for nearly a decade, Wrogan reigned supreme from the emperor's castle in Floraine, which he now called Deathsgate. He fortified the city until it seemed an impenetrable fortress, and with the continent now under the Dark Brother's yoke, Wrogan began preaching that soon Dibhor would use the Lord Father's Gift of Creation to call forth a monstrous Beast of Destruction that would consume the entire world at the End of Days."

Thom gave a shudder, and Royne fixed him with a sneer.

"However," Lughus continued, "not everyone was willing to bow down to the Warlock, just as they were not willing to bow down to the Calendral Emperor. Occasionally, men still rebelled, despite Wrogan's cruelty, while others attempted to worship in secret. In Baronbrock, a farmer's son named Aiden Galadin and his wife, Elisa, gave birth to their first and only son, Caleb. It was said that when Aiden held his son in his hands for the first time, he was so overcome by the love of his family that he swore an Oath to the Lady of Light that he would not allow his son to grow up in a world overrun with Dibhor's darkness. He beat his father's plowshares into a sword and, with the help of only a handful of his friends, attacked the castle of the Dibhorite governor and cut him down."

"So it was that Aiden and his friends began their war against Wrogan's men, attacking them unawares and then disappearing into thin air. They

21

began by freeing towns throughout the interior of Baronbrock and then crossed over into the other realms. Men from every nation across Termain soon joined with them, rich and poor, commoner and noble, including Halford Drude. Soon, people began calling Aiden, Halford, and their men the Guardians of the Light, and although they were a small group—no more than three thousand men at the most—the Dibhorites began to fear them."

"Unfortunately, since the Guardians never had enough men to hold any of the towns that they freed, Wrogan's armies would often simply retake them once Aiden moved on to help others in need. Finally, Aiden decided that the only way to end Wrogan's reign of terror was to defeat the Warlock himself. So, in the autumn of Wrogan's twelfth year of rule, the Guardians stole into Calendral and attacked Deathsgate."

Royne and Thom snickered quietly and exchanged a glance. Discussing the stories of the heroes and their great battles seemed to stir something in Lughus's blood. Two years ago, he had begged Rastis to allow Hob to teach him basic swordplay. However, only after the boy had completed an exhaustive study of the traditional knightly virtues did the old man finally give his consent.

"Very good, Lughus," Rastis said. "I know you're capable of leading us through a blow-by-blow account of the battle, but if you boys want to make the Coronation Feast, we'll have to save that for another time."

"Yes, sir." Lughus grinned in spite of himself.

"Now, Thom, we started with you. Why don't you finish the story?"

"The Beast?" Thom asked with renewed vigor at the prospect of attending the celebrations. "Is that what you mean?"

"Yes, from where Lughus left off. Go on."

Thom cleared his throat and sat up straighter in his chair. "It did not take long for the Guardians to take Deathsgate, though they lost over half their number securing the fortress. While the main battle was being waged at the gates, St. Aiden and Halford Drude pursued Kalius Wrogan, who, at the first signs of the assault, had fled up the mountain paths overlooking the city. There in a clearing, Wrogan and his acolytes began performing a dark ritual that was to summon forth the Beast of Dibhor to ravage the world."

Thom paused. "No one knows what the Beast looked like, but apparently, it was some sort of monster large enough to shake the whole mountain."

"Or it could also just be a metaphor," Royne muttered.

"At any rate," Thom continued, "they say that Wrogan and his acolytes slew themselves to complete the summoning ritual"—the chubby boy shuddered—"and called forth the Beast. The legend says that Aiden fought the creature, but it proved nearly impossible to wound. Finally, when Aiden was near death, the Lady of Light appeared to him. Her heart broke at the sight of humanity's suffering, and she determined to use her Gift of Creation to undo the evil Dibhor had wrought with his. With the help of St. Aiden, she banished the Beast to the Abyss and locked it away with a silver key made from a fallen star, the Key of Salvation."

"Which is *most certainly* a metaphor," Royne muttered again.

"Shut up, Royne." Lughus smirked.

Thom continued. "When the battle was over, and the Beast was defeated, Aiden finally succumbed to his wounds. Like Royne said, his body was returned to his wife and son in Baronbrock, and a cathedral was built over his tomb. The people of old Calendral, nobles, soldiers, common folk, all, saw that Kalius Wrogan was gone and quickly turned on the remaining Dibhorites and returned to worshipping the Kinship, though without Dibhor. Aiden Galadin was named the first saint, and the people began looking to the Guardians and Halford Drude for leadership. Together, they razed Deathsgate to the ground and built Castle Testament in its place. They renamed the city Titanis, Old Calendral came to be known as Andoch, and the provinces were granted the sovereignty to govern themselves as they saw fit."

"With the remaining armies of Calendral free of the Warlock's tyranny and now loyal to King Halford I, the remaining Guardians were free to return to their homes, though many stayed to help the new King. Together, they created the Council of Five and planned to establish the greatest kingdom the world had ever seen. The Hierophant would reestablish the Church of the Kinship, the Warlord would lead the King's armies, the Chancellor managed the day-to-day governing of the realm, and the Loremaster chronicled the history of the Order and all learning across Termain."

Thom took a deep breath. "And I think that's it."

"For about three hundred years," Royne added.

"Until the Siege of Three," Lughus finished.

"True," Rastis said, "but I suppose you've had enough history for today, and I'm sure you're hungry."

"Especially Thom," Royne muttered.

"Shut up," Thom hissed.

Rastis rolled his eyes and sighed. "Before you go, however—if you can leave off each other for a moment—there is something else I needed to speak to you about."

Together, the boys sat up straight. Their heads bowed apologetically. "Of course, Rastis."

Rastis drew a long pull on his pipe and let the smoke drift slowly from one side of his mouth up to the ceiling. "It will not be long," he began. "Before your time as apprentices will be over and it will be time for your full initiation into the Order of the Guardians. To prepare you for that, there are things that I would have you do."

"What is the Rite of Initiation, Rastis?" Thom asked suddenly. "Does it mean we'll be anointed with titles like you and Hob?"

"Thom, you know that he can't tell you that," Lughus muttered, "and besides, some men serve the Order for their whole lives without ever being anointed."

Royne shook his head. "But maybe they can make an exception for you, Thom, and anoint you 'The Idiot.'"

"Shut up."

Rastis gave a sigh before continuing. "In a week's time, Lughus, you will begin a pilgrimage to St. Aiden's Cathedral in the barony of Galadin."

"In Baronbrock?"

"Yes," Rastis said, "there you will study the holy relics and spend a year in service to Provincial Hierophant Andresen at the court of Baron Arcis. Thom, you will travel with him for a time, but once you reach the Brock, you will instead make your way to Highboard and the court of my nephew, the Lord-Baron, where he will make the necessary preparations to see you safely north and west to Wrathorn."

"Wrathorn?" Thom repeated, turning white. "With the barbarian clans?"

"You will be recording a history of Clan Brindlebairne, Hob's people," Rastis said. "And I would suggest you not be so inconsiderate as to refer to them as 'barbarians' within his hearing."

Thom bowed his head in contrition as great tears began welling in his eyes. "I didn't mean it."

Rastis sighed. "I know, Thom," he said. "But in any case, Hob's hope is that the history you write will help dissuade such false generalizations. To date, the Brindlebairnes are the only clan of the Wrathorn to convert to the worship of the Kinship."

"What about me, Rastis?" Royne asked. "Where am I to go?"

Rastis cleared the teapot and the empty teacups from the tabletop. "You'll stay here, Royne," he said. "With Lughus and Thom gone, I'll have even greater need of you."

A shadow fell across Royne's features, but he bit his lip. "Yes, sir," he finally said.

Rastis turned away from the table and began emptying his pipe over the glowing coals in the stove. "Now go on, boys," he said with a smile. "Enjoy the feast. It's not every day that a new King is crowned. I'll see each of you again before week's end with more instructions."

"Yes, Rastis."

One after another, the boys nodded and departed from the Loremaster's chambers and silently made their way through the first floor library to the tower's main entryway. It was not until they were closing the heavy oaken doors behind them that Thom finally spoke, breaking the silence. "You know, I don't think I'm very hungry," he said.

CHAPTER 2:
THE PRISONER

Snow crunched softly underfoot as the raven-haired girl tiptoed carefully into the center of the copse of holly trees. The dark, waxy leaves and bright red berries that encircled the hilltop stood like the walls of a long-lost fairy tower borne from the rhythmic melodies of a Wrathorn folksong—not the deep, sonorous war chants of the mercenaries, but the clear, impassioned ballads of the wandering skalds. The air within the ring of tree trunks, while cold, was spared the biting chill of the wind so the girl loosened her thick woolen muffler and breathed in deeply, savoring the taste of the frozen plains. She scooped up a handful of snow in her mitten and let it slowly melt against her lips, invigorating after the long hike to the ancient mound.

The nearby cry of a falcon sent the girl's blue-eyed gaze searching the gray northern sky, and she watched as the noble bird alighted upon a low branch directly before her. In the face of such regal bearing, she curtsied, bowing her head in a sign of respect, and was delighted when the bird, watching her closely with its golden eyes, returned the courtesy. All at once, the branches of the holly trees swayed, and between their gray trunks, other creatures of the north-lands arrived upon the scene. A massive brown bear lumbered lazily into the circle and curled up at the base of one of the trees. A gray wolf crept up silently on padded feet and sat down benignly between two bright pheasants and a small gaggle of geese. A doe and a massive hart appeared, huddling together in the cold while a flight of winter finches landed as one upon the great buck's rack. A musk ox tramped in, followed by a trio of hares, a red fox, a badger, a beaver, and a lynx. Last but not least, a massive Spirit Hound of Perindal at the edge of the circle trotted in nobly to lie at the raven girl's feet. It shut its dark green eyes and sighed as she reached down and ran her fingers through its thick, golden fur.

Suddenly, the hilltop, the holly trees, and the animals all faded back into fancy at the sound of a smarmy voice.

"Watch this."

A black-feathered arrow whistled through the air to pierce the target's center circle with a decided thump and a polite cheer. Alan Beinn rested the tip of his longbow on the ground at his feet and raised his head proudly before the collection of young nobles gathered around. In the late afternoon sun, the velvet, silk, and brocade of their fine clothing stood out against the drab surroundings of the castle yard.

"Great shot, my lord!"

"Yes, amazing!"

"Wonderful!"

"Good luck with that one, Sir Donal," Alan leered.

"I'll certainly need it, my lord," the other boy nodded. He was large, broad-shouldered, and strong. In his thick, heavy hands, the slender yew bow looked likely to break.

Moira and Ellen continued to clap politely while Nora and Caryn received Alan with doe-eyed fawning as he returned to his seat between them. Brigid peered over in her customary diffidence, quietly mourning the loss of her animals and her holly trees upon their snow-topped hill. Her bright blue eyes grew wide with feigned interest as they turned away from her idyllic inner world to the reality of the one without. From her left, another young man, tall, dark-eyed, and handsome, leaned toward her.

"Your cousin is a fine archer, my lady."

Brigid thought about asking if all bull's-eyes were painted as large as Alan's but instead turned her head to hide behind the long, dark cascade of her hair. She toyed idly with the lacey sleeve of her periwinkle dress and mildly nodded her agreement.

"He is, Sir Reid."

She could sense the young man beaming at her use of the title. Though not yet a knight, it had become the custom among Alan and his friends to refer to each other by the titles that they would one day inherit, and Sir Reid, son of one of Dwerin's most powerful lords, would inherit a great one, as Brigid's mother regularly reminded her.

A few feet in front of them, Donal prepared for his shot. At the far side of the green, the target stood like a headstone over a giant's grave. As Reid continued to lean toward her, comfortably unaware of her discomfort, Brigid wondered by how much Donal was intending to miss. When he finally released the arrow, the party watched as it sailed well high of the target to bounce against the mortar of the castle's inner wall. A passing servant leaped up in alarm, but remained silent when he saw the arrow's source among the party of young nobles.

Donal shrugged. "I've no skill as an archer."

Alan sighed sympathetically and raised his snubbed nose. "Victory in battle does not always go to the strongest, Sir Donal." Alan nodded sagely. "You may be deadly with your sword, my friend, but killing a man with a bow requires *precision*. Am I right, Sir Reid?"

"You are, my lord," Reid said. "Certainly, you are your father's son."

Alan received the compliment with a another nod.

"Is the Sheriff very good?" Nora asked blithely.

"Haven't you heard the stories?" Caryn asked.

"The common folk say the Sheriff can hit a falcon's eye in flight," Donal answered.

"A falcon's eye!" Ellen exclaimed.

Donal nodded. "Thank the Brethren the Sheriff is here to protect the realm since the archduke died."

"He'll make sure that your kingdom is kept safe until you come of age, Lady Brigid," Sir Reid told her, "or until you find a husband."

Brigid nodded, though her mind was remembering a different falcon. "I'm certain," she said. Without looking, she could sense the other girls' mooning and longed to return to her daydream or, at the very least, her chambers. However, her mother insisted she spend more time being social, which it turned out meant suffering the young Reid's advances and watching the four giggly tarts swoon every time the Young Sheriff picked his nose.

Thankfully, Alan changed the subject to bring the attention back to himself. "Speaking of my father," he said, plucking at his bow, "would anyone like to know a secret?"

"What kind of secret?" Ellen smiled.

"I like secrets," Caryn simpered.

Brigid suppressed an impatient sigh.

Alan took Caryn's hand in his. "Oh, I know all sorts of secrets," he teased. "Some just for you, Lady Caryn, and some for you, Lady Ellen, and others for you, Lady Nora."

"I want to know a secret too," Moira pouted, puffing up her lips.

"Oh, believe me, my lady, I have plenty of secrets for you too," Alan laughed and leaped to his feet. "But this secret can be for all of us, and to find out what it is." He took a few steps backward. "You'll have to follow me."

The young ladies giggled at one another and followed their young lord, Donal dogging them from behind, eager to be a party to their games. Reid offered his arm to Brigid in a show of gallantry, and despite herself, she meekly accepted. Leaving the cushioned chairs and archery equipment for the servants, Alan led the party across the lawn to the castle's southwest tower.

Blackstone was a stalwart, highland castle as old as Dwerin itself. Built in the days of the Calendral Empire, the castle had seen its share of battles over the years, though its thick granite walls and solid watchtowers were as strong today as ever in the past. Brigid had lived nearly her entire life within its confines, only passing through the main gates for the rare sojourn with her mother down the mountain path to the city below. Her father had taken to ward enough of his vassal's daughters to provide her with plenty of companions, should she want them (which she usually did not after her mother's careful vetting). However, Brigid learned at an early age to find solace in worlds of her own making. For in the ethereal waters of her imagination, she could fashion a land of her own design just as Father Alantir had done at the beginning of time.

The guards stationed just inside the tower stiffened and saluted as Alan passed by. The Young Sheriff acknowledged their fealty with a nod and led his followers to the rear of the tower and a broad stone stairway. Here, he stopped.

"Now," he began, "who remembers being awakened by a commotion in the dead of night three days past?"

Caryn, Ellen, and Moira erupted into giggles as Nora turned scarlet. Donal smugly pretended not to notice.

"Well, perhaps not Nora and Donal." Alan grinned. "But anyone else? No?"

The party shook their heads.

"I do," Brigid said at last. She spent enough of her daylight hours dreaming away that she often had trouble sleeping at night.

"My dear cousin," Alan addressed her, holding out his hand, "my apologies, Sir Reid, but I must borrow her for a family matter."

"Certainly, sir," Reid nodded.

"But my Lord Sheriff," Caryn whined, "when do we get to hear the secret?"

"Patience, my lady, patience. Before you can understand the secret, it may be necessary to provide you all with a bit of a history lesson," Alan said. "Come, Brigid."

Brigid stepped lightly across the flagstones and, with little choice, took her cousin's clammy hand. Alan began the ascent one step at a time, lecturing as he went, and Brigid felt an uneasy feeling in the pit of her stomach. Her cousin only spoke to her when he felt it necessary to suit his elaborate, self-absorbed dramas.

"You see," he began, "when my dear cousin's father, Archduke Danford, fell in battle against Grantis, leaving our dear Archduchess and Lady Brigid here all alone, my father and our other uncles decided that they would help them bear the burden of leadership until Brigid was old enough to rule"— he paused and grinned—"or old enough to marry."

The ladies fell into giggling again, and Brigid flushed with a mixture of anger and embarrassment. She wanted to pull her hand away but felt Alan's grip tighten as he continued his lesson. "They took command in order of age and rank. Young Uncle Nealen would lead the armies, Uncle Graham became admiral of the fleet, bookish Uncle Waylon manages the mines, and as sheriff, my father does everything else to keep the realm from falling apart. It has been like this for five years, and though there is not one among us who does not miss the archduke, Dwerin has prospered. However..." He stopped suddenly and gazed dramatically into Brigid's eyes, as if what he was about to say deeply pained him. "My dear cousin, I'm afraid one of our uncles has been very naughty."

Ellen gasped.

"What happened?" Nora asked.

"Are you ready for the secret?"

"Tell us!"

"Yes, tell us!"

Alan sighed heavily and continued up the stairs. "Three nights ago, an assassin broke into my father's bedchamber while he slept and tried to kill him."

"No!"

"Oh no!"

"The scoundrel!"

Even Brigid was surprised. "Is Uncle Darren all right?"

Alan held out his hands. "Fear not, my friends," he said as if apologizing for having alarmed them. "Your lord is fine. Thank the Brethren that father is a light sleeper. He stirred at the first sound of the assassin's intrusion and was able to turn the fool's blade just as he was about to strike, suffering only a small scratch."

"The Lady be praised!" Nora declared.

"Yes, certainly," Alan said.

"But," Brigid asked, "how does this concern our uncles?"

It was no secret that Brigid's father and his four brothers bore little love for one another. To find all five in a room together was a rarity, even when Archduke Tolliver, Brigid's grandfather, was alive. However, would any one of them go so far as kinslaying? According to the hierophants, even Dibhor did not take up arms against his Brethren directly, nor they him. And no matter what evil he may have wrought in the time of St. Aiden, the Lord Father decreed that his punishment should only be banishment to the Abyss, not execution.

Alan seemed to have been awaiting this question. He crept up beside Caryn to act out the scene. "Just as the fool of an assassin made to strike, the man whispered in father's ear." He drew an imaginary dagger from his belt and brought his face close to the girl's ear. "'Your brother sends his love!'" the Young Sheriff said and thrust his phantom blade into Caryn's bodice to set her squealing. The rest of the group laughed and clapped as Caryn chased Alan up the steps, swatting away playfully at his antics. However, as soon as they reached the two guardsmen at the top of the staircase, Alan waved a hand, and the party halted.

"Good day, my lord," the men said together, averting their eyes to stare at the floor.

Alan eyed them smugly. "Father hasn't killed him yet, has he?"

"No, sir," one of the men said. "Not yet, sir."

31

"He's still in there," said the other, "in his chains."

Reid and Donal exchanged a glance, and for once, the four giggly girls were silent. Brigid realized suddenly where Alan led them.

"Open the door," Alan commanded.

The guards exchanged a glance. "My lord," the first one began hesitantly, "your lord father…"

"Sir," added the second, "this man is dangerous…"

"So?"

"My lord," the first said suddenly with a glance at the other, "we fear for your safety."

"Oh, nonsense!" Alan scoffed. "You said he was chained. Now do as I commanded, or you'll find out it was your own damn safety that you should have been worrying about."

Reluctantly, the guards saluted and did as they were told, unbarring the heavy oak door.

"You'll wait out here," Alan told them.

"But, my lord—"

"I command it!"

"Yes, my lord."

Alan turned back to the group. "Follow me."

For the first time Brigid could remember, Alan's followers showed the slightest bit of hesitancy.

"In there?" Ellen said.

"Of course," Alan grinned.

"With the man who tried to murder your father?" Moira asked.

"You heard the guards. He's chained. He'll be perfectly harmless."

Still, no one moved. Alan seemed to be growing impatient. "Donal, Reid," he said, taking Caryn and Ellen roughly by the arms, "Usher the ladies forth. We'll protect them."

"Yes, sir." Donal followed with Nora and Moira in tow.

"My lady, I'll protect you," Reid promised, offering Brigid his arm. She was hesitant to take it, though her hesitancy was not due to the prisoner.

Inside, the room was dim, lit only by three slender shafts of light seeping in through narrow slits of windows. The rank odor of rotted straw wafted through the room as their feet turned over clumps of the stuff strewn about the floor. To the right of the door, a round wooden table and two chairs sat against the wall, but otherwise, the room was unfurnished. As her eyes adjusted to the darkness, Brigid noticed something long and slender hanging from a heavy iron chain that reached all the way up to the rafters above.

"Listen for my knock," Alan called to the guardsmen once the party had all entered, and before the men could reply, he shut the door. At once, the girls uttered meek whines of protest.

"Oh, shut up," Alan snapped.

He strode up to the object dangling in the center of the room, and for the first time, Brigid recognized it as a man. Heavy iron bindings fastened around his ankles and suspended him upside-down five feet above the floor.

"Wake up!" Alan spat and gave the hanging torso a sharp shove that set him swinging like a pendulum. "Donal"—he waved—"on the table. There's a light."

As Donal struggled to light the small oil lamp, Alan gave the prisoner another shove. Finally, the man yawned and stretched his arms out below him. The manacles chaining his wrists jingled in the gloom.

"Visitors! What a pleasure!"

At last, the lamp sparked to life in Donal's hands, and he passed it to Alan, still standing at the hanging man's side.

"Just look at him." The Young Sheriff grinned. "What a dirty sod."

Brigid watched Alan raise and lower the lamp along the man's body to give them all a better look. He was long, lithe, and clad all in dark colors— black, brown, or gray perhaps, but dark enough in any case to have made it harder to see him without the light. His hands and his feet were bare, and two of the nails on his left hand were bruised and bloody. Thick brown hair hung from the top of his head and a coarse, scruffy beard and mustache sprouted from his upper lip and along the line of his jaw. At best guess, he appeared to be about thirty, though the skin of his face was flushed from hanging, and black and blue bruise patterns encircled his large golden eyes, making it a bit difficult to guess his exact age. Still, even after such harsh treatment, he did not appear altogether unpleasant, for even now, he was smiling.

"When the Lord Sheriff asked if my accommodations were to my liking, I told him that it would be the height of hospitality for him to send up a whore," the hanged man said pleasantly. "Little did I know he would send me four."

"Silence!" Alan hissed. He landed a heavy slap across the prisoner's face, sending him swinging again. A look of amusement spread across the man's features, though he remained silent. "Do you know who I am?" Alan asked.

"Are you asking me?" the prisoner said after a moment.

Alan glowered at him. "Who else?"

"Well, you told me to be silent before, so I could not be certain."

Alan ground his teeth and slapped the prisoner a second time. "Do you know who I am!" he screamed.

The man sighed. "If I'm not mistaken, you are the Lord Sheriff's rotten son," he said, "which makes those two boys your arse-kissers, those four giggly girls your playthings, and the pretty mouse in the corner your cousin, the archduke's daughter."

"How dare you call my lady a mouse!" Reid shouted indignantly.

Brigid blushed and examined the floor. She felt the prisoner's eyes upon her and immediately felt her cheeks turning red. "My apologies to the lady if I have offered offense. I certainly meant no insult." He paused, "To her."

Alan answered with another slap. A trickle of blood dripped down from the man's lip, and he wiped it on his shoulder with a laugh.

"Look," he said, "I can't just hang around here all day playing guessing games. Is there a reason for your visit, or did you just want to hit me?"

"My lord," Alan seethed.

"What?"

"Would you like to hit me, *my lord*?"

The prisoner laughed. "Certainly, but I find I'm not free at the moment."

Alan grimaced in frustration and stormed over to the small table, picking about the objects strewn about its surface. From the various bloody rags and oddly shaped blades whose functions Brigid preferred not to wonder about, Alan selected a slender leather belt with a pair of long-bladed daggers dangling in their sheathes. With a sharp intake of breath, Brigid glanced back at the prisoner only to find his unsettling, amused gaze fixed on her once again. A chill ran down her spine, for something about them seemed familiar, like the eyes of the falcon in her daydream. Hurriedly, she looked away as Alan returned to his grim drama, his hand playfully toying with the hilt of one of the blades.

Tentatively, Reid cleared his throat. "Alan," he said softly, "your father will be angry if you kill him."

"Yes, and you do know that those are sharp?" the prisoner added. "They're not like the blunted toys you noble boys play at war with in the yard."

Alan ignored him and unsheathed the dagger. The folded steel waves along its surface shimmered in the lamplight down to the glimmering, golden hilt. Even in her daydreams, Brigid had never thought any jewelry to look as beautiful.

"Who is ready for another secret?" Alan said coldly. "I told you I've got plenty."

The party remained silent.

"No one?" the Young Sheriff gasped. "Come now!"

"Oh get on with it," the prisoner muttered.

Alan flashed a smile, testing the point of the blade. "Not only was this assassin sent by one of my dear, faithful uncles…" he said, siding up with the prisoner. Slowly, gently, he rested the gleaming edge of the blade along the hanging man's arm. "But he's a Guardian too!"

"From Andoch?"

"How do you know?"

Alan raised an eyebrow. "Just watch."

A splash of red blood splattered across the floor, mingling with the clumps of straw and dried remnants of the past three days' worth of torture. Brigid winced as the hanging man grimaced and twisted the manacles to clutch his bleeding forearm. Moira and Nora turned pale at the sight and leaned unsteadily on Donal's shoulders.

"That'll have healed before tomorrow morning." Alan leered in satisfaction. "Isn't that right, fool? You Guardians can suffer longer than a normal man and heal faster too, if the old stories are to be believed."

"Hand me the blade, and we'll compare," the prisoner winced. "You're not a Guardian, are you?"

Alan slapped him and turned back to his followers. "Father let me watch while he questioned him yesterday. Look"—he pulled back the sleeve from the prisoner's good arm—"Father sliced all along the skin right here, and they're all just scars now."

"Scars, perhaps, though I would not call them just."

Donal's brow furrowed with confusion, "But, my lord," he asked, "I thought Dwerin and Andoch were allies. Why would the King send one of his Guardians to kill your father?"

Alan was speechless. However, Brigid could think of a few reasons, perhaps not for the King, but for the servants, the townsfolk, or the sobbing peasant girls she saw out of her window being dragged to the keep some nights.

"Well," Alan finally said, "maybe he's a defector."

"A Blackguard, my lord," Reid corrected. "That's what they call Guardians who defect. Blackguards. They're outlaws, and the Guardians behead them on sight." Brigid felt him pull her closer toward him but managed to slip subtly away. "Be careful, my lady," he told her.

The prisoner caught Brigid's eye and raised an eyebrow. She turned her head and let her hair screen her from both Reid's unnecessary closeness and the prisoner's gaze.

Alan waved the blade at the dangling man. "A Blackguard? Is that what you are?" he asked. "A Blackguard? No wonder one of my uncles hired you. You were supposed to upset the alliance with the new king by slaying my father!"

"You're very quick to change your mind. Am I to be a Blackguard today and a Guardian again tomorrow? In that case, perhaps then you can let me go. This King may be angry if you kill one of his men."

Alan grinned. "You're avoiding the question, so it *must* be so."

The prisoner gave an upside-down shrug. "Must it?"

"Is it?"

"I can't say."

"Or won't say?"

"Perhaps I don't know."

"Oh, you most certainly do." Alan smiled wickedly. "So now it is as simple as finding out which of my uncles would have opposed the alliance and sent you!"

"Truly, you are clever," the prisoner said. "You should inform your father at once! Although, I seem to remember hearing him tell you that you were not to come here alone. Didn't he also say something about not breathing a word of this to anyone?"

"Shut up, you," Alan spat and sliced the man's other arm. The prisoner grimaced and hugged both of his arms to his chest. Blood trickled through his fingers as he applied pressure to the wounds. However, Brigid knew that it was the prisoner's barb that had struck home, for the wave of anxiety emanating from her peers was palpable.

"My lord," Caryn asked hesitantly, "will the Lord Sheriff be angry if he finds us here?"

Ellen turned as pale as Nora and Moira. Donal, too, suddenly looked very anxious. Reid tightened his grip on Brigid's arm. "Alan, perhaps we should go."

Alan was reluctant but soon felt the effects of his followers' mounting uncertainty. He sheathed the dagger. "Fine," he said, tightening the belt and daggers around his waist, "But I'm keeping these."

The prisoner's eyes narrowed, and when he spoke, his voice was changed. There was no hint of sarcasm, no touch of levity. It was clear, cold, and commanding, and Brigid felt her skin prickle at the sound.

"May the Father, the Brothers, and the Lady of Light herself help you if you do."

For once, Alan's blind faith in the force of his own will seemed to waver beneath the hanging man's gaze. A long moment passed in silence until again Reid whispered, "Alan, we should go..."

At long last, Alan forced his lips into a wicked grin, spun on his heel, and blew out the lamp. Then, with the mania of false nonchalance, he bounced back merrily to the door and knocked for the guards to open it. "I imagine my father will be back to see you tonight, Blackguard," he said, leading his followers through the doorway. "Enjoy your prison until then."

One by one, the nobles ushered out—the four ladies, Donal, and finally, Brigid and Reid. With a resounding thud, the guards shut the door.

"You are to say nothing of this to my father," Alan sneered. "Not one word."

"Of course not, my lord," the guards said, bowing their heads.

"Good," Alan sighed and, returning once again to his captive audience, took Moira and Caryn by the arms. "Now who feels like a game of blind man's bluff?" he asked, leading a hasty descent to the base of the tower. "We should have just enough time to play before supper." Donal, Nora, and Ellen followed, and with a gallant bow, Reid led Brigid after them. However, as her foot touched the flagstone of the very first step, she could have sworn she heard the prisoner whispering after her.

"Until next time, Mouse," he said.

CHAPTER 3:
OAKHEART & ACORN

The stars were shining when Geoffrey awoke in the small hollow along the hillside. Below, the ransacked wreckage of the small caravan littered the roadside dotted here and there with the fresh corpses of Geoffrey's fellow travelers. The caravan guards in their chain mail had been the lucky ones when the bandits set upon them. They were picked off cleanly from far away, an arrow to the heart of each. If they had lived longer, they could have at least suffered alongside the rest of the travelers, perhaps earning the payment that they had demanded in advance. Instead, they died mercifully, spared from the carnage of wanton murder, rape, and looting that the common folk endured before the bandits finished butchering every man, woman, and child.

Save perhaps one. The old man-at-arms was still fighting. Even after Geoffrey himself had been felled by an arrow while trying to flee, he could still remember seeing the old man swinging his cudgel like a champion and driving the enemies before him with his shield, his gray beard speckled red.

Geoffrey pressed his hand against the side of his tunic, and when he raised it in front of his face, it glistened in the starlight with blood. At least, he thought, he was beyond feeling the pain in his side. Thank the Brethren for that. He could spend his final moments in peace, his thoughts on Annabel and the children. At twelve, Karl would be old enough to help, though he still had much to learn about running a farm. However, experience was the best teacher, they said, and in time, Fredrick and Greta would also grow up to be able to carry their share of the burden. Besides, Oliver and Cousin Martin would remember them as well. Oliver would welcome the boys as additional farmhands, and as a lay preacher of Church of the Kinship—a cousin—Martin would help see the family through their troubles. Blind as he was, Old Amos, Geoffrey's father, would certainly do what he could to help his son's widow and his grandchildren too.

Geoffrey swallowed a great bitterness in his throat. If only he had not needed the plow horse to carry his sacks of oats to market, he could have left the old nag to them as well. Instead, it had been led off with the other beasts of burden, probably to be served in some bandit's stew.

A loud, low sound echoed a few feet away. Geoffrey braced upward in fright to see the ghostly outline of a barn owl soar down the hillside and disappear among the branches of the forest beyond the road. His heart thundered in his chest, and his hair and whiskers stood on end.

And yet, despite the suddenness of his movement, he still felt no pain.

Again, Geoffrey reached inside his bloody tunic and felt along the flesh of his left side. To his amazement, he felt nothing. No pain, no puncture, not even the broken shaft of the arrow that had burned like a viper's sting as it bit into his flesh. He could even taste the dried blood on his lips, but for all he could tell, the wound was gone, healed, and scarred over in a matter of...hours? Minutes?

He gazed around him, not at the stars or the forest or at the wreckage below but near at hand. How had he gotten here? When, in the midst of the battle, had he had the good sense to climb up and hide within the hollowed side of the hill? Geoffrey wiped the blood from his hands and rubbed his eyes. He took another deep breath and looked up in the direction from which the owl had flown. At the crest of the hill, he saw the broken remains of a tree stump and, sitting against it, the broken remains of the old man.

Tentatively, Geoffrey climbed up and knelt before the man's body. Goose-feathered bandit arrows pierced him in a dozen places— before, behind, and on either side, and on the grass around him lay the bloody, broken shafts of perhaps a half dozen more. A round wooden shield rested face down on the ground at his left hand, and at his right, a stout, wooden cudgel gave testament to the old warrior's glorious last stand. Though he already knew that the man's spirit had long since departed, Geoffrey touched the old man's chest to check for any remaining sign of life—ragged breathing, a weak heartbeat—but as he suspected, there was none. Thus, with the quiet resignation that marks one for whom death is all too familiar, Geoffrey closed the old man's eyes and offered a prayer to the Kinship that they might receive the fallen warrior's spirit in the life beyond.

Without warning, a large flight of sparrows took wing all at once from the forest and fled across the dark sky overhead. In a flash, Geoffrey dropped down low behind the old man's tree stump, wondering if the birds were fleeing the hungry barn owl or perhaps some greater threat. His heart beat faster, and he glanced down more than once at the old man's idle arms. Finally, with a reticent sigh, he took up the wooden shield and gripped the leather-wrapped handle of the club.

"Forgive me," he whispered to the old man's body, "and please don't think me a thief." His eyes searched the eaves of the forest along the roadside. "I'm no warrior, but…if there are more of them out there…" The night suddenly seemed darker. Geoffrey shook his head. "I'm sorry," he said and, leaving the old man's body, crept swiftly down the hill.

Less than three days ago, Geoffrey and his plow horse, two covered wagons carrying families, two boys leading a pony, and a half dozen other yeomen, peasants, and drifters had set off from the market in Granmouth. Together, they hoped to find safety in numbers—and in the guards, they pooled their coin to hire—along the road. Most travelers were making for Dwermouth at the far end of the Spade, the swath of land lying between the forks of the river Hydra. However, a few, including Geoffrey himself, would turn aside along the way, heading home to any of the small farming communities that dotted the grassy plains. They were but a single day's journey from Geoffrey's village of Pyle when the bandits attacked.

The moon was low in the western sky as Geoffrey hustled along the roadside. He tried to keep low and move swiftly, using the undergrowth for cover. He was not sure if this would make him any less visible in the moonlight; however, if there were bandits hidden in the forest eaves watching the road, perhaps they might overlook a single peasant stumbling along foolishly through the brush and brambles.

He was still uncertain as to how long he had been unconscious, though it was clearly long enough for the bandits to thoroughly salvage what they could from the slaughtered travelers and disappear. With a sigh, Geoffrey wondered if anyone else had survived the massacre, then suddenly cursed himself for not having bothered to search for any living among the corpses before making his escape. Then again, what possibly could he have done to help anyone? He was no healer any more than he was a warrior. He was Geoffrey the Plowman, a simple farmer from the village of Pyle. What could he have possibly done had the bandits still been out there? The only blades he'd ever held were the one he used to cut his bread and the other attached to his plow. He was just as likely to cut himself as he was an enemy. At once, his mind flashed an image of the attack, a man torn open across the midsection, his organs spilling out into a glistening, red heap.

A bulging root caught the toe of Geoffrey's boot, and he nearly tumbled into the roadside dirt. When he finally righted himself, Geoffrey paused, leaned over onto the old man's club, and heaved the contents of his stomach out onto a leafy pile of greens. It had been hours and hours since he had eaten, but he continued to wretch long after there was nothing left.

"Lady, save us!" Geoffrey stammered, his eyes burning with tears. "Forgive me for being so weak." For another few moments, he rested, trying to think of other things. He thought again of his wife and his children, of how happy they made him to still be alive. Then he remembered the families in the caravan on their way to Dwermouth, and visions of their awful fates flashed before his eyes. "St. Aiden, protect us." He breathed in heavily and forced himself to hurry on.

The Spade had always been a dangerous country to live in, even when Geoffrey was a boy. Situated as it was between two arms of a river that provided the natural borders for two separate realms, the ownership of the land was constantly under dispute and, as a result, always seemed under attack. In the years where Grantis seized control, the armies of Dwerin invaded from the west. In the years opposite, when Dwerin had succeeded in taking over, Grantis attacked out of the east. In either case, neither realm had ever succeeded in establishing formal fiefs and vassalages, let alone the taxes and tributes that came with them. Thus, for those willing to risk it, a farmer in the Spade could rightly call himself a freeman, and the entire bounty of his harvest was his to keep or sell as he pleased so long as he did not flaunt his liberty too flagrantly at the market or show any preference for one realm over the other. For Geoffrey and many of his fellows, this meant rotating his visits to the market in the same manner in which he rotated his crops. The spring harvest he sold in the Grantisi town of Granmouth in the east while the autumn harvest he sold at the Dwerin port of Dwermouth in the west. Of course, both towns required that standard taxes be paid for the right to sell "foreign" goods, but to most men of the Spade, it was a small price to pay for freedom. For they were an independent and diverse people descending from the fair-skinned folk of the mountains, the olive-toned people of the Republic and, like Geoffrey, from the rich brown shades of the Kordish Empire to the south. Yet in spite of these varied origins, they had developed a strong sense of identity that while neither Dwerin nor Grantisi, bonded them together as one.

However, since the archduke of Dwerin fell five years past in battle with the Grantisi Fifth Legion, the fighting between the two nations had steadily declined, and control of the Spade left them in an even greater state of ambivalence. For, the Ironmen of Dwerin had turned their attention to the internal strife that was the result of their sovereign's death while in Grantis, any actions the Republic hoped to take to establish formal control of the region was stymied by bureaucracy and squabbling of ambitious senators. In either case, though, with the fighting at a standstill, the services of the many mercenary soldiers hired by both sides were no longer needed. Entire companies of soldiers of fortune, released from their contracts, were left penniless to make their own way. As such, it did not take long for poverty and idleness to give rise to banditry, and without Dwerin lords or Grantisi senators to protect whatever holdings they might have carved out for themselves in the Spade, the farmers were on their own.

At sunrise, Geoffrey reached the road marker, where he would have left the caravan to turn north toward Pyle. Sensing the journey's end was near, he allowed himself a brief moment to rest and searched the woodlands for something to eat. The night's march had exhausted him, and his entire body seemed coated in a thick film of sweat and dried blood. *If I don't at least try to clean myself up,* he thought, *They're likely to take me for one of the Warlock's Army of Dead!* Fortunately, wild blackberries grew all over the wilds in the Spade, and along the roadside, he discovered a small stream. The water tasted of mud and sand, but after the night's long journey, he drank deeply and sat down to wash as best as he was able.

Geoffrey took a moment to look over the old man's arms now that it was light. Both were crafted from the same white wood, lightweight but very hard. The shield, perfectly round in shape, was coated on the underside with a thick sheet of soft leather while two leather straps and an iron handle held it in place when readied. The outer surface bore countless tiny pits and pockmarks, but although Geoffrey had seen the old man turn aside blows from axe and sword and arrow, none had left behind more than a small scratch or nick. As Geoffrey admired its craftsmanship, he noticed an emblem, which though slightly faded with age, still remained clearly visible. It was a single red acorn, and although something about it seemed extremely familiar, it did not belong to any house Geoffrey could recall on either side of the Spade.

The cudgel, at first glance, seemed like nothing more than a bough broken down from a tree, roughly shaped to be wielded more easily in war. However, when struck against a stone or the trunk of a tree, it felt more like iron than mere wood. The blunt, fighting end was stained in places with dried, rusty blotches from the old man's last stand, but like the shield, it bore little other scarring. The handle was wrapped tightly with the same soft leather as the inside of the shield, ending in a wide loop for the wielder's wrist. Burned into the wrist strap were some symbols Geoffrey recognized as letters though he could not read them.

The caravan had met the old man on the road shortly after setting out. He was walking the road alone, and one of the other travelers had called out and invited him to come along. He seemed about sixty years of age yet surprisingly spry. His shoulders were broad and muscular, and when one of the wagons got stuck in a muddy rut along the roadside, the old man proved his strength by helping the others roll it out. He spoke very little along the way, grunting only once that he was making for Dwermouth to meet a friend. Yet despite his gruff demeanor, he seemed to welcome the company, particularly the children. More than once, Geoffrey caught the old man laughing as he watched them at play.

But now the old man was dead. They were all dead. And somehow, he was still alive. The sun had fully risen when Geoffrey shouldered the club and set off again northward, away from the road, toward Pyle and home.

It was just noon when he reached the southern edge of Oliver's fields. Erik, Oliver's youngest boy, was out playing and saw Geoffrey from a distance, shield and club in hand. Immediately, he went off running, replaced moments later by Oliver himself and his two eldest sons armed with spades and a fork.

"Holy Brothers!" Oliver gasped when he recognized him. "Geoffrey?" He rushed out to take him by the arm.

"Oliver," Geoffrey said, leaning heavily on his friend's shoulder. "Thank the Father!"

Oliver waved a hand, and his son Nickolas took Geoffrey's other arm. "Axel," he told the elder boy, "fetch Cousin Martin and tell him to come at once. Then run to Annabel and tell her Geoffrey's returned." The boy ran off, and Oliver and Nickolas ushered Geoffrey through the fields toward their house. "Lady save us." Oliver sighed. "Are you wounded? You're covered in blood."

Geoffrey halted them and stood on his own. "I'm...not harmed," he said. "Just tired and glad to be home. I ran nearly all night."

"What happened?" Oliver asked. He motioned to the cudgel and the shield. "And where did you get those?"

"Bandits and a dead man."

When they reached Oliver's cottage, they sat Geoffrey down on the log outside the door that served as a bench. Agnes, Oliver's wife, rushed out to meet them. Nickolas ran into the house to fetch water.

"Lord Alantir, Oliver! What's going on?" Agnes prattled. "Erik sees a bandit out in the fields, and here's Geoffrey looking like death! What's happened? Where's Axel?"

Oliver gently held her by the arms as Erik and his two sisters, Bethany and Laura, crowded around the cottage door. "Everything's fine, love," he said calmly. "Axel's just gone to fetch Annabel and Cousin Martin. Geoffrey met trouble on the road."

"Bandits!" the peasant woman exclaimed. "St. Aiden, preserve us!"

"Here you are, Geoffrey," Nickolas said, returning.

Geoffrey drank the water graciously while Nickolas stared with excitement at the acorn shield and club. "Wow!" he breathed. "Geoffrey, could I hold them?"

Before Geoffrey could answer, Oliver swatted his son's shoulder. "Oi!" he grunted. "You leave that be. You don't know where they've been!"

"Cracking skulls, looks like," Nickolas muttered. "Geoffrey, what a find!"

A moment later, Axel returned, followed closely by a man in course brown robes and a thick, homely peasant woman with her brown hair bound beneath a wimple.

"Geoffrey!" Annabel shouted with tears streaming down her face. "Lady keep us. What's happened?"

44

Geoffrey hugged her tightly in his strong, farmer's arms, easing up only for fear that he might crush her to death. "Hush now, darling. I'm fine. I'm fine," he said. "But tell me, where are the children?"

"Karl's watching the younger two at home," she said, kissing him. "Oh my lords, Geoffrey! You look as if you've crawled out of a grave!"

The man in robes drew nearer, reluctant to interject. "Are you hurt, Geoffrey?" he finally asked. "Let me take a look at you, if you please." He was a rather young man, thin and curly-haired, clad in the simple garb of a country lay preacher in service of the Kinship. He set down the burlap satchel he had brought with him and began sorting through various pouches of medicinal herbs for making poultices.

"I'm fine, Cousin Martin. I'm fine," Geoffrey said, releasing Annabel from his embrace, "Just...weary."

"Nonsense," Martin said. "Let me at least have a look."

Geoffrey did as Martin bid him and took off his soiled tunic. Despite the dirt and crusted, dried blood, there was not a mark on him save for a raw, circular scar that stood out against his brown skin.

"Where did you get that?" Annabel asked.

Geoffrey shook his head. "I'm...I'm not certain," he said.

Martin prodded at the scar tissue with his finger. "It looks like it was made by an arrow," he observed. "But it looks as if it's been healed for some time."

Geoffrey shrugged. "I don't know."

Oliver eyed him skeptically but remained silent. At length, Martin sighed. "Well, my friend, you look well enough to me."

"Can you tell us anything else about what happened?" Oliver asked.

At his side, Agnes swatted at him, nodding tersely at the children gathered around.

"Or if you'd rather talk later, it can wait."

Geoffrey shrugged and sat down again.

"Nickolas," Oliver said, "take your brother and sisters inside."

The boy groaned. "Dad..."

"Move."

"What about Axel?"

"Axel's older than you. Now go."

"Fine." Nickolas sighed and did as he was told.

When he was gone, Geoffrey took a deep breath and rubbed his eyes. He didn't feel much like talking, like remembering, but the rest of the village had a right to know of any trouble. The life of a farmer was not one of solitude. From planting and harvest to bandits and blight, the villagers all shared one fate, whether weal or woe. "There's not much to tell," he said at last. "I sold what I could of what remained from the harvest and put in with a caravan out of Granmouth. Things were quiet for two days, and then last night, arrows started flying at us from out of the forest. Before long, a whole mob of brutes appeared and put anyone left to the sword. As far as I know, I'm the only one who escaped." He sighed. "They took the bloody plow horse and all the money I made at market too."

Annabel's eyes fell. "At least you have your life."

"Aye," Oliver said. "The horse is a great loss, but we can always borrow one."

"I suppose," Geoffrey said.

"What about the shield, Geoffrey?" Axel asked. "And the club?"

"It's called a *targe*," Nickolas said, appearing in the window of the cottage.

"Hey!" Oliver snapped. "Inside, I said!"

Nickolas withdrew with a sigh.

Geoffrey held the club aloft. "One of the men traveling with us had them. He was the only one who tried to fight." He thought of the old man's body leaning against the tree. "When he fell, I thought I should take them with me, just in case." He paused and glanced up with concern at the cousin. "Do you think that's all right, Martin? I don't want his spirit upset with me from beyond the grave."

"I don't see why not?" Martin said. "You say the man fell fighting the bandits. I think he'd understand that you were in need, although I promise to pray for his soul and light a candle for him all the same."

Geoffrey nodded graciously.

"What is that? An acorn?" Oliver asked. "Can't say I know that sign."

"Aye," Geoffrey said, "I was wondering that myself."

"It looks too plain to belong to a nobleman," Oliver said. "Do you know it, Martin?"

"Not that I can recall," the parson said. "However"—he motioned toward Geoffrey's club—"may I have a better look at that?"

Geoffrey slipped his wrist from the leather strap and held it out to him. The young man tested the weight of the weapon and inspected the grain of the wood. Then handing it back to Geoffrey, he lifted the shield, and his eyes widened with surprise at its light weight.

"Geoffrey, I could be mistaken," he said, knocking against the wood with his knuckles. "But based on what I've read...I believe this might be Holy Oak."

"What?" those gathered muttered in disbelief. "Holy Oak?"

Martin's brow creased in thought. "I'm not certain, but it makes sense, for they say the acorn of a Holy Oak is as large as a pumpkin and red as blood."

Oliver shook his head. "Will wonders never cease?" he said. "Holy Oak sown by Brother Tengale himself. Imagine if it's true! That man must have been some warrior to have arms like those."

"Well, they say all great warriors name their weapons," Geoffrey said, holding the club out in front of him, "The cudgel's name is Oakheart."

"How do you know that?" Oliver asked.

"It says it," Geoffrey told him, pointing to the letters burned into the leather wrist strap. "Right here. Oakheart."

Annabel glanced at him quizzically. "Since when have you known how to read?"

The sudden realization left Geoffrey speechless. "I...I don't know," he said at last. "I suppose...since just now."

CHAPTER 4:
THE PRINCE & THE TOWER

The dew-laden grass muffled the heavy footfalls of the horses as they silently paced through the towering birches of the White Forest. Despite the oppressive darkness and the occasional sounds common to the wild in the early hours after midnight—owl calls, wolf cries, the rustling of small creatures among the undergrowth—not one made any attempt to break away from the group or uttered any whinny of fear. Though they were not the armored destriers or the noble palfreys of the mounted knights, the coursers of the light cavalry were just as well trained. The animals' full faith lay in the steadfast resolve of their leather-clad riders, guiding them by the bridles from a few steps ahead. For many, the bonds between them had been forged since childhood, learning the magnificent dance of mounted combat not as horse and man but as one unified creature, and when they faced death upon the battlefield, they did so unwaveringly together.

Days like today.

At the head of the column, Prince Beledain halted, and the long line behind him slowed to a stop. He ran his hand down Igno's nose and idly flicked one of the tiny bells on the horse's bridle with his finger. There were dozens more along the stirrups and the saddle, but not one of them made a sound, for the tiny hammers within each had all been removed. Privately, Bel did not care much for them or the gaudy way they glittered in the sunlight against the red chestnut sheen of Igno's fur. However, the bells had been a gift from the men of the light cavalry after his first major battle, and as much as he might not like the flashy outfit, Igno would wear it proudly for as long as Bel remained in command, for he was their Silent Prince of Bells, silver for each man who rode with him, and gold to remember any who fell behind.

There will be more gold ones by day's end, he thought with a sigh. He turned back toward the stalwart young woman behind him, his lieutenant and cousin, Lady Valerie.

"We'll wait here for now," he said softly. "The edge of the valley's not much further. Dermont planned to attack at dawn, so we should be ready to charge at first light."

"Aye, sir," Val grinned with anticipation. "It'll be done, my prince."

"Val…"

"It'll be done…Cousin."

Bel smiled at her stumbling speech. Though at twenty-four, she was five years his senior and had earned her knighthood long before him, it was only after Bel had been placed in command of the skirmishers that she was finally able to put her combat training to real use. For until her younger cousin, no other officer was willing to risk the life of a lady knight who was not only the daughter of General Leon Tremont but niece to the king of Valendia himself.

"Val, how often must I tell you?" he said quietly. "Family before the chain of command."

"As you say."

"As my father says, and I have before, but it seems to do no good with you." He smiled and glanced up into the lofty branches of the trees. "My guess is that we're still two hours from dawn, though it's hard to tell in this forest. Set watches and let the men have their ease until then but insist that they be *quiet*."

"Of course."

All night, Bel had led their men through utter darkness south and then east from the valley where his elder brother Dermont and the main part of Valendian host were encamped west of the great birch forest known as the White Wood. Then at midnight, they turned northward into the forest and walked their mounts through the winding woodland paths only to find themselves positioned behind the Gasparan lines, ready to ride down the enemy reserve force while they sat around their morning cookfires like a flock of sheep.

When Val had gone, Bel hitched Igno's reins around a low tree branch, chewed a piece of dried venison from his saddlebag, and held out a carrot for the horse. If all went according to plan, the sun would rise on what would be Valendia's decisive victory and set on five generations of bloody civil war.

Nearly a century ago, King Durante of Montevale and his wife, Queen Solana, gave birth to twin brothers, identical in look and bearing and, as they aged, identical in ambition as well. Since it was never clear which brother was the elder, when their father died, both made claims to the throne and refused to acknowledge the rights of the other. As a result, Valente seized control of the southern half of the kingdom with its fields and valleys while Gaspar claimed the highlands of the north. The gray searoan stallion that was the symbol of the Montevalen kings since the days of Old Calendral became divided was torn asunder to become the Black Horse of Valendia in the south and the White Horse of Gasparn in the North.

But soon, by the will of the Brethren, Gasparn's King Marius would abdicate, and Bel's father Cedric would reign over a unified Montevale. He only hoped Dermont would be gracious when he accepted the Gasparn surrender, for in the twelve months since the death of Marius's only son, Gislain, Gasparn morale had steadily declined. To treat them with anything but honor after the death of their greatest hero would be to rub salt in an open wound.

Even the men of Valendia respected the Snow Prince Gislain, though they called him by a different name. Five years ago, when Bel's young uncle Talvert laid siege to the Gasparn fortress at Whitemane, Gislain and his men fell upon them from the mountains in the middle of a snowstorm, freeing the city and decimating Bel's uncle's entire force. Even Lord Talvert was lucky to escape with his life. From that day forth, the Valendians referred to him as the Avalanche.

But now Gislain was dead, not gloriously in battle, but from a festered wound, and with an aging king and no male heir, the men of Gasparn seemed to have lost the will to fight. Perhaps at long last, the War of the Horses would finally be over and Montevale could at last be at peace.

However, dreams of gold did not put food in a poor man's mouth, as Bel's father always said. There was still the present to contend with: a battle, and with it, the very real possibility of death. Bel tested the blade of his longsword, inspected the string of his short bow for fraying, and ensured that his buckler and quiver of arrows were secure behind his saddle and within arm's reach. The hours just before a battle were the strangest sort of anticipation, an odd blending of excitement and fear, and such routines as checking his equipment helped him to focus, for not only would he be responsible for his own safety but for the lives of the soldiers under his command.

Let's hope this is the last time then, Bel thought. *The last time I lead men and women to their deaths.* With a sigh, he patted Igno fondly on the flank and flipped open the saddlebag to retrieve another piece of venison when, suddenly, he felt the cold touch of a naked blade against his neck.

"Move," said a whisper, "and you're dead."

In the darkness, Bel took a long, slow breath. "I'm ready."

He felt the blade press more firmly into his skin and then disappear with a cackle of laughter.

Bel's heart began to beat again as he recognized the voice. "You!" He gasped.

"I'm ready!" the merry voice mocked him before erupting once more into fits.

"Lilia!" Bel hissed, straining in the dark to see her. "Lilia, Shut up!"

"I'm ready!" She laughed. "Who says that?"

Bel shook his head and tried to avoid the contagion of the young woman's laughter. "It's not funny!" he said. "Really, Lilia. The Gasparan reserve force is camped just beyond the edge of the forest, and they outnumber us five to one. If they find out we're here, if they hear you, we're all dead!"

"Well, it's a good thing I'm ready!"

As much as he fought it, Bel could not keep the smile from playing about the corners of his lips. At last, he could just make her out when she appeared from out of nowhere at his side.

"It's not funny," he said again.

"Yes," she told him, sliding her slender arms around his neck. "It is."

Even in the darkness, Bel knew he was blushing. "Lilia, please, you need to be quiet," he said again, "I mean it."

"Then make me," she whispered and pressed her lips to his.

For a fleeting instant, he tried to resist, but it was no use. Gently, he brought his arms up around the small of her back and pulled her closer, savoring the taste of her mouth and the sweetness of her tongue. When she finally released him, he breathed a heavy sigh.

"We shouldn't do this," he said. "Not now."

With a playful smile, Lilia shook her fingers through his dark hair and gazed coquettishly into his hazel eyes. She bent forward to kiss him again, and as he opened his mouth to meet hers, she laughed and slipped suddenly away from his grasp.

"Oh, it's all right," she teased. "I passed Val on my way up here. She knows what we're at."

"That's exactly why we shouldn't do it," he said. "You're exactly the reason why in King Alderic's time women in Valendia weren't allowed to fight."

"And he almost lost the war too, didn't he?" she asked, stepping around to let the red coarser nuzzle her shoulder. "Good thing your old grandfather Ignacio had the sense to change that," she said. "Isn't that right, Igno?"

"I think he was just tired of hiring mercenaries out of Wrathorn," Bel said. "Particularly once the Gasparns began offering to pay them more."

"The Wrathorn have always allowed their women to fight. They even have women chiefs, some say." She sighed and kissed the red horse on the nose.

"No wonder he didn't start," Bel whispered. "He smelled you."

"Of course he did," Lilia whispered. "You know," she added, "we should put your Igno here to my Ban. Imagine the foal the two of them would make! We could lie down beside them too while they were at it. Unless, of course, you gelded him like all you noble butchers do."

"No." Bel sighed. "He's not."

"Good thing," Lilia said, padding softly back to hug him. "You know what they say about the man who gelds his horse?"

"Gelds himself. Yes, yes. I've heard it."

Even in the darkness, he knew she was smiling.

"So where is Banshee? I don't see her."

"Of course, you don't. She's a black horse, and it's the middle of the night." Her breath was warm against his neck. "But she's right there, all ready for war."

At last, Bel allowed himself to relax and raised a hand to run his fingers through Lilia's shaggy brown hair, twisted into a multitude of little braids to match Banshee's mane and tail. *The horse and rider are one,* he thought, recalling his father's words.

"I want to ride into the battle beside you," she whispered. "If I'm going to die, I want the last thing I see to be you."

Bel held her closer, breathing in the earthy scent of her as he kissed her on the brow. "But what if I fall before you?" he asked.

"You won't.

"How do you know?"

"Because, my Silent Prince," she said, touching her finger to his lips. "I won't let you." Her brown eyes caught a glimmer of starlight through the treetops. "But even if I don't, as I hear it, you're ready."

"Oh, shut up." Bel smiled in spite of himself.

Again, he sought to silence her with another kiss, her slender torso rising against his as he pulled her closer, and he remembered the first time he saw her. It was last spring, not long after his brother had granted him command of the light cavalry with orders to patrol a stretch of the Bloodline—the invisible border that divided north and south. At dusk one evening, they came upon a large column of Gasparn skirmishers hoping to sneak south to pillage the Valendian supply caravans funneling food and fresh gear to the frontlines. At that time, all but a few of the bells on Bel's harness were silver, though, after that day, a good many turned to gold. The sun had long since set by the time the battle was over, and the grassy plain underfoot had turned dark with the blood of man and horse. Bel was picking his way through the carnage, looking for survivors and granting the gift of mercy to dying foes, when suddenly he found her. She was lying on her back beneath an overturned wagon—a pretty girl of an age with him frozen in deadly combat with a pair of enemy corpses, each with a dagger in his belly pressed to the hilt. Blood as thick as tree sap covered her from head to boots, pooling between the plates of her boiled leather and mixing with the sooty, black patterns of war paint on her skin.

Taking her for dead, Bel climbed beneath the wagon to pull her body out for burial, quietly mourning yet another golden bell. Yet as soon as he made to touch her wrist, her body snapped like a bowstring. Her legs lashed out and wrapped around him, dragging him down to the ground, and before he knew it, she had him pinned with a dagger at his throat. Her chest heaved with fury, and she snarled, bearing her teeth like a frenzied beast mere inches from his face. Death loomed like a shadow in the depths of her eyes, yet in spite of that, covered in blood and gore, he found her all the more beautiful and terrible to behold—like flowers upon a grave. So it was he named her the Blood Blossom of the Battlefield, a flower that thrived not on water but on blood. And in spite of the single bead of crimson that welled up from beneath her dagger's point, he craned his neck to meet her maddened gaze and, there, beneath the wagon, kissed her on the mouth.

It was that same spirit, that selfsame animal ferocity, that made her so deadly in battle, and that so intoxicated him now. Bel's mouth traveled from her lips to her jawline to the side of her neck while his hands untied the leather bindings of her cuirass and let it fall to the forest floor. Underneath, she wore only a thin linen shirt tucked into her leather breeches. His fingers slipped beneath it and traced lightly along the lines of her ribs to palm the supple white flesh of her breasts. Their tips hardened like little stones while her hands tugged impatiently at the buckles of his jerkin. As he paused to unbuckle the clasps, she shrugged out of her shirt and loosened the laces of her leather breaches before, together, they lay down on the soft moss of the forest floor. Again, she pulled his lips to smother hers before allowing his mouth the freedom to travel on its own down her collar, along her breast, and finally end its journey on the rough cord of skin along the lower edge of her ribs. It was a scar, the only mark she had upon her beneath the wagon on that first day, the worst of all the wounds she had suffered in spite of all those that she had given. Bel kissed it, and her breath quickened.

"Paint me."

He climbed up to lie beside her. "What?"

"I want you to paint me," she said softly, sweetly.

"Now?"

"I can't do it myself in the dark without it looking all smeary, and what man is going to run in terror from that? I want you to do it. Then you can have me."

"You know it'll just get all smeary anyway then."

"Do you not *want* to have me?"

"Did you mix the paint?"

Bel watched Lilia's pale shadow crawl a few paces away to the tree where Banshee was tied. When she returned, she pulled off her boots and leather breeches, and Bel did the same with his.

It had been the tradition of the light cavalry since Bel's great-grandfather's time. When King Alderic began hiring mercenaries from the Wrathorn clans to supplement his losses, he found many of them rather well suited to the skirmishing companies. They were unafraid to wade into battle lightly armored, showed skill at hit-and-run attacks, and possessed a natural affinity for horses. However, beyond simply their martial prowess, the Wrathorn brought with them many of their tribal customs too, such as their belief that to paint the body in the image of their pagan gods was to receive the favor of the divine.

Dipping their fingers into the wet paint pot, the Silent Prince and the Blood Blossom painted each other with signs and symbols sacred to the Spirit of the Wild Horse. Patterns of tiny horseshoes galloped over their shoulders and down their backs while thick spiraling rivers meandered around their forearms and thighs. Crescent moons marked each of their biceps and the sides of their faces and around their eyes. Then as one last measure of protection, Lilia took Bel by the hand and poured the last few drops of paint between their palms, squeezed them together, and pressed their blackened handprints over the other's heart. With these final brands in place, Bel gently slipped his arms around her waist and brought his head closer to her for another kiss. Yet to his surprise, he found her hesitant.

"Wait."

"What is it?" he asked.

"Don't die," she whispered. "Promise me you won't die."

"I thought you weren't worried about me?" He smiled grimly.

"I lied. Promise me."

"You know I can't do that," he said. "But I'll take back what I said before."

"What's that?"

"I'm not ready yet."

With a forlorn smile, Lilia ran her inky fingers through his hair, clasped them around his neck, and pulled him down with her to lie on the grass. Bel breathed a heavy sigh and kissed the side of her neck and her cheek as her hands reached down and found him, guiding him to her below. When the moment had passed, they lay together for some time, wrapped in each other's arms before, with one last kiss, they donned their leathers and parted, separately leading their horses back to the column through the dark.

"Good morning, cousin," Val whispered when she recognized him approaching from the gloom. The night was fading fast, only to be replaced by a thick morning fog. "Should I ready the men?"

Bel felt a touch of guilt but cast it aside for now. There would be time for such things after the battle, if he lived that long. "Very good, Val," he said. "Thank you."

"I'll have them form the line." She smiled, offering Igno a light pat on the flank. "So long as you save me the space at your other side, would you?"

"Of course," he said, ignoring her use of the word "other."

Not long after Val departed, Lilia appeared out of the darkness atop her Banshee, followed by a handful of the other distinguished riders. Their short bows rested across their laps while behind their saddles hung an assortment of swords, handaxes, and daggers.

"Good morning, my prince," Lilia said.

"Lilia"—he returned her greeting, and to the other men nodded— "Briden, Jarvy, Horn."

"Prince Bel," they said, urging their horses up to begin forming the line.

"The forest ends just over the edge of the hill there," Bel whispered. "When Dermont sounds the attack, we'll charge and take out their reserves."

"Aye." Jarvy nodded as other riders appeared from out of the fog to join the line. He was an older man with ruddy, wind-burned skin, and thin gray hair that matched his horse, Piper. "When I was on watch before, my lord, I crept up to have a look. They're all gathered 'round like chickens in a roost down the valley about five hundred yards."

"And we'll be the foxes to pluck every feathery arse." Lilia grinned.

Val rode back on her dappled mare, Gale, her broad shoulders and square jaw set for war.

"Galdorn must truly favor you, cousin," she said, falling in beside him. "To travel all night through darkness and come up on their rear like this."

Briden Sheradon, the standard-bearer, was a boy not yet sixteen and the youngest son of a minor lord. Perpetually wide-eyed, he unfurled the banner of Valendia and held it aloft. "The black horse on a field of white," he said with a practiced ceremony.

"But today, let's turn the ground red." Jarvy smirked.

The other riders grunted in hearty agreement, though were the enemy not so near at hand, they would have raised a cheer.

Bel was pleased. He sensed the electricity that passed between his brothers-in-arms and recognized the wolfish gleam that shone in their eyes. They were hungry.

"Who commands below?" Val asked him. She slipped her arm into her shield and fingered the hilt of her heavy, flanged mace.

"Raylon Jace," Bel said, "the Snow Bear."

Lilia rolled her eyes and shook her head. "I'll never understand why you nobles insist on giving these names to everything." She grinned. "Sir Raylon Jace the Snow Bear, Sir Beledain Tremont the Silent Prince, Sir Valerie Tremont the Iron Fist..."

"Norwen Wrolanger, the Painted Beast." The rider beside her bristled beneath his thick black mustache. He was a big man, the son of a Wrathorn mercenary and a Valendian soldier, so although his real name was Harmen, he was known as Horn.

"Leon the Black Lion, Talvert the Summer Storm, Ignarius the Red Wave..." Jarvy counted on his fingers. "Sir Mason Ringol the Stone Giant, Sir Darius Ringol the Blood Giant..."

"Gorfred Klein the Ruddy Axe, Kilgan Dorn the Blade Song..."

"Cedric Tremont the Laughing Prince," Briden piped up, "now the Laughing King."

"Aye, all men must earn their names," Bel said, though it had been some time since his father had laughed.

"The Blue Sunrise..."

"The Valley Breeze..."

"The Lightening Colt..."

"The Blood Blossom." Lilia coughed.

"Who's that?" Briden asked.

"Nobody," Bel said, avoiding Lilia's eye. "At any rate, the names are a tradition going back to the old days. The Guardians in Andoch are the same, though their titles pass on from man to man. A lot of the old stories don't even refer to them by their proper names, merely 'The Watcher' or 'The Lancer.'"

"The Herald, the Shield, the Archer..." Val added. "King Cedric used to read us stories about them when we were children," she told Beledain. "Your brothers and me."

"I think there's one called the Bard," Briden said. "When my granddad used to tell me stories, they always began with 'As the Bard tells it...'"

"Aye," Jarvy said, "the Bard is the source of all the greatest tales, and his songs spoke not only of great deeds past and present but of the future as well."

I wouldn't mind hearing that sort of song right now, Bel thought. He glanced up into the forest ceiling and at long last noticed tiny glimmers of light through the leafy canopy. "I'm going to rally the line," he told Val, nudging Igno forward a few paces ahead. "Listen for Dermont's horn, and if it sounds, be ready to ride as soon as I return."

"Aye, cousin." Val and the riders nearby drew their weapons.

"Briden," Bel said to the boy, "with me."

"Yes, sir," Briden nodded, spurring Magpie, his piebald mare, to follow.

By now, the entire line of skirmishers was in position with their weapons drawn and ready. Horses of every coat and color pawed the earth, grunted, and shook their manes, clearly aware of their riders' nervous excitement. Man and beast, they made him proud, for as much as they were his, he was theirs.

When they reached the final rider, Bel stopped and turned Igno about. "Are you nervous?" he asked the standard-bearer as they began trotting slowly back down the line.

The young man shrugged his shoulders uncomfortably. "I don't know," he muttered. "I've already seen two skirmishes. I guess it would be silly to be afraid now."

Bel shook his head. "It's not silly." He began trotting slowly back down the line, nodding encouragingly to his squad leaders, acknowledging whispered cheers from the other riders. "I'd think there was something wrong with you if you were not."

Briden followed closely. "Are you afraid, my lord?" he whispered. "If you don't mind my asking."

"Every man's afraid. It's what you do with that fear that makes you brave, or so my father says." Bel smirked. "Just trust in old Maggie here and hold that standard high. Jarvy and Horn will ride beside you, and they're both proven heroes of the company."

"Aye, sir," Briden repeated. "Jarvy and Horn."

"They'll watch your back for you," Bel said kindly, "and so will I."

The young man's eyes went wide. "Yes, sir," he said. "Thank you, sir."

"I just had your silver bell attached to my saddle. I'm not ready to trade it for a gold one yet."

By the time they rejoined the line, the other riders had fallen silent. Bel led Igno into the space between Banshee and Gale while Briden took his place close by with the other men.

"All right, my prince?" Lilia called softly.

In answer, Bel offered her a silent nod and furtively touched his leather breastplate where just beneath it, her handprint marked his heart. With a smile, she did the same.

More time passed, though how long, Bel was uncertain. The fog continued to gather in thick, curling tendrils as they waited.

"It'll be a gray morning," Jarvy whispered in the stillness. "Perhaps rain."

As if in answer, the deep, mournful tone of a war horn sounded in the distance.

Val smiled. "Then let us bring the thunder!"

Bel readied his bow and set an arrow to the string. "When we reach the edge of the forest, we'll let loose a volley," he shouted. "Then, on my signal, we charge!"

"For the Black Horse!" Horn bellowed.

"For the Silent Prince!" Lilia and Briden cried.

"Valendia! Valendia!"

"Ride!"

As one, the line of horses climbed the low hillock to the eaves of the forest and paused at the tree line to fire. The peak of a pavilion and the shadowy gleams of cookfires were only just visible through the morning mists, but as the arrows rained down upon the encampment, cries of shock and pain rang out as half-shrouded figures scrambled to arm themselves.

"On my signal!" Bel shouted, shouldering his bow. He armed his buckler, drew his blade, and paused only but a moment as the other horsemen did the same. "Together as one," he cried, raising his sword, "we ride!"

The thunder of hoofbeats shook the edge of the valley as the light cavalry plunged into the fog to fall upon the Gasparan reserves, cutting wide swathes in the unsuspecting enemies as they struggled to understand exactly what was happening around them. Bel's sword whirled through the ranks of scurrying footmen like a cold, red wind. Beside him, Lilia screamed with bloodlust, wielding a short sword in each hand, and Val's iron fist crushed skullcaps like eggshells as Jarvy and Horn made way for Briden bearing the banner of the Black Horse. From all across the battlefield, Bel's riders shouted their war cries.

"For the Black Horse!"

"For the Silent Prince!"

It was impossible to tell how many of the Gasparn soldiers were cut down within the first few minutes, but at last, their commander, Raylon Jace, was able to establish some semblance of order. As the first drops of rain fell upon the field, his men finally rallied together to mount a defense, for they knew full well now that they were fighting for their very lives. With shouts, threats, and angry curses, they turned to fight.

Although from the backs of their horses, the riders had the advantage of height and reach, they could no longer move as swiftly as the rain steadily worsened and the soft grass of the valley turned into deep, viscid mud. It was not long after that the fighting grew just as thick. Yet Bel led his men onward, deeper into improvised Gasparn lines. He hammered away at a pikeman to knock aside his spear and cleaved the man's collarbone in two with his sword. Blood ran in rivers when he drew out the blade and turned to face his next opponent.

The battle raged on, and the riders of the light cavalry began to separate from their initial line into pairs and trios in order to engage their opponents a few at a time. Bel cursed, knowing full well that if his men were drawn too far apart, they could be swarmed by their opponents, pulled from their saddles, and easily overcome. Quickly, he turned hoping to find Briden and the standard just in time to see a Wrathorn mercenary swing a giant maul up at his face. In desperation, Bel raised his buckler to block the blow, but the small shield splintered, and he was knocked from Igno's saddle to the ground. The fall caught him off guard, but otherwise, he was unharmed, and as he raised his sword to face the painted mercenary, he counted himself lucky, for the sheer force of the man's blow could have shattered an ox's skull.

With a cry of primal rage, the barbarian screamed and swatted at Bel with his maul, throwing his entire weight behind every attack; yet each time, whether by chance or skill, Bel narrowly dodged, stepping back just out of reach. At last, roaring with fury, the mercenary raised his hammer high and brought it down in one mighty, earth-shattering swing—and overextended himself. With his heart thundering in his chest, Bel swung his sword and sheered through both of the man's arms at the elbows. The Wrathorn warrior barely had time to register his horror at the sight of his bloody stumps when Val trotted past and finished him with a blow from her mace. The cousins exchanged a silent nod before Val turned to engage more foes, and Bel waded back into the fray to recover his horse.

As soon as he felt the absence of his rider, Igno spurred into a crimson frenzy, snorting, stomping the ground, and knocking over forgotten pots of porridge into the smoldering remains of campfires. A lone Gasparn soldier foolishly reached out to grasp the stallion's reins, only to have his face caved in by an ironshod hoof. Globs of blood and broken teeth spewed forth from the ruin of his shattered face as Igno reared back on his hind legs and cried havoc across the battlefield. Bel fought to reach him, carving a path through the mud and enemy soldiers, but before he could make it, he spied Lilia ride up on Banshee and reach out a hand to calm the raging stallion. As soon as he caught her scent, the red horse calmed, and Bel watched as she led Igno by the bridle from the battlefield, her brown eyes smoldering like torches at the sight of the empty saddle.

The sudden clatter of hoofbeats brought Bel's attention back to the battle, followed by a flash of pain across his shoulder that forced him to one knee. An armored knight in gleaming full plate armor and mounted upon a great white destrier had struck him as he passed. His shield and surcoat bore the same device: a white bear on a dark blue field, and as he brought his horse about, Raylon Jace, the Snow Bear, leveled his sword.

"Come, Silent Prince!" the knight taunted through the narrow slit of his helm. "Let me hear you scream!"

Bel felt along the length of the wound and was relieved to find it only a scratch. From the safety of his steel casing, the Snow Bear meant to toy with him, carving him up with little wounds so as to make him suffer. *The Bear might like to play with his food*, Bel thought, gripping his sword in both hands. *But he'll get no such satisfaction from me.*

With a flourish, the enemy commander raised his blade and spurred his horse to charge. Bel readied himself for the attack and, at the last moment, leaped aside just in time to dodge the horseman's blow and counter with one of his own. Unfortunately, he only succeeded in denting the Snow Bear's shield, and a moment later, the armored knight turned his horse around for another pass. Again, Bel sidestepped and swung his sword, slashing through the fine embroidered surcoat; yet the sharp edge merely scratched harmlessly against the knight's breastplate and the prince had barely enough time to parry the Snow Bear's attack.

As the enemy knight paused to bring his horse around, Bel tried to maneuver away for better positioning, but found his boot stuck fast in the mud. The Snow Bear smiled, readying his blade for one final charge, but before he could strike, he faltered at the sound of a scream that froze even Bel's bones to the marrow.

Galloping at full tilt, Lilia drove Banshee straight through the fray, knocking aside men from both armies in her effort to reach the prince's side. Seeing that his opponent was distracted, Bel let his blade fall to the ground and grabbed hold of the Snow Bear's sword arm while Lilia, leaping from Banshee's saddle to the white destrier's back, drew a dagger from her belt and slipped its point into the seam between the knight's gorget. Once, twice, three times, she struck, each thrust answering with a fountain of red gore.

When the gauntlet finally fell limp in his hands, Bel released it, and the heavy corpse slid from the saddle to sink in the mud. He retrieved his sword and struggled to catch his breath. Lilia, awash in the Snow Bear's blood, laughed like a madwoman and slipped down from the knight's saddle to forcefully smother the prince's lips.

"Where's Igno?" Bel shouted when she released him.

"He's fine," she told him as Banshee drew up behind her. With a slap, she sent Jace's white destrier charging off riderless across the field and Lilia swung back up into Banshee's saddle. "Get behind me," she said. "I'll take you to him."

"Afterwards…" He gasped, sucking air. "The battle…"

"Look around you, my prince!" she cackled maniacally. "We've won!"

"What?" Bel's eyes went wide as he gazed around him.

But for a few stragglers here and there, it was as she said, for at the sight of their commander's fall, the Gasparan soldiers of the reserve had broken and begun to flee.

Away across the field, Briden tossed the standard to Val, and raising it high above her head, she rode around the field. At the sight of the Banner of the Black Horse, the scattered riders—some mounted, others afoot—raised their fists and cheered. From the back of her black coarser, Lilia offered Bel a red hand.

"Come, my prince! My blood is still too hot!" she shouted through the steady rain. "And with no more men to kill, there's only one way for you to cool it down! Quickly, before your Blood Blossom bursts!"

Bel shook his head, grinning from ear to ear. "You're insane!" he shouted, climbing up behind her.

Lilia laughed even louder and gave Banshee a light nudge with her spurs. "Am I to take that as a yes, then?"

"Later," he said with a quick kiss to her cheek. "If the war truly is over, we should have all the time we want."

"Until your brother calls for you to wait upon him so he can regale you with tales of his great victory," she told him. "Tell me, has he ever been wounded, watching the battle from beneath that pavilion of his?"

"Dermont commands more than just a unit of archers or heavy horse," Bel quieted her. "He leads the entire army *and* issues orders to those my uncles command at Roanshead and Ebon Keep."

Igno stood tied to a low-hanging branch not far, Bel realized, from where he and Lilia had lain together a few hours earlier. "That doesn't mean he shouldn't lead his men into battle," she said, "Your father led his own charge. Your grandfather too. So did Larius. So do you…"

With a sigh, Bel kissed her tenderly and slipped from Banshee's back to the ground. Igno gave a soft snort as Bel patted his shoulder and, pulling the reins free from the tree branch, climbed up into his saddle. Lilia eyed him, waiting for him to speak. That was another one of the things that drew him to her, he realized. She let him have his time to think. This time, however, as long as she might wait, he had no answer to give.

"Let's just return to the men," he finally said. "If the battle in the valley is still being waged, Dermont might have need of us. We should regroup and ride down to join him."

Lilia arched her eyebrows but remained silent and together they rode back to the battlefield. As soon as they were in sight, Val hailed them and waved out in the direction of the valley to where a processional of armored knights approached them through the rain. At once, the horsemen of the light cavalry hurried to gather their ranks.

"A gray horse on a green field," Lilia observed.

"It's the old flag of Montevale"—Bel nodded—"the searoan."

"It means truce," Val said. "It seems they wish to speak to us."

Bel gave a nod. "Briden, I'll need you with me. Jarvy, Horn, Rallo, Wendell, you too." He raised his voice so that the entire company could hear him. "Perhaps they've come to tell us that we can all go home?"

Collectively, they cheered as Bel, Lilia, Val, Briden, and the others rode out.

When the bearers of the Montevalen flag recognized the light cavalry envoy, they reined in their horses and formed a line. There were eight of them, heavily armored knights encased in full-plate armor draped with tabards of fine embroidery, and as the skirmishers drew near, the leader of the procession plodded his horse forward a few paces to meet them and removed his helmet.

His shield bore the image of a brown tern upon a field of yellow. Raindrops made little tinkling sounds as they dripped upon his gilded armor.

"I am Lord Giles Pronet of Velmont," he said. "Are you Beledain Tremont, the one they call the Silent Prince of Bells?"

"Do you not see his harness?" Lilia muttered, shaking her head. "Ass." Val cleared her throat and glared at her.

Bel nudged Igno forward. "I am."

Giles Pronet was a long time answering as he made a show of his skepticism, looking Bel up and down. At length, he spoke, "My lord-general has asked that I offer you his compliments regarding your attack upon our reserve force. He bid me say that you showed great ingenuity and forthright determination."

"You may offer him my thanks for his kind words," Bel began but stopped short when Pronet interrupted him, holding up a gauntleted hand.

"As a show of his respect, he has also bid me offer you safe passage through the valley should you wish to join with your brother as he retreats south."

Bel felt as if he had just been kicked by a horse.

"What?" Lilia said, "Retreats?"

"Did you not hear me?" Giles Pronet asked smugly. "You may have fought well through your use of guile, but when our heavy horse made their charge, Prince Dermont's ranks scattered like a flock of sparrows. He and his knights simply fled the field, though I can't say that I blame them, for our lord-general knows the virtues of true cavalry"—the nobleman's lips twisted into sneer—"and by cavalry, I mean armored knights of bearing. Not a mob of leather-clad highwaymen slinking through the forest."

"Prince Dermont had near thirteen thousand men all told," Jarvy said. "Your army fielded less than half that." He turned toward Bel. "It could all just be a ruse, my lord."

"Aye," Lilia spat, "how do we know what you say is true?"

"I say it's a load of shite," Horn growled. His heavy charger, Bastard, gave a snort and stomped the dirt, sensing his rider's anger.

"So you let your men speak for you?" Pronet leered at Bel. "Is that why they call you the Silent Prince? It seems my lord-general greatly overestimated you. He had heard you were a knight of honor. He shall be most disappointed when I tell him you are little more than deaf-mute leading a band of dirty thugs."

In a flash, Lilia drew a short sword, and the line of Gasparan knights followed in unison.

"Foolish girl," Val whispered as her hand slid subtly to the hilt of her mace. "It's a banner of truce."

"Then he should mind his tongue," Lilia said. "They say 'war' and 'words' both start out the same."

Pronet laughed in amusement. "Surely, if you prefer to fight, I can just tell my lord-general that you refused his offer."

At last, Bel spoke, "My men ask a valid question," he said. "And as yet, you have not offered any proof by way of an answer. How do we know, then, that it is as you say?"

Pronet sighed and waved a hand. Behind him, one of the knights nudged his horse forth and unfurled a tattered standard. It was the same as that carried by Briden but with a golden crown sewn upon the black horse's brow. "Is this not the mark of your brother?"

Val bowed her head. Not only did the loss of the banner appear to confirm Pronet's words, but to have lost a standard was also a mark of great shame.

A shadow fell over Bel's features. "Who is this new lord of yours? Have the men of the White Horse found a way to bring Prince Gislain back from the dead?"

"Not unless you've found a way to bring back your brother Larius, though I imagine it would be quite a waste, considering…" Pronet waited, but when he saw that Bel would not rise to his goading, he continued. "My lord-general is Sir Marcus Harding, Guardian of Andoch, though sometimes men know him simply as 'the Tower.'"

"Dibhor's bloody cock," Horn cursed.

"Indeed." Giles Pronet nodded.

Bel breathed a sigh. "Then you may offer the Tower my compliments as well," he said softly. "For sure enough, his was the greater victory."

"So I will," Pronet crooned. "But I grow weary of this prattle. Will you accept his gift of mercy or not? From what I see here, you amount to—what? Two hundred light horse, a third of whom are women? Our army suffered less than a hundred casualties against your brother. By all means, refuse and let our lord-general crush you too."

"We may be women," Val said. "But we fight for our own lands."

"Aye," Lilia joined. "We don't need the bloody Guardians to fight our battles for us."

"Valendia employs mercenaries, as does Gasparn. Must we only hire Wrathorn savages or pirates from the Sorgund Isles? Surely not, and as I understand it, it was the Guardians who approached King Marius with the offer of assistance, so impressed was King Kredor by the tales of our late Gislain."

"I can only wonder at the price your king must have paid," Jarvy said.

"Probably sold the young princess off to be 'crowned' by King Kredor, the Council, and half the wretched Order." Lilia sneered.

"You'd best mind that sharp tongue, girl," Pronet snapped. "Or I'll find a new use for it after my men and I slaughter your companions."

"You're welcome to try," she spat, raising her blade. "My tongue's not all I have that's sharp."

"Enough!" Bel shouted. Lilia and Pronet both stood down and allowed him to continue, "You tell your general that we will accept his offer with my thanks and ride south to join my brother, but only as long as he agrees to extend the same mercy to any wounded that my brother was forced to leave behind."

"My lord-general has already seen to it," Pronet said, replacing his helm. "And he bid me inform you that his surgeons will treat your wounded as they will our own, for after all, when he succeeds in defeating your brother, they will be citizens of the White Horse."

"That remains yet to be seen," Bel said. "But again, he has my thanks."

With a flippant wave of his hand, Pronet and the other Gasparn knights turned their horses about and rode off together across the plain. As Bel watched them go, his stomach churned with bile at the news of the Valendian defeat. So much for ending the war, he thought, so much for peace. With a heavy sigh and a heavy heart, he gently tugged at Igno's reins and addressed his men. "Val, form up the column. Horn and Wendell, gather what men you need to make litters for the wounded. All others with me. Let's be gone from this place."

CHAPTER 5:
DEPARTURE

Over the course of the week that followed King Kredor's coronation, the Loremaster's apprentices made the necessary preparations for their respective journeys.

Thom spent hours reading accounts of the customs of the various clans of Wrathorn, though he soon discovered that the authors of such texts, mostly evangelists sent in search of converts, did not carry much empathy for the "savage" or "heathen" practices of the animistic clansmen. As a result, he spent long hours shadowing Hob while he went about his duties, listening to the burly scribe laugh and tell stories, hoping for a better understanding of what to expect. However, the more Hob talked of clan wars, snowstorms, and bears the size of small houses, the less Thom wanted to learn.

In preparation for this journey to Baronbrock, Lughus spent most of his time rereading the old accounts of St. Aiden and the Beast. The version of the tale that was most widely known and accepted was that described in the *Scrolls of the Hierophants*, the holy text of the Church of the Kinship. As he sought out information on the relics housed within the cathedral—a fragment of Aiden's hauberk, the nosepiece from his helm, a scrap of parchment bearing the handprints of the hero's wife and son—none interested him more than the descriptions of Luminaire, the magical sword said to be entombed with the bones of the saint himself. According to the Hierophants, the sword, forged from the blade of Aiden's plowshare, glowed with white flame and could sunder solid stone as if it were soft cheese. It would flash whenever a man told a falsehood, it was impossible to mar or break, and if an unworthy man tried to wield it, it would burn all the flesh from his hand. Many illuminated drawings showed the Warlock's dead soldiers burning with holy fire as they fled in terror before Aiden's wrath. Though not every story corroborated the Hierophants' descriptions (one account, for instance, claimed that the sword had not been made from Aiden's plowshares but was, in fact, a gift from a Dwerin artisan freed from the servitude of a Dibhorite Lord), the mere possibility that such a blade existed filled Lughus's heart with excitement.

Royne, meanwhile, remained sullen. He resented the fact that Lughus and Thom were being sent out into the world beyond Castle Testament while he was doomed to remain behind. For half the week, he sat alone in the dusty storerooms of the tower's fifth floor, brooding over an old history of the Siege of Three, considering what it would be like to run away from Titanis and its stupid towers to become a Blackguard. Of course, he realized the futility of such rash actions since until he was fully initiated into the Order, he was technically free to leave anyway. In fact, there were even times when those who passed the Rite of Initiation were granted leave under certain circumstances (inheritance of a fiefdom, appointment at a nobleman's court, a marriage arranged by the Guardian King). Rarely was this the case with men of the Loremaster's Tower, yet it still happened from time to time. Only the Anointed were completely barred from leaving, for the Oath of Fealty demanded service unto death, and to renege on such a vow rendered one's life forfeit—and rightly so if even a half of what the legends told of them was true.

It was widely believed that during St. Aiden's lifetime, he possessed the miraculous ability to heal the sick and the wounded with a mere touch of his hand. After his death in battle against Kalius Wrogan, stories soon began to circulate that many of the remaining Guardians and their heirs were also capable of this and many other extraordinary things (most of which Royne knew were clearly preposterous). Some possessed unmatched skill with a variety of arms, others could endure wounds that would have easily slain lesser men, and still more could remain untouched by either poison or plague. However, although often gifted with unusually long life, one enemy that they could not stand against forever was old age. Thus, as time passed and the Guardians in Andoch became steadily more organized, the Guardians under Halford Drude began training new generations of men to protect the fledgling kingdom. Most would serve the Guardian King as soldiers in the standing army; however, those that showed particular promise would be assigned a place among the towers of the Order's councilors and, if they were lucky, would eventually inherit the title and auspices of one of their superiors. In this manner, the Order would continue to flourish and would remain at the ready to defend the folk of Termain against the threat of any new darkness.

However, in the early days of the Order, it was not Andoch alone that was home to the Guardians as was the case today, for those of Aiden's men who chose to return home following the fall of the Warlock often took on protégés of their own, anointing these successors with rank and title as well. Often, these men became the stuff of legend across Termain as champions, heroes, and local saints, and many an early Bard tale told of wandering knights errant descended from these men. For three hundred years, the Order was marked by this duel development until the Siege of Three brought the era of the "Wandering Guardians" to a sudden, violent end and formally established Andoch as the Order's only home.

As Aiden and his men began to take back parcels of land in their home province of Baronbrock, the folk living on those lands would band together to protect themselves once Aiden's warriors moved on. Over the course of the rebellion, these settlements grew into towns and then cities. They formed alliances with one another for mutual protection from the Dibhorites but remained independent in their governance. After Wrogan's final defeat, the fourteen independent city-states (or baronies) banded together to become the single nation of Baronbrock. To lead the new nation, the fourteen barons elected one among them to become Lord-Baron serving as arbitrator between the other thirteen and the head of state comparable to the Andochan Guardian King. The Lord-Baron would retain control of his home barony but would also assume the seat of power in the capital city of Highboard.

Though united under one banner, the baronies were fiercely independent, and as they grew and prospered, border disputes, skirmishes, and even wars were not uncommon. The Barony of Galadin, named in honor of its most famous son and later led by his descendants, often remained neutral, keeping the peace while the other baronies bickered and made war with one another. As a result, for much of Baronbrock's history to that point, the Lord-Baron was often a Galadin, and the barony itself was home to many of the so-called Wandering Guardians—the successors of Aiden's closest friends who joined him in his initial uprising. The Galadin Barons endeavored to maintain the peace among the other thirteen; however, to do so often proved impossible, and before long, many of their peers cried accusations of favoritism, particularly in regard to trade. Eventually, when the Baron of Marthaine grew angry over the verdict of one of the Lord-Baron's arbitrations, he sent his soldiers to attack Highboard, and the Lord-Baron was slain.

In response, before the Lord-Baron had even been entombed, three Wandering Guardians singlehandedly laid siege to Baron Marthaine's castle at Harrier's Keep. According to legend, they positioned themselves outside of each of the castle's three gates and slew any soldiers set against them, one by one or en masse. By the end of the first week, the three Guardians—the Marshal, the Vanguard, and the Blade—had reduced the castle's forces by half. When a messenger was finally able to slip free to recall the Marthaine soldiers sacking Highboard, the vengeful Guardians disappeared, though not before it was discovered that Baron Marthaine, too, was dead.

As a result of "The Siege of Three," people across Termain, particularly nobles, regents, and other heads of state, came to fear the Wandering Guardians, labeling them "Blackguards." At last, the Council of Five responded to their appeals and decreed that henceforth any man who was Anointed under the title of a Guardian must present himself within a year and a day to swear an Oath of Fealty to Andoch, dedicating his life to the Order and his service to the will of the Guardian King. If he did not, he would be considered an enemy of the Order, the Brethren, and the people of Termain and would be punished accordingly by death. While for a time, many men resisted, the majority complied; though some—including the fabled Three—still refused and remained outlaws to this very day.

What nonsense! Royne thought bitterly. *Fanciful propaganda and romantic tragedy!* He closed the yellow leaves of parchment with a light clap only to see Lughus standing above him in the doorway.

"The Siege of Three," he said. "That's one of my favorites."

"I'm not at all surprised."

Lughus ignored the slight and set down the stack of books he carried atop one of the dusty crates against the wall. "I thought you were above such fanciful dribble." He smirked, folding his arms.

Royne tossed the book aside onto the floor, inviting a small cloud of dust. "I am," he said.

Lughus sighed. "Royne, what are you doing up here?"

The lanky apprentice shrugged. "I didn't want to be in the way with you and Thom so busy with your preparations," he leered. "Speaking of which, what brings you up here?"

Lughus shrugged and sat down beside his friend. "I just needed a break from Thom's sobs," he said. "He's convinced that the Wrathorn are going to roast him alive."

"Then why is Rastis sending him?"

"I don't know. Why's he sending me to Baronbrock?"

"Don't tell me you don't want to go," Royne said. "With all your talk of adventures and excitement, you can't pretend you're not excited to visit the tomb of your bloody hero."

"No, but somehow, when I imagined it, I always believed it would be the three of us traveling the world together."

"Like the Three."

"I suppose so. Like the Three."

Royne sighed. "Well, that was stupid. You know as well as I do that Thom's not made for adventuring, nor am I, for that matter. Believe me. I don't envy you two the journey. Baronbrock's a long way off and Wrathorn even farther."

"Well, you seem rather bitter for staying behind."

Royne shook his head. "I never said I wasn't relieved," he said. "I'm just…not looking forward to being alone."

Lughus sighed, and a heavy silence fell upon the lofty tower room. In the spire top above, even the owls and rooks were quiet. "Look," Lughus said at last. "By week's end, Thom and I will have left this place to be gone for at least a year. If you're so damned worried about being left alone, then why hide up here brooding when we could at least have a last bit of fun?"

"Fun and foolishness both start out the same. I have no interest in either."

Lughus shook his golden head. "Fine," he said, collecting his things from the barrel top. "I've work to do." He turned to go.

"Rastis said you're to plot your own course, right? I hope you're not planning on going over land."

"Why?"

"Because you'd have to cross the northwest horn of the Firriny Mountains."

72

"True. It's the quickest route."

"As the crow flies maybe." Royne smirked. "But from what I can tell, you don't have wings, and flapping your arms won't help you cross the mountain chasms or avoid the bandits who make camp along the borderlands."

"Then what do you suggest?" Lughus asked. "You're so smart. Show us."

With a heavy sigh, Royne stretched his arms and slowly got to his feet. "All right," he conceded. "Go get Thom, and we'll go over the maps together. I'll meet you downstairs."

By the following morning, Royne had helped Lughus and Thom plot their course. They would not risk the mountains to the north but instead ride the Imperial River south and east to the Andochan port city of Galdoran on the Calendral Sea. From there, they could book passage on a ship heading north to the barony of Nordren and trek the rest of the way to Galadin. When they approached Rastis with the plan, the old Loremaster agreed. Hob would talk to some of the barge masters in the city's Riverton district to see if any would be willing to carry two passengers as far south as Lenard's Crossing, where Rastis would arrange for a guide to see them the rest of the way.

With the details of the journey settled thusly, the boys were free to enjoy their last few days together as they pleased, and on the eve of the departure, Rastis even allowed them to spend their day in the city wandering the inns, the shops, and the markets. It was a rare treat, and the three apprentices began to sense that it was only with reluctance that the old Loremaster was sundering their odd bibliophilic family. He had even given them money to use to purchase traveling clothes—even Royne, who was staying behind.

"Your habits are fine for studying in the library and reading by the fire," he had said, handing each of them a small purse. "But not very practical for the river and the open road."

Titanis was the largest city on the entire continent, for beyond the limits of its outer walls, the city's poorest district, the Groundlings, extended far out into the countryside in a sea of lean-tos, tents, and hovels that, in the warmer months occasionally grew so large as to encroach upon the local farmers' fields. Even without this seasonal tide of humanity, however, the city proper, safely guarded by a forty-foot curtain wall, was no less impressive with four independent districts, numerous castles and fortified estates, and an extensive collection of holy sites of religious pilgrimage. There was the Riverton District along the banks of the Imperial, Weston on the east bank. Finally, within a second set of walls that rose like an island from the center of Easton was Nobleton, which housed the nobles' estates, the Cathedral of the Kinship, and Castle Testament with its Keystone and Nine Towers. As the three apprentices crossed from Nobleton into Easton, it surprised them how little of the city they had actually seen, and they could not help but find it strange that two of them were to be sent away to learn when there was so much that remained unstudied and unknown here at home.

Not long after they passed through the Nobleton gates (or keyholes as the locals called them) into Easton, they discovered a tailor's shop where Lughus and Thom each purchased two new tunics, pairs of breaches, sets of small clothes, a plain woolen surcoat, a new pair of boots, and a thick woolen cloak with a hood, though, in spite of Royne's teasing, Thom had insisted on buying one lined with rabbit fur.

When they went to pay for it all, however, they discovered that Rastis had given them far more money than was necessary, and since Royne had not needed to buy anything at all, they decided to celebrate their final night together with a proper supper at a cheerful little inn nearby. The image on its signboard branded the place as "The Book & the Barrel," and although none of the boys had ever been there before, the name had its own appeal for three apprentices of the Loremaster.

Since it was the month of Falcontide, the great central hearth was cold, but the late afternoon sunlight streaming in through the large, open windows was just as inviting as any fire. Long oaken tables, simple but charming, ran the length of a common room, at the rear of which stood a polished bartop and an open doorway to the kitchen. The enticing aroma of a bubbling stewpot and roasted chicken wafted in from beyond. As it was not quite the hour of supper for the shopkeeps and other townsfolk, the room was relatively empty save for a pair of toothless old men smoking pipes over a game of draughts, the portly barman, and his wife.

"Loremaster's apprentices, I see," the barman said with a friendly grin. His cheeks glistened with sweat from the kitchens, and the apron around his bulging middle was stained with spots of grease.

"Welcome to The Book & the Barrel," he said with a practiced flair. "My name is Walter, my dear wife, Mary, does the cooking, and in the corner, as always, are Old Bob and Ed. Now I know what you're thinking, but don't worry. They're harmless."

The boys glanced over just in time to see one of the two old codgers slide a piece across the game board at a snail's pace. The barman winked. "So what'll it be? Rabbit stew, roast chicken, a pint of ale?"

Thom's eyes glimmered with delight. "All three!"

"Good man." He grinned. "I guarantee you've had nothing near as good locked away up in that Tower!"

The jolly barman made good on his promise, and as the sun set, the boys discovered that they were not the only ones among the Loremaster's Tower drawn in by the inn's name; rather, it seemed a veritable home away from home for many among their sect of the Order, for soon scribes, scholars, sages, conspicuously attired in their burgundy habits, wandered in from the streets to sit reading over a bowl of stew or a pint of ale.

"I suppose this is something else we can look forward to when we return," Lughus observed.

"What do you mean?" Royne smirked. "After you two leave, I'm coming here every night of the week."

"Rub it in. Why don't you?" Thom sighed enviously.

"Don't worry, Thom," Lughus said. "They say the Wrathorn hunt deer the size of horses."

"Think about who you're talking to," Royne sniggered. "In a year's time, he'll have picked the forests clean!"

"Shut up, Royne!" Thom squealed.

"Aye," Lughus agreed. "You know Thom's no hunter!"

Time passed, though none of the boys could tell whether fast or slow as they ordered a third round and took turns telling stories of their collective past—jokes they had played on one another, stories that they used to read, fights with the Warlord's cadets. However, before long, a touch of sadness seemed to seep in with their ale, and without a word, they knew it was time to return home to the tower.

Their footsteps echoed in the darkness of the cobblestone streets as together they made their way back to the castle. Not one of them said a word, unable and unwilling as they were to understand the unusual feelings of loss and grief that hung like millstones around their necks.

"Our clothes should be there by now," Thom said, attempting to force an end to the awkward silence. "The tailor said he'd have someone deliver them."

Lughus nodded. "I can't believe you insisted on the fur."

"Why?" Thom muttered. "It's soft."

"Aye, it reminds him of his mother," Royne smirked. "What kind is it? Wild boar? One of those great northern buffalo?"

Somehow Thom just didn't have the heart to get angry.

"You know I don't mean it," Royne said quietly. "When I tease you?"

"I know," Thom nodded.

Walking between them, Lughus patted his friends on the shoulders, and together, they made their way through the keyhole to Nobleton. The streets were relatively empty at this time of night, though it was still early enough that folk might take the air without breaching curfew. However, when they reached the other side, they stopped. Along one side of the gateway, a figure was slumped against the wheel of an oxcart, its head drooping heavily onto its chest.

"Aiden's flaming sword," Lughus swore. "It's Pryce."

"What's wrong with him?" Thom asked.

Royne eyed the brawny cadet slumped on his bottom against the stone of the inner wall. "He's drunk!"

Thom giggled. "Really? I didn't know the cadets were allowed to go out in the city."

"Well, clearly you forget, Thom," Royne mocked, remembering their last fight in the tower. "Pryce goes wherever he wants, though that doesn't mean he always remembers where he's been."

"To think"—Lughus sighed—"he'll be a knight one day."

"You never know." Thom shrugged. "Perhaps he'll die in battle."

"Thom!"

"What? He might!"

"Hush! Both of you!"

While the other two watched, Royne carefully tiptoed away to their longtime tormentor's side and waved a hand before his eyes. When Pryce remained unmoved, Royne quickly knelt to remove something from the cadet's waist and, hiding it within the folds of his habit, hurried back to his friends.

"Let's go!" He grinned.

"What did you do, Royne?" Lughus whispered.

"Don't worry about it."

"Royne…"

"I said don't worry about it."

Lughus shook his head. "That's exactly why I'm worried."

The Loremaster's Tower was dark upon their return, except for the soft gleam of the sconces lining the wall of the staircase leading up to the higher floors. The door to Rastis's chamber was shut tight, but a small glimmer of light shining from beneath it and the faint odor of pipe smoke told them that the old man was still awake. Just as Thom had suggested, the parcels containing their new clothes sat waiting on their beds with two weather-beaten rucksacks.

Once more, the awkward sense of grief washed over them, and for a long moment, the three apprentices stood outside of their small cells, unable to speak. At length, it was Royne who finally broke the silence.

"Well," he said, "good night."

"Good night," Lughus said.

"Good night," said Thom.

Before sunrise the next morning, Hob woke them. Lughus and Thom, dressed in one of their new sets of clothes, packed the others away with their habits in the rucksacks, and with Royne in tow, made their way in silence down the spiral stair. When they saw Rastis waiting for them, his pipe in one hand and a taper in the other, Thom quietly began to weep.

"Boys," the Loremaster said.

"Good morning," Lughus and Royne muttered. Thom made a noise that may have been a greeting but came out sounding more like a stifled sob.

Rastis smiled sadly. "Partings are always sad times," he said. "But for every departure, there must be a return. Simply believe that you will see each other again, and someday, it will be so."

The boys nodded. Thom's shoulders shook with a muffled cry.

"When you reach Lenard's Crossing, a friend of mine named Crodane will meet you at the sign of the Kingfisher. He's a native of Baronbrock, and he's promised to see you the rest of the way there."

"Yes, sir."

"Finally," Rastis told them, "I want you to have these."

He nodded to Hob, and the Wrathorn steward offered Lughus and Thom each a thick sheaf of parchment wrapped in oiled leather, a handful of quills, and a large bottle of ink sealed with wax.

"Now," the old man said, "as you know, the Loremasters are the smallest sect of the Order of the Guardians, but our task is no less important than those sworn to the Warlord, the Chancellor, or the Hierophant. One guards us in war, one guards us in peace, one guards us in faith, but we—*we* guard our history, our identity. *We* guard the Truth."

"Now, as you travel, I'd like you to record whatever you see, whatever you hear within the pages of these journals. Learn to know men not only by what they appear on the surface but by their words and their deeds. And write it down. When you come to a new place, learn not only to admire the great halls of its nobles or the beauty of its cathedrals but also the squalor of the poor and the suffering of the destitute. And write it down. And as you learn more of yourself, about who you are, about what you think, and what you believe, for better or for worse, in triumph or in shame, write it down. *For, evil often hides in the shadows of darkness, beneath Dibhor's black cloak of Deceit, and only when guided by the Lady's Light of Truth, can the Guardian hope to defeat it.*"

"From the *Scrolls of the Hierophants*," Royne said softly.

Thom stopped sobbing long enough to ask a question. "Does that"—he paused, rubbing his eyes—"does that mean we've just been granted the Rite of Initiation?"

Rastis burst suddenly into merry laughter. "Alantir, no! We'll talk about that when you get back." He grinned, holding his pipe between his teeth. "You'll be ready by then. I'll warrant. If not before." Together, the boys smiled sadly, and the old man gripped the two travelers by the shoulder. "Be safe," he told them meaningfully. "You'll be in my thoughts every moment you're away."

"Thank you, sir," Lughus and Thom said together. "Goodbye."

Rastis looked beyond them. "Royne?"

"Yes, sir."

"After you and Hob see them off, I'll have some things I need you to copy for me."

"Aye, sir." Royne nodded, though he could hardly hear his own voice.

"Take care," Rastis said one final time, and at a nod from the old man, Hob led the three apprentices out into the pre-dawn streets.

Not a word was said between them as they left the Loremaster's Tower behind and passed from Nobleton to Easton and finally to the stone levees of

Riverton built upon the banks of the Imperial. Here, Hob led them to a wide, flat-bellied barge where a band of rivermen were loading the last of their cargo.

"Hobart, you old dog"—the master of the barge grinned—"we was beginning to think you weren't going to show." He motioned toward Lughus and Thom. "These the boys?"

"Aye, they are, Landen, you old mudskipper." Hob grinned, handing the master a jingling purse of coins. "And you'd better treat them well, or I'll hear of it."

"No worries, matey," he said. "We'll be off in a minute, lads. Time enough to say your goodbyes."

"Aye," Hob said. "Safe journeys, Landen."

"You can tell the old man I won't let his coin go to waste."

When the master of the barge had gone, Hob turned back to Lughus and Thom. "Take care of yourselves," he said earnestly. "Stick together and watch out for each other."

"Aye, Hob," Lughus said, "we will."

Thom nodded his head, though he seemed unable to speak for his weeping.

"Like Rastis said, Crodane will meet you at the Crossing and see you the rest of the way to Galadin." He smiled kindly. "He's a good sort, and he'll keep you safe."

"Aye."

"And if old Fergus is with him, tell him I said hello too."

The boys nodded together one last time in silence, and with a wistful grin, the giant scribe slapped each of them on the shoulder in turn. "Take care, lads," he said one last time and, with a nod to Royne, walked to the end of the dock to wait.

For a long moment, the three friends stood in silence but for the sound of Thom's quiet sobs.

"Well," Royne said at last, "I guess this is it."

"I wish you were coming with us," Lughus said.

Another moment passed, and as the first rays of the rising sun appeared in the east, the bargemen finished loading the last of their cargo. At the Cathedral of the Kinship, the great bronze bell tolled to mark the dawn.

"Well," Lughus said, "we should go."

"And I've got things to copy when I get back," Royne complained, though he knew full well that the old man's task was only designed to give his mind something else to occupy it in his grief.

"Take care of yourself," Lughus said, offering his hand.

"You too," Royne returned. "Look after each other."

Lughus gave a nod. "We will."

With his head buried in his hands, Thom's shoulders shook with great, inconsolable sobs.

"So long, Goldimop. Farewell, Thom Fatty."

"Goodbye, Royne."

Quietly, the boys turned to go their separate ways—Lughus and Thom to join the men at the barge and Royne to return with Hob. However, all of a sudden, the lanky apprentice stopped short with a jolt and whirled around.

"Oh yes." He grinned. "How could I forget?" Carefully, Royne withdrew an object from the folds of his habit and tossed it to Lughus across the dock. "For protection along the way," he smirked.

"Royne," Lughus said, sliding the blade from its sheath, "this is a cadet's dagger."

"Aye, so it is." Royne shrugged. "But you're better with a blade than Pryce is, anyway."

With a smirk, Lughus snapped the dagger back in its sheath and slipped it into his belt. "Thanks," he said. "It means a lot."

"To Pryce, I'm sure." Royne grinned, backing down the docks toward Hob. "Though, hopefully, you won't need it!"

CHAPTER 6:
THE NOBLE FEAST

"Darling, you know how ghastly I find it when you slouch."

"I'm sorry, Mother."

Lady Josephine sighed in exasperation and exchanged a glance with her aged handmaiden Livonia. Livonia shrugged sympathetically as she carefully polished Josephine's fingernails.

"Oh, my dove," Brigid's mother said at last, "what are we ever going to do with you?"

Brigid straightened her back, lifted her chin, and folded her hands in her lap.

The archduchess carefully inspected her daughter. Her long, dark hair had been carefully braided into two thick plaits, and then each rolled into a large bun on the back of her head. Thin strands of tiny pearls had been woven along her crown beneath a thin silver circlet set with a large blue star sapphire that rested in the center of her brow. Her snowy-white gown was trimmed in an embroidered pattern of tiny, azure flowers that matched the color of her surcoat and gathered at the waist with a girdle of silver rings. Around her shoulders, she wore a dark blue mantle trimmed with white rabbit fur and clasped at her throat was a brooch fashioned in the shape of a silver anvil, the symbol of the archduke of Dwerin.

"Livonia, I know that blue always matches well with her eyes, but I think we should avoid dressing her in so much white in the future," Josephine said at last. "She's far too pale as it is, and the white only draws more attention to it."

"Yes, madam."

"We still want her skin to look fair and clear, mind you," the archduchess added. "But at this rate, people with mistake her for a little corpse."

Brigid suppressed a sigh. For over an hour, she had been sitting in the same position, perched on the edge of a heavy oak chair carved with elaborate, serpentine creatures. The work of some long-dead master craftsman, not only was it breathtakingly beautiful, but just like every other aspect of her mother's private apartments in the keep at Blackstone, Brigid found it both cold and incredibly uncomfortable. The small of her back ached with pain, and she had to constantly wiggle her toes to keep her legs from falling asleep as the edge of the seat dug into the backs of her knees. For once, however, it made her thankful for the gown's absurd length since it kept her mother from noticing her fidgeting.

At long last, Livonia finished with her mother's hands, dipped them in fragrant water, and held up a glass for Josephine to admire herself. Though she was just now beginning to show signs of age, Josephine still looked exquisitely beautiful. Her flaxen hair shone brilliantly in the dusky light of the sconces, a mountain of cascading yellow curls. Her crimson lips glistened as they spread into a smile of sensual delight, and her long eyelashes flickered coquettishly around her dark eyes. Her gown shone like polished copper beneath a surcoat of forest green, all cut to accentuate the fine curvature of her bosom and hips. Her jewelry matched that of her daughter, though instead of silver, she wore gold, and around her shoulders, her cloak was lined with the fur of a black wolf.

"Now how do I look?"

She stood up from her seat and made a quick turn.

Not for the first time today, Brigid considered her mother. Physically, she could only be described as beautiful, perfection in grace and form. As the setting sun outside the window fell upon the polished nugget of amber set in Josephine's golden circlet, her very person seemed to radiate with light.

"Like the fairies' queen," Brigid said at last, and she meant it.

The archduchess was pleased. "You hear that, Livonia?" She smiled. "At least she knows what a proper woman should look like. We can take that for a positive sign."

"The Lady be praised," the old woman agreed.

Brigid said nothing. Though the subject of their conversation, she was not meant to participate. However, she was used to this. It was the same with Alan and his entourage. She may be present or even the focus of their gathering, they may speak a kind word to her or include her in one of their games, but it was always only for appearances. For all intents and purposes, she could have just as easily been substituted by a new tapestry or an exotic bird or even a small dog—something new to talk about, something new to gather around, and occasionally something new to haggle over. She was the ultimate conversation piece.

It was in those moments that Brigid chose to disappear, receding within her mind's eye to the frozen Wrathorn hilltop with its animals or a Caledonian ruin along the banks of the Imperial River in Andoch. Lately, she envisioned herself upon the deck of a Sorgund longship sailing along the coast. It was those moments that she longed for, escaping the confines of Blackstone Castle where her purpose was to sit, look pretty, and remain quiet as a…

Mouse.

"Brigid!" Josephine snapped. "And just when it seemed we were finally making progress. Do not slouch!"

Brigid snapped to attention. "I'm sorry, Mother."

"How, my darling girl, do you ever expect to attract a man with such poor posture?" Brigid's mother scolded. "You're sixteen. There are some girls your age who are already married and having babies. Holy St. Aiden, why can you not learn to sit straight?"

"I'm sorry," she said, though she could not help but be thankful that she was not one of those girls.

"Brigid, my dove, watch me," the archduchess returned to her seat, her back rigidly straight, a delighted smile upon her bright lips. "Now look at my breasts. When you sit with proper posture, it thrusts out your chest and makes your bust appear that much larger. Do you see?"

Brigid nodded, though she could feel herself blushing.

"At last, some color in your cheeks." Josephine sighed. "I should embarrass you more often." She continued her lesson. "Darling, hear me. Men love only with their eyes, and if you can fool their eyes, you can fool their hearts. Now I know that you're young and you're still growing, but for now, it does not hurt to rely upon deception. Do you understand?"

"Yes, Mother."

"Good," she said, "but I had better not look over at you tonight and see you slouching."

"No, Mother."

"And for pity's sake, laugh from time to time, or at the very least smile. You can't expect young Reid to fancy you for long if you don't make at least some show of interest."

"Yes, Mother."

"Hold his hand, smile when he speaks, laugh at his jokes, and if no one is watching and he should try to, for the Lady's sake, let him kiss you." Josephine shook her head in exasperation. "Holy St. Aiden, Livonia, this girl! Your title will buy you a lot, my dove, but if you act like a dead fish around every handsome young man who comes your way, that pride of yours will only serve to tie you to a fat, old, and ugly one!" She sighed and glanced out of the window. "Now it's time enough for us to go."

"Yes, Mother."

Josephine led Brigid and Livonia down the spiraling stair from their apartments atop the keep all the way to the first-floor hallway that led to the rear entry of the great hall. As they drew nearer, the sound of laughter flittered in the air, filling Josephine with effervescent excitement and Brigid with darker dread. She had come to hate feasts and feasting; the food was often far too rich for her taste and far more than she could ever stomach. The wine flowed freely, transforming even the more tolerable members of the gentry into a slobbering pack of licentious sots, and perhaps worst of all was the continuous commentary Brigid would endure while Josephine publicly decried her daughter's many faults—at least until the undivided attention of the company's most handsome, rich, and powerful men muddled the archduchess enough for her to forget that she had ever become a mother.

Yet as much as she might dislike it, Brigid knew that she was trapped. For tonight marked the first night of Harvestide, the thirteenth month of the Termainian calendar, and though for the peasants working the land, this meant only twenty-eight more days of backbreaking labor until the Feast of the Father on an extra day, the twenty-ninth, for the nobles who owned the few fertile lands among Dwerin's rocky soil, the whole month was a time of celebration, to enjoy the fruits of their tenants' tireless efforts convincing crops to grow.

When Josephine entered the hall, the assembly stood in her honor. Even the Sheriff, ensconced in the grandeur of his office, bowed his head in a show of grand deference as he helped her to the central chair at the high table. At once, Alan rushed forth to wrest a flagon of wine from a passing servant to fill his aunt's goblet while the remainder of the gathered nobility looked on with sycophantic envy. After the great lady had been seated, Brigid entered alone and made her way unnoticed to the vacant chair at her mother's right hand. As she approached, the young Reid, positioned conspicuously at her right, forced himself to look away from the glory of the archduchess and hurriedly helped Brigid to her seat.

"My lady," he whispered, pursing his wet lips to kiss the back of her hand.

"Thank you," Brigid said quietly, though she neither meant it nor was she sure that it was the proper reply.

"You look beautiful," Reid told her. "Just like your mother. I swear it is the sun and the moon between the two of you!"

Truer words were never spoken, Brigid thought, though, to the young man, she simply said, "Thank you."

The young man smiled and fixed her with a meaningful gaze. "They say the day has its virtues," he said. "Though there are also many pleasant things about the night."

Brigid smiled as her mother had instructed but said nothing. Something about the look in his eye sent a shiver of anxiety down her back, and for the first time that she could remember, she felt relieved when her uncle raised a hand to speak.

Darren Beinn was not a large man in either height or girth; however, his mere presence seemed to stir in others a vague measure of uneasiness, an unspoken suggestion of the consequences of his displeasure. The Sheriff's hair and pointed beard were as dark as Brigid's, though they lacked the luminous sheen of her raven tresses, and in its place, his bore the thin coating of grease that also marked his son. He was dressed all in black striped with gold but for a thin cloth of gold mantle lined with fur. Around his neck, he wore a long gold chain bearing the medallion of his office, and on his right hand, the archduke's signet ring had been placed for safekeeping. As he gazed out over the great hall, his lips pulled back slowly, twisting with reluctance into a tight leer. It was the same ghastly grin of self-satisfaction that Alan often wore, though with more than twenty years of practice and the weight of real authority. One smile from Uncle Darren was enough to remind Brigid why he was the one of her father's brothers, whom she had always feared the most.

"My dear family, friends, and loyal retainers," Darren Beinn began, "on this, the first night of Harvestide, let us count ourselves lucky to be in the presence of such radiance as our beloved Archduchess Josephine. Truly, the memory of her beauty on this night will be enough to warm the hearts of many throughout the entire winter season!" Alan's father nodded ceremoniously toward Brigid's mother and raised his glass. "My lady," he said, "to you!"

Those gathered in the hall cheered in agreement as the guardsmen bounced the butts of their pikes upon the floor. Josephine blessed them with a smile and raised her own glass. "Thank you, my Lord Sheriff! As always, your presence and your words fill us with delight," she said and led the congregation as they drank.

Brigid was never surprised by the fondness men had for her mother nor by the fact that Josephine was often just as fond of them. Even before the archduke's death, Brigid could recall her mother being visited throughout the year by a steady flow of amorous suitors, though they often hid their true intentions beneath the guise of state affairs or behind the presence of their noble wives. The lucky ones would leave Blackstone with satisfaction while others the archduchess spurned would leave in tears. And when Brigid's father returned from time to time after his long campaigns fighting Grantis over the borderlands in the south, those same noble suitors would appear again, hoping to curry favor with the man that many of them had already gifted with a pair of horns. Whether Archduke Danford ever suspected his wife or cared, Brigid never knew. There had never been much love between her parents, and with the exception perhaps of the two occasions on which they conceived Brigid and another stillborn son, Josephine and Danford spent their nights miles apart. Perhaps it was the border war that parted them, perhaps it what something else; however, when news of the archduke's death reached Blackstone, it seemed the passing of a saint for all of Josephine's ostentatious weeping.

After the toast, the servants filed in bearing dishes laden with traditional harvest fare: roast beef, mutton, and venison; great slabs of fresh ham; stuffed chickens, ducks, and other fowl; an assortment of local vegetables, potatoes, and fresh fish caught that morning in the nearby mountain streams; breads, pies, puddings, and pastries of all sizes. Truly, the peasant farmers and the servant cooks had clearly outdone themselves, and if doing so had not become an expectation, the nobility might have thanked them.

When the servant brought forth slices of the roast, Reid leaned forward and used his dagger to cut Brigid's meat. As always, he made an effort to be closer to her than was necessarily required, but before she could subtly lean away, Brigid felt the weight of her mother's gaze and instead sat still as Reid's arm lightly brushed against her shoulder.

"How gallant," Josephine observed, "what a joy it is to see that the finer qualities are still present, nay thriving, in a young knight."

Reid blushed scarlet. "The joy is mine, your grace," he said.

"And so humble," the archduchess beamed, "you know, Sir Reid, Brigid and I were just discussing your finer qualities this morning actually, and I must say, you made my shy daughter positively overflow with descriptions of your valor."

Brigid felt her heart shrivel just as she knew Reid's was growing bolder. Beneath the table, she felt her mother's fine white fingers grip her hand implicitly; however, as meek as her mother might think of her, Brigid refused to join Josephine in her simpering. *He's not even been knighted yet,* Brigid thought bitterly. *He's not* Sir *Anything.*

At last, the archduchess was forced to fill her daughter's awkward silence. "Do you see, Sir Reid?" She grinned. "You leave her speechless."

Reid returned Josephine's smile, though his eyes, Brigid noticed, were not on her teeth. "Then I suppose I should be glad for it," he said. "Lady Brigid is very beautiful, your grace, though I cannot say that I am much surprised considering her mother."

Josephine laughed aloud, and a few of the men nearby fell silent to savor the sound. "What a silver tongue you've got, my young cavalier!" she exclaimed as Reid's cheeks turned even redder. "Perhaps I had best be more careful after all leaving my daughter in the hands of such a handsome man as you!" She winked. "Or perhaps not."

For the first time in her life, Brigid was thankful for Alan. From the other end of the high table, Alan's angry shout at one of the servants spared Brigid any more of her mother's attention as Josephine turned to watch with quiet amusement while her nephew lambasted the poor man with his forked tongue. Brigid pitied the unfortunate soul but could not help but feel grateful for his timely blunder, spilling a thimbleful of wine on Alan's cuff. Had she any money, she would have given the man a gold piece.

Reid, too, had become distracted as, on his right, Donal and his father had engaged him in a conversation about the proper way to whet a sword. With her sudden but, no doubt, brief moment of freedom, Brigid pushed the food around on her plate and quietly withdrew into the recesses of her own mind, escaping the feast, escaping the company, escaping the castle entirely.

The moon shone brightly in the sky above while the waves lapped gently against the sides of the longship. From her position in the stern, Brigid gazed across the main deck at the long, curling neck of the figurehead mounted at the bow. Its face, carved into the likeness of the Sorgundian Sea Dragon, gazed menacingly out across the midnight sea, its eyes seeming to smolder in its wooden face.

Brigid let the sound of the water soothe away the anxiety, the embarrassment of the outside world and let the cool ocean breeze toy playfully with her hair, drawing her further into the sanctity of her private world. She gripped the wheel, eyed the star men called the Lady's Lantern shining directly above her in the center of the sky, and all of a sudden, the single, enormous sail of the longship unfurled, and the oars began to row on their own accord.

As the dragonhead cut through the water, it sent forth a fine mist of spray, at once cold and invigorating. Brigid gazed to starboard at some unknown impulse and was surprised to see a pod of dolphins, Galdorn's Vassals as they were sometimes known, leaping alongside her, keeping pace, their chirps of laughter filling her breast with joy. They raced into the open waters, far from any sight of land, as the moonlight lit the white cordage rigging the sails like silver.

At last, the pod pulled ahead, and Brigid acknowledged their victory with a bow and a wave of her hand. The leader of the group leaped high in the air, rolled into a flip, and landed with a soft splash before lifting his tail high out of the water to return her salute. As the dolphins swam on into the distance, Brigid watched them go until a quiet flutter from above brought her gaze up to the top of the single sail's spar. It was the falcon, her falcon, the one with the golden eyes.

Brigid watched for a moment, gripped by a quiet uncertainty. Not once had the strange bird appeared within her daydreams since the last time, the dream on the snow-covered hilltop. Remembering that day, she stepped out onto the deck and, again, bowed low in respect. Without hesitation, the falcon returned the greeting, regarded her with its golden eyes, and fluttered down beside her to land upon the ship's wheel. Brigid stood motionless, amazed to be suddenly so near it. She examined the fine patterns of its speckled feathers and the golden light that emanated from its eyes. She slowly raised her hand as if to touch it, when without warning, the strange creature looked at her and spoke.

Mouse...

A strange sensation woke her from her reverie, and it took a moment to realize that Reid had suddenly placed his hand upon hers where it rested on her lap. With a shudder, she sat up sharply and, without thinking, thrust his hand away with a slap. She glanced over at once only to meet his startled gaze, alive with mingling anger, shame, and doubt. He quickly turned his head away and did not speak to her for the remainder of the meal, preferring instead to hide in conversation with Donal and his father.

When the potboys finally made their rounds to clear the empty plates and platters, a handful of serving men arrived to move aside the center tables and clear the room. Together, the sated guests took to their feet, and a trio of bards ushered in, strumming a merry tune. In the center of it all, Josephine descended from the high table to dance with the other noble ladies of the court while all eyes watched, enraptured. Her skin shone with a brilliant flush, and Brigid felt a wash of relief, knowing that the archduchess had now drunk enough to forget her. After the first song ended, the Sheriff and a few of his most trusted retainers withdrew to converse in the conspicuous privacy of the hall's eastern wall, for no holiday could be void of politics, while Alan and the rest of the younger knights and noblemen called for more wine before rejoining the ladies in their dancing. Reid's lower lip stuck out sullenly in resentment and dejection, avoiding even the slightest glance anywhere in Brigid's general vicinity. Instead, he followed behind Alan and Donal as they followed the other girls in the *saltarello*.

And suddenly, all at once, Brigid realized that she was alone, utterly alone, and forgotten. Not even the servants seemed to notice as she sat slouching in her chair, watching the company at their play. Yet instead of feeling lonely or isolated, for the first time all evening, she felt free—free of the unwelcome attentions of the court, free of her required posturing, free to be herself. If she wanted to, she thought, she might slip out of the hall altogether—back to the safety of her room, out into the moonlight of the yard, anywhere—and no one would ever even notice. All she had to do was throw caution to the wind and try.

However, even at the thought, her blood ran cold with anxiety. She had been trained at an early age to know her place and to do as she was told—not only by the archduchess herself but by a steady stream of nurses, nannies, tutors, and her mother's ever-present handmaid, Livonia. Once, when she was only five years old, while Josephine was attending to one of her many suitors, Brigid stole away from their apartments in the keep and made her way down to the kennels to see a new litter of puppies. For the rest of the afternoon, she sat happily beside the nursing mother, petting the pups' soft fur and cradling them in her arms. That night, when she returned to her room, smelling of dogs and hay, Josephine was furious, and as punishment, she gave orders that every one of the puppies was to be drowned. However, the lesson Brigid learned from that experience was not the one her mother intended regarding proper conduct and noble duty, but rather that living beneath the shadow of the archduchess, she would never truly be free.

Thinking now on the memory, Brigid was filled with a sudden longing to escape, and the bard's songs took on an eerie, manic quality as Josephine and the others danced wildly in circles, laughing, singing, and shouting aloud in the tumult of their revelry. *They'll never even know*, she thought. *Not one of them will ever notice…*

For the rest of that song and another, Brigid continued to debate with herself, watching as her mother leaned on the arm of a handsome young man and called for another cask to be brought up from the cellars. Only then, as the servants rushed to obey the archduchess's command, did Brigid finally make her move.

She was halfway across the hall before she realized that she had been right; not a single person noticed as she slipped from her seat at the high table or even raised an eye, for they were far too busy carousing to detect the pale shadow that passed so swiftly before their eyes. Even Josephine was too busy to notice her daughter pass within arm's reach, simpering as salaciously as she was at the other men around her, far too focused on such amorous matters to distinguish the passage of one tiny mouse.

Four large braziers lit the entryway to the keep, but with the exception of the guardsmen playing cards in the alcove, it was empty. Brigid scurried quietly along the edge of the room, rushing past dusty tapestries bearing the mark of the Anvil of Dwerin. Her limbs tingled, and she smiled, drunk with the exhilaration of her adventure. She had just about reached the heavy wooden doors to the courtyard when, all of a sudden, she heard footsteps clattering upon the flagstones behind her. Quickly, she slipped behind one of the tapestries and held her breath as Alan and Donal swaggered out of the great hall, sweaty, red-faced, and laughing while Reid tramped gloomily after them.

"You're right, Alan," Donal cried, falling back against the wall and sliding down to sit on the floor. "I can hardly look at your aunt without feeling my blood get hot."

"I told you." Alan laughed. "She does herself up well for a feast."

"I'll say, and I always thought her fine anyway."

"So she is." Alan leered. "And you know what the best part about her is?"

"I think I'd have a hard time deciding." Donal grinned. "But tell me."

"We're not related by blood," Alan said smugly. "Which means it would be perfectly acceptable for me to, as we archers might say, draw back her bow to fit her with my arrow?"

Donal made a great show of laughter, and so Alan carried on, convinced of his own cleverness. "Were I a swordsman, though"—he smirked—"I might just run her through instead."

Again Donal erupted into brutish guffaws, though still, Reid remained silent.

"And what's wrong with you, good Sir Knight? Still pining over Lady Frigid?"

Reid turned his head away sullenly.

"Oh, bloody St. Aiden." Alan sighed. "Would you stop looking so morose? How many times do I have to tell you?" He leaped lightly along the floor and threw a consoling arm around Reid's shoulders. "My father and yours have already settled the matter, with the archduchess party to the bargain. Mark me, by winter's end, the fresh fruit of luscious Lady Josephine's sweet, sultry thighs will be squirming about beneath you in the bridal bed." He grinned. "But if you insist on sulking about like a weeping, washerwoman, by the Brethren, next time you find yourself alone with her, simply thrust her to the wall and take what time will reward you with anyway!"

Reid sighed and folded his arms. "Alan, I'm not in the mood for your wordplay," he said. "And I'm not so sure you should say such things about your cousin."

"Fine. No wordplay. In any case, I should rest my tongue for Lady Josephine later tonight." He laughed. "Though as for Lady Frigid, I say have at her, whether she likes it or not. It would be good for both of you. Trust me. There's nothing worse than a woman who doesn't know her business, right, Donal?"

"As you say, Alan."

"If you don't break her in a bit, then you're only setting yourself up for misery." He let go of Reid's shoulder and paced back at an unsteady totter to continue his lecture. "Honestly, let me speak to you from my own experience. Look at Caryn or...Nora...or... whomever. Just look at any one of them! You get them underneath you, and all they want to do is wiggle and giggle. Warlock's balls! If they weren't so willing, we wouldn't even bother with them!" He paused to steady himself against the wall, "For, let me tell you. There's a place in town just outside of the walls where the women *really* know their craft! Each one is an artisan, a master in the Guild of Love! Am I right, Donal?"

"That you are, Alan!"

"Of course, I am." Alan laughed. "Though, trust me, it couldn't hurt to at least have a go at Lady Frigid just so you know what you're getting into. Try her once, and if her ice doesn't melt, well then, keep her for her title, and I'll take you to the place where you can forget the rest."

Reid hung his head, "I don't know."

"Oh, come now." Alan sighed. "Yes, she's bony and pale, and my father and I have often thought her somewhat simple, but really, you'll only need to tumble with her to get a baby in her belly, and then after that, you can rut with whoever you want."

Behind the tapestry, Brigid's blood burned with the raging inferno of the Abyss. Years of repressed resentment and suppressed scorn brought bitter, angry tears to her eyes while her mind filled suddenly with images of violence, of bloody carnage as she slew Alan, Reid, Donal, her uncle, her mother, and all the rest a hundred times over in a hundred different ways. Her rage grew so intense that in her anguish, she began to fear herself more than she feared any of them.

At length, Reid sighed heavily. "Let's go back," he said. "We'll be missed."

"Fine," Alan said. "My throat's gone dry again with all this talk as it is, but I want you to remember what I said."

Brigid listened as Alan, Donal, and Reid staggered back to the party, back to the assembly of her enemies. For another few moments, she hid in silence behind the dusty tapestry, rubbing the stinging tears from her eyes and trying to stifle her shuddering sobs. *I am a mouse*, she whispered in despair. *A mouse trapped all alone in a castle full of cats, a prisoner in my own home...*

And without warning, an idea sprang forth from deep within her that at once tempered her anger and made her smile with grim resolution. She rubbed at her eyes one last time to stop the flow of tears and sprang silently from concealment to traverse the flagstones to the main doors. Away in the alcove, the guards were still at their game, and as always, not one of them noticed her as she ran out under cover of darkness to the inner ward.

Outside, the night was quiet and still. At the gateway to the middle ward, she spied another two guardsmen at their posts; however, they were far enough away not to notice her as she scurried along the western wall to the southwest tower.

A single wall sconce lit the tower's interior, though not a soul was to be seen. However, from the far side of the room, the sound of muffled laughter spilled softly from an adjacent room. More guards, she guessed, were taking a break from the monotony of their duties while their betters were busy dancing and drinking. Regardless, Brigid took their absence as a blessing and hurried on, fueled by reckless abandon, to the long winding stair. It was completely dark above owing to the absent guards, and guided by the moonlight, Brigid stealthily climbed the staircase to the bolted doorway and stopped.

Frigid, am I? she thought. *If I'm cold, it's only that which you made me.* With one last bracing breath, she lifted the bolt, pushed open the door, and gave herself over to the utter blackness of the cell, shutting the door behind her. Her foot struck something lying on the floor that sounded like metal clinking against metal, but otherwise, there was utter silence.

"Hello?" she whispered softly to the gloom, "Hello, Prisoner?"

In answer, a sudden flash of light scattered the darkness, and the oil lamp on the table flared to life. Seated comfortably in one of the chairs, the prisoner grinned at her while the lamp's small flame cast the long shadow of his dangling chains against the far wall. He was thinner than when last she saw him and bore the marks of even greater abuse; however, his golden eyes still smoldered in their sockets like those of the falcon in her dreams.

"Hello, Mouse," he said softly. "I knew you would return." He motioned languidly toward the second vacant chair. "Come. Let us talk a bit."

CHAPTER 7:
THE WRATH OF A FARMER

"What do you mean you don't know?"

Geoffrey rested the blade of his shovel against the wall of the hole and wiped the sweat from his brow. He shrugged. "I just don't know."

Oliver sighed noisily and plunged his shovel beneath the surface of the muddy water that puddled around their feet and lifted a great clump of dirt into the bucket that sat between them.

"Okay, Nickolas!"

At once, the bucket rose swiftly above them only to return moments later void of its former slop. Without a word, Geoffrey took up his shovel again and went back to work. Oliver, however, was not yet through with his questions.

"You don't find it odd?"

"What?"

"You know."

Geoffrey breathed a heavy sigh and poured another load of dirt into the bucket. "Of course I do, but sitting around thinking about it's not going to get my crops ready for Harvestide anymore than it's going to dig this well."

Oliver shook his head. "To be able to read just like that!" He snapped his fingers. "You say Cousin Martin even tested you on it too?"

"He made me read a passage from *The Scrolls of the Hierophants*."

"And you did?"

"Word for word."

"Remarkable!"

Together, the farmers finished another load of mud, and while Oliver sent the bucket rising upward to the surface, Geoffrey twisted his back and stretched against the stiffness. "I wouldn't call it remarkable," he muttered. "Lots of men read."

"Aye, by learning"—Oliver grinned—"how many others you heard of can do it after a night out in the forest? I don't know what's more unbelievable. That or the part about surviving a bandit attack unscathed."

"Not unscathed."

"What? That scar on your belly? The one you said healed all on its own? Truly, Brother Tengale himself must favor you, my friend."

"Well, he has a strange way of showing it." Geoffrey sighed. "My horse stolen, the money gone, and now the well gone dry..."

"Aye, but you're alive. Your children are healthy, your family is safe, and we'll be harvesting the wheat any day now."

"Except for what we lost to the field mice."

"We *always* lose some to the field mice, and the birds, and the blight," Oliver said. "You know, you should learn to count your blessings."

Geoffrey stomped on the blade of his shovel, levering a heavy clump of mud out of the water and into the bucket. "I just have a bad feeling," he said. "It's just...it don't none of it seem right. I mean... what if it's a curse?"

Oliver added another shovelful of mud to the bucket with a plop. "Bah!" he grunted. "You're bloody mad."

Geoffrey sighed. "I mean it."

"Rubbish."

Geoffrey let the tip of his shovel dip into the water with a loud splash and leaned against the handle. "Fine, you don't believe me? Then listen to this," he said. "Every night since I got back from Granmouth, I've hardly slept a wink because every time I close my eyes, I see nothing but horrible visions of bandits and battles and people of all sorts being hacked to pieces. It's like having to relive that night on the road again and again and again." He paused and shook his head. "Last night, I dreamed I was walking into a town with a nice little tavern, big red rooster on its sign! Pleasantest looking place in all the world! So I open the door to go inside, and who is there to greet me? An entire village's worth of corpses! Men, women, children even! Some of them were missing arms. Others were missing legs. Some of them burned black as pitch!

It was horrible! Dreadful! When I woke up screaming so loud, Annabel nearly fell out of bed!"

"Geoffrey," Oliver said gently, "it was just a dream."

"Well, it didn't feel like one," Geoffrey said. "It felt real." He picked up his spade and, with disgruntled fervor, resumed his digging. For a long moment, Oliver remained silent until at last, he thrust his shovel into the mud and breathed another sigh. "Well," he said, "it's almost midday. I say we take a break for a bit and let the boys have a go. I could use something to eat."

Geoffrey added one last load to the bucket, tugged at the rope to signal Nickolas, and nodded. "So be it."

The sun was directly overhead when they sat down beside the diggings and lowered Oliver's elder sons down into the hole to take their turn. A few feet away, Oliver's youngest son Erik and Geoffrey's oldest boy Karl had begun sorting through the mud and dirt to collect rocks for the base of the well. Exhausted from a long morning of digging, Oliver lay down on his back to stretch and called out to them. "Since it looks like you boys have collected enough stones," he said, "maybe after lunch you wouldn't mind walking the fields to hunt some of the mice?"

The boys exchanged a happy glance. "Is it all right, Dad?" Karl asked, his brown cow eyes alight with excitement.

Geoffrey smiled. *Thank the Lady they take after their mother*, he thought. "Of course," he said at last, rustling his son's hair, "Kill enough, and you just might save the whole village from starving."

"Can I use that club you found?" He grinned. "Oakheart."

At a tug from below, Geoffrey slowly drew the bucket up from the hole and tossed the muddy contents out with a loud slop. "Son, I think you'd do better just using a stick," he said, lowering the bucket back down into the hole. "That club's head is so big around. You're likely to smash more stalks of wheat than you will mouse heads."

Karl sighed with disappointment. "All right, Dad."

"All right, Dad," Geoffrey mimicked, rustling his son's hair with a dirty hand. "Have fun."

"Come on, Erik!" Karl called as the two boys ran off.

Oliver sat up and squinted in the sun, watching them go. "It's hard to believe we were their age once."

Once more, Geoffrey pulled up the bucket and lowered it down again. "Spend more time with my father." He laughed. "In no time at all, you'll feel a beardless boy again." He dropped his voice in imitation. "'No, no, my son. What do you think you're doing? You don't plant crops that close together! I know I'm blind, but is that a turnip, or is that your head?'"

"Old Amos has his charms." Oliver laughed. "Last time I saw him, he told me I'd grown much more handsome since the last time we met. Back then, he said he could still see my face, and now he couldn't see it at all!"

"That's my father," Geoffrey said, shaking his head. He stared off across the fields of wheat, nearly ripe for the Harvestide threshing, when suddenly something caught his eye. "What's this now?" he asked aloud.

"Huh?"

"The boys are coming back."

Oliver held up a hand to shield his eyes from the sun. "Is that Oscar with them too?"

"Looks like."

Oliver called down into the hole. "Hey, boys, hold on. Climb up for a moment."

Together, the two farmers helped the young men out of the unfinished well just as Karl, Erik, and a cluster of other men arrived armed with farming tools of every shape and size. Geoffrey felt a cold shiver run through him as from some new instinct. Something was wrong. Their expressions told him that much, but what? He wiped the mud from his hands onto his trousers.

"What is it?" he asked.

Oscar's eyes darted around the field, and when he spoke, his voice was a whisper.

"It's Damon," he said. "Raleigh says he saw men hanging around his house. Men no one's ever seen before. Men who came on horses."

"How many?"

"Three."

"Bandits?" Oliver asked.

Damon's farm was the furthest along the western end of Pyle. If the bandits from the forest north of the trade road had come east, his farm would have been the first they met.

Oscar shrugged. "Don't know for certain, but Raleigh says they were armed."

Geoffrey chewed his lip. "Are you sure that there are only three of them?"

"I don't know. Daren and Raleigh are still down watching them now. Luther and Garth are running to tell Cousin Martin and the northern farms. Ronalt and I came south, and these others followed along."

"Has anyone seen Damon or Linda?" Oliver asked. "Or their children?"

The men exchanged empty glances with one another and shook their heads, "No."

A spark of fury kindled within Geoffrey's breast, and to his great surprise, his blood began to boil. It was as if, while digging the well, instead of uncovering a shallow pool, they had somehow tapped into the ocean. He turned back to the two younger boys. "Karl, Erik, run to our house and bring me the shield and the club. Go quickly."

"What do you think we should do, Geoffrey?" Oscar asked.

Geoffrey was torn. Part of him wanted to tell them all to run, to lock themselves in their cottages and pray to the Brethren that they would be spared. However, another part—the part that had sent the boys to fetch the weapons—felt very different. It was the same part of him that somehow knew that something was wrong. It was the part of him that somehow knew that Damon was already dead.

He avoided any answer until the boys returned carrying Oakheart and the Acorn. With a long, slow breath, he slipped his hand into the leather bindings of the shield and gripped the handle of the cudgel.

"Run home now and see to your mothers," he told them, but to the assembly of men said, "Let's go have a look."

Together, they crossed the fields heading westward, and by the time they reached the center of the village, Geoffrey had somehow emerged as the leader. Oliver stood steadfastly at his right hand, and though silent, his face burned with questions about what his friend had planned. At length, they met Raleigh and the other men crouched low behind a rickety fence on the outskirts of Damon's cottage.

Geoffrey glanced at Raleigh's thin, bearded face. The man's skin had gone ghostly pale, and he slowly shook his head from side to side with anxiety. From the direction of Damon's cottage, the farmers could hear the sound of ribald laughter and smashing pottery. In structure, the house was the same as any of the others in town: a long, low building crafted of waddle and daub, the interior of which would be separated into two rooms by a single, thin wall. The front door, though mostly shut, hung crookedly on its hinges, and to the left of the cottage, three skinny nags were tied to iron spikes thrust into the ground.

"What should we do?"

"What *can* we do?"

"Perhaps we should wait for Cousin Martin?"

"And then what?"

Without a word, Geoffrey climbed over the fence and made his way to the front of the cottage. He glanced back at the frightened farmers and Oliver's look of alarm. "What are you doing?" his friend whispered harshly, but Geoffrey did not hear him. With a deep breath, he opened the door.

Inside, he found three men clad in moldy leather lamellar seated around Damon's table, an assortment of wineskins and hunks of food before them. One man was short and bearded with dark stains in the whiskers around his mouth. Another wore a small steel cap, and a long scar ran from his right ear to his eye. The last was an older balding man with yellow eyes. In the corner near the hearth, Damon's wife Linda stood expressionless, mildly turning a piece of meat on a spit over a small fire. Her hair looked as if a small animal had been living in it, and one whole side of her dress had been torn to her waist, exposing a heavy sagging breast. Her nose was crusted with dried blood, and bright purple bruises stood out in blotches on her skin. On the floor in the corner, Damon's body lay in a glistening pool of blood. There was no sign of the two children, though the door to the second room was shut.

When Geoffrey's eyes met the bandits' glares, time stood still as the four men gazed at one another with mingling expressions of wonder, anger, doubt, and fear. The heat of the fireplace was warm against his skin. His knuckles turned white, tightening their grip around the cudgel, and all at once, time came flooding back.

In a flash, the bandit with the scar stood and made to draw his sword, but Geoffrey threw him back, bashing him in the neck with the edge of the targe, and followed through with a heavy blow from the cudgel. Since the age of ten, Geoffrey had worked the lands of the Spade, and after thirty years more, the hard, physical labor had made him very strong—stronger than he, himself, even knew. When Oakheart struck the scarred man along the crown of the skull, blood and brain matter splattered the cottage wall with a resounding *crack!*

Immediately, the bearded bandit drew a dagger and leaped to his feet, throwing himself over the tabletop in rage at the plowman, but again, Geoffrey drove the red acorn back into the man's face, and as he fell prone, flattened his head with the club.

At the sight of the sudden, violent deaths of his companions, the bald man went white and ran for the door. However, in his attempt to dodge a blow from Geoffrey's cudgel, he tripped and fell into the grass just outside of the doorway. Oliver and the other farmers readied their spades while the bald man groaned in a frenzied panic, and as they watched on, Geoffrey returned silently through the doorway and used his boot to roll the man onto his back. The final bandit gazed up at Geoffrey with his yellow eyes, and his face twisted in horror and fear as the plowman slowly raised Oakheart high in the air. In an instant, Geoffrey's mind flashed images of all the sufferings he had known and those that his fellow villagers had endured: the sack of the caravan to Damon's family now to his own mother's death when he was still but a child. His stomach burned at the endless trail of injustices, the violence inflicted upon the weak by the strong. Enough was enough. He brought Oakheart down and planted the yellow-eyed face into the ground.

"No more," he whispered softly. "No more."

For a long moment, the other men of the village stood together, struck dumb in astonishment, when, suddenly, Cousin Martin and the men of the northern farms appeared. Speechless with wonder, Martin gazed at Geoffrey, whose eyes still had not left the bandit's broken head. However, with only a moment's pause, the cousin hurried past through the open door of Damon's house. All at once, the spell was broken, and the other men were able to move. Some followed Martin inside. Others stood around in disbelief. Oliver ran to his friend's side.

"Geoffrey!"

At long last, Geoffrey turned away from his red handiwork, blinked his eyes, and let the club and shield slip free from his arms.

"Geoffrey! Are you all right?"

Slowly the farmer reached up and wiped a thick glaze of sweat and splattered blood from his brow and wiped it on his trousers. "The children," he said wearily, "where are the children?"

As if in answer, Cousin Martin returned, leading Linda from the house, followed closely by Oscar carrying Damon's daughter and infant son. Raleigh covered Linda in his tunic, and together, they followed Martin away from the scene of carnage.

"They're safe, Geoffrey. You saved them," Oliver told him. "Are you all right?"

Geoffrey breathed a heavy sigh. "I don't know," he said.

CHAPTER 8:
THE SHAME OF DEFEAT

After the battle, the light cavalry crossed the bloody sea of corpses that once filled the ranks of Dermont's army while, from far across the field, the soldiers of the enemy encampment watched on in silence. Although Bel's plan to intercept the enemy reserves had been a great success—defeating a force five times larger than his own—the victory felt empty, for as they rode away in retreat, he counted nearly ten Valendian dead upon the battlefield for each fallen Gasparan. What could have possibly happened to have led to such a rout? After five generations of fighting, the war had seemed so close to being over, yet once again, it had slipped away like light snow upon the breeze. He wondered now if the sons and daughters of a sixth generation would be doomed to perish in the name of his long-dead ancestors' lust for power. Truly, the Brethren were punishing Montevale; brother should never make war on brother. Whether two horses were divided or one reunited, peace could be the only answer. However, in light of his most recent defeat, it was unlikely that Dermont would feel the same.

The men and horses of the light cavalry were weary. Not only had they fought for their lives against a much larger force, but they had traveled all through the night in order to do so. After seeing to the travel requirements of the wounded, it took another few hours for Bel's riders to finally reach the remaining Valendian soldiers in their flight through the valleys of the southwest. Now the horses were beginning to drag with fatigue, and men nearly fell from their saddles from exhaustion. Bel's men needed rest, and soon. He had not even had time to clean the blood and mud from his gear, leaving it up to rain to do it for him. As Bel left his riders at the rear of the column and rode off to find his brother, he tried to estimate the number of survivors. Of the nearly eleven hundred infantry and archers that marched across the Bloodline afoot, less than two thousand were limping back, most of whom Bel recognized by their captains and their banners as having belonged to the reserve. Of the twelve hundred armored knights that rode north, more than half that number rode south; however, like Lord Giles Pronet the Princox, as Lilia had named him, the only stains that marred their tabards were from the rain. Bel's green eyes burned with silent fury as he searched for Dermont, but the general was nowhere to be found. At length, he ignored the hails of the knights at the head of the column and rode back to one of the archer divisions of the reserve.

Beneath a brown banner bearing a trio of black arrows, Sir Norton Wherling, the Standing Stone, rode amount alongside the bowmen under his command. His frizzled gray hair curled out from beneath the brim of his rusted kettle helm. The old man's leathery face drooped gloomily from the back of his mare. Though a knight of a noble family, the Wherling lands had never earned enough for the aging lord to afford the arms and armor of the heavy cavalry. However, what Sir Norton lacked in funds, he made up for in mettle.

"Prince Beledain"—Sir Norton nodded and tipped his helm as Bel rode alongside him—"I'm glad to see you and your men made it out alive." His voice dropped. "There's many as were not so lucky."

"So I see," Bel said, "what happened? Where is my brother?"

"Forgive me, my lord, but I cannot answer the first question since I am not quite certain myself," the veteran replied stiffly. "As for the second, your brother rode on ahead nearly an hour ago with three hundred heavy horse riding with him."

"Three hundred *with* him?" the prince repeated. "But it looks as if a full six hundred still ride at the head of the column."

"Seven."

"Seven hundred?" Bel shook his head. "How did we lose nine thousand infantry yet not a single heavy knight?"

"You'll have to ask Prince Dermont, my lord," Sir Norton said. "I remember watching as the infantry were sent in to attack. At first, they seemed to be gaining ground because the Gasparns suddenly began to fall back.

However, when the men were sent on to pursue, they ventured too far from the cavalry and from us in the reserves. Meanwhile, the Gasparan heavy horse rode round to flank our infantry from the side and tilted for the charge just as the Gasparns fleeing on foot turned to counterattack. It was a slaughter. Shortly thereafter, we were ordered to retreat."

Bel ground his teeth. "Why didn't Dermont send our horse against theirs?"

"I cannot say, my lord. It is not my place to question the will of a prince and a general."

Bel remained quiet. *Dermont, what have you done?* he wondered.

"Who is in command?" he asked after a moment.

"Lord Harren, I believe. He had command of the reserves." Sir Norton paused. "Though as prince, I should think it would be you…"

"Thank you," Bel said, ignoring the older man's implication, and rode off to the head of the column, steeling himself to face the awkward conventions of court. Beneath him, however, he could sense Igno's weariness.

"We'll rest soon," he whispered. "I promise."

Without Briden and the standard, it took a moment for the armored horsemen to recognize him as more than a common messenger. A few nodded cordially or called a greeting, though most others simply ignored him or bent their helmeted heads to whisper some comment between them. Bel paid it no mind. Before assuming command of the light company, he had trained hard to be one of them; he could fight just as well in heavy plate and unseat nearly anyone in the joust. Yet war was much different from inside an iron shell, slower and more distant. It could easily make a man feel invincible and numb him to the realities of battle. Furthermore, commanding heavy cavalry meant commanding knights and nobles, men who most often achieved their positions as either sycophants or bullies. The former never had any will to fight, while the latter could not follow orders.

Lord Jarret Harren, leading the column in retreat, was both. The elder patriarch of a wealthy house, Lord Harren had risen to his position through a blend of courtly pandering and passive-aggressive intimidation. As Bel rode up, he realized once again from the lord's expression that he had not had time to clean the blood, mud, and war paint from himself after the battle, nor had he any time to see to his own shoulder wound. Harren's armor glimmered with gold highlights and silver tracery swirling intricate patterns along every plate and joint. Standing together side by side, they were a study in contrasts.

The lord greeted Bel with a practiced smile that masked not only his disgust at the prince's appearance but also his irritation at being assigned to what he most certainly viewed as an ignoble command.

"Why, Prince Beledain!" he exclaimed, feigning a mixture of surprise and delight. He slowed his little palfrey to a halt, and the entire column came to stop behind him. "Thank the Kinship that you have survived! Your brother and I feared for your safety."

"I am here," Bel said simply, "though I see that Dermont is not."

"Prince Dermont rode ahead to return to Tremontane Castle upon the Sires," Harren said, "though he left a message for you in hopes that you would return. Would you like to hear it?"

"Please."

"You are to return with all haste to meet him as soon as possible. He suggested that you gather an escort and ride ahead on your own and leave your men under my command."

"Thank you, Lord Harren," Bel said. "But my men are weary, and our horses are nearly spent."

"Of course," the smiling noble said. "However, if you'd like to be on your way, I'm certain that we can find other horses that are more rested."

Bel suppressed a sardonic grin. Some men of the light cavalry, Horn more than likely, Lilia for certain, would have knocked out a few of Lord Harren's teeth at the audacity of such a suggestion. "As generous as that offer is," Bel said politely, "my men need time to rest as well. By your leave, we would welcome the chance to do so."

The prospect of the prince requesting his leave in the sight of other knights in the column was too much for Lord Harren to refuse; however, he hesitated.

"Do you think it safe to stop so soon? Might the enemy not attempt to assault us further?"

Bel had considered that himself, wondering how far the Tower's gift of safe passage would extend. As they rode to catch up to the army, he had his three fastest riders, Lilia, Rallo, and a girl named Sparrow, hang back at intervals to wait and watch for any sign of pursuit. However, as far as they could tell, the

Gasparns had contented themselves with the blood that the Valendians paid in the field.

"I believe it is safe," he finally said, "though we will, of course, set watches."

"Ah yes," Harren nodded, "watchers! I suppose that is wise. Although..." The lord's lips spread with a sly grin as a sudden thought crossed his mind. "I give you my leave, Prince Beledain, and for what's more, I will do you one better," he said. "I will leave you Sir Norton Wherling and the remainder of the foot to act as your watchers while you rest. Meanwhile, I will ride on with my fellow horsemen as your brother requests. Should we reach him before you, I will tell him that the slower pace of the infantry has caused your delay."

Bel might have laughed. Though he would welcome the infantrymen as his "watchers," he recognized the nobleman's blatant cowardice and longing for the creature comforts awaiting for him at home. Perhaps sending the heavy horse would not have changed the tide of battle after all with so many men like Lord Harren who took the field that morning not to fight but rather to witness the spectacle of the war's end—to be able to say to their political rivals and simpering courtiers, "I was there!"

In any case, Bel simply nodded. "Thank you, my lord."

Harren inclined his head smugly and turned back to the column. "Heavy horse!" he shouted. "On me!"

Bel stood still as the knights and their retinues paraded by. They were certainly a sight to behold. When they had finally passed, however, and the remaining men of the infantry reached him, he called out to Sir Norton and raised a hand.

"Hold here, Sir Norton," he said, "Lord Harren had left you and the rest of the infantry under my command."

"Thank the Brethren," the older man said. "I'm your man, my lord."

"My men are weary, and our horses are nearly spent," Bel said. "Can I trust you to set watches while we take a few hours to rest?"

"Of course, sir. Leave it to me."

Bel nodded gratefully. As the veteran warrior began barking orders, he rode back to the rear of the column, where Val waited anxiously with his men.

"Make camp!" he shouted to them, "See to your horses and to the wounded. Then get some sleep. We'll move in a few hours' time if we're ready."

Sixteen bells had tarnished from silver to gold, and he would not risk any of the others—man or horse—in the name of expediency.

"Wendell," Bel added in an aside, "after you see to the wounded and you have a minute…"

"I'll make time, sir," Wendell replied.

"Don't on my account. See to the others first."

"Aye, sir."

For a time, Wendell had studied to become a cousin of the Kinship, and though incomplete, his limited training often served as the closest thing the light company had to a surgeon. Though he was wounded himself by the Snow Bear's blade, Bel could manage enough on his own for now. It was for the men who could no longer ride their horses but, instead, dragged behind them on stretchers that Wendell skills would be most needed.

Again, Igno snorted with weariness, and Bel, with a touch of guilt, reached out to pat the side of his neck.

"Soon, my friend," he whispered.

As the order went around to make camp, he watched the riders rope spikes to their horses' bridles and anchor them into the soft wet turf before removing their saddles and other gear. Only once their mounts were secure would they see to their own needs, wrapping themselves in wool blankets against the rain. After the rigors of the battle and subsequent march, however, nearly every horse and rider fell instantly asleep.

They think their victory hollow in the face of Dermont's defeat, Bel thought quietly, watching the raindrops flick against Igno's silent bells. Slowly, he took a deep breath and looked up just as Val, Lilia, and Briden trotted near.

"Do you need anything else of me, my lord?" Val asked.

It was a long time before the prince spoke. "Nine thousand men, Val," he said. "We lost nine thousand men."

"Cousin"—she sighed—"the Gasparns were led by the Tower. I remember more than a few Bard's tales about him. Some might think us lucky to have lost so few."

"At least our nobles and knights are safe," he jeered. "Better to lose a few conscripted rabble than the high lords who draw the bloody levees." He shook his head bitterly. "According to that capon Harren, Dermont rode for the Steeds and requires us to follow with all haste."

"So we make camp?" Val asked.

"Dermont did not risk his horse. I will not risk mine."

"As you say, cousin."

Bel sighed. How many times over the past hundred years, he wondered, had one side held victory within its grasp only to see it slip away, leaving another generation of fathers, brothers, sons, and daughters to die in this absurd conflict?

"This is madness," he said aloud. "Complete and utter madness. The War of the Horses? It should be the War of the Fools."

All of a sudden, Val cleared her throat, and with a shock, Bel shut his mouth, realizing at once that exhaustion and frustration had together made the Silent Prince's tongue loose. *Why should I hide it from them? They probably know me better than I know myself.* He turned back to his retainers and smiled weakly, "Get some rest. All of you. Please."

With a quick salute, Val and Briden nodded and turned to make camp. However, Lilia lingered a moment longer, and although she said nothing, Bel read the question in her eyes.

"I'm all right," he told her gently, "Go on."

She raised an eyebrow to make him aware of her skepticism, but in the end, she turned Banshee around to follow after Val. As much as Bel suddenly wanted to hold her, he knew better than to do so in the open field. He was certain that Val knew about them and that others may have had their suspicions, but he held on to the vain hope that the majority of the others would only think their relationship was that of an officer and a skilled retainer.

Since Valendia began accepting women soldiers in Bel's grandfather's time, there had been a number of well-known stories told of scandalous affairs among the ranks. Not only did such relationships have the potential to weaken the chain of command, but they also had the potential to breed resentment among the remainder of the rank and file, who would soon begin seeing signs of favoritism, regardless of whether or not they were true. Furthermore, the social class distinction added yet another complication to

Bel's relationship with Lilia, and there were plenty of popular tales to discourage this, too, nearly all of which ended in shame, death, or general misery. Yet in spite of the stories and the very real consequences that they warned against, Bel also knew that resisting his feelings for Lilia was futile. Noble or commoner, captain or command, it did not matter.

When the last skirmisher had staked his horse, Bel saw Igno and tried to push these thoughts out of his mind as he attempted to clean away the blood and grime from the battle with rainwater. Luckily, Wendell arrived soon after to tend to Bel's shoulder and give his report regarding the condition of the wounded. Only afterward, at long last, did Bel finally wrap himself in his cloak, cover his face beneath his blanket, and find something akin to sleep.

When he awoke, the storm had passed, and the sun hung low near the western horizon. Quickly, Bel's riders and the reserve infantry formed their ranks to march again, and together, they traveled southward through the mountain vales that, before the war, had granted the old realm its name. The sky steadily grew clearer with the setting sun, and one by one, the stars winked to life in the vast, indigo dome above and brought with them a sense of quiet peace after the disaster of the morning's battle. It was midnight when the small army made camp for the second time, and though weary from the last stretch of the march, the prevailing mood among the soldiers as they sat around their cookfires had improved slightly from one of despair to a type of melancholic acceptance.

Though Bel and Val often left the men to eat their meals in private, free of the unconscious reserve that often accompanied an officer's presence, Lilia convinced them to join the rest as they supped. While on the march, Sir Norton's archers had taken a number of wild rabbits and a few of the fat mountain grouse that sometimes roamed the valleys, so many of the soldiers even had a bit of stew to go along with the dried biscuits and trail rations that comprised their usual fare. Jarvy, the elderly cavalryman, was a consummate storyteller, and as the riders sat around their campfires, he regaled them with tales not only from Montevale but also Wrathorn animal fables and even a few Sorgund fish stories. Bel did not fail to notice, however, that the older man was careful to avoid recounting any of the Bard's tales about the Guardians.

When the meal was over, Bel met with Val and Norton to split the watches among the riders and the infantrymen. There would be watches to guard as well as to mind the horses while they slept or grazed throughout the night. Once these were settled, Beledain left the camps of the cavalrymen to check on Wendell and the wounded before ending his rounds with a brief walk among Sir Norton's archers to learn names and shake hands. Lilia and Briden followed with him.

Throughout the long march into the night, the young standard-bearer had quietly become the Silent Prince's shadow, carrying the unfurled banner of the Black Horse with him wherever they rode. When they stopped to make camp this second time, Bel turned his back for but a moment only to find Briden in the midst of seeing to Igno's feed and care. Though it was common for even minor knights to be attended by squires or stewards, Bel had never had any desire for one, preferring instead to take care of his needs himself. However, as his father always said, to reject an honest kindness is to invite eternal scorn. If the boy insisted upon serving in such a manner, Bel would allow it; however, he would make it clear that he did not expect it.

When he had completed his rounds and the sentries were set, Bel made his way back to where Briden had placed his things, unrolled his soggy blanket, and lay down. No sooner had he done so, however, when he heard the quiet patter of feet nearby, and he was unsurprised to find Lilia creeping toward him in the darkness.

"I won't stay," she whispered before he could protest. "I know."

Something about the way she said it, void of any resentment, made him feel terrible. He sat up and reached out for her hand, pulling her down beside him.

"How's your shoulder?" she asked, gently leaning her head upon it.

"Better now." He heard her stifled laugh and slipped an arm around her waist.

For some time, they sat in silence, and Bel wondered at it. So much of their time together seemed to lie within the heat of a moment—before a battle, a short stop along during a long march, the bloody fray of the battlefield itself; intensity and passion raged like a sudden, violent thunderstorm appearing and disappearing in the matter of a heartbeat. And though they had occasionally known brief, quiet moments of tenderness too, merely sitting beside her now beneath the stars was somehow more fulfilling than any of the rest. With a deep sigh, he shut his eyes, kissed her forehead, and before long felt himself nodding off.

Lilia must have noticed it too. "I should go," she whispered reluctantly. "Too many eyes, and you need your sleep."

Bel said nothing. More than anything, he wanted her to stay but knew that what she said was true.

At length, she kissed him and smiled in the darkness before slipping away, "Good night, my Silent Prince."

The remainder of the journey back to Tremontane Castle passed uneventfully, leaving Bel with plenty of time to think about what he would say when he finally encountered Dermont. Though Sir Norton had not said as much, Bel knew that the defeat had occurred as a result of his brother's pride. When he ordered his lines of footmen to attack all at once, Bel knew that his brother had expected a short, sudden slaughter as the Gasparns were either overrun by or fled from the swarming Valendian infantry. However, in his rush to run down a seemingly terrified, fleeing enemy, he allowed the Gasparan heavy horse to flank the footmen and trample them like dust.

However, every commander was subject to mistakes in judgment, and he could forgive Dermont's overconfidence—he, himself, had fully expected the war to end that morning. Yet, to abandon nine thousand men? To not even attempt to relieve them?

Since taking command of the armies of Valendia two summers past, Dermont's tenure as lord-general seemed charmed. In his first major offensive, he succeeded in sacking the Gasparan castle of Whitemane, which for nearly two decades had marked the only secure advancement either country had made in crossing the Bloodline as well as the sight of Bel's Uncle Talvert's defeat at the hands of Prince Gislain. Without their southernmost citadel, the Gasparns would be required to maintain significantly longer supply lines to support their soldiers at the front. As it turned out, however, they would not need to as Dermont and his uncles continued to march the Valendians northward, pushing the Bloodline back by over twenty leagues.

When winter set in, the fighting slowed for a short time, and the lords of the White Horse in their highland citadels began planning a spring counter-offensive under the command of the Avalanche himself. When the snows melted, the Gasparns mounted their attack, and although they did succeed for a short time in returning the Bloodline to its former state, it was in this bloody springtime that Prince Gislain received the wound that would eventually kill him and that Bel, at the age of only eighteen, was elevated to lead Dermont's light cavalry and quickly established himself as a resourceful and quietly charismatic field commander. By all accounts, the Gasparan death knell had sounded.

No, defeat was not something that Valendians were much accustomed to, and when Dermont saw the tide of the battle turning, perhaps he had simply panicked. That, too, Bel could understand and even sympathize with. What he could not understand, and therefore not forgive, was Dermont's decision not to send his own knights to engage the Gasparns, why he instead chose to sound the retreat and utterly abandon the infantry. However, as Bel's father said, never condemn a man until first hearing him speak. He would hear Dermont's account of the battle before jumping to any conclusions.

Not that Bel's opinions on the matter would mean much anyway. As the eldest son and heir to King Cedric, Dermont's word was law.

The remnants of the army rode on, and at long last, just after midday, the walls of Tremontane Castle were finally in sight. Built in the better days of Montevale before the War of the Horses, the castle consisted of three round towers, each situated atop one of the high hills that folk referred to as the Steeds, for it was believed that they marked the burial sites of the first three searoans that the Brother Galdorn gave to man at the beginning of the world: Daravain the Stallion, Rowana the Mare, and Corlindus the Colt. Each of the fortresses housed its own complement of men and was connected to the others by massive stone walls upon which four horses could ride side by side. In the center of the eastern wall, an enormous barbican, known as the Gate of Levantis, guarded the only known entrance to the courtyard, and high atop its battlements, the banner of the Black Horse billowed in the breeze.

Bel ordered Val and Sir Norton to bivouac in the fields northwest of the city and selected an escort to accompany him to the castle—Briden, Horn, Jarvy, and in spite of certain misgivings, Bel chose Lilia. Together, they rode across the fields to the single, snaking roadway that wound along the slopes of the Sires to the High Gate.

As the cadre of horses trotted along the cobblestones, Bel felt the awkward nostalgia of a homecoming. Since accepting his command, he had only returned to Tremontane once, last Horsetide when his father had requested that he and Dermont join him for the Feast of Galdorn. Bel did so, but without the company of his men. Now riding at the head of his entire command, fresh from the field of battle, he felt uncomfortably exposed as townsfolk stopped to stare at them, whispering excitedly or cheering as they noticed Igno's silent bells.

When they finally reached the massive, ironbound doors of the castle gates, the heavily armored sentries stepped forward carrying their halberds to greet them as from somewhere above in the gatehouse, another squad of soldiers began turning the large winch to raise the iron portcullis separating them from the inner ward.

"Welcome home, Prince Beledain!" a familiar voice called as Bel and his followers rode through.

Bel glanced across the courtyard to where yet another cadre of men had assembled to meet him; however, these were clad in the formal trappings of King Cedric's household guard. "It's good to see you, Sir Emory." Bel smiled as the leader approached and dropped to one knee. At once, a groom ran forward to take hold of Igno's bridle as the Silent Prince leaped from the red horse's back.

"After what we've heard of the battle, I'm glad to find you still standing, my prince," the old knight said.

"I might say the same to you." Bel smiled kindly, hoisting the elder man to his feet. Sir Emory Knott had been King Cedric's seneschal for as long as Bel could remember. Far longer, in Bel's opinion, for any absurd kneeling.

Sir Emory bore a nasty scar running the length of his left cheek, which gave his smile a somewhat ghoulish appearance. However, Bel had always found it strangely comforting. That scar, King Cedric once told him, was a reminder of how much the seneschal was willing to sacrifice to keep their family safe. He smiled now.

"It seems every time we turn around, more messengers arrive with news of your great deeds," the old knight said. "Makes me proud to have had the honor of showing you how to sit that horse." "The honor was all mine, believe me," Bel said. "A lesser man than you would have given up as many times as I fell out of the saddle."

"Well, your father said that if I couldn't teach a Black Horse to ride, then you must have been a changeling sent from the White, and I'd best get to the

Bloodline to ask for his real son back." The seneschal grinned. "Lucky for us it turned out right in the end, eh? I'd hate to have to ride out against you."

Bel shrugged off the compliment. "I have good men," he said, nodding toward the riders behind him. "Speaking of which, is there any space for them here at the castle?"

"For these four?"

"And Lady Val."

"The Iron Fist! Certainly," Sir Emory said, "I'll have the stewards prepare the servants' chambers beneath your old apartments, and I'll have a set of finer rooms made up for Lady Valerie as well." The old knight shook his head. "To think, you've got your own guard now. You make me proud, my prince, mighty proud."

"Oh, leave off, old man," said a voice. "Can't you see you're making the boy blush?"

Bel glanced up to see a tall, broad-shouldered man descending the wide, stone staircase that led down from the western tower, the Stallion. His fine white tunic was embroidered with a pattern of tiny black horseshoes over which he wore a snowy, white surcoat bearing the emblem of the Black Horse with the added insignia of the lord-general's golden crown. The very same, Bel recalled that had adorned the tattered banner Giles Pronet had waved at him as he delivered the Tower's terms. His dark beard and hair were neatly trimmed, and around his shoulders, he wore a thick cloak of black fur. Onyx stones set in the silver hilt of a longsword glittered in the afternoon sun.

"The Silent Prince!" Dermont announced as he stepped forward to embrace Bel. "Though perhaps we should change it to the 'Tardy Prince.'"

"I'm sorry," Bel said. "If we pushed the horses any further, they would all be dead. The infantry at least allowed us time to rest."

Dermont cast the apology aside with a wave of his hand. "No matter. That fop Harren told me he left you to mind the foot, though not in so many words," he glanced over Bel's squad, "I don't see Val with you. Tell me. She's not..."

"No, no. She's fine," Bel said, "I left her in command of the camp with Sir Norton. We had a lot of wounded to see to."

Dermont gave a nod. "Sir Emory, send for Lady Val after you see to my brother's men and horses."

"Of course, my prince."

"Find them a place where they can bathe too." He winked. "If they're going to be hanging around the castle, we can't have them looking like they've just crawled out of a grave."

"Aye, my lord."

Bel watched in silence as the seneschal hurried to obey, leading Bel's soldiers and their horses to the long row of paddocks that lined the perimeter of the inner ward. The riders of the light company were a motley crew when compared to the folk of the castle. Perhaps that was why he had stayed away so long. He breathed a heavy sigh.

"What a mess, eh?" Dermont whispered a moment later. "If Lord Kilbane hadn't died already on the battlefield, I'd have had him beheaded on the spot. Bastard led my infantry into a bloody deathtrap."

"Lord Kilbane?"

"Aye, it was all a ruse. The Gasparn infantry made as if to flee the field, and Kilbane took the bait. I sent word for him not to pursue, but he didn't listen, and he ended up cutting himself off from the rest of our forces. I'd have sent the heavy horse, but by then, it was far too late. Better to withdraw, regroup, and plan for the next assault. The nobles can always raise more levees, and if they cannot, well, the Wrathorn are always willing to fight for coin."

Bel bit his lip. "Could you not have sent the heavy horse to charge them from the rear?" he asked, "Outflank the flankers?"

Dermont shook his head. "Kilbane was too far out of reach," he said. "Bastard can't follow my orders, then he can suffer the consequences. In any case, he paid for it."

And nine thousand others too… Bel thought bitterly.

"Ah well"—his brother sighed—"the war goes on."

"So it does."

Dermont continued to mutter his frustrations, and Bel nodded accordingly, though he could not help but find his brother's cavalier attitude toward the outcome of the battle disquieting. Before long, he found his attention wavering from Dermont's monologue to where his soldiers were installing their horses in the stables. He saw Briden's stiffness as he unsaddled Magpie, glaring at the groom's attentions to Igno, watched Horn beam with pride as he introduced Sir Emory to Bastard, and saw Jarvy singing softly into Piper's ear as he combed out her mane. *So many dead*, he thought. *So many silver tarnished to gold.* He shook his head and, with a sigh, spied Lilia slip lithely from Banshee's saddle. When she caught Bel's eyes on her, she furtively pulled a face and smiled.

"So is that your common girl?"

Ice water rushed suddenly through Bel's veins. "What?"

Dermont grinned, watching her. "Too skinny and not much to speak of in the way of tits," he mused. "But she's got a pretty face and sits a horse well." He snorted a laugh and leered. "I bet there's sweetness between her legs, eh?"

The Silent Prince swallowed a ball of fire.

"I'd ask to take a turn with her, but I hear she's gelded other men for trying."

"Only twice," Bel finally managed.

"You'd think one would have been enough."

"Some men never learn."

All of a sudden, Dermont broke into a loud fit of laughter. "Oh, don't worry, little brother. She's all yours!" He grinned, throwing an arm around Bel's shoulders. "Fire and Blood! You should see your face!"

"How did you know?" Bel whispered as his brother began ushering him along toward the steps of the Stallion.

"You can't be a good king without good spies," Dermont said. "And before you start worrying, know that you can count on me to be as silent as you on this matter. As far as I'm concerned, you can fuck any girl you want, willing, or not! Leave a trail of bastards from here to Dwerin, just as long as you keep fighting like you did before Kilbain's blunder."

"You already know about the battle with the reserves?"

"Why else do you think I wanted you here so soon but to help me plan a way to raze this bloody Tower?" He grinned. "We have much to think on. However, I suppose before we get to it, you should first say hello to father. He was atop the walls as you rode in. Let's go find out if he still recognizes you."

CHAPTER 9:
LENARD'S CROSSING

As the bargemen pushed hard against the muddy riverbed with their long poles and brought the barge to a complete stop, Lughus gazed along the wharf at the town of Lenard's Crossing, his eyes alight with the spirit of adventure. Beside him, Thom lurched suddenly against the rail, his face an unhealthy shade of green, but there was nothing left in his stomach to bring up. Still, considering he had spent most of the past nine days lying on deck moaning like a dying sea creature, Lughus saw the mere fact that Thom was upright to be a significant improvement. The Brethren only knew how Thom was ever going to survive among the Wrathorn clans of the North.

Lughus himself had taken to the river with ease, so much so that, at times, the bargemen had allowed him to help as they guided the great floating platform downstream. His eagerness to learn and record the details of their craft in writing instantly ingratiated him with the crew, and although there were plenty of collections of Sorgund fish stories among the books of the Loremaster's Tower, Lughus quickly learned that the inland rivermen were just as capable of telling tales as their brethren who sailed the seas.

With a cry of "Ho!" the sailors slapped the gangplank against the pier with a resounding thud and began off-loading the cargo they had taken from the capital. Thom swallowed noisily and took a deep breath. "Can we get off now?"

Lughus shook his golden head and helped his friend shoulder his pack. "You're going to have to get used to this, Thom," he said. "There's still a long way left to go before we reach the sea, let alone Baronbrock."

"Let's just go ashore," Thom muttered. His rucksack, bulging out from his back, made him look very much like a giant turtle. "I want to feel solid ground beneath my feet."

Lughus shouldered his own pack, and together, he and Thom made their way down the gangplank to the dock. The master of the barge grinned at the sight of them and paused in his work with the cargo to see them off.

"Well, call me the Warlock!" he beamed. "I've made the dead walk!"

Thom slouched miserably and, in a Royne-like voice, muttered, "Just a story..."

Lughus stifled a grin. "Thank you, sir." He held out his hand, and the old sailor crushed it in his own callused grip, "For your kindness and for the safe passage."

"Take care of yourselves, boys." The man winked. "You know where you're headed?"

"The Kingfisher," Lughus said.

"Aye, it's in the town proper, away from the docks," the master told them. "You'll know it by the sign, though if you'd like, I can send one of the lads to show you."

Lughus shook his head, "I'm sure we can find it."

The master nodded. "We'll be here for another day or two before heading back to Titanis should you find yourself in a bind." He turned back to the cargo and hoisted a large sack onto his shoulder. "Farewell and fair journeys!"

Lenard's Crossing was a small river town roughly halfway between Titanis and Galdoran, Andoch's large port city on the Sea of Calendral. The banks on either side of the Imperial River were lined with small docks, piers, and jetties, and ferries crossed back and forth constantly from the farmers' fields and watermills on the south bank to the town proper on the north. After leaving the bargemen behind, Lughus and Thom traversed the wharf connecting to the town center, passing as they did, dozens of vendors shouting their wares and plying their trades. Most were simple fisherman, peddling the morning's catch—trout, perch, pike, salmon, great baskets of crayfish, and long, writhing eels; however, there were also a number of farmers ferried over from the south bank with barrels full of fresh produce and a few local hunters with great slabs of venison, flanks of forest boar, ducks, geese, swans, and other river fowl. A trapper sold furs from half a dozen animals, an old man whittled icons of the

Brethren out of linden wood, and from somewhere further inland, the strike of a hammer on an anvil resounded throughout the town.

Lughus eyed it all with wonder. Having spent so little time out of the confines of the Keystone and the Loremaster's Tower, the dockside market was an altogether different world. Even on those rare occasions when he and Thom and Royne had been permitted to venture out of Nobleton, the folk of Titanis were vastly different from the common folk of the river town. Less refined, of course, but more hearty, like comparing a set of new boots to a pair of old ones. He could only wonder at what their lives were like—their hopes, their fears, their pursuits, and their diversions. Nothing he had read had ever told him as much, and he wondered if perhaps this was one of the lessons Rastis had intended for him to learn.

For Thom's part, between the feel of solid ground beneath his feet and the sights and smells of the vendors, he was soon much refreshed, and some of the sickly green pallor had faded from his freckled cheeks. He purchased a spicy, dried sausage from a hunter and a small icon of Brother Galdorn from the old man, perhaps hoping that the Lord of the Sea would hold some influence on the effects of nausea and seasickness as well.

"Thank the Brethren!" Thom gasped, munching away happily. "I feel I'm half-starved after the food those bargemen eat."

"I'm not so sure you should be buying anything right now," Lughus told him. "That's all the coin we have."

"Oh rubbish, we've got plenty of money," he said, "loads and loads."

Lughus shot his chubby friend a cold glance. "Do you want to shout that any louder, Thom? I think there are some fishermen out on the river who didn't hear you."

"Calm down, Goldimop." Thom laughed merrily and strode on ahead. "Let's just find this Kingfisher. After this sausage, I'm going to need a proper drink."

"I'd sooner find this Crodane," Lughus muttered.

His hand brushed the hilt of Pryce's dagger tucked safely into his belt, and he hurried after.

As they left the wooden planks of the wharf for the sturdy cobblestones of the town's narrow streets, the stench of fish was replaced with the more familiar smells of urban shops and trades: the sweet aroma of tannin from a leatherworker's stall, the scent of fresh lumber piled in a carpenter's yard, the odor of smoldering coal from the blacksmith's forge. People of all types scurried here and there, buying, selling, and haggling over prices. There were wealthier folk who spoke through their servants and poor folk who begged on the corners for spare copper coins. Cadres of wandering mercenaries for hire milled about along the roadside, some offering their services for protection by river or by road, an old crippled sailor hobbled by leaning on a crutch, and Lughus watched as a boy half his age ran cackling with laughter from a red-faced pie-man whom he had just robbed.

At length, the thoroughfare ended in a wide, circular plaza from which the entire southern half of the town down to the riverbank might be observed. A tall statue of a grim-faced man with a beard stood menacingly from atop a dais in its center, and at its rear was a large wattle and daub building bearing the mark of a river bird on its signboard.

"I guess this is it," Lughus said.

"Is that a kingfisher?" Thom asked, pointing up at the sign, "So that's what they look like. I don't think I've ever actually seen one."

Lughus sighed and shook his golden head, "Let's just go in."

The front door opened into a large rectangular common room filled with round wooden tables and a long bar running the whole length of the eastern wall. The smell of fisherman's stew and spilled ale greeted them while the locals, eying them with suspicion through steaming bowls and frothy pints, did not. In the corner, a young groom sat on an empty barrel picking his nose while two homely barmaids wandered from table to table delivering food and drink this way and that. To the left of the doorway, a short staircase led upwards to a long hall lined with rooms for rent. While waiting for someone to receive them, Lughus glanced around, wondering which of the men, if any, was Crodane. Finally, after what seemed an eternity, the barman called out to one of the serving women and nodded toward the two boys.

With a look of disdain, she rolled her eyes and approached with feigned hospitality. "What do you want?"

Lughus glanced around cautiously. This was certainly not The Book & the Barrel. "We're to meet someone here," he said. "Another traveler. A man named Crodane."

"Don't know him," the woman said. "Though that don't mean he ain't here."

"I see," Lughus said.

"Is that all you need?" she asked impatiently, "I've got hungry mouths to feed."

Thom glanced questioningly at Lughus. Without having to ask, Lughus knew what his friend was thinking. He sighed. "Is it all right if we wait here?" he asked. "We'd have some of that stew."

"As you like." The woman waved a hand in the general direction of the common room and went back to making her rounds.

Lughus led Thom through the tables, careful not to bump into any of the patrons taking their meals. They found an empty table in the back corner from which they could still watch the front door. Not that it mattered much, Lughus thought, since they had no idea what Crodane looked like anyway. Still, as he mildly cast his gaze over the faces of the other patrons, he was happy to have his back to the wall, especially when he realized that nearly half of them were armed.

In the capital, only certain people—members of the Order, kingsmen, and household guards —were allowed to openly carry any weapon larger than a dagger to use at meals. It seemed that Lenard's Crossing was not nearly as strict regarding arms and armor. Within the inn alone, men wore light shirts of chain, boiled leather cuirasses, and took their meals with their sword hilts and axe handles resting against the tabletop beside them. It filled Lughus with an even greater sense of anxiety and impatience at the absence of their guide.

Thom, however, seemed oblivious to all of this. Though often frightened of his own shadow, the murky stew and stale ale filled him with an almost manic glee after nine days of seasickness on the barge. He was ignorant to the sullen indignities of the wait staff or the way that the men laughed or jeered every time he spoke.

"So," Thom began, finishing his second bowl of stew, "when we meet this Crodane, do you think we'll stay here tonight, or will we set out again right away? Because I, for one, vote we at least spend one night here. It'd be nice to sleep in a bed again after rolling around on the barge like that. I don't know how these sailors do it."

"Thom," Lughus said quietly, "half the time, the barge was traveling so slow you could barely tell it was moving."

"Well, I have a delicate constitution. I can't help that." He sighed. "I just hope the ride down to Galdoran is not nearly as rough."

Lughus furtively scanned the faces of the crowd. "Will you please stop talking so loud?" he whispered. "I'd rather not have the whole world know our purpose."

"Oh, phish-posh." Thom laughed and swatted at Lughus's head with a hammy hand. "Why would anyone care about us? What possible interest could anyone have in two apprentice scribblers to the bloody Loremaster? Unless they want to kidnap us and force us to read them bedtime stories every night or maybe write down their memoirs for their illiterate posterity."

"Shut up, Thom!" Lughus hissed through clenched teeth. He made to kick his friend under the table but missed. "Order some more food if it keeps your mouth shut! Perindal's Sword, you're dense. Shut up!"

"You shut up, Goldimop!" Thom shot back.

He ripped off a piece of stale bread from the side of his trencher and tossed it at Lughus's head. Lughus anticipated Thom's attack and lashed out to slap away the chubby boy's hand, sending the stew-sodden glob flying across the common room, where it landed with a splash in a frothy pint of ale. In an instant, the entire room fell silent, and all eyes turned toward the two boys in a mixture of amusement and anticipation.

Lughus watched anxiously as the owner of the pint slowly stood up from his seat and turned to face them. He was clad in mottled shades of brown, patched in a few places with bits of other colored cloth over which he wore a lamellar cuirass of boiled leather. His ruddy, pock-marked face twisted with contempt, framed by twisted locks of greasy black hair flecked with gray, and with a quiet grunt, his two fellows at the table rose to their feet. Though armed, they bore no insignia or the device of any lord, labeling them mercenaries, sellswords, hired blades.

"Thom, you idiot," Lughus whispered.

As the three men crossed the floor of the common room, Lughus could hear Thom's heavy breathing beside him, and beneath the table, he fingered the silver pommel of Pryce's dagger.

"Teach 'em a lesson, Stokes," a voice laughed from the direction of the bar.

"Aye, carve the fat one up like a stuck pig!"

The lead man, Stokes, tossed his tankard down upon the boys' tabletop with a heavy thud. A fine mist of spray sloshed over the side. "Something appears to have fallen in my cup," the mercenary said.

Lughus cast Thom an angry look, but the big boy was not paying attention, staring silently at the floor and resigning himself to whatever fate was to come.

"I'm sorry about your ale," Lughus said at last. "My friend and I are more than willing to make amends by buying another round for you and your friends."

Stokes raised his eyebrows and exchanged a glance with his fellows. The man on the left, shorter, thicker, and with a mustache, shrugged apathetically, while on the right, a thin man in a rusty, steel cap, barked a laugh.

"Well," Stokes shrugged, "it seems we was all but done drinking anyhow."

Lughus eyed the mercenary with suspicion. "Then accept our apologies. We meant no harm."

The man on the left grinned, revealing a set of crooked, yellow teeth. The thin man gave another laugh. Stokes suppressed a grin of his own and rested his hands comfortably upon the hilt of the rusty longsword in his belt. "You know," he began, "I would, but the lads and I—we're not the forgiving type."

"I see," Lughus said simply. "And I'm sorry to hear that. However, I don't see how else we can resolve this."

"Well, that is the question, isn't it?"

Finally, Thom found his voice. "Surely, you wouldn't just kill us?" he said shrilly. "There are laws! And it was an accident! We meant no harm!"

"Aye, no harm." Stokes smirked. "But you sorely hurt my feelings."

"That's no grounds for murder!" Thom whined.

"No," Lughus agreed coolly. He suddenly thought of Royne and the fight in the tower with Pryce and his cronies. A cold resignation began to spread throughout his limbs, replacing the unnerving disquiet of fear. He eyed Stokes looming down on him from across the table, but when he met the mercenary's gaze, he saw him for what he really was. He saw Pryce. He saw a bully.

"It's no grounds for murder." Lughus sighed. "But it is grounds for satisfaction should he press it, which I'm certain he will."

Stokes's smile spread wider, and a cold light kindled in his eyes. "Aye, so I will," he called out over the amused mutterings of the common room. "The fat ginger there offered insult, and I demand satisfaction."

Thom's face grew paler, and he began to sweat. His breath came even quicker, and Lughus began to worry that his friend was going to faint. All around them, the other patrons of the Kingfisher began to snicker and laugh openly, and a few even cheered Stokes's name. However, as angry as Lughus had been at Thom mere moments ago, he would not allow his friend to suffer—or even die—for the amusement of a belligerent pack of drunken thugs.

"Fine," Lughus said quietly, struggling to keep his voice steady. "But Thom's no fighter. If dueling's what you aim at, then you'll have to face me."

"Alright," Stoke grinned, "I bleed you or I bleed him. It's all one to me."

Outside the tavern, the town square filled as the patrons of the Kingfisher filed out laughing and jeering in the late afternoon sun. Word spread quickly, and a small crowd gathered to watch the spectacle, and even the waiting staff of the pub appeared in the doorway to watch Stokes carve up the fresh-faced lads who talked so pretty. Two members of the town watch had even wandered over to see what the fuss was about; however, with a word from one of Stokes's friends, they simply nodded, laughed, and joined the other onlookers leaning on their pikes.

At one end of the square, Lughus removed his cloak, folded it in half, and handed it to Thom without looking at him. The chubby boy was already crying, whispering, "I'm sorry. I'm sorry," over and over again.

Lughus nodded in answer but said nothing. His heart thundered in his chest, and his fingertips tingled with a mixture of fear and doubt as he drew Pryce's dagger.

Nearly a year ago, Rastis had allowed him to participate in the tourney celebrating the Feast of Perindal, a day marked by jousts, melees, and other celebrations of martial prowess. Though he lacked the formal training of a nobleman, soldier, or cadet, Lughus had managed to defeat every opponent set against him in the junior tournament. In the first round, he bested a raw recruit from among the kingsmen. In the second, he defeated Marl Sandon of the cadets, and in the third round, he defeated a young knight two years his elder before facing Pryce in the final round to win the day. However, as it was only a tourney, those swords had been blunted, and his opponents mere boys near enough his own age. Now he was to fight a grown man.

At the far end of the square, Stokes stood with his companions. The mercenary, too, had removed his cloak and tied his lank hair back to keep it out of his eyes. At last, he drew his rusty longsword and stepped forward. "I hope you're ready," he called.

Thom's sobbing grew louder, though it was barely audible over the ribald snickering of the mob. Lughus ignored it and raised the long dagger in front of him. "I'm ready," he lied.

Stokes laughed and raised his own blade, calling out to the crowd. "Quite the bloody sword he's got there! It's near as long as the one I've got down me trousers!"

The crowd erupted with amusement, and Lughus did his best not to blush as Stokes turned back to face him.

"It is sharp, I hope. Not just a toy?"

"Come closer, and I'll show you," Lughus said coldly.

His cheeks burned with embarrassment as the crowd erupted into laughter. *What a fool I am*, he thought. *A complete and utter fool…*

A few more voices shouted bawdy jokes or sarcastic jeers, and Lughus glanced around himself, suddenly very conscious of the disdain with which the assembled people—people whom he had never even met—seemed to regard him. He wondered at the ways of the common folk that they could so readily wish for a stranger's blood. His mind leaped to the stories of the great heroes, the great romances and Bard's tales that he had spent his young life reading in the Loremaster's Tower. He thought of the adventures of Sir Borlan the Wave, or the wanderings of Sir Grandon the Eye, or the legends of the Blessed St. Aiden himself, and he knew there would be no grandeur to mark his own fall. There would be no great tale of triumph or woe. He would die here as a fool and nothing more, a nameless corpse who met a bloody end simply for the entertainment of a mob.

So much for adventure, he thought miserably. *So much for heroes.*

"You demanded satisfaction for your wounded honor," he called out to the mercenary, struggling to keep his voice steady. "Then stop stalling and come claim it."

Stokes raised his eyebrows as the crowd made sounds of mock admiration. "In due time, boy," he said. "But I'll at least give you a sporting chance." He raised his voice over the mob. "Would anyone mind loaning the boy there a proper sword?" He crowed. "I promise to return it shortly"—the mercenary winked—"and clean."

"He can borrow mine."

Lughus turned around to face the speaker. He was clad in faded shades of grays, greens, and browns, and beneath his plain woolen surcoat, he wore a light chain habergeon spotted with rust. His dark brown hair and beard, though perhaps somewhat scruffy with the addition of a few days' stubble, were still well-kept, and when placed alongside his long nose and deep-set blue eyes, granted his features a certain canine bearing of nobility, like a foxhound that has just caught the scent.

The crowd quieted as the man stepped up beside Lughus and drew his sword.

"Who the blazes are you?" Stokes asked uncertainly, glancing at his fellows.

"Merely a wanderer," the man said calmly. "My name is Crodane."

Lughus's heart skipped a beat; however, it was Thom who spoke.

"Crodane?" He gasped through his sobbing. "We were waiting for you!"

Crodane kept his gaze leveled at Stokes standing uncertainly across the square. "I'm sorry," he said without emotion. "I was delayed."

"Well"—Stokes shrugged, wagging his sword impatiently—"if you'll loan the boy your sword, we can take care of things here."

"Or perhaps, you and your lads would like to make things more…interesting," Crodane said. "There are three of you, grown men all. Experienced. Veterans." He raised his voice so that the entire crowd might hear. "I'll stand with the boy. Why not make it interesting? Two against three?"

The assemblage of townsfolk laughed and cheered with anticipation at the prospect of a greater show. Watching Stokes gut a nameless fool was one thing, but a proper melee with at least a few seasoned warriors was another. Stokes and his fellows, however, gave pause.

"We've no quarrel with you, friend," the mercenary finally said.

"That may be," Crodane said. "But I have business with this boy, and if he dies, my business goes unfinished. At least if I stand with him, we live together or die together, and one way or another, my business will be fulfilled."

Again, Stokes looked to his fellows, but by now, the crowd was growing restless with the delay; they came to see a fight, not the wagging of tongues.

"Get on with it, Stokes!" someone shouted.

"Aye, enough talk!" grunted another.

At length, Stokes spat on the ground and nodded. "Fine," he said, as his friends removed their cloaks and readied their weapons, "The three of us against the two of you."

"So be it," Crodane said and, with a curt nod, readied his stance. With a deep breath, Lughus squared his feet beside him and swallowed the lump in his throat. Behind them, Thom renewed his sobbing, though not nearly as loud or as pathetic as it had been before.

"I'm sorry," Lughus whispered to the guide.

"You owe me no apology," Crodane replied as the mercenaries lined up in front of them.

Stokes held his blade out before him while his thin friend in the cap raised his sword high above his head, wiggling the tip about in little circles, and the man with the mustache hefted a heavy axe over one shoulder like a headsman ready to strike.

Crodane lowered his sword and turned his wrists so that the blade pointed down at the ground behind him. The form of the Dragon, Lughus knew from his days of sparring with Hob, a deceptive stance but powerful.

"Watch the body, not the blade," the guide said quietly. "They will have reach on you, so if you engage, step into them as close as you can to take away their advantage. Otherwise, stay clear and use your offhand to block your body and your face. If I knock a man down or put him off-balance, strike swiftly under his arm or at his throat." He turned his icy gaze to meet Lughus's wide, gray eyes. "Do not hesitate! For, you can be certain that they will not."

Lughus took a deep breath, wiped the sweat from his hands on his tunic, and readied Pryce's dagger.

"Yes, sir," he said.

"I will not let you die today," Crodane said simply. "Know this and have no fear."

Stokes eyed his fellows and called out, "Ready?"

Crodane glanced at Lughus and shouted a reply, "By your leave."

A cheer went up from the crowd, and Stokes spat on the ground at his feet. "So be it."

Shouting his battle cry, the thin man charged headlong at Crodane and brought his sword down with all of his strength; however, the blade found only air as Crodane sidestepped to his left and swung his own sword around in a wide arc, slicing the mercenary from shoulder to navel. Blood sprang forth in a red fountain, gathering in the crenels between the cobblestones at Lughus's feet. He felt his hold on the dagger slacken as his stomach churned at the gory sight, and he had barely enough time to leap out of harm's way as Stokes and his mustachioed friend leaped into the fray to avenge their fallen comrade. Crodane took a step forward as Lughus stepped back, wrenching his sword from the thin man's corpse just in time to parry a blow from the mustache man's axe.

"You bastards!" the mercenary cried, twisting his axe head to tangle up with Crodane's blade just as Stokes rushed in with his sword.

Yet instead of retreating to avoid Stokes's blow, Crodane dove forward, driving his shoulder into the axman and knocking him off his feet. The slash from Stokes's sword still stuck flesh and tore a deep gash in Crodane's left shoulder; however, as the mustachioed man fell backward, Crodane slipped his sword free just in time to parry Stokes's second blow.

As the axman hit the cobblestones, Lughus knew it was his turn to act. Ignoring the promise of more blood and death, he leaped forward onto the fallen mercenary and drove the point of Pryce's dagger into the soft flesh beneath the man's arm all the way up to the hilt. The mercenary's body gave a sharp shudder, and he cried out in agony, his mouth already red with his own blood, and when Lughus withdrew his blade from the dying man's side, a red lake spread out beneath them. The cobbles turned slippery as blood continued to leak from the corpses, and as he tried to rise again to his feet, Lughus fell heavily on his side, jarring his left wrist on the slick stones. Behind him, he could hear the sound of Thom's retching.

At the sight of his second comrade's demise, Stokes's face twisted in frenzied rage and terror. His sword strokes came faster and faster, hammering from on high; however, Crodane parried each blow in turn. Finally, the mercenary's pace slackened as his endurance waned. He gathered his strength for one final blow, but it was then that Crodane made his move. Sidestepping to the right, he turned his blade and brought it up horizontally across the mercenary's midsection, doubling him over as the blade cut upward through the boiled leather scales of his lamellar deep into his belly. Stokes dropped to his knees, and as his shoulders slumped forward, Crodane slipped his sword free from the mercenary's innards and brought it down to separate his head from his neck.

The crowd broke out in a mixture of cheers, muttering, and disgust. The momentary diversion of the duel now over, the assembled spectators began to disperse to return to their personal business. For a moment, Crodane eyed the two watchmen carefully; however, neither seemed to have any intention of challenging the lawful nature of the affair.

"I suppose someone will have to clean this up," one of them muttered.

"Glad it's not me," said the other.

Lughus collected himself and staggered to his feet, his knees and his tunic soaked with blood. Thom leaned forward onto his knees, traces of vomit and saliva trailing from the corners of his mouth, and emptied his stomach again. Crodane wiped his sword clean on the corner of one of the mercenaries' discarded cloaks and returned it to his sheath.

"You're unharmed?" he asked Lughus.

Lughus nodded slowly, though his face was pale, and his feet felt unsteady as the horrid odor of Thom's vomit mingled with the dead men's emptying bowels.

"That was your first time," Crodane remarked, "killing a man?"

Lughus nodded and found Pryce's dagger where he had dropped it when he fell.

Crodane tossed him a scrap of a cloak. "Here," he said, "for the blade."

Lughus took a deep breath and wiped the dagger clean while Crodane picked among the bodies, comparing Stokes's sword to the thin man's. When Lughus returned the bloody cloth, Crodane wiped the blood from the better of the two and offered it to him.

"It gets easier," the swordsman said, his blue eyes ablaze beneath his thick brow. "It shouldn't, but it does."

Lughus took the sword and slipped it into his belt but said nothing.

At length, Thom collected himself and hobbled up beside them. "Lady save us," he said. "I've never seen so much blood."

"Pray you never do again," Crodane said. "Though I make no promises if you're the boy Rastis is sending to join the Wrathorn." He ignored Thom's sudden whimper. "Come. I had hoped to spend the night at the Kingfisher. We have much to talk about. However, now I think it would be best if we were gone. Dead men have a way of attracting unwanted attention."

Lughus nodded. "As you say."

"Aye," Thom agreed, "you've already proven yourself a friend as far as I'm concerned."

Crodane snorted. "Have I?" he asked. "I would think I've merely proven myself a killer, or at least quite capable in that regard." He smiled as Thom gave a start. "But no, I am no threat to you."

"Then we shall follow you," Lughus said, "cautiously."

He eyed Thom significantly, recalling their argument of what he could hardly believe was barely an hour before.

Crodane's lips twisted into a wry smirk. "Very well." He made his way to the edge of the square. "I have a currach stowed along the riverbank southeast of here. Let's hurry to it and be gone. Beneath the cover of darkness, there will be fewer chances of being seen." He set off at a brisk pace, his long legs striding across the cobblestones.

"Why is that suddenly an issue?" Thom asked as he and Lughus followed along. "And aren't you wounded? Yes, there. On your shoulder?"

Crodane sniffed and shook his head. "A scratch. By the morning, it will be gone," he said. "And as for your other question, consider the corpses lying back there in the square. If misadventure can find you when your enemies are not watching, then it's best always to assume that they are."

"But we have no enemies," Thom whined, "and I am not a lover of boats."

"Shut up, Thom," Lughus muttered. "You've gotten us into enough trouble for one day."

The two boys followed in silence as the swordsman led the way through the village to the edge of the wharf, passing through throngs of dockworkers, fishermen, and other assorted townsfolk as they packed up their stalls, stowed their goods, or wandered off to any of the various dockside taverns. Word had already spread of the melee in front of the Kingfisher, and more than once, Lughus overheard one man or another regaling his fellows with the gossip. He gathered his cloak around him as if to shield himself from any recognition and followed silently behind Crodane.

When they reached the end of the wharf and stepped down into the soggy grasses of the riverbank, they traveled downstream another half mile as the sounds of civilization were soon replaced by the gurgling of the river and the steady, rhythmic chirping of crickets and frogs. Beneath a scattering of beech trees, Crodane stopped to uncover a small boat loaded with two large sacks of supplies from beneath a covering of burlap and fallen leaves.

"Here we are," he said. "Now let's be gone."

CHAPTER 10:
THE COUNCIL OF FIVE

Royne lay with his head tilted back and his eyes shut, dozing ambivalently in the setting sun. On the table before him, his book lay closed, and his tin tankard sat empty, though he felt little enough motivation to remedy either. In the week and a half, since Lughus and Thom had left, he had made good on his promise to spend his time at The Book & the Barrel in town.

For the first few days, Rastis had tried to keep him busy, having him copy old fading manuscripts to stave off the overwhelming sense of loss at being left behind. He had even granted Royne a certain degree of autonomy that included the freedom to roam Nobleton and Easton as long as his regular duties were still completed.

As the only apprentice remaining in the tower, Royne fully expected his work to increase threefold, to be locked away in his cell to slowly go blind as he squinted by candlelight to copy faded manuscript after faded manuscript, illuminated tome after illuminated tome. Instead, he was surprised to find the opposite and steadily began feeling overwhelmed by a great sense of restless idleness. He found himself suddenly bored by even his favorite books, yet unable to find the enthusiasm to tackle anything new. He lurked around the study rooms and dormitories, hoping that perhaps one of the scribes or scholars would have need of his assistance, only to be disappointed when they did not. He would have asked Rastis for more work; however, since the day Lughus and Thom left, the old man had seemed to disappear. Hob claimed he had been called to meetings at the Keystone as the new King grew acclimated to his role as leader of the Council of Five, and when the Loremaster finally did return to his tower late into the night, Royne chose not to bother him.

Thus, every day at dusk, after a long day of idleness, he would wander down to The Book & the Barrel and reflect upon his lack of accomplishments. He had made good use of the money that Rastis had given him that last day with Lughus and Thom, though after nine days' worth of meals and ale, the coin was finally coming to an end. He would have to wait until being elevated to the rank of scribe before he would actually receive any sort of stipend for his work as a copyist or record keeper.

At last, Royne sat up straight and took his empty bowl and tankard up to Walter and Mary at the bar.

"How now, Royne?" the bartender said with a nod. He filled a tankard from one of the large casks lining the back wall and slid it down to Old Bob at the end of the bar. "You sticking around for another or heading home?"

Royne slipped his book back into the wide pocket of his habit. He made a mental tally of the coin he had remaining and sighed. "I think I'll head home," he said. "What do I owe you?"

Walter and his wife exchanged a glance.

"Nothing," Mary said kindly.

"Aye," Walter added, "tonight's on me."

"You don't have to do that," Royne said, shaking his head.

Walter shrugged. "I don't," he said, "But I am." He filled another tankard and passed it down to Ed. "Hob told us about your old mates being sent off."

"We want you to think of us as some new ones," Mary said, ladling stew into a tray full of bowls.

Royne sighed. "Hob often talks too much."

"That he does." Walter laughed. "Now go on. Get out of here. You can pay tomorrow."

Finally, Royne consented. "Thanks," he said.

The shopkeepers in Easton were closing up for the night as Royne made his way back through the keyhole into Nobleton. He allowed himself a quiet chuckle as he passed the spot where he had relieved Pryce of his dagger and imagined the first cadet's face when he awoke to discover it gone. The blade was to the Cadet what the book was to the apprentice. If discovered, Pryce would probably lose his position as the captain of the Cadets. However,

Royne felt no remorse. To Pryce, the blade was merely a ceremonial trinket; to Lughus—though not a sword—it could at least mean some measure of protection from the dangers of the world. By Royne's calculations, his friends should have arrived in Lenard's Crossing by now. He wondered if they had met their guide yet, and though not the religious type, Royne offered a silent prayer to Perindal that Lughus had not yet had any reason to unsheathe Pryce's dagger.

The sudden passage of a nobleman's carriage brought Royne to an abrupt halt, and he had to leap backward to avoid having his toes crushed beneath the wheels. He shot the driver an angry look, but if the man noticed, he paid it no mind, and Royne was forced to mutter impotently the rest of the way back to the tower. When he entered, he was surprised to see the light coming from the open door of the Loremaster's chambers, and it was with great relief that he listened to the scribe at the front desk tell him that Rastis had left word that he wanted to see him.

Immediately, Royne strode across the tower floor to answer the Loremaster's summons. He could only hope that the meeting would result in some task, regardless of how menial or trivial it may be. He would willingly count the vowels in all fourteen volumes of *The Historie of the Baronies of the Brock* if it meant the end of wretched, idle monotony.

When he reached Rastis's door, he heard the sound of familiar voices within. He knocked against the doorframe and poked his head inside to see Rastis and Hob sitting around the Loremaster's table.

"Come in, Royne," Rastis said.

Hob offered him a quick nod of greeting and stood up to leave. Rastis relit the bowl of his pipe, inhaled deeply, and released a small cloud of smoke. "So you'll see to it?" he asked the Wrathorn scribe. "I know I don't have to tell you how important this is, Hobart."

"You can count on me, sir," Hob said. "I only wish there was another way."

"I'm afraid there is not." The old man smiled. "May the Lady protect you, my friend."

"And you, Rastis." Hob nodded and withdrew. However, as he passed Royne in the doorway, he patted him on the shoulder with a beefy hand. "Congratulations." He grinned.

"Come in and sit down, Royne," Rastis said once Hob's footsteps receded. "Would you like some tea? I can heat some if you'd like."

Royne sat at the table in the same place he had occupied on the day of King Kredor's coronation and tried to ignore the two vacant seats on either side. "I'm fine, sir," he said, "but thank you."

Rastis nodded silently and smoked his pipe. Fragrant wisps of gray smoke wafted about the room. At length, he sighed. "Hobart and I were just discussing a number of important issues that appear to have fallen into our laps at this time," he said. "And as such, he will no longer be able to serve in the same capacity as he did previously as my steward and scribe."

"You mean Hob's leaving too?" Royne said suddenly.

"No, of course not," Rastis said calmly. "I mean only that I require Hob's particular services in a number of…other matters. You can rest assured that he's not leaving the city, though you may not see him around as often."

Royne's mind buzzed with curiosity. It was well-known that Hobart was a Foundling—a man anointed as a Guardian by a Blackguard who only afterward swore allegiance to the King. Before that, he was simply a Wrathorn mercenary like any other. He fought and drank and sold his blade wherever it was needed. If those were the "particular services" that Rastis was alluding to, Royne could only wonder what use they would be to the bookish old Loremaster. Were Thom there now, he would have simply blurted out the question, and though Rastis would not answer it, the manner of the old man's refusal might at least offer a hint.

Still, Royne was not Thom, and so he simply nodded. "I see," he said.

"In any case," the Loremaster continued, "Though I understand that you have not formally been initiated into the Order, I have decided to elevate you to the rank of scribe so that you might attend me at meetings of the Council of Five and serve in all other capacities as my new steward."

Royne sat up straight in shock. "What?"

Rastis allowed himself a quiet laugh. He stood up from the table, walked over to his desk, and handed Royne a parcel wrapped in twine. When the apprentice opened it, he found that it contained two new burgundy habits striped around the cuffs and the hood with a thin band of white. They were the uniform of a Loremaster's scribe.

Royne shook his head in confusion and looked up to meet the old man's gaze. "I don't understand," he said. "Is this why I was made to stay behind?"

Rastis shrugged and returned to his seat. "In part"—he puffed at his pipe—"let us say that it was one of many." He grinned. "Royne, among the apprentices, you have always possessed the most critical and analytical mind. You are never satisfied until you have rooted out every ounce of truth from a thing and examined it from every angle and from every perspective, even if it meant critiquing the words of the King himself."

Royne nodded bashfully. "Thank you."

"Now do not misunderstand me," Rastis continued. "I do not at all intend my compliment to you as a slight in any way to Lughus or Thom. They, too, have strengths where you, or I, or Hob, or any other, might have flaws. However, that is why they were selected for their tasks and why you were made to remain behind for yours."

Royne nodded again in agreement and smiled in spite of himself at the white stripes along the new robes.

"Thank you, sir," he said again. "I will do my best."

Rastis puffed at his pipe. His smile faded, and he eyed Royne gravely.

"I hope so," he said. "I fear there are dark days ahead." He slid a small silver object across the tabletop. It was a cloak pin shaped like a writing quill.

"Hob left that for you," Rastis said. "It marks you as my steward."

Royne placed it among his new robes. "Thank you," he said again.

Rastis sighed and folded his hands across the table. "Tomorrow morning, the council will convene again, and I will need you to accompany me to the Keystone."

"Yes, sir."

"Until tomorrow, then."

"Yes, sir. Until tomorrow."

"Good night, my boy."

The following morning, Royne was up at dawn. Hurriedly, he dressed in his new robes and woke the tower's servants, Milo and Gordy, to prepare Rastis's breakfast. Royne had always suspected that neither man had ever liked him on account of how little of their food he ate, let alone enjoyed, so he was not surprised when they feigned sleep to ignore his calls. However, when he flashed the silver steward's pin, they reluctantly rolled from their bunks and wandered off to the kitchens to prepare Rastis's usual morning meal: two runny eggs, two slices of dry toast, and a slice of bacon glistening with grease. The old man insisted on brewing his own tea.

"Hob often tipped us in silver by way of a thank you," Milo said, handing Royne the breakfast tray.

"Did he now?" Royne grinned. "I'll tell him you miss him when next I see him."

The sullen cook turned away with a sneer. "Snotty prick," he muttered.

Royne stifled a laugh and hurried merrily down the stairs to the Loremaster's chamber. By the time he arrived, Rastis had already woken and sat smoking his first pipe of the day beside the embers of his fire and brooding over *The Book of Histories*. When he saw Royne appear with his breakfast, he breathed a long spindle of smoke from the corner of his mouth and flipped the heavy book shut.

"Ah," he said, "thank you, son." He dipped a piece of toast into the runny yellow goo that Gordy claimed was once an egg. "Have you eaten?"

Royne nodded. "While I waited."

"Good," Rastis said. "Sit down."

Royne sided into his usual seat. "Is it customary for the council to meet this early?" he asked.

"It's not customary for the council to meet much at all, sadly," Rastis said. The kettle on the fire behind him began to whistle, and the old man paused to pour his tea before continuing, "Recently, however, the King and his new adviser have decided that, if meet we must, then the early morning hours are the best time for it so as to leave the bulk of the daylight hours for more pressing matters, or so some would believe."

Royne wanted to ask what the old man meant and if not in meetings with the council, where Rastis had been for such long hours over the past week. However, he was rather surprised by the taciturn Loremaster's sudden candor, and so instead, he decided to hold his tongue. The old man read him like a book.

"Royne," he said, "I am certain that you will find today to be a most eye-opening experience."

When Rastis finished with his breakfast, Royne ran the empty tray back upstairs to the kitchens, and the old man made ready to go. As the Loremaster's steward, it would be Royne's job to carry the massive, leather-bound tome of his office to the council chamber in the Keystone. As he held it in his hands, his heart felt light, imagining the secrets that must certainly lie within. He was gripped by a tremendous longing to pry it open—if only but for a peek—but forced himself to maintain self-control. For to trespass on the secrets reserved only for his master would be the height of sacrilege.

As the sun was clearing the horizon, the old Loremaster and the young scribe made their way across the courtyard of Castle Testament to the keep. Although Royne had lived for as long as he could remember within the castle's walls, he could count on both of his hands the number of times that he had stood within the gilded majesty of the Keystone's throne room. Towering pillars of white marble reached high up into the lofty ceilings bearing massive braziers shaped into the likeness of enormous golden keys that set the gleaming floor tiles shining like sunlight upon the snow. For a moment, Royne was wary of setting foot upon it, lest some speck of dust or dirt from his boot mar its pristine surface. Rastis, however, continued undeterred to the raised stone dais upon which rested the throne of the Guardian King. Carved from holy oak and adorned with soft cushions of scarlet cloth, the sight of it gave Royne pause—despite the many jokes he'd made over the years about the massive chair recording the history of Kings' fat asses.

Beyond the high seat, a series of passageways channeled off to other parts of the keep, and it was here that the old Loremaster continued on.

"Come along, Royne," he said with half a smile. "I'd expect such dawdling from Lughus and Thom, but I always thought you to be unimpressed by such things."

"Apologies, sir," the lanky scribe muttered bashfully and hurried along behind.

At the end of one of the long corridors, Rastis stopped before a heavy oaken door and knocked. Two men clad in the massive great armor of the keep's private guard shambled heavily through the doorway, looking more like metal golems than mere men. They saluted Rastis automatically as he passed but remained in the passage outside to receive the remaining councilors.

The room that lay beyond the sentries was hardly what Royne would have expected as the meeting place for the most prestigious men of the Order, for apart from the fine, stained-glass windows that, in the early light of the morning, painted the room with myriad colors, it contained only a large wooden cabinet and a long wooden table upon which sat three silver candelabras, again, fashioned in the likeness of keys.

Ushering him inside, Rastis rested his hand on Royne's spare shoulder and pointed. "Once the meeting begins," he whispered, "I'll sit there to record the minutes, and you'll have to stand behind me against the wall. Try to keep from making eye contact with any of the others, and unless spoken to directly, avoid making any sound louder than a cough, regardless of what you hear."

"Yes, sir," Royne nodded.

"If I break a quill or need more parchment, you can find it in the cabinet on the top shelf. You'll see where when the Hierophant's steward retrieves another flagon." He winked. "Old Hagan likes his drink."

The young scribe suppressed a nervous laugh. "Yes, sir," he said again.

"You'll do fine," Rastis told him. "Though I'd avoid correcting the King if, for some reason, he happens to mistake his history…"

"I won't say a word, Rastis," Royne said. "I promise."

"I'm only joking, my boy." The Loremaster smiled. "But listen closely. I want you to—"

Rastis cut himself off as the door opened, and Rordan Baird, the Chancellor, strode into the room, followed closely by one of his courtiers carrying a large leather case in one arm and in the other, the ceremonial lantern of the chancellery.

"Rastis," the Chancellor said with a polite nod.

"Hello, Rordan," Rastis said, "I hope the morning finds you well."

He motioned to Royne, and together, they sidled around the table to the Loremaster's place while the Chancellor took his place at the foot. Baird was a very slight man, Royne noticed, though his every motion seemed punctuated by an air of direct confidence, like the precise, staccato movements of a farmer reaping grain. His attendant, a dour, pinch-faced lad of perhaps eighteen, hurriedly uncovered the flap to a broad leather case and stacked a small tower of wide ledgers upon the table at his master's left.

"Thank you, Maurice," he said briefly and turned back toward Rastis. "The day finds me well indeed, Loremaster, though I hope that you will find our discussion this morning satisfying enough to keep it brief."

"So do I," Rastis said politely, and Royne wondered at the implications of the Chancellor's comment.

Though he had seen the Chancellor at ceremonies and in the courtyard from time to time, he had never actually met him, nor did he have the feeling that Rordan Baird had any interest in meeting him now. His dark, pointed beard bobbed up and down as he reviewed his ledgers, occasionally pausing to make notes. The Chancellor and his men, the courtiers, constables, counselors, and commissioners, oversaw Andoch's civil legislature, legal courts, and trade regulations. As such, they prided themselves on their efficiency and expediency, likening themselves to the oarsmen of an ancient imperial war galley of Old Calendral. For just as it was only through orderly precision that the rowers could make the great ship advance, so it was with a great nation such as Andoch. And if civil service required that the men of the Chancellor's Tower be chained to their ledgers like galley slaves chained to their oars, it was a sacrifice each man made for the greater good.

The chamber door opened again, and a blonde, smooth-faced young celebrant of the Order entered, leading the way for the portly old man following behind him. Hagan Shawn, the Grand Hierophant of the Order, waited while his assistant pulled his chair out from the table for him, took the old man's staff, and removed his miter.

"Good morning," the high priest said abruptly as he took his
seat.

"Good morning, Grand Hierophant," the Chancellor nodded.

"Hello, Hagan," Rastis said.

Royne watched the Grand Hierophant out of the corner of his eye. The old man sat stiffly upright in his seat across the table from Rastis. A glossy film of perspiration settled upon his brow, and the purity of his fine, white robes made his ruddy complexion seem nearly as dark as the Loremaster's burgundy. He was not overly fat but rather thick and blockish of form, though his heavy jowls and cheeks came together in lips that pursed together like the mouth of a great fish. Over the course of his lifetime in the Loremaster's Tower, Royne, Lughus, and Thom had been formally introduced to the Hierophant at least seven or eight times at various ceremonies or festivals, yet each time the old man regarded them as if it were the first.

The Hierophant knocked lightly on the table near the Chancellor.

"Thank you for agreeing to assist us with the tithes again this year," he said lowly. "With the yearly contributions from the provincials, the cousins, and the handmaids, I do not know what we would do without your courtiers and their teams of collectors."

The Chancellor looked up from his ledger. "Harvestide is a busy time for all of us." Baird nodded sympathetically. "From noble to commoner, the people often forget how much work must be done in the wake of all their festivals and feasting. My men are glad to be of assistance."

"May the Lord-Father bless them for their industriousness," Hagan Shawn replied.

He turned to his assistant, waggled a finger, and with a polite nod, the youth withdrew to the cabinet along the wall and retrieved a tray laden with crystal glasses and a tall flagon of a deep red wine. Royne watched idly, noticing the shelf Rastis had mentioned stacked with sheaves of parchment, extra quills, and inkpots; however, when the Celebrant set the tray on the table and poured for his master, Royne noticed that there were six glasses instead of five. The Loremaster appeared to have noticed it, too, but said nothing.

The door opened a fourth time with a boisterous hail of laughter as Dandon Rood, the Warlord, slapped a meaty hand upon the shoulder of one of the sentries at some prior joke and tramped heavily into the room to take his seat between the Hierophant and the Chancellor. Even without the polished plate of his great battle armor, Rood was an enormous man, broad-shouldered, heavy-jawed, and strong of arm. He was near sixty years of age, but with the exception of a widening paunch at his midsection and gray patches of hair around his temples, he bore no signs yet of any enfeeblement. He was outfitted formally in his courtly regalia, a fine crimson surcoat and a short cloak of cloth of silver, soft white leggings, and calf-skin boots lined with white rabbit fur. In his belt, he carried a dagger, seeing no need to carry his massive great sword, Duty, within the confines of the Keystone, and left it safely and ceremoniously in the hands of his attendant.

Royne's jaw tightened. It was Pryce.

Newly clad in the attire of a Warlord's partisan, Pryce regarded Royne with a smug look of condescension. In the place where once the cadet had worn a dagger, the partisan now wore his own sword in addition to carrying the Warlord's. Royne ground his teeth in silence.

"Good morning, all!" the Warlord said, pouring himself a glass of wine from the tray.

The Chancellor and the Hierophant offered their greetings.

"Morning, Dandy," Rastis said.

"Well, Rastis, you were right about sending Harding," the Warlord said after a drink. "Word just reached me last night. It was an absolute routing.

The Valendians lost nearly ten thousand men. Mark my words, The War of the Horses will be over in no time at all."

"His majesty will be happy to hear it," the Hierophant said. "He wants a united Montevale. Gasparn's request for our aid might suggest that there may be some measure of redemption for those kinslayers after all. I'm surprised that neither side has requested that I send a provincial. You know, those—" He would have continued, but for the door opening one final time.

"His Majesty, the King!" one of the sentries shouted, and reflexively, the council members stood.

King Kredor Drude hurried into the room with brusque ceremony, and up close, at least to Royne, the King bore little resemblance to the resplendent hero he appeared on his coronation day. He wore neither armor nor any cloak but rather a simple, unadorned surcoat of crimson velvet, simple leather breeches, and a linen shirt. In his belt, he carried a long dagger but otherwise bore neither sword nor scepter, and his fine dark hair fell loose upon his shoulders, unfettered by his crown. At such a close distance, Royne was able to guess Kredor's age at thereabout thirty, and his face seemed one used to laughter, though of a sardonic or ironic sort as opposed to more common expressions of joy or mirth. In one smooth motion, he slid heavily into his seat at the head of the table, swept up a crystal goblet, and poured. Two young pages clad in red-and-white motley—sandy-haired twins with rosy cheeks shining like apples—carried small, silver tambourines that jingled lightly as they pranced after him, accompanied by yet another gentleman. He was of an age with the king and finely arrayed in robes of crimson silk and gold embroidery, but in contrast to the fiery shades of Andochan red of his clothing, the man's white-blond hair, pallid complexion, and pale-blue eyes made him seem carved from a block of ice. Royne had never seen him before, though when he took the chair at the Kredor's left hand, it was immediately clear that whoever he was, he was a person of great import to the Guardian King.

"Well, Rastis," the young King grinned, "I hope you find today's meeting well worth waking up at such an ungodly hour. I should say there are things enough to do as it is, but then again, you are the Loremaster, and none doubt your wisdom."

"Thank you, Your Majesty," Rastis said.

Kredor nodded magnanimously. "But come," he said, "the council convenes. What shall we talk about?"

The King settled his gaze upon each of the council members in turn; however, the Chancellor, the Hierophant, and the Warlord each remained silent. Only once the monarch's eye fell upon him did Rastis clear his throat to speak. "Your Majesty," he began, "after your father passed on his title to you, I had the honor of spending many long days and nights at his side as age and illness slowly claimed him."

"And you were a great comfort to him, I'm certain," Kredor said.

"It was my duty not only as his adviser but as his friend," he said simply. "In any case, as we spoke, there was one issue of which we spoke that, as I understand it, was a point of contention between the two of you for some time."

"Ah yes"—Kredor nodded—"the Protectorate."

"The Protectorate," Rastis repeated.

Royne tried to remain still and keep his expression impassive. However, out of the corner of his eye, he noticed the other councilors squirm awkwardly in their seats. The Warlord coughed into his fist, and the Chancellor breathed a heavy sigh. Hagan Shawn, the Hierophant, folded his hands across his lap and licked his lips, staring into his goblet at the shallow remains of his drink. Only the sixth man remained unaffected.

Royne tried to remember what he had read of the Protectorate. It had something to do with the consolidation of power for the mutual defense of Termain, a way to defend the entire continent when faced with a unified foreign threat. From what he could recall offhand, only twice in the Order's history had it ever been put into use. The First Protectorate, little more than a century after the fall of Kalius Wrogan, was to combat the armada of the Empress of Tulondis from across the Nomaric Ocean, and the Second Protectorate, merely a few centuries ago, was to defend against an invasion from Kord on the southern continent. However, in both cases, the Protectorate was implemented only at the request of the sovereign leaders of the other nations of Termain—Dwerin, Grantis, Montevale, Baronbrock. Together, they jointly named the Guardian King of Andoch as the high commander of their allied defenses so as to present a unified force. Yet as far as Royne knew, neither Tulondis nor Kord (nor anyone else, for that matter) posed any threat to Termain at this time.

At length, King Kredor leaned wearily on one elbow and ran his finger along the rim of his cup. "All right, Rastis," he said, "Out with it."

Rastis made a note with his quill. "Your Majesty," he said, "I understand the sacred duties that the Drudes feel to safeguard the realms of Termain. However, with all due respect, you must understand that from a historical standpoint, the very concept of the Protectorate is contradictory to the ideals upon which our very Order was founded."

"In what way, Loremaster?" Kredor said.

As Rastis spoke, his voice was clear and strong, and Royne could sense that, in his own manner, the old man was making his stand.

"When St. Aiden fell in battle defeating Kalius Wrogan, the people of Old Calendral were lost and frightened. The Warlock was dead, but so was the Saint. So they begged the Guardians for assistance, and Halford Drude, your noble ancestor, acquiesced to their wishes and promised to guard and protect the people but only as king of Andoch. Each of the remaining provinces was granted the autonomy that had been denied them previously under both the Calendral emperors and the Warlock, and with the assistance of the fledgling Order, the clans and villages of each new realm banded together to establish their own rulers and their own system of governance. For not only was St. Aiden fighting against the evil of Dibhor but also the tyranny that men like Landus Veirne and Kalius Wrogan often inflict upon one another."

"Tyranny, my fellow councilors," Rastis continued, "was perhaps the concept most feared by our predecessors at the outset of the Order, for they knew well the dangers of a single, autocratic ruler. We are quick to vilify Landus Veirne, as we rightly should, but let us not also forget the sins of his forbearers: Emperor Nantos, who put a thousand children to the sword fearing one may have been his own bastard, Emperor Forius, who instituted the policy of Divine Homage, granting his nobles the right to take to bed any common man's wife with impunity, Emperor Siverus, who imprisoned the men of Dwerin in their own mines and released them only after they paid their own weight in gold. The list goes on and on."

"Yet"—Rastis sighed—"these were men believed to be chosen by the Brethren themselves, and if those blessed by the gods were so susceptible to sin, what hope do the rest of us have?"

Hagan Shawn shook his head. "That was the corrupting influence of Dibhor," he said tersely. "As has been noted by the faithful long ago. Since the time of St. Aiden, the rights of the nobility have been free of this taint, and with the exception of but a few who embraced sin by their own volition, the divinity of the nobility has been pure and true."

"You are the expert on religious matters, Lord Hierophant," Rastis said. "I simply speak in terms of history."

King Kredor smiled. "Then what are you suggesting, Rastis? Do you suggest that I, too, will become a tyrant?"

"I do not suggest it," Rastis said. "However, as a friend to your father, I watched you grow into the man that you are today as my King. Thus, I am doubly concerned with the safety of your person, your majesty, for just as I have always feared you might come to harm in battle, I find that politics is no less dangerous, perhaps not to the body, but to the soul."

Kredor nodded but remained silent, and inwardly, Royne smiled. *Well said, Rastis. Well said.*

The old man continued, "Regardless, our forbearers knew the dangers of a single ruler, and as such, it is for that reason that we all sit gathered together here and now. The Protectorate was meant solely as a military agreement in a time of war instituted to organize soldiers against a common threat. However, in either of the past instances of this policy, the Guardian King was recognized solely as a military leader backed closely by the Warlord and the most honored generals of the other realms. True governance, the day-to-day management of the realms remained in the hands of the respective leaders, the archduke, the Lord-Baron, the Montevalen and Grantisi Kings."

"I say, Rastis," the Chancellor remarked. "Now that you mention Grantis, I must admit that much of what you speak of smacks of the Republic. I hope at our next meeting you do not intend to suggest we follow their example and declare war on the gentry."

"Of course not, Rordan." Rastis smiled, ignoring the slight. "You know that I would never advocate a war under any circumstances. History is far too full of wars and many other sad things besides. Plagues, famine, sackings, and raids. How sad that men never seem to record happy things, the weddings, festivals, good harvests, the kind deeds one man does for another." He paused and shook his head. "In fact, when I was a boy, I often found history to be rather depressing. However, now that I am an old man, I realize that the reason for this is that these dark things are unnatural. For we do not often think about breathing or waking in the morning, we simply do them, such as it is with good deeds. History, if anything, is a record of the unnatural, so we can learn from these…anomalies and not repeat them. Sadly, it appears that we have yet to learn the lesson of war."

"I hardly think the Warlord would agree with you," the Hierophant muttered.

"On the contrary," Dandon Rood said, "any day my sword remains sheathed is a good one. A true warrior fights only when he must, not because he wants to."

The Chancellor sighed wearily. "If we could return to the matter at hand…"

Rastis nodded. "Then I will make my point," he said. "For thirteen hundred years, the Drudes have served Termain as the Guardian Kings of Andoch, and as a part of the Order, they have served as arbitrators and protectors to ensure the safety of all men in all the realms. Twice under the policy of the Protectorate, they led us to victory over the encroachment of a foreign threat at the behest of the leadership of the other realms. To seek the Protectorate now in a time of peace would be, in my opinion, very dangerous not only to Termain but to the person of the Guardian King himself. For, correct me if I am wrong, Lord Hierophant, but Dibhor likes nothing more than to corrupt that which by nature is good, often through confounding our pure intentions. We should continue to guide the other realms as we always have: through example, arbitration, and right action. Not through the Protectorate. We enter our neighbors' homes when invited, not by breaking down their doors."

"So the Loremaster believes it wise then to do nothing?"

Royne started and glanced in the direction of the speaker. It was the pale man with the eyes of ice. Once again, he wondered at the man's identity, for he was clearly not a member of the council, nor did he seem in any way affiliated with the Order. Whoever he was, though, Royne's breast swelled with mounting antipathy for the man. Who was he to dare interrupt the Loremaster? Such a thing was unthinkable, unforgivable. Yet, strangely, no one else seemed to share in his outrage. Instead, the man was simply allowed to continue.

"Consider, Loremaster, the state of the other realms at this time," he mused, counting on his long white fingers. "Dwerin has been without an archduke for a full five years now, leaving behind not a son to inherit but a daughter who is little more than a girl. Montevale has been at civil war now for nearly a century, embroiled in a conflict built upon kinslaying. Grantis is governed by a senate of fools who have rejected the Kinship in exchange for the blasphemy of the southern continent and their Sign of Four, and in Baronbrock, despite the best efforts of thy noble brother's son, Rastis, the baronies squabble over trade routes and tariffs, willing to go to war with their neighbors over a handful of coppers. This, of course, is to say nothing about the Wrathorn clans that worship their sticks and stones and live like droves of wild beasts stalking the lands of the North or the Sorgund corsairs marauding along the coasts. Is this not the tyranny of men as well? Is this not what the Guardians are meant to protect us from? Must we wait for Kord or Tulondis to attack our shores when the insidiousness of corruption is already destroying Termain from within? I doubt the Order would turn a blind eye to such dangers."

Rastis's eyes flashed. "You seem to know a great deal about the duties of our Order, Natharis, for not being one of us."

The pale man smiled and bowed his head. "As the personal adviser to the King, it is my duty to know such things," he said. "Certainly, you of all people can recognize the importance of knowledge."

Royne's fists clenched involuntarily. Natharis Tainne, he recognized now, was King Kredor's oldest and closest friend. Though not a warrior like the King, Tainne had made a name for himself among the Andochan nobility and throughout the realm, though for what exactly, Royne did not know. For although the Guardians made their home in Andoch and were a symbol of its power, in essence, their purpose was to serve the Andochan people from the least to the greatest. The Chancellor's men acted as civil servants, the Hierophants were to be servants to the faithful, the Warlord's men functioned as generals and elite warriors serving as protectors of the populace, and the Loremaster's men served as advisers and teachers. Even the King, in theory, was a servant, providing his people with leadership, direction, and protection as was his duty. However, like any other realm, Andoch still had its nobles, its poor, and its middle class. It maintained its own system of justice, its own economy, and its own secular culture. It was in that world that Natharis Tainne had thrived.

At length, the Hierophant cleared his throat. "Your Majesty, fellow councilors," he said slowly, "I believe Lord Tainne speaks the truth. From the standpoint of the church, I have been greatly distressed of late to see the wanton abandonment of the Brothers by the other realms, and I admit that I often find myself fearing for the lot of our fellow men's souls."

Fearing reduction in your yearly tithes more like, Royne thought to himself.

"But I must admit," the Warlord said, "is the Protectorate truly the answer? I find it difficult to believe that the other realms would accept such a proposal in a time of peace, and if they reject it, what then? We cannot demand their allegiance. Would the Guardians truly go to battle against the very folk we were sworn to protect?"

King Kredor grinned. "Oh, come now, Dandy! That's a bloody great sword you carry to keep it all the time in its sheath. Don't tell me the Warlord fears war?"

Royne watched as Dandon Rood stiffened. "By no means, Your Majesty," he said, "However, consider the men of our Order. Though not the majority, a great many of our number do not hail from Andoch originally. Would a man fight against the men of his own homeland if called to do so?"

Kredor smiled. "I don't know. Would you, Rastis?"

Rastis's face bore no expression; however, Royne could sense the Loremaster's anger. "My loyalty is to the Order and to the people of Termain, my King, as you well know," he said quietly. "And as for war, I believe I already made known my feelings on the subject."

"Oh, calm yourself, old man. I jest," Kredor said. "However, make no mistake. These are precarious times for the people of Termain, and as the Guardian King, I cannot merely stand aside and watch as they all fall to ruin. What would the Brethren think of a King who abandons his duties? And as such, though I do intend to consolidate power beneath the banner of the Protectorate, I do not intend to lead the nation into a prolonged war. Even now, steps have been taken to ensure a bloodless, diplomatic solution to the problem. In fact, many other realms seem to regard our offer to intercede as a welcome relief. Already, an alliance has been reached with Dwerin, and Marius of Gasparn has pledged us Montevale so long as we help him to bring an end to the War of the Horses. Beyond that, Rastis knows full well of our means by which to pacify the baronies of the Brock while the Wrathorn and the Sorgunders can just as easily be bought—those we don't hang as criminals, of course."

"But what of the Republic?" the Warlord asked.

The King shrugged. "I admit it. Grantis will almost certainly come to open blows, but since the Senate has openly embraced the Sign of Four, who is to say that this is not the first stage of what may one day be a full-scale Kordish invasion? This leaves only Castone on the far edge of the continent, but the Keepers of the Lighthouse have forsworn the use of arms and armor, and as he studied with them in his youth, Lord Tainne is confident that they would welcome our pledge of protection in the event of war."

"Dandon, you referred to ours as a 'time of peace,' but, my friend, I assure you that the battle rages on already. And if no one raises a hand to safeguard the people of Termain from themselves, then we may as well invite the armies of the other continents to our shores. For, as Grantis has shown us, they need not send soldiers to take our lives or to corrupt our souls. Already, the Beinns are readying for war against the Senate to avenge their fallen archduke. It is my intention, and that of the Andochan noble houses, to back them."

The Warlord stuttered, "But, Your Majesty, Harvestide will soon be upon us, and shortly thereafter, autumn will pass quickly into winter. Should we not wait until the spring as is customary? The preparations alone to muster the armies could take weeks, even months!"

"Perhaps for your Guardians, Warlord Rood." Natharis Tainne smiled. "However, the nobles and the kingsmen have been readying these summer months and more. Should we send a token force by sea to join Dwerin's armies preparing to march out to retake the Spade, we can fortify the castles along our border with Grantis and be well-placed to attack immediately following the spring thaw. The legions of the Senate will be forced to fight a war on two fronts whilst our fleet joins the Dwerin armada to cut off any aid from the heathen Kordish to the south. By this time next year, should the Brethren will it, the entire continent of Termain could be safely under the protection of the Guardian King and his retainers. It will be the beginning of a new age, a golden age of peace and prosperity for all!"

Royne fought with all his willpower not to give in to a sudden urge to laugh. Tainne was a madman! Dwerin, with its mines, forges, and foundries, produced the continent's finest arms and armor; however, soldiers couldn't eat ore any more than mountains could grow grain, and though fertile, the farmlands of Andoch could certainly not produce enough grain to feed *two* armies. Even if the Dwerin forces miraculously captured the Spade before winter, the Grantisi would certainly be wise enough to destroy any remaining stores they could not take with them in their retreat.

What a fine pair of leaders! Royne thought. *Lord Fop and King Boor!* Add to them Chancellor Abacus and Hierophant Sot, and the meeting of the council seemed a gathering of fools.

Regardless of the young steward's personal feelings, however, King Kredor nodded with approval at Lord Tainne's words and returned his attention to Rastis. "Natharis has the right of it, dear Loremaster, and that is why the Protectorate is necessary. For the safety of all Termain and its people, I will bring them under one rule, under one king. You say Baronbrock and Montevale and the others will not accept it, but I assure you, Rastis, they will"—he paused— "for the Grantisi defeat will show them, as it will show us all, that when met with the will of the divine, there is no other choice."

Royne shot a furtive glance at the King in an attempt to gauge the full implications of that statement from the sovereign's visage. However, Kredor's face was a mask of stalwart determination. It filled the young steward with uncertainty.

"To say it again," Kredor proclaimed, "as King, my office affords me full command of the Andochan armies, and as Natharis suggested, I intend to use them to back Dwerin against Grantis. It is my sincerest hope, however, that the Order will provide me with unified support in this endeavor and in all others as well. After all, Warlord Rood, the men will have need of your officers to command them."

Royne eyed Rastis, but the old man merely scratched away with his quill, impassively recording the minutes.

The Chancellor cleared his throat and paged quickly through one of his ledgers. "As it stands now," he said, "I see the benefits of His Majesty's suggestion outweighing the costs. Generally speaking, endeavors such as these serve to stimulate trade, and should we strengthen relations with Dwerin and its mines, the long-term benefits might outweigh any short-term costs. Furthermore, should Grantis be forced in their defeat to…make certain amends...their farmlands will help to replenish any of our stores spent in support of the ironmen. Thus, I motion that the Order supports the King."

The Hierophant agreed. "I believe my opinions on this matter are already known," he said. "But again, for the sake of reassurance, I will remind the Council of the Order's sworn duty to safeguard the people of Termain and not simply their physical welfare, but more importantly, the security of their immortal souls, for we cannot stand by idly and watch as they fall victim to the blasphemy of the Sign of Four." He breathed a heavy sigh. "I second the Chancellor's motion."

Dandon Rood shifted uncomfortably in his seat, and Royne watched as the big man's eyes roamed from the tabletop to Rastis and back again as if he were hoping for the Loremaster to speak. However, Royne knew, just as Rastis did, that voicing any further disagreement would be a futile effort. The old man remained silent, and to Royne's surprise, the Warlord did as well.

"Then I believe the motion carries." King Kredor nodded at last. "Excellent." He smiled and drained the remaining wine from his glass. "Now, is there any other business to attend to, or shall we adjourn? We've got plenty to do with missives to write and soldiers to muster and whatnot..." he turned to Rastis, grinning. "What say you, old man? Any other concerns you'd like to bring before the council, or can we get on with it?"

Rastis returned the King's smile politely, but Royne knew that it was merely for show, "Not at this time, Your Majesty."

Kredor glanced around the table at the other councilors. Already, the Hierophant was rising from his seat.

"Then I suppose that that will be all for today then. Warlord Rood, I will speak to you further before the week's end regarding our initial plans and orders for the field commanders..."

"Aye, Your Majesty," the Warlord said with a bow. "I will convene my justiciars and determine those best suited."

"Very good," said the King. "We must send out best."

Beside him, Natharis Tainne cleared his throat quietly, and the King paused. "Oh yes, Loremaster, one last, private word if you please?"

"Of course, Your Majesty," Rastis said mildly as the Chancellor, the Hierophant, and their attendants withdrew.

When they had gone, the Warlord drained his goblet and set it on the table with a solid thud. For a fleeting moment, Royne thought he saw the old soldier exchange a quick glance with the Loremaster, but he remained silent and, with a quick wave of his hand, motioned for Pryce to follow him out.

Royne shifted uneasily on his feet, uncertain of whether or not he should stay for the King's "private word." However, neither Natharis Tainne nor either one of the sandy twins made any move to depart, and in spite of the demands of the King's hectic schedule, Kredor seemed in no great hurry to speak. He simply refilled his goblet from the decanter, swirled his cup, and took a deep gulp.

Rastis, meanwhile, sat unmoving in his seat at the table, his posture straight but calm, his hands folded atop the stack of parchment upon which he had kept the minutes of the council session, and slowly, it dawned on Royne that whatever it was that the King intended to speak of, the Loremaster was already more than aware.

Perhaps Kredor knew it too, for only after a second sip from his goblet did the King finally speak. "I see that you have finally replaced your Wrathorn with something more appropriate." He observed. "Tell me, what is your new steward's name?"

Rastis caught Royne's eye and motioned him forward, and though it was against his natural inclinations, Royne dropped to one knee.

"This is Royne, one of my apprentices," Rastis said. "Recently raised to scribe, though he has yet to take the rite."

The King nodded magnanimously. "Rise, son, and be welcome."

"Thank you, Your Majesty," Royne muttered and returned to his place behind Rastis.

"I seem to recall, Loremaster, that you had more than just this one apprentice," Kredor said. "And speaking of old Hobart, wherever has the old boy gotten himself to these days?"

"Hobart has unfortunately undertaken some new duties for me that have rendered him incapable of serving as my steward any longer," Rastis said simply. "And as for my other two apprentices, I had decided that to begin preparing them for full initiation into the Order, it would be in their best interests for them to continue their studies beyond the borders of Andoch so that they may gain a greater understanding of the Order's duties across Termain."

"I see," King Kredor said, pursing his lips. "Natharis tells me they set off down the Imperial…what was it? Eight? Nine days ago?"

"Lord Tainne is correct," the old man said. "They left by barge at dawn's first light."

"I see," the King said. "But tell me, Rastis, is it really true that one of the boys was the heir to Baron Arcis Galadin of the Brock?"

What?

Royne's breath caught in his chest, and he struggled not to cough. Lord Arcis, he well knew, was one of the most powerful of the barons in Baronbrock and the direct descendant of St. Aiden himself—the last of his line, in fact.

"As you alluded to in the council meeting," Rastis said simply, "yes, he is."

At once, King Kredor's eyes flashed, and his gaze became as steel. He cast a quick glance back at Natharis Tainne. However, the adviser's face was as stoic and impassive as the Loremaster's.

"I hope, old man," the King said at last, "that you intend to inform us of where you sent him!"

"Certainly"—Rastis shrugged—"I sent him home."

"You sent him *home?*"

A sudden chill rolled down Royne's spine, and his hands felt numb. *Blood and fire, Rastis,* he thought. *What have you done?*

Rastis continued, unaffected. "The boy's place with us was never meant to be permanent," he said simply. "And as Arcis Galadin's condition grows worse, he will desire to see his heir installed."

"So he will," Kredor said, "which might have provided an excellent opportunity to prevent future bloodshed."

"I'm not quite sure that I know what you mean, Your Majesty."

"Forgive me if I find that rather hard to believe, Loremaster."

Rastis breathed a heavy sigh. "As I mentioned earlier," he said, "the Order of the Guardians was founded not only in opposition to the Warlock but as a means of safeguarding the people of Termain against the Darkness of Dibhor, against injustice, against tyranny. What, Your Majesty, is tyranny if not the denial of freedom, the denial of choice? Arcis Galadin entrusted his grandson to my keeping so as to keep him safe until he came of age. I have done that. However, were I to force him to forswear all that he is due and to live a life of servitude to the Order, I would be no less a tyrant than a

Calendral Emperor. Furthermore, the boy has undergone no Rite of Initiation, nor has he been anointed with rank and title requiring him to swear the Oath of Fealty. Thus, it will be—it *must* be—the boy's choice whether to return to us or to stay in Baronbrock and assume his role there."

"That may be," Kredor said, "though his presence here might well have meant the difference between the peaceful submission of the Brock and prolonged, open warfare. I would hate to have all that blood on my hands for such a rash decision."

"I have made my choice, Your Majesty," Rastis said. "Come what may, I must accept the consequences, whatever they might be. However, as you reminded us in the meeting, I will count myself fortunate in knowing that the power to muster the armies of Andoch and declare war on our neighbors resides solely in the hands of the Guardian King. That, at least, is one choice I will not have to make."

At once, Kredor's face drained of color, and his knuckles went white, gripping the arms of his chair. Once more, he glanced at the adviser seated at his side, but Natharis Tainne offered no words of counsel to the young King. He simply folded his pale, white hands upon the tabletop before him and fixed the old Loremaster with a serpentine stare.

That's it! Royne realized, gazing at the pallid lord, *Pale as a viper's underbelly and the cold dead eyes of an adder!*

Never had Royne experienced a heavier silence, nor could he ever recall seeing men exert so much effort to appear so apathetic. Yet, somehow, he sensed that he had just witnessed something of great magnitude as if somehow the Loremaster had thrown down a gauntlet, had drawn a line in the sand, and he—as the old man's Steward, had been invited to act as the old man's second in the resulting duel of wills. Whole minutes seemed to pass without a word or even a sound until suddenly, one of the pageboys dropped his tambourine, and the spell was broken as the instrument clattered noisily upon the flagstones.

Kredor whirled on him. "Boy!"

The page approached Kredor cautiously, his head bowed in deference. The King shook his head in exacerbation and slapped the boy hard across his face. The second twin immediately began to giggle with laughter until Kredor summoned him too with a snap of his fingers and struck him dumb with a second blow. Rastis shook his head and breathed an audible sigh, not bothering to hide his disapproval.

"Lord Vendik's sons," Natharis Tainne declared, "His Majesty took them on after their father's death." His lips spread into a subtle leer. "You see, Rastis," he said, "you're not the only one with a habit of collecting orphans."

Kredor dismissed the pages back to their places to sob in silence before turning once more to face the old Loremaster. "You know, Rastis," he said, "if it were not for the long years of loyal service and friendship that you provided for my father and grandfather, one might consider an act such as this as a stone's throw from treason."

Royne's eyes went wide. *Treason! By the Gods, has everyone gone mad?* He glanced at Rastis, but if the old man was concerned, he did not show it. He simply cleared his throat and sat up straighter in his chair. "I suppose it might be considered an act of treason," he said, "Though to others, it might appear an act of great faith, if not one of wisdom."

Royne felt a bead of sweat carefully glide down his neck and continue onward down his spine.

At length, King Kredor shook his head and breathed a heavy sigh. "Natharis," he said, "send word to Constable Harlow down in Galdoran. He should be more than capable of finding the boy and returning him to us."

"Yes, Your Majesty," Tainne said. "I'll send both riders and birds at once."

Kredor sighed and turned back to Rastis. "You know," he said, "when my father chose to anoint me as the next King, he told me that, above all others, I could count on you. How disappointed I am to find that I cannot take him at his word. You may return to your tower."

CHAPTER 11:
THE MOUSE & THE FALCON

"Will you sit, my lady?" The prisoner grinned. Brigid's blood turned to ice, and all of a sudden, she began to feel faint. When she spoke, her voice was but a whisper. "How did you free yourself?" she asked.

He raised an eyebrow. "I might ask you the same question."

Her eyes widened with the prisoner's smile, and she wondered at her own rash decision in coming here.

"This was a mistake," she whispered and at once made to turn for the door.

At once, the prisoner leaped to his feet, gasping involuntarily against some wound hidden beneath the folds of his clothing.

"Please don't," he said. "Please, I swear by the Lady of Light that I will not harm you."

Something about his tone of voice gave her pause, and she glanced back at him inquisitively. His shoulders hunched awkwardly, and he swayed slightly on his feet as if the slightest wind could knock him over. Once more, her eyes met his, the two smoldering orbs from her daydreams, and she sighed.

"Please," he said again.

Tentatively, Brigid nodded and slowly crept forward to the table. The prisoner sank back heavily into his chair but managed to thrust out a foot to kick the other out for her.

"Thank you."

"You are most welcome."

With the slightest hesitation, she assumed the proffered seat at the table and, against every inclination, tried to avoid staring, for if this man, this criminal, could maintain some sense of decorum in spite of his situation, then surely, it would be the height of discourtesy for her not to do the same. However, as the moments passed and the silence lengthened, for he seemed in no hurry now to speak, her curiosity soon got the better of her, and timidly, she cast her gaze upon him up close.

He was handsome, as she had noticed before, and his dark brown hair and beard, though another week longer and even more unkempt, looked as though they were used to being neat and tidy. The same could be said for his clothing, which despite its tears, cuts, and bloodstains, seemed from its stitching to have been well-made and reliable for one used to the lifestyle of the traveling adventurer. The buttons and buckles were finely crafted, and the leather, though worn, seemed supple. Remembering now the baldric and the fine pair of daggers that Alan had stolen, Brigid wondered how an outlaw could ever have come into possession of such finery—even if he was gifted in the ways of the Guardians. Her blue eyes widened with wonder; it did not escape the prisoner's notice.

"I must look dreadful," he said, uttering a soft, voiceless laugh. "Do I frighten you, Mouse?"

With a shock of anxiety, she folded her hands in her lap and sat up straight in her chair. "No," she whispered.

Once more, the prisoner laughed, louder this time, though not unkindly. "You're lying," he said, "But I thank you for trying to be polite."

Brigid blushed, and her eyes fell on the tiny flame dancing at the end of the oil lamp. *Why did I come here?* she wondered. Her sudden rage at Alan and the others had gone cold, dissipated like snowflakes on the wind, leaving her once more alone with her despair. If the prisoner decided to go back on his word and kill her after all, she would not beg him to spare her life. *Why would I? It's hardly mine as it is.* She breathed a heavy sigh.

"May I ask you a question?" the prisoner said, breaking what had become a long, heavy silence. He did not wait for her to answer, "Why were you crying?"

Brigid looked up at him in surprise, caught his piercing eyes, and quickly looked away.

The prisoner sighed and shook his head. "My dear Mouse, you are in a very dangerous place."

Her eyes flashed with the remnants of her latent anger, "You are the one in the cage."

"Am I? I see no chains." He held up his wrists and motioned toward the door. "And but for you sitting there, the way looks clear, especially with so many of the castle folk occupied at the keep." He smiled wolfishly and stretched his limbs, showing that in spite of his wounds, he was still quite capable. "No, Mouse. It is *you* who is in the cage."

Brigid felt her throat tighten as she realized the truth of the prisoner's claim. The ice water in her veins coursed through her, welling up in pools beneath her bright blue eyes and glistened with fear.

"You are right," she whispered as the first crystalline tear escaped down her cheek. "I am the true prisoner."

Now it was the prisoner's turn to look away; he leaped up from the table, turned his back to her sobbing, and walked a few paces into the shadows. "I'm sorry," his voice called softly. "It was not my intention to upset you so. I admit that I am a peculiar man. I have spent so much of my time in the dark that I often forget the ways of ordinary people who walk in the light. Forgive me. It breaks my heart to see such beauty in such distress."

Brigid wiped her eyes. "It's just..." She shook her head and sighed. "I am in a cage, as you say, and I am alone with no hope and no chance of escape."

A long moment passed in silence, and Brigid went back to staring at the dancing flame. The prisoner remained shrouded in darkness until, once again, he whispered to her.

"Would you like to know how it was that I came to free myself?" he asked.

She stared into the darkness and caught the white flash of his wolfish grin. "How you freed yourself?" she repeated.

"It's actually quite easy, with practice." He motioned toward the door at a small lump of shadow on the floor. "Those are the manacles." He nodded. "You tripped over them as you came in. Bring them here."

Hesitantly, Brigid stood up and retrieved the thick iron chain from the floor. The prisoner left the darkness and held out his hand. However, as she offered him the iron bindings, he swung the cuffs around their wrists, and before she knew it, he had locked their arms together. She glanced up to meet his look of golden-eyed amusement with a show of defiance to mask her fear.

The prisoner ignored her anger and, with his other hand, reached into the folds of his clothing and withdrew a thin piece of twisted metal no larger than a needle.

"Now give me your other hand," he said.

Brigid stood still and merely glared.

"Please"—the prisoner sighed—"I swore by the Brethren that I would not harm you."

"And I should trust the word of a murderer?"

"To the best of your knowledge, have I actually killed anyone?" he asked. "It seems you should at least have to kill someone before being labeled a murderer."

"You meant to kill my uncle."

"Did I?" The prisoner laughed.

In a flash, his free hand shot out like a viper and caught hers. She felt him slip the piece of metal between her fingers and then guide it down smoothly to the lock of the binding around her wrist. Gently yet firmly, he guided her fingers as they fished with the metal needle around the mechanism of the lock until, with a soft click, the manacle opened, and she slipped her wrist free. His grasp loosened around her other hand, and she leaped away from him, rubbing at the flesh where the metal had closed around it. The prisoner unlocked his own wrist and tossed the chains away again onto the floor.

"How dare you!" Brigid hissed, though she could feel herself blushing. "How dare you touch me!"

"Such venom, Mouse"—the prisoner smiled—"would that I were, Sir Reid."

Brigid felt the fires of rage spark to life again in her breast, and she remembered Alan's talk of the "bargain." Her jaw tightened, and her fists clenched. The prisoner noticed this as well.

"So I see the young knight's advances are not as welcome as he would believe," he said.

"I do not wish to marry him," Brigid declared.

"Then don't."

Her eyes examined the flagstones. "I do not think that I have much choice."

The prisoner shook his head in disbelief, smiling his wolfish smile. "I can't for the life of me imagine why not?" He mused. "You are, after all, the daughter of the archduke of Dwerin and the rightful heir to these lands. Every man, woman, and child in that keep owes fealty to you, the Sheriff and your mother included. What right have they to decide who you should marry?"

Brigid avoided having to answer. "You said you did not come here to kill my uncle?" she remembered, changing the subject. "If that is true, then why *did* you come here?"

The prisoner raised an eyebrow. "I seem to recall merely answering your accusation with a question. I laid claim to nothing of the sort. However"—he smiled—"I will admit it. I did not come here to kill your wretched uncle, despite how much he may deserve it."

"But you were captured in his very bedchamber, trying to cut his throat!"

"I would be a pretty poor assassin if I could not do such a simple thing as cut a man's throat out while he was asleep."

"So you admit to being a murderer?"

"I admit to having sometimes worked as an assassin but also as a soldier and occasionally as a mercenary. I've also worked as a hunter, a caravan guard, and on at least one occasion long ago, I was employed as an apprentice to a butcher." He shrugged. "Each role often involves killing to some degree. Does that make each one a murderer in your eyes? If the answer is yes, then by all means, I am a murderer. However, so are all of the others."

"You're using cleverness to avoid answering my question."

"Just as you did mine."

Brigid flushed with frustration. "If you did not intend to kill my uncle, then why would you allow yourself to be captured? Why endure the horrible things he has done to you if you are innocent? And if you can free yourself as easily as you have shown me, then why ever would you choose to stay?"

The prisoner uttered his voiceless laugh and returned to his seat at the table. "Very good, Mouse," he said. "Unlike your foolish cousin, you are astute enough to ask the right questions." He nodded toward her vacant chair.

"My name is Brigid," she said as she sat down, "Brigid Beinn."

"I know," he said simply. "It is a beautiful name for a beautiful lady. However, I prefer Mouse—so long as it does not vex you as it seemed to vex noble Reid."

An involuntary smile escaped her lips at the memory. "I suppose 'Mouse' is fine."

The prisoner's eyes flashed. "You should smile more often." he grinned. "The Wrathorn believe it frightens Death away. That's why you hear so many of them laughing and singing in the midst of battle."

"You know about the Wrathorn?" Brigid asked.

"My dear Mouse," he said smugly, "I know lots of things."

She smiled again, briefly. "I imagine you've had many adventures if it's true that you were a soldier and all those things," she observed. "You must have traveled all over Termain."

"And a little beyond." The prisoner smiled. "A man with no home cannot but be a traveler."

Brigid sighed and removed the silver circlet from her brow. In the light of the lamp, the star sapphire gleamed magnificently. "I wish I could leave here," she said. "Not that any of them would even notice I was gone. When I left the feast, not one person even looked up as I passed. To them, I am more 'air' than 'heir.'"

The prisoner smiled. "Well said."

"You asked why I was crying before," Brigid said softly. "I was not crying because I was sad, not really. I was crying because I was angry—at my mother, my uncle, my rotten cousin, Reid, even my father—at all of them. Blackstone is a wretched place, and Dwerin is a wretched land. I'm not as blind as they may think. I see things. I see how cruel Alan is to the servants and to the girls. I know about the horrid things my uncle does in the middle of the night to you and to others. When I leave here, I will go back to my chamber and have to cover my ears against my mother's cries of passion in the next room while she…tumbles with whatever man she's chosen as her plaything for tonight, just as I have since I was a child before my father was even in his grave. The nobles feast on dishes that would feed half the town while the poor folk who work the land go hungry with what's left after they pay their tithes." She shook her head bitterly. "And all the while, I am made to sit straight and never slouch, watching while Alan plays at war with his bow and Reid paws at me with his creeping fingers until the day when I can be married off and put on display like some trophy in the treasury." Brigid clenched her teeth; she could feel the tears beginning to burn again in the depths of her brilliant blue eyes.

"I was crying because I was so angry that I frightened myself," she continued, her voice rising in the stillness. "Angry enough that I came here to set you free and beg you to kill them all!"

Her voice echoed, rising to the rafters of the tower, and for a moment, she feared that the guards downstairs might have heard. Neither she nor the prisoner spoke for some minutes, though while she strained her ears for footsteps, he merely sat quietly, staring into the flame.

When, at last, the prisoner finally broke the silence, his voice was soft. "I will not do this for you."

Brigid felt her throat thicken, and a tear trickled down her fair cheek. "I know."

"Make no mistake." The prisoner smiled grimly. "It is well within my power to do as you ask." He caught her eye. "But I would not want that for you, for although I would be the blade to do the actual killing, it would only be by the exercise of your will."

"I know." She bit her lip as more tears came.

"They say that Dwerin, like its people, is a land of iron and stone, and from noble to peasant, the names of the Brethren are uttered far more often in anger, oath, or passion than in prayer," he told her. "But the Brethren do not look favorably upon the kinslayer, regardless of what land they call home, and I would not have you be cursed."

Brigid swallowed a lump in her throat. "I know," she said a third time.

"However," he added with a sigh, "I will not abandon you either."

Brigid glanced up in surprise, her eyes shining in the lamp-light with tears. The prisoner reached out, gently took her hand, and knelt. "For all your bloody thoughts," he said, "I believe that you have a good heart, and although you are angry at your mother or your uncle or your cousin, and rightfully so, you do not truly wish to have their blood on your hands, else you would not have been frightened." He caught her gaze and held her blue eyes in the shadow of his gold. "They have treated you horribly and may have designs on mistreating you further, but they are merely the symptoms of a greater illness that afflicts not only Dwerin but all Termain. It is this illness that truly vexes you, if you do indeed accept your role as the rightful heir, for it is a disease called Injustice and part of a larger plague called Evil, and that, my dear Mouse, is a foe that I will happily fight alongside you, for it is my enemy too."

Brigid wiped her eyes and watched as the prisoner let go of her hand and walked over to collect the manacles. "But how?" she asked.

"I came here to accomplish a task." He walked over to his dangling chain, leaped up to grab hold of it, and flipped himself nimbly upside-down, locking the iron bindings around his ankles. "Once it is done," he continued, slipping into the manacles, "I will leave here, and I will take you with me."

Her eyes widened. "You would?"

"There are many mice running around the woodpiles of this world, my lady, and you and I are but two of them." He grinned. "If you wish it, I will take you to meet the others, and perhaps, together, we might find a way to cure Dwerin of its disease. Until that time, however, take heart, for you are not alone, not anymore."

Brigid nodded silently and stood up from the table.

"Now, as much as I've enjoyed your company, my lady, I think now it would be best if you go. Your dear uncle often enjoys torturing me for show and what better opportunity for an audience than a feast?" He laughed. "Like father like son, I suppose. Just remember to blow out the lamp on your way."

For a moment longer, Brigid lingered, watching as he clapped the manacles around his wrists and folded his arms bat-like across his chest. *What a peculiar man*, she thought. *Quite extraordinary...*

At length, she put out the light and carefully felt her way along the wall to the unbarred door, yet once more, she paused. "I do not like to call you 'prisoner,'" she whispered to the darkness. "Do you have a true name I can call you?"

"True names are dangerous things—and powerful. Best to be careful with true names."

"Then if not your true name, is there something else I might call you?" she asked. "Anything at all?"

"Well," he said at last, "I suppose that if I have named you 'Mouse,' then it is only fair that you name me what you will as well."

"I..." She paused. "All right."

She heard his voiceless laugh. "So what shall it be then?"

Brigid sighed. There could only be one name for him.

"Falcon," she whispered, "I will call you 'Falcon.'"

The moonlight flashed briefly on the prisoner's upside-down smile. "Falcon it shall be then." He grinned. "Good night, friend Mouse."

For the first time in a long time, Brigid realized suddenly that she did not feel afraid. In fact, she wondered if what she was feeling could be labeled as contentment or even joy. In any case, though, just as he had said, she no longer felt alone.

"Good night, Falcon," she said softly, "my friend."

CHAPTER 12:
THE FEAST OF HARVESTIDE

Geoffrey crouched beneath the low-hanging branch of a maple tree and peered down the hillside toward the rocky inlet below. Not far from the shore, a wooden watchtower overlooked an old longhouse surrounded by a palisade wall. Armed men stalked about here and there impatiently, staring every few minutes out to sea in hopes of sighting a sail.

The Guardians may have dwindled over the years in number, skill, and virtue; however, that did not mean that they were entirely gone. Some still followed the old ways of the road, wandering the lands, safeguarding the common folk, and rooting out the darkness Dibhor cast upon the world. And by Perindal's Sword, even the Warlock himself knew that slavery was wrong.

Good, Geoffrey thought. The men's impatience meant that the captives must still be inside, that the slave ship had not yet arrived to take them off to the Sorgund Isles or beyond. He had heard of slavers attacking wagon trains of Wayfolk, nomadic wanderers and traders who roamed from village to village across Termain; however, the rumors had been hard to confirm. Kidnap folk from a village and their friends and neighbors were bound to make a fuss, but kidnap people who had little enough of either, and there was a significantly lower chance of getting caught, at least by landed knights or city guards. Thankfully, Geoffrey and his companions were neither.

Beside him, another man sat poised like a hunting hound ready to spring, a naked longsword held lightly in his hands. He was younger, perhaps twenty-three or twenty-four, but the youthful passions seemed long gone from him, and for all his dour brooding, it seemed he could have lived at least twice as many years. Still, in the few weeks that Geoffrey had known him, the newcomer had more than demonstrated his prowess in the arts of war.

"Regnar!"

The word was but a whisper inches away from Geoffrey's ear. His right hand tightened on Oakheart, and his left whirled around to guard himself with the Acorn. His heart thundered in his chest, and beside him, the swordsman leaped to his feet in alarm.

"Fire and blood!" Geoffrey cursed aloud, though the voice was not his own. "Gareth, you bastard!"

The source of the whisper was another young man, little more than a boy, and in this one, the exuberance of youth was alive and in full bloom. He leaped nimbly from the swordsman's reflexive strike and grinned mischievously from ear to ear.

"My apologies, old man," the limber youth replied, his golden eyes ablaze with inner fire. "I've done as you asked. There are sixteen of them. Those two up there in the tower, four more on patrol to the south, two on a hilltop to the north, and you can't see them from here, but there are two more asleep under a canvas lean-to just before that dune. The other four are inside the longhouse minding the captives."

"That's only fourteen," the swordsman whispered.

The boy let out a sigh. "Fine," he confessed. "Two more set out to hunt, and I ran into them not far from here. Since the others won't be looking for them to return for a little while, I decided to take care of them myself."

Geoffrey sighed with impatience. "You fool," his other voice said wearily, "I told you not to kill anyone yet."

"Calm down, Greybeard. I was quiet." He patted the hilts of his daggers. "Neither one ever had any chance to make a sound. Whisper for the one and Shade for the other."

The swordsman sheathed his long blade and returned his gaze to the longhouse.

Geoffrey shook his head and stroked his beard. "Can the two on the northern hill see the four to the south?" he said at last.

The boy shook his head. "No, but those in the tower might."

"All right," Geoffrey told him, "if those daggers are as quiet as you claim, then see if you can climb that tower and rid us of those two." He turned toward the swordsman. "Think you can handle the two on the hill and the two by the dune?"

"I'd rather take the four to the south," he said quietly. "I don't care much for killing men in their sleep, even slavers."

"Fine," Geoffrey relented. "You take the south, and I'll handle the north. We'll watch the tower for the boy and go once he has it under control." He sighed and shook his head. It was going to take work to get these two into proper shape; too much of the soldier in one and not enough in the other. He rested Oakheart upon his shoulder. "Let's go."

"Let's go?"

"Aye," Geoffrey said, "let's go."

"Love, what are you talking about?"

Geoffrey opened his eyes and looked up at the thatching of his cottage's roof. The soft, rhythmic chirping of crickets sounded in the darkness outside of the small bedroom. Lying beside him, Annabel eyed him curiously.

"Sorry, what?" Geoffrey whispered.

"You said, 'Let's go?'" She arched an eyebrow in amusement. "Where on all the Father's creation would you want to go at this hour?"

Geoffrey smiled in spite of himself. "I must have been dreaming."

Annabel slipped her hand into his and kissed him on the cheek. Around them in the quiet of the cottage's single bedroom, Geoffrey could make out the sleeping forms of his children and took comfort as he listened to the sound of their breathing.

"They were so excited for the festival tomorrow, I thought they'd never go to sleep," Annabel said.

"Aye"—Geoffrey sighed in agreement—"it makes the months of long work worth it, seeing the looks on their faces."

Annabel nodded and rested her head against Geoffrey's shoulder, her soft brown braid against his cheek. For four weeks, he and his fellow farmers had worked the wheat fields from before dawn until long past dusk, harvesting, threshing, winnowing while Annabel and the rest of the women and children tied the stalks into sheaves, brewed ale, and prepared stores for the winter. Some they would keep for themselves while the bulk of it would go to the great communal storehouse in the center of the town to be milled into flour and divided equally among the families of the village throughout the winter by Cousin Martin.

Although the lands of the Spade did not see the heavy snows of Wrathorn, Baronbrock, and Montevale, the southern winter still brought with it bitter cold, disease, and starvation, Geoffrey had hoped to use the money from his spring crop to buy a few more chickens or perhaps a goat or a few sheep; however, he preferred not to think about that now. At least he had been able to find a replacement for his plow horse.

At sunup, Geoffrey rose from bed and went out to see his new horse. Greta, Geoffrey's young daughter, had taken to calling her Daisy, and before long, the rest of the family had too. She was not a fine creature and had not yet taken to farm work, but she was docile and sweet. Geoffrey forked feed into Daisy's pen and gently patted her muzzle, allowing himself to linger on the idea that at least in his care, the horse would find a much better, if no less wearisome, life of hard work and toil. Still, the life of a farmer's horse, like that of the farmer, was an honest one.

And today would be the day to celebrate that, for it was the final day in the month of Harvestide—the Feast of the Father, as it was called, when the common folk took a break from their long months of labor to honor the Lord Alantir with a grand harvest feast. Garth had offered up one of his aging sows for slaughter, and Raleigh and his sons had been able to track down a deer for roasted venison. Oscar and his wife made large wheels of cheese from goat's milk, and Oliver and Agnes would bring parsnips roasted in honey. Annabel had spent the day before baking rastons, and in years past, Ronalt and his wife had brought big crocks of jam made from wild blackberries. Indeed, with these and more contributions from the other folk of Pyle, there promised to be plenty of good food, good beer, dancing, and singing long into the night.

Yet, in spite of all that, in spite of the promise of everything the holiday had to offer, Geoffrey still did not feel much like celebrating. In the wake of the bandit attack on Damon's family, an undercurrent of fear spread throughout the village like a chill wind, and many feared that three dead bandits would only attract more live ones. Geoffrey could not help but feel partially responsible for the sense of impending danger, and though he did not necessarily regret taking action to save Damon's family, he still felt riddled with guilt. Oliver and Annabel both told him that such thoughts were foolishness, that all he needed to do was think about what worse fates might have lain in store for Damon's wife and children had Geoffrey not decided to act. However, he also sensed subtle anxiety in the looks and the glances, the kind words and the greetings of his fellow men of Pyle, a type of reluctant resentment that, in saving one family, Geoffrey had unintentionally doomed them all.

The memory of that day was but another bough to add to the great bonfire of confusion that seemed to have engulfed Geoffrey's life of late. With each passing day since his encounter with the bandits on the road home from Granmouth, things seemed to make less and less sense. It began with this reading business, as if a candle had suddenly flickered to life in his mind, and what once seemed merely squiggles and dots blotted upon a piece of parchment had become words, stories, and ideas. Cousin Martin had insisted upon loaning him a book—some giant tome about animals and herbs—but although Geoffrey had agreed to take it home with him, he had yet to crack the cover. It was all too much, too frightening.

Then as if the reading weren't enough, he'd started having these nightmares now, too—visions so clear that they seemed more out of memory than dream. Sometimes they were merely images: a castle's keep, a ruined tower, a crowded marketplace by the sea; other times, he heard voices and spoke to strange people he knew but did not know, as in the dream that had awoken him this morning.

"Regnar!" Geoffrey said aloud as the memory came flooding back to him. "That was the name!" He leaned upon the pitchfork and idly patted Daisy's flank as she munched away at her feed. "The lad with the daggers was Gareth," he told the horse, "and the last one—him with the sword—I don't know his name, but I've seen him before too." His brow creased, and he chewed his bottom lip, "I wonder if Regnar was the old man's name?"

Daisy made no reply other than an idle swish of her tail, and Geoffrey smiled in spite of himself. "That's why I like you, Daisy," he said. "You know how to listen."

"Well, the horse has you there," said a voice.

At once, Geoffrey whirled around to face the speaker, only to see his old father standing in the doorway of the stall, leaning heavily on his cane. Somewhere out in the village, a rooster was crowing.

"Da, what are you doing here? I told you we'd send Karl and Freddy to collect you."

"To collect me? Bah! I don't need collecting!" Swinging his cane before him, Old Amos shuffled his way along the stable and came to sit on an old barrel. "I get around just fine, thank you very much, and besides, I felt like walking."

"Alone in the dark?"

"I'm blind, turnip-head! It's always dark!"

Geoffrey sighed and shook his head but remained silent. Amos lived alone in the same small, one-room shack Geoffrey had grown up in on the northern edge of the village. At least once a month, Annabel made a futile attempt to lure the old man into moving in with the rest of the family; however, each time, he refused.

Amos folded his hands upon the crook of his cane. "I smell a horse," he said. "I thought you lost yours."

Geoffrey turned back to Daisy. "I got another one," he said.

"How?"

"I bought it."

"With what money? And from whom?"

Geoffrey hesitated. "With blood," he nearly said but kept silent. He had decided not to tell his father about the recent activities relating to the bandits. Even though it had been almost thirty years since Geoffrey's mother had been killed, he knew that the memories still brought the old man pain, as much as he tried not to show it.

"Da, please," Geoffrey said, "It's a long story, and I still have work to do before the festival."

Amos sighed. "You must think I'm pretty stupid, don't you?"

Geoffrey leaned the pitchfork up against the wall. "Of course not," he said. "Why would you say that?"

Amos shrugged, pawed at his tunic for his pocket, and set to lighting his pipe. "Don't you have work to do?" he said.

At midday, Geoffrey, Annabel, Old Amos, and the children made their way to what passed for Pyle's village square since here could be found the storehouse, the mill, and the small chapel dedicated to worship of the Brethren. Long wooden tables had been fashioned for the day, bountifully laden with holiday fare, and before them, Geoffrey and his family joined the assembly of their neighbors, accepting their pleasant greetings.

Cousin Martin regarded them happily from atop the chapel stairs and, after a few kind words of opening, led the villagers in a hymn in praise of the

Lord-Father to give thanks for all that the land had provided. In his private thoughts, Geoffrey also gave thanks for the lives of his family and friends and offered a silent prayer to the Lady for guiding him home safely on the road in what now seemed a lifetime ago. Lastly, he offered a prayer for the old man— Regnar— and hoped that his soul had found peace with the Kinship in the Realm of the Blessed.

Such a sad thing that so many must die before knowing peace! Geoffrey thought, gazing over the congregation at Damon's widow, standing waiflike on the outskirts of the crowd and clutching her two children to her. He wondered that the will of the gods should include such senseless barbarity and needless suffering as men seemed so wont to inflict on one another. Surely, if the Brethren were truly as compassionate and as loving as the hierophants claimed, they would never have allowed such evil in the world, such violence, such hate.

"And on this, the Feast of the Father, we praise you, Lord Alantir, and all your works," Martin intoned, "and we ask that in your mercy you safeguard our families and friends in the coming winter that we might continue to thrive like these fruits of our labors, for your glory and the greater Kinship among Gods and Men."

"May it be so," the villagers replied together.

"May it be so," Cousin Martin repeated and would have continued with the service when suddenly his voice trailed off at a low sound like thunder rolling in from the south.

Geoffrey turned and raised a hand to his brow to peer through the sunlight. At least two dozen riders led a small line of large ox-drawn wagons along the village's main thoroughfare. At the head of the column leading them rode a man in full chain mail with a steel helm fashioned in the likeness of boar.

"What's that sound?" Old Amos called.

"Lady save us," Geoffrey muttered.

"Should we send the women and children away?" Oliver whispered.

"It's too late."

"I hear horses," Old Amos said forlornly, "lots of them."

The riders made their way to the village square outside of the chapel and arranged themselves in a wide arc, and some dormant memory put Geoffrey in mind of cavalry just before a charge. However, these were no knights. For, with the exception of the man in the boar helm, they were clad mostly in a mishmash of boiled leather mixed here and there with the odd piece of chain or rusty plate. Their weapons varied even further, ranging from sickles and woodcutter's axes to the odd longsword and flanged mace. *Scavengers*, Geoffrey thought, carrion beasts disguised as men.

From beside the man in the boar's head helm, one of the riders, short, lean, and grinning, steered his horse forward and raised a hand in greeting, or perhaps, warning.

"Greetings, good folk and true, and a happy Lord's Day to all!" he shouted. "And might I add how kind it is for you all to come out to greet us as such!"

A few of the other riders snorted with laughter. Annabel pulled Fredrick and Greta close to her. Old Amos released a heavy sigh.

"We are the men of the Red Boar Brigade under the command of my lord and captain, Bruse Mathon," the rider removed his arming cap and bowed his head in the direction of his leader. From his saddle, the captain's expression remained cold and hard as stone beneath the shadow of his helm, and Geoffrey felt a torrent of fear grip him at the sight of the man's face. Its dispassion invoked dread.

Cousin Martin stepped forward from beneath the eaves of the Chapel doors. "Then, in honor of the Lord's Day, be welcome in Pyle," he said tentatively, "as long as you intend to keep the Lord's Peace."

"Of course we do, Cousin"—the mercenary smiled—"as long as you've done as asked." He slipped lightly from his saddle and whistled. The men atop the oxcarts began to move, driving the great beasts of burden up toward the center of the courtyard, forcing the assembled villagers to stand back unless they be trod upon.

Martin tried to remain calm, though already, Geoffrey heard a few of the women muffling quiet sobs. "My apologies, sir," he began. "However, you'll have to excuse me. For I don't know what exactly it is that you mean. What were we to have been asked?"

The man ignored Martin's question and nodded toward the village's storehouse. "Is that where you keep it all?" he grunted.

Oliver exchanged a look with Geoffrey, and a few other villagers whispered in alarm.

Cousin Martin descended the stairs of the chapel and hurried to the bandit's side. "Please, sir," he begged. "I do not know what it is you mean. Why have you come here?"

The mercenary shrugged, feigning concern at Martin's confusion. "Why, for the tribute, of course!"

"Tribute?" Martin repeated.

"Aye, the fair tribute to my Lord Mathon for keeping this here village safe from the bandits and the other rogues that wander the Spade."

Martin rubbed the crown of his tonsure. "I'm afraid I don't understand."

"The stores and supplies you are to pay to us for the winter!" He grinned. "Surely, you remember the messengers we sent nary a month ago? Three men, all mounted?"

A chill ran down Geoffrey's spine as he felt the eyes of his friends and neighbors fall upon him.

"Come to that," the mercenary replied, his feigned cordiality fading. "Those men never returned to us. I wonder what could have befallen them?"

Cousin Martin breathed a heavy sigh. "Would that I knew," he said at last, his voice level. "But the lands of the Spade are indeed dangerous these days, as you say."

The mercenary eyed the preacher coldly. "Aye. So they are."

Martin's eyes fell to the ground, and his shoulders slumped in dejection.

"So that's the storehouse, then?" the mercenary asked again, motioning.

"Yes, sir. Yes, it is."

While half of the mercenaries emptied the storehouse of its supplies, the remaining riders dismounted and helped themselves to the villagers' feast. The man who spoke, whose name seemed to be Karthan, gave orders to Martin, and soon, many of the other villagers were forced to serve as attendants. As best as he was able, the good cousin attempted to placate the warriors to prevent what was clearly wholesale theft from escalating to wanton murder. Martin was not a violent man, nor strong, nor anything approaching the qualities of the great heroes from the legends or the Bard's songs; however, as he stood impotently watching the affair, Geoffrey though no man could ever doubt the preacher's courage.

As the afternoon wore on, the meat soon ran low as the bandits gorged themselves on a feast meant to feed the whole village. As a result, Karthan ordered a great bonfire built, and half a dozen of the villagers' egg-laying chickens were slaughtered and roasted over a spit along with Oscar's milk-goat. Geoffrey's heart turned black with anguish and shame, and he often found himself staring into the haughty features of Lord Mathon's face.

Without a word, the captain had dismounted his horse and seated himself alone at one of the wooden tables. No man among his company sat with him, nor did he utter a single word to anyone. The villagers acting as servants would approach, and if he had an interest, he would accept a serving with a slight nod. However, he made no outward show of enjoyment, nor would he in any way acknowledge or join in on his followers' gluttonous mirth. Rather, he seemed somewhat weary of the whole affair, as if he found the whole business of widespread theft and extortion simply far too tedious.

At length, when the wagons had finally been loaded, and the storehouse lay bare, the mercenaries reluctantly left the last few bits and bones of the feast and returned to their horses to depart. The farmers, though doleful and weary, felt an inkling of hope that with the loss of their hard-earned food and feast, they might at least keep their lives.

"You've been a most gracious host, Cousin," Karthan said, blowing his nose into his fingers and wiping it on the hem of his smock, "Most gracious."

"You are welcome," Martin said, uncertain what else to say.

"Aye," Karthan said, "however, there's one more thing we'll be needing before we go."

Martin tried to remain stoic. "What is that?"

Karthan coughed and spit a thick wad of filth on the ground. "You see," he said, "we lost three men here, and worthless as it turns out they may have been, that's three empty holes in our lines."

Martin took a deep breath. "I'm not certain what you mean." Karthan turned his back to him and looked up at his lord. Bruse Mathon's brow furrowed, and raising a finger, he pointed—at Oliver's eldest boys, Axel and Nickolas, and then to Geoffrey's firstborn son, Karl. Karthan nodded, and the captain began trotting off alone down the thoroughfare to the south.

"All right, lads," Karthan said, "take them."

Half a dozen men of the brigade slipped down from their saddles and roughly grabbed each of the boys, bound their hands, and draped them over the side of a horse. Geoffrey and Oliver shouted in protest and tried to push their way to their sons' sides as Annabel, Agnes, and a few of the other women erupted in wails of dismay. However, in a flash, Karthan grabbed Martin by the cowl, threw him to the ground, and pressed the blade of his dagger to the cousin's throat.

"We'll have none of this!" he shouted wickedly. "Or the preacher here will be the first to die!"

The other farmers reached out to subdue Geoffrey and Oliver, and the women fought to suppress their sobs.

"You should feel honored," Karthan snapped. "We're taking your bloody brats to turn them into men! They'll ride among us as warriors, not swineherds and shit-shovelers like the rest of you!" He turned back toward the rest of the bandits, nodded, and the column formed behind the oxcarts now heavy with Pyle's winter stores. A rider drew up beside Karthan leading his horse.

"Thanks for the hospitality, Cousin," Karthan sneered and, without a word, slit Martin's throat from ear to ear.

The villagers watched in horror, and Geoffrey's heart felt as if it would burst. The arms restraining him loosened, but all he could do was fall down to his knees in the dirt.

Karthan leaped up into his saddle, wheeled his horse around, and nodded toward the bonfire.

"Burn the chapel down," he commanded and rode off to the front of the bandit host.

CHAPTER 13:
THE BLACK HORSE

King Cedric Tremont leaned heavily upon the parapet, gazing into the darkness of the western horizon while the north wind howled along the ramparts, sweeping through the old man's hair and beard like cobwebs in an ancient bell tower. Reverently, he closed his eyes and breathed in deeply, gulping down the chill breeze like water from a mountain spring. His cheeks flushed with cold, and the white skin on his long, bony hands gleamed in the moonlight like paper. Beledain watched his father's lips slowly spread into a smile of melancholic contentment. He stepped closer and wrapped an arm around the old king's spare shoulders.

"Are you all right, father?" he said. "It's not too cold for you?"

King Cedric exhaled slowly, and only then did he open his eyes. "That's the north wind, son," he said, "The Tremont wind. Our wind."

"I know," Bel said gently. "But I don't want you to catch a cold."

"Never fear, never fear," the old king said, "I'm fine." He stood up straight, coughed a deep, airy wheeze, and leaned upon his cane. "Will you walk another round?" he asked his son. "I've missed your company these long months."

Bel nodded and slipped his arm through his father's to steady him as they began the slow walk from the parapets of the Stallion, Daravain, along the walls north and east to the Colt, Corlindus. "You should be careful how much time you spend up here," Bel said. "They say you're out here by sunrise every morning until long after dark."

"Perhaps"—King Cedric shrugged—"I often lose track of time."

"Father, you should be resting."

"A king must protect his people, my son," the old man said. "The strength may have fled my sword arm, and I may no longer be able to sit a horse, but I have not yet gone blind. I can, at the very least, offer my eyes in service to the realm. On clearer days, when I stand atop the Mare, I can even make out the cold southern shores of the sea."

Bel sighed. "Father..."

"If it means that much to you," King Cedric told him, "perhaps tomorrow, I will stay inside."

"You know that by tomorrow you will have forgotten."

The old king smiled. "I remember the days when you were so quiet that your mother worried that you had been born simple. Now you return to us after these many long months, and I find you've grown up to become a nagging old nursemaid! Tell me, when you inspect your men, do you always check to see that they've washed behind their ears?"

Bel laughed quietly and shook his head. "Fine," he said, "I'll say no more."

They walked the rest of the way to the northern tower in silence, though more than once, Bel felt a tightness in his throat. For nearly two weeks now, he had walked the walls with his father, making round after round from tower to tower long into the night. Some infirmity of forgetfulness had taken hold of the old king's mind, and now every night when Bel went to meet with him, it was almost exactly the same as it had been the very first time.

The last time Bel was home, for the feast of Galdorn, his father's illness had already begun to take root; however, it seemed merely the senility of age. King Cedric was nearly seventy years old, and though that did not make him ancient by any means, the hardships he had endured in his later years weighed upon him like heavy chains.

As Bel's father stepped from his grasp to rest against the northern parapet, Bel swallowed a lump in his throat and prepared for the part of their conversation's routine that he had come to dread. He had tried on earlier nights to change the direction of their speech together; however, somehow, the king would always bring it back around. There was something about the tower itself that reminded him of buried thoughts, open wounds, and old woes.

"Corlindus the Colt," King Cedric observed quietly, "Son of the Stallion and the Mare."

Bel leaned against the stonework beside him and nodded in silence.

"You know," the old man observed, "by the end of Harvestide, your brother's son would have been five years old."

Bel bit his lip and stared off into the darkness with his father. "I know," he whispered.

The old king sighed. "Larius once told me that if the boy had lived, they were going to name him Balthis. Now that would have made a fine name for a king. King Balthis the Black Horse. It sounds nice, very regal."

"It does," Bel agreed. "You know, Father, it's cold. Perhaps we should go inside."

King Cedric shook his head. "I like it out here. When the wind blows, it helps me to remember what it was like to ride." He closed his eyes, and his lips spread into a wistful smile. "By the Brethren, Celeste was a fine horse. Do you remember? Whiter than the false horse of the north."

"I remember," Bel agreed, "she was certainly beautiful."

"I had hoped that one day she would have a foal that we could gift your brother's son, to Balthis, when he was old enough." He sighed. "But that damned Gislain went and slew her out from under me before we had the chance. I did not feel much like riding anymore after that. A rider without a horse is like a bird without wings."

"Like you always say." Bel smiled weakly.

"Do I?" The king chuckled. "I so often forget. Perhaps I should request that the Guardians send me one of their scribes. It would be good to have someone close at hand to write these things down."

"I'll remember them for you, Father." Bel could feel the burning in his eyes.

Cedric nodded forlornly and returned to his vigil. "Now what was it I was saying?"

Bel remained silent. He could not handle another night of reminiscing over sad days he had spent years trying to forget.

"Come, Father," he said, reaching out to take King Cedric by the arm. "It's far too cold for you to be out here. Let's go."

The old man shook away from his son like an impetuous child. "You go in if you're so cold," he said, furrowing his brow. "I say I like it out here."

"It's the middle of the night," Bel said. He motioned to where the fragments of the army were encamped. Their campfires had all gone dark.

"Leave the watch to the guards for just this once," Bel said. "You can get back to it in the morning."

King Cedric's lip curled in defiance. "I was speaking now of your brother, and I would rather you not interrupt me. I have a hard enough time remembering as it is!" He turned back to the parapet and gazed off into the night. "Don't treat me like I'm a child. I may have relinquished command of the armies to Dermont, but I am still your king."

Beledain swallowed the lump in his throat. "I'm sorry," he finally said. "I just…Father, I fear that your grief will destroy you."

King Cedric sighed heavily but did not turn. "It already has, my son," he said at last. "It already has."

Bel was silent.

"Now go inside," the king commanded. "I still wish to walk a bit."

"I can stay—"

"No," the old man interrupted, "I would rather be alone."

The prince gnashed his teeth in frustration but bowed his head in obedience all the same. He made his way to the door leading into the Colt. "Good night, Father," he called.

"Good night, my son," the old king said.

Bel shut the door behind him and made his way through the fortress tower down to the bottom and left through the main entrance to the courtyard. He felt tired and wretched and longed to saddle Igno and ride off down the hillsides out into the open plains. However, at home in Castle Tremontane, he was no longer the Silent Prince, captain of Lord-General Dermont's Light Cavalry, but merely Prince Beledain of House Tremont, and he no longer had the freedom to come and go by his own will. Still, he made his way quietly to where Igno was stabled and took his time brushing the red sorrel and combing out his mane. The belled saddle sat idly atop an empty barrel, and in the light of the lanterns that hung from the stable's ceilings, he could see that Briden had been at it, polishing the gold and silver until they shined brighter than the stars. Bel sighed heavily when he saw it and wondered just how long Dermont intended to keep him here, wondered how long it would be until he could ride out again with his men and find a way to end the bloody war.

When he had finished caring for Igno, Bel gently rubbed the horse's nose to say good night and at long last returned to his old apartments in the Stallion's tower. Once inside his bedchamber, he prodded the dormant embers in his small hearth to life, and the room was soon aglow in the flickering light of his tiny flame. Bel pulled off his princely, black-and-white surcoat, tossed it absently on a chair, and lit another candle on the small tabletop beside his bed. He was just about to lie down to sleep when there came a soft knock at the door.

"Come in," he called out and allowed himself to fall backward onto the soft furs covering his mattress, "and bar it behind you."

A moment later, Lilia appeared. She was dressed, like the other riders Bel had brought with him to the castle, in the clean, black-and-white tabards that Sir Emory had given them to identify them as the prince's personal guard. "I've been waiting for you for ages." She leaned her sword against the wall and bent down to kiss his brow. "How am I supposed to guard you if I don't know where you are?"

"I was with my father," he said, "walking the walls."

Lilia slipped out of her tabard, stepped out of her boots, and clambered onto the mattress beside him.

"Who's on watch tonight down in the camp?" Bel asked.

"Val handled it," Lilia said. "I don't know."

Bel rubbed his eyes. "Val should be captain for all the times she has to take care of things for me." He sighed. "I hate being here."

Lilia smiled and slipped out of her breeches, her long linen shirt hanging like a gown to her knees. "I don't know," she said, swinging her legs over the edge of the bed beside him. She pulled him into a sitting position and carefully helped him out of his princely finery. "When was the last time we slept together in a real bed and not some forest hollow?" She grinned.

Bel smiled wearily. "Never."

"Aye, never," she said and kissed him.

He kicked off his boots and his trousers while she blew out the candle, and by the light of the small fire, they curled up beside one another beneath the blankets and furs. Bel held her close to him and let the misery of his family's past sufferings slowly dissipate.

"Your shoulders are as taut as a bowstring," Lilia whispered in the firelight.

"He's losing his mind," he whispered.

Beneath the furs, she ran her fingertips lightly along his arm. "We can go for a ride tomorrow, if you'd like."

Bel laughed cynically. "I'd have to ask Dermont for permission first."

"What's it to him? You're just as much a prince as he is."

"Yes, but he's still older, and I still serve at his command."

Lilia sighed heavily, and Bel understood the words she left unsaid.

"You know," he told her. "He knows about you, about us."

There was a long silence. "I'm sorry," she whispered at last.

"I'm not," Bel told her. "Besides, he said he doesn't care."

She sighed and changed the subject. "I think Val might have her eye on a man."

"What?" Bel said. "Why do you say that?"

"The other day, she asked me about the best way to seduce someone."

"She asked you?"

"She said if I could seduce a prince, a normal man would be no problem."

Bel smiled. He could sense the light in the hearth beginning to go out, but he was reluctant to stir, to leave her side. "What did you tell her?"

"To bat her eyes and puff out her lips and whisper soft words into his ear."

"Never once"—the prince laughed—"have I ever seen you do any of those things."

"Well, you're not a normal man, are you?" She laughed.

"I seem to remember the one time I whispered 'soft words' into your ear. It made you angry," he said.

There was a brief silence, and Lilia shifted her weight in the bed. "I was angry because you were prattling on about impossibilities," she said.

"Impossibilities?"

"How easily you seem to forget your rank and title."

"What has that to do with it?"

"Everything."

"It doesn't change the way that I feel about you."

She sighed. "I know."

Bel held her close and buried his nose in her wild brown hair. His hands slipped beneath her linen shirt, and she pressed them against her chest. He wanted to whisper to her again, to speak the words he carried in his heart.

"Don't say it," she warned. "Saying it will only make it hurt worse in the end."

"I'm not planning on there being any end."

"Of course, you're not."

Bel shook his head and rolled her over beneath the blankets to face him. "Why are you so afraid?"

"I'm not," she said, "believe me."

"Do you worry about a child?"

She laughed. "Of course not. I keep track of my moons."

"Then what is it? You know I would never leave you."

"Exactly."

Bel shook his head in frustration. "You're impossible."

Lilia laughed softly in the shadows and clambered over to him. "Then stop asking foolish questions"—she smiled, her eyes aglow in the dying firelight— "and kiss me."

"As you command," Bel smirked. With a deft movement, he grabbed her by the wrists and pulled her to him. At once, he could feel the tension in his shoulders ease and shift to other areas of his body. He pressed her arms to her sides and basked in the feral light shining from her eyes as her lips glistened with want. His mind conjured the memory of their recent battle with the Snow Bear and how, like two wild beasts, they had brought him down together. It awakened his hunger and made him ravenous. His blood warmed, and he kissed her deeply and urgently, and on her lips, he almost tasted the blood of their freshest kill.

At length, flushed and gasping, Lilia reluctantly lifted her head to breathe, freeing Bel's mouth to trace upon her neck and shoulder. He could sense the ardent smile playing wantonly upon her lips as his fingertips found the soft flesh beneath the hem of her shirt and began a slow migration upward from the small of her back. She released a throaty murmur at the delicate sensation, and the fingers of her one hand curled involuntarily in his thick dark hair while the other tugged maddeningly at his shirt.

Finally, with a rasping breath, he paused to pull the offensive garment over his head and watched as, with a grin of mischievous glee, she did the same. As always, his eyes relished the sight of her— lithe and languid, like one of the mountain lions that prowled the Gasparan steppe. The lean muscles of her body tensed with arousal; her pert breasts taut with need. When she pressed his lips to them, she could not contain the throaty moan that escaped her as his tongue teased her, tormenting her with delight. True enough, Bel ached for her with a fervor driven by the magnitude of his love; yet, while she resisted putting her thoughts and passion into words, he knew in moments such as these that Lilia's ardor was more than a match for his.

With a movement that was at once swift and slow, she shifted her body over his and forced him down to the mattress. His senses flared at the touch of her bare flesh against him, and every subtle shift or movement sent bolts of lightning radiating throughout his skin. His hands slid over the knotty scar at her side to settle firmly upon her hips. In another flurry of motion, she shifted her weight and pressed her hips forcefully against his, bringing him with her as she rolled onto her back and guided him between her legs.

When, at long last, their passion reached its apex, Bel felt her back arch beneath him, and her fingernails rake across his shoulders, igniting his own explosion of delight. Lilia's lips parted as if to cry out, but his mouth silenced the quivering murmur that escaped her lips as he held her ever tighter in a lover's embrace.

With a tuft of gray smoke, the last glowing ember in the hearth went dark, and Bel and Lilia finally lay still, wrapped together beneath their heap of furs. With a deep sigh of contentment, he held her close, reveling in her warmth, and gently pressed a kiss to her crown before following her to sleep.

The sun was already high in the eastern sky when Bel awoke the following morning. Lilia still slept soundly, her fair flesh bright against the dark shades of the animal furs. In spite of the late hour, he could not bring himself to rise. Instead, he lay back, taking comfort in the quiet sounds of his Blood Blossom beside him at rest. For, like some rare forest creature, she was always in motion, and only in darkness beside him in sleep would she ever lie still. He examined her hands resting softly beneath her chin, their thin, wiry fingers curled together in peace. The skin of her left hand was slightly less callused than that of her right, but both marked her as a practiced hand with a blade. Her knuckles and wrists were speckled in places with tiny, insignificant scars—reminders of past battles, skirmishes, and even brawls—but he smiled at the irony of her fingernails, chewed down to the quick—a wild cat without her claws.

At the sound of a sudden knock on the chamber door, her eyes flashed open with a start, and she was in motion again. She lurched upright and gathered a bearskin around her like a cloak.

"Who calls?" Bel shouted.

"Prince Beledain," Briden's voice sounded reluctantly, "are...are you within?"

Lilia shot Bel a glance and silently burrowed beneath the furs and blankets as he slipped quickly into his shirt and hose.

"I'll be there in a moment, Briden."

"Yes, sir."

Bel stepped into his boots and strode across the room to unbolt the door. Briden stood pale and freckled, looking somehow more gangly than usual in his black-and-white tabard. "I'm sorry to wake you, sir," he said. "But Prince Dermont sent word that he wants to speak with you."

"Finally," Bel said, rubbing his eyes. For all Dermont's talk of discussing strategy together, Bel quickly felt left out, particularly after yesterday morning when a rider arrived in such haste that his poor horse was dying from exhaustion and had to put to peace. No doubt one of Dermont's enigmatic spies, Bel thought. "Thank you, Briden." He nodded to the standard-bearer. "I'll be there shortly."

"You're welcome, sir."

"And, Briden," Bel added, remembering, "thanks for seeing to my saddle. It looks grand."

"It's my honor, sir," Briden grinned.

Bel closed the door and barred it as Lilia slipped from beneath the cover of the furs. "So the Black Plague calls, and you must answer, eh?"

Bel gathered his things and continued dressing. "Please don't call him that," he said mildly. "You know I don't like it."

"Would you prefer 'The Prince of Corpses'?" Lilia asked, raising an eyebrow. "What was it you told me once? All men earn their titles?"

"So my father says." Bel sighed reluctantly.

She stood up from the bed, kissed his cheek, and gathered her clothes from the night before.

Dermont had earned his titles in the weeks preceding his victory at Whitemane. To weaken the besieged city, he gathered together corpses from one of the coastal towns where men had recently been dying of a horrific disease known as Dibhor's Curse and had his men launch them with siege artillery over the besieged fortress's walls. Within a few days, the plague had begun to spread—not just among the Gasparan soldiers but also among the hundreds of common folk who sought refuge within. So while Dermont and his armies waited patiently from outside, the people inside Whitemane watched helplessly as the flesh fell from their living bodies in globs of putrefied decay, and their eyes shed tears of blood before, finally, the disease liquefied their brains. As a result, hearing his brother's titles aloud was enough to make Bel sick to his stomach.

When they were both dressed, Bel walked Lilia down to the small cell she had been granted down the hall from where Briden and the men billeted. Lilia took his hand, and Bel pulled her close for one final kiss.

"Ask him about the ride," she said. "Call it reconnoitering. Who knows? Perhaps we'd chance upon a pack of White Horses south of the Bloodline. You know that my blade is always thirsty."

"Such bloodlust." He smirked and idly touched the pommel of her sword, where it hung at the ready in her belt. "What is it that drives you so?"

"For everyone I kill, that's one less that tries to kill me or you for that matter. It's simple survival. Kill or be killed." She sighed. "Why you go about unarmed with the Black, with you-know-who so close at hand, is beyond me."

"A man who bears arms in his own home is a man who shall never know peace," Bel recited.

"Your father?"

"I remember so he doesn't have to." He shrugged. "At any rate, find Briden, Horn, and Jarvy and check in with Val. If Dermont allows it, I'd like to ride out as soon as possible, so we'll have to be ready to muster the men out of their leisure in the town."

"Yes, my prince"—she smiled—"and good luck."

From his section of the Stallion, it was only a few short flights of stairs to where Dermont would be waiting for him in what had traditionally been the king's solar. However, since King Cedric ceded control of the military to his second and now eldest son, the solar had been requisitioned as Dermont's throne room in-waiting.

The heavy oak door leading into the solar bore the images of a trio of intricately carved horses rearing up on their hind legs overlooking the sea: Daravain, Rowana, and Corlindus yet again. The armored sentries that stood watch beside it offered Bel a show of fealty and allowed him to step forward to knock on the door. Almost immediately, Dermont's voice rang out clearly.

"Come!"

Bel pushed his way through the door and allowed it to shut behind him. He clasped his hands behind the small of his back and stood rigidly straight. "Brother," he said.

At the rear of the room, before the large, gilded fireplace, Dermont's high seat sat vacant. However, gathered around it sat the lord-general's closest advisers, who also happened to be his closest friends: Inen Vilnois the Golden Garron, Vaston Delon the Boiling Sea, Wilmar Danelis the Sundering Hand, and finally, Dermont's seneschal, Kurlan Malacco the Death Knell. Their fine clothing and bejeweled sword hilts glittered in the light that streamed in from the long, paned windows that lined the walls of the room; however, Bel knew full well that these men were not the simpering nobles in the vein of Lord Harren and Giles Pronet. They were fighters, men trained in the arts of war from the time they were children, and though they may have come from fine families with mountains of ancestral gold, they were as skilled as they were deadly. For they had been raised just like Bel and his brothers, to spend their lives embroiled in yet another generation of civil war.

Dermont himself stood with his back to the door, leaning forward over the broad, circular table in the center of the room. Rolls of parchment and oiled skins covered the table's surface and spilled over its side onto the stone floor.

"About time you show up," he said without turning, though Bel could sense his brother's latent irritation, "It's near midday."

"I'm sorry, brother," Bel apologized. "I was walking the walls with Father late into the night."

He tried to avoid making eye contact with any of the men seated at the table. Somehow, no matter how many battles he fought, no matter how many men he bested in combat when Bel found himself surrounded by Dermont and his friends, his blood turned cold. He could never forget the way they used to torment him as a child, Dermont's little brother, who never spoke a word. He remembered how they used to knock him down and kick him until the day Larius found out and beat Dermont across his backside with the flat of his sword. From then on, they never touched him, but their words and their cold glares were more than enough.

Dermont laughed and glanced back at him over his shoulder. "Next time, just have the guards wrestle the old fool back to his chambers." He leered. "He'll have forgotten the whole thing by the morning, at any rate."

Dermont's friends joined in his laughter, and Bel felt his cheeks flush with anger, but he said nothing.

"At any rate, it's good that you're here now," Dermont continued. "We were just discussing what to do with you."

"My men are rested and eager to return to patrolling the Bloodline." Bel nodded, adding, "As long as that is what you wish."

Dermont exchanged an amused glance with Kurlan Malacco. "Oh, I do indeed," he said. "Though when they do so, it will be under the command of Lady Valerie, not you."

Bel felt a sharp pain in his stomach as if he had just been kicked by a horse. "Val certainly deserves a command of her own," he said at last. "But does that mean that I am to be relieved?"

"Only temporarily, little brother." Dermont smirked. "I have something else I'd like you to do first. Then once you're done, you're welcome to whatever command you like. Read this."

He handed Bel a roll of parchment and slowly made his way back to his chair. Bel stood before the table, reading and then rereading the message.

"The Tower took Roanshead?" Bel asked. "When?"

Dermont leaned on his arm. "Four days ago," he said, "the rider who arrived yesterday brought word."

"What of Uncle Leonis?"

"Ransomed"—Dermont shrugged—"forgive me if I leave it to you to tell Val. However, you can tell her of her temporary promotion too, so…" He sighed. "Hopefully, she'll take it well."

Bel's jaw clenched involuntarily, and his chest tightened. "Forgive me if I do not share in your optimism," he growled.

He felt the eyes of Dermont's advisers fall upon him and remembered the familiar threats of violence carried by those dread stares.

Finally, Dermont released a heavy sigh, "Leave us."

With a show of hesitation, the Golden Garron, Boiling Sea, and Sundering Hand stood up from their chairs and left the room. The Death Knell lingered behind a moment longer until, finally, he stood and left the brothers too.

"I hope you intend to pay the ransom," Bel said the moment the seneschal was gone.

"Of course," Dermont argued, "but in time. There are others who need to be ransomed first."

"Before your own uncle! Your own blood!"

"Yes," Dermont declared, meeting Bel's green-eyed stare with his own. "It does not make me happy to admit it, but there are more important things than family at stake here. I am trying to win this war."

"Dermont," Bel shook his head bitterly, "did you not learn anything from our first meeting with the Tower? Nine thousand men! Nine thousand men lost their lives! Add that to the tally over close on one hundred years and see if winning the war is worth that price, let alone Uncle Leonis or Larius."

"Larius took his own life out of despair." Dermont sighed without emotion and scribbled idly upon a piece of parchment. "He was not a casualty of the war. If anything, he was a deserter."

Bel could hardly believe his ears. "How dare you!" he roared. "Larius was our brother! Our Brother! How *dare* you!"

"How dare me? How dare Larius! How dare *you*!" Dermont shouted. His hand went to the hilt of his sword, and for a moment, he stood tense, ready to draw; but, as Bel's eyes widened in wild-eyed horror, Dermont appeared to come back to his senses. "Forgive me," he said at last.

Bel said nothing.

"I will send for Uncle Leonis as soon as possible," Dermont said softly. "But I have an important task that I believe can only be completed by you. Please"—he sighed—"will you hear me?"

Bel rubbed a bead of sweat from his brow. He was not accustomed to shouting in anger. His fingers trembled like the spindly legs of a newborn foal. Finally, he nodded. "I will hear you."

Dermont took a deep breath. "King Marius the White Horse intends to hold a tourney on the Feast of Perindal to test the mettle of the greatest horsemen in Gasparan lands," he said. "He intends to form an elite cavalry unit to be placed under the personal command of the Tower, Harding, the Andochan dog. Apparently, any man who can afford both horse and armor is welcome to enter the jousts." Dermont shook his head and laughed. "I imagine the False King is even willing to knight commoners; he's that desperate for men."

Bel did not share in Dermont's mirth. Most of the light cavalry were common, and those that were not, like Briden, were often the younger sons of lesser nobles who could not afford the costs of plate. Regardless, Bel knew they could fight just as well—and often better—than any of the wealthier, trueborn noblemen.

"At any rate," Dermont continued, "I want you to pose as a man of Gasparn, say you grew up in Rosewood or some other border town, then prove yourself in the tournament and infiltrate the Tower's band."

Bel shook his head in disbelief. "I'm no spy," he said. "Besides, they're sure to be heavy horse. I haven't worn chain, let alone plate, since assuming my command."

"The Gasparns have lost just as many men as we have over the years, and rarely are new knights trained adequately enough to manage proper arms. Often what pass for nobles knights up north are merely jumped-up merchant's sons or house guards riding plow horses and pretending that they're worthy of sharing a table with their betters! They should be no problem for a rider as skilled as you."

Bel shook his head. Now he laughed. "Dermont, you cannot be serious. Why would you possibly send me?"

"Two reasons," Dermont said, counting on his fingers. "Firstly, whether light or heavy, you are still the finest horseman in all *our* lands. I've seen you in tourneys and on the field since you could first sit a horse. No man can stand against you, and I mean that. Humbly"—he smiled—"secondly, you have a way about you that for some reason endears you to the other men, particularly the common men, and they respect you for it. You know their ways. Understand their hearts and minds. Just take one glance at that saddle of yours. Your men—even my men—would follow you wherever you chose to lead," Dermont said earnestly. "They fear me, but they love you. You will need that quality to endear you to the Tower."

Bel ignored his brother's compliments. "Why would the love of our men mean anything in this matter with the Tower?"

Dermont sighed. "Because," he said hesitantly, "because the Tower, like you, has a knack for inspiring confidence if the old stories are to be believed. They love him and respect him, just as he does them in return. You can use this to your advantage. For you are the same way, and after you gain acceptance into his ranks, which I am all but certain you will, I want you to gain the Tower's confidence, and use it to feed us information. Then, eventually, when the time is right, I want you to kill him."

"What?"

"You will gain the Tower's confidence, and then when I command it, you will kill him."

Bel laughed in disbelief. "First, you ask me to play the part of the spy, and now the assassin? Brother, I'm no murderer. Besides, if your intention is merely to kill him, why waste time gaining his trust?"

"And risk Andoch lending more than merely advisory support? Certainly not. However, if the war goes poorly over time, the Guardians will believe that they have simply sided with a weak ally, and when we win the war, they may no longer see us as any real threat."

"Then why kill the Tower?"

"Is there any army more incompetent than the one that cannot protect its leader? Your killing the Tower will provide the final nail in the coffin of the Andochan-Gasparan alliance."

"Dermont, I cannot do this," Bel pleaded. "I am not an assassin."

"No," Dermont told him. "But in this, you will be. The Tower is the only thing keeping the White Horse alive. If we topple him, we win. You say you want this war to end? You want to keep more men from dying? Then you will do this. You will kill the Tower."

"What you ask me, Dermont, I cannot do," Bel said bitterly. In his mind, he heard Lilia's voice whispering his brother's titles, and his chest tightened with shame. "I would sooner sue for a divided land of peace than a united Montevale bought with treachery and blood." "The War of the Horses began with treachery and blood. It may as well end with it."

"Brother, I will not do this."

Dermont's voice dropped to a cold whisper, and his green eyes seemed to burn with an eerie glow, "You will do as I command. I am your lord-general, and soon, I will be your king. Though you may be my brother, as a soldier and a subject, you must obey. You must."

Bel shook his head in frustration. "Dermont, you realize that if I am forced to follow the Tower into battle, I will be forced to kill our own soldiers, our own countrymen," Bel pleaded. "I may even be forced to kill the men of my own command."

Dermont threw his hands up in exasperation. "So be it!" he snapped. "I doubt that it will ever happen, but if so, they will be nothing less than a sacrifice necessary for the good of the realm, like any other dead men."

Bel shook his head in adamant refusal. "I cannot do this."

"No, brother," Dermont declared, his voice wickedly calm and cold. "You will, or I will see your common girl raped and tortured, then dragged across the valley behind her own accursed horse."

If Bel had worn his sword in that instant, he would have branded himself a kinslayer. Yet with an equal amount of relief and regret, he stood rigid as a statue, clenching his empty fists until his arms began to shake.

Dermont sat back in his chair and watched his brother's silent anguish with an air of quiet satisfaction, content with the knowledge that he had won. "Think on *that* whenever you find yourself wavering," he leered. "Now shut your mouth, Silent Prince, and do as you are told."

CHAPTER 14:
THE IMPERIAL RIVER

Long into the night, the curragh slipped in silence down the banks of the Imperial River, leaving scarcely a ripple in its wake but for the occasional whisper of the single oar dipping below the surface. Crodane was a skilled ferryman, and as he guided the small craft southwards, even Thom seemed to forget his earlier maritime discomfort. Instead, he braced himself firmly between the two burlap sacks in the stern and gave himself over to sleep, his small carven figure of the Brother Galdorn clutched tightly between his plump, white fingers.

For Lughus, however, the prospect of any real rest seemed as distant as any dream. He sat still, rigidly upright in the prow, staring off into the misted shadows of the dark river. The Imperial grew wider the further away they sailed from Lenard's Crossing, and the trees and undergrowth lining the riverbanks grew steadily thicker and more gloomy. Occasionally, bats flew by overhead hunting insects, and from time to time, an owl, lost somewhere among the treetops, hummed its low call. Frogs chirped, hidden among the cattails, and somewhere in the distance, Lughus swore he heard a wolf howl. Upon his lap, naked in the moonlight, lay Pryce's long dagger and Stokes's rusted sword.

In many ways, Lughus felt rather foolish, thinking back on the excited naiveté with which he had greeted the previous dawn and the prospect of adventure. For too long had he deluded himself with romantic ideals of adventure and daring, imaging his own journey alike to the great epics of the earlier generations of Guardians or the fanciful tales of the Bard. Little did he anticipate the magnitude of taking another man's life or how closely he would come to losing his own. He could almost hear Royne's sigh of disappointment or the way he would shake his head in silent reproach.

Lughus knew that in good faith, he could not hold Thom solely accountable for the events of the day. For the life of an apprentice was in many ways one of knowledge without experience, a sheltered life in the tower spent more often in the company of books than of people. To expect anything but Thom's foolery would be like expecting a fish to know how to fly or a songbird to know how to swim. No, Thom alone did not bear the burden of blame. Thom's hands had not yet bathed in the red horror of another man's blood.

Nothing Lughus had read had prepared him for the magnitude of the act, to bear the burden of knowing that in that short moment, in that single, swift strike, he—Lughus—would become now and forever, the instrument of that man's doom. He had deprived a man of his life and stolen away all the days of his future without even knowing the man's name.

"You fought well."

Lughus's breath caught at the sound of the voice, the sudden harshness that broke the muted stillness of the night. He glanced behind him to see the swordsman at his oar, mildly regarding the far riverbank.

"Thank you," Lughus finally said, adding, "I suppose."

Crodane dipped the blade of the oar beneath the surface with a quiet sweep. Lughus's eyes fell upon the bright blade of Pryce's dagger, and again, he recalled the seemingly endless font of blood. He turned his head away to examine the shifting current of the dark water.

"Many men falter at their first true fray, and few of those, if any, live to see another," Crodane said softly. "However, you stood your ground and proved your mettle."

"And a man lies dead by my hand," Lughus said.

"Would you prefer the tables turned?"

The boy remained silent.

Again, Crodane's paddle slipped beneath the surface of the river. "I could tell from your stance that you've had at least some training in the arts of war," he said. "Am I right?"

"Rastis's steward, Hob—Hobart, Rastis allowed me to learn from him. He's Wrathorn and worked as a mercenary before joining the Order."

"Hob!" the swordsman said merrily, barking with laughter. "Don't tell me Old Hobart's still following Rastis around after all these years! And a steward no less!"

Lughus returned Pryce's dagger to its sheath, "So you did know him? He said as much."

"Aye, I knew Hobart." Crodane nodded. "Though this was back in Baronbrock when he was simply another Wrathorn sellsword in service to Rastis's brother, even before he was anointed 'the Ox.'" He shook his head. "Well, if Hob taught you, that would explain why you were leaning so far forward. The Wrathorn prefer their bloody mauls and bearded axes. Asking a Wrathorn to teach you the ways of the sword would be like asking a giant to teach you how to sew with a needle."

"He taught me the five guards," Lughus protested.

"And I'm sure he taught them well, or as well as he was able for one who is not a swordsman," Crodane said, "But Hob was not the only one who instructed you, was he? Who's the master-at-arms now instructing the cadets?"

"Sir Neran Weiss, but I wasn't allowed to practice with them."

"But someone else did teach you?"

Lughus shrugged. "I suppose," he said, "one of the cavaliers, Marcus Harding, the Tower, had a fondness for learning, and whenever he was in the city, he would often borrow books from the library and meet with Rastis and the elder sages. Once, he caught me practicing footwork in one of the study rooms and asked me to show him what else I knew. He was never in Titanis for very long before being sent out on a campaign, but when he was, he would ask me what I had learned since. He said that if a soldier could also be a scholar, he saw no reason why a scholar could not also be a soldier."

"Indeed," Crodane agreed. "But though a wise man and a great warrior, the Tower is a horseman and a lancer, not a swordsman who fights on foot."

Stirrings of resentment knotted in Lughus's breast. "I thought you said that I fought well."

"You did," Crodane replied. "But if you seek to master the ways of the sword, you still have much to learn."

Lughus sighed and turned his back on the swordsman. He felt so weary, yet some lingering anxiety still promised to keep him from sleep. "I'm not certain that I want to learn swordplay," he said, "if the only purpose of such knowledge is to take another man's life."

A long moment passed in silence as Crodane steered the currach out further into the center of the channel and braced the oar against the rail, allowing the current to carry the boat downstream on its own accord. "Lughus," he said, "hear this now."

Lughus turned around carefully in his seat in the prow as Crodane carefully drew his blade from its sheath and held it out across his palms.

"Tell me," Crodane said, "what is this?"

Lughus inspected the sword. It was long, long enough to be wielded in one hand or two, with a thin blood groove running half the length of the blade. Its wide, straight crossbar was unadorned, and neither precious stones nor gold embellishments decorated its pommel. It was a simple weapon and old, bearing the tiny nicks and pockmarks of innumerable battles, yet clearly, the steel was strong and meticulously cared for. In the silvery light of the Harvestide moon, the fine weapon radiated an antique beauty all its own.

"What is this?" Crodane asked again.

"It's a sword."

"And what is a sword?"

Lughus hesitated, and his brow furrowed in confusion. "I'm not quite sure I know what you mean," he said.

Crodane's steely, blue eyes shone with a strange fervor. "A sword is not simply a piece of sharpened steel meant only for war or killing, to glut the field of battle with red gore and carnage," he said, "nor is it as innocent as a tradesman's tool like the plowman's spade or the woodcutter's axe, though for many it may draw a meal or carve out a wage. No," he said, "a sword is more. A sword *is* the man who wields it. It is his will given substance, his heart given form, and his soul revealed to all the world. To master the sword is to master oneself, to know oneself."

"Lughus," Crodane continued, "what you say is true. A sword may take life, but it can also give life, and when a man draws a sword, he makes a choice to do one or the other. For, while my blade may have taken the lives of those men in the town today, it also gave life to you and to Thom, and that is something that I do not regret," he said sternly, "nor should you."

Lughus caught Crodane's gaze and understood from it the earnestness with which the swordsman spoke.

"Do you understand?"

Slowly, Lughus nodded. "Yes."

Lughus's eyes lingered upon the blade of Crodane's sword until, all of a sudden, the swordsman returned it to its sheath.

"Good," Crodane said, taking up his oar again. "Baronbrock is still a long ways away. If you decide that you should wish it, while we travel, I can teach you the way of the sword." He slipped the blade of the paddle beneath the surface, and somewhere along the riverbank, a bullfrog croaked. "At any rate," Crodane said, his voice softening to a whisper, "For now, I suggest you take a lesson from Thom and try to sleep."

Lughus could not recall the next day how long it took before sleep finally claimed him; however, the sun had already climbed nearly halfway to its zenith when he awoke. Thom, from his seat in the stern, was packed tightly between Crodane's burlap sacks like an enormous hen roosting. Still, whether through the intercession of Brother Galdorn or Crodane's skill with the oar, he appeared to have finally developed sea legs enough for river travel.

"Oi, look who's finally awake," Thom said.

Lughus sat up straight and stretched. Somehow he had managed to slump down in the base of the boat with his back braced against the pointed nose of the prow. He grimaced against the cramp in his shoulders from having slept in such an awkward position, which he suddenly realized was only slightly more uncomfortable than the soggy, wet splotches on his side and on his rear end from where river water collecting in the bottom of the boat had soaked him through in the night.

Thom giggled with laughter. "It almost looks like you wet yourself!"

Lughus rubbed his eyes and ran a hand through his hair. "Unless I've found a way to piss out my ass, I don't see how that's possible," he muttered sullenly.

"There're dried stores in those sacks," Crodane said, "If you're hungry."

Thom cooed with pleasure while Lughus continued to rouse himself awake. "Where are we?" he asked. He gazed from one bank to the other, both of which were lined with an assortment of forest trees, their leaves just beginning to show the first signs of changing color.

"We are nearly thirty miles south of Lenard's Crossing," Crodane said. "I hope to add another twenty before nightfall. Then, we can stop and make camp."

"Fifty miles!" Lughus said, "So soon!"

"We're traveling downstream, and the current is a bit swifter than usual for this time of year."

"Still..." He was about to ask if Crodane had bothered himself to sleep when suddenly Thom emerged from one of the burlap sacks with a hunk of bread and a piece of dried venison jerky.

"Ah ha!" Thom exclaimed.

Lughus rolled his eyes at his friend but could not help but smile. "It seems you've lost your fear of boats," he said.

Thom grinned merrily as he munched away at his breakfast and held up the little statuette by way of an answer. "If there's time, I'd like to visit the temple in Galdoran to show my thanks," he said. "I figure it's only proper."

"It's customary to visit the Cathedral before taking to ship," Crodane said, "and it may take a day or two to book passage north."

"Have you traveled much, then?" Thom asked.

"Oh yes," the swordsman said, "a great deal."

"That's strange," Thom said. "I always thought that most of the Anointed held administrative roles in the cities, except for them sent out by the Warlord to command the armies on campaign."

"What are you talking about, Thom?" Lughus asked.

"His shoulder," Thom said, nodding toward Crodane, "you said yesterday it would be healed by the morning, and well, it doesn't seem to be bothering you now. So," he beamed, teeth stained brown from jerky juice, "my guess is that you're one of the Anointed."

"Or perhaps the wound was simply not nearly as grave as you believed it." Crodane's lips twisted into a smirk, and he returned his attention to his oar. "Besides, what do you know of the Anointed?"

"Well, the stories. The songs"—Thom shrugged—"I don't know. They all talk about the Anointed ones being able to heal themselves, and heal the sick or the dying, and do all sorts of extraordinary things."

"Sounds like fairy stories and Bard's tales to me," Crodane said. "Next, you'll be asking about dragons and unicorns, or worse, magic!"

"Well," Thom said, "You've traveled. You've never seen anything of the sort?"

"I'm sorry to disappoint you," Crodane said, "but no, at least not in my experience."

"Not at all?" Thom asked dejectedly, "Truly? But..."

Lughus tried to hide his own disappointment by changing the subject. "Rastis had a saying that 'a man who claims he knows it all only proves himself a fool, yet any man who seeks to know it all only dooms himself to failure'," he told Crodane. "He said that this is the very reason behind the Council of Five. Each councilor stands for one of the Five Holy Virtues that the Order holds true, faith from the Hierophant, fellowship from the Chancellor, courage from the Warlord, wisdom from the Loremaster, and fidelity from the King, and while all men should strive to live by these principles, no single man alone is perfect." Lughus paused. "So Rastis encouraged Thom and I and the other apprentice—our friend, Royne—to learn what we could about many things but focus on what we most loved. Thom studied music, herbs, beasts, and birds. Royne studied philosophy, politics, mathematics, and astronomy. And I studied law, building, romances, and theology. We all studied history, though Royne was probably best at it."

"Aye, and he loved nothing more than proving it," Thom said fondly. "But Rastis said that a master carpenter, a master painter, and a master swordsman have more in common with each other than they do with others in their field." The chubby boy began stroking an imaginary beard and waved his hand as if holding Rastis's long- stemmed pipe. "'There are many pathways through the Forest of Ignorance, but only one Palace of Wisdom on the other side.'"

"True enough," Crodane agreed.

"So..." Thom began again, "are you one of the Anointed? You are, aren't you?"

"Thom," Lughus said, "even if he is anointed, you know it's not polite to ask about such things, nor are they allowed to speak of it. Think of how cross Rastis was with you for pestering Hob."

"All right," Thom said, "fine. But you are a member of the Order, at least? What do you do? You're good with a sword. Are you sworn to the Warlord?"

"Thom..." Lughus said.

"Or are you one of the Chancellor's constables? Do you hunt Blackguards?"

"Thom..."

"I'm still not clear on what it means to be initiated and what it means to be anointed. I just don't understand the need for all the secrets."

"Thom!"

"Lughus!"

"Shut up."

"You shut up!"

"Look," Crodane broke in suddenly, "on the western bank of the river. Do you see the stone circle there?"

The boys quieted in their bickering long enough to look. "It looks like the remains of a tower," Thom said.

"In your studies of history, do you recall the last great war with the southern continent? Five hundred years ago during the reign of King Darius Drude II?"

Thom bit his lip in thought.

Lughus nodded. "I remember. The Kordish armies overran Grantis and executed their king. Then they pushed on into Andoch around the horns of the Firriny Mountains."

Crodane nodded. "That stone circle marks the limit of their push north into the interior of Termain."

"It was also one of but two times that the nations of Termain fought together against a common foe," Lughus added.

"True," Crodane said, "at any rate, there are plenty of other ruins along the banks of the Imperial—some far older than that one. If you'd like—and you can keep off bickering with each other—I can point them out to you along the way."

Lughus exchanged a nod of truce with Thom, and the swordsman shook his head at them with a grin.

Throughout the rest of the day, Crodane made good on his offer, noting every time they passed various points of interest along the river. Occasionally, if neither Lughus nor Thom was familiar with the story behind a place, the swordsman would regale them mildly with a local legend, a bit of history, or a description of the various flora and fauna native to the Imperial. They passed a standing stone said to mark the remains of a witch who served the Warlock and a small settlement of fishermen whose ancestors had lived along the same small bend of the river since the days of Old Calendral. Crodane pointed out the kingfisher, the emperor heron, and the little red-and-white songbirds known as troubadours or "trubs." They passed a nest of river otters, watched a doe and her fawn trot down to the river's edge to drink, and learned of the various types of fish that swam only but a few feet below them.

"We should be writing this down!" Thom said to Lughus, though no sooner had he clumsily wetted his quill with ink than the motion of the currach made him feel nauseous. However, Crodane assured him that he would have a chance to record all of it later that night when they stopped to make camp.

Though he knew he should know better than to be surprised at the wisdom of the Loremaster, Lughus was impressed and comforted by the old man's choice of guides. Not only did Crodane seem as knowledgeable as would befit a scholar or a historian, but he was also patient and kind, answering Thom's multitude of questions and listening to (or at least feigning interest in) his endless prattle. Besides, Thom's loquaciousness was only a further testament to the swordsman's character, as Thom seemed to have forgotten his former fears.

Lughus, too, in spite of his earlier designs to be cautious, could not help but feel an increasing predilection for the man, a growing interest and trust that only improved at dusk when they stopped to make camp.

"Thom, do you know how to build a fire?" Crodane asked as they slid the currach up out of the water onto the riverbank beside a gnarly old willow tree.

Lughus leaped out into the water to assist him, though, to his amazement, the swordsman did not seem nearly as weary as would be expected after rowing the small boat without pause all through the night.

Thom carefully tiptoed out of the boat, careful not to slip in the mud. "I believe I can do it," Thom said, "though I've never built a fire outdoors before."

"Then best you learn before heading north," Crodane said shortly. "You'll find flint and steel in here." He lightly grasped the two sacks from the stern of the boat and tossed them on the land.

"What do you need me to do?" Lughus asked.

Crodane walked up further onto the river bank away from the water's edge. "You," he said, waving his arm, "should stand over there and draw your sword."

Lughus's eyes widened, and Thom's face went pale. "What?"

Crodane drew his own blade. "Unless you have decided that you have no wish to learn?"

Lughus ignored Thom's questioning glance. "No," Lughus said and took his place where Crodane had indicated, "though don't you need to rest?"

"Those who live by the blade need be prepared to use it at all times," Crodane said simply. "Now you say Hob taught you the five guards. Show me."

"Eagle"—Lughus raised the sword high above his head— "Lion"—he dropped his hands and raised the tip of the blade before him—"Wolf"—he let the point fall forward to point toward the ground—"Bear"—he raised the hilt to the right of his head and extended the blade before him—"and Dragon," Lughus said turning his hands and lowering them to his side so that the blade pointed backward behind him.

"Your feet are too far apart, and you're still leaning too far forward."

"I'm sorry."

"Don't be. Fix it."

Lughus adjusted his feet and began again, "Eagle...Lion..."

"Hold the sword straighter."

"Eagle..."

"*Straighter*, and make sure your right heel is in line with your left foot."

"Eagle...Lion..."

"Stop," Crodane said. He raised his sword aloft, mirroring Lughus's stance. "Watch me. Begin with the Guard of the Eagle."

Lughus watched Crodane's posture and the rigidly nimble yet natural posture with which he stood. Lughus adjusted his own positioning to emulate his instructor. "Eagle," he said.

Crodane nodded curtly. "Better, but hold the blade straight."

Darkness had fallen when Lughus had finally shown enough precision in his stances to meet Crodane's satisfaction, but already he felt his ability, and his confidence, grow. Crodane was able to explain in detail the reasoning behind each stance and the type of attacks and defensive maneuvers most suitable when adopting or defending against each one. Already, Lughus could feel his familiarity with his new blade growing, and as he adopted each of the guards, he tried to think of the sword not simply as an object he held in his hand but rather—as Crodane had said—an extension of his own arm. When the two finally rejoined Thom for an evening meal of dried foodstuffs, Lughus already looked forward to Crodane's next lesson and hoped that it would include an opportunity to test his new knowledge and spar.

"How long do you think it'll take to reach Galdoran?" Thom asked later.

He sat upon his bedroll like a great boulder with his legs folded beneath him, his journal, inkwells, and quills arranged neatly before him. In the firelight, an illustration of a large, bewhiskered catfish stood out on the open page with notations regarding its size and habits. Lughus nodded at Thom with approval; the drawing did not lack skill.

Crodane poked at the fire with a stick and sat down stiffly at the base of the willow, leaning his sword within reach against the trunk.

"Depending upon the weather," he said, "Perhaps a week."

"When we get there, let's stay at an inn with a bathhouse," Thom said. "I feel like I haven't bathed in at least two weeks."

Lughus unrolled his own blanket and lay down, drawing his cloak around him. "You can take a swim in the river tomorrow before we set out again if you like," he said.

"The water's too cold, and besides," Thom said, pausing to yawn, "things live in it."

Lughus sighed but otherwise kept his mouth shut. It was nice to be able to stretch out flat on a bedroll rather than trying to sleep curled up in the curragh or out on the open, rolling deck of the barge, and between the swaying branches of the old willow, he could occasionally make out the twinkling lights of the stars. Slowly, he felt the embers of adventure beginning to rekindle in his breast.

"Should we set a watch?" he whispered softly to Crodane.

The swordsman folded his arms across his chest and closed his eyes. "No," he said, "Fergus is out there. He'll keep watch."

Lughus's brow furrowed. "Fergus? Hob mentioned him. Who is he?"

Crodane drew the hood of his cloak up over his head. "A friend," he said.

CHAPTER 15:
A QUESTION OF TREASON

"You sent them into danger," Royne said, his voice airy with disbelief. "You may have even sent them to their deaths!"

Rastis, chewing on the stem of his pipe, looked up from *The Book of Histories* and carefully closed its ancient cover. He eyed Royne curiously. "You have questions?"

"Aye," Royne said, the first tremors of frustration reverberating in chest, "I do."

"Then ask them," Rastis said calmly.

Royne chewed his lip and shook his head bitterly. They had only just returned from the meeting with the council, and the old man had not spoken a word about it since their return. He merely sat down by the fire in his quarters, lit his pipe, and returned to his reading, only just remembering to tell Royne that he was dismissed. However, the young steward did not want to go. Never in his childhood could Royne ever recall having been angry with the old Loremaster, yet in but a matter of a few weeks, it seemed that every new day Rastis said or did something else to draw his ire.

"The Galadin boy the King mentioned, the one you sent away," Royne began. "It's Lughus."

Rastis nodded simply. "It is."

The old man's candor took him slightly aback. "Does he know?" he asked.

"When he left here, he did not." The old man shrugged. "However, it may very well be that he knows now."

Royne's mind raced over the pages of history he had read concerning Baronbrock and the Galadins. Descended from St. Aiden himself, the Galadins were one of the most powerful of the Baronies of the Brock, though it seemed that Arcis Galadin, the current baron, would be the last of the line following the death of his only daughter. Royne ground his teeth and shook his head—fifteen years ago. Lughus would have been scarcely a year old. Royne could only imagine his friend's reaction, finding out that he was descended in a direct line from the warrior saint and not some orphan vagabond or nobleman's bastard like himself and Thom.

Royne clenched his fist. "And now the King is sending Willum Harlow to bring him back? The Hammer? The man's a bloody bounty hunter."

Rastis took a pull from his pipe. "Harlow is one of the Chancellor's constables, chief constable in fact, and also an anointed member of the Order honored with both rank and title," he said, "As the Chancellor is the keeper of the law, those in his service are often tasked with bringing fugitives to justice."

"Aye, but Lughus is no fugitive," Royne said angrily, "let alone a bloody Blackguard!"

Rastis turned a page and continued his reading. "Not to my knowledge, no."

Royne felt his temper flare. He wanted to reach out and toss the bloody book into the fire—anything to get the old man to look at him, to answer his questions. Royne struggled to contain his rising irritation. "What does the King even want with him, and why did you really send him away? Is it because they say that Arcis Galadin is dying? Is Lughus to come into his own? If he is a Galadin, why was he even here in the first place and not in Baronbrock?" The questions were coming all at once. His chest tightened, and inwardly, he reprimanded himself for, yet again, prattling on like Thom. "Aiden's Flame!" he said at last, slamming his fist into his other palm. "Rastis, what have you done?"

Slowly, Rastis ran a hand through his beard and puffed deeply at his pipe. He closed the book. "Sit down, Royne," he said.

"I think I'd rather stand."

"Fine," the old man gave a heavy sigh and rubbed his eyes. "I understand that you are angry," he said wearily. "And that you are worried for your friends. However, do not think for a moment that, at any time, I have willingly sent your friends into harm's way." He paused. "Believe me. I am no less concerned with their safety than you are."

"Then why have you sent them away?" Royne asked.

"If you won't sit down," he said, "then at least shut the door."

Royne quickly did as he was asked and returned to stand before the Loremaster, folding his arms sullenly across his chest.

Rastis took a slow pull from his pipe. "As you well know," he said, "I, too, was born in the Brock in the barony of Glendaro. My brother was once the Lord-Baron, and now that honor belongs to my nephew."

Royne nodded. He had known that; however, Rastis had always been the Loremaster of the Guardians, and as such, his loyalties lie with the Order and, by association, with the Guardian King, not to the land of his birth.

"However," Rastis continued, "I knew Arcis Galadin and his family, and as is befitting of his lineage, the Galadins and the Order have always held each other in very high esteem."

"Not sure how true that holds today, considering the meeting," Royne grumbled.

"You are not incorrect," Rastis sighed, "though, unfortunately, a break with the Order would be but the next in line of a series of misfortunes to befall the Galadins, one that began with a tragedy so great that it threatened to be the end of the bloodline, the end of *St. Aiden's* bloodline."

Royne nodded, thinking. "Something to do with the Marthaines. Though it's unclear exactly what. Something about marriage, an effort to force the two families to peace."

Rastis hesitated. "Yes," he said at last, "however, regardless of the details, after the deaths of his wife and his daughter, Arcis feared for his grandson's life, and as recompense for what he believed my brother's negligence, I was asked to safeguard the boy until he came of age for fear that others may try to harm him."

"Then why didn't you tell Lughus any of this?" Royne asked and, after considering it, sat down at the chair across from the old man.

"Royne," Rastis said, "until recently, there was only one person other than myself and Baron Galadin who knew the truth about Lughus, and I would trust his silence on the matter more than my own. Even Hobart did not know the whole story."

"Then how did the King find out?"

"That I do not know," Rastis said, "though I began to suspect it some time ago, even before King Valder was laid to rest and Prince Kredor was crowned. The prince was always an ambitious man, and ambitious men often attract others like them."

"Tainne," Royne said.

Rastis inclined his head and dropped his voice. "If you recall, it was Tainne who informed his majesty about the boys' departure, though they have many other allies among the nobility and among the Order, Lord Hanson Fowler, Lord Basilar Gendrik, Lord Marcel Pryce, the Hierophant, the Chancellor, and many, many more. King Valder himself was not without certain concerns about his son and his friends, though he would not voice them readily. I remember a time not long after Prince Kredor's victory over Clan Thorwick. Valder remarked once that Kredor would be an excellent king in a time of war, so long as the Brethren granted him one. And in fairness, such a thing has its virtues. For it is the prerogative of the Guardians to defend the realms, all of them, but not necessarily to reign over them." The old man paused to draw from his pipe. "However, as Arcis Galadin's condition worsens—another tragedy for the Galadins, and for all of Baronbrock—I knew that if I did not send Lughus soon, then—"

Royne scowled. "They would have tried to use Lughus as ransom."

"Arcis Galadin is a good man," Rastis said mildly, "even his enemies respect him. Were he to speak out in favor of the Protectorate, it would lend significant weight to the prince's—excuse me, the King's—claim. And though you will find few as honorable as the baron of Galadin, the son of his only daughter, the last of their line, might mean considerably more to him than principle."

Royne stood abruptly from the table and shoved his chair underneath it with a bang. "Those bastards!" he hissed. His blood grew hot with resentment, and a burning sensation churned in his innards. So much for the glory of the Guardians! So much for the Five Holy Virtues! For over twelve hundred years, the Guardians had appeared as the subject of innumerable legends, histories, and poems. They were the Light of the Lady Callah that drove away the Darkness of Dibhor, the epitome of all that was thought to be good. Royne had never considered himself to be an idealist, quite the contrary, and often, it was his skepticism that tempered the romantic ideals of Lughus or the epic poems loved by Thom. However, there was something so disgusting about the truth of things that now that he knew he was right, he suddenly wished he was wrong.

"Bloody hypocrites," he snarled, "I knew that King was rotten from the first he was crowned! Stories of the bloody Warlock! He's a fool! A mad fool!"

Rastis ignored Royne's outburst and merely smoked his pipe. "So you see now why I sent Lughus away," he said softly.

"Aye," Royne said, "I see it. He is not going to Galadin to further his studies. He's getting away from the bloody council and that rotten, ignorant bastard of a k—"

"For his own protection," the old man cut in as the volume of Royne's voice grew, "and to be formally recognized as Arcis Galadin's heir, though, as I said, it is ultimately Lughus's choice. If he instead decides to return to the Order, then so be it."

Royne took a deep breath. He returned to his chair and felt his lips twist into an involuntary smirk at the thought of Lughus as a Baron; however, it suddenly made sense. St. Aiden was always depicted in iconography and in the legendary accounts as a man ensconced in gold, and like other noble families, the Galadins carried certain physical traits through the generations. Who'd have thought that the old Goldimop was a mark of noble birth? He recalled *The History of the Baronies of the Brock*. The Galadins all bore "hair as golden as the sun."

"What about Thom, then?" Royne said after a moment. "He's not heir to the throne of Tulondis or some such now, is he? Or how about a dragon in human form? It would certainly explain his appetite."

The old man raised his eyebrows, holding the stem of his pipe between his teeth. "Not to my knowledge," he said. "But I thought that if Lughus had to go, it may help to have a friend along for the journey, at least for a time. Hobart was serious about Thom visiting the Wrathorn, and with Thom's love of music, feasting, beasts, and birds, I thought it would be good for him since the northern clans share those loves as well. However, most importantly, I am sending him to meet an old friend of mine, a very old friend."

"As long as he can overcome his fear," Royne said.

"All the more reason for him to go then." Rastis took another long pull on his pipe and released a wispy cloud of fragrant smoke into the air above his head. He stroked his beard pensively. "I only hope that they'll have taken to ship for the Brock before word reaches Harlow," he said, "for the King will not simply use pigeons. For something like this, he will send a kite, perhaps two, to be sure…"

Calendral Kites, Royne knew, were the special birds of prey reserved for the Guardian King. However, unlike the trained hunting fowl of the general nobility, the kites were bigger, faster, and far more intelligent. Royne recalled a time once when he, Lughus, and Thom had been granted the opportunity to see them up close and to feed them. Thom, in particular, was delighted. However, his delight soon turned to horror when one of the birds nearly bit his hand; they were remarkably ill-tempered but carried messages incredible distances very quickly. *Certainly faster than a barge upon the river might sail…*

"Do not lose hope yet, my boy!" the old man said as Royne hung his head. "Nine days by the river is a significant head start, even on a barge, and Crodane is with them. I trust that he will keep them safe."

Royne gave a weak nod. "How can you be certain?"

"Few things are ever certain," the old man said. "But I have hope."

Royne watched the wisps of pipe smoke spindle up to the ceiling and disappeared. That was true; as cynical as he might normally be, Royne knew that Rastis was right. He could not give up hope, or else, he would essentially be abandoning his friends. No, he would not lose hope. At length, he spoke, "Rastis, I believe I owe you an apology."

The old man arched an eyebrow. "Why is that?"

Royne folded his hands on the tabletop and sighed. "I'm sorry for what I said before when I was angry," he said, "for what I said about sending them to their deaths."

Rastis shook off the apology with a wave of his hand. "You were concerned about your friends because you care for them," he said, "but just remember, so do I."

"Yes, sir," Royne said. He stood up from the table. "At any rate, I'll leave you to your work." He remembered his steward's pin. "Is there anything else you need, though? Tea? Bread?"

"No, thank you," Rastis said. "However, Royne, I believe that it is my turn to apologize to you."

Royne shook his head. "I understand why I was left behind." Rastis raised an eyebrow. "But do you really?"

"I believe so," he said. "You told me that you had need of my mind. You needed someone logical and analytical, and after that meeting today, I think that perhaps I can see why."

"And why is that?"

Royne sighed. "It's like the fortunetellers and the magicians that you see sometimes at the summer fairs," he said at last. "You know it's not real, that it's all just a trick. However, sometimes, it takes an extra set of eyes to see past the deception, and from what I observed, you seem to be surrounded by liars."

"Well, you're certainly not guarded with your opinions," Rastis said, "though be careful not to pass judgment too swiftly. For the *Scrolls of the Hierophants* speak of eyes as well, remember."

Royne nodded penitently. "'Man is but a single eye gazing out upon eternity,'" he quoted.

"Correct. So be cautious."

"Yes, sir," Royne said, though inwardly his heart swelled with pride. "I'll stay silent, but I promise to keep a sharp eye."

"Good," Rastis said. "However, that is not exactly what I wanted to apologize for." The old man paused, shook his head, and stroked his beard. "For you see, by sending Lughus and Thom away from the danger, I have, by default, chosen to keep you nearer to it?"

A sick feeling spread through Royne's stomach, and his insides felt suddenly hollow. The color drained from his cheeks. He had not thought about it, but it was true. Whatever conflict was brewing between Rastis and the King, Royne would, by his own recent admission, help the old man to see it through, and although he did not consider himself to be brave or anything at all resembling heroic, he did consider himself to be loyal. "I know," he finally said, "but I intend to do what I can to aid you, Rastis, if it pleases the King or not."

Rastis sighed wistfully. "I sincerely appreciate it, Royne, and it means a great deal to me. However, I would advise you not to say such things aloud, lest you seek to end up accused of treason too," he said, "and the last thing in the world that I would want for you, my boy, would be a place kneeling beside me at the block."

Royne scoffed. "Those were just words. Even in times of strife, the Order has never censured a member of the council before. If you were forbidden from speaking your mind, how else could a councilor possibly counsel? Surely, the King would have to be mad to accuse you of treason."

Rastis laughed, and a great cloud of sweet-smelling pipe smoke drifted slowly up to the ceiling. "Perhaps he would be if I had limited my defiance to mere words." He smiled forlornly. "However, for better or for worse, I willingly set into motion a series of events in direct opposition to what I anticipated would be the King's decree, sending Lughus and Thom to Baronbrock was but one instance. Perhaps I misjudged your abilities, Royne, because that sounds to me like the very definition of treason!"

"What do you mean?" Royne asked.

The old man sighed. "I'm not quite sure I know any more myself, Royne, and I find myself beset by many doubts and fears that I would not burden you with—if only to keep you innocent of the charges I may soon bear. Suffice it to say, however, that these are troubling times for the Order and for all Termain. Kredor's empire, should it come to pass, is but the first in a long line of tragedies looming before us, and should we hope to avoid them, we must bend every effort in doing so."

"Whatever the course may be, Rastis," Royne said, "I am with you. First and last."

CHAPTER 16:
HOPE

When Brigid awoke the morning after the feast, the birds nesting on the ledge below her window were sounding their morning calls. The morning sunlight shone in through the shutters casting the room in the soft blue light of dawn. She breathed a heavy sigh, rolled over in her tangle of blankets, and curled into a comfortable ball. For once, she did not awake fretting over another long day of following Alan and his sycophantic train of fools, nor did she dread the prospect of taking meals with her vain mother, sitting shamefacedly as Josephine provided commentary for her every move. She did not even fear the inevitable confrontation with Reid over the awkward moment last night when she had slapped his hand. None of it seemed of any consequence to her anymore, she realized, and for the first time in a long time, her heart felt glad.

She gave another sigh and smiled, running her fingers through her long, thick hair. Free of its customary tresses, it fell like strands of dark silk, spilling out onto her pillow like water. Perhaps today, she would refuse when her mother sent her servants in to plait it, and when she stood later in the yard watching the boys at their training, the swift mountain winds would flow through it, and she could pretend again to be standing upon the deck of her imagined ship, racing the pod of dolphins along the shore. She would be sure to win next time, for it was, after all, her daydream.

She laughed in spite of herself; what foolishness it was to lose to a mere figment of her own mind! She shut her eyes again and pictured half a dozen of her other favorite escapes: the Sorgundian longship, the Wrathorn hill, a forest in Baronbrock, a barge on the Imperial River, a lighthouse in Castone, and a wild horse trail cutting through the valleys of Montevale. She wondered suddenly if the prisoner had ever seen them and to what extent her imaginings—based largely on fragments of stories she had read or old fables she remembered from her nursemaids—matched any of their real-life forms. She would have to ask him—her friend, the Falcon.

That thought alone brought with it a particularly unique brand of happiness. Never before had she made a friend of her own. Caryn, Nora, and the other girls—if indeed she could consider them friends—were not Brigid's choice of companions, but rather Josephine's, each one selected based on a combination of family connections, physical beauty, wealth, and agreeableness. In short, they were the type of young women Brigid's mother would have chosen for herself. They were to be tasteful accoutrements— rings, ribbons, and bangles to further accentuate the gloriousness of the crown.

But the Falcon—Brigid thought, burying her smile in a pillow; he was hers and hers alone. He was clever and witty and gallant and handsome. He knew things about the world both inside and outside of Blackstone, knew the truth about Alan and her uncle and her mother, and perhaps most exciting of all, he had promised to take her with him when he finally escaped. She wondered quickly what purpose kept him here and how soon it would be before they could be gone. She wanted to run across the grounds to his donjon tower and ask him but knew that daylight brought with it an even greater chance of getting caught.

And then what? What would her uncle or her mother do? What would they say if she were to suddenly storm into the great hall and demand the prisoner be released?

Brigid sighed. Probably ignore her, as they had ever done.

That realization seemed to bring her feet back safely to the ground. She rolled over onto her other side, and suddenly, the mattress beneath her seemed uncomfortable and the blankets too hot. Her moment of reckless frivolity had passed. The new day had dawned, and it was time to get up.

Brigid slipped from the blankets and threw on her dressing gown as she tiptoed silently across the cold stone floor to her wardrobe. On days like this, her mother often stayed in bed until well past midday, sleeping off the effects of the wine and the memory of her late-night company. For Brigid, this allowed a greater degree of freedom—so long as she could avoid Livonia the Scold. That wretched old woman had spent enough of her life at Josephine's side to anticipate the mercurial mood swings and absurdities that were so much a part of the archduchess's day and the source of so much of Brigid's strife.

Hurriedly, she clad herself in her favorite dress: a plane cotton gown of grayish blue—the same color as the sky before a thunderstorm. Josephine hated the dress and said it looked like something a lowborn shepherdess would wear, but Brigid liked it because it was soft and less bulky than the other gowns her mother forced her to wear with their foolish trains and billowy sleeves. If the dress made her look like a peasant, then all the better. Better to be poor and happy than noble and miserable. Her hair she let fall loose around her shoulders and down her back—tresses be damned—and donning her light shoes, she scurried out into the hallway just outside of her room.

The tapers in the iron wall sconces were nearing the ends of their wicks after a long night's burn, and the sentry at the top of the staircase seemed near as spent. Brigid nearly frightened the life out of him when he suddenly recognized her and snapped to attention with a start. "Good morning, my lady," he said hurriedly, tapping the butt of his pike against the flagstones. He averted his eyes obediently, staring into the tapers across from his post.

Brigid paused, realizing that it was perhaps the first time she had left her apartments unattended, let alone spoken to one of the guards. She eyed the man nervously in his chain mail. On his breast, his tabard bore the mark of the golden anvil, *her* mark, one of *her* soldiers—at least in theory. "Good morning, sir," she said at last, slightly surprised at the sound of her own voice. "Thank you for keeping watch over us these long nights."

The guardsman glanced quickly at her out of the corner of his eye. He seemed nervous, Brigid thought. Perhaps he wondered if she had seen him dozing and was now attempting to discern any sarcasm or condescension in her tone. Finally, his own silence seemed to make him uneasy. "It's my duty, my lady," he said.

"Well, I thank you for it all the same," she smiled, "Do you have a name?"

"A name?"

"Your name."

"Hodges, my lady." He saluted again and stared uncomfortably up at the ceiling, "At your service."

Brigid smiled. "May I get past you, Hodges?" she asked.

The guard's eyes widened, and his ruddy, whiskered cheeks shone red. "Begging your pardon, miss," he said hurriedly, stepping back a few paces. "I meant no disrespect…hindering you on your way."

"It's quite all right," she said. "Thank you."

"Of course, my lady," the man said. "Good day."

Brigid hurried past him down the stairs. "Good day!"

As she skipped down the rest of the way, she began to feel inklings of the same reckless excitement that had gripped her when she first awoke. Her heart felt much lighter again, and the chilly morning air that filled the lofty mountain fortress seemed more invigorating than cold. When she finally reached the base of the stairs behind the great hall, where her mother had made her grand entrance at the feast, Brigid was pleased to find that the room was empty. A few tables still bore half-filled tankards or dirty plates, and a row of empty barrels sat upright along the eastern wall. However, for the most part, the room had been cleared. She stepped lightly over the floor, following the same route she had traveled in her escape the night before, leaping from the high table to the wall and out into the entryway and its dark braziers. Another guard sat on duty in the tiny alcove by the heavy doors. Like the man upstairs, he looked in his thirties with a simple countenance and a messy, unkempt bit of scruff that might have passed as a beard.

"Hello," Brigid called out to him.

The guardsman hurriedly got to his feet. "My lady," he said.

"I hope the day finds you well." She smiled.

"It does indeed, miss," he said, "and I hope it does fine by you too."

"It does, sir," Brigid said. "Thank you."

"You're welcome, my lady," the man said.

Brigid sighed and looked forlornly at the heavy wooden doors that led out into the inner ward. "Would you be able to open the doors for me?" she asked the guard sweetly.

The guardsman shifted his weight hesitantly. "My apologies, miss," he said. "But I'm afraid I had better not."

For a second, she lost her nerve, nodded, and began to turn. However, some sudden urge, this new, unknown boldness, kept her rooted at the spot. "Might I ask, sir," she said suddenly. "Why not?"

The guardsman bit his lip. "Well, ma'am...er...miss...my lady"—he coughed—"your lady mother or your uncle—"

"Neither of whom are here."

"Well, no, but..."

Brigid lowered her eyes in feigned dejection. "Please," she said, "I only wish to walk a bit around the ward."

The guard shifted his weight uneasily and leaned on his pike.

Finally, he sighed. "Yes, my lady."

Slowly, the guardsman lifted the heavy wooden beam barring the door and cautiously pushed one of the two doors open. Brigid curtsied politely and tried to subdue the rush of joy she felt at her success. She walked quickly out into the soft green grass of the yard and halfway down the northern wall before she allowed the smile to flower upon her lips. For a time, at least, she was free.

Her steps were light as she traversed the perimeter of the inner ward, nodding courteously to the two other sentries guarding the gate to the outer ward until, finally, she came to a stop at the base of the Falcon's tower. The door was shut but unguarded, and although a great part of her wanted to rush inside and up the stairs to greet him, she knew that to do so would be unwise. Instead, she continued her walk, pausing every so often to notice the petals of a wild mountain flower or study the thick coating of moss on a rock. For the world seemed new and fresh today, more familiar, more real, and for her part, Brigid felt as if she were suddenly an integral part of the whole and not merely an impassive observer.

After some time, however, she began to sense the rest of the castle's company stir and knew that before long, her mother—though more likely Livonia—would come to collect her. Rather than face their looks of condescending disapproval, she walked one last time past the Falcon's prison, gently gliding her fingertips across the wooden door, and decided to return to the keep. However, as she entered through the entryway past the attentive sentry, she stopped suddenly, and her breath caught in her throat. In the center of the floor, surrounded by dusty old tapestries, Alan stood miserably leaning up against the wall. He wiped his mouth with a handkerchief, and Brigid noticed that his skin was a peculiar shade of pale.

"Brigid!" he started when he saw her.

Brigid nodded and curtsied politely. Her fingers tingled with anxiety as she recalled the horrid things she overheard the last time that Alan spoke. "Good morning, cousin," she said at last, "how are you this morning?"

Alan scoffed and pressed the handkerchief to his mouth. "Perfect," he said shortly, "I was just…seeing to some things in the stables."

Brigid suppressed a flash of disgust—more like passed out there after conscripting some poor servant girl to tup. She said nothing, only nodded and made to hurry past him back to the great hall. However, as she passed, his arm lashed out and snatched her wrist. Suddenly, she was overwhelmed with the stench of spilled wine and vomit.

"Wait," Alan said wickedly, "I have a secret for you." He twisted her wrist and tried to pull her toward him. "It's quite interesting." He leered. "Trust me."

Brigid stood rigidly in fear, struggling to slip from Alan's grasp. His clammy fingers felt like melting icicles. "I don't want to know any of your secrets," she whispered.

Alan tottered unsteadily on his feet, and he brought the handkerchief up to his mouth. Brigid took it as a chance to slip from his grasp and leap away across the flagstones.

"I'll let Reid tell you then." Her cousin laughed.

Brigid stopped. When she turned to face him, her countenance bore no trace of the fiery inferno raging within her. "You know," she said in a tone of honey and venom, "before you came to live here, there was a crow that used to roost atop the gate to the outer ward. All day, it would puff itself up and squawk and squawk and squawk away. Then one day, a falcon heard its call, flew down from the mountainside, and tore it to pieces." Her lips twisted into a wry grin. "Every time I hear your voice, I think of that crow."

Alan was too stunned to speak. He lurched forward and sat down in a heap at one of the long tables. He folded his arms on the tabletop in front of him, spit on the floor, and impotently muttered, "Bitch."

Brigid stifled a laugh as a shock of elfin glee ran through her, setting her hands and knees tingling. Without a word, she backed away hurriedly from her besotted cousin through the side hallway to the staircase that would return her to her rooms. As soon as her foot touched the bottom stair, her laughter burst forth in great shuddering gasps, doubling her over. The thrill of even such a small victory over Alan was nearly too much for her to bear, and she struggled to contain her giggling for fear that she was going mad. However, the fact remained. She had stood up to Alan.

At the third-floor landing, Brigid paused to catch her breath and reestablish her composure. Her mother might very well be awake now, and though she may still not have been out of bed, it was certain that Livonia would be seeing to her affairs. *And I'll once again be a mouse*, Brigid thought. Yet she had tasted what it was like to be a falcon, even if but for a few hours, and it was not a sensation she would soon forget.

A guardsman stood at the top of the stairs, though he was not the same man as before. His eyes stared off into space, away from her, at the ancient gray mortar between the thick stones of the castle wall. He knew his place, and though her breathless dash upstairs may have been unseemly, he knew better than to stare. She was about to wish him good morning when, suddenly, the man started, slammed the butt of his pike against the floor, and snapped sharply to attention.

For a split second, Brigid wondered if it was she that he was saluting when suddenly a velvety whisper from the direction of her mother's chamber sent an icy chill down her spine.

"Good morning, Lady Brigid."

Brigid whirled around to see her uncle, the Sheriff, still dressed in the same finery as the night before. In an instant, she lost all trace of her former boldness and was once again the mousey young girl with blue eyes and raven hair. Her breath caught in her throat, and her head bowed submissively.

"Or perhaps I should say good day," the Sheriff purred. He shut the door to her mother's chamber behind him and clasped his hands behind his back.

"Good morning, my Lord Sheriff," she stuttered, her voice but a whisper. "I hope the day finds you well."

"It does indeed, child." Her uncle sighed. "Though I find it is already half gone." He smiled. "Your mother is within if you await her. She has some important news to discuss with you today, though I'll allow her the privilege of informing you of such happiness. My apologies if I have dominated her attention over long."

Brigid remained still, though her stomach suddenly felt sickened, and the healthy flush drained from her cheeks.

"Good day, my lady," the Sheriff said, siding past her to the stairway, "and let me be the first to give you joy."

"Good day," she whispered after him, though she stood rooted to the same spot listening to her uncle's footsteps clattering heavily upon the stone stairs. When the sound of her uncle's passing had died way, she fled for the safety of her own chambers and, once inside, shut and locked the door. Barely had she done so, however, when without warning, a cold, iron fist clenched tightly in her dark hair.

"There you are, you foolish girl!" Livonia snapped. "You've had me worried sick! The Lady and Lords only know what could have befallen you alone and unattended!"

"I'm sorry!" Brigid gasped in pain as the old woman wrenched her head back. "Please, madam, I'm sorry!"

"Aye, you will be sorry, you dreamy-eyed fool! I've half a mind to slap you, you stupid girl!"

"Please! I'm sorry!"

Livonia twisted her fingers and threw Brigid forward, letting her fall to the floor. Brigid's scalp burned at the roots where the hag had gripped her. She shut her eyes as tears of molten anger collected in her eyes. Her fist clenched, and for a moment, she envisioned herself rising from the floor to strike back, wondering how many of the old woman's rotting teeth she could knock out in a single blow.

"Now get up," Livonia said. "Your uncle's just been here, and we've got to see you properly dressed."

"Why?" Brigid asked.

Livonia answered her with a stinging slap.

"Don't question me," the hag said. "You do as I say."

Brigid pressed a hand to the side of her face. Her bright eyes smoldered with a cold blue fire, but the crone merely laughed and began searching through Brigid's armoire. "Your mother and your uncle have asked me to see that you're ready, so that's what we do. It's not to me to question the will of the archduchess nor the Sheriff either. However," she added, grinning wickedly, "if I had to wager, I'd say a certain empty-headed young maiden may find herself without a different head by year's end."

Brigid's blood froze in her veins, and the old woman cackled maniacally at what she believed was her own cleverness. "I will not marry Reid," she swore, leaping to her feet.

Livonia laughed.

"I know that's what they intend," Brigid said.

"It's not my place to presume their intentions one way or another, nor is it yours."

"Well, if that is what they intend, I will not do it."

"No," Livonia said matter-of-factly, "you'll do as you're told, same as always, same as I will." She held out the sleeve of one of the armoire's gowns, inspected it, and shook her head in dissatisfaction. "Ain't no one questions the will of the archduchess, save perhaps your uncle."

Brigid thought again of the Falcon, of his promise to take her with him. Her blood grew hot, and again, she wondered at his errand and how much longer she would have to wait. Still, the thought of her secret friend made her bold. "They say, one day, I'll be the next archduchess," she said suddenly, casting a glance out of the window in the direction of the Falcon's tower, "When I ask you to throw yourself from the top of the keep will you follow that order without question as well?"

As soon as the words passed her lips, Brigid regretted the hasty remark. She winced instinctively, bracing herself for the worst. However, she felt no blow strike her cheek. No gnarled fingers twisted violently through her hair. Instead, she watched as the old woman's chapped lips twisted into a wry grin. "I certainly will," Livonia said, "assuming that day ever comes."

CHAPTER 17:
DESPAIR

"What do we do now?"

The precise source of the question was unclear, but it mattered not who spoke it, for it was the question on every man's mind. However, the silence was the only answer the men of Pyle had to offer, gathered together in the courtyard where only a few hours ago, they had assembled to praise Alantir, the Lord-Father, for a successful harvest and another summer of relative peace.

Geoffrey stood apart with his back to the others, gazing at the smoldering ruin of the village chapel. For the most part, the fire had burned itself out, though in the muted shades of dusk light, a few bright embers remained to emit serpentine spindles of acrid smoke, and where once the chapel's altar had stood, there was now only a warped, broken icon, twisted and scorched as if by the lightless flames of the shadowy Abyss. The ground at his feet was dark with Cousin Martin's blood, his body having already been taken to one of the nearby hovels to be seen to by the women. By the grace of the Kinship, Martin's soul would already be safely under their protection and at peace. However, after the day's events, Geoffrey was having a hard time believing that the gods were gracious, let alone good.

"Aiden's flame!" someone cursed. "First Damon, now Martin, who's next?"

"*All of us*, that's who," another voice cried bitterly. "Without the stores, not one of us will survive the cold of the coming months, let alone have enough seed to begin planting for next year!"

"You should have never killed those men, Geoffrey!"

"Aye, 'tis always a sin to kill a messenger!"

Geoffrey turned around to face the accusatory stares of his friends and neighbors. All his life, he had known them, yet suddenly, they appeared cold and unfamiliar, like old stones. "I'm sorry," he said.

"Aye, you should be!" shouted a man, who Geoffrey slowly recognized as Oscar.

"You can shove your apologies up your ass, I say," said a man resembling Raleigh. "You've doomed us all!"

Suddenly, there was a flurry of movement as Oliver, crouching red-eyed and mute on the edge of the assembly, burst forth, flailing his arms in a desperate attempt to drive his fist into Raleigh's face. Other men hurried to separate them.

"Steady on, Oliver!" "He's gone mad!"

Oliver slipped free and backed off to stand at Geoffrey's side. "They've taken our sons!" he hissed.

"Aye," Raleigh growled, "but at least your boys will have plenty to eat with the bandits whilst mine are starved!"

Oliver made another leap, and the men converged a second time to halt the violence with limited success. Soon, other men began to push and shove, tempers flared, and harsh oaths flew like volleys of arrows from neighbor to neighbor. Geoffrey stirred from his own numb grief to try to hold Oliver back while Oscar joined Raleigh in taunting Oliver. A few men called out to let the two of them fight, and very soon, other voices joined them. Oliver struggled against Geoffrey's grasp, spitting and snarling, tears streaming down his cheeks. Oscar and Raleigh shouted further curses and leered maliciously, making ready. Someone shoved Geoffrey from behind, and he felt his grip slacken on Oliver as the men converged.

"*Enough!*"

The voice was loud and low, slicing through the clamor of the mob like the crack of a whip. Men froze like children caught in the act of mischief.

"Dibhor take you all! I said *enough!*"

At the edge of the courtyard, Old Amos, Geoffrey's father, stood like a watchtower. Though not by any means a large man, with his spindly legs and wispy, white beard, the old man's voice sent shivers down the younger men's spines, for it was the voice of an elder, and it carried with it the weight of aged authority.

"Have you all gone *mad*?" Amos growled, pounding his cane against the ground in wrath. "By the bloody Brethren, I've never seen such out-and-out stupidity, and I'm *blind*!"

A cold silence fell over the assembly of men. Heads drooped in shame, and teeth gnashed in despair.

"We're sorry," Oscar muttered softly, "We—"

"*Shut your mouth!*" Amos snapped and, with a swift crack, slapped the nearest man across the shins with his cane, knocking him to the ground. "It's my turn to speak!" he said. "And you will *all* listen!"

"Now, you fools, you utter asses," he began again, slowly making his way into the center of them. "I will not stand by while you destroy yourselves, your families, and this whole bloody village out of dumb, animal stupidity. I will not, and as the oldest man in the village, I think having lived this long without dying has at least earned me the right to speak."

Geoffrey watched his father take a deep breath and steady himself. He could not remember a time when the old man had ever been *this* angry, not even when, as a boy, Geoffrey broke the blade of their plow. The veins stood out from the old man's face and arms like ancient tree roots, and the skin of his forehead was steaming in the chill of the autumn dusk.

"All of you, I'm sure, remember the last war, some of you may even remember the war before that, and I was a young man for the one before that one when it was old Archduke Tolliver as led Dwerin against the legionaries of the Grantisi Senate. Then as since, both sides fought for control of these lands, hoping to install lords of their own and gain tribute from all the farmers of the Spade, never mind the fact that men had tilled these fields for generations by their own accord."

"And what happens in wartime? You wake one morning to go out to the field only to find an army camp and a third of your crops taken as 'tribute' for the cause. A week later, you go out to find another camp of soldiers from the other side, and another third of your crops was gone. Then come next season, you're plowing your fields only to turn up dead men's bones with the usual rocks and stones."

"I think it was Grantis who won the war that time, not that it matters, and we had a few years of what the lords away in their castles might call peace.

There was talk of Grantis building a fort and setting up a local lord, as there always is, and messengers were sent expecting us all to bend the knee. Though, of course, all of us then knew better that the end of the season of war never, ever means peace. It means simply the trading of one injustice for another. It means the replacement of looting armies with thieving bandits, tithes for tribute, and one measure of misery for another. Sometimes the lords would send aid, sometimes they wouldn't, but it never really matters because, before long, the war would be on again as one side tried to reclaim what they lost and those once labeled bandit return to being hired soldiers."

"Twice more, the cycle has repeated since then, and in that time, I've lost countless bushels of crops, a barn's worth of livestock, half a village of friends, and my wife."

Amos paused, leaned on his cane, and sighed heavily. "The life of a farmer is a life of hardship," he said. "And often a life of suffering and a life of pain. However"—he tapped his cane—"the only way for anyone of us to make it through is to stand by each other. For who was it that helped me to rebuild my house? Who was it that helped me to plow my fields without a horse? Who was it that helped me to raise my son? My friends and my neighbors. The people of this village. To this day, we store our crops for the winter together in the storehouse. We share the bounty of our labors. Why? Because together, we live. Alone, we die."

"It is true. We are in a bad state. We've got little food. We've lost loved ones, including my own grandson. We're all grieving." He paused and let his words hang for a moment on the air. "But if you turn on each other now, then you, and your families, are all doomed."

A heavy silence fell over the group, and men continued to bow their heads for fear of meeting each other's eyes. At length, Old Amos sighed heavily and, in a calmer, kinder tone, said, "It's been a very long day, and standing around now is not going to make any of it better. For now, I think we should all go home to our families. Think on what I've said, and we'll meet again to discuss what to do in the morning."

One by one, the men of Pyle shuffled off to their homes, weighed down by their heavy hearts. However, Geoffrey could not find it in himself to leave the ruin of the chapel or the bloodstained ground from where Martin fell. At once, he felt driven to act, to do something, though his mind seemed clouded, muddled by feelings ranging from guilt and sorrow to rage and grief. Karl was gone, taken by the bandits to fill the empty place in their ranks.

It was not unheard of, nor uncommon, for the bandit troops to take young men and boys. Like a shepherd breeding sheep to replace the numbers of his flock gone for mutton or to market, the bandits often used their years of peace to train new recruits for the next war. What better way to prepare them for the coming battles than to practice terrorizing the villages of farmers who would not fight back? However, the thought of Karl as a mercenary—as a bandit, was more than Geoffrey could bear, and he fought off the darker feelings within him that would have preferred the boy's death to a life of pillaging and murder.

Darkness had fallen by the time the courtyard of the ruined chapel had finally cleared, leaving only Geoffrey, Oliver, and Old Amos standing like pillars of stone. Oliver looked as one left for dead, pale and tattered, his eyes red and burning with grief. Geoffrey knew that, like him, his friend was gathering his courage to return home to a cottage suddenly made emptier.

Somewhere in the fields, crickets chirped and a barn owl sounded its cry. The last of the chapel's embers went out with a whisper of smoke and dissolved upon the breeze. Slowly, the quiet tap of Amos's cane grew nearer, and from behind him, Geoffrey heard the old man's voice.

"So," he said quietly, "what do you intend to do?"

Oliver remained silent. Geoffrey sighed. "I don't know."

Amos's cane tapped forward, and out of the corner of his eye, Geoffrey could sense his father standing at his right, regarding the ruined chapel as if he still had sight.

"Do you remember," Amos said slowly, "when your mother was taken?"

Geoffrey took a deep breath, "I try not to."

Amos sighed. "Nor do I." He paused to clear his throat with a cough. "But there's not a moment goes by that I'm successful."

Geoffrey said nothing.

"I often wonder if I could not have done something, anything, to save her," he said. "All these years, every hour of every day, I wonder, and for a long time, I would say to myself, 'You're just a farmer. What could you possibly have done?' As if that will somehow justify it all, as if that could somehow ease the pain." Amos sighed. "Let me tell you, it doesn't."

Geoffrey rubbed his eyes. "Da, you were already wounded in the attack."

"Aye, but not badly. Men have fought with worse."

Geoffrey shook his head. "Fighting men, perhaps. Knights and soldiers. Like you said, you're just a farmer."

Suddenly, Old Amos tapped his cane for emphasis. "Aye," he said, "but there's the rub."

"What do you mean?"

"St. Aiden."

Geoffrey sighed. He was weary and in despair. "What about him?" he asked irritably.

Amos ignored his son's tone. "St. Aiden," he said, holding up a finger to emphasize his point, "St. Aiden was just a farmer, a farmer who began by fighting for his wife and his son."

Geoffrey shook his head in frustration. "I am not St. Aiden."

"And I wasn't suggesting that," Amos said. "For starters, they say he was very handsome, and unfortunately, you're your father's son." He smirked. "But he *was* a farmer, and he fought."

Geoffrey's eyes widened, and his head snapped up to catch Amos's dull eyes in his stare, "You're mad!"

"Am I now?" Amos said bitterly. "I know about you at Damon's house and the men you fought and killed. I know all about it. I may be blind, but I can still hear and speak."

"So what about it?" Geoffrey snapped.

"Well, it's the first anyone here has fought back since I can remember."

"And look what happened today because of it!"

Amos spit on the ground in disgust. "Don't be an ass," he said. "Do you think it would have been any worse otherwise? They said themselves that the three men were messengers to inform us of their bloody 'tribute.'"

Geoffrey took a step away and punched the air in frustration. "At least they might not have taken the boys!"

"Oh, I see," Amos said. "So then you're content to just let it go then? To leave Karl and Oliver's boys to their fate?"

Oliver looked up miserably at the mention of his name.

Geoffrey sighed heavily with despair. "The village isn't going to hunt down an entire troop of mercenaries."

"Aye, *they* won't."

"You just said that we have to stand together!"

"We do, as a village. We'll decide tomorrow how best to defend the village in case they return and how to prepare ourselves for the winter. We'll gather what seed we have remaining and begin planting. As I said, all of this has happened before. In the meantime, you and Oliver can go find your sons."

Geoffrey shook his head in disbelief. "You're a madman! Oliver and I? Alone?"

"You wouldn't abandon Karl to the bandits, would you?"

"No," Geoffrey said, grinding his teeth, "but at least right now, he's alive."

"Oh, so you're fine with him becoming one of them?"

"No, of course not, but what do you expect me to do? Fight them? Thirty armed men? If we go after them, they may just kill the boys, and then they'll come back and slaughter everyone else!"

"Perhaps."

"None of us are warriors. It would be ruin." Geoffrey sighed. "Look, it's as you said; we can talk about what to do in the morning."

"You know, you're right," Amos said venomously. "We're all just farmers!" He slashed wildly with his cane in the direction of his son but stuck only air, "At least we've a few less mouths to worry about feeding!" He turned in anger and hurried off in the darkness. "Good night, *farmer*."

Geoffrey watched bitterly as the old man's slight shape disappeared. Slowly, Oliver came over and stood beside him. "You say that old man-at-arms killed thirty men?" he asked. "All by himself?"

Geoffrey nodded. "He did."

"Well, that's good," Oliver said, "because there were around thirty men in the Red Boars, and I doubt it'll be more than just you and me."

Geoffrey's eyes widened. "What? You agree with him?"

"Aye," Oliver said, "the village. They'll look after each other, and they'll look after our families while we're gone."

Geoffrey nearly laughed. "You've gone mad too."

"Damn it, Geoffrey," Oliver shouted, "these are our sons!"

Geoffrey sighed heavily, "I know."

Oliver shook his head in frustration, walked off a few paces in the direction of his house, and stopped. "You can stay behind if you'd like, but I'm going," he shouted, "and don't worry. If I meet Karl, I'll be sure to tell him that his father loves him!"

CHAPTER 18:
THE TOURNAMENT

Beneath the overhang of the black-and-white pavilion, Bel sat watching as, at either end of the lists, two heavily armored knights made ready. In the grandstand between them, the elder noblemen and ladies sat wrapped in soft furs and embroidered brocade enjoying the spectacle of the contest of arms and warm cups of hippocras. The air was chill, and a few light snow flurries fell softly upon the grass, but the winds were calm.

A tiny snowflake drifted from on high and alighted on the cold steel of Bel's gauntlet. He had only once been this far north before when Dermont had sent him to scout the lands surrounding the castle town of Snowden far to the west, and he had forgotten how much earlier winter came in the highlands of Gasparn. Barely half the Month of the Hound had passed, and in Valendia, there would still be another month or two of cold rain before the snows came. Bel flexed the fingers of his swordhand and sighed, watching his breath hang in the air. His entire body felt heavy and only in part from the weight of the plate and chain he wore.

"My wager's on the Talon, my lord," Jarvy said amiably. "Young Lord Praid has a fine horse, but the Talondaires come from a long line of great horsemen."

Bel nodded idly, lifted his great helm, and placed it on his head. "Larius fought the old Lord Praid at the Battle of Woodbridge. It was one of his first great victories."

"Aye, so it was, my lord," Jarvy said, his voice dropping, "though I believe that the young Sir Winfred out of Rosewood would see it more as a tragic Gasparan defeat."

"Yes," Bel said hesitantly, "I suppose he—I suppose *I* would."

Jarvy nodded and sent Bel a quick wink. "You'll get the hang of it, sir," he said. "Soon, it'll be as natural as breathing."

"I'm not sure I relish the idea of becoming a natural liar," Bel said. He began rising to his feet, and the old skirmisher hurried to his aid.

"Don't think of it as lying then, my lord," Jarvy said. "Think of it as just another ruse, like last summer when you had Horn and Rallo pose as wagoners to draw out the skirmishers attacking our lines to Whitemane."

Bel sighed. "I suppose so."

Out on the field, the two combatants readied their lances and, at the word of the Knight of the Field, spurred their mounts to a charge. Bel turned away before the tilt was decided and made for where their horses were staked behind the tent. Jarvy hurried after, though not before the Talon's lance shattered Lord Praid's shield. Bel adjusted his scabbard and smoothed the front of his tabard: a yellow sun upon a field of light gray, the same as the caparisons draped beneath the saddle of the black horse.

"Whoa, Banshee," he whispered, stepping into the stirrup to climb into his saddle.

Jarvy patted the nose of the second horse, his own Piper, hitched by the reins to the small wooden cart that had carried them north. They had only just arrived in time for the festival and had little time to find proper stabling. However, both horses were used to life in the open, and Jarvy pointed out that keeping their mounts close at hand would be beneficial in the event that the ruse failed and they would need a quick escape.

"My name is Sir Briden Winfred. My father Warwick was a retainer to Lord Solidar of Rosewood," he repeated. "My name is Sir Briden Winfred. My father, Warwick, was a retainer to Lord Solidar of Rosewood. My name is…"

"Very good, my lord," Jarvy said. "Just keep that up, and you'll be fine."

Bel smiled weakly behind the steel faceplate of his helm. The decision to involve Jarvy in this endeavor had not been an easy one, for Bel did not relish the idea of dragging anyone else along with him on Dermont's mad command. However, he had no skill in the arts of deception outside of tactical movements on the battlefield, and Jarvy's knack for telling stories and natural charisma suggested a certain talent for manipulating the truth. It was at the older man's suggestion that Bel adopted his alias. Briden would be a name familiar enough to draw Bel's attention if called, and Winfred was the name of an actual family from Rosewood. Though situated as it was so close to the Bloodline, the Winfreds could just as easily have been loyal to Valendia as to Gasparan. However, with Lord Solidar dead and Rosewood now in ruins, no one would be able to confirm or deny Bel's false claim. Such as it was, more than once already on the long journey northward had Jarvy's silver tongue helped to speed them on their way.

A cheer went up from the crowd as the riders made ready for another pass. Bel upon Banshee, with Jarvy walking alongside, passed through the assortment of colored tents belonging to the other competing knights. Most were small, like Bel's, and attended by only a single groom or kipper, and only about half of the tents bore any recognizable coat of arms. So many men had died over the course of the past hundred years that battlefield knighthoods were not at all uncommon. A man who may have once been only a lowly member of a lord's house guard may soon find himself serving as a seneschal, should he fight well enough to outlive his fellows. Thus, as Dermont had suspected, none seemed the least suspicious of a landless minor knight attached to the long-dead lord of a ruined village.

Beyond the tents belonging to the combatants, the crowds of men grew thicker and thicker as knights and their retinues were replaced by tightly packed mobs of peasants competing for a better view of the competition. Though guardsmen in black tunics bearing the mark of the white horse stood to watch to ensure that the rabble was kept under control. A few large barrels of ale had been set up by some of the local brewers, and a number of homely alewives mingled about, offering men swigs from large clay jugs.

"This way, my lord," Jarvy muttered, motioning to a gated paddock that had been constructed at the end of the tourney field. A few of the guardsmen nodded toward the old skirmisher at their approach.

"Boys," Jarvy said by way of greeting.

"You'll be up next, my lord," one of the men nodded to Bel, "as soon as this run's over."

Bel inclined his head by way of reply and felt his helmet shift ever so slightly, despite his arming cap. It was not enough to impair his vision (at least, any more than usual for a great helm), but it was just enough to be annoying. "Where are the lances?" Bel asked.

"Just there, sir, on the rack with the shields," Jarvy nodded into the field. "They'll load three of each onto the rack once your bout begins. You'll have three turns through the lists, and if one of you is unhorsed, you'll dismount and take to arms until one of you submits. Same as we do it in the south, sir."

"So it seems."

On the third pass, Lord Talondaire's lance struck home squarely in the center of Lord Praid's chest. Talondaire reined in his mount, preparing to continue the fight on foot; however, whether unconscious or dead, Praid's limp form was already being dragged from the field by another handful of men bearing the mark of the White Horse. Noble and commoner alike sounded a cheer, and the Knight of the Talon rode forth and removed his helm in deference before the old man seated in luxury at the center of the grandstand. Bel could only assume this was King Marius himself.

"Well," Jarvy said quietly to Bel as the servants swung open the paddock and hurried out onto the field to make ready for the next bout, "I guess that'll be our turn."

"I suppose," Bel said calmly, "and in the event that I fall, Jarvy, I want you to know that I'm glad to have you with me."

Jarvy nodded and cast Bel another wink. "I'm sure you'll do fine, my lord," he said. "Just be sure to take care of that horse. Herself would be none too pleased to find it come to any harm."

Bel allowed a smile in spite of himself. "You have that right."

"Good luck."

When the field had been cleared and the nobles refreshed with another round of hippocras, Jarvy scurried to the rack bearing the lances, and Bel guided Banshee to meet his opponent at the center of the field beneath the king's seat.

"Sir Briden Winfred of Rosewood and Sir Willoughby Forne of Brockton!" a herald shouted as Bel and his opponent, another knight clad in a tabard quartered with tawny and white, slipped from their saddles and knelt before the noble spectators and the king.

Never in life had Bel ever seen King Marius, and though he dared not stare, he could not help but steal a covert glance now at his father's northern nemesis. Marius was younger than Cedric by perhaps a decade or so and heartier of build, though the slope of his broad shoulders also told of the weariness of war. His beard was short, though full, and mottled like a magpie, and a few small patches of dark hair yet remained just above his ears. He was richly adorned in fine sable cloth trimmed with ermine and bearing the emblem of the white horse. Upon his brow, he wore a simple silver circlet, and upon his hip rested a silver blade wrapped in a scabbard of supple, white leather, its hilt fashioned in the shape of a horseshoe and encrusted with pearls. However, none of the king's finery could compete with the radiance of the young woman seated at the king's right hand.

In both Valendia and Gasparn, Princess Marina was known to all as the Winter Rose, and looking upon her now, Bel had no need to wonder why. Her fair skin shone as clear as newly fallen snow, framed by thick, fiery waves of red hair. Her green eyes stood out like two great pines upon a mountainside, and her soft crimson lips seemed to sweeten the northern air with a breath of loveliness each time she exhaled. Like her father, she wore thick furs of ermine, though the gown they lined was ivory set with pearls, and across her lap, she warmed herself with a blanket sewn from the hides of white rabbits and a black bear. For a moment, Bel forgot himself, regarding her, until with a flash of panic, her eyes met his, and he returned his gaze to the cold, hard ground. However, flustered, he failed to notice if the Tower, or anyone bearing the mark of Andoch, was in attendance as well.

"Arise," the herald commanded, "and prepare for your first pass through the lists."

Bel took a deep breath, replaced his helm, and climbed back into Banshee's saddle. He offered his opponent a salutary nod; however, Sir Willoughby, upon his fine white palfrey, regarded him with a look of mild repugnance and rode off to retrieve his first lance from his man at the far side of the field. Silently, Bel returned to his own end and, without a word, accepted Jarvy's proffered lance and wheeled Banshee around for the first charge. The great black mare snorted and pawed restlessly at the dirt with her hoof, and Bel wondered briefly if it would have been better to have brought Igno, after all, in spite of Lilia's concerns that even without the belled saddle, men would recognize the Silent Prince of Valendia on his red coarser. Banshee was strong-willed, unpredictable, and wild—much like her rider.

Bel cleared his throat and pushed those thoughts, those memories, from his mind. He needed to focus on the task at hand.

A cheer went up from the crowd as the herald standing at the front of the king's grandstand raised an arm. "Sir Briden" and Sir Willoughby raised their lances and prepared to charge.

"Good luck, my lord," Jarvy called.

The herald lowered his arm. Bel urged Banshee onward with his spurs, and the black mare took off at a gallop, steadily gaining speed. Bel's heart pounded in his chest like the drums of a Sorgund galley. He lowered his lance and braced for the impact of Sir Willoughby's charge.

The force of the blow nearly unhorsed him. However, when Bel reached the end of the tourney wall and pulled up on Banshee's reins to slow her speed, it was Sir Willoughby who wobbled unsteadily in his saddle, his shield splintered and useless from the force of Bel's blow.

"Three points to Sir Briden for a perfect hit to the boss!" the Herald exclaimed over the buoyant applause of the crowd.

Bel took a deep breath, tossed his broken lance to one of the tourney attendants, and wheeled his horse around to return to Jarvy at the other end of the field, inclining his helmet graciously to his opponent as they passed. This time, Sir Willoughby returned the courtesy.

"Fine work, my lord, fine work," Jarvy said, grinning like a fox as he readied another lance. "Once more like that, and you'll have him unhorsed!"

Bel armed himself as the herald announced their second pass. He could feel his old habits returning, those he had learned long ago under Sir Emory's tutelage, teaching him to ride and run the ring joust. He remembered the hours upon hours spent practicing with the quintain and how when he struck the target off center, and the heavy arm swung round to knock him from Igno's back, Larius was always there to help him back up into the saddle, just as Dermont and his friends were there to mock him and laugh.

The blow from Sir Willoughby's lance smashed against the center of Bel's shield before it turned aside and grazed his upper arm. Bel's own blow had nowhere near the same force as his first tilt but still struck his opponent on the shoulder of his shield arm.

"Three points to Sir Willoughby of Brocton for a strike to the boss and one point to Sir Briden of Rosewood!"

Bel shook his head and tossed his splintered lance to the attendant as Banshee bucked and pawed at the turf restlessly. "Whoa, Ban," Bel whispered, tightening his grip on the reins, "settle."

He took a deep breath and exhaled slowly, attempting to clear his mind. If ever there was a time for flights of melancholic reverie or for wallowing in past grief, it was not now.

Bel returned to his place in the field and, without a word, retrieved his final lance from Jarvy. "If you score another hit like the first, my lord," Jarvy said, "you'll win the bout by points. However," he paused, replacing Bel's broken shield, "if you miss, you'll both dismount and have to settle it on foot."

Bel nodded, readied his arms, and as the herald lowered his arm, he again spurred Banshee to a charge. The black mare's hooves echoed with the sound of thunder; Bel lowered his lance. Sir Willoughby's shield crumpled as if it had been made of reeds, and Bel's lance drove onward, striking his opponent in the center of his breastplate. Willoughby's feet twisted in his stirrups as the force of the blow threw him backward in the saddle, and though he did not fall, his lance dropped from his hand and onto the grass. For the first time, Bel noticed the cheers rising from the crowd.

"Three points for Sir Briden!" the herald shouted. "And with seven points, Sir Briden Winfred of Rosewood wins and will advance to the next round!"

Bel steered Banshee around and rode around to the front of the grandstand, then removed his great helm and bowed his head reverently toward the Gasparan king. The assembled nobles offered him their applause, and Bel could not help but steal another look at the princess, smiling and clapping her hands. Quickly, he looked away only to notice the absence of anyone bearing the emblem of Andoch seated anywhere in the vicinity of the king.

When the applause settled, Bel returned his helmet to his head and rode back to where Jarvy awaited him at the edge of the field. Sir Willoughby's kipper and a group of tourney attendants had taken hold of the defeated knight's palfrey and were now struggling to help him from his saddle to his feet. Splotches of red appeared upon the knight's tabard as the servants hurried from the field toward the knights' tents, and one of them ran ahead, calling for a surgeon.

"Fine run, my lord, fine run," Jarvy said, taking Banshee by the bridle. "Shall I fetch the spoils from Sir Willoughby now or wait until they are better situated?"

Though his victory entitled him to claim Willoughby's horse and arms as his prize, Bel dismounted, removed his helm, and shook his head. "I cannot see what use I could possibly have for them," he said. "One set of armor is more than enough. No, let the man keep them."

Jarvy's eyebrows arched in surprise, but when he spoke, he simply nodded. "As you wish, my lord," he said, "do you think his wound very grave?"

"Bleeding from the impact of the lance, I imagine," Bel said. "Nothing more. Though, a broken rib will leave him in pain for a time." They reached the end of the tourney ground. Another knight was waiting with the tourney attendants for his bout. A few of the men cheered Bel as he approached, and the next knight offered him a courteous nod. Bel returned the gestures humbly but hurried onward to return to his tent and free himself of the heavy armor. For in spite of his victory, his next turn in the lists would not be until at least the following day, and the apparent absence of the Tower from his due place seated beside the king made Bel wonder where else the great lord-general could possibly be.

"You haven't noticed the Tower yet, have you?" he asked.

"Not yet, my lord," Jarvy said, "I'd have thought he'd have been in the box beside the king in a place of honor, considering the whole tourney's being put on in his name. However, not so."

"I see."

"They say he's a very tall man, hence the title, and he rides a bloody searoan, given him as a reward from King Marius for the victory over your brother."

"It seems someone like that would be difficult to miss."

"If you'd like," Jarvy began, "after I see to Banshee and your armor, I can scout around and see if I can learn anything more about him?"

"I imagine 'scouting' includes having a few pints of ale and watching the rest of the tourney." Bel smiled.

"Aye, sir. Well, there's that too." The older man smirked. "But it would also give me a chance to size up some of the men you may face later on in the lists. And, seeing as you don't care much for this sort of thing…"

"Get me out of this armor, Jarvy, and you can do as you like," Bel said, "But be careful and report in from time to time."

"Thank you, my lord. I'll be sure to do that."

When Jarvy had gone, Bel withdrew to the privacy of his pavilion. He had never much cared for tourneys or festivals or the like, at least not after experiencing the realities of war firsthand. He often wondered that so many men—battle-hardened veterans like himself, would be so willing to mingle celebration with combat, that reenacting the arts of war could appeal to anyone after a hundred years of constant conflict.

The remains of the small breakfast Jarvy had prepared that morning remained untouched upon the large, flat-topped wooden chest. Bel picked at it now, tearing off a hunk of hard bread and cheese, and decided to check on Banshee and Jarvy's Piper, tied off with the cart they had been forced to bring with them to haul the tourney gear north.

Away at the lists, a cheer rose up from the crowd. Bel patted Banshee's nose as Piper snorted and drew nearer. Bel tore the remains of the bread in two and offered it to the horses, feeling a perfunctory twinge of guilt and longing at the absence of Igno, separated as they were, for the first time in the horse's life. Still, he knew that Lilia would look after him. The red horse knew her, and he seemed to trust her.

Lilia. The sudden thought of her only deepened his sense of loss and tightened his chest. Their parting had not been easy, nor had it been pleasant.

After meeting with Dermont, Bel called together the men of the light cavalry to inform them of his temporary departure. In light of Andoch's recent support of Gasparn, Dermont had instructed him to tell them Prince Beledain was being sent to seek support from the senators of the Republic of Grantis, hoping to capitalize on the long-standing tension between the two neighbors to the southwest, rumors that now spoke of open war. Lady Valerie was to assume command of the skirmishers in his absence, which was at least some consolation, and they would resume patrolling the Bloodline and disrupting the enemy supply lines. Only afterward, and against Dermont's wishes, did he inform Val of the truth. However, she was to be the only one who knew, and would have been, until later that evening when Lilia cornered him and insisted that she, Jarvy, and Briden be allowed to accompany him to Grantis as his honor guard.

All afternoon, he had avoided her, walking the walls with his father or visiting Larius's tomb. However, he knew that, eventually, he would have to face her and that most likely the notion that she would accompany him was already being assumed. He did not relish telling her that not only would she not be going with him but also that she was being "reassigned" to serve under Sir Emory in the king's household guard and would thus not return to the light cavalry. "To ensure her safety," Dermont had explained to him, "we would not want her coming to any harm while you were gone."

Involuntarily, Bel kicked at a clod of dirt and clenched his fist. His jaw hurt suddenly as he realized he had been grinding his teeth, and when he looked around, he noticed that somehow in his ruminating, he had wandered away from his pavilion, leaving the horses and all of his possessions unguarded.

"Blood and fire," he swore aloud.

Thankfully, both Banshee and Piper were still staked in their places beside the cart. Yet to Bel's apprehension, a third horse, a sprightly white palfrey, stood beside them, led by a man in a drab woolen surcoat spotted with rust.

"Can I help you?" Bel uttered, hurrying up.

The man turned and regarded Beledain, light-blue eyes beneath a weary, careworn brow. "Sir Briden?"

"Yes," Bel said stiffly.

"This is Snowflake," the man said, patting the palfrey's nose. "Sir Willoughby's man offers you his master's congratulations on your victory."

"I thank Sir Willoughby," Bel said, "but I already have a horse." "So it appears," the man said. "Two of them, and now you have a third."

Bel eyed the white mare. She was a pretty thing with tawny ribbons braided into her mane and tail, and seldom were pretty things well suited for war. "I would ask that you inform Sir Willoughby that he may keep his horse," Bel finally said. "But I take it that you are not Sir Willoughby's man."

"I am not." The man smiled, a day's worth of whiskers standing out sharply from his cheeks. "I am called Sir Galen Helm."

Bel nodded in greeting and tried to remember if he had ever heard of Sir Galen or his title, struggling to maintain an appearance of calm beneath the façade of Sir Briden. He hoped against hope that Jarvy would choose now to check in, but to no avail.

"Then, Sir Galen," Bel said, with another nod, "it is good to meet you. Do you intend to take the lists?"

Sir Galen folded his arms across his chest and glanced idly across the field. "I'm afraid not," he said wearily. "Tourneys are for the young, the bold, and the ambitious. They hold little interest for a middle-aged knight of middling rank such as I am." He smiled. "Though you seemed quite skilled out there today."

"Thank you." Bel nodded yet again and suddenly realized that, in his awkwardness, he must look a fool, bobbing his head like a chicken. "Can I offer you some wine or…something," he said, hurrying to the flap of the pavilion.

"No, though I thank you for it," Sir Galen said, "I simply wished to meet you and offer my congratulations."

"Well, thank you again," Bel said, again wondering where Jarvy had gotten to.

"If you'd like, I can return Snowflake here to Sir Willoughby," Sir Galen said, patting the white horse's nose again. "Though are you certain that you will not accept? Few would turn away such a prize."

"I have no need for her," Bel said, "And there is no need to compound Sir Willoughby's losses."

Sir Galen nodded. "A skilled horseman and a gracious victor." He observed with a smile. "I'll hope for your continued success in the tourney, Sir Briden."

Bel returned the nod and again thought of chickens.

"I'll return the horse," Sir Galen said "Good luck."

Bel watched the elder knight go, silently admonishing himself for his own foolishness in wandering the campgrounds. He made a mental note to keep Jarvy closer at hand and to confine himself to the interior of his pavilion for the remainder of the tourney. However, supposing he did prove himself worthy enough to join the ranks of the Tower's elite cavalry, the Brethren only knew how he could possibly maintain the deception. Jarvy may serve as his kipper now, but as a mere servant or a camp follower trailing the heavy cavalry on a campaign, the old skirmisher would be accompanying him less and less.

"He's sending you to your death," Lilia had said, "and though you won't admit it, you know it's true. He hates you."

Bel pressed his lips together in silence, doubting his own words before they even left his mouth. "Dermont is my brother," he said. "He doesn't hate me."

Lilia shook her head in frustration. "He does. He hates you because he fears you," she said, "because the people love you, and they hate him."

"The nobles love him."

"Just because they kiss his arse does not mean that they love him. They flock to him like whores to a rich merchant. Don't confuse that with love."

"You seem to know a lot about love for one who so hates to hear the word spoken aloud."

In retrospect, Bel thought, that was an unwise thing to say.

Over the coming days, Bel fought two more bouts in the lists, and on both days, and in spite of Jarvy's scouting, the Tower was still nowhere to be found, conspicuously absent from the king's grandstand. Still, if frustrating, Bel's growing irritation seemed to fan the fires of his military prowess. His first opponent, a Sir Ledford Gaines known as the Iron Gate, collapsed in the first turn, unhorsed and unconscious as Bel's lance caught him squarely in the chest. His second, young Lord Renault Defour, though unhorsed in the third turn, was unharmed, and Bel was forced to dismount and face him on foot. Defour was a fine swordsman according to the polite rules of tourney combat, rules that, in many ways, rendered any practical experience of battle somewhat null. Still, in the end, Bel was able to disarm the young lord and progress, with not more than a score of others, to the fourth and final round of the tournament, an honor, Jarvy informed him afterward, that guaranteed him a place among the Tower's elite.

In the privacy of his pavilion, Bel shed his armor and allowed himself a moment of relief. The first part of his mission was over. Sir Briden of Rosewood had proven himself worthy of the Tower's command. However, he knew that it was not truly a victory but rather an invitation into greater danger with an increasingly complex web of deception and an even more tenuous margin of error. But for now, at least, as Jarvy again pointed out, he had done it. Barring any unforeseen circumstances, he was now the Tower's man.

"If that is so, though, then why continue with the nonsense of this tourney at all?" Bel asked. "Surely it's proven its intention."

"A tourney's got to have one victor," Jarvy said. "Twenty men can't share the honor, else it means nothing. Besides, it gives them a chance to determine who is chief among them."

"The Tower is chief among them."

"Aye, but after that," Jarvy said, "if Horn hadn't knocked Feron Tallshanks in the teeth last spring, who do you think'd be riding into battle in the line beside you? Horn or Feron?"

Bel sighed. "But how about you, then, Jarvy? I've never known you to brawl. If what you say is true, then how is it you've been at my side since I first took command?"

Jarvy's lips spread into a wide grin, and he tapped the side of his nose. "There's more than one way to prove your mettle," the older man said. "Some have strength, some have cleverness…"

"And some a silver tongue."

"Aye, sir, that they do." Jarvy smiled. "Why else do you think Herself suggested you bring me along?"

Before Bel could reply, however, a call from outside the pavilion made him start.

"Sir Briden of Rosewood?" a voice called.

"See who it is," Bel whispered to Jarvy.

A few moments later, Jarvy returned with another man. He was simply clad in traveling garb of burlap and sackcloth with splatters of dried mud decorating the hem of his old cloak and the worn soles of his boots. His hair, black and unkempt, framed a blotchy young face notable only for its drab, dark eyes and crooked nose, a mark no doubt of a tendency toward pugnacity. The smell of dried ale and piss told of a tendency toward drink.

"Sir…Briden?" the man said with a grin.

Bel, seated, inclined his head. He did not like the man's grin, nor was he very inclined to like the man. "Who are you?" Bel asked.

The man snorted a laugh and folded his arms across his chest. "My name is Canton," he said. "I was supposed to meet you on the road north from…Rosewood, was it?"

Out of the corner of his eye, Bel saw Jarvy's hand slide smoothly to his own dagger. Apparently, Canton saw it too.

"We'll have none of that, old man," he said. "None of that at all."

"What is it that you want?" Bel asked coldly. "Speak plain."

Canton cleared his throat and spit. "I work for your brother," he said. "I'm to be your contact whilst you're in the north here. On occasion, I, or one of the other lads, will check in with you or your man there to get word to where it needs to go. You know, messages and the like."

Bel felt a knot forming in the pit of his chest. "You're one of Dermont's spies," he said.

"Can't say I know anyone of that name," Canton said bitterly, "or leastwise, I forgot it long ago, as should you."

Bel exchanged a glance with Jarvy. "Why have we not heard from you before?" he asked.

"Like I said," Canton snorted, "I missed you on the road. Then, of course, I figured there was no point in bothering if you didn't make it through the tourney since you'd just be turning around to go right back home again. But it looks like you made it after all, so I'm here now."

Bel said nothing, but his silence seemed to somehow amuse the spy.

"At any rate," Canton said, "I simply wanted to introduce myself and let you know that my boys and I will be keeping an eye out."

"I'll sleep soundly tonight, then," Jarvy muttered.

"You do that," Canton said. "Now I'd best be gone. You got another visitor coming."

Bel stood up, and Jarvy peered through the flap of the pavilion as Canton stepped through.

"You're certain you won't sell the horse?" Canton called back to them as Bel recognized Sir Galen approaching. "My master will be most displeased."

"For the last time," Jarvy said smoothly, "no!"

"More's the pity," Canton grunted, "then goodbye."

Sir Galen stood quietly as Canton staggered off. Jarvy shook his head after him and turned to the knight, his features a mask of weariness. "May I help you, my lord?"

"I simply wished to offer Sir Briden my congratulations," he said. "Ah! There he is."

Bel stepped forward from the tent. "Sir Galen." He nodded and fought the urge to wince. No more chickens.

"Sir Briden"—Sir Galen nodded in return—"good show today. Your duel with Young Defour made for quite the spectacle."

"Thank you," Bel said. Quickly, he exchanged a glance with Jarvy before turning back to Sir Galen. "Please, sir, this is the second time you've called upon me with kind words. Would you sit and perhaps take some wine?"

Sir Galen sighed. "I suppose that it would be improper to refuse you again," he said. "I thank you."

Bel directed Sir Galen into the pavilion, where Jarvy hurriedly arranged a second chair and filled two cups with wine. "Was Sir Willoughby pleased to have his horse returned to him?" Bel asked.

Sir Galen accepted Jarvy's proffered cup. "He was," Sir Galen said, seating himself, "though I believe it was his younger sister who was even more delighted. It was she that named the mare."

Bel returned to his own seat and took a small sip from his own cup as Sir Galen drank from his. Bel was never a very good judge of wine, having little experience of it on the battlefield, and he hoped that Sir Galen would find it acceptable. It must have been, however, since the knight made no comment to the contrary, nor any comment at all. Jarvy cleared his throat, and Bel, a twinge of anxiety beginning to stir within his breast, tried to think of a topic of conversation befitting a polite host and his guest.

However, after a lengthening silence, it was Sir Galen who spoke first. Again, the knight sighed and took a small sip from his cup. "Sir Briden," he said, "do you mind if I ask you something?"

Bel took a sip from his own cup, reminding himself quietly not to drink too quickly. He returned his attention to Sir Galen. "Of course."

Sir Galen leaned forward. "Over the course of the last few days, I have noticed a number of the younger knights and young ladies gathering with some of the elders at various estates, halls, and inns within the city. Unfortunately, as a knight of some rank not participating in the competitions, it has fallen to me to 'tip it the civil,' as men say, and attend many of these banquets and such. However, I have noticed, or should I say, failed to notice, your presence."

Bel was hesitant. At first, he regarded the observation with some apprehension, though from Sir Galen's manner and tone, he could tell that the comment was not meant to be taken as a slight. In fact, Bel quickly realized it was an honest question that, if anything, seemed perhaps voiced with a degree of honest concern. As such, Bel sighed. He would return it with an honest answer.

"To be perfectly candid, Sir Galen"—Bel sighed—"I'll admit that I am not one for the frivolity or the carousing of most of the nobility."

Sir Galen nodded without emotion, but Bel felt suddenly like further explanation was necessary. He took another sip from his glass. "Were you present at the sacking of Rosewood?" he asked, "When the Black Horse took the town?"

"I was not, I'm afraid. I was far away."

Bel stared into his glass. He had no need for deception now; he could speak mostly from his own memory. "It was shortly after Prince Dermont, the…Plague Prince, took command of the military forces of Valendia. I may not look it, young as I may be, though I've seen my share of battles, though Rosewood…I was younger, less experienced then." Bel paused. "At any rate, it was the twelfth of Salmontide—Lover's Night, and Lord Solidar and his family were hosting a feast for his minor knights and retainers when the Black Horse attacked. The snows had not yet melted, and no one suspected that the Valendian forces would be willing to resume the war until after the thaw, which I believe was why the Plague Prince chose that time to attack."

"With the celebrations at the lord's keep, the town was defended by only a token force, and the Valendians assumed control in a matter of minutes, looting, sacking, pillaging, and more, as you know, results from a sacking."

Sir Galen nodded. "Aye. I know."

"At the keep, the top retainers saw no other choice but to bar the doors and hope that word would reach King Marius that the Black Horse had crossed the Bloodline and that the battle had resumed. However, rather than lay siege or offer ransom or the like, the Plague Prince ordered his men and any townsfolk not dead or too wounded to gather wood and set it in great piles surrounding the keep."

"Then," Bel said, "the Plague Prince himself set it on fire."

"By the Brethren," Sir Galen said quietly.

Jarvy cleared his throat and bowed his head somberly.

Bel took another sip of his drink. "Once the roof caught fire, the nobles unbarred the doors and tried to flee. However, the Valendians simply cut them down. Some of the lucky ones escaped though."

"Like you," Sir Galen said.

"Aye," Bel said, returning somewhat suddenly to the present, "my father and I…" He glanced unconsciously at Jarvy. "We escaped, though he was wounded. He raised me to knighthood just before he died."

Sir Galen remained grave, staring into his wine somberly.

"So," Bel took a sip from his cup, "that is why I do not care much for carousing."

"Dibhor dances merrily upon the graves of those who spurn him," Sir Galen said, "or so the hierophants say."

Bel nodded.

Sir Galen drained his wine and stood up from his seat. "Well then, Sir Briden," he said, "I should probably take my leave of you now."

Jarvy hurried to take the knight's empty cup while Bel stood up to see him out to the tourney grounds.

"I'm sorry if I turned the mood dour," Bel said quickly, "it was not my intention to—"

Sir Galen cast off the apology with a wave of his hand. "Don't be foolish." He smiled. "It's nice to find a young man with a sense of reality about him for once. Many of these others seem to regard war as a final step in accomplishing their own preordained glory. A knight with sense is a rare thing, and I look forward to seeing you in the future."

Bel nodded, smiling at the elder knight with genuine fellowship. "Thank you, sir," he said. "I do as well."

"Farewell then, Sir Briden," Sir Galen said. "Enjoy your victories, and I wish you continued success in the remainder of the tournament." He leaned close. "From what I hear, the king intends to forego the joust and have the final twenty combatants compete in a mounted melee instead. Due in part, perhaps, to your prolonged duel with Lord Defour"—he smiled—"though it's just as likely that after three days of sitting out of doors, the nobles are beginning to complain of the cold."

"Truly?" Bel asked. "A melee?" Jarvy's eyes widened beneath the shadow of the pavilion. Melees were a bad business, carrying with them a greater chance of injury to both man and horse. It seemed a senseless risk to take with the Tower's new men.

From his tone, Sir Galen appeared to share Bel's sentiment. "At least it will speed this madness along to its conclusion," he said. "There is, so I hear, a war on."

CHAPTER 19:
GALDORAN

The next day's ride down the river in the currach continued as pleasantly as the first. Soon, the trees of the forest south of Lenard's Crossing gave way to open fields and woodlands while the shores along the riverbanks grew thicker with tall grasses and reeds where tall wading birds hunted frogs among the shallows. The pike heron, or so the birds were called, was the symbol of the Shoran house of nobles, Crodane told them, who drew levies from much of the river lands along the southern Imperial's shores. Their line stretched back as far as St. Aiden's days, and it was said that the first Lord Shoran was himself a Guardian, one of the first of the Anointed, who had followed the saint to war.

"He was known as the Tiller," the swordsman said, "though I do not believe any of the Shorans have born that name for nearly five hundred years. Eventually, the title itself died out altogether in the last war against the Kords."

"How did the title survive outside of the family?" Lughus asked.

"Guardian titles do not always pass on by heredity, and many, if not most, of the Guardians, are not noble by birth. In fact, most are often battlefield commissions, transferred from a Guardian upon his death to his squire or another surviving warrior who has proven his worth. Usually, the inheritance is marked by a symbol, like the Loremaster's tome or the Warlord's sword, an heirloom usually reaching back as far as Aiden's time. In the case of the Tillers, I believe it was a leather baldric known as Galdorn's Girdle. In any case, such a treasure is not something any family, noble or common, would easily part with. However, in the case of the noble, such things, heirlooms, titles, roots reaching back to St. Aiden, often add to the family's political sway. Thus, Guardians of noble birth often endeavor to keep the title alongside the hereditary name, as in the case of the Kings of the line of Halford Drude. Could you imagine an Andochan king who did not wield Testament?"

Lughus considered it. "Rastis never told us any of this," he said, "and I've never seen anything written about it in any of the tales I've read."

"Aye," Crodane said, "and I've probably said more than I should. As you pointed out yesterday, the ways of the Anointed are not to be spoken of."

"So all the Anointed Guardians carry heirlooms?" Thom asked.

Crodane nodded. "Aye, all except for the Bards, though they've become as legendary as their stories."

Thom winked at Lughus mischievously. "So what's your heirloom?" he asked Crodane. "Your mail? Your sword?"

"Thom..." Lughus muttered, and Crodane suddenly barked with laughter.

"Why don't we go back to identifying old ruins, beasts, and birds?" He grinned.

They carried on. Just before midday, they spied a bevy of otters digging for shellfish among the mud, and Thom was delighted by their playfulness. Floating upon their backs with the current, the otters arranged their meals before them on their long, flat stomachs like serving platters in the hall of a great lord. A few floated by the currach nearly within reach, though when Thom reached out suddenly to try to pet one, the small boat lurched hard to one side and had Lughus not been quick enough to snatch his friend's flailing arm and pull him back, they easily would have capsized. For the rest of the afternoon, Thom sat braced once again in his place in the stern mumbling prayers to Brother Galdorn, his statue clenched, white-knuckled, in his chubby hand. Only once did he speak above a whisper to point out what he thought was a black bear lounging beneath a mass of brambles, though, he admitted, it could just as easily have been a very large stone.

But for a few local fishermen paddling about the river in their tiny, one-man coracles, there was little traffic upon the river over the remainder of the day, and Crodane was able to barter with one of the men so that, at nightfall, they had fresh fish to dine upon for their evening meal when they stopped to make camp.

Once again, however, before they stopped to rest and to eat, Crodane instructed Lughus on the Five Guards and, afterward, guided him through a number of other drills. Though simple maneuvers designed for the practice of footwork—steps advancing, steps retreating, steps to one side or another, and lunges (much of which he had already had some instruction of from Hob)— Lughus found that when refined under Crodane's scrutiny, even the most basic of movements, when accomplished with focus and precision, could leave him both physically exhausted and mentally strained.

He was almost thankful, then, on the third day of their journey, when after a gloomy morning, the skies opened, and the rain began to pour. The current grew swifter and choppy, and as it did so, Thom's face grew white, then green, and his stomach churned. More than once, Crodane had to fight to keep the small boat from toppling over while Lughus tried as best he could to bail out the inches of rainwater that collected in the bottom. Finally, late in the afternoon, they paused briefly to allow a particularly heavy downpour to pass. While they waited, Crodane fashioned another makeshift oar from a fallen tree branch and from another limb, cut a long straight bough to function like one of the bargemen's poles.

Surely, Lughus thought, once they began again and the rain continued to fall, surely, they would forego swordplay that night in favor of rest and sleep. However, he was wrong.

"Your enemies will not hold on account of rain," Crodane said, standing with his sword drawn, his face shadowed beneath the drawn hood of his cowl, "nor will they pause for weariness, nor illness, nor grief; if anything, these will be the very moments when they choose to attack. Therefore, you must learn to defend yourself even under the worst conditions and at the worst of times."

The next few days offered plenty of opportunity for such practice as the rain continued to fall almost continuously, heavy and hard. The surface of the Imperial swelled and flooded up over the banks, turning murky and brown as it sucked at the soggy mud cascading down from its shores. Logs and branches knocked loose from wind and heavy downpour, soon offered further hazards, and from his place in the prow, Lughus was tasked with using the bargepole to push away any of the smaller debris that did not require Crodane to paddle around.

In spite of the fifty miles they made the first day and the forty or so on the second, the rain significantly hampered their progress, and by the end of the week, they were scarcely more than halfway from Lenard's Crossing to Galdoran. Finally, at long last, midway through the eighth day of their journey, the rain began to slacken, and by the dawn of the ninth day, it ceased altogether.

"Thank the Brethren," Thom said as they began again, "I take back what I said before about an inn with a bathhouse. I think I've had enough water running down my back to last me through the end of the year."

Lughus twisted his cloak up and attempted to wring out some of the rainwater over the side of the boat. "I actually wish I would have packed one of my habits so I would at least have something dry to wear." He sighed. "So much for new clothes."

"Your habits would only draw unwanted attention," Crodane said. "Besides, those clothes seem well-made, and even when wet, wool will still keep you warm. They'll be dry by nightfall, I'll warrant, and if not, tonight we should be able to keep a fire, and you can dry them then. Perhaps I can snare a rabbit, or if Fergus is still following us, perhaps he can take a deer."

"Fergus," Lughus said, "you mentioned him before."

"Aye," Thom agreed, "Hob told us to pass along his 'hello!' when we left Titanis."

Crodane nodded. "He's been following us since Lenard's Crossing, and he'll do so until we reach Galdoran. Once we take a ship, though, he'll head north and meet us again when we reach Baronbrock. He doesn't care much for cities, or perhaps I should say, people feel somewhat uncomfortable around him."

"Why?" Thom asked. "Who is he? Is he a Guardian?"

Crodane shook his head. "He's a friend," he said. "You'll meet him eventually." He paused and turned to Lughus. "You've actually met him before, though, at the time, you were very, very small."

Lughus raised his eyebrows. "What do you mean?"

Crodane hesitated, and his brow furrowed as he seemed to be considering the right words to speak. He breathed a heavy sigh and set his oar against the rail. "You see..." he began and suddenly stopped. His eyes peered anxiously past Lughus's shoulder up to the opposite shore.

Lughus glanced behind him, though he saw nothing. "What?" he asked. "What is it?"

Crodane took up his paddle and began steering the boat in toward the riverbank. He brought it to a stop behind a thick patch of cattails.

"What is it?" Lughus asked again.

"Silence," Crodane whispered. "Keep your heads down." Without a sound, he drew his sword.

Thom's face went pale.

Lughus felt his heart quicken, and unconsciously, his right hand went to the hilt of Stokes's sword, and his left loosened Pryce's dagger in its sheath. Crodane crouched rigidly, as unmoving as a statue, his head tilted slightly, again adopting the poise of a hunting hound seeking a scent. Suddenly, there was the hurried sound of hooves, and Thom gasped. Lughus shot him a harsh glare of silent rebuke.

Above them, on the shore beyond the curtain of cattails, a horse snorted and tromped at the ground.

"What's the matter?" a voice called. "Why'd you stop?"

"I thought I saw something out on the river," came the answer, "looked like a little boat."

The first voice scoffed, coughed, and spit noisily. "Imagine that!"

"Shut it," said the second. "I saw it a second ago, and now it's gone."

"Who gives a shit? It was probably just some accursed fisherman."

"Might be, but who knows? They told us to watch the river."

Crodane remained motionless, and Lughus held his breath. At length, what seemed an eternity of silence finally passed, and the first voice spoke.

"Come on," it said. "Let's get out of here. My arse is hurting from the ride."

"You sure that's all it's hurting from?" the second voice said with a laugh.

"As sure as your wife was last I paid her a visit. Come on, let's go."

The currach stayed motionless among the cattails long after the sound of the riders' fading hooves had died away heading north. Finally, Crodane returned his blade to its scabbard, took up his oar, and began paddling swiftly downstream. "Lughus," he said, nodding to the makeshift paddle, "take the other oar."

Lughus did as he was instructed, and soon, the curragh was coursing down the river with speed.

"What was that all about?" Thom asked. "Who were those men?"

"I'd rather not find out," Crodane said. "But hush now. I'd like to see how far we can make it before nightfall."

They spoke barely a word for the remainder of the day, though as the hours wore on, Lughus found his questions multiplying like rabbits in the spring. As he worked his oar, he found himself constantly scanning along the riverbanks, though whereas previously he had looked for ruins or birds, he now watched for men on horseback and strained his ears for the sound of hooves. Crodane had made mention of "enemies" upon their first meeting in Lenard's Crossing, and though his heart burned with questions demanding answers, he remained silent, trusting in the swordsman's greater knowledge of the world outside the Loremaster's Tower.

That night, when they pulled ashore to make camp, Lughus was relieved when Crodane told him that they would leave their practice for another day. His arms ached from rowing; they had stopped only twice when they chanced upon a number of tradesmen's barges floating slowly down the river and chose to drift past them leisurely so as not to seem unusual or become the subject of gossip once the boats finally reached the dockyards of Galdoran.

Yet when the swordsman went off alone into the wilds under the pretense of finding some food worthy of "a proper meal after the days of rain," Lughus could not help but feel on edge, and after Thom built a small fire and the two of them stood around it in silence chasing the last bits of damp from their clothes, he made sure to keep his dagger and sword drawn and within reach. Thankfully, Crodane was not gone long, and when he returned, he carried a fat brown rabbit and a handful of wild herbs.

"I'd like to leave before dawn tomorrow," he said after they had finished the meal. "And if you wouldn't mind, Lughus, I'd like you to help row as often as you can. If at all possible, I'd like to reach Galdoran the day after next."

"Yes, sir," Lughus said. "But—"

"Sorry," Thom interrupted. "But are you ever going to tell us about that business with the riders today? Because I, for one, would at least like to know what is going on. Are we in danger?"

Crodane sighed and looked away from the boys' questioning eyes. "Thom," he began, "I would not be evasive if it were not for your own well-being. However, you'll simply need to believe me when I tell you that the less you know about this matter, the safer you will be in the event of the worst."

Thom glanced at Lughus. "Well, that doesn't make me feel any more at ease," he muttered.

"I'm sorry," Crodane said, though with some finality. "Now I suggest that you boys try to get some sleep."

The swordsman spoke no more for the remainder of the journey, though thankfully, they met no more riders upon the shore. The traffic upon the river, however, steadily increased the nearer they drew to the port, from barges to skiffs to a few large keelboats—all carrying cargo from the capital or the estates of the interior either to be traded within the port city or to be exported to the other realms.

Finally, shortly after nightfall on their eleventh day out from Lenard's Crossing, nearly three weeks after they had said goodbye to Rastis and Royne, the great Andochan port city of Galdoran came into sight, and the first leg of their journey appeared to be approaching its end.

Neither Lughus nor Thom had ever been to Galdoran, though they had heard it mentioned often enough in books as well as by the other elder scribes and scholars who called the Loremaster's Tower home. Built upon the Imperial River delta, Galdoran was an old city built in the days of the Empire of Calendral. In fact, many of the city's major landmarks had been constructed before Kalius Wrogan and St. Aiden had even been born, as evidenced, Lughus noted, by the classical architectural style indicative of the Imperial Era recognizable in such buildings as the Alluvial Castle or Andoch's island prison known as Lockton-on-the-Breakers. However, there were newer buildings, too, built within the last five hundred years or so, such as the Cathedral of the Tides, whose bell tower marked the highest point in the city save for the great lighthouse on the southern point of the coast known as the Eye of Galdorn.

All this Thom and Lughus spied from the currach as Crodane steered the small boat downstream toward the interior of the city where the riverboats docked and awaited customs agents under the jurisdiction of Chancellor's agents and the city's lords. However, since they would simply be abandoning their little boat, as they would no longer need it, they would not have to wait, and barring any unforeseen complications at the gates, they would be free to enter the city.

"I'm just glad to be back safely in a place guarded by the kingsmen," Thom said as they passed a number of the city watchmen stationed at the gates in their red Andochan tabards. "I've had enough of wild places and lawless men like Stokes and that lot at the Kingfisher."

"I would not let your guard down so soon," Crodane said quietly as they passed the guardsmen by. "There are still plenty of ways to find trouble in a city, perhaps even more so than on the road."

"And it looks like there is no law barring common men and mercenaries from carrying arms in Galdoran either," Lughus said.

"No," Crodane said, "that is something unique to the capital. Here, any man may carry a weapon with him anywhere outside of the Gate of Gold separating Highdeck from Seaside."

"Where the nobles' estates are built?" Thom asked.

"Aye," Lughus said, "and the Alluvial Castle."

Crodane nodded. "For now, though, let's find an inn. There will be time to see the city in the morning."

From the river wharf, they made their way through the gates to the district on the western bank of the Imperial River known as Waverton. Though not as fine or as affluent as Galdoran's eastern district of Seaside or the Easton district of Titanis around The Book & the Barrel, Waverton was not unpleasant. Most of the houses were two-story structures of wattle and daub, though here and there, a stout stone and mortar house could still be found. The streets had been paved with cobblestones, and many were lined with tall braziers to provide some illumination at night. As they followed Crodane to find an inn, the boys noticed a large number of taverns and public houses, and the sound of ribald merriment and folk songs spilled out into the streets from within. A few of them, Thom pointed out to Lughus, seemed guarded by women with painted faces and bodices that seemed fit to burst, and the chubby boy erupted with juvenile giggling when Lughus, blushing, informed him that they were probably whores.

At length, Crodane led them to a small inn called the Sunfish, its signboard bearing the print of a blue fish overtop a yellow sun, and inside the smoke-filled common room, the boys dined on fisherman's stew and peasant bread. The locals, for the most part, who appeared to be simple fishermen out for a pint with their mates, were significantly more genial than the folk of the Kingfisher, and since few among them carried blades longer than a dagger or a scaling knife, the patrons seemed content to leave the man with the longsword and the two boys accompanying him to eat their meal in peace.

Afterward, when they had withdrawn to the privacy of the small room the three of them were to share, Crodane stoked the fire in the fireplace, and Thom and Lughus climbed into two of the quartet of bunked beds. "Tomorrow," the swordsman said. "I will begin searching for a ship bound for the Brock. If you still seek to visit the Cathedral, then it might be as good a time as any. However, I would advise you not to venture outside of the city walls or to speak too loudly regarding your studies with the Loremaster or anything relating to our larger purpose. I would hate for the events of Lenard's Crossing to repeat themselves." He smirked. "I will meet you back here before tomorrow evening."

"I'll be sure he doesn't do anything stupid." Thom giggled.

Lughus ignored him. "Will you need money?" he asked. "For passage on a ship?"

Crodane shook his head. "It's taken care of," he said. "Now enjoy the beds while they last. Soon enough, we'll be off again and onboard a ship where there'll be no stopping on land in the evening to make camp! I'll be down in the common room for a time if you have need of me. I have a few questions I'd like to see if the locals can answer and hear any news that may have occurred over the fortnight past. Good night!"

It was midmorning the following day before Lughus and Thom had finally roused themselves from their beds. After three weeks of sleeping in the open, even the lumpy mattresses and course blankets of the Sunfish were a joy compared to the sway of the boat and the pouring rain. Crodane was nowhere to be found in their room or down in the common area, though he had left orders with the innkeeper to provide the boys with breakfast once they were awake.

In the street outside of the Sunfish, a strong ocean breeze was blowing in from the southwest, and high above the rooftops, white gulls sounded their calls. Thom took a deep breath.

"The air smells different here," he said. "And I don't mean the rotting fish."

However, Lughus did not answer; he stood motionless, staring out far over the rooftops to the east.

"What's wrong with you?" Thom asked.

Lughus simply pointed, and Thom joined him in his awe. "It must have been too dark to see it last night," Lughus said.

"I know it's foolish." Thom nodded. "But it's as if it goes on forever."

Lughus sighed and felt his heart stirred yet again by the winds of adventure, for there before him, past a veritable forest of mastheads and brightly colored sails, stretching ever onward into the horizon, was the sea. "I've never seen anything like it," he said.

An old man, stinking of ale and fish guts, hobbled by on his cane, watching the boys with the same expression on his face with which he might observe the birthing of a three-headed goat. "You stare long enough, you'll fall in," he muttered bitterly and pushed past them into the Sunfish for a breakfast of eel pie and cheap ale. "Bloody fools."

"Old toad," Thom muttered when he was certain the man was out of earshot.

Lughus sighed. "At any rate," he said, "the Cathedral of the Tides?"

Thom nodded. "Sounds good to me."

From the Sunfish, the boys followed the streets of Waverton in the direction of the cathedral's bell tower, visible above the rooftops from any point in the city. Galdoran, during the day, was a lively place full of all the sights and sounds that any large seaside port could possibly have to offer. As they made their way to the cathedral across the enormous stone bridge crossing over the Imperial into Seaside, Lughus and Thom noticed merchants and storefronts hocking all manner of wares. There were fishwives selling fish, butchers butchering meats, cloth dyers dying cloth, a tailor, a haberdasher, a weaver, a silversmith, a woodcarver, a bowyer, a cooper, a sailmaker, a blacksmith who fashioned only blades, another blacksmith who crafted only household wares, and still another blacksmith who only made parts for ships. There were men who issued loans, men who issued permits for trade, men who recruited men for work on merchant ships, men who recruited men for the Andochan army, men who collected money from imports, men who collected money from exports, and men who somehow seemed to be collecting money for just about everything.

Soon, the wares—and often the people selling them—became even more diverse, and suddenly, Lughus realized that they must be nearing Galdoran's great Markethouse. Here, many of the stalls bore the arms of famous crafting guilds from across Termain, usually coupled with the arms of a noble patron and the arms of their native realm. A thick crowd of men stood around a stall belonging to a Dwerin swordsmith as a hawker sang of the virtues of mountain steel. Another mob of onlookers gathered around an assortment of merchants out of Baronbrock who seemed to traffic mostly in cloth and leather goods, though there was an armorsmith selling fine coats of ringmail and steel helms fashioned into a variety of shapes. Near a large group of paddocks, a man from Montevale was putting on a show with a beautiful honey-colored horse. The man waved his hand to highlight the horse's shoulders and the muscles of its legs, then lifted its lips to show off its teeth and gums. A handful of Sorgundian sailors with long braids and tattoos offered jewelry and other trinkets, though they claimed that aboard their ship, they kept their "private stock" of "special wares" should any buyer be serious enough to pay them a visit. A group of Wrathorn painted for war muttered at each other aggressively in a blend of the Termainian speech and their own strange northern tongue. A few of the northmen were selling furs; however, most appeared to be selling themselves—as mercenaries, bodyguards, or any other manner of hired thug.

"You should go talk to them," Lughus urged Thom, trying to hide a smile. "Ask them about home."

"Perhaps on our way back from the Cathedral," Thom muttered, "if they're still here."

"I'm only joking, Thom." Lughus grinned. "Besides, I'd rather not risk upsetting one of them."

Thom nodded, though he did not laugh. "Funny you mention that," he said as they walked on. "Because, well...I wanted to apologize."

Lughus watched as the Dwerin hawker tested the blade of the sword, using it to slice cleanly through some manner of gourd. "Apologize for what?" he asked. "For Lenard's Crossing? You already did. In fact, that's mostly what I remember from the fight. You sputtering apologies over and over again through tears."

Thom cringed at the memory. "All I can remember is the blood."

"Yeah," Lughus said softly. "I remember that too."

Thom paused, breathed a heavy sigh, and carried on. "I just want to say that I'm sorry," he said. "Sorry for being so weak and for crying all the time and...everything else along the way. I mean...I nearly got you killed, and should that have happened, well, I hope that they would have killed me afterward too—"

"Shut up, Thom."

"No, I mean it," Thom said, "because I would never have been able to live with myself knowing that it was my foolishness and cowardice that caused your death. So can you forgive me?"

Lughus stopped walking and breathed a heavy sigh. "Thom," he said, "you and Royne are my brothers, no matter what, and there's nothing that is ever going to change that. How do you think I would have felt if I'd have done nothing while Stokes and his fellow bullies carved you to pieces?" He sighed. "And if I've been unkind to you lately, then I'm sorry too. It's just been a rather trying couple of weeks. Thank the Brethren we have Crodane to guide us, else I think we'd both have died long ago."

By way of reply, Thom drew up his hood and reached out to pat Lughus fondly on the shoulder.

"Thom," Lughus asked as together they began walking again, "are you crying?"

"Shut up."

"Aiden's Flame, Thom…"

"They're happy tears!"

At long last, they reached the Cathedral of the Tides, and since there was no service going on, the boys were free to explore the magnificent building on their own; however, they parted ways so that they might offer their thanks to Brother Galdorn in peace. Lughus sat for a while in the rear of the cathedral, examining the stained-glass windows on each of the five walls that turned the brilliant sunlight shades of blue, green, yellow, and white and the frescos depicting Galdorn aiding Father Alantir in the creation of the seas and its creatures. In each of the corners of the room was a large marble statue of a rearing horse—a searoan for certain, and at the front of the cathedral, Thom knelt before the altar behind which towered the enormous marble statue of the Brother himself.

"Watch over him," Lughus thought quietly, gazing from Thom up to the benevolent face of the Sea Lord, "and watch over Royne too. Please."

A sound from outside of the cathedral suddenly drew Lughus's attention, and since Thom still seemed to be lost in prayer, Lughus quietly slipped through the cathedral's main doors (left open so as to provide some manner of breeze for the acolytes of the Hierophant as they tended to their work inside) and went out to hear what the fuss was about.

It was a crier, an official herald dressed in a tabard bearing the Andochan arms and carrying a scepter fashioned in the manner of Callah's Key.

"Good folk of Galdoran," the herald cried, waving dramatically with his scepter. "By issue of His Majesty, King Kredor Drude II, Sovereign Lord of Andoch, First of the Guardians, Bearer of the Key of Salvation, and Wielder of Testament, Halford Drude's famous sword, the holy nation of Andoch has pledged itself to the aid of the mountain Duchy of Dwerin and the noble Archduchess Josephine Beinn, widow of the Archduke Danford Beinn, in defense of their lands against the hostile encroachment from the heathen Senate of the Republic of Grantis! Effective immediately, all properties belonging to citizens of the Republic of Gratis, all goods sold on behalf of the citizens of the Republic of Grantis, and all ships in the service of the Republic of Grantis shall be seized in the name of the throne!"

"Aiden's Flame," Lughus whispered.

He glanced around him as other listeners began to gossip feverishly at the news when suddenly there was a loud crash from the direction of the marketplace and a stall bearing the arms of Grantis was overturned. At once, looters began making off with its goods. Somewhere else nearby, another Grantisi stall was overturned. Lughus hurried back up the stone stairs of the cathedral to find Thom. If the kingsmen did not regain control of the looting quickly, the entire market could erupt into a riot.

"Thom!" Lughus shouted, his voice echoing from the nave to the apse, but to his horror, the other boy was gone. Lughus quickly ran to the base of the altar where he had last seen his friend kneeling in prayer. "Thom!" he called again.

An acolyte scarcely a year older than Lughus appeared from the sacristy and eyed him tersely.

"Have you seen a chubby boy with red hair?" Lughus asked him.

The acolyte sighed with annoyance. "No," he said, "and stop shouting."

Lughus shook his head in frustration. Even in Titanis, the acolytes were generally worthless. "Cupbearers," Royne called them since all they ever seemed to do was refill the Hierophant's goblet.

"Lughus!"

Lughus turned around to see Thom, pale-faced and sweating, hurrying toward him from the doors.

"We've got to go!" Thom said.

"I know," Lughus said. "They're overturning carts in the market. Apparently, we're going to war with Grantis."

"What?" Thom asked, struggling to catch his breath. "Is that why all the kingsmen are out there?"

"They are?"

"Yeah, a bunch of them. But it seems like things are back under control."

"Still," Lughus said, heading for the door, "there could be trouble. We should get back."

"Aye, and hurry," Thom said, gasping after him, "before Crodane does."

As Thom had said, the guardsmen in their red cloaks had arrived to restore order in the marketplace, and a number of men had already been rounded up and were now under guard, a few of them bearing the marks of a brawl. Lughus led Thom down a side street away from the Markethouse; however, they did not slow their pace until they were safely on the other side of the bridge.

"War with Grantis," Lughus said again, "strange."

"Aye," Thom said, "but more importantly, we have to get our things and get out of the inn."

"What are you talking about, Thom?" Lughus said. "And what is this about Crodane?"

"We need to get away from him as soon as possible!" Thom said, clutching a stitch in his side, "In the cathedral just now...I saw..."

"Wait, wait," Lughus said, noticing suddenly the strange looks that the townsfolk were giving them, "Not now. You can tell me when we get there."

Back at the Sunfish, the common room was filled with men taking their noontime meal, and as the boys ran in, red-faced and breathing hard, the old man with the cane from that morning chewed at the stem of his pipe, shook his head at them, and muttered. "Now here's a couple of rare birds..." However, neither Lughus nor Thom heard, their footsteps clattering noisily up the staircase to their room on the second floor.

"Now what, Thom, what in the bloody Abyss is going on?"

Thom shut the door behind him and bolted it. "Crodane is a bloody Blackguard!" he shouted.

Lughus sat down on the edge of his bed and ran a hand through his hair. The golden locks began to curl under the sweat of exertion. He wiped them from his eyes and sighed incredulously. "Thom, you cannot possibly be serious."

"I am!" Thom gasped. Bright beads of sweat streamed down his forehead, and he had to steady himself against the bed frame to keep from falling over. His breaths came in great shuddering gulps.

"I don't believe you," Lughus said simply.

Thom sat down on the opposite mattress and wiped his face on his sleeve, leaving it soaked with perspiration. "In the cathedral," he said slowly, "in the cathedral, I ran into a man bearing the seal of the Chancellor, not the robes mind you, just the seal, as a cloak pin." "So what? I saw one of the Hierophant's acolytes. Who cares?"

"So what?" Thom reached out to slap Lughus on the back of the head but missed. "Don't you remember? The Chancellor's men aren't all coin counters like old Rordan Baird," he said. "The Chancellor bears the Light of Justice!"

Lughus shook his head. "So he was probably a constable there to keep the peace when the herald made his proclamation. What does that have to do with Crodane?"

Thom waved his hand at Lughus again and once again missed.

"Cut it out, Thom!"

"Lughus, he carried a mace on his belt shaped like a hammer, and he said his name was Harlow," Thom said, waving his arms for emphasis. "*Constable William Harlow*," he said, "as in Harlow the *Hammer?*"

"The Hammer?" Lughus felt a strange anxiety in the pit of his stomach. There were stories about the Hammers leading back to the Siege of Three. Following the Mandate of Allegiance, many of the Chancellor's constables—or at least those with titles—were often tasked with hunting down Wandering Guardians who refused to bend the knee. "What did he say?" Lughus asked.

Thom took a deep breath. "He asked if I was who I am, and of course, I said yes."

"Okay."

"Then he asked if you were with me, but when I looked around, you were gone, so I said no."

"All right."

"Then he asked us how we got here, and I said a man named Crodane brought us."

"Did you ask him what he wanted with us?"

"Just listen," Thom said. "When I mentioned Crodane, he suddenly seemed to get really angry like Scholar Varen got that time when I spilled ink all over his boots. I thought he was going to start screaming at me, but instead, he asks me if Crodane is still in the city, and I tell him that he was out at the docks looking to book passage for us on a ship to Baronbrock."

A chill ran up Lughus's spine. "Thom, you shouldn't have said anything like that! Didn't you learn anything from last time?!"

"No, Lughus, I did right for once! Just listen." He took another deep breath. "So Harlow tells me to get you and get to the Guardhouse—the Sandstone, he called it—as fast as we can. He said he'd take us there himself, but he had to rally his men. He says Crodane is a Blackguard and that he's extremely dangerous! We're lucky to be alive!"

Lughus's eyes suddenly flashed with anger, and before he knew what he was doing, he leaped from the bed and rushed at Thom, jabbing him in the gut with his fists. "Shut up, Thom Fatty!" he snapped. "You're crazy!"

"Quit it!" Thom squealed. "I'm not!"

Lughus punched him again. "Shut up!"

"I'm not! I'm not!" Thom cried. "Listen! He said that Rastis and the King were sending you to Baronbrock because of something about you having family there. Crodane was to guide us because he was supposed to be a friend of your father and a member of the Order, but only after we left did they learn that your father was dead and that Crodane was the bloody murderer!"

"Shut up, Thom!" Lughus shouted. "Shut up!"

"I'm not lying! That's what he said! Why would I lie about that?" "Because you're a coward, and you don't want to go to Wrathorn!" Thom shook his head. "You're right. I am a coward, and I don't want to go," he said. "But I'm not lying. For the love of the Lady, Lughus, Harlow is a bloody constable!"

"So what? Constables never lie or get their facts wrong?"

Thom sighed heavily and took a few breaths to relax. When he spoke, his voice was soft and calm. "Think about *him*," he said. "Think about...*Crodane*. Think about his shoulder. Think about the riders on the riverbank. Think about all the stuff he knows about the Order. He even told us stuff that we're not supposed to know about the Anointed."

"Only because you asked him to!"

"So what? Like Rastis or Hob never refused!"

"And what is this lie about my family?" Lughus said. "You know very well that I haven't got any. How would Harlow, if that's even who it was, your man with a hammer and a cloak pin, how would he know who we are or anything about Rastis? And why wouldn't he have spoken to me about any of it?"

"I don't know. Maybe he didn't see you? I looked back where you were sitting, and the next thing I knew, you were gone!" Thom sighed. "But I suppose if we meet him at the guardhouse, he can tell us more."

Lughus shook his head. "I don't believe this, Thom," he said. "For one thing, when have you ever known Rastis to make a mistake? Or Hob? Hob knew Crodane. If he suspected anything, he would have said."

"You know Hob! There's a reason why he's the oldest scribe in the Tower!" Thom said. "And as for Rastis making mistakes, don't you remember the time he mistook tea leaves for his pipeweed? I never heard a man cough like that in all my life!"

"Mixing up jars of dried leaves is hardly the same as being duped by a murderer!"

"I'm just saying, Rastis isn't perfect."

"He's never claimed to be."

Thom shook his head and ran a hand through his bob of ginger hair. "Why won't you believe this? Because you finally found someone willing to teach you to fight with a sword? So you can fancy yourself St. Aiden or some other hero and get yourself noticed by the Warlord?"

"Shut up, Thom. You know that's not true."

"What's not true? That you'd much rather fancy yourself a partisan over a scribe?"

"You know that's nonsense!"

"What do I know?" Thom squealed. "At least you know Crodane knows how to use a blade. He cut Stokes and those others down easy enough. Who knows how many others he's put to the sword? Oh yes, your father!"

"I said shut up, you fat bastard!" Lughus shouted and struck Thom a blow to the gut, this time harder, this time for real. The chubby boy lost his wind with a grunt and rolled down from the mattress onto the floor. Immediately, Lughus felt his whole body cringe with guilt. With a repentant sigh, he reached down to help Thom back to his feet but was surprised when Thom swatted at him with his arm, pushing him away.

"Don't touch me!" Thom gasped.

Lughus sighed. "Thom, I'm sorry."

Thom struggled to his hands and knees. "I don't care!"

"Thom..."

"Get away, Goldimop!" Thom forced himself upright, took a deep breath, and staggered over to retrieve his pack from the corner of the room. "I'm going to the Sandstone and Constable Harlow," he said shortly, biting back his tears. "You can stay here with the murderer if you like, and if he kills you, see if I care!"

Lughus sighed and waved his hands apologetically as the other boy unbolted the door. "Thom, I'm sorry," Lughus said again. "Just wait." He reached out to put his hand on Thom's shoulder only to find it slapped away.

"Get away from me!" Thom snapped, scurrying out into the hallway. "You're just as bad a bully as Pryce!" He slammed the door shut after him with one last shout, "Goodbye!"

CHAPTER 20:
THE STEWARD

Over the remainder of Harvestide and on into the Month of the Hound, Royne's duties as a Scribe and as Rastis's Steward quickly fell into a routine. The Loremaster, as Royne well knew, was both a creature of habit and a man of simple tastes: eggs and toast for breakfast, sausage rolls and gravy for dinner, a pipe and a pot of tea for dessert. Each meal was also accompanied by a bit of reading material, though on some occasions, the old man would invite Royne to sit with him, and the two would discuss Royne's studies. Rastis had provided him with a detailed list of recommended titles and suggested reading, ranging from old philosophical musings about the nature of the Kinship to a treatise on the trade customs among the Sorgund Isles. There was an epic poem out of Dwerin describing the deeds of a blacksmith named Garm who forged a magic sword out of a fallen star, and a dusty old tome dating back to the days of Old Calendral describing the manner in which the future could be discerned by examining the patterns in a flight of various flocks of birds. Both of which, of course, Royne found completely preposterous.

Yet when discussing the matter later, it was for that very reason—the alleged absurdity—that was behind the inclusion of *Heroden's Augury* and *The Star of Garm* on the Loremaster's list. For, to understand the ways of man, Rastis said, one cannot only limit himself to the study of the truth that is proven but also to the falsehood—however egregious—that is still believed.

"Knowledge is a man in a dark room who carries but a single candle," the Loremaster said. "He may discern the shapes of all things that fall within the light. However, he may only attempt to interpret that which lies beyond in shadow. We may not be able to know for certain what lies out there in the dark, Royne, but it would be a tragic mistake to assume that, beyond a doubt, there is nothing else there. The future holds many secrets, as do the past and the present. Yet I think we can both agree that for all our Truths, there are still times when we find ourselves standing alone in the night."

It was comments like these that Royne found the most maddening, for they had not spoken of the council meeting again since when last it met—and for all intents and purposes—it did not appear that the Five would assemble again soon between the mustering of the Guardians, the kingsmen, and the levies of the Andochan nobility, and the celebrations in honor of the Feast of the Brother Perindal.

This year the holiday took on an added degree of splendor due in no small part to the impending war. Brother Perindal was known as the patron of honorable warriors, and as such, his feast day was marked from Dwerin to Castone by displays of martial prowess; however, as the home of the Order and the seat of both the Grand Hierophant and the Guardian King, holidays in Andoch were expected to maintain a level of intensity appropriate of the monarchical theocracy.

So as the King's soldiers and the Warlord's captains began preparing to support the Brothers Beinn in their conflict with the legions of the Grantisi senate, Titanis seemed a city besieged by warriors willing to test their mettle and hopefully find gainful employ—a fact that left Royne in a state of embittered distress, particularly after the festivals were over and the soldiers of fortune still had not left.

"They're bloody everywhere!" he muttered bitterly to the bottom of his pint of ale, "like flies on filth!"

One of the perks of his elevation from apprentice to scribe and steward had been a weekly stipend for any custom his copying or illuminating services may have drawn, an amount that, though meager, was enough to provide him with an excuse to visit The Book & the Barrel. Yet sadly, when he looked across the tavern's common room, it was no longer occupied with simply sages and scholars but was now crowded with new men outfitted in lamellar made from boiled leather and hauberks of metal scales or mail. Where once men of learning sat debating theories or arguing over translations of *The Scrolls of the Hierophants*, thick-armed brutes told bawdy stories and ribald jokes, boasting about battles Royne was certain had never truly happened outside of their small, thuggish brains after they had been pickled in mead. Once, a fistfight had even broken out—an event Old Bob said had not occurred since three years past when Scholar Jessup spilled a pot of gin and ruined Scholar Unwin's copy of *The Kordish Rose*. At least the law was still the law, and the drunken sots were forbidden from openly carrying their weapons. Else what ended with a few bruises, a broken barstool, and three smashed clay plates might have been much worse.

"I thought their lot only hung around places like The Wyvern," Royne muttered to Walter, "or any of those other piss-pots over in Weston or down in Riverton by the docks."

The hostler shrugged and replaced Royne's tankard with a full one. "Who am I to scoff at a bit of business?" he said. "As long as they behave."

Royne sighed and raised his cowl. "The bouts ended last week. When in the Abyss are they leaving?"

"I assume it won't be long now. Just as soon as King Kredor and Warlord Rood order the march off to war," Walter said, pausing to wipe one of the tabletops clean with a rag, "though I assume you'd know more about that, then I would, young steward."

"Not likely."

"Well," Walter said, "no matter how crowded it gets, we'll always make sure there's a place for you." He grinned. "And Hob, for that matter, wherever it is he's got himself to."

"Thanks," Royne said politely, though he chose to ignore Walter's unasked question regarding the whereabouts of Royne's predecessor, for he himself did not know. Rastis had told him that the Wrathorn scribe was not planning on leaving the city; however, between his size, his beard, and his manner, he could not possibly imagine where Hobart could possibly have been hiding.

A call for more ale from across the room sent Walter off again in a tizzy and allowed Royne to return to his brooding. He had endeavored to make good on his word to Lughus and Thom, returning to the tavern on most nights. There had been no word from Galdoran or the Hammer, at least as far as Royne knew, and though he very well knew it to be an absurd superstition, when he was sitting in The Book & the Barrel at the very same table where the three of them had spent their last hours, the many miles between them seemed a little less far.

Royne sighed and took a heavy sip of ale, reminding himself to take it slow. More than once, he had accidentally stood up to return to the tower only to find that, without realizing it, he had gotten drunk. Life in the tower had not allowed him to become as accustomed to ale as most, though in the fast few weeks, he felt he had done a decent job of making up for it some. As long as he did not allow his wits to grow too dull or drink enough to neglect his duties, he was fine. Hob drank like a fish most nights, and Rastis never seemed to mind a certain propensity to imbibe in his former Steward.

Royne settled back in his chair. The ale had finally had its effect, and he found it much easier now to ignore the other patrons of the tavern, choosing instead to turn his eye inward to indulge his often-suppressed sense of self-loathing.

An orphan, a bastard, and a baron in exile—what a combination the Loremaster's apprentices had made! What could the old man have been thinking when he plucked them up from the gutters so long ago?

Yet Lughus and Thom were gone, and here he still was, orphaned again. Royne suddenly felt the illusory walls of childhood collapsing all around him, and by some impossible, preternatural sense, he knew that very soon, the time would come for him to make a choice, a choice that would—not by some mystical force or fate, but by logic—ultimately determine his fate.

Still, he would see this business of Rastis's through, whatever its end—treason or not. He owed the old man that much and more; however, the more he saw the inner workings of the Order, the more disconnected he felt.

Since the time of St. Aiden, the Order of the Guardians had stood (like its castle of the same name) as a testament to enlightened leadership, truth, and the greatest virtues exhibited by men. True, the reality did not always match the legendary tales of adventure that Lughus so loved or the poetic folksongs Thom sang (as Royne was often quick to point out). However, men of the Order still tried to live right, and that, often, was enough. Within the Cathedral of the Kinship, each of the building's five walls was adorned with a central grand window of leaded glass depicting an event from the life of St. Aiden. Looking down upon him carved just above the window was a likeness of a different member of the Kinship—the father, the sister, or one of the three brothers—while beneath each scene was a different verse from the

Scrolls of the Hierophants identifying which of the Five Holy Virtues was exhibited at that moment by the saint. It was around these Five Virtues that the Council of Five was structured, and for these Five Virtues that the corresponding councilors were meant to stand: faith from the Hierophant, fellowship from the Chancellor, courage from the Warlord, wisdom from the Loremaster, and fidelity from the King.

However, though Royne had never really put much stock in religion or in virtue, he appreciated the idea behind such things: the rituals, the symbolism, the suggestion that when men lived their lives in accordance with such principles, the entire world could benefit. Yet now, when he thought of the current council (with the exception of Rastis, of course), they seemed less the holy saviors guiding men to greater glory, but rather…he could not find the right word…false? Foolish? Fallen?

Royne knew that he could not serve such men. He could not serve a King like Kredor, a boorish brute who, like so many nobles, was concerned not with the welfare of the nation or its people but his own motives and own glory.

The Protectorate! How preposterous! And to demand it at that beneath the guise of holiness and sacred duty? Madness, absolute madness. No, Royne could not, would not, serve such a King.

Yet a baron…

If he eluded Harlow the Hammer and safely reached the Brock, Lughus stood to be named heir to Arcis, Baron of Galadin, and would one day inherit the title himself. Baron Lughus Galadin would be a descendant of St. Aiden, ward of the Loremaster—a man like that might singlehandedly be the spark to ignite Baronbrock's Golden Age. For Lughus, like himself, had been raised to believe in the Five Holy Virtues—and though Royne's natural cynicism often tarnished his belief, Lughus's quiet devotion to the heroic romances had, for better or for worse, made him the very embodiment of such things (if somewhat idealistic and naive). However, his studies under Rastis's tutelage had not just been limited to the legends, the war stories, and the epics, but also—and Royne understood it clearly now—a smattering of rhetoric, of law, and (of course) history. All this, coupled with Lughus's natural character—his courage, his compassion, his humility—not only prepared him to become an enlightened ruler but a veritable Philosopher-King!

Yet these same qualities, while good for the land and its people, would draw the ire of those other members of the elite: greedy, conniving men focused only on where they may have had less and obsessed with the prospect of gaining more. It seemed now to Royne no mere chance that Lughus had often come into conflict with Pryce but rather a precedent for what was yet to come. Pryce, the entitled son of an Andochan noble whose father through political maneuvering bought him a place at the Warlord's side, was unfortunately not an exception to the manners of the aristocracy but rather the rule for all their kind.

"All the more reason for it!" Royne said aloud as the idea slowly took form. From their place at the end of the bar, Old Bob and Ed eyed him curiously and shook their heads, but he was too excited to care. As history had shown time and time again, Men of Vice hate nothing more than Men of Virtue. Lughus would need someone to stand at his side, someone to watch his back. Who better than a misanthrope? A cynical bastard? A brother? Royne could not imagine, nor would he trust, anyone other than himself.

"So be it."

Royne drained his tankard dry and returned it to the tabletop with a solid *thunk!* to seal it. As soon as he finished his business with Rastis, he determined, once and for all, to leave the Order. He would join Lughus, his friend, his brother—even if it meant turning Blackguard. Yet by rights, he should still be free to depart with impunity. Perhaps, he suddenly realized, this was the reason Rastis named him a scribe without the Rite of Initiation.

Royne stood up from the table, possessed now with a greater sense of purpose (though also, perhaps, a bit muddled with ale). He threw Walter a wave, left a pile of coins on the table, and hurried out to the streets of Easton to return to the Loremaster's Tower.

The air had grown colder in the past weeks, and autumn had fully set in. He thrust his hands within the wide, flared sleeves of his habit and bowed his cowled head against the chill, imagining how similar he must look in the darkness to a poor country cousin undergoing his Trial of Silence. The Hierophant and his lot could learn a thing or two from their lay brethren, he laughed cynically.

At the gates of the castle, Royne paused at the hail from the red-cloaked kingsmen on watch and gestured with a wave of his hand at his habit so that they would let him pass. There were significantly more guards on duty these days, as if the legions of Grantis were knocking at the gates. Royne often wondered how the senators had reacted to Kredor's formal declaration of war, particularly since the young King had worn his crown for less than a month when the missive had been signed. How long had he been plotting away in that thick skull of his? And how long had he been in cahoots with the Beinns? Royne had been reading more and more about the archdukes of Dwerin recently. Men as cold as steel. Iron ran deep through their mountains and through their veins. They would make great allies in a time of war, though what they offered in steel, soldiers, and ships, they cost in food. Mountains made for poor farming, and those peasants who did not work in the mines, more often raised herds of goats and sheep. Man might live on mutton, but for bread and beer, he needed grain; and for that, the archdukes perennially turned their eyes upon the fertile lands of the Spade. Securing the Spade for Dwerin ensured their acceptance of the Protectorate. That, at least, Royne would admit, was a wise idea, which was why he knew that it could not have been Kredor's; it could only have been the artifice of Natharis Tainne.

Tainne—there was another one. At first, Royne had wanted to simply write him off as another dandy nobleman, another fop in finery. However, the more he thought of the King's personal adviser, the more he grew uncertain. There was something extremely unsettling about the man's eyes. Never before had he seen any like them— eyes the color of a drowned corpse with pupils like tiny pinholes gazing out at you from the darkness of the Abyss. He shuddered at the memory. There was a mystery. For the nobleman's presence at the meeting had been an insult, and but for Rastis, it passed completely without notice or remark. Surely, Tainne could not simply be another noble lapdog like Marcel Pryce or Rordan Baird following at Kredor's heels begging for scraps. He was something else. He was an unknown, and that made him dangerous. Ambitious men attract ambitious men, Rastis had said, but how often do men place limits on their ambitions?

In any event, Royne made a mental note to investigate the "personal adviser." A noble house like the Tainnes should appear on record in numerous annals in the library or at least occupy an entry in the *Heraldic Registry*. He would ask Rastis when he brought his breakfast in the morning.

However, when Royne pushed open the portal to the tower, he was met with a great surprise. For standing at the central desk of the library stood three of the elder scribes, wide-eyed and agitated, stuttering and mumbling awkwardly regarding the manner in which the books were organized, and seated before them, as impassive as always, was none other than Natharis Tainne.

A shudder of anxiety poured like cold water down Royne's spine. Any lingering effects of the ale disappeared as he instantly sobered.

"Ah, here we are," one of the scribes, Jevan, said as he spied Royne in the doorway. "This here is the Loremaster's steward, Scribe Royne. He should be able to answer all your questions, my lord."

Royne made another mental note, this one to kick Jevan in the groin when next he caught him alone. However, he kept his face unassuming as he approached and felt the weight of those unnaturally pale eyes upon him.

"Thank you, gentlemen," Natharis Tainne said. "You may return to your duties, and hopefully, this matter will have resolved itself very soon."

The three scribes bowed their heads and, without looking at him, brushed past Royne in their haste to reach the tower stairs.

Now, alone with Lord Tainne, Royne felt his heart quicken. He forced a deferential smile. "My lord Tainne," he said, "how may I be of service?"

"Ah yes, Young Royne," the lord said, "I remember you now. It has been some time since the last meeting."

"Too long," Royne said politely.

Lord Tainne breathed a heavy sigh and stood up from the chair. "You seem a capable fellow," he said, "Else, you would not have been selected to replace Scribe Hobart as the Loremaster's steward, correct? Perhaps then, you can help me."

Royne's eyes glanced quickly to the door to Rastis's quarters. After serving his dinner, Rastis had released Royne for the rest of the evening, leaving him to his own devices. However, though it was late, it was not nearly late enough for the old man to have gone to bed. Yet his door was closed. Had he been called away to a meeting? Why had he not sent for Royne at The Book & the Barrel? Surely, Rastis would never have allowed Tainne to wander about the library unattended, questioning scribes and such.

Royne suppressed his irritation. "How may I be of service?" he asked again.

Tainne folded his arms across his chest and gazed upward at the bookshelves lining the walls. "I'm afraid that, at the moment, I find myself a bit out of sorts, and perhaps you might help me to get my bearings," he sighed, "In my youth, I had the good fortune to study at the Lighthouse in Castone, but truly your collection here appears even more extensive."

"Thank you, my lord," Royne said. "But what is it I can help you with?"

"Well, with a few things actually," Tainne said, "first, I have a list of titles that I am going to need you to find for me, as well as a number of old maps that I believe you will find in the archives." He paused at Royne's start. "Don't worry. I know that they are kept under lock and key. I'll ensure that you're granted access."

Royne hesitated, "Yes, my lord, though you will have to speak to the Loremaster first."

Tainne smiled. "I understand."

Royne cleared his throat. "The books should be no problem, though."

"Good." Lord Tainne nodded. "Now, speaking of the Loremaster, I imagine that although you were only his steward for a matter of weeks, he relied on you to aid him in the completion of his duties?"

"Well, my lord, I saw to his meals and did a bit of copying here and there," Royne said. He did not like the direction the conversation was heading. *Damn it all, Rastis, where are you?*

Tainne's eyes flashed. "Did he ever ask you to record any of his correspondence or to record any of his letters?"

Royne felt a sudden rush of anger and wondered at the frankness of the lord's question. He fought against his growing resentment. "No, my lord," he said mildly. "He did not."

Natharis Tainne sighed with disappointment, and his brow furrowed. "Never?" he asked again.

"Never, my lord."

Tainne shook his head. "Then I'm afraid, my young steward, that I have some information that may likely come as a shock."

Royne straightened but remained silent.

"It is with no pleasure that I inform you," the nobleman bowed his head sadly, regretfully, and Royne felt the sudden urge to punch him. "Earlier this evening, a messenger arrived from Galdoran with what appears to be damning evidence suggesting that our dear Loremaster has been trafficking with Blackguards."

Royne's heart froze. "That's impossible," he said. "Forgive me, my lord."

Natharis Tainne sighed, walked a few paces and, to Royne's amazement and discomfort, gently placed his hand on the boy's spare shoulder. "The message includes the account of one of your fellow apprentices, a boy named Thom. In it, he states that he and your friend Lughus were guided south to the port city by a man by the name of Crodane."

Royne felt his hands beginning to shake. The Hammer had found them.

Tainne gave Royne's shoulder a sympathetic squeeze. "This Crodane is a known Blackguard, one of the most dangerous of all," he said. "And according to your friend Thom, he claimed to be an old friend to the Loremaster and, sadly, to your Wrathorn predecessor, Hob."

Royne's stomach tied into a knot. *Curse you, Thom Fatty!* he thought. *Curse you for the treacherous, cowardly bastard that you are!*

"Needless to say," Tainne concluded, "King Kredor was left with little choice but to arrest the Loremaster on the grounds of high treason and for conspiring with enemies of the realm. We're still trying to locate Hobart Brindlebairne, though by all accounts, he is still somewhere in the city."

"And"—Royne paused, aware that suddenly there were tears in his eyes—"and the other apprentices? What of them?"

"The apprentice Thom," Tainne said, "is currently under the protection of Constable Harlow. He's safe."

Royne ground his teeth. "And Lughus?"

"Unfortunately, it appears that the boy Lughus is still the captive of the Blackguard."

Royne sighed, though he was unsure if it was with relief or greater fear. Would Rastis have truly sent Lughus off in the company of a Blackguard, or was this just an excuse for Kredor to get Rastis out of the way? And what was Thom doing, wrapped up in all this? Or Hob for that matter?

"However," Natharis Tainne continued, "in the interim, King Kredor has asked me to act as Loremaster, and since I am not formally a member of your Order, I was hoping that as *my* steward, you could help me to discover the depth of Rastis's treachery and in doing so help me to help Harlow save your friend." He paused. "What say you?"

Royne took a deep breath and stepped away from the nobleman's grasp, rubbing the tears from his eyes. When he spoke, his voice was clear and full of purpose, at least enough, Royne hoped, to mask the lie.

"Of course."

CHAPTER 21:
DIVINITY

As Livonia suggested, Brigid's impending marriage to the young Sir Reid was soon the subject of whispered conversation among the denizens of Blackstone Keep, from servant to noble, yet at no time did anyone, not her mother nor her uncle nor Young Reid himself, bother to ascertain her interest in the matter nor her consent. Moira, Caryn, and the other girls (who Brigid had recently begun to collectively refer to in her thoughts as "the Drove" for their incessant, sheep-like blathering and the docile readiness with which they would lie down for Alan and his friends) seemed even more giggly and unsubtle than usual, speaking about her in what Brigid suspected they believed was tactfully ambiguous, prattling on about some lucky person's impending delights.

It was at these times that Brigid's daydreams often took on a darker tone, envisioning battles and bloody duels, with a figure shrouded in darkness but for two shining blades that flashed in the light of the harvest moon like a great black bird with silver talons.

It had been nearly a month since that night when Brigid had spoken with the Falcon, and though in all that time, she had not once been able to return to him, there were very few moments when he was not in her thoughts.

She longed to see him, to hear his voice, and with every day that passed, she feared more and more for his safety, wondering if her horrid uncle had finally grown tired of torturing her poor friend and intended to finish him off. It hurt her to think of the pain that he must have endured, though, at the same time, the thought gave her the strength to bear her own struggles. After all, she would remind herself, he had promised to take her with him, to free her from this horrible place. Surely, he would not abandon her. He would not, could not, leave her behind to be offered like some prize pony to Reid.

The very thought of her potential husband turned Brigid's stomach, and the sight of him sent shivers like drops of icy water down her back. To be bound to him in marriage was to be relegated to a life of soulless exhibition, where she would exist purely as an object of conquest, of opulent social mobility. To be the possessor of the daughter of the archduke was to have subsumed a piece of the archduke himself, to rise even higher in the social ladder, taking one step closer to the crown itself, and though it was a crown Brigid did not necessarily desire nor care for, she would not sacrifice her dignity to Sir Reid or to anyone.

Or so she promised herself, though, in reality, it was not as simple. Between her mother and her uncle and all the others, her enemies were many, and without the Falcon, she was but one, a lone mouse lost in a den of wolves.

So in the meantime, as Livonia the Crone had commanded, Brigid would do as she was told, sitting with her mother as she tried on different outfits, sitting with the other girls as the boys played at archery, sitting at a table for the harvest celebrations, sitting, sitting, sitting. However, in all the sitting, thankfully, whether by mere chance or through some feigned sense of propriety, she had not once had to suffer the presence of her husband-to-be on her own. For Brigid had not forgotten what had been said between Alan, Donal, and Reid that night when she had hidden behind the tapestries, and for all Reid's displays of chivalry, she sensed an undercurrent of something darker in his eye and his every gesture. It was the same prurient air with which Alan often observed the poor servant girls and the same as his father now adopted when regarding her mother. The Falcon had sworn to watch over her, but how could he possibly do so locked in his donjon across the ward?

What made the whole ordeal even worse, however, was that, in spite of the fact that all arrangements seemed to have been made, there was yet to be any type of formal, public announcement of the betrothal—and even more maddening, not even an informal, private one between Brigid and her mother. Apparently, the archduchess had more pressing matters to attend to than a discussion concerning her daughter's future.

Brigid sighed, glanced up idly into the cloudy, gray-blue sky, and mildly entreated Brother Tengale to send rain—Alan, Donal, Reid, and an assortment of other young men, whose names she did not know, where, again, as the Falcon had said, "playing at war" in the yard. There had been a strange incursion of other young nobles to Blackstone of late, and as a result, Alan's flair for the theatric and need to sustain his illusory, overinflated sense of self-worth had resulted in a series of "contests of skill," where he habitually asserted his titular dominance over his peers. Accordingly, the young ladies of the Drove, who had also seemed to multiply, were expected, though never requested, to attend.

So yet again, Brigid sat among the bleating herd while Reid and Donal led the new boys in exercises of swordplay while Alan, who for today had donned a suit of shimmering mail and a finely embroidered tabard bearing the crest of Dwerin, rode around them upon a sprightly dappled palfrey doing his best to adopt the attitude of a seasoned general inspecting his troops. Blackstone's proper master-at-arms, Sir Ogden Shute, to whom the task of training would normally belong, was nowhere in sight, though this was not surprising as Alan and Sir Ogden did not often see eye to eye on most things, including Alan's martial abilities. However, the knight's loyalty to the Sheriff allowed him to maintain his position, despite the son's continual calls for his removal.

Brigid watched her cousin atop his horse and observed the manner in which his bascinet seemed to bobble back and forth comically over his eyes. She did not know if he remembered their exchange in the entry hall on the morning after the first Harvestide Feast, though he had not spoken to her directly or attempted to draw her into his mummery since. She imagined how delightful it would be if he were suddenly thrown from the back of his horse, landing face down in a pile of dung; then she remembered the suffering that had ensued the last time and the savage beating the Young Sheriff had inflicted upon one of the grooms with his riding crop. Still, there was always the chance that such a fall would break his neck...

At the sound of giggling, Brigid's vision of Alan's fall was interrupted, and she became aware of Reid smiling at her from across the yard. When he winked, she looked away, pretending not to notice, just as Alan ordered his sparring soldiers, his noble retainers, to pause.

"Now change partners and start again," he commanded, drawing his sword. The horse slowed to a trot, and as the boys began their awkward, measured sparring, the Young Sheriff addressed them. "It has been spoken of that very soon Dwerin, to honor our ties to the Guardian King in Andoch, will renew the assault on the vile Republic of Grantis to the south, the nation of murderers responsible not only for the death of our dear deceased archduke but has assaulted the very order of nature through their abolishment of the divine right of the nobility!"

At the end of the line of boys, he paused, quickly slid his sword back into his scabbard, and clumsily turned the horse around before continuing. "Yet take heart, men," he said, drawing the sword again with a theatrical flourish, "for those same insults that the Grantisi have come to hold so dear will only hasten their collapse before the might of Dwerin"—he paused—"and also Andoch."

"Consider it for a moment," he beseeched them. "Consider first the matter of faith! When a man believes in an ideal, we say he has conviction. He has fervor. He has fidelity!" Alan paused and sheathed his sword, only to draw it again. "But what do we say to a man who changes his mind? Who abandons his ideals? Hmmm? Him, we call him fickle or faithless. Him, we call wavering and womanly. Him, we call a coward! Yet this is what the *entire nation* of Grantis has done by abandoning the Kinship and accepting the witchery of the southern heathens! Now how could this manner of a man possibly stand strong against the strengthened resolve of the men of Dwerin and Andoch?" he asked. "What hope could they possibly have?"

The blatant hypocrisy of Alan's claim nearly made Brigid laugh aloud. Like Dwerin, Baronbrock and Montevale tolerated the presence of a provincial hierophant and his retinue under the command of the Grand Hierophant in Titanis, though his duties were only to serve the people in their day-to-day (or as was more likely the case in Dwerin, seasonal or holiday-specific) religious needs. Dwerin's provincial, the venerable Hierophant Toombs, fulfilled his duties from Orandal, the city of mines and foundries commanded by Brigid's Uncle Waylon on the far end of the mountain range to the west. Toombs had held his position long enough to have blessed each of her uncles upon their birth, and it was said that the last time he ventured from the sanctity of the Orandal Cathedral was to preside over the nuptials of the late archduke and the Lady Josephine. Even now, despite the alliance with Andoch, the relationship between the nobility and their spiritual leader appeared to be the same as their approach to their own token religion: out of sight and out of mind. Again, Alan returned his sword to its scabbard and continued.

"Yet as if this cowardice were not enough, the foolish heathens have worsened their condition even further!" He sighed heavily and shook his head to emphasize his disbelief. "For not only has Grantis sold away their souls, but their nobility as well! They've abandoned those to whom the very gods of the Kinship themselves have chosen by divine right to guide them, to protect them, and to rule them and replaced them with an assembly of common men! Baseborn senators jumped up from the lower ranks of the groundlings and masquerading as if they possessed the faculties of their betters to lead!"

Beside Brigid, one of the new girls was swooning. "The Young Sheriff's words are like honey," she breathed.

Caryn batted her eyes. "The purest sweetness drips from his tongue," she simpered. "With any luck, you will not have long to wait before you taste it."

The new girl stifled a giggle. "Oh, I hope to," she said hungrily. "Believe me."

Brigid felt her stomach turn, and in an uncharacteristic show of outward antipathy, she fixed the two girls with a gaze of mingling disgust and disbelief. To her surprise, the young ladies reddened and looked down uncomfortably at the grass beneath their feet.

The boys finished their round of sparring; however, rather than have them begin again, Alan seemed content to have them merely stand deferentially and listen to the rest of his speech. He drew his sword again and raised it high above his head. "What, may I ask you, differentiates the common from the noble? Hmmm?" he asked. "I will tell you!" He spurred his horse and quickly rode to the other end of the yard, thrusting his sword up high into the air. "Divinity!" he shouted shrilly, "Divinity!"

The young ladies clapped politely while Donal and Reid led the other young men banging their sparring swords against their practice shields in a show of martial appreciation. Suddenly, it all struck Brigid as the height of absurdity, and again, to her surprise, she found herself smirking in an outward show of incredulity. She looked around to see if anyone else had the same reaction as she but to no avail.

Alan continued. "Look at yourselves," he said. "The blood that flows in your veins is the blood of the utmost humanity has to offer. Its purity manifests in natural strength and martial prowess among you noble men all and as the paramount of beauty and virtue in you fine ladies! Ours is the blood that builds great cities and great nations! Ours is the will that brings the greatest of triumphs and lays low any who oppose us with one fell sweep!" he threw back his head and laughed. "Now how, I ask you, could the baseborn senate of Grantis hope to stand against the will of the noble? How could they possibly hope to compete with armies commanded by those blessed by the gods?"

Suddenly, he drove the horse quickly around to the other end of the ward in a wide loop only to stop suddenly in the direct center, surrounded by his noble retainers on one side and, on the other, the assemblage of young ladies. Alarmingly, Brigid saw that his eyes were alight with mounting, hysterical passion as he drank in the attention of his captive audience and the sound of his own voice. She felt, all of a sudden, somewhat afraid.

"You there!" Alan called, pointing with his sword. "You there! Step forward!"

Brigid followed the line of his arm to where two of the castle guardsmen stood standing with their halberds outside of the entryway to the keep. For a moment, the two men exchanged an uncertain glance, and then the nearer of the two called out in reply.

"Me, my lord?"

Alan laughed and rolled his eyes at his fellows. "Yes, you," he called back, "you bloody twit. Step forward"—he pointed to a spot on the grass with his sword—"here."

Brigid's blood turned to ice water as she feared what Alan was planning to do. The poor guardsman knew better than to ask questions, however, and as he made his way to the place where Alan indicated, something about him struck Brigid as familiar. She had met him once in the hallway, standing guard by the stairs outside her and her mother's rooms. Hodges, she remembered, that was his name.

"Look sharp, guardsman." Alan leered when Hodges had reached his place in the grass. "We'll have no slouches on my watch."

"No, my lord," Hodges said, standing straight.

"'No, my lord'?" Alan repeated. "You dare disagree with me?"

"No, my lord, I mean, yes, my lord."

"So you do disagree?"

Hodges looked visibly flustered. "Of course not, my lord," he said suddenly. "I only mean that you'll tolerate no slouches, my lord."

Alan rode up and rapped the top of Hodges's nasal helm with the flat of his sword. "How dare you presume to tell me what I will and will not tolerate!" he spat and quickly winked conspiratorially at his peers. Somewhere one of the boys sniggered. Brigid's fist clenched in anger, and she fought to contain the tears of rage she felt burning in her eyes. Hodges was twice Alan's age, and with but a few words, the Young Sheriff had already brought him low. But he was not done yet.

"Remove your helmet, guardsman," Alan said, "and your cap."

"Aye, my lord."

Hodges hurried to comply and returned stiffly to attention. As soon as he had done so, Alan adopted the demeanor of a man inspecting a tapestry, a horse, or a piece of fruit. Then with a chuckle, he ran the tip of his sword through the wispy patch where Hodges's hair was thinning as the other nobles looked on merrily.

"There," Alan said with satisfaction, "just look at him. Baseborn and common. Probably can't even read." He paused and tapped Hodges's shoulder with his blade. "Can you read, guardsman?"

"Not well, my lord."

"So you don't."

"I suppose not, my lord."

Alan laughed and shook his head. "Now"—he turned his attention back to the nobles— "just look at him." He sighed. "The wide, low brow, the flat, bulbous nose, a jaw like a bloody lantern, brutish, bestial, and base..." He wheeled his horse around. "Yet send him to Grantis, and he can be a senator! A leader of the people!" He laughed hysterically. "Oh, please!"

Brigid dropped her eyes to the grass. She could not bear to watch any more.

Alan sheathed his sword and drew it again. "Without the noble," he said, "a man such as this is no man but an animal! A beast! It is by our will and our pleasure alone that they are not grazing in the fields like cattle or snuffing through the dirt like boars! It is the will of the nobleman that holds a nation together and the commoner who is but fodder to ensure the will of the nobleman. It is our will alone that will allow—nay, ensure—that Dwerin will triumph in this war, and if this man or a thousand or even ten thousand like him should fall in the field, do not mourn them. For their sacrifice is but a trifling to our divinity!"

"For Dwerin!" Reid shouted, raising his sword.

"For Dwerin!" the other nobles cheered.

"For the Sheriff!" Alan rallied them.

"For the Sheriff!"

"Back to your place," Alan spat at Hodges.

He pulled up on his reins, hoping to persuade the palfrey to rear, but when she refused, he instead raised his sword high above his head again and, digging his spurs mercilessly into the horse's flank, charged onward in a wide circle around the perimeter of the inner ward. Laughing and giggling, the young men and women of the court began to chase mirthfully after him.

Brigid watched them go, her fists quaking with shame and horror at those who were said to be her peers. She glanced up at the tower donjon and recalled what the Falcon had told her about the injustice that had overcome Dwerin as the true source for all her bloody thoughts. She remembered the crow from her childhood, the one who reminded her of Alan, and the way it met its end. "All falcons must have talons," she said aloud and ran off back toward the doorway into the keep. Hodges and the other guardsman had already resumed their posts.

"Hodges!" she called, surprised for a moment at the volume of her own voice.

"My lady." Hodges and his fellow nodded courteously, though Brigid could sense a hoarse tremor in the man's voice. Her blue eyes flashed with a vengeance at the poor guardsman's shame.

"I'm going inside," she said, "if anyone asks, you can tell them that I've taken ill. I sense a foul-smelling wind every time the Young Sheriff opens his mouth!"

"Yes, my lady," Hodges said, meeting his fellow guard's glance with a look of alarm.

"Actually, you'd best forget the part about the wind."

"Yes, my lady."

Brigid shook her head and sighed. "I'm sorry, Hodges," she said. "Alan is an ass."

Hodges nodded and pushed back on the heavy oaken door into the keep. "There you are, my lady," he said.

Brigid hurried inside. "Thank you," she said, "and Hodges?"

"Yes, my lady?"

"I want you to know that should the worst ever come to pass, I would mourn you," she said. "I would mourn you and any other man who fell in service of our home more than I would for any one of that whole rotten lot."

"I believe it, my lady," Hodges said simply and, nodding toward his partner, added, "We all do."

Brigid nodded appreciatively and hurried inside.

At the far end of the great hall, she raced up the stairs two at a time, gripping the edge of her gown so as not to fall. It made her sick to wear it, and as soon as her business was concluded, she would return to her quarters and change. Let Livonia try to berate her for doing so or for tearing out her wretched plaits. She would knock the last of the old crone's rotten teeth out.

Anger carried her as far as the second floor and the long hall, where Alan and his selected companions called home. Brigid paused and trod softly out into the hallway, warily straining her ears for the sound of any passing servants. It had been years since she had been on this floor. Funny, she thought, considering that by right, every inch of Blackstone belonged to her. Still, she knew that pressing her claim would mean nothing to Alan or her mother and, least of all, to her uncle. She needed to be cautious, silent, and swift.

"Like a mouse." She grinned.

The door to Alan's quarters was at the end of the hall, and empty as it was, it was unlocked. Bracing herself for whatever might lay beyond, Brigid took a deep breath and entered, shutting the door behind her. Almost immediately, she regretted that she did.

The smell was atrocious: spilled wine mixed with sweat and vomit in the chamber pot. Brigid wondered that the servants had not yet cleaned any of it, though with Alan's ever-shifting moods, perhaps they were waiting for him to order it rather than risk his wrath for tidying when he would have rather they had not. She stepped lightly over pieces of clothing and empty wine casks strewn at random upon the floor and tried to avert her eyes from the disheveled bedclothes. Her eye could not help but notice a series of rusty brown stains among the linens or the riding crop shoved halfway beneath a pillow, and she felt sick in her stomach at the memory of one of the new maids bent double at her household chores. Thankfully, before she happened upon any further marks of her cousin's unsavory appetites, she discovered what it was she was looking for. Looped over an iron wall sconce hung the prisoner's daggers, safely sheathed in their leather baldric.

With great care, Brigid tiptoed toward them, a shudder of vengeful glee tickling her spine. She remembered when first she'd seen them, glimmering in the soft lamplight of the Falcon's cell. They were just as beautiful now, so much so that, at first, she was hesitant to touch them. When she did, carefully sliding one of the blades from its sheath, she was amazed, for it barely made any sound. Her heart beat faster in her chest as she peered closer at the rippling pattern of the folded steel blade, holding it with some reverence in the pale afternoon light of Alan's bedroom window. Here was a masterpiece— masterpieces, for there were two of them, a matched pair, the work of some great artisan, a true artificer of the forge.

A sound from the hall suddenly startled her, and she nearly cut herself on the blade. There will be time for appreciation later, Brigid thought, once she had smuggled them safely back to her room. She lifted the belt from the sconce and wrapped belt, blades, and all within the folds of a black, hooded half-cloak that she hoped was clean and scurried silently back out to the hall— only to collide head-long into her soon-to-be betrothed, the young Sir Reid.

"Brigid!" he started in amazement.

Brigid's heart stopped, and she nearly dropped her cloth bundle as she leaped back in fright, "Reid! What are you doing here?"

"This is my room," he said, nodding to the door next to Alan's. "When I came inside after you, I thought you'd gone to your chambers." He grinned. "What a surprise to find you here! Were you looking for me too?"

"No, I—" Brigid's pulse quickened as she tried to think of something to say. "I should go," she finally said. However, before she could get away, Reid's hand shot out and held her fast by the wrist.

"Brigid, wait," he said gently. "Don't go."

Brigid felt ill at his touch. "Reid, please. This is unseemly."

"In a minute, in a minute," Reid said. "Please, I've wanted to speak with you alone for so long, but there never seems to be the right moment."

She tried to slip free from his grasp, but his grip tightened. "Reid, I must go."

"Brigid, please," he said, "I need to speak with you." He pushed open the door to his room and pulled her along behind him.

"Reid, let me go!" Brigid said sternly. She wanted to scream but wondered if she did, what good it would do. Would her mother or her uncle be angrier at her for stealing the daggers or at Reid? More likely, they would assume she came to Reid's room voluntarily.

"Reid," she said again, "You *must* let me go."

Reid ignored her, pulled her inside, and shut the door. "You know." He smiled, trying to catch her eyes with his. "We're to be married."

Brigid looked away. "No one has told me as much."

With his free hand, Reid lightly ran his fingers through her hair and touched the side of her cheek. Cold fear filled the pit of Brigid's stomach, and she felt her eyes welling up with tears. "Reid," she said softly, "Let me go."

"Oh, Brigid"—he breathed, drawing nearer—"kiss me." He brought his lips closer to hers, and she turned away.

His eyes widened in surprise.

"No," Brigid said.

He pushed her back roughly against the door and tried to kiss her a second time, but again, she turned away.

"No!"

Reid twisted her wrist, and Brigid felt a searing flash of pain. The cloak and daggers fell from her other hand to the floor, and she slapped him smartly across the face; however, this only served to make him angrier. He twisted her wrist more violently and held her face tightly in his grip.

"Yes!" he said and forced his lips over hers.

Brigid clenched her teeth and fought as he tried to force his tongue into her mouth. His hand slipped from her wrist up to her torso and roughly squeezed her breast while the other began grasping at the folds of her dress, trying to find its way underneath, and for once, Brigid was thankful for the cumbersome layers of heavy, embroidered cloth. Tears streamed down her cheeks as she fought with every ounce of her strength, but Reid was significantly stronger, and she knew that if she did not escape soon, she would not be able to resist him for long. In one final effort, she clenched her fist and brought it up with all her might into his groin. The blow knocked him backward, and as he fell, she spied a golden hilt protruding from the folds of the cloak on the floor. In a flash, Brigid grabbed hold of it, and just as her betrothed was about to renew his assault, she thrust the blade into his stomach up the hilt.

Reid's eyes bulged in their sockets in a mixture of shock and pain, and his mouth gaped wide, soundlessly, wordlessly.

"You bastard!" Brigid hissed, her voice shaking through her sobs. She pulled the dagger free from Reid's innards and thrust it in a second time, twisting the blade sharply. "I told you," she cried. "*Let me go!*"

Red spittle collected across Sir Reid's gaping mouth as he gasped for air. Yet as much as he might breathe, it could not save him, and before long, his body went limp and fell back heavily upon the floor, crimson rivers streaming freely from his wounds. Brigid gaped down at Reid's body and noticed her right arm wielding the dagger coated up to the elbow in sticky red blood. Her chest shook with heavy sobs, but she knew that she must escape; she must get away. She wiped the dagger and her hands on the blanket over Reid's mattress and, without a second thought, ran upstairs to her bedroom and locked the door.

Brigid's heart thundered in her chest, and her wrist, where Reid had twisted it, was swollen and burned like fire. Blood splatter ran down the front of her dress, and in her haste up the staircase she could not remember if she had passed anyone. Even a passing glance would have noticed the blood! Hurriedly, she stripped down to her shrift and hid the gore-stained garment and the daggers beneath the mattress of her bed before attempting as best she could to clean her hands in the washbasin, emptying the dirty water afterward in her chamber pot.

Outside her window, she could hear Alan and the others still at their games. With any luck, it would be hours before anyone discovered what had become of Sir Reid, time enough, hopefully, for her to come up with a plan. If only she could get to the Falcon. Surely, he would know what to do. But there was no way that she could get to his tower in broad daylight, no way that she could ever hope to avoid being noticed by the guards.

She sat down on the edge of her bed and buried her face in her hands. "Lady, save me," she whispered. *Was it murder?* she wondered. She had only acted in defense. Surely anyone would have seen that? Or would they? If it was true that she and Reid were to be married, would anyone have seen Reid's behavior as anything but claiming his right?

That thought made her skin crawl and her stomach turn with disgust. The thought that any man could claim her as his property, his plaything—husband or not—made her anger flare. She thought suddenly of Alan's riding crop and the catalog of horrors she did not even want to imagine he inflicted on any of the poor servant girls in his room. No—her room! For Blackstone was her castle by right!

"Never," Brigid swore aloud as tears welled in her eyes, "never will I be with any man who I do not love and who does not love me in return," for she knew that for all his talk, Reid did not love her. He simply coveted her—her title, her castle, her body, and, one day, her children. She would have killed him a hundred times over before she allowed him any of those things, though that did not make the magnitude of actually having done so only once any less grievous.

Brigid lay on her bed and wept, her breaths coming in great, shuddering sobs. At least, she thought bitterly, she had spared her mother the trouble of announcing the betrothal.

CHAPTER 22:
THE CONTEST OF THE SPADE

Geoffrey's legs felt weak as he clambered up the hill alongside the forest road. At least the pain had subsided, like dipping your hand in an icy stream. After a while, you just ceased to feel the cold, and were it not for the multitude of feathered shafts springing out like pennants from his chest and the way his breathing came only in short, quivering gasps, he might not have believed that his end was nigh. Yet he still had some time. Time enough, he only hoped, to see things through.

The first two he discovered were already too far gone. The first, a young boy of perhaps fourteen, had been felled by a single thrust to the abdomen. Red blood dribbled still from the corners of his mouth, but sadly, he was dead before Geoffrey could finish speaking the last words. Such a shame. He seemed a strong lad used to a life of hard work and toil, and he was about the proper age. The life would have suited him.

The second was a girl of perhaps twenty, probably a milkmaid or a farmer's daughter. It was rare to pass a title on to a woman, but his time was running out, and his vision was becoming more blurry. Yet she, too, was already dead, cut down by a pair of arrows to the chest in the opening volley, only to bleed out in the madness of what followed. Thankfully, none of the bandits had gotten to her to add to her suffering in those last few moments before she died.

A sudden resurgence of pain brought Geoffrey to his knees, and he had to lean heavily on Oakheart to keep from collapsing altogether. The metallic taste of blood appeared upon his tongue and on his lips as he spit a great glob of crimson among the grass. When the call of a barn owl overhead brought him back to his senses, he knew he must hurry.

Near the crest of the hill, he spied a third figure; and this one, it seemed, was still moving. A single arrow pierced the man's side. Though painful, it was a wound that most fighting men could—if the gods were good—survive. However, in spite of the delirium of his wounds, Geoffrey could tell that the man was no warrior. True, he was strong enough, with arms thick as the boughs of a tree and shoulders like an ox, but it was clear that those muscles had been raised by the plow rather than forged with steel. Plus, the man was old. Forty perhaps? When he took up with the Marshal and the Blade in those days so long ago, his voice had not even broken. This man could already have a wife and children of his own. He'd be completely unsuited for a life on the road.

Another flash of pain brought Geoffrey to his knees, and he realized time was almost spent. He had no choice. Unless he wished the title to die off with him, the man would have to do. He must speak the words soon, or else, they would both die.

Geoffrey awoke in the hollow beneath the copse of beech trees where he and Oliver had stopped to make camp. Through the multicolored canopy of autumn leaves, he could see the sun was already on the rise. Oliver sat nearby, bleary-eyed and dour, stoking the small campfire they had built just a few hours earlier.

Two days had passed since the Red Boars raided the village, and though neither Geoffrey nor Oliver had any skill as a tracker, the wheels of the oxcarts, weighed down as they were with Pyle's winter stores, had left a clear trail to follow along the muddy paths of the forest road.

The bandits had been traveling toward Grantis, stopping only twice to rest. Since they were both mounted and had at least a twelve-hour head start of the farmers following on foot, Geoffrey believed that it was unlikely that he and Oliver would catch up with them before they reached their roost, not that the bandits were in any real hurry. Since they were the source of terror on the road, they had no need to fear any other.

It was just before dawn when Geoffrey and Oliver discovered the trail of the oxcarts had left the road to turn south by way of a forest path, and the two farmers decided to pause for a few hours of rest before facing the forest and what might lie in wait within—whether beast or bandit. Geoffrey suspected that the Red Boars had taken up residence in one of the many abandoned forts along the coastal plains on the far side of the forest. While selling his crops at the market, he had often heard other farmers speak of the coastal plains and their fertility. In times of war, those farmers were often the first to find their harvests taken by soldiers by land or raiding parties from the sea. Dwerin or Grantisi, it did not matter. Supplies were always running short, and an army had plenty of mouths to feed. Eventually, the farmers gave up their lands, and either headed further inland to settlements like Pyle or left the Spade altogether, seeking work beyond the borders in one nation or another.

But regardless of whether Geoffrey and Oliver caught up with the Red Boars on the road or at their fort, Geoffrey still had no clear idea what the two of them alone could possibly hope to do.

"Do you want some of this?" Oliver asked, noticing Geoffrey had awakened. He unwrapped a bundle of oatcakes from its cloth wrapping, broke one in half, and offered it.

Geoffrey rubbed the sleep from his eyes, accepted the proffered breakfast, and ate. He sensed the lingering memories of another nightmare and, hoping to drive it away, attempted conversation.

"So," he said, "they turned south."

Oliver nodded. "I suppose so," he said shortly.

Geoffrey sighed. He knew his friend was still angry with him for his reluctance to pursue the bandits; for nearly the entirety of their journey, he had seemed unwilling to speak more than a few short words at any given time. But today was a new day.

"Any thoughts on what we should do when we meet them?" he asked. "Do we have a plan?"

"No."

"Do you think we should?"

"I don't know."

Geoffrey shook his head. "This is madness."

Abruptly, Oliver kicked a clod of dirt over their small fire and hopped to his feet.

"You can go back then," he said shortly. "Chances are it's a fool's errand anyway. Go back to the village if you want to live."

However, Geoffrey remained, and before long, they were trekking southward through the woods along the beaten track. Geoffrey carried

Oakheart in his right hand, resting it solidly on his shoulder, while Acorn hung loosely strapped to his left forearm. Oliver carried one of the rusty swords taken from the three dead scouts at Damon's farm, though when he swung it on occasion, he wielded it more like a hoe or a spade than a weapon.

By mid-afternoon, the two farmers reached the edge of the forest, and before them—for many miles—stretched the lowlands that eventually ended at the shores of the Spade's southern coast. The dirt path widened steadily into what could more easily pass as a proper road, meandering hither and thither around clumps of large gray standing stones strewn about the countryside like the discarded toys of a giant child. Geoffrey wondered what force could have plucked up such massive stones—taller than a man in some cases and wider around than an ox. For the mountains of Dwerin were a long ways off, and there were no quarries to speak of nearby, at least as far as Geoffrey knew.

It was while inspecting one of these boulders that they discovered the body. It belonged to a man, that much was for certain, though much of his features were difficult to discern; his end had not been kind. His face had been smashed in by some blunt force, and any hair he once might have had been taken, cut free in a long, jagged strip that ran the length of his scalp. His clothing, blood-soaked and torn, had already been picked over. Though unarmed and unarmored, miscellaneous bits of assorted gear lay around him, as haphazardly tossed away as the great rocks—a leather vambrace cracked with age, a dented iron cap, and a crude dagger fashioned from a trowel.

"Aiden's Flame!" Oliver exclaimed. "What do you think happened to him?

Geoffrey knelt and examined the corpse, noticing now a trail of blood leading out away from the boulder. There, wide swaths of grass had been matted down, and the unmistakable shape of hoofprints stood out in the mud. Slowly, the man's story became clearer.

"He was a scout," Geoffrey said. "He came in over the woodlands to the east, and by the looks of it, the Red Boars gave chase and rode him down. They must have dragged him for a time before they finally did him in. Probably stripped him for gear, too, I'd warrant. Soldiers always have better gear than the brutish knaves that often join up with the bandits. A mercenary's little more than a bully who steals a sword off a dead man and fancies himself a warrior." The closeness of that sentiment suddenly caused Geoffrey to fall silent, and he remembered the old man-at-arms.

Oliver eyed the body curiously. "Soldier, you say? How do you get that? And what do you mean 'scout'? Who'd he be scouting for?"

"Or a border guard or some such. It's all one, really." Geoffrey chewed his lip and carefully turned the body over onto its side, revealing a cloak that, before the bloodstains, appeared to have been the color of sage. "Matches the undergrowth quite well, doesn't it?" Geoffrey said. "Be hard to see someone far off covered in that." Oliver's eyes widened, and Geoffrey continued, "But if that's not enough, then"—he paused to point at the underside of the dead man's arm—"there's this."

"A tattoo," Oliver muttered, "What is that? A goat?"

"I think it's a wolf."

"A legionnaire then? Out of Grantis?"

"'It's not birth but worth as leads the Wolf Pack.'" Geoffrey nodded. "Isn't that what they say? Looks like the war may be on again."

Oliver shook his head bitterly. "He could just be a deserter."

"Then why'd they kill him? Why not ask him to join? He'd probably be a better hand than those louts as followed Karthan and Mathon or those men that killed Damon."

"It still doesn't make sense why they would have killed him."

Geoffrey shrugged. "I don't know. They killed Cousin Martin without so much as a word." He sighed. "Do they need a reason?"

Oliver's face darkened. "By the Brethren, Geoffrey. The things that go on in your head. How do you know all this? About the scouts and all?"

Geoffrey knelt and drew the edge of the cloak up to cover the dead man's remains. "It just came to me," he said at last, "like I always knew it. Same as reading. Same as when I…" He paused, and his voice fell to a whisper, "Same as when I killed those men."

Oliver breathed a heavy sigh. "We should press on."

"Aye," Geoffrey said, "that we should."

Suddenly, the sound of an arrow in flight knocked Oliver flat, and Geoffrey dropped low, raising Acorn up before him for cover.

"All right, Oliver?" he whispered harshly.

Oliver lay beside the corpse, afraid to move lest another arrow let fly. "Lady save us!" he gasped by way of a reply.

Geoffrey tightened his grip on Oakheart and slowly crept to his friend's side as the clatter of hooves drew near the beaten track.

"Show yourselves!" a voice demanded, clear and strong. "Else, the next arrow to take flight will not be in warning!"

Geoffrey made to move from behind the boulder as Oliver lurched to his knees and caught him by the arm.

"Are you mad?" he asked.

The voice called a second time, close at hand. "Come out from behind there! I will not ask again."

Geoffrey met Oliver's stricken glance with a reticent shrug, shook himself free, and stepped out into sight. Two men a-horse, skirmishers in light chainmail byrnies, waited at the ready. One held an arrow notched and drawn, while the other eyed him menacingly with a sword in hand. Both wore cloaks of drab yellow wool pinned over their right shoulders with iron brooches shaped into the likeness of an anvil.

"Who are you?" the man with the sword demanded. "Speak quickly."

"Just farmers, sir," Geoffrey stammered as Oliver crawled out slowly from behind the rock, "from the village to the north." He was reluctant to offer Pyle's name so handily.

"And do the farmers of the Spade often go about thusly armed these days?" asked the rider.

"Not often, sir," Geoffrey said, helping Oliver to his feet. "Though these are dangerous times."

"Indeed."

Geoffrey's eyes furtively searched the men's faces. They were men of Dwerin. The sign of the anvil told him that much, but what were they doing here? Had the war truly begun again?

"Pardon us, sir," Geoffrey began again after a moment. "But we're no friend to the Wolf Pack, if you be wondering." Nor were they particularly friendly to the Iron Men either, he couldn't help but think. Still, he bowed his head deferentially. "We mean you no harm."

The riders exchanged a glance, and at a nod from the swordsman, the archer lowered his bow, dismounted, and began surveying the area where they stood, reminding Geoffrey of Oscar's pigs after mushrooms.

The remaining rider kept his gaze level on the farmers. "What can you tell us about these lands?" he said. "I assume with your village so near, you must know something of the area."

"Not much, I'm afraid," Geoffrey said. "We rarely venture though the northern wood for fear of the bandits."

"Then what brings you out here now?"

Oliver cast Geoffrey a sidelong glance but remained silent. At length, Geoffrey suppressed his own uncertainty and spoke. "Well"— he sighed— "bandits actually."

"Bandits?" the rider said shortly. The archer reached the boulders behind them, and Geoffrey glanced quickly over his shoulder as his heart quickened.

"Why are you following bandits?" the rider asked again. "Alone?"

Geoffrey sighed. "Well, sir, you see, three days past, the Feast of the Father, mind you, these bandits came upon our village and stole all our winter stores." He paused. "They also took three young lads to join their ranks—our sons. We've tracked them since."

The rider's eye narrowed. After a long moment, he sheathed his sword. "I mourn your loss," he said, "though I cannot say whether I find two men, and farmers at that, following what seems by their tracks to be at least a score of mounted brigands very brave or very foolish."

Geoffrey avoided Oliver's eye. "Perhaps both," he said.

"Have you any idea where they were headed?"

"No clear idea, sir. Though we figured they were headed back to their camp to hide the stores, but—"

"But?"

Geoffrey paused. A sudden thought occurred to him. Again, an idea formed within his mind like something out of memory, though not one of his own. "But," he continued, "there used to be an old motte-and-bailey a ways to the south of here left over from one of the last wars. Ashfort, I think it was called. It was one of a string of places along the Spade, though most have since been burned.

Again, Oliver eyed him curiously, but Geoffrey knew he had no answer to his friend's unasked question.

Suddenly, the archer called from behind them. "We've got a dead wolf back here."

"That's what we was looking at when you saw us," Geoffrey said.

The rider fixed his gaze on the horizon to the east allowing his gaze to travel to the south. "Ashfort, you say?" his eyebrows narrowed.

"Aye, sir."

The rider nodded. "Mason," he called to the archer.

"Aye, Captain?"

"Mount up."

"Yes, sir."

As the archer returned to his horse, the captain turned his attention back to Geoffrey. "My name is Barrow," he said, "My men and I have been tasked with scouting these lands in advance of our armies led by Lords Devon Walsh and Padraig Reid."

Geoffrey bowed his head. "I'm Geoffrey, and this is Oliver," he said. "Both men of the village of Pyle."

"Well, Geoffrey of Pyle," Captain Barrow said, "I suppose that you had best come along with us."

Oliver began to protest, but Geoffrey stayed him with a hand. "Sir," he said, "we only wish to find our sons."

"I understand that," Barrow said, "though to let you go off alone would be to send you to your deaths, or in the case that you have been lying to us, to send you back to the Wolf Pack as informers hoping to curry favor. No," he said sternly, "you shall come with us for now to where my men are camped. I would like to know more about this area and these bandits that you seek, and in particular, I would like to know of this Ashfort." He turned his horse, and Mason, the archer, rode out to follow the farmers from behind. "And who knows?" Barrow added. "Perhaps we may find ourselves of complimentary purposes?"

At length, Geoffrey sighed. "We have no choice?"

"There is always a choice," Barrow said. "We could fight, though I dislike killing a man for such a trifling purpose."

CHAPTER 23:
THE TOWER'S GUARD

Nearly two weeks passed before the men of the Tower's Guard first mustered in the field outside of Reginal in the very spot where once King Marius's grandstand had stood for the tourney. In that time, the air grew steadily colder, and a light glazing of frost turned the soft blanket of grass and mud into a rigid field of tiny, crystalline spears and frozen dirt.

The delay following the tourney was the inevitable result of the mounted melee when the two dozen men to triumph in the lists were set upon one another in what—to Bel at least—seemed an even more meaningless display of martial posturing than the joust. Each man among the twenty-four was assigned at random to one of two squads of twelve to stage a mock-battle that would highlight the individual prowess of each warrior and provide an afternoon's entertainment for the elder knights and young ladies among the nobility. Any man unhorsed would be disqualified, and the fighting continued until only one team remained.

Bel wondered that a general of such renown as the Tower would indulge in such a senseless act. Melees were dangerous affairs, and though on the surface, appeared as if they were only for show—with full armor and blunted weapons—men could still end up dead, for a sword without an edge was still made of steel, and a fractured skull or a broken limb could easily erase any honor the victors may have previously won.

Such as it was, there were two of the company would not be joining the other men in the field when they were finally called to assembly. However, Bel had been spared any injury, as fate would have it, due to what could

293

either be considered an act of great wisdom or great cowardice, though perhaps it could best be attributed to pure, dumb luck and blind chance. For, it came to him without thinking, as the result of frustration and defiance as he stood alongside the other eleven of his squad listening to them argue over tactics and the rights of command.

That was another reason Bel preferred to fight with the common men, he realized. Knights and lordlings fought only for their own glory beneath the guise of serving a lady or a king. Commoners, however, fought as a unit, often banding together to defend their friends and neighbors.

In the case of the melee, the crux of the conflict came down to Lord Hadley and Lord Talondaire. Both demanded the right of honor for the squad and the position of command. Hadley, the elder of the two, commanded a personal force of two hundred men-at-arms and oversaw the administration of three great fiefs of land. The Young Talon, however, though slightly less landed, boasted a closer connection by blood to the king. The remaining riders—knights of lesser and varying rank and birth, some simply elevated house guards (like "Sir Briden" to Lord Solidor), stood meekly by in silence, reluctant to support one or the other of the lords.

Suddenly, from the grandstand, the herald summoned the combatants to take the field; however, even when he called them forth a second time, none of the men moved.

Bel, cast aside like his fellows by either lord, felt frustration burning in his breast when, as Hadley and Talondaire intensified their private war of words, the herald sounded his call a third time. Bel—as Sir Briden Winfred, rode out alone to take the field.

From the noble grandstand to the mob of peasants gathered on the periphery of the field, the sight of a lone rider set the spectators to whispering, and as Bel led Banshee out onto the grass to the patch of ground directly in front of the king's box, he could feel the eyes of the other riders—Lords Hadley and Talondaire, in particular—glaring at him in vexation.

The herald, uncertain for a moment what to do, paused to find Bel's name. "Sir...Sir...Briden Winfred of...of Rosewood!" he announced, scanning over his notes.

His heart in his throat, Bel dismounted, removed his helmet, and bent his knee. All at once, he realized the full magnitude of his impulsiveness, and he felt himself blushing scarlet as he stared into the grass, averting his eyes from the king.

The herald cleared his throat. "Sir Briden," he said, "I assume you with to speak? Tell us. Is there some reason for this delay? Why have your fellows not yet taken the field?"

Bel took a deep breath and wondered where Jarvy was, knowing the old skirmisher was probably somewhere among the peasants watching. The silence lengthened, and his pulse quickened like the cavalry spurred to a charge. "Forgive me, Your Majesty," he said softly, struggling to keep his voice level. "However, if this contest is to determine the ranking among the Tower's chosen men, then..." He paused. "If it pleases His Majesty and the lord-general, then I offer myself, unhorsed as you see me, to be first to be named least among my peers."

A great murmuring went up from the crowd, and incredulous whispers spread like a pail of water poured over a fire. At length, a different voice called out from the grandstand. "Sir Knight, your trials in the lists have proven you a horseman of some worth," said the speaker. "Do you not wish to gain further honor?"

Bel swallowed a lump in his throat. "Certainly, my lord," he said. "Though if these men are to ride beside me on the battlefield and to serve the Lord Tower as my brothers, then I would gladly yield to any man among them in their pursuit of glory."

Again, the sound of murmurs washed like a wave over the crowd, and though Bel kept his eyes averted, he recognized a figure clad in armor seated at the king's right-hand opposite of the princess. It was this man who had spoken.

"As you wish, Sir Briden," he said, "you may stand aside in the area beside the grandstand reserved for the fallen."

"Yes, my lord," Bel said and, donning his helmet, led Banshee away while the crowd sat shocked in bewilderment. However, the delay had given the two squads of horsemen time to resolve their disagreements and line up abashedly for the opening charge.

"Clever move, my lord." Jarvy had grinned later when the melee had finally been decided, and the wounded staggered (or were carried) from the field to return to their pavilions. The last men mounted, the Young Talon and another knight named Sir Linton Traver, both of Bel's squad, would be honored at the castle at sundown during the king's feast.

Bel shook his head. "I'm not so certain," he said. "Perhaps all I've done is label myself a coward." Not a man among the others had said a word to him throughout the melee or in the field afterward. "In truth, I had no wish to fight in the first place, and as it happened, I did not."

Jarvy shrugged. "Perhaps," he said, "to some, it might seem that way. However, I heard no talk of cowardice, but rather, it seemed most praised you for your knightly sense of humility and of fellowship. Just like in the stories, they said."

Bel sighed and, not for the first time, longed to return home, longed to ride out on Igno across the southern plains, free from the steel prison of his armor and lies. The Blood Blossom would ride alongside him on her Banshee to the small field by the standing stone where they had said their last farewells, where he had finally convinced her to accept his promise. "At least the Tower was in attendance," he said at last, pushing those thoughts out of his head, "though I didn't get a good look at him."

"Nor I," said Jarvy, "though it's a wonder if anyone did, seated as he was beside the majesty of the king and the beauty of the princess. I'd say it's easy to get lost in those two shadows."

And so it seemed that evening at the feast as well, when Bel arrived as required with the other knights to be honored before the assembly of Gasparan nobility. The castle at Reginal, built atop the uneven lands of the Montevalen highlands, consisted of a series of concentric rings of stout, stone walls, each protected by a series of towers and heavy iron gates, and in the very center of the fortress stood the great tower where King Marius, his family, and their most trusted retainers dwelled. It was a place Bel realized, in which no one in his family had set foot freely for a hundred years.

By the time knights of the Tower's Guard were ushered into the king's great hall, the meal had already been served, and most of the nobles had moved on to puddings, sweet liquors, and dancing. One by one, the herald called out their names in the order of achievement decided in the melee. As Bel stood waiting beside the others, he glanced around the room from noble to noble and from the king to the fair princess, though the lord-general himself, it seemed, was once again not in attendance.

However, it appeared that Jarvy had been correct in what he had mentioned about the rumors regarding Bel's hasty action. For when the herald, lastly, announced "Sir Briden's" name, many of the nobles hailed him with what seemed honest sincerity, rather than the polite applause often used to cover derisive whispers. Sir Galen Helm later confirmed the matter further as Bel attempted to hide quietly in the corner, and across the hall, he caught the elder knight's eye.

"Sir Galen"—Bel nodded at the knight's approach—"I hope the evening finds you well."

"So it does, Sir Briden," Sir Galen said kindly, "and may I congratulate you on another fine showing today. You keep putting on displays like that, and by midsummer, you'll be commanding a round tower on the Bloodline."

Bel accepted the complement with a nod but otherwise remained silent. The more he saw of Sir Galen, the greater he felt a deepening sense of guilt. For he was coming to like the Gasparan knight, and he did not relish the thought that one day they might meet on the battlefield once Bel finally returned to Valendia.

"I'm not certain if disqualifying myself from the melee somehow labels me fit for command," Bel finally said with half a smile, "probably the opposite, in fact."

Sir Galen grinned. "I don't know about that. It seemed to me as if your actions pointed out the absurdity of the entire affair." He paused to take a sip from his wine goblet. "You know, Lord Hadley's leg is broken. In spite of everything, he'll not be able to ride alongside you after all. A Sir Egan Something-or-Other is out too, though he was on the squad opposite you. Broken arm. The heralds are checking the results of the lists to see who qualifies next to replace them."

Bel shook his head. "That's a shame."

"So it is," said Sir Galen. "But those are the risks, which is why I prefer not to mingle fighting with frivolity."

"Any man who plays at war only proves he's still a child," Bel intoned, catching himself just as he was about to finish with, "As my father says."

Sir Galen nodded in agreement. "Well spoken."

Bel took a sip of wine to mask his blushing.

"So," the knight began again, "was that it?"

"I'm sorry?" Bel asked.

"Your bold concession today," Sir Galen clarified. "Was it the result of honor, humility, jesting? What was it that made you act as such?"

Bel sighed. A servant walked by with a platter of roasted walnuts, and Sir Galen selected a few. "I suppose," Bel began once the servant had gone, "that it was a combination of matters."

Sir Galen popped a walnut into his mouth and crunched noisily. "Such as what?"

Bel bit his lip in thought, suddenly feeling somewhat exposed, and for the first time, he wondered at Sir Galen's questions and his motives. However, for better or for worse, when under duress, Bel found deception foreign to him, and he could not help but answer honestly.

"Well," he said, "speaking of Lord Hadley, it seemed that he and Lord Talondaire became involved in a disagreement over who should assume command of our squad. And though I mean no disrespect to either lord, I found it all rather foolish for men of the same side to be prattling on as such," he paused, "I told you when last we spoke about what happened in Rosewood. Well, there was a group of men-at-arms on foot," Bel cleared his throat, remembering, "Watchmen known to me, commoners on guard. There were only four of them, but they fought together with pike and shield as one, and though in the end they were captured—and later beheaded by Vaston Delon, who had command of the Plague Prince's vanguard—for a time, they held their own against at least a score of armored horsemen."

Sir Galen nodded. "They say that it's cavalry that wins wars," he said. "Heavy horse thundering across the plane. However"—he paused to take a sip—"in the fighting between Grantis and Dwerin, the legions of the senate have often been able to turn away many a mounted charge. In fact, without knights or nobles, the Grantisi make use of very little cavalry aside from light horses used mainly as skirmishers or scouts—much like the younger Valendian prince, the one they call the Prince of Bells."

Bel fought to keep his composure. "My name is Briden Winfred..." he began repeating over and over again in his mind.

"At any rate," Sir Galen continued, "if I've learned anything over the course of my career, it's that discipline, fellowship, and trust are the principles that make fine warriors, as I imagine was the case with your pikemen. History is full of examples." The knight sighed. "Show me a soldier who seeks only his own glory, and there also will you find a graveyard glutted with men who mistakenly called him their friend."

Or brother. Bel could not help but think, though he said nothing.

Sir Galen emptied his goblet, shook his head, and patted Bel on the shoulder. "Well, Sir Briden, I will leave you be." He smiled. "Though, as always, I enjoy talking to you. However, I have noticed a number of young ladies who appear to have been watching you these last ten minutes or more from the dais near the minstrel gallery, and the fractious muttering of an old soldier is the poorest of company by comparison."

Bel glanced in the direction Sir Galen indicated and blushed at the coquettish smiles of the young ladies. His chest, knotted with a trail of longing, reached far across the Bloodline to the south. "You often speak as if you were an old man," he said quickly, turning away. "Though I've not noticed any gray among your hair."

The elder knight laughed quietly and unconsciously ran a hand along the crown of his close-cropped, sandy head. "I might say the same of you." He grinned. "At any rate, enjoy the feast, and we shall see each other again very soon. Farewell!"

Yet it was a full two weeks before Bel saw Sir Galen again, out upon the Reginal plain. As the men of the Tower's Guard mustered on the field, their commander arrived to meet them upon his great searoan stallion, Tempest. Only once before had Bel seen a searoan, and from a distance—Squall, that belonged to the Snow Prince Gislain. However, "belonging" was perhaps not the proper word. For according to the stories, the searoans of Galdorn, like the spirit hounds of Perindal, were no normal beasts but rather blessed by the Brethren upon their creation with wits matching those of a man.

Both horse and rider bore polished plate embellished with silver leaf that shone brighter than the sun. Upon his right shoulder, the commander wore a small crest bearing the arms of Andoch, but his black tabard, like the kite shield he carried on his left arm, bore the White Horse of Gasparn. A simple long sword rested in its sheath strapped to his baldric, and in his right hand, he carried his lance. According to the stories, neither the point nor the shaft had ever broken, and as was appropriate for a man called the Tower, the weapon's name was Spire.

Yet none of these things explained Bel's awe or the reason that the sight of the captain made him gasp suddenly in surprise. For when the general, Sir

Marcus Harding, removed his helmet and gazed out sternly upon the men of his new command, he did so with Sir Galen Helm's light-blue eyes.

"Be welcome, men," the Tower said. "My name is Marcus Harding, and though I have met most of you already, let me congratulate you again on your performance in the joust and in the melee. His Majesty King Marius was quite pleased with the display and in the wake of the Battle of the White Wood this past Falcontide against Prince Dermont the Black Plague, a battle that I know many of you were present for, the tourney rallied the support of both the common and the noble, and they stand united behind us now in our efforts to end this war."

"However," he said, "therein lies our task, and the road ahead of us is long, and as the winter months approach, covered in snow."

Beside Bel, another knight muttered, "What makes an Andochan think he knows the first thing about snow?" Bel did not know his name, but his tabard bore a scarlet rooster on a white field.

The rider next in line, whose arms were a blue lily on a silver field, agreed. "Shame enough to have a foreigner leading us in the first place," he said. "If we're not careful, we'll have women fighting like the south."

"To be honest, though," said the first, "I rather like facing an army full of women. It makes the taking of prisoners that much sweeter…"

Bel tried to keep his attention on the Tower as he continued speaking—of quarters, camp followers, billeting for pages and squires—but the snide chatter of his false-friends stirred his ire, and without thinking, he muttered under his breath, "Bastards."

The two knights exchanged a glance. "*Pardon me?*" hissed the Knight of Lilies.

Bel fixed the two noblemen with a glare of disgust before returning his attention to the Tower.

"You see, Gurney," said the Knight of the Rooster. "It's as I told you. He's that Sir Briden who dropped out of the melee."

"Ah yes," the Knight of Lilies replied. "Now I remember. Though you know what they say, 'First to fall in the tourney field, first to fall in the battle.' I, for one, doubt it will be long."

"Sir Gurney, Sir Briden, Sir Trenton?" the Tower's voice called out suddenly. "Are there questions?"

"No, my lord," said Sir Gurney.

Bel shook his head. "No, my lord."

Sir Trenton, the Knight of the Rooster, paused. "Actually, my lord," he said, "I was just asking Sir Briden about the melee, and since I did not have the opportunity to see how he fights, I was inquiring if he might like to face me in a friendly duel."

The Tower's eyes narrowed, but at the far end of the line of horsemen, the first rider, Lord Talondaire urged his horse forward. "My lord Tower," he said, "it does seem a fine idea, and to be honest, Sir Trenton speaks the truth. How are we to rely on Sir Briden in battle if not one of us have seen how he fights?"

Sir Gurney and a few others voiced their support.

At length, the Tower sighed wearily, and when he spoke, his voice shook. "No wonder that after a hundred years, you men of Gasparn were but a hair's breath away from losing this war," he declared. "No wonder your king and country so lament the loss of Prince Gislain. For truly, he seems to have been the last real fighting man among you, more concerned as you are with strutting like roosters than battle. And hear me now, gentlemen, I have little patience for pissing contests and duels." He nudged his mount forward, and the great horse began trotting from one end of the line of riders to the other.

As the Tower passed him, the Young Talon raised a hand. "My lord," he grunted, "You do us all a disservice!"

The horse stopped short, and the Tower turned in his saddle. "I do you all a what?"

"A disservice," Talondaire said, "we have already proven ourselves to you in the tourney. We deserve more courtesy than that."

One by one, the other knights dropped their eyes to the ground. The lordling had fired a stone over the Tower's wall, and now he must face the counterassault alone. Sir Harding turned Tempest around and slowly approached the young knight. However, when he spoke, his voice was soft, hardly more than a whisper.

"How old are you, Lord Talon?" he asked.

"One and twenty."

"And how many battles have you fought in over the course of those years?"

Talondaire averted his gaze from the Tower's eye. "I had the honor of fighting in the Battle of the White Wood, and then later, I rode beside Lord

Giles Pronet when he commanded the reserve force as your lordship captured the Black Lion at Roanshead. I fought in a number of skirmishes against bandits on my father's lands and took first in a number of tourneys. Including this most recent one. I also have the pleasure of naming King Marius himself as my mother's second cousin."

The Tower brought Tempest up alongside Talondaire's palfrey. "So the answer to my question," he said, "is but two."

"I suppose it is," the young noble said, adding, "my lord."

The Tower turned away and returned to his place in the center of the line. "Lord Talondaire," he said, "please take the place on the other side of Sir Briden."

The Young Talon looked up at the general, his eyes seething with rage.

"Go on."

Talondaire grunted and wheeled his horse around, swiftly galloping to his new place at Bel's left. No one else said a single word.

Sir Marcus cleared his throat. "Gentlemen," he began again, "tell me. What is the function of the heavy cavalry?" The general scanned the line of riders. "Sir Linton?"

In the place where Lord Talondaire once stood, the other victor of the melee spoke, "The charge."

"In most armies, yes," Harding said, "the knights line up along the battlefield, and in one great rush level their lances and ride head-long into the ranks of the enemy infantry. The sight and sound alone are often enough to cause the enemy ranks to break and run while the riders simply ride them down." He paused. "However, what if the enemy doesn't break? What if their infantry holds strong? Or what if the field has been sown ahead of time with caltrops or the men you face employ tactics like the Grantisi tortoiseshell, or they employ longbowmen like in Baronbrock, firing off volleys and retreating behind palisades?"

None of the men had any reply.

"Gentlemen," the Tower continued, "an army that believes in brute force over brains can only win for so long. For clearly, your enemies in Valendia do not intend to simply line up and charge away at each other like two bulls fighting over a mate. The Plague Prince already proved that by using corpses to sack Whitemane without even breaching its walls. You cannot expect him to change his methods, sitting as he does beneath his pavilion, safe and sound, behind his reserves. Nor does this mean, however, that we must become like him, trading honor for victory, slaughtering ten thousand women and babes for the purposes of defeating no more than a thousand defenders. Yet we must fight *wiser*. We must rely on our wits. Now follow me."

Bel and the other knights followed behind the Tower as he led them further out across the field away from the city. There, long lances trailing pennants had been driven into the earth. "Now," the Talon said, "you will recognize on each pennant the arms under which you fought in the tournament. Find your place and take up your lance."

As the riders did as they were told, the formation began to take shape, and Bel soon recognized it as a large, solid triangle with the Tower atop Tempest in the very middle. "This," he said, "shall be out first formation, which we will know as the Sky, and the three points of the triangle, where Sir Briden, Sir Linton, and Sir Ballard are standing, shall be known as the Sun, the Moon, and the Stars. Now when we ride, we ride together *in formation*, following the lead of the point I call out." He paused. "So when I say we ride for the Moon, you will know which direction to face your mount. Understand?"

Grunts of assent sounded among the men, though not without an undercurrent of skepticism. However, the general ignored it. "Sky Formation!" he shouted, his deep voice echoing across the plane. "To the Moon!"

Slowly, the triangle moved following Sir Linton, though the riders struggled to maintain their individual horse's pace. After a hundred yards, Harding shouted again, "To the Sun!"

Like a capsizing vessel, the formation turned to follow Bel. Bel bit his lip, urging Banshee on at an even pace, and he tried to feel the locations of the nearest horsemen without turning. At length, the general called out again, "To the Stars!" and so forth for the rest of the afternoon.

However, by the time the Tower finally called the men to a halt, the triangle had, for the most part, maintained its shape, and though a few of the men seemed to mutter under their breath, most were silent.

"Good work, men, though we still have a long way yet to go!" he shouted. "The Sky Formation was a tactical pattern utilized by the Imperial Horse-Lords in the Days of Old Calendral long ago. From this position, we can turn at any direction, charging and withdrawing to charge again like a hammer striking against an anvil, and easily reform into any number of other formations as the situation demands. However, we will save those and many other drills for another day, though rest assured, learn them we will: cavalry formations, infantry formations, and many more. But, for now, you may return to your pavilions or your lodgings in the city, and tomorrow, we will begin again."

With a collective sigh, the riders of the Tower's Guard broke ranks and went their separate ways. Bel hung back a bit to watch the Knights of Lilies and Rooster and Lord Talondaire. When they had gone on ahead, Bel nudged Banshee onward to return to where he and Jarvy were still staying among the few remaining tents. A moment later, Bel heard a snort and looked to his left to see Marcus Harding and Tempest beside him.

"Sir Briden," Harding said.

"My lord," Bel said swiftly, saluting after the Gasparan fashion.

Harding returned the salute with a wave. "I wanted to apologize for the farce," he said, "Though if it is any consolation, you were not the only man to meet Sir Galen Helm."

"There is no need to apologize, my lord," Bel said. "Though, to be honest, I shall miss Sir Galen. I had grown rather fond of the old knight."

"And he of you," the Tower laughed, "though I find that on many occasions, the true measure of a man can only be taken when he believes that no one is watching."

"True," Bel said, "my father used to say something similar." "Actually, it is along those same lines that I wish to speak to you."

Bel felt a stab of terror. "My father?"

"No," Sir Marcus said, "about the true measure of a man." Bel blushed. "Oh."

The Tower brought Tempest to a halt. "Sir Gurney and Sir Trenton," he said, "you know that now you will have only become their target. Perhaps for Lord Talondaire too."

Bel nodded. "Yes, I know."

Sir Marcus sighed. "I know I told them that I do not abide dueling," he said. "However, I think that it may be a good idea if you... perhaps arranged something with them in private."

Bel paused. "You *want* me to fight them?"

Harding nudged Tempest, and Bel and Banshee followed. "No," the general said. "However, I do want you in this unit, and a great part of that depends upon cohesion. To move as one, to fight as one, each man must have the respect and the trust of the others, as we spoke of at the feast. My concern is that if the other men do not find a way to respect you, they will try to ruin you and therefore destroy the entire company."

"I see," Bel said.

"So," Harding said, "do you think that possible? I have the sense that your experiences at Rosewood alone have granted you significantly more experience of real combat than any of those three, and I would hate to have to cut you loose for such an absurd reason."

"Yes, my lord," Bel said. "I will see it done."

"Good," the Tower said. "Then I look forward to seeing matters resolved."

CHAPTER 24:
THE SANDSTONE

Galdoran's main guardhouse, the Sandstone, was a solid rectangular building that, in spite of its name, had been built upon a foundation of dull gray masonry topped with a second story of wattle and daub, which in many ways gave it more of the appearance of a craftsmen's guildhall or a market house than a barracks for the red-cloaked kingsmen of the city watch. Upon first entering, Thom was surprised to find a row of long wooden tables set before a central hearth, and were he not so preoccupied with his own abject fear, he might otherwise have found the room to be rather pleasant.

Only two men were on duty when he arrived, sitting idly at one of the tables playing dice, and when Thom entered and asked after the constable, they paused at their game only long enough to inform him that the Hammer was out, but if he liked, he was welcome to await his return in one of the wooden chairs near the front corner of the hall.

With exaggerated gratitude born of anxiety, Thom did as the guardsmen instructed and set to watching the door impatiently for either the constable's return or Lughus's eminent arrival, for he knew that sooner or later, Goldimop would come after him, as always, if only out of guilt over pummeling him during their fight.

In truth, Lughus had not hurt him nearly as much as he had let on; however, after a lifetime together, Thom knew his friend and his ways better than he understood his own. He knew that Lughus would never simply run out on Crodane without first speaking with him, without allowing the man at least some chance at an even say. So for their own good, then, Thom knew he had to act, to force Lughus to forego stalling, to forego propriety, and act before it was too late. For a Blackguard was not someone to trifle with. They were the worst possible villains, save perhaps the Warlock himself. Treacherous, vile, cruel, and Thom knew that if they did not get to safety with all possible haste, they would never get another chance to escape.

A Blackguard! The word alone was like the cry of a wolf on a moonless night. There were plenty of songs and stories about Blackguards—and most of them were frightening. Even the best of them, where the villains still met their end at the hand of a loyal Guardian hero, was enough to give Thom nightmares as a child. There was the tale of Daren Buck the Spear, who led an army of rogues against the Baron of Crofton in the Brock and burned seven villages before Sir Lendis Porin the Candle finally brought him to justice. Then there was Narwen Straver the Wagon, who turned slaver, kidnapping good folk from the villages along the Andochan coast to sell to wealthy scoundrels out of Tulondis and Kord at the markets of the Sorgund Isles. Thank the Brethren, the legends say he incurred the wrath of Galdorn himself and was lost in a storm at sea. The Hand that slew Lord Willowood and his whole family while a guest of honor in their home, the Hare that ran off with Lord Abern's only daughter, the Clover who took to banditry and terrorized the highlands south of the Firranies—all villains, all thieves, all murderers, and all of them, thankfully, dead. For the only good Blackguard was a dead one, as the men of the Order always said, and it fell to the constables to make certain of it.

Not for the first time, Thom was very glad not to belong to the Chancellor's Tower. True, it was only a small number of men—only those anointed with rank and title—that were ever actually sent to hunt the Blackguards (most constables seemed to do little more than collect tithes or organize patrol rosters for the kingsmen of the local garrisons), but the thought of having to hunt down such dangerous men was far too unnerving. As an apprentice to the Loremaster, the worst one had to fear on a day-to-day basis was a paper cut.

Thom took a deep breath and wiped his sweaty hands on the hem of his cloak. His stomach was beginning to ache, and he was considering whether or not to interrupt the dice game to ask one of the guards to direct him to the privy. He wondered how long he had been waiting and how much longer it would be until Lughus and the Hammer arrived. "Lady save us," he whispered quietly and began digging through his rucksack for a snack—only to discover that in his haste, his little figurine of Galdorn must have somehow fallen out of his pack.

For a split second, Thom's vision went black, and he felt his forehead growing hot and moist with sweat. He wondered if the Brother would take offense to his carelessness or if the loss of the statue was a sign that the gods had abandoned him. What if, as punishment, Galdorn had delayed Lughus long enough for Crodane to catch him or confounded the Hammer enough to allow the Blackguard to escape?

"O Brother," Thom whispered, his voice catching in his throat, "Forgive me…" His chest heaved with every breath, and he fought to keep from sobbing openly in front of the guards.

At least, he reminded himself, for right now, *he* was safe. No man, a Blackguard or not, would be foolish enough to try to break into a guardhouse. Besides, why would Crodane be after him? Thom had not gone out of his way to inform the Hammer that he had been their guide. If anyone, it was Lughus that Crodane was interested in, for he had already killed Lughus's father (or so Harlow had warned). Thom was a nobody tagging along. Surely, Crodane would not trouble himself with killing him?

Besides, Galdoran was home port to half the Andochan fleet, readying now for war, as well as the casting off point to reach the prison isle on Lockton. It was utter foolishness for Crodane to have brought them all the way to the city as it was. And to think, Thom scoffed, trying not to focus on the acidic churning of his stomach. He had once thought Crodane rather clever.

Before long, the two kingsmen finished their game and began another followed by another, but still, neither Lughus nor the constable had appeared. A full hour must have passed, and the pain in Thom's stomach was now making him worry that he was going to either soil his pants or vomit on the floor. The edge of his cloak was clammy with sweat from his hands, and wet circles soaked his tunic around his underarms. When, suddenly, the door to the guard house opened, much to his disappointment, it was only another pair of red-cloaked guards.

"Who goes?" one of the guardsmen called, pausing to glance over his shoulder as he boggled the dice in a wooden cup.

"It's us."

The new guards removed their nasal helms and set them on the table, one of them pausing long enough to notice Thom.

"Who's that?"

"Waiting for the Hammer," said one of the dice players.

The guardsman nodded and turned away from Thom to pour himself a cup out of a clay pitcher on the tabletop. "He may be waiting a while," the man said. "Harlow caught the scent, and you know how he gets when he's vexed."

"Good thing for us he told us to mind the place here," said the other dice player.

"Aye," said the new guard. He wiped his brow with the edge of his cloak and took a long drink. "We're only back on account Conad took a slash to the arm from this one. Thanks be the surgeon says it's only a flesh wound."

"Bled something awful, though," said his partner. "Two fucking Blackguards is as many days. Can you believe it?"

"At least Conad'll make it through. With thems as going off to Dwerin for the war and poor Treva cut down by the big fella the other day, I'd hate to lose anymore men."

"Aye, else, it'll be double shifts for the likes of us through to the end of the winter."

"Fucking Blackguards."

"Anyway, the Hammer told us to head back here after seeing to Conad. Told us to watch for two boys. I assume that fat one over there's one of them."

"Mayhaps," one of the dice players said, "no one tells us nothing."

One of the newly arrived red cloaks flicked his wrist and knocked the wooden cups of dice over, scattering them over the floor. "Bastard!" growled the players; however, the guard simply laughed and refilled his drink.

Forgotten again, Thom listened closely as the guards gossiped. From what he could gather, after the trouble in the marketplace was settled, Constable Harlow and a dozen kingsmen headed to the docks where the Hammer had heard a report that another Blackguard was sneaking around (and Thom remembered now how suddenly the Hammer had fled at the mention of Crodane seeking passage on a ship). The men began searching ships and talking to crewmen, piecing together a description of one man in particular that Harlow seemed to know.

"Crodane, the Hammer calls him. Said he was a soldier to one of the Barons in the Brock. Harlow remembered him from back when he was still serving under old Commissioner Dowden who was ambassador to the Lord-Baron in Highboard."

"Crodane? What kind of name is that? Sounds more like a bird than a man."

"Well, you should see him fly," the first guardsman continued. "We did. Walking down the wharf, Harlow gets this odd look in his eye, and his face went pale, see. When up on the gangplank to one of the ships is this man."

"What did he look like?" asked a dice player.

"Tall with brown hair, scruffy looking. He carried a longsword and wore an old mail hauberk. Looked like a mercenary when I first saw him."

Thom's stomach lurched. "It *was* him."

"Bloody fools, those Blackguards. Too proud to bend the knee, so they live like vagabonds wandering about the streets or preying on the weak. Worse than bandits. And to think, you ever heard of an Anointed who didn't live like a king in Titanis? I'd sell me own mum to be anointed."

Thom's ears perked up, and were he not so afraid, he would have smiled. "I knew it," he whispered to himself. "He *was* anointed. The fact that he was a Blackguard just proves it."

"Aye, I'd sell your mum too but can't say as I'd get much for her."

"Shut up and finish the story."

"All right, all right," said the soldier. "So the Hammer, he calls him. Shouts out some old taunt or something I didn't quite get. Anyways, for a long moment, they just stand there, staring at each other, and neither one moved. Then all of a sudden, the Blackguard draws his blade and cuts a rope on the ship, and barrels start rolling everywhere. Sailors are running about shouting, and Harlow sends us lads after him while he himself heads down the dock to try and cut him off. But, instead of going for the Hammer and trying to fight him like the big fella the other day, this Crodane charges the twelve of us."

"All twelve?"

"Aye, all twelve!"

"And still, you couldn't take him?"

"Well, there's the thing. Conad's in front, and he goes for him, but in a flash, the Blackie knocked his sword out of his hand and had him on the ground wounded, bleeding all over. On the gangplank, he had the advantage because he was higher and the way we filed in, we could only have tried to take him two at a time. So we backed up, hoping the sailors, pissed as they were about their cargo, would try and get him from behind. Before they could though, he leaped off to the dock, probably a good eight feet, and off he runs into the streets knocking over carts and crates as he went. Harlow sent the other lads after him and told us to see to Conad."

"And the Hammer's still after him?"

"Aye, but from the sound of it, it was the bloody riots all over again with all the carts he was overturning. People started looting and shouting Grantis this and heathens that."

From his chair on the other side of the room, Thom piped up. "Excuse me?" he said. "Excuse me, sirs?"

The kingsmen paused and exchanged a glance. "The Hammer's still not back, sweetheart," one of the dice players said. "We'll let you know when he is."

"I know he's not back," Thom said. "But that man, Crodane. *I* can tell you where he is."

"Can you now?" said another soldier. "And how would you know that?"

"Because I was the one who told the Hammer where to find him in the first place," Thom said smugly.

"Oh really," said another soldier. "And how'd you know that?"

Thom hopped out of his chair and walked over to their table. Up close, he could see that the men were smiling at him, though he could not tell if their smiles were out of kindness or mockery. He chose to believe the former. "Well," he said, "my friend and I—his name is Lughus—we're apprentices to the Loremaster in the capital, or we were until Rastis sent us off to learn more. Lughus was to go to Baronbrock, and I was to..." Thom paused. "Anyway, that's beside the point. Rastis hired Crodane as our guide on account that he's Rastis *Glendaro*, like the barony in the Brock. I imagine the Hammer knows him if he was working for the ambassador like you said."

One of the guards stifled a laugh.

"Darling," said another, "how old are you?"

Thom's eyebrows furrowed. "Six and ten," he said, "why?"

"Well," said the red cloak, "I've never seen a girl your age with a set of tits that big before!"

The other soldiers erupted with laughter, and suddenly, Thom dearly regretted his former boldness. He fought the urge to cry.

"I'm a boy," he muttered.

"Sure, you are," said another guardsman. "Pay no mind to him. His eyes are bad."

"And his ears," snickered another.

A thick lump formed in Thom's throat. "I'm trying to be helpful," he said. "Crodane is at the Sunfish, or he will be, come dark. He was supposed to meet us there tonight."

"Well," said another guardsman, "we'll be sure to tell the Hammer. You can go back to your seat."

Thom nodded miserably, but as he was about to turn, another guard called him back. "Wait, a second here," the man said. "Did you say you was an apprentice to Rastis Glendaro?"

Thom shook his head and failed to notice the guard wink at his fellows.

"Well, if that's true," the man said, rising from the table, "then we'd be ignoring our duties if we didn't do our utmost to keep you safe."

"Aye," said another. "And think how angry the Hammer would be if we didn't show you the proper hospitality."

Thom felt uncertain. He didn't like the tone of the man's voice. "I'm fine waiting here," he said, "though I thank you."

"Nonsense," said the guardsman, "we'll show you to the special room." He stood up from the table and lifted a heavy ring of keys from on the table next to his dice cup. "Come on."

Thom breathed a heavy sigh. His eyes traveled from one man's face to another, and though he did not like the look of them, he felt he had no choice but to follow.

The guardsman led Thom through a door on the side of the room that opened into a hallway. "That there's the Hammer's office," he said as they passed on their way to another door at the end of the hall. "Though until he returns, you can wait in here."

"What is this room?" Thom asked.

"It's the waiting area," the guard said, unlocking the door. "It's where men await transfer out to Lockton."

"Lockton?" Thom repeated as the guard ushered him into the dimly lit room. "But that's the *prison!*"

"Trust me, lad." The guard smiled, and Thom heard a snicker as the faces of the other red cloaks appeared in the doorway from the main hall grinning with mirth. "There's no safer place in all of Galdoran."

"No!" Thom squealed, but it was too late. The guard gave him a rough shove from behind that sent him bounding over onto the cold stone floor of an open cell. Peals of laughter echoed from the hallway, and with a heavy clang, the door slammed shut behind him, trapping him inside. "You can't do this!" he cried. "Please! I need to speak with the Hammer! I need to speak with the Hammer!"

"We'll be sure to tell him." The guardsman laughed.

Thom babbled something incoherently and broke down into heavy, shuddering sobs. His hands brushed a clump of wet, sodden hay strewn about the floor, and in the dim light of the single, barred window, he spied the outline of an overturned bucket. The smell of urine burned his nostrils, and he felt his body tightening up, readying itself to vomit.

"You see that, Magnus," the man said, rattling the bars of the adjacent cell. "We've gone and brought you a little girlfriend."

"Go fuck yourself," a voice growled from the darkness.

Thom's eyes widened and searched the room, slowly adjusting to the lack of light. In the cell next to him, lounging against the bars, an enormous figure sat shrouded in darkness.

The guardsman laughed. "I forgot how funny you look in there, shorn like a sheep!" he said, fumbling with the front of his trousers. "So funny that I nearly pissed myself."

There was the sound of a splash, and Thom heard shuffling as the prisoner beside him muttered something and leaped to his feet. Thom was amazed. He was taller than Hob and at least as muscular.

"You fucking bastard!" he shouted, "You try to piss on me again, and I swear to the gods that when I get out of here, I'll cut your fucking cock off and shove it down your throat!"

The guard was undeterred. He buttoned his trousers and grinned at the prisoner through the bars. "You know, Magnus," he said, "it's true what they say. A Wrathorn without his beard is like a bull without his bollocks."

"Oi! Yarley!" called one of the other guards from the hallway. "It sounds like they're coming back!"

"I had to take a piss." The guardsman took a step back toward the door. "We'll let the Hammer know you came to call, my lady," he said to Thom, "until he's ready to see you, though, enjoy your new friend. Magnus here knows loads about Blackguards, don't you?"

The prisoner remained silent, and another call sounded from the hall. "Good night, ladies," the guard said and shut the door.

Thom's sobs grew louder and more violent in the darkness. Lying on his belly among the straw, he could feel wetness soaking into the cloth over his knees. His eyes burned from the terrible odor of the cells and from weeping. All he had wanted was to be safe and to do the right thing, yet it seemed that no matter what, he was ridiculed and bullied. In Titanis, it was always Pryce who would go out of his way to pick on him. Then it was those men in Lenard's Crossing at the Kingfisher. Today, it was Lughus—his friend—who had attacked him for trying to save his life, no less. And now, guards of the kingsmen, for no other reason than their own amusement, locked him up like a common criminal in a cell that reeked of shit and piss. In his misery, his stomach gave a great lurch, and he heaved forth its contents, splattering the slimy stones of the floor with vomit. In the cell next to him, Thom heard the other prisoner—Magnus—sigh.

"Great Bear's bloody cock. You did *not* just throw up in here."

Thom gave a heavy cough, cleared his throat, and spit on the floor. "I'm sorry," he stammered, gasping for air.

Magnus growled under his breath and, without warning, began pounding with his fists against the bars—a sound so loud that Thom nearly wet himself.

"Let me out of here!" the prisoner shouted. "I am Magnus Bloodbeard, and I swear in the name of my ancestors that when I get out of here, I will slay every last one of you and drink wine out of your fucking skulls!"

Thom's heart thundered in his chest with fright. He gave a great, heaving sob, and his breath escaped in a loud, miserable wail.

"Would you stop crying!" Magnus shouted.

"I'm sorry!" Thom whimpered.

"Then stop!"

"I can't!"

Magnus returned to his seat on the floor in exacerbation and pressed the palms of his hands to his ears. Out of cold, abject terror, Thom fought to control himself and, after a few minutes, seemed to have gained at least some measure of success. His wailing had settled to a loud sniffling accompanied by an occasional whimper. Out of the corner of his eye, he saw Magnus lower his hands.

"By the gods, you're fat," he said.

Thom wiped a thick river of snot from his upper lip. "I know," he said miserably.

Time passed. The light through the window was becoming steadily weaker, and the shadows lengthened. Thom lay on his back like an overturned turtle. The Hammer had not returned—or at least not called for him. Again, he wondered at the misery that seemed to accompany his life. Somehow, he sensed, Lughus was not coming. He was gone, either killed by Crodane or run off on his own, leaving Thom to rot. To think that only a few short hours ago, Lughus had named him not simply his friend but his brother. Is this how brothers treat each other?

"Is this how brothers treat each other?" he whispered aloud.

"My brothers killed each other over which one of them got to fuck a peasant girl first after a raid," Magnus observed in the darkness, "Lucky for the girl, the other men simply killed her. Slit her throat. But at least she got to die without being raped."

Thom said nothing. Every word the other prisoner uttered felt like another little needle poking into him. But Magnus, if he was aware of that fact, continued the conversation undeterred.

"What is your name?"

Thom said nothing. He shut his eyes, hoping to give off the appearance that he had merely uttered nonsense in his sleep.

"Boy!" Magnus called again. He reached through the bars and roughly shook Thom's foot. "I said, boy! What is your name?"

Thom took a deep breath. "Thom," he said, "they call me Thom Fatty."

Magnus suddenly broke into laughter, and Thom wondered that he could reach an even lower depth of shame than he already had.

"Thom Fatty?" Magnus grinned. "If a man asks you your name, why in the world would you ever call yourself that?"

"That's what they call me," Thom whimpered, "because I'm fat."

"Aye, but you don't hear other men name themselves Bob Shithole or Walter No-cock." He laughed and shook his head. "What a stupid thing to name yourself."

Thom sighed miserably.

"Well, boy," Magnus continued, "what have you done for them to put you in here?"

"Nothing."

"What's that?"

"Nothing."

"Nothing? Not stealing sweet rolls or making off with some hostler's pies?"

Thom shook his head, and only then realized that in the darkness, Magnus probably wouldn't have noticed.

"No," he said.

"So if you don't deserve to be in here, then why'd you let them?"

"I don't know."

"Well, that's stupid."

Thom felt a flash of anger in spite of his fear. "Well, what have *you* done?"

Magnus snorted a laugh. "Lots of things," he said, "everything. Pick a crime, and I've probably done it. Murder, thieving, smuggling, any of it and all." He paused. "Though in this case, it seems your friend the Hammer locked me up simply for being drunk and choosing the wrong bunch of mates to fall in with—though rest assured I plan to settle accounts with them once I get out of here."

Thom gave a shudder. He'd escaped one villain only to find another.

Magnus picked at his teeth and spit on the floor. "In fairness, though, I did kill one of his men in the process. Split his bloody head open, helm and all."

Thom thought back to what the kingsmen had been talking about. "Are you the other Blackguard?" he asked.

"So they say, but the word means nothing to me."

"It means you were anointed by the Order of the Guardians, and you refused to pledge yourself to the king."

"Does it now?" Magnus snorted with amusement. "So to be called a Blackguard is a complement? I'll be sure to call myself such the next time a man asks me my name. For the only thing I'll pledge to the Guardians is the edge of my fucking axe—as any true Wrathorn should."

Thom swallowed a lump in his throat. "You're Wrathorn?"

"I am, or at least I was."

Thom peered into the darkness, and though he could not make out Magnus's features clearly, he could tell from his silhouette that— as the guard had mentioned—Magnus's hair had been cropped short, and he had no beard. In what little had been written about the Wrathorn and their ways, one thing was known for certain. A Wrathorn man's beard was the mark of his manhood, and as such, they were cared for meticulously—braided, oiled, bejeweled. Even among the "civilized" like Hob, shaving was tantamount to castration—and as such was often a punishment inflicted upon Wrathorn prisoners of war. It was said that the captives taken in King Kredor's battle with the Thorwick Clan were all publically shorn before being executed, and many of the Andochan knights afterward would pin the braids of the vanquished to their armor as souvenirs. Pryce had once bragged about having one, though neither he nor his father had fought in the battle.

"I was supposed to go to Wrathorn to write a book about your people," Thom muttered.

Magnus laughed. "Good luck with that. The only use they have for books and paper is for wiping bums. If anything's worth remembering, we put it in a song. Easier to remember and no need to know how to read."

At long last, Thom heard the sound of footsteps, and with a loud squeal, the iron lock on the barracks door turned, revealing a red-cloaked kingsman, though not the same one as before. "Boy!" he called from the doorway. "Is there a boy here who is apprentice to the Loremaster?"

Magnus leaned against the bars. "Look around you, you cunt," he said to the guard. "You've got two options, and do I look like a boy?"

The guard eyed Magnus with disgust but remained silent as he unlocked the door to Thom's cell. "The constable wishes to speak with you," he told Thom.

Thom rubbed his eyes and stood up in the darkness, remembering, then, the filth that had soiled his clothes. He did his best to rub himself clean, but as he followed the guard into the hallway, he could still faintly smell the odors of the cell.

"Hey, guard!" Thom heard Magnus yell as the kingsmen was locking the door behind him. "How about some food, eh?"

"Oh," the guard said, "did I forget to bring it with me? No matter, they'll just bring it to you in the morning."

"Aye, they'd better. I'll need something for dessert after I eat your fucking heart!"

In the hours that had passed while Thom was in the cell, the number of guards in the Sandstone had more than doubled, and ahead of him in the main hall, they sat lining the tables for the evening meal. Thom's mouth watered as the scent of beef stock and brown bread reached his nostrils, and his stomach yearned tragically for but a single cup of broth. However, the guardsman stopped short of the hall just outside of the door to the Hammer's quarters and, at the response to his knock, ushered Thom into the room.

It was often said that though the Chancellor bore the Light of Justice, it was the Hammer, who enforced the rule of law. The first man to bear the title in the days of St. Aiden was a man by the name of Yorick Burns, a carpenter (hence the Hammer), and like Aiden, a man who fought back against the injustices of the Warlock after his own village was put to the torch. After Kalius Wrogan's defeat, Burns was one of the many who remained in Andoch to assist Halford Drude in the creation of the new realm, seeking any Dibhorites that still wandered free and enforcing the new King's justice in what was, by some historical accounts, a free but lawless land. Willum Harlow, the current man to bear the title of the Hammer, was, like his predecessor, a staunch believer in justice and an enforcer of the law. Early in his career, as the kingsmen had said, he made a name for himself in Baronbrock as an assistant to the Andochan ambassador, aiding the Lord-Baron in brokering the Galadin-Marthaine Peace. Then, after being elevated to the rank of constable, Harlow fought against pirates out of the Sorgund Isles terrorizing the southern coast. So successful was in delivering justice that their hanged corpses were said to have lined the shores thicker than the pennants upon a tourney ground.

Twice since, Harlow was offered and turned down further promotion, preferring the action of the field rather than the politics of court. This prompted the Chancellor to create the rank of "chief constable" to award him the honor due to him and to acknowledge his authority in matters of law where the simple word of a constable may not suffice. It was this man who had approached Thom at the cathedral and this man who he stood before now.

When Thom entered, the Hammer was silent, seated at his desk reading a roll of parchment. He was not a large man, nor was he small, but rather squarely average—unassuming even, dressed as he was in the simple garb of a member of the middle class (comfortable, functional, practical) in hues of black and gray that matched the peppery hair sprouting from his temples. Were it not for the chain mail hauberk beneath his tunic and the insignia of his office stitched over the right side of his breast, one might easily mistake him for a merchant or a clerk.

His face was long and somewhat hollow, with narrow cheeks, a long, thin nose, and a heavy brow shadowing two dark eyes. Neither beard nor mustache framed his thin lips, which seemed unnaturally straight and unused to either smile or frown, while the point of his chin seemed sharp enough to cut stone.

When he finished reading, he sighed and glanced at the young man seated at the small table against the wall to his right. "Send word to Lockton that we will be sending them the barbarian after all. I had thought to have him sent to Titanis to face execution before the King. However, the Marshal will make for a much better prize."

"Yes, my lord." The young man nodded, scratching furiously with his quill.

He was a scribe, Thom could tell by his robes, but not one known to him. However, this was not necessarily surprising since, often, the scholars and sages assigned to other cities across Andoch trained apprentices of their own. Thom had simply been lucky enough to study with Rastis.

"You had best tell Commissioner Barnabus that he will need to send someone to assume command of the kingsmen here while I am gone," Harlow continued. "Send word to Lord Chandren at the castle and Admiral Franik on the *Lion* as well. Between the three of them, I'm sure they can find a temporary solution. I will stay through the evening to ensure that the city has returned to order and that this damned looting has finally stopped. However, at dawn's first light, I intend to depart to continue the pursuit."

"Yes, my lord."

The Hammer sighed and, for the first time, turned his attention to Thom. "I see you failed to bring your friend," he observed.

"I'm sorry, my lord," Thom stammered. "I thought he would follow me here, but…" He shrugged. "You've not had any word from him, have you?"

"I have not," said the constable. "Though I have seen him, still in the company of the Blackguard, I might add. For all we know now, he may very well be dead. Considering your failure to bring him here, I hope, for the sake of your conscience, that this is not the case."

Thom's chest heaved with a deep gasp. "Surely, he can't be dead!" he cried.

"There is no telling what a Blackguard might do, particularly when cornered," the Hammer said simply. "Thus, I suggest you double your efforts to cooperate with me in our hunt. I would hate to have the death of one of my own fellow constables on my head, and though I know very little of how the Loremaster operates, I doubt that you would care to shoulder that burden either."

"Of course not, my lord!" Thom gasped. "I mean, of course, I'll help you how I can."

"Then I need you to explain to me, in full detail, all that has transpired since you left the capital. Leave nothing out."

"Of course, sir," Thom said.

He waited for a moment while Harlow spoke quickly to his scribe, instructing him to record Thom's story word for word, and with a nod, Thom began. He spoke first of their assignments and the ride on the barge, followed by the brief stop in Lenard's Crossing and the duel with the mercenaries. Next, he spoke of the days in the currach on the river and, finally, of their arrival in Galdoran the previous night. Throughout the tale, the Hammer remained silent, regarding each word Thom spoke without expression. Something about this put Thom in mind of Royne when the lanky apprentice was in one of his particularly cynical moods, and he couldn't help but feel a latent resentment, as if somehow Harlow was forcing him to submit to a test. Before long, he began to sweat, and yet again, his stomach tied up in knots. When he finally finished with an abbreviated account of the argument at the Sunfish, Thom took a deep breath.

"I suppose that's it."

The Hammer exchanged a glance with the scribe. "You recorded everything?" he asked.

The scribe nodded. "Yes, my lord."

Harlow returned his attention to Thom. "I will need you to sign your name to the transcript of your statement asserting that it is true."

"Yes, my lord," Thom said. The scribe offered him the quill, and carefully, Thom signed. Suddenly, he remembered his rucksack and his own writing paper, left hours ago in the main hall while he waited for the constable to return before they put him in the cell. He wondered if Harlow was fully aware of the way the guards had treated him—bullying him and mocking him, forcing him to sit for hours behind bars beside a criminal.

"Tomorrow," the Hammer continued after Thom returned the quill to the scribe, "I will be leading a number of men north in pursuit of your friend and the Blackguard. While I am gone, you will stay here in the Sandstone and await my return. If the Brethren are kind, you will not have to wait long, and I will then personally escort you and your friend back to Titanis."

"Back to Titanis!" Thom gasped. His heart leaped with joy. "You mean, I won't have to go to Wrathorn?"

Harlow seemed suddenly annoyed by Thom's outburst. "My orders say to return you, so that is what I intend to do."

The constant ache that had gripped Thom's insides for the past month eased, and he sighed with great relief. "Bless you, my lord." He could not help but smile. "Thank you."

"Yes," the Hammer said. "However, while I am gone, I would ask that you remain in your cell."

Thom stopped. "I'm sorry. What?"

"As you were told, a cell is the safest place for you."

"Next to the barbarian murderer?"

"The Wrathorn Blackguard will be gone in a day or two," Harlow said, "and I assure you that locked in his cell, he can do you no harm."

Thom's former relief was instantly forgotten, replaced once again with fear. "This is a barracks. Surely, there is another place for me to stay!"

"This is a barracks, a barracks of the King's soldiers, and you are not a member of the watch, are you, apprentice?"

"No, but—" Thom's heart thundered in his chest. "It was unkind for the men to put me in there in the first place. I am not a criminal. I am an apprentice to the Loremaster. The kingsmen have no right to treat me so unkindly. No right at all."

The scribe shook his head disapprovingly; however, the Hammer simply folded his hands atop his desk.

"You say the kingsmen were unkind to you."

Thom was reticent. "I do."

"Kingsmen, who act as the representative of the King himself," Harlow said, "am I to believe then that you are suggesting that the King himself was unkind to you?"

Thom's eyes went wide. "Of course not!"

"Then go. I have no more time to waste on you. We will speak again when I have your friend. Farewell."

Before Thom knew what was happening, the red-cloaked guard had entered the room and shuffled him out into the hall. Part of him thought fleetingly about continuing his protest, hoping that the guards would have pity and perhaps allow him to join them in the hall; however, when he recalled that they were the very ones who devised locking him up in the first place, he gave up. There was no use in complaining, for not a single person cared for Thom, not ever. Even he no longer felt like pitying himself. He wondered why the Brethren had allowed him to live such a worthless, wretched existence and why a man like the Loremaster would ever have agreed to take him in. He suddenly felt very weary, so weary that when they reached the cells, he went into his and lay down in the straw without a word. Even the rancid smell of piss and vomit no longer bothered him, nor did the presence of the Wrathorn Blackguard. He just wanted to sleep, and perhaps in the morning, he would not wake up.

Yet wake he did, some hours later, though it could not have been much more than an hour after dawn. He still lay in his cell, the surface of the flagstones cold and covered by a thin patina of greasy film. Two red-cloaked kingsmen brought him a small bowl of burnt porridge and a cup of dingy water, which they set upon the ground between the bars.

"Wake up, Titty-Boy! Breakfast!"

Thom recognized the guard who spoke as the man who threw him in the cell. The other was one of the dice players. Despite how repulsive the white, pasty gruel appeared, Thom realized that he had not eaten since the previous day. He scurried across the floor, eager for the meal. However, before he could reach it, the guard kicked it with his boot, tipping it over into the straw.

"Whoops!"

322

Thom stared at the overturned bowl longingly as the porridge spread slowly along the crenels on the floor.

"Look at him," the guard said to the other. "Bet you a silver, he still eats it."

The other guard laughed. "You're wicked, Yarley. You know he's not a prisoner."

The guard, Yarley, shrugged. "So what? The Hammer's gone after the other one. Why not have some fun?" He knelt on the ground in front of Thom's cell. "Come on, Piggy. Eat it. Go on, give it a try."

Thom continued to stare at the porridge and followed it on his hands and knees as it continued to spread across the dirty floor toward the bars separating his own and the Wrathorn's cell. His eyes burned, and he could feel the tears welling in his eyes. He *was* hungry, pathetic, and miserable. Yarley leaned down closer. "Come on," he called gently. "Come on, darling. Think about how good that porridge must taste. So warm, so tasty. Go on, try it."

Thom reached out his finger and dipped it in the porridge. It *was* warm.

"That's right," Yarley continued, "Come on, darling—"

All at once, there was a sudden flash of movement and a great popping sound, like the noise a fresh log makes when thrown on a fire. Thom's eyes snapped up from the porridge. Less than a foot away from him, he saw Yarley's eyes bulging from their sockets like hard-boiled eggs. His face contorted in agony, and though his mouth opened as if he was shouting, no sounds came out. In tormenting Thom, the guard forgot himself and drew too close to the bars—close enough for Magus to reach out around him and hug him, crushing him in his powerful arms.

The second guard stood agape at the agonizing horror of his friend's death. Yarley's limbs shook in a frenzy of final, involuntary spasms and suddenly fell limp. "Lady save us! The bastard's loose!" the remaining guardsman shouted and ran out down the hall to raise the alarm.

Magus released Yarley and let his body drop like a stone to the floor. "I told you I'd kill you, you fuck!" he growled and spit on the corpse.

Thom felt numb as so many powerful emotions swelled within him. Time stood still as he stared at the tiny red blood blisters that had appeared all over Yarley's nose and the way his tongue lolled like a giant slug out of the side of his mouth.

"Toss us the keys if you can reach them!" Magnus snarled. "Hurry! Do it now!"

Thom shook his head and wiped his eyes. "What?"

"The keys!" Magus shouted. "On his belt! Get them and give them here, or I will kill you next!"

Hurriedly, Thom did as he was told. For a split second, he was hesitant to touch the corpse, but the Wrathorn's might was more than enough motivation to overcome his fear of the dead. Once he had the keys, Thom passed them through the bars, and Magnus freed himself from his cell. Already, the other kingsmen were hurrying back to them from the hall. Magnus searched Yarley's body for a weapon and took up the dead man's dagger. Thom scurried to the rear of his cell and cowered in the corner.

"Lady save me!" he whispered over and over, hiding his eyes and plugging his ears against the ghastly sounds, "Lady save me! Lady save me! Lady save me!" When he finally opened his eyes again, the bloody bodies of another three kingsmen had joined Yarley's corpse on the floor. One had its throat opened from ear to ear, a second's chest had been punctured in half a dozen places seeping red gore, and a third lay still twitching its final death throes. Surrounding all three, a great red sea steadily spread.

Warm urine trickled down Thom's leg, and his jaw locked, preparing for him to be sick. Through the open doorway, he could still hear the sounds of battle with Magnus roaring and shouting curses above the clamoring din. Thom's heart beat faster and faster, and with every new scream, he found it more and more difficult to catch his breath.

And just as suddenly as it had begun, the fighting stopped, and there was silence. The whole ordeal had taken less than five minutes.

Still, Thom remained in his cell, uncertain of the results of the battle. For all he knew, no one was left alive, and he began to wonder if that were the case, if anyone would ever find him.

At length, there was a heavy stumbling in the hallway, and shortly thereafter, Magnus appeared, painted with blood from head to toe. He carried a bloody sword in one hand and a flanged iron mace in the other. He pushed his way through the door, stepping over the corpses, and allowed himself to fall back in exhaustion against the wall before sliding down to the floor. Thom watched him, wide-eyed and terror-stricken, wondering if the Blackguard had come to either die or claim him as his next victim. To his surprise, Magnus dropped the weapons and tossed the key ring back through the bars.

Thom eyed the big man curiously.

"Let yourself out," the Wrathorn said. "Just give me a moment to rest, and we'll be gone." He took another deep breath and wiped his bloody hands on his tunic. The sun must have fully risen, and in the full light of the window above them, Thom could see the barbarian clearly. He was taller than Hobart, though a bit younger, and from the scruff just beginning to grow in on his shorn scalp and whiskers, Thom could tell that the Wrathorn's hair was reddish-brown. The skin of his arms bore both the scars of numerous battles and an odd assortment of swirling tattoos traced in black ink. His tunic and trousers, soaked now with blood, had been shoddily stitched from simple sailcloth, and from the shade of his tanned features, Thom guessed that he was a man accustomed to the sea.

Hesitantly, Thom unlocked the door to his cell. "What do you mean, 'we'll be gone'?" he asked.

Magnus yawned, wiped his fingers again, and rubbed his eyes—eyes like flint. "My axe is here somewhere, and I want it back," he said. "We'll also need new clothes if we're to make it out of here unnoticed. Food, wine, probably money, and other loot too. We'll need it."

Thom shook his head in agitation and rubbed his hands together furiously. "No, no," he said, "I mean, what is this 'we'? Why do you keep saying 'we'?"

Magnus pointed at Thom and then back at himself. "You," he said slowly, "and me."

"What?"

"*You* are coming with *me*. If you're to write a book about the Wrathorn, I'll see you do it right. Else, I'll snap your neck like that one over there," the sight of Yarley's corpse brought a smile to Magnus's lips, "You see how his head went like that? What a piece of shite."

Thom breathed a great sigh and, for what seemed the thousandth time in but a few short days, resigned himself to his fate.

"Yes, sir."

Magnus burst into laughter at Thom's inflated wretchedness, only to abruptly pause. "Did you piss yourself?" he asked.

CHAPTER 25:
CRODANE

In his room at the Sunfish, Lughus sat upon the edge of his bed, staring into the darkness of the empty hearth. Streaks of afternoon light somehow found their way through the grimy windowpanes, and somewhere outside, a seagull laughed at the ringing of a ship's bell.

Lughus sighed. On his back over the top of his cloak, he had donned his leather rucksack, and across his lap rested Pryce's dagger and Stokes's blade. Strange, he realized, that this assortment of things should amount to all his worldly possessions and that two of them, he still could not bring himself to refer to as his own.

It had been nearly an hour since Thom had gone, and although Lughus's first impulse was to follow (at least to apologize for lashing out at him), something about running off just did not seem right. The utter randomness of it all bothered him, though no less than the oddity of coincidence, and if studying history had taught him anything, it was that life was anything but random. There was an order to all things set into place by Father Alantir himself when he first called forth the other Brethren into being out of the swirling chaos of the primordial Abyss. Lughus needed to focus on that order now, that divine truth. He needed to think first and then act, not the other way around.

Thom was driven by emotion, by passion, and while this had its place and was often its own form of strength, it could also be a crippling weakness. Bard's tales and history both bore witness to countless tales about the dangers of impulsiveness, men who charged off too eager for battle only to leave their homes undefended, over-zealous generals who, in their lust for victory, spread themselves too thin, heroes so driven by love and affection that their great romance led only to tragedy and despair.

Royne, on the other hand, would consider the cold, hard facts, pure logic, causes, and effects. To Royne, people were not people; they were numbers, variables, calculated into the larger arithmetic formula to arrive at the most probable conclusion. Yet this, too, had its limitations, as espoused by history, for kings who saw their people as nothing more than pawns often fell from grace to cruelty, strategists who wantonly sacrificed their soldiers for the ends to justify the means, a political marriage to join two houses that only served to darken the unhappy couple's souls.

No, Lughus thought, perhaps neither would do. Perhaps order itself was an illusion? But then, what was left? Chaos? No, surely not. There must be something in all the nothing. There must be a reason. There must somewhere be a Truth. Perhaps there was a balance, a middle ground between logic and emotion. Was it impossible to imagine that one might temper the other like in the forging of a good blade?

Lughus sighed and rubbed his eyes, wondering if perhaps he should be recording all this in his journal. Sometimes the mere act of writing, the act of inscribing what seemed nonsensical musings, helped to bring light to the dark.

Why would Rastis, and Hob as well, place Thom and him in the bloodstained hands of a villain? The answer was simple and obvious: they would not—unless, of course, they, too, were deceived. Then again, how often did anyone ever deceive the Loremaster? Not once could Lughus ever recall—from history or legend—a moment where the Loremaster had ever fallen victim to such gross deception. However, Lughus thought back to his first meeting with Crodane, what seemed now so long ago in Lenard's Crossing. There was something the swordsman made mention of, something that Rastis may not have told them—something that Crodane knew but had not said.

And now a man claiming to be a constable appears at random with strange tales of Crodane not only being a Blackguard but even more insane, the murderer of Lughus's own father? Madness.

Lughus shook his golden head. Only on rare occasions did he ever take the time to think about his father or his mother or anything about the life he may otherwise have led. For as long as he could remember, they had existed only as phantoms. It was Rastis, Hob, and an assortment of other scholars, maids, and servants who had raised Royne, Thom, and him. They were his family, not two people whose names he had never heard or whose faces he had never seen. He felt the first touch of resentment rising within him, and rising from the bed, he thrust his dagger and his sword into his belt.

Maybe, Lughus thought, he should go after Thom, if only to ensure his safety. He had been gone a long time. The mayhem in the marketplace had made Lughus nervous, as had the sudden announcement of war. Andoch seldom involved itself in the bickering between the other realms, and if anything, the King and the council sent representatives from the Order to serve as moderators to broker peace. However, between Sir Marcus being sent off to Montevale and now the King's Army mustering in support of Dwerin, Lughus could not help but wonder what would become of Termain if the Order had begun taking sides.

What a strange place the world was outside of the Loremaster's Tower, at times exciting, at times upsetting, equally like and unlike any of the legends he thus far devoted his life to reading. Yet perhaps that was the true nature of an adventure; perhaps that was the real reason why Rastis had chosen to send him.

A commotion in the hallways brought Lughus's hand to his hilt, and as he paused reflectively at this new reflex, the door to the room opened, and Crodane hurried in.

"Good. You're ready," he said. "We must go immediately. Where's Thom?"

"Thom's gone," Lughus said.

"What do you mean gone?" Crodane asked, striding past to take up his burlap sacks. Feeling their weight, he doffed them again and began emptying the contents of one into the other. "Where has he gotten to?"

Lughus stood by awkwardly. "He said a man approached him at the Cathedral." He fixed his gaze on the swordsman. "A constable. A man named Willum Harlow. The Hammer."

To Lughus's surprise, Crodane's lips twisted into a wry grin. "And what did this Hammer fellow tell him?"

Lughus took a deep breath, his hand still resting on his hilt. "A lot of things," he said.

"I see," the swordsman said, "I suppose then that he told you I was a Blackguard, a horrible villain, and a murderer."

Lughus felt his blood freeze in his veins. "He also said you killed my father."

Crodane sighed, tossing the empty sack toward the fireplace, and shouldered the full one. "What the Hammer told Thom is true," he said simply. "Though I am certain that he did not tell the tale in full."

Lughus felt his nerve waiver. The simple honesty of the swordsman's reply had disarmed him, and suddenly, half a dozen emotions swelled within him all at once. Crodane, however, did not waste any time.

"In any event, we must go," he said, "we must get across the bridge to reach the north gate and leave the city before the Hammer is able to spread the word among the kingsmen. If we tarry, they'll be watching for us."

Lughus shook his head in confusion. "Wait!" he said. "You don't deny the Hammer's claims?"

"I'll not deny the truth," Crodane said plainly.

Lughus's chest tightened, and his eyes grew wide with disbelief, "You're a Blackguard, and you killed my father?"

"And would again were I given the chance."

Lughus drew his sword.

Crodane barked in amusement. "The space in this room is too confined for the longsword, particularly standing as you are by the bed frame. You would have done better to have drawn the dagger."

Lughus's cheeks flushed with anger and embarrassment. "Silence, Blackguard," he said, "and defend yourself."

Crodane sighed, "No."

The sword suddenly felt very heavy in his hand. "Then I'll have to kill you," he said.

"Then I suppose you will, for I'll not fight you."

Lughus breathed a heavy sigh and felt his eyes beginning to burn. He swallowed the lump in his throat. "Why not?" he asked. "If you intend to kill me too, then why prolong it?"

The swordsman raised an eyebrow. "If I had any intention of killing you, I would have simply let those men at the Crossing do so and be done with it." He sighed. "But come, Lughus, we have no time for this. We must be gone."

Lughus shook his head in disbelief. "Why would I go anywhere with you?"

Crodane's blue eyes flashed. "Because you must," he said, "please."

"You're mad! You're a bloody Blackguard, and you just admitted to killing my father!"

"Boy, if you knew your father, you would not be so quick to stand for him."

"Then tell me!"

Crodane took a step closer, and Lughus raised the tip of his sword.

"Lughus, there is no time."

"Then fight or run, but I'll not go with you!"

"And I cannot go anywhere without you."

That caught Lughus by surprise. "Why?" he asked.

Crodane sighed. "Please," he said, "if you come with me, I promise to tell you everything once it is safe."

"That's a fool's bargain, and I'll not trust a word you say."

"Fine," Crodane lamented. "If you will not trust me, then think on Rastis. Would the old man have sent you to me if I intended you harm? If you trust Rastis, you'll go with me, at least to the crossroads. Please!"

Lughus paused. He did trust Rastis; he had been thinking the selfsame thing but a few moments ago.

"After we escape the city, I will tell you everything, Lughus, I promise," Crodane added. "And if you are still not satisfied, I swear to you that I will return *with you* to the Hammer and submit to the judgment of the Order."

"They will kill you."

"Then so be it."

Lughus was reticent; however, there was something about the whole business that did not make sense, what it was, he could not quite identify, but it was enough to raise his doubts. Rastis would not have sent him into harm, nor would he have entrusted his wards to a man that he did not trust. The same could be said for Hob. As a foundling, Hob could have easily born the label of Blackguard as well, for it was a former Blackguard, the Ox, who had anointed him. Still, there was one last thing to consider.

"What about Thom?" Lughus asked. "He's at the Sandstone."

Crodane sighed heavily. "Then I'm afraid we must leave him behind," he said. "But I can assure you, he will be safe. The kingsmen will not harm him. He has done nothing wrong. However, you and I must still go, and soon."

Lughus continued to consider it. Thom would never agree to go anyway. Besides, he may still be angry after their fight. No, if Lughus was going to chance the Blackguard's offer, the Sandstone was the safest place for Thom to be. He would not play dice with his friend's fate as well.

"Please, Lughus, we *must* go now."

At length, Lughus returned his sword to his belt. "I have your word," he reminded the swordsman. "If I'm not satisfied, then we return."

Crodane nodded. "So be it," he said. "Let's go."

The crowd in the Sunfish had grown considerably as the work day came to a close, and men stopped off on their way home for a drink. The air was abuzz with news of the impending war with Grantis, as well as talk of the trouble in the markets and news of a scuffle with the kingsmen by the wharf. While Lughus eavesdropped on the rumors, Crodane left a pile of coin with the innkeeper, and before long, they made their way out again into the streets.

"So you made it to the cathedral then?" Crodane asked as they passed a duo of guards on patrol. The swordsman offered them a casual nod, and the men ignored him sullenly and moved on. Lughus's pulse quickened, and he marveled at his own madness in agreeing to go along.

"We did," he finally said. "Did you find a ship, or was that a lie too?"

Crodane barked a laugh. "A few," he said, "though we'll be traveling by foot now, I'm afraid." He paused, "And for the record, I have never once lied to you."

"Omission is its own form of deception," Lughus observed.

"True enough," the swordsman conceded.

As they reached the great bridge in the center of the city, the red cloaks seemed to grow in number, and Lughus wondered whether it was due to the rioting and the looting or something else, for he had a feeling that the trouble at the wharf involved his guide, and he wondered if suddenly the Hammer should appear and try to stop them, would he run?

"We'll have to hurry across the bridge here before we reach the north gate," Crodane whispered. "Try to stay close, and we'll lose ourselves among the crowd. They may be searching for us as it is, and I'd rather avoid bloodshed."

"That seems off for a Blackguard," Lughus muttered.

"And what would you know of such things, living your whole life locked in the Keystone?" Crodane whispered, "Let us hurry."

At the north gate, a group of kingsmen stood on watch, funneling the traffic out of the city into two separate queues: one for wagons and riders, the other for folk on foot. Meanwhile, along the wall beside the gatehouse, a group of laborers, under the watchful eye of a man wearing the robes of a Chancellor's courtier, were unloading carts of confiscated trade goods bearing the insignia of the Republic. The Grantisi merchants themselves knelt with their hands behind their heads while another red-cloaked kingsman paced around them in a circle, idly swinging his mace.

"Is this your King's justice," Crodane whispered, "or simple thievery? I thought it was the duty of the Guardians to protect the common folk in times of trouble, regardless of realm."

Lughus bit his lip sullenly, remembering the wanton looting in the market and the sound of carts being overturned. At least here, the guards had maintained control; however, somehow, that did not necessarily make it seem any better.

When at last they reached the portcullis, another pair of kingsmen eyed them briefly and, much to Lughus's surprise, simply waved them on.

"Why did they not stop us?" Lughus asked. "We're both armed. They didn't even check our packs for goods."

"There's no law against carrying weapons in Galdoran, remember?" Crodane said. "And armed men leaving the city, if anything, is a blessing in the eyes of a guard. No, those men there." He paused, pointing back to the merchants on their knees. "Dark hair, dark eyes, olive skin, they're Grantisi— or at least look enough like it to be robbed."

Outside of the gate, the road was still crowded with wagons and carts waiting to enter the city or getting ready to depart. Atop an embankment, to the left of the road, a large stable for the boarding of both riding horses and draft animals overlooked the banks of the Imperial while on the right stood a small tavern called the River Rose. As they passed it by, Lughus spied a copy of the Proclamation of War nailed to a posting board beside other miscellaneous notices and calls for laborers.

"I still can't believe any of this business about the war," he said, "Rastis would never stand for it."

"Aye, but Rastis is one man, and the council sits four more," Crodane replied, "There are dark days ahead if the wisdom of the Loremaster goes unheeded."

"Strange you award him such respect, considering you betrayed the Order."

"I betrayed no one. Though in a sense, you could say it is the Order that betrayed itself."

"What do you mean?" Lughus asked when, suddenly, Crodane's arm subtly shot out and brought him to a halt.

In the doorway of the tavern, two more red-cloaked kingsmen suddenly appeared. Near the paddock to the stables, two more stood searching among the stalls.

"Stay calm," Crodane whispered. "The Hammer is inside that tavern."

Lughus's pulse quickened. "How do you know that?"

Crodane did not answer. Instead, he stood still along the roadside watching the influx of travelers on foot, by wagon, and by horse. Suddenly, there was a flurry of movement, and a man in dark clothing burst forth from the tavern door. Beside him, Crodane stood like a hunting hound, ready to spring. His blue gaze traversed the thirty yards or so that separated them from the tavern, and somehow, in spite of the passing traffic, Lughus could sense the two men's eyes meet.

"I swore you an oath to return you to the Hammer if you are not satisfied with what I have to say," Crodane said quickly. "Will you honor your part to go with me at least as far as the crossroads?"

Reluctantly, Lughus conceded. "I"—he sighed—"I suppose."

"Then ready yourself," Crodane whispered, "and thank you."

Without further warning, the swordsman leaped forward and knocked a passing rider off his horse. "My apologies!" Crodane shouted, hopping up into the saddle. He offered Lughus his hand, and grinding his teeth in consternation, the boy accepted and climbed up behind the swordsman on the horse.

Crodane spurred the beast forward as voices began shouting in agitation from the tavern, and at the stables, the other two red-cloaked kingsmen began running toward them in alarm. Lughus felt his heart thundering in his chest in time with the horse's hoofbeats, and the edge of his cloak flapped out behind him as they picked up speed.

Faster, they charged through the crowds as wagons, carts, and folk on foot scurried to clear their path. The horse was not a fine creature, nor was she very fast; however, even carrying two, the dappled mare could still outrun a man on foot, least of all a kingsman weighed down by a byrnie of metal scales.

At the far edge of the stable's enclosure toward the open road, Lughus felt his nerves tighten as Crodane drew his sword. Before them, slowly plodding along, two men led an ox-drawn wagon heavily laden with hogsheads of ale. At the sound of the speeding hooves, the brewers ran to cower at the roadside, and with a quick swipe of his blade, the swordsman slashed the ropes that kept the barrels bound and sent them rolling out, forcing any pursuers to dive out of the way.

"That should buy us some time at least," Crodane barked, glancing swiftly behind them.

Already, the giant casks were wreaking havoc among the traffic of the road, and only a single red-cloaked kingsman made it through the gauntlet. However, he quickly gave up his pursuit, knowing better than to attempt to carry on alone.

Before long, the north gate, the stables, and the river were far behind, and in the western sky, the sun steadily sank toward the far horizon. From the east, a cool, salty breeze blew in from the sea. Again, Lughus wondered at his own madness in fleeing the guards. Everything sensible about him told him he was walking further into doom, yet at the same time, his heart seemed to urge him onward, if only to find out the truth, the truth about the swordsman, about his father, and about himself.

At last, when Galdoran stood but a tiny set of glimmering lights on the horizon, they reached the crossroads where the road running north split. To the northwest, it would continue onward toward Lenard's Crossing and beyond it to Titanis; to the northeast, it grew into the coastal road running all the way along Andoch's eastern coast to the border with the Brock. Without even needing to be reminded, Crodane brought the horse to a stop, and when he and Lughus had both slipped from the saddle, he slapped the horse on the flank. It ran off again south to return to its master.

"Time is short," Crodane said, "and surely, the Hammer and his men are already in pursuit. However, you've been more than patient, and I owe you answers."

Lughus backed away and leveled his gaze at Crodane; to his surprise, the swordsman looked away. "Tell me of my father. You admit that you killed him, that you'd do it again," he said. "Tell me why."

334

Crodane breathed a heavy sigh and walked a few paces in a wide ark around the wooden post of the road sign. "All right," he muttered, and for the first time since Lughus met him, he seemed to show hesitancy, even weakness. "Where do I begin?"

"I assume the beginning," Lughus replied, surprised to hear himself speaking with such venom at someone his elder. "Though if you want to avoid the Hammer, I suggest you speak quickly."

Slowly, Crodane nodded and halted in his pacing. "You say Rastis told you nothing of this?" he asked.

"Never."

"Left the burden all to me then," he said, "as it should be, I suppose."

"Speak," Lughus commanded impatiently, "I'm weary of this stalling, and with the Hammer behind us, there is no time for further delay."

At length, the swordsman gave a resolute nod, and his blue eyes blazed. "Fine," he said, "though listen close. For this is not an easy tale to tell."

"I was born the son of a fine craftsman in the employ of Baron Arcis Galadin of the Brock," Crodane began. "My father was an artisan of great skill, and it was said that he was one of the few men capable of working Holy Oak in all the land. Baron Galadin took notice of him, and after commissioning his services for work in both the Cathedral of St. Aiden and the castle, he decided to keep him on permanently."

"I was just a boy when we moved into the Houndstooth, that is, Baron Galadin's castle, though I will never forget it, nor will you, I hope. It's not the same as the Keystone or the Alluvial. It's simpler, stronger, built upon a rocky crag overlooking the town proper with squat round towers marking the corners of the walls along the outer bailey, and taller, thinner turrets marking the walls of the inner ward. In the center, rising high above it all is the great keep. If ever there was a place that one could feel safe, it was within those walls!"

"As it was, the Baron's seneschal was a man named Wolfram of Parth, a big man and strong, but always quick with a laugh and light on his feet. He and my father became fast friends, and noticing my interest, it was Parth who first taught me the ways of the sword."

"But how does this concern, my father?" Lughus asked.

Crodane waved his hand and nodded. "I'm getting to that," he said. "Also in the castle, of course, with Baron Galadin, lived his family—his wife, Lady

Emelia, and his daughter, Luinelen." The swordsman paused and, from beneath his furrowed eyebrows, caught Lughus's eye. "Luinelen was your mother."

Lughus felt a heavy weight suddenly fill his chest. "What do you mean, my mother?" he asked.

Crodane took a deep breath, "Your mother was the daughter of Baron Arcis Galadin, which makes you his grandson and heir—and a direct descendant of St. Aiden Galadin himself."

For a long moment, Lughus stood still, staring at the dust of the roadway swirling about Crodane's feet. His hands felt numb and tingly, and the tips of his fingers seemed to pulsate in time with his heartbeat. "You can't be serious?" Lughus laughed in disbelief. "This is madness." However, the swordsman's eyes betrayed no hint of laughter, only earnestness and a heavy sadness that made the boy look away for fear that the man might weep.

"It's true," he said, and from around his neck, he drew a small object tied with a leather string. "Here"—he held out his hand— "this was your mother's signet ring. Consider it yours, and consider it proof."

Lughus accepted the ring and held it between two fingers. In the dusk light, a tiny golden hound rampant glimmered upon a field of blue.

"The Golden Hound of Galadin," the swordsman said. "Set in Baronial Blue."

"A Spirit Hound," Lughus whispered.

It was an image he had seen a hundred times in a hundred books. It was the seal of Galadin, the seal of the Blessed Saint. Yet now, it seemed something more. The fine cut of the gold band seemed made for the thin, dainty finger of a woman's hand, and attached to that hand would be a slender arm, a round shoulder, and a body Lughus did not know. However, in his mind's eye, he perceived a vision of light, a kind voice, and a soft, loving touch.

"You look just like her," Crodane said. "The dark gold of your hair, the shape of your eye, your nose, your chin. They're all hers, and your grandfather's, and all the Galadins before you." He paused and shook his head. "You know, I saw you arrive on the barge at Lenard's Crossing, long before you and Thom even reached the inn. But I couldn't approach. The very sight of you reminded me so much of her."

Lughus ran a hand through his hair and rubbed his eyes. His legs felt weak. Somehow, he knew the swordsman was not lying, but that did not make his words any easier to accept. "What happened to her?" he said at last. He tried to remember his studies of Baronbrock, but his mind felt muddled, and he found it difficult to think. "What was she like?"

"What was she like?" Crodane smiled. "What was she like?" He paused and gave a short laugh. "She was"—his grin widened—"she was very funny, though most wouldn't know it, probably because she was so clever. And, of course, she was very beautiful. Men talk of the archduchess of Dwerin—Lady Josephine—that was the daughter of Old Lord Pike, but Josephine was like a moth to your mother's flame. There was a harshness, a coldness to Josephine's beauty, but your mother, by the gods, she was like the sun! I think I can safely say that she was the kindest person I've ever met in all my life."

Lughus bit his lip. "Then you knew her well?"

"I did. For, as Sir Wolfram was your grandfather's seneschal, as his brightest pupil, your mother's safety became my responsibility." He paused to breathe a great sigh and turned away. "But I failed."

"How?"

"Your father."

Lughus's brow furrowed. "What do you mean?"

"She died by your father's hand."

"What?" Lughus said aghast, "What do you mean? Why?"

"Your father's name was Gaston Marthaine."

"Marthaine?"

"Yes," Crodane said, "son of Roland Marthaine."

Lughus shook his head. "The Marthaines and the Galadins have been enemies for a thousand years," he said, "since before the Siege of Three. Why would a Galadin marry a Marthaine?"

Crodane glanced off at the horizon, remembering the Hammer. "Listen," he said, "I will tell you more, about your mother and your father, about Rastis, myself, and all the tragedies that drove you from the Brock, but we have tarried here for far too long." He sighed. "Now you know some of my tale, at least, and though one of the Anointed, my oath of honor lies not with Andoch but the Galadins of the Brock. You, Lughus Galadin, have nothing to fear from me, not now nor ever, but rather in recompense for my failure to protect your mother, the safety of her only son is my duty for all the days of my life. Will that suffice enough for you to come with me? So that I might see you safely installed as heir to Baron Arcis, your grandfather?"

Lughus clenched his fists to keep his hands from shaking, then took a deep breath and slowly placed the leather strand bearing his mother's signet ring around his neck.

"Lead on."

CHAPTER 26:
WHISPER & SHADE

Three days and four nights passed following the death of Young Reid before Brigid had been permitted to leave her room, though, in all that time, not a single person had bothered to tell her why. She had gathered from Livonia's occasional visit to bring her meals that the hall outside her room had been placed under heavy guard, and not simply the usual watchmen who patrolled the grounds, but men in plate and chain armed with kite shields and bearded axes. The old crone said nothing as to the reason (nor did she say much at all, for once), and Brigid soon feared the worst, for she knew Reid's fate could not remain undiscovered; he was far too conspicuous a figure among the court of Blackstone to remain unsought after for long, and in her haste to escape the scene of carnage, she could easily have been careless. Perhaps the blood splatter that soaked her dress had, in her flight, left a trail behind her on the floor all the way to her room. The bloody garment remained, stains and all, where she had stowed it with the Falcon's daggers beneath her bed.

For better or worse, her imprisonment had also awarded her plenty of time to think about him and to stare out of the window across the ward at his tower. She wondered how she would escape with him now or if her actions to save herself from Reid's assault had doomed her to remain forever a prisoner in her own castle, locked away in despair.

The injustice of it all brought tears to her eyes, tears of anger. Her arm was still swollen from when Reid wrenched it, and it throbbed with pain.

Livonia noticed on one occasion when bringing her dinner, and Brigid was forced to concoct a story about slipping in spilled water from her washbasin.

"Foolish girl," the old woman scolded, "you're lucky the cold weather's coming, else your lady mother would be right cross with you for having to wear long sleeves to hide the bruising."

According to Livonia, however, the archduchess was far too busy with another matter to request her daughter be brought to her presence for inspection, a matter that, for some reason, required that Brigid be confined to her quarters.

What would they do to her, Brigid wondered? Most members of the nobility, those few fortunate people who by some strange accident of birth had been—as Alan had put it—touched by the divine, often seemed to regard themselves as the very masters of life and death, threatening the common folk of the castle with the hangman's noose for even so menial a thing as a spilled cup of wine. How often had Alan had grown men beaten or broken for lesser things? And if what Brigid overheard was true, his father, their uncles, and even her own father were worse. She remembered one day two years past when Alan paraded his entourage up along the ramparts of the outer ward so they might watch as down below in the town square, three peasants—two men and a woman—were hanged. The woman and the younger of the two men had apparently failed to seek the Sheriff's permission before they were married, and the other man, the girl's father, was forced to share in the blame. The memory still made Brigid sick to her stomach when she thought about it, and though she averted her eyes during the final moments, she would never forget Alan's gleeful laughter at the sound of their necks cracking.

Yet if the will of the nobility could be so swift, unmerciful, and fickle in regard to the common folk, what happened when one noble killed another? Would there be a trial or a duel or some other strange ordeal otherwise masquerading as justice? Did the sole female heir of a dead archduke outrank the son of one of Dwerin's great military commanders, particularly now that the war with Grantis had been renewed? Not likely, Brigid thought miserably, no more than it would matter that she had only acted to defend herself.

On the morning of the fourth day after Young Reid's death, Brigid was summoned to appear in the great hall before her mother, her uncle, and the other members of Blackstone's court and household staff. As she stood by while Livonia dressed her (like a child might a doll, Brigid could not help thinking), she felt the tips of her fingers tingling with numbness, and her skin—as the old crone was quick to point out—seemed to grow increasingly pale.

"Thankfully," Livonia said in irritation, "you've the periwinkle blue to wear today, though I can't say your mother will be too pleased in her scarlet and tawny. You'll not please the eye seated beside her. If only you'd not taken so much after the Beinns, you might look more like your mother—and act like her too, perhaps."

"I don't want to act like her," Brigid mumbled without thinking.

Livonia answered with a smart slap. "At least now you've got some color in your cheeks," the old woman sneered.

Brigid felt the sting of the old woman's gnarled hand but was too preoccupied to offer much more in return than a cold stare and a single crystalline tear. What would come of this audience with her mother? Would a backhand from an old woman be but the first of many ordeals? Regardless, come what may, Brigid resolved to face her fate with dignity and grace; she would take solace in the fact that for once in her absurd, sheltered life in the castle, she had taken a stand. In her heart, she knew that Reid had left her no choice, that in attempting to force himself on her, he proved himself her enemy, and in accordance with the ways of war, she had cut him down. She had shown herself at the very least, that in the face of wrong, she would not simply consent.

And if doing so earned her a noose and a gibbet of her own, then she resolved to spite Death with a Wrathorn smile, just like the Falcon said.

When Livonia had finished and was satisfied that the archduchess would find her daughter's appearance acceptable enough, Brigid followed the old woman to the great hall. Upon her arrival, she found that most of the court had already assembled and she stopped short, hoping to avoid drawing attention to herself; however, to no avail. All eyes fell upon her at once, and as she glanced uncomfortably around the court, she noticed the usual sea of familiar unfamiliar faces. There was Lord Redden Kilkon of Castle Cragland, Lord Friedan Garnold of Garhold, Sir Donal Pind the elder, Sir Geralt Lotan, the archduchess's elderly seneschal, Sir Ogden Schute, the master-at-arms, Sir Envard Upton, Sir Vernon Pult, Sir Aren Plaice, and half a dozen other landless knights whose names Brigid never learned. Beside each man sat an ornamental beauty—a wife, a daughter, a courtly lover, whose simpering smiles and delicate laughter always seemed to Brigid either the hallmarks of madwomen or the futile resignation of slaves.

In addition to the lords and ladies, favored courtiers and the chief officers of Blackstone's staff were also in attendance, for though they bore no mark of nobility, the services they provided for the day-to-day functioning of the castle, rendered them about as worthy as could be expected from those of common birth. Uncommon commoners, the Lord Sheriff had once quipped—Norben Welch, the chief herald; Jonad, the seer newly arrived from Andoch; Forghan Lutus, the chamberlain; Jan Vaston, the master of wardrobe; Dawson, the Blackstone steward; Parcon, the Blackstone butler; and a wide assortment of more: minstrels, merchants, a trio of cousins, important servants, and a handful of guards. It seemed all would bear witness when the archduchess and the Sheriff decided Brigid's fate.

At length, Livonia put an end to Brigid's gawking with a rough pinch to her swollen arm and ushered her forward to sit at her mother's left. For at the archduchess's right sat the Lord Sheriff, and beside him sat Alan. However, as she assumed her seat and Livonia scurried off to stand at Josephine's shoulder, Brigid spied across the gallery something that caught her breath, for standing among the courtiers was a man with golden eyes.

In an instant, Brigid felt her senses leave her, and for a moment, she feared that she might faint. That it was him—the Falcon—she was certain, for although he had clearly been cleaned and fed, there was no mistaking those eyes. She felt her heart go all aflutter and her cheeks flush; he was far more handsome free of his cell, more dashing. But what was he doing here now? Before she had the chance to risk a second glance, the chief herald called the hall to attention and announced that her grace, the archduchess, was to speak.

As always, Lady Josephine was resplendent, and as the morning sun shone through the leaded glass of the great hall's eastern windows, the archduchess seemed to glow with a radiance of her own. She was dressed in a fine gown the tawny color of the changing forest leaves, with a sash of deepest scarlet around her waist. Her mantle had been stitched from the soft pelts of the red foxes that roamed the mountain steppes, with a tiny fox head adorning each of her shoulders like epaulets. Her pendant, fashioned in the shape of Dwerin's anvil, was forged of solid gold, while upon her brow, she wore a circlet encrusted with garnets and pearls.

With all eyes upon her, the archduchess smiled, and the cold stone walls of the great hall of Blackstone turned warm and sweet as honey. "Now that my daughter has finally joined us," she said, masking her impatience, "we may begin."

Brigid ignored the slight but allowed herself to slouch as her mother began again.

"For some time now," she began, "I have noticed a quiet excitement here among us at Blackstone, and as I understand it, a sense of great anticipation has occupied each of our hearts." She paused and glanced significantly among the assembly, enticing the court's delight and inviting their enthusiasm. "And so it seems that if there is one word that could capture the single source of all our hopes and joys, then that one word is 'betrothal.'"

At this, a low murmur passed over the crowd, and from the nobles to the court officials to the servants in the wings, Brigid felt the myriad eyes upon her. A chill ran down her spine. Was Reid not dead? Had he miraculously overcome two blade thrusts to the stomach, and had they discovered a way to return to him his teeming blood? Or had he somehow returned by the unholy grace of the Warlock to plague her forever like some ghoul from a fairy story, to wreak foul vengeance upon her for refusing his nefarious advances? Her blue eyes grew wide in fear, and she struggled to resist the urge to stare into the crowd of nobles for the Falcon's golden gaze, to beseech him, to implore him to help her escape before Josephine could finish passing her sentence.

At last, when the archduchess deemed the drama had reached an acceptable level, she continued. "Five years past," she said, pausing to issue a melancholy sigh, "My beloved husband and your honored Archduke Danford Beinn met his end at the hands of the Grantisi dogs who threatened our lands through illegal occupation of the Spade. But now, as you are all well aware, with the help of the Guardian-King, Kredor Drude of Andoch, we have officially begun a campaign to retake what is rightfully ours and to avenge our fallen lord."

The assembly broke into a sudden outburst of applause and cheers; Josephine allowed it for a moment and then raised a hand for silence.

"However," she continued, "once our efforts are complete, it is true that we will again be whole in land. But what of our hearts? For the return of the Spade will not return the archduke to us, and it seems that without a true man to rule us and ensure our further defense, our vengeance—our victory— will ring hollow."

Again, Brigid gathered what memories she could of her father. He was so seldom at home that as time went on, she found it increasingly difficult to conjure up an image of his face, and as always, she wondered what type of man he truly was, what type of ruler, and what first drove him away from her mother to incite the years of vindictive antagonism that characterized her parents' relationship for the duration of Brigid's early life. Josephine was the object of desire for every man who met her; what was it that incited Lord Danford's revulsion?

Then again, Brigid thought, mother and daughter were not on the best of terms either, and though the Archduchess enjoyed posing as the Queen of Love from the fairy stories, Brigid had learned long ago that her mother's heart was stone.

"As such," Josephine continued, "I believe that it is time, perhaps, that we cease dwelling upon the tragedies of the past and instead look to Dwerin's future, that we look toward the crowning of a new archduke."

Brigid felt a great lump form in her throat, and she fought to remain calm, for, while every muscle in her body wanted to rise from her seat and run as fast and as far away as she could, she resolved to remain calm and face what was to come. After all, she thought again, the Falcon would soon take her away. He promised.

And at that thought, her breath caught in her throat. Was that the very reason for his miraculous appearance? Had he concluded his business? Was the time for an escape to be now? If only she could have known! She would have found a way to smuggle the daggers with her, for surely the knights of the court would never simply allow them to go. Brigid steeled herself for whatever was to come.

With a dramatic sweep of her gown, the archduchess rose from her high seat. "In the absence of my husband," she said, her voice heavy with spurious grief, "there have been many fine friends to see to the needs of both myself and my daughter. For sadly, in these times, two young women alone in the world may easily fall prey to villainy and deceit. However, of all my advocates, my advisers, and my loyal retainers, though all have proven both bold and true, none has been dearer to me than my dear late husband's dearer brother, our Lord Sheriff!"

At this, Brigid's uncle, Alan's father, rose from his chair and—to the hearty applause of the court, knelt and kissed Josephine's proffered hand before rising again to stand at her side.

The sudden upwelling of so many powerful emotions nearly caused Brigid to swoon. At once, she felt both relief and despair, amusement and disgust, for it was not she who would marry, it was not she who was to become betrothed, but rather, her mother, Lady Josephine, to her uncle, the Sheriff, which meant...

Brigid's brow furrowed. What did it mean? If her uncle married her mother, how could she then name him the next archduke? True, he was the eldest of the surviving Beinn brothers, but Brigid was also her father's daughter. Did a brother's claim outweigh a daughter's if the brother married the widow? Would Alan then become heir to the archduke's throne and usurp Brigid's right? And what of Brigid's other uncles? The four were to share the governance of Dwerin as equals. Would the others accept Darren's elevation to the throne? Brigid shook her head. The trivialities of right and lineage. These were the true concerns of nobles while the soldiers fought the wars and the peasants worked the mines or tended herds. Is this what it mean to be "touched by divinity," as Alan said? Wishing others dead as means to acquiring more? Is that what it meant to be noble?

She thought about these things as her mother, and her uncle continued to speak—of plans, of love, of ceremonies, and slowly Brigid realized that her earlier fears would not come to pass. In fact, it appeared that Young Reid's absence had not even been noticed, nor had he been mentioned in the least. Though, of course, that fact simply brought with it further questions, greater mysteries, and deeper intrigue.

The Falcon would know, she thought; he must, for a man did not go from captive to courtier so easily (if ever). How desperate she was to speak with him, to know the truth, yet she could not even look across the hall at him for fear of betraying their secret acquaintance. At long last, the speeches came to an end, and the archduchess allowed the Sheriff to assume control over the meeting. Meanwhile, she and the other ladies of the court withdrew to Josephine's bower to discuss the impending marriage and to avoid interfering with the more manly concerns of the court: trade, taxes, matters of justice, and of course, the war. Messages had arrived from Graham and Nealen Beinn,

Admiral and Castellan, respectively, regarding relations with the Andochan military and the few early engagements with the Grantisi enemy.

Brigid followed benignly after her mother and the other ladies; though as she rose from her seat, she could not help but chance another glance at the Falcon and, in doing so, met the full force of his gaze. Her heart swelled; it *was* him, for although his face bore an austere expression appropriate to a castle court, she recognized the selfsame spark of mild amusement alight in his golden eyes as if the court and all its fine people were the butts of a private joke to which only she and he were aware. She did her best to hide her blushing, but at a chiding glare from Livonia, Brigid hurried on her way and prepared herself to once again sit.

The remainder of the morning on into the afternoon passed beneath a façade of friendship and a shroud of luxury. Josephine and the other fine ladies of the court sat in a circle, pretending to sew while Brigid and the young "maidens" of the Drove sat among them so as to learn the ways of proper behavior by example. The conversation began, of course, with the competitive fawning over the impending wedding as each noblewoman attempted to outdo the former in what to Brigid seemed an escalating storm of melodrama.

The archduchess on her divan absorbed each compliment with the satisfied smile of an empress out of Old Calendral. At her feet, Brigid sat in silence like a little dog, returning quietly to her role as yet another ornament to her mother's grace, and receding, once again, into her private world of dream.

It was night, and the air was brisk—cool enough that with every breath she took, a tiny wisp appeared upon the breeze like a wayward ghost. Brigid stood before the window of her bedroom gazing out at the Falcon's tower, its spire rising like an arrow to pierce the full moon. Clad in her favorite dress, the simple one her mother hated so, Brigid donned a thick woolen cloak of midnight blue and raised the cowl. Somewhere in the town outside of Blackstone, a bell struck the hour with a deep, resonant gong followed by the much nearer sound of a pair of wings fluttering in the darkness just outside her window. As she drew closer to examine the source, she perceived the glow of a pair of golden eyes.

"It is time."

A hand extended from the gloom, born of a figure enveloped in shadow. When she accepted, the hand closed over her own, gently but firmly, and led her over the windowsill. Before she knew it, she was traversing the uneven black stones of the keep's face, guided carefully by the shadowed figure all the way down to the soft green grass of the inner ward where watchmen bearing torches meandered about like fireflies. Brigid held her breath and faded back against the tower wall to where the darkness was thickest. Her guide put a finger to his lips, slipped free from her grasp, and without a sound, darted out into the night.

Once more, she was alone; however, she was not afraid, for she knew that the shadow man was still near and that he would protect her. So she simply waited and watched as, one by one, the torchlights went out, snuffed like candles in the wind. Before long, her guide returned again to her side. She slipped her hand into his, and they carried on.

Across the grounds, they sped without a sound through the gates to the outer ward past the stables and the barracks to the main castle gatehouse beyond which lie escape and freedom. But upon their approach, a new figure appeared and barred their passage further—an armored guardian clad in heavy plate with red eyes that shined ominously through the visor of his steel helm.

From her side, the Falcon (for she knew it was he who was her guide) leaped forth and drew his twin blades in a flash of silver and gold. The gate guard raised his heavy gisarme and charged, but the Falcon artfully dodged the blow and counterattacked, his daggers slashing like the talons of his namesake swooping down upon its prey. One blade flashed along the armored breastplate sending up sparks as metal struck metal, but the second blade found its mark, and in the light of the moon, the walls of the gatehouse were splattered with crimson spray. However, the wound was not grievous, and the armored figure stood his ground as the Falcon backed a few paces to secure his footing before the duel renewed.

But before the combat could be resolved, the dream disappeared, and Brigid returned to the present, sitting at her mother's side, for, suddenly, at a lull in the conversation, the archduchess voiced a question that tied knots in Brigid's insides.

"Have you all heard the news concerning Young Reid?" Lady Josephine asked blithely.

Among the gathered sycophants, a polite murmuring implied that they had not. Brigid examined the floor.

"Yes," the archduchess said, "it seems that with the war, Young Master Reid has been elevated to full knighthood. Isn't that splendid?"

The ladies clucked with admiration, and the Drove squealed with delight.

"Oh, how grand!"

"Such a gallant young man!"

"I almost pity the Grantisi now!"

Josephine smiled. "Unfortunately, however, with his knighthood, the young man had to hurry away to join his father in the Spade." She sighed. "So I must admit my own disappointment, for he was such a handsome young man, and my dear Brigid was so terribly smitten with him." The archduchess raised a shapely arm and lightly ran a finger along her daughter's cheek as if to wipe away an invisible tear. "Sit up straight, darling," she added in a whisper.

Brigid did as she was told but remained silent and kept her gaze averted, for she was certain that all eyes were upon her, hoping to bask in the drama of what could only be—in their eyes—the greatest of all sorrows. Still, in spite of Josephine's deception, Brigid believed that things had suddenly become much clearer.

No one knew—or at least no one was supposed to know—that Reid was dead, which meant, Brigid suspected, that no one knew that she was to blame either. Life at Blackstone would simply carry on, free of scandal and free of fear, until a time when a proper lie could be crafted to appease the elder Reid. Perhaps he would be waylaid by bandits or spies of Grantis on his way to meet his father? Perhaps he would lose his way and be eaten by a bear? Perhaps he might even be thrown from his horse down a mountain ravine? The lie could take any form, and poor, desperate peasants could easily be found who would corroborate the story or point accusatory fingers at their fellows when threatened or bribed.

What a strange place Blackstone was, Brigid wondered, where it seemed that nothing was ever truly what it seemed, where clean was dirty, and gold was mere coal. Was the whole world like this, or was the castle of the archduke simply unique? Was there ever a place in all Termain where men still cared for Truth?

As the afternoon wore on, the ladies were released to return to their own quarters to change their clothes for dinner. Since the announcement of the betrothal, the evening meal would mark but the first in a long series of opulent feasts and social engagements. Livonia saw Brigid back to her room and, with a few obligatory chidings, locked her within, promising to attend to her dressing in due course, for the archduchess's appearance would require the crone's utmost devotion for such an occasion.

So, weary from an afternoon of idleness, Brigid sat down upon the corner of her bed and turned her eyes once again upon the Falcon's tower. Yet now she smiled, for as the donjon had since become her beacon of freedom, it now stood vacant. The prisoner was no longer imprisoned. Where could he be? She wondered.

To her surprise, the answer came in the form of a sudden movement from behind the curtains, and before her very eyes, the shape of a man came into view. Brigid leaped to her feet in alarm.

"Hello, Mouse," the Falcon said.

For a moment, Brigid stood speechless. Her heart thumped in her chest, and her mind raced suddenly over all the things that, for weeks, she had wanted to say to him. However, in the end, all she could muster was a weak "Hello."

The Falcon touched the tips of his fingers together and offered her a slight bow. "I apologize for intruding upon you such as this," he said as the corners of his lips curled in quiet amusement. "However, I thought it prudent to make certain of your safety, for I hear there is another assassin loose in Blackstone."

Brigid swallowed a lump in her throat. "You know?" she gasped. "But how?"

The Falcon grinned. "My dear Mouse," he said, "how else do you think it is that I am not still rotting in that tower?"

Brigid took a deep breath and walked a few paces away from him. It was strange. Despite how much she had wanted to see him again since that first night of Harvestide feasting, the Falcon's sudden materialization in her quarters made her nervous. She recalled how easily he had taken care of the locks on his manacles; a simple locked door must have been be no problem.

Without looking, she reflected upon his appearance. He was still thin, and his cheeks now seemed a bit hollow, though that was to be expected after the near starvation associated with imprisonment. But he did not seem to be much weighed down by any wounds resulting from the torture that he no doubt was forced to endure at the hands of the Sheriff or the arbitrary tantrums of his son; in fact, quite the contrary. His hair and beard had been neatly trimmed, and the simple black and gray doublet he wore was well-made and new. He was handsome, that was certain, with a roguish flair that outside of the donjon seemed all the more dashing, and though much older than her, she recalled that he had once named her beautiful and now wondered if he said so out of benign politeness, or if he really meant it. Regardless, the longer she kept silent, the more she felt like a fool, and she prayed to the Lady that she was not blushing.

"I see," she stammered at last and folded her arms to keep from nervous fidgeting, "how is it then that you were able to free yourself?"

"Oh, that was simple," he said. "Your uncle simply unlocked the door and let me out."

She shook her head. "I'm sorry?"

The Falcon smiled gently. "I can see that I have made you uncomfortable," he said. "I apologize, Mouse, truly. As I said, my ways are strange. I simply wanted to make certain you were safe and to inform you that, should you still wish it, I am still willing to help you escape with me once I finish my business. Pardon my intrusion."

Brigid shook her head. "No," she said, "I am simply...surprised. You may stay a moment, if you please." Her heart beat faster. "I would like to know what you came to tell me. Truthfully, I still intend to go with you, to leave Blackstone and...follow you." She took a deep breath and felt very foolish.

If he noticed her self-consciousness, the Falcon did not show it. "Well," he said, "a few days ago, your uncle came into the tower all in an uproar demanding to know how I freed myself. Now you know and I know that I could easily do so; however, I did not speak a word of this to anyone, and though it may sound strange, Mouse, I did not believe for a moment that you would have betrayed me either."

"I said nothing to no one," Brigid said quickly.

"I know," he continued. "So for once, I admit, I was a bit surprised, which does *on occasion* still happen, though rarely, and when I informed the Sheriff that I had no idea what it was he was talking about, he was...at first, rather reluctant to believe me."

"Then how are you free?"

The Falcon smiled and walked back to the window. "Well, that is a bit funny," he said, leaning against the sill. "Do you recall what it was I told your uncle just as he caught me in his chamber?"

Brigid thought for a moment. "Alan said something about our uncles sending their regards?"

"Precisely," he said, "and it is this statement that had kept me alive for so very long."

"What do you mean?"

For a moment, the Falcon was hesitant. "How much do you know of your uncles, Lady Mouse, or of the importance Dwerin holds among the other realms of Termain?"

Brigid shrugged. "I know that Dwerin possesses richer mines than any other nation," she said. "And that the arms and armor we produce are considered the best in all the lands."

"True."

"And as for my uncles and my father, I know that they never held much love for one another, but after my father's death, they divided the responsibilities of the realm so that each might be responsible for a different part of the nation until such time as I was married and a new archduke could be named."

"True as well," he said. "But what else do you know of your father's death or of the alliance with Andoch that came afterward?"

"What do you mean?"

The Falcon shrugged his shoulders and paused, choosing his words carefully. "What if I was to tell you," he finally said, "that your father did not die in battle by the hand of an enemy, but rather, in his sleep by the treacherous machinations of his brothers?"

Brigid thought for a moment and recalled Josephine's cavalier attitude in concocting the lies about Reid's death. "I suppose it's quite possible," she said.

The Falcon gave a smirk. "A much cooler response that I might expect for a young lady learning the truth about her father's murder."

"I'm sorry." Brigid bowed her head. "I must seem very cold. It's only that...I hardly knew him. He and my mother did not get along well, and, as for my uncles..." she sighed, "If the Lord Sheriff and his son are any indications of what the other three are like, then I would not think them above cruelty either."

"They are not."

"I am not blind," she told him. "I know that my family is…not good."

The Falcon folded his arms, and she felt the gaze of his golden eyes upon her. "Yet somehow," he said, arching an eyebrow, "you are."

Brigid looked up and caught his glance, then quickly looked away. "You're wrong," she said.

"Rarely is that the case." He grinned.

"No," Brigid sighed heavily, and her voice dropped to a whisper. "I did it," she said. "It was I who killed Reid."

The Falcon's smile faded, though he did not look surprised. "So I suspected, and so I feared," he said.

Her icy-blue eyes seemed ready to melt. "I suppose then that I, too, should be labeled a murderer."

The Falcon shrugged and gave a heavy sigh. "Listen here, Mouse," he said. "Killing is not something that comes easy, but it is not always the same as murder."

Brigid shook her head, and a tear escaped her eye, leaving a glistening trail down her fair cheek. "I didn't mean to," she said, "at least, not on purpose. I…I had no choice."

The Falcon stood up from the window and walked to her side. "Hush, Mouse," he said gently and tentatively placed an arm around her shoulders, "I do not believe you did."

Brigid started at his touch, and her mind suddenly felt very muddled as she struggled to understand what it was she was feeling. Another tear escaped her eye, and then another, and another, and before she knew it, her eyes stung with bitter anguish, and her shoulders shook with heavy sobs. The Falcon drew his other arm around her and very softly patted her on the back.

Why was she crying? Brigid wondered, and why could she not seem to stop? And now the Falcon! Was he hugging her? Did this mean he liked her? Again, she tried to stop her tears but found that they only flowed more freely.

"There, there, Mouse," the Falcon whispered in her ear. "All will be well."

She breathed a heavy sigh and let her head fall against his shoulder, and she realized that she could not remember the last time anyone—least of all her mother—had ever actually hugged her. Yet here was a man who, in barely any time at all, had shown her more kindness than anyone that she could remember. All of a sudden, she felt immensely alone, so desperately alone, and the only one who seemed at all to care for her was this man, a man who, by his own admission, was a murderer. Why did he care what happened to her? What could he possibly hope to gain from being so kind to her? Did he think of her as she had often thought of him? At this, she raised her head, wondering whether or not she should try to kiss him. She had done so from time to time in her daydreams, and he *was* handsome and dashing, like a hero out of a story...

But when she gazed up into his golden eyes, it was not lust with which he looked back at her (for she remembered—and feared—that passion from Reid), nor did she sense it was love (of which she was aware, she knew very little); however, it was *something*, something that stayed her from kissing him and told her that should she try it, he would refuse. For within the smoldering golden glow, his eyes seemed to speak to her without words, to tell a story of their own. It was not that he did not care for her—quite the opposite—but rather that his care for her was not born out of desire or out of romance but out of simple, honest, compassion. And though there was something about him that she still found very dashing, she no longer felt the same strange feelings toward him as she had before. She returned her cheek to his shoulder.

"Would you like to tell me what happened?" he asked gently. "Or would you rather I guess?"

Brigid took a deep breath; she no longer felt anxious or worried but rather free to simply be herself. "He tried"—she sighed—"he tried to force me."

The Falcon's jaw tightened. "Bastard," he cursed. "Are you unharmed?"

Brigid nodded. "My arm is swollen, but otherwise, I'm fine."

"Show me your arm," he said.

Reluctantly, Brigid slipped free from his embrace and rolled back her sleeve. It was indeed swollen, much more now than she recalled. Gently, the Falcon touched it with his fingertips and asked her to rotate her wrist and bend her elbow.

"How much do you know about the Guardians?" he asked, returning to his customary geniality, "Apart from the fact that they live in Andoch and seem to enjoy giving each other funny names."

"Little, I'm afraid," she replied, "although, I suppose, they are Dwerin's allies."

The Falcon smirked. "Yes, 'suppose' is the key there." He paused and rubbed the palms of his hands together. "Have you heard the old stories? About St. Aiden and the Gift of the Guardians?" he asked.

"I know about St. Aiden," she said, "and when Alan cut you, he said you would be healed by morning."

"And so I was, though that doesn't mean the little bastard didn't hurt me." He grinned. "However, do you know why it is that those with the Gift—the Anointed, they sometimes call them—all heal so quickly?"

Brigid shook her head.

"Then here," he said. "Close your eyes."

She did as he told her and, once again, felt his fingers trace along the swelling. Suddenly, she became aware of a strange, cooling sensation as if he had poured a glass of water down her arm.

"Now open them."

She did, and to her surprise, the pain was gone.

"How did you do that?" she asked. "You can heal?"

The Falcon smiled. "Not exactly," he said, and rolling back the sleeve of his own arm, Brigid could see now that the elbow was as red and swollen as hers had been but a few moments ago.

"Those with the Gift heal quicker than normal men so that they might heal the wounds of others," he said. "For me, this should be healed by tomorrow."

Brigid could scarcely believe her eyes. "And all the Guardians have this Gift?"

"All those they refer to as the Anointed," the Falcon said, "Or those they call Blackguards, like me."

"And you say you'll have healed by morning?"

"Most likely, though, of course, some wounds take longer than others, and some can't be healed at all," he told her. "There's no healing a missing hand or a missing foot, and were I to try to heal a mortal wound, I might heal it, though it would surely kill me." He paused. "Of course, in that situation, there are other consequences as well."

Brigid shook her head in amazement. "Remarkable!"

"And also, a rather guarded secret." The Falcon smirked, raising an eyebrow.

Brigid smiled. "I understand."

"Good," the Falcon said, "and it's nice to see you smile again."

"It frightens Death away," she said, "I remember."

"So you do."

And suddenly, Brigid remembered something else. "Speaking of," she said, "I have something of yours." She hurried over to her bed and lifted the mattress revealing her bloody dress and the Falcon's blades.

"Reid's, I hope?" the Falcon said.

Brigid nodded. "Yes," she said, "but I found these." She offered the leather baldric, the daggers' hilts glimmering in the light of the window. "Your talons, Lord Falcon, safe from the clutches of my wretched cousin."

Much to her distress, however, the Falcon's face fell. "Is this what led to your encounter with Sir Reid?" he asked.

"I was returning with them to my room when Reid caught me," Brigid admitted reluctantly.

"Exactly," the Falcon said, "but what if he was not alone? What if that oaf Donal or some other horrid cur had been with him?" He shook his head, and she was surprised to see his face contort into a grimace. "You should not have taken such a risk on my account, Mouse," he said again. "You know well the vile passions of your cousin and his friends. You should not have done this. It was extremely foolish."

His reprimand cut deeply. "I am not a fool. But I thought—"

"You thought wrong."

Brigid was silent. "I'm sorry," she said at last.

At length, the Falcon shook his head and sighed. "Mouse, forgive me," he said. "Far be it for me to reprimand anyone for impulsiveness, recklessness even—Old Regnar would die of laughter if he could hear me now! And do not believe for a moment that I think you a fool. Rather, I do not wish to be the cause should you come to any harm. I would find it very difficult should the blood staining that dress have been yours! Friends do not come easily for one such as me, and I admit to have considered you among the ranks of those few—with your permission, of course."

Brigid reddened with embarrassment. "To speak truly, you are…probably the only friend I have."

"I very much doubt that." He smiled. "But all I ask is that you be careful, and we'll have no more talk of foolishness. At least they're safe and free from the Young Sheriff's clutches." He leaned back against the windowsill again.

"And since the three of you have already made some acquaintance, allow me to introduce you formally."

"To whom?"

The Falcon motioned her over to his side and, in a flash, drew each of the blades. "Now, at first glance," the Falcon observed, "you might have assumed that the blades are exact copies. However"—he traced his finger along the flat, folded steel of each blade and then handed both to her—"what do you notice?"

Brigid carefully inspected each of the daggers, testing their weight in her hands.

"What do you notice?" he asked again.

Brigid took a deep breath. "This one feels slightly lighter," she said. "And this other one here. The blade does not reflect the light near as much."

"Aye"—the Falcon smiled—"you're right." He held out his hand for the lighter blade. "This one," he said, "is called Whisper." He spun the dagger in his hand and returned it silently to its sheath. "The other," he said, holding out his hand again, "is called Shade."

Brigid smiled at the names. "They're beautiful."

"So they are," he said, returning the blades and belt to her. "And if you do not mind, I'd like to leave them in your care for the time being."

"You want to leave them with me?"

"For safekeeping," he said, "if you'll have them."

"You're certain?"

"It's the last place they will look."

Brigid nodded. "Why do you say that? Quite frankly, I'm surprised that they have not suspected me in regard to Sir Reid."

"Oh, they won't look to you for that," he said. "As far as they know, it's a new assassin sent from your other uncles, just as they believe I was."

Brigid's eyes narrowed. "What do you mean?"

"As I told you, five years ago, your uncles conspired to kill your father, and with the help of some friends out of Andoch, they succeeded. Since my arrival, and perhaps as a result of our many pleasant conversations in the tower, the Sheriff, has come to believe that history is now attempting to repeat itself." He paused. "And though, as I said, I would rather you had not taken the risk in recovering what is rightfully mine, I must concede, my dear Mouse, that it was your victory over Young Reid that provided the stroke of luck I needed. For with another assassin on the loose, your uncle believes that he has convinced me that my former employers, who he, of course, believes to be his brothers, have left me to rot and that it would be in my best interests to betray them. As a result, he has offered me freedom in exchange for my services. However, where he sought to use me as his puppet, he has yet to realize that, in truth, *I* am the master dangling him upon the strings."

"But what does that mean?" Brigid said. "What have you done? Is that why he is marrying my mother?"

"Politics is a dirty business, my dear Mouse," the Falcon said. "And I would rather spare you the exact details. Suffice it to say, though, that your other uncles will be most displeased with the Sheriff 's designs at archdukedom, and it will not be long before they are at each other's throats. They will make for confounding allies to the Guardian-King of Andoch when rather than fighting a common enemy, they are too busy fighting among themselves. Furthermore, should they destroy each other and Dwerin find itself without a ruler, I know a certain young lady who could easily appear out of exile to assume the throne that is rightfully hers, perhaps not simply as an archduchess but something more regal. How about a mountain queen or some such? A young woman who cares for the concerns of the common people, who would stand strong against injustice and fight against evil. Do you know anyone like that, Mouse?"

Brigid smiled and shook her head. "You must be joking," she said.

"Usually, but not in this."

"Forgive me if I do not know what to say." She blushed. "That is much to think on."

"Then think on it," the Falcon said, "for as I said, there are many mice in the woodpiles of the world. We are not without friends."

"I will," Brigid said. "But speaking of archduchesses, Livonia may call for me soon. She is sneaky and wicked, and I fear she will find you here."

"True, she is all those things, but she will not find me," he replied simply. "And if you will give it to me, I will dispose of that bloody dress for you when I go, if only to ensure that she will not find it."

Brigid recalled the dress and sighed suddenly with relief. "Thank you! For a moment, I thought to throw it out the window, but I knew the guards would only find it."

"The fireplace would have been a better option." He grinned.

"I suppose that's true..." She blushed. "I was...frightened and not thinking clearly."

"No one will find it now," the Falcon said. He folded the bloody dress over his arm and, in a flash, unlocked the chamber door. "And fear not, Lady Mouse," he said, making ready to depart, "when last we spoke, you mentioned a cage. But know this. You are not in a cage but a room with a hundred doors. Choose any that you like, and I will be there to guide you through"—he grinned—"even if, at first, you find them locked."

Brigid smiled. "Goodbye."

"Farewell, my dear, and again, fear not. We will speak again soon."

CHAPTER 27:
THE KING'S HUNT

Natharis Tainne's elevation to the role of "acting" Loremaster appeared to pass with scarcely any furor. In truth, some changes were made, though small ones (for instance, the Loremaster's quarters had been restored to the fifth floor of the tower as opposed to the much simpler, smaller area Rastis preferred on the first); however, for the most part, activity in the tower continued as usual. Scribes still scribed, scholars still studied, sages still behaved sagaciously, and whether out of fear, futility, or apathy, most saw Rastis's removal and replacement as merely substituting one straw man for another. For the learned men of the Order were primarily an independent lot, often preferring the company of long-dead ghosts from the pages of history books to each other (let alone the rest of the general masses of humanity), so whether it was Rastis Glendaro or Natharis Tainne that bore the Book of Histories made little difference to them.

This indifference, this general lack of concern, Royne could not help but see as a betrayal, and he understood suddenly the solitary nature so common to leadership and the reasons, therefore, why—as was generally uncommon—Rastis had personally overseen the education of the three apprentices assigned to Titanis.

Of all the divisions of the Council of Five, it was true that the Loremaster's was the smallest; however, more noteworthy was the fact that it also laid claim to fewer anointed Guardians than any other as well. In fact, Royne could count no more than six total all across Termain, including

Rastis and the foundling Hob (who frankly would have been much more suited to follow the Warlord).

The reason, Royne conjectured, must be found in the nature of the work and the Loremaster's guiding virtue. Most scribes, scholars, and sages pursued knowledge, and in all the lands, there were few (if any) who could match their understanding of myriad esoteric subjects.

Yet, knowledge alone did not make *wisdom*, for wisdom required something more—application, experience, and example. Wisdom was not found locked atop a tower gazing out over the heads of one's fellow man, as Royne had until recently believed. Rather, wisdom belonged on the cobbles, on the roadside, in the hills and dells, in the markets, and in the town squares. It belonged to both the king and the beggar and could be found in the halls of every palace and the smoke-filled common rooms of every public house if one only knew where to look. Wisdom drove men to write books; knowledge simply filled them up, and a dusty old tome sitting on a shelf was worth nothing until someone opened its pages to read it. Knowledge simply existed. Wisdom required action.

And it was action now that Royne needed, for it was time to put his knowledge to work. It was for this reason that Rastis had kept him behind, and for this reason that Rastis had named him scribe and steward, for there was no doubt in Royne's mind that the old man had anticipated his own arrest, or for that matter, that he had anticipated everything that for the past few months had transpired. He knew that Kredor intended upon pressing the Protectorate just as he knew that Lughus needed to flee, and now that Rastis was locked away, it was up to Royne (and Hob wherever he was!) to see Rastis's plans through to the end.

However, *what* exactly was the end? And *why* was it so important? If Royne was going to see things through, he was first going to have to figure out *what* those things were. If only Rastis had told him, he might have some direction, some plan. However, for now, and for the first time in his life, Royne was going to have to content himself with playing the fool in order to serve a man whom he knew was his enemy, Natharis Tainne.

Natharis Tainne, Royne realized very quickly, was an extremely knowledgeable man. Serving as Tainne's steward, Royne had seen him match wits with some of the Tower's most honored sages and, in every case, laid them all low. For just as it was common among the men of the Warlord's Tower to face one another in a sparring match or a friendly duel, so it was among the Loremaster's men to subtly test one another through seemingly innocent lines of questioning. A question about a historical event here, an intentionally wrong date there, a misquoted passage, or a disproven theory, all passed off as truth—it was a game they often played, and a game that, based on Royne's observations, Natharis Tainne was very much accustomed to winning.

As King Kredor had alluded at the last council meeting, Tainne had studied with the monks of the Lighthouse far off on the eastern peninsula of Castone. The Keepers, or so the monks were formally known, were an organization that predated the founding of the Order of the Guardians, stretching back to the days of Old Calendral. Though they were forced into hiding for their opposition to the policies of Emperor Veirne, the Keepers returned to their studies following the Rise of the Warlock and Aiden's Rebellion. However, in spite of their self-imposed isolation in far-off Castone and a denigrated social ranking in a post-imperial world, the Lighthouse remained the nearest thing the Loremaster's Tower had to a rival.

It made sense to Royne for Lord Tainne to have studied with the Keepers, for he was certainly not a man of war like his friend, the King. Kredor was brash, overbearing, loud, and reveled in the sound of his own voice. Natharis Tainne, on the other hand, was reserved, courtly, quiet even, but his mere presence seemed to add a certain chill to a room. When he spoke, his voice was like a dagger to Kredor's battering ram; one might knock down a castle door, but the other, if used properly, would simply pick the lock, and for a man who was no warrior, something about the nobleman struck Royne as particularly dangerous, which is why, at least for the time being, Royne knew that he could not do anything to overtly challenge either the "acting" Loremaster or the King, as much as he might want to.

Tainne had to know that Royne's loyalty was to Rastis, yet for some reason, Royne suspected that the nobleman desired to keep him close at hand. Perhaps Tainne believed he knew something about what Rastis was up to, which of course, he did not, though he was not about to confirm or deny that fact for the benefit of his enemy. He would allow Tainne to believe he knew something he did not know, and perhaps one day, he would learn what it was he did not know, just in time for Tainne to give up and believe that he did, in fact, not know it.

Oh, how dizzying the games of intrigue could become, how tangled the webs of deceit! Were it not for the fact that Rastis was locked away in the Judge's Tower, the young scribe might almost have found the whole business rather fun. Almost.

As if Royne's stewardship to Natharis Tainne was not in and of itself unsavory enough, it also awarded the young scribe the displeasure of an almost continuous audience with the King. For as Kredor's best friend and top adviser, Lord Tainne's presence was imperative as the King's proverbial right hand; however, as steward to the now "acting" Loremaster, Royne was granted access to nearly all of the inner workings of Kredor's political machinations, another fact that Royne could not help but believe Rastis had somehow contrived long before his arrest.

In terms of the Protectorate, Kredor and Tainne were already moving quickly. In spite of Kredor's claim to merely "support" Dwerin against the Grantisi senate, the soldiers of the Andochan standing army, the kingsmen, were assembling in Galdoran and at the fortresses of Crownwood and Longspire along the Andochan-Grantis border to the southwest. The nobles were rallying their own knights and retainers, and Warlord Rood had already assigned commands to his chosen cavaliers and justiciars. The Hierophant and his prelates preached sacrifice and service at home while, in the other realms, Hagan Shawn's provincials spoke of the first Guardians, the glories of the Guardian Realm of Andoch, and the blasphemies of the Sign of Four. The Chancellor's men gathered taxes and sold confiscated Grantisi trade goods for a considerable profit due to the sudden scarcity of such imports (Grantisi wine, in particular, was suddenly worth its weight in gold). Meanwhile, in Dwerin, the forges sang with the sound of the hammer striking the anvil, and Duke Nealen Beinn ordered the first forays into the Spade to avenge his fallen brother, the archduke. Indeed, all seemed well for the new King and his adviser, much to Royne's chagrin, so in celebration, it was deemed appropriate for Kredor to indulge in his favorite pastime, the Hunt.

Thus, in the miserable autumn drizzle, Royne was forced to follow his new master, tramping around in the mud in search of a boar or a bear or whatever might lose enough blood to sate the passions of the King. He only hoped that whatever creature they happened upon might, in its frenzied fight for its life, find a way to take Kredor along with it. Tainne, however, seemed to have no intentions of dirtying his white hands. He was content to walk unarmed at the

King's side while the hounds and the cadre of royal hunters flushed the undergrowth along the eaves of the Firriny Mountains north of the city in search of prey.

Try as he might, Royne was unable to hear what it was they spoke of. Rather, he was forced to stand just out of earshot with the half-dozen silent, armored men assigned as the King's personal guard, who made for quite a contrast to the two cherubim pages in their motley dancing about incessantly, bickering with one another, and jingling their tambourines. Before long, Royne longed to slap them himself. As irritating as they were, though, they were still mildly tolerable in comparison to the other presence that he was forced to endure: Pryce.

It seemed that with the Warlord's justiciars already in command of troop deployment afield and the cavaliers in charge of drilling kingsmen and the nobles' conscripts in the cities, the Warlord had suddenly found himself without purpose, for although Dandon Rood was a man of action and one who preferred to lead his men into battle personally, his place on the Council of Five (or Four, as was the case without Rastis) required that he remain in Titanis. Rather than sit and stew in idleness atop his tower while a battle raged hundreds of miles away, he accepted the King's invitation to hunt with relish.

Much to Royne's surprise, though, he rather enjoyed the Warlord's company. For although a soldier through and through (which often—if anything—predisposed Royne against a person), Rood was the only member of the council or the Andochan court to offer any overt protest against Rastis's arrest and imprisonment. He simply refused to believe that there was anything nefarious in the Loremaster's nature, and though it may have seemed like Rastis had acted against the King, Rood believed that the old Loremaster had only done so with the best intentions of the King, the realm, and the Order in mind. Still, at his core, Dandon Rood was a soldier, and in the face of the combined weight of the Chancellor, the Hierophant, and the King, the Warlord was forced to accept the political defeat and simply follow orders. Perhaps as a result of this loss, he seemed to go out of his way to be kind to Royne in the weeks that followed.

Pryce was an entirely different matter, and, if anything, he redoubled his efforts at antagonizing Royne. He reveled in Rastis's fall from favor, and he spoke of it loudly and often whenever the opportunity presented itself (as long as his master was out of earshot).

"Once Broken, always broken," he would intone, citing the derogatory nomenclature sometimes applied to the men of the Brock, "for one who's supposed to be wise, the old fool sure proved himself quite stupid going against the King."

More than once, Royne was thankful that he had not been armed for the hunt either, else he would have shot Pryce in the back with a crossbow or shanked him from behind with a pike. Still, in the company of the King's retinue, it was difficult for Pryce to do more than make unsubtle observations such as these, so direct physical bullying would be out of the question. The physical maladies of the wilderness were enough of a trial for Royne anyhow.

Never in his life had Royne been hunting, and as he had long suspected, to finally do so was not something that he enjoyed in the least. For one thing, he was not fond of the outdoors. The sights and smells of nature did not at all agree with him, but more often sent him into coughing or sneezing fits and headaches.

If that alone was not enough, there was the weather to compound his misery. Being the middle of autumn, the air was rather cool; however, walking through the forest trails made him warm, and soon, he would begin to sweat. Yet just when he decided to take off his cloak, the wind would blow, and he would be cold again when, suddenly, the sun would reveal itself from behind a cloud, and he would once again be too hot, and so on and so on.

Worst of all, though, was the main objective of the hunt, namely, killing something, or at least in Royne's case, watching some poor creature be killed, for only the King, the Warlord, and the royal hunters would do the actual killing. Even Kredor's hounds were trained only to subdue or corner a beast, and the remainder of the party—a handful of servants, the motley twins, Pryce, and Royne himself—were not outfitted for the hunt (though Pryce wore his sword), while Natharis Tainne seemed to regard the whole affair as dispassionately as a walk through the Nobleton gardens.

As Royne followed along, ignoring Pryce and the bumbling pages, he, again, strained his ears in an attempt to overhear what the King and his special adviser discussed concerning Grantis, Dwerin, and the Protectorate. Clearly, they had provided more than a token force to support Dwerin, mobilizing whole armies to bring the Senate to its knees before the snows thawed. In either case, with a new aristocratic government in place (perhaps overseen by Lord Tainne or Marcel Pryce should no one else suitable be found), Grantis would join Dwerin as a staunch Andochan ally. Then come spring, if the Tower had not settled the War of the Horses in Montevale, soldiers could be sent (in spite of King Marius's protests) to force a resolution to the conflict. However, truth be told, the recent correspondence Lord Tainne had begun with the Valendian prince in the south seemed promising as well. In any event, whichever side won the war mattered little as long as the victor was willing to support the Protectorate, and as it stood, both sides seemed to care more about defeating the other than they did about offering fealty to the Guardian-King.

Of the "civilized" realms, that left only Baronbrock, at which point the King's mood soured, and Royne suppressed an inward surge of glee, for there had yet been no new news from the Hammer, which meant that for the time being at least, Lughus was still free.

"If only the child had been born a girl," Lord Tainne observed, "all could be resolved quite nicely. Imagine joining the bloodlines of the Drudes and the Galadins after thirteen hundred years. Such a thing would usher in a new era to the dynasty of Drudish Kings."

Kredor tromped along through the undergrowth, watching as a ways off ahead, the Warlord and one of the royal hunters paused to inspect the scoring along the base of a large oak tree. Royne crept a bit closer.

"Can't say I'd mind if the girl had the look of her mother," the King said, "unlike that mute waif Darren Beinn wants to pass off on us."

"Still," Tainne observed, "she may not look like Josephine, but the girl is reportedly quite fair, and according to the Sheriff, she's also quite...docile. However"—he paused—"if you'd prefer, the archduchess and the Sheriff are as yet unwed. I'm sure that if you desired it, the remaining Beinns would not protest. From what I understand, they are, in fact, quite annoyed with Darren's attempt to upset the balance of power. You could cut down one and ensure the loyalty of the other three..."

"Josephine? Ha! She's fair, no doubt, but aging, and free enough with her favors as it is. A woman like that would leave a man wondering if his heirs were his own."

Natharis Tainne nodded. "True, but an heir you must have. If not the young Beinn girl or her mother, then why not Marius's daughter, the Winter Rose?"

Kredor laughed. "King of the bloody continent, and these are my options? A whore, a half-wit, and a northern girl who most assuredly smells of horse? Lucky me."

Tainne sighed. "No one said you need be faithful, merely that you get them with child—children, male preferably."

"Male, certainly," the King corrected. "No point in any other, else all we hope to accomplish here could quickly be undone."

"Perhaps then you should simply try your hand with all three, and the lucky one who bears a boy wins the crown as queen?" Lord Tainne shrugged. "It is not unheard of. In fact, it was common among the Emperors in the early days of Calendral. If we intend to follow their example in other matters, why not in this as well?"

Royne's brow furrowed. So the protectorate *was* simply a path to an empire. Why remain simply King Kredor Dude II when he could be Emperor Kredor Drude I? Kredor was, as Rastis had said, quite ambitious, and if history taught any one lesson, it was that the more a man already had, the greater his desires. It was only natural that the king of a country would seek dominion over a continent, just as the king of a continent would seek to rule the world. Guarding against such a thing was, in fact, the reason for the last two Protectorates to defend against Tulondis and Kord. Still, the very idea of such a thing never made sense to Royne. What possibly could a person hope to gain through the constant pursuit of *gain* itself? It would be like trying to fill in a hole as deep as the Abyss.

None of this was surprising in the least but merely confirmed what Rastis, Royne, and most blind men would have already seen. What struck Royne, though, was the rather cavalier attitude with which the King and his adviser so openly discussed their scheme. It was like a thief visiting a homeowner to let him know in advance which items he intended to steal. Clearly, they saw no room for failure.

Kredor took a deep breath. "Come spring," he said, "we'll invite them all to the castle—the archduchess, her daughter, and the horse princess. I'll have a look then." He snorted. "Maybe more than a look if the opportunity presents itself, and we'll see about things from there."

Pryce smiled at the King's comment, and Royne hoped Kredor would turn suddenly and catch him eavesdropping. The stewards might be present for the conversation, but unless ordered otherwise, they were to turn deaf ears to the words of their betters. Apparently, Pryce's noble lineage had not taught him that.

"For now, though, just let me be, Tainney," Kredor said. "We'll have no more talk of weddings until the spring."

"Certainly, Your Majesty," Lord Tainne said, "I only seek the best for you."

"I know, Natharis, and I thank you for that," Kredor said, patting the "acting" Loremaster on the shoulder. At that moment, Dandon Rood waved a hand, and he and the hunter began pushing on through the wilds. The King, Lord Tainne, and the rest of the party followed after.

"Speaking of seeking," Kredor began, "have you found…"

"Nothing for certain yet. My steward and I have been searching the archives, yet thus far, we have discovered nothing."

Royne suppressed a sigh. Perhaps he may have discovered something, he thought, if Tainne had told him exactly what it was he was looking for. Instead, he had merely been forced to stumble blindly through old manuscripts from the Order's founding. Most spoke in lofty verse of Aiden's final battle with Wrogan and the Beast, a rather pointless study considering it was a folktale every man, woman, and child in Titanis could recite by heart. Still, it did allow Royne the opportunity to wander the archives a bit on his own. In addition to all the books, there were a number of old artifacts from the Guardians of the past, many of whose titles were no longer borne. Lughus would have gone mad to know that in the locked storerooms but a floor below where they slept were half a dozen Guardian weapons: a few swords, a mace, a kite shield. Thom, too, were he not a naively treacherous bastard, would have jiggled with excitement to see the ancient lute thought to have belonged to one of the Bards.

Kredor sighed. "So we still know nothing?"

"Nothing more than what we already knew, which I say is still rather considerable. The Keepers know much and more, but"— Lord Tainne sighed—"there is still the one book that I have yet to investigate."

"And the old man?"

Natharis Tainne shrugged. "He refuses to speak."

Royne's ears perked up. Beside him, the twins began slapping each other with their tambourines, and the older boy glared at them to be silent.

"Have you tried forcing him?" the King asked.

Royne's fist clenched involuntarily.

"I do not think that would be wise," Lord Tainne said. He nodded toward the Warlord. "Disgraced or not, the old man still has friends, and besides, his will is exceptionally strong."

"So it seems." King Kredor sighed. "Tell me, have you asked…" The King turned, and quickly, Royne looked away.

"I believe he knows nothing," Tainne whispered quietly, "nor do I think him very wise, else it would have been him sent alongside the Galadin boy. It is most likely that he was left as a sacrifice to deceive us and perhaps save the other two."

Royne's insides twisted with anger and resentment, and he fought to keep his temper under control. He stared into the bushes feigning ignorance, a steady stream of obscenities running silently through his mind.

"Still, I say we ask him," Kredor said, "Or better yet, we ask him to ask the old man."

"I had toyed with that idea myself."

"Or else we could just torture him. It saves time."

"I suppose there may be some sense in that as well."

"Only *some* sense, Tainney?" Kredor smirked. "Were you not my friend, I would have you flogged for such a comment."

"My apologies, Your Majesty."

"No matter," Kredor said and, turning, called, "Young steward!" Pryce stepped forward eagerly. "Yes, Your Majesty!"

"Not you."

Under normal circumstances, Royne would have laughed at Pryce's expense but not this time. His anger had stifled any sense of mirth. He took a deep breath. "Yes, Your Majesty?"

"Walk behind me with your master for a moment."

"Yes, Your Majesty." Royne hurried up to meet them, though against all inclination.

At length, King Kredor spoke. "I hope that you have enjoyed your stewardship to Loremaster Tainne," he said, "though I am certain you miss old Rastis too?"

Royne thought carefully. "Lord Tainne has been...very kind."

"Good," Kredor said, "you should know that Lord Tainne and I are doing all we can to rescue your friend from the Blackguard, though why Rastis would have allowed this in the first place is quite upsetting."

"It is as you say, Your Majesty," he said. "Very upsetting."

"If you only knew." Kredor sighed. "However, there is one thing that has been causing a great deal of difficulty in our search, something that—truth be told—you may be able to help us with."

Royne forced a smile. "I will do my best, your majesty."

"That's a good lad." Kredor grinned. "Tell me then. Since you began your duties in service to Lord Tainne, have you noticed your hands a little idle?"

Royne's brow furrowed. "My hands, Your Majesty?" he said.

The King nodded. "Look at Master Pryce, for instance. What do you notice is different between you two"—he suppressed a laugh—"apart from the obvious."

Suddenly, Royne's fingers tingled nervously, and a chill ran down his spine as he noticed the other steward carrying the Warlord's great sword, Duty, in its beautifully adorned scabbard.

"*The Book of Histories*!" he gasped in genuine surprise. "It's gone!"

Kredor and Tainne exchanged a look. "Exactly," the King remarked, "and has been for some time now."

Royne's mind raced as he struggled to remember when last he saw the book, and he cursed himself inwardly for failing to notice its absence before. Yet he did not yet know whether to feel joy or sorrow at its loss. Clearly, Rastis had done something with the book, or if not Rastis, then surely Hob, but what?

"I'm only going to ask you this once, boy," King Kredor said, "and I expect you to tell me the truth." From beside him, Royne could feel the unnatural stare of Lord Tainne's pallid eyes. "Do you know what Rastis has done with the book?"

Royne took a deep breath and shook his head. "No, Your Majesty," he said, "I do not."

Without warning, there was a great commotion, and all of a sudden, men were shouting in utter panic as something heavy crashed through the wilderness with a shrill cry of rage and terror. Royne was knocked aside into the dirt and mud while somewhere close by, the motley twins shrieked in

369

unison. King Kredor, spouting obscenities, called for his hunters and his hounds, as Pryce and Natharis Tainne scattered into the brush.

Frantically, instinctively, Royne curled up into a ball and shielded his head with his arms, taking cover beneath the overhang of a large thorn bush. Something large snorted fiercely nearby, stomping the ground with its feet and digging through the undergrowth in a frenzy. Again, the twins screamed in fear, and the creature charged through the woodlands in the direction of their cries.

"Aiden's Flame!" Royne gasped.

He forced himself deeper beneath the jagged branches, wincing as thorns raked his hands and brow, and when he turned his head as the beast lumbered past again, he felt the sharp sting of another branch of thorns tearing into his scalp.

Madness! Complete madness! What sane man would willingly risk his life for idle sport!

"Give me the damned spear, you bloody fool!" Kredor shouted from scarcely a few feet away. "Curse it all, you worthless bastards!"

Royne cautiously peered from the branches just as King Kredor drew his sword. Ahead of him, an enormous boar dug into the brush, its tusks throwing great clumps of dirt left and right as it pursued some prey, and a sick feeling filled the pit of Royne's stomach as he no longer discerned the screaming twins. The King's armored guards hurried clumsily through the bushes to defend him, yet Kredor irritably waved them off with his hand.

The King rushed the creature from behind and swung his heirloom sword, Testament, stabbing downward from above. The blade pierced the pig's flesh in a great torrent of blood and squealing. At once, the boar shuddered in agony and rage, turning around to face its tormentor and flailing wildly with its great tusks. However, Kredor turned with it, forcing the blade even deeper, all the way to the hilt, before diving headlong into the bushes to save himself.

In one final maddened effort, the boar charged after him, only to trip and roll forward in its death throes straight into Royne's bush. Blood poured in a great deluge from the place where the King had pierced the beast, and as the sticky red gore washed over him and the dying creature emptied its bowels, Royne's stomach churned, and his vision went dark.

When he opened his eyes again, his head throbbed with pain, and his robes felt heavy and wet. His hands twitched as he rubbed his eyes, and he would have fallen back over again had a sturdy arm not held him up.

"Steady on there, lad," Dandon Rood said gently. "Don't fear. None of this blood is yours, at least not that I can tell."

Behind his shoulder, Pryce's lips twisted into a mocking sneer. "All right, Royne?" he asked with false concern. "How about that pile of filth? Is that the boar's too, or did you mess yourself? There's no shame in it if you did."

If he weren't so weak and the Warlord not watching, Royne would have thrown a handful of the steaming feces at the other steward's head. However, for now, he ignored him and glanced around. The hunters and the King's personal guard clustered around the carcass of the giant boar while here and there, the hunting hounds barked at one another and sniffed the dead creature's blood. Somewhere off a ways, one of the motley twins was bawling.

"How is he, Dandy?" another voice called. In spite of his ordeal, Royne recognized it immediately as belonging to the King.

"Apart from a few cuts and scrapes from the bushes, he's unharmed," the Warlord said. "How about the other?"

"There is nothing I can do for him," said Natharis Tainne. "He is already dead."

Royne coughed. "Who?" he asked.

The Warlord's face grew ashen, and Royne looked past him to where the King stood beside his adviser. It was immediately clear why there was the sound of only one twin crying. The other lie grotesquely twisted in a heap, his motley now a single shade of red and the little tambourine smashed and covered in gore. Royne's stomach lurched involuntarily, and his throat burned as he forced the contents of his stomach back down.

"Bloody Abyss," he gasped.

Tainne left the dead boy's side and came near to check on Royne. "Some of these scratches along your forehead may leave scars," he said impassively, "though nothing serious. Can you stand?"

"I think so," Royne said. He rubbed his eyes, took a deep breath, and, leaning on the Warlord for support, slowly got to his feet.

"See," Dandon Rood said, "I always said those scribblers are made of sterner stuff that one might think, isn't that right?"

Royne nodded wearily, and the Warlord patted him on the shoulder before heading off to see to the singular twin. Pryce followed behind him, but not without one final leer.

"It appears you owe King Kredor your life," Natharis Tainne observed.

Royne took a long, deep breath. He was not quite certain that was true, but he was also not about to argue. "He has my thanks."

"I should think he deserves considerably more than that."

Royne nodded. "Yes, my lord, though he is already my King. I owe him much and more as it is. What else could I possibly offer?"

"Perhaps..." Lord Tainne said, then suddenly paused, and Royne noticed the nobleman's eyes take on a strange, pallid glow. "Perhaps there is another way you could show your gratitude to the King," Tainne said, a smile tugging at the corners of his lips, "for King Kredor and I greatly desire *The Book of Histories*, and though we cannot find where it is hidden there is one person who most certainly knows..."

CHAPTER 28:
CAPTAIN BARROW

Captain Wilfred Barrow was a somber man in his late thirties with the marked bearing of a professional soldier. His every action seemed governed by an unconscious sense of timely precision and an adherence to a strict regimen of self-disciple and duty, which, out of habit, made itself known in the very features of the captain's face—a long, narrow jaw, aquiline nose, and a furrowed brow that curled pensively over a pair of dark piercing eyes. Still, he was not overly severe, nor was he unkind in his demand that Geoffrey and Oliver remain with him, merely insistent. Most importantly, however, he did not treat the farmers like most soldiers—as simply his inferiors—but regarded them with a measure of respect that Geoffrey believed marked him as an honorable man.

All through the remainder of the afternoon, the two farmers followed along behind the captain while Mason, the archer, circled around in a wide arc behind them and to either side. Barrow remained silent much of the time, but when Geoffrey finally built up the nerve to ask, the captain confirmed that the war for the Spade had indeed begun again; however, this time, the Guardian-King in Andoch had decided to lend his support to Dwerin in punishment, most believed, for the Grantisi Senate's dissolution of the nobility and abandonment of the Kinship as their sole faith. As such, Nealen Beinn, Castellan of Dwerin and youngest brother to the dead archduke, had rallied his soldiers behind his two most honored generals, Devon Walsh, and Padraig Reid.

Upon hearing this, Oliver breathed a heavy sigh of despair. "If it's not bandits, then it's soldiers," Geoffrey heard him mutter, "Old Amos was right."

When the sun touched the horizon in the western sky, Barrow halted at the edge of a small, craggy hillock, and Geoffrey became aware of the faint odor of horse dung and campfire playing upon the wind. A sentry dressed in the same manner as the two mounted scouts appeared from behind a cluster of wild blackberry bushes, bow drawn at the ready, but upon recognizing his captain, lowered his weapon and saluted.

Barrow nodded to the sentry and turned to his companion. "Mason," he called, "see our guests are fed. I must speak with the others."

"Aye, sir." The archer nodded, and the captain rode off.

The skirmishers had set up camp along the far side of the hill with two other sentries posted at intervals along the edges and another at the hilltop, where a large alder tree grew from an odd angle along the northwestern slope. From what Geoffrey could gather, the scouts in total numbered perhaps four and twenty, though all were outfitted for battle with bow, buckler, and falchion. Most also carried metal nasal helms, and instead of boiled leather, many of the soldiers wore short-sleeved byrnies of ringmail, which was not necessarily a surprise considering Dwerin's mineral wealth. Even the horses bore some measure of armament, usually in the form of a metal or leather chamfron and a light mail crinet.

As for the men themselves, they seemed no different than any other soldiers Geoffrey could recall encountering over his life. They sat around their fires on large stones and fallen logs, eating hastily cooked meals, arguing, laughing, and poking fun at one another over half a dozen private jokes. Some spoke of women, others old battles, and a few huddled together, rattling wooden cups of bone dice.

Mason dismounted, took his horse by the bridle, and led Geoffrey and Oliver through the camp. A few men offered the archer greetings or jeers, their eyes silently questioning the reason for the two peasants following behind. At length, they reached the largest of the campfires, where a fat soldier with crooked teeth stirred a large iron pot of brown stew.

"Oi there, Ernald," Mason said, staking his horse in the ground nearby, "what's cooking tonight?"

The man looked up and blinked. Geoffrey could see now a long, jagged scar running the length of the cook's face from just behind his ear along the line of his jaw. "Stew."

Mason patted his horse on the flank and returned to the fireside. "I can see that, you knob." He snorted. "But what kind?"

Ernald's eyebrows furrowed, and he eyed Mason in confusion. "Stew." He shrugged.

"Fine then." Mason motioned for Geoffrey and Oliver to sit. "Three bowls of stew then."

Ernald nodded and ladled spoonfuls of watery brown liquid into wooden bowls. Geoffrey and Oliver wondered briefly at the nature of the bits of things floating in their bowls but, in the end, gave into hunger, for they had not eaten since the oatcakes they shared that morning.

Free of the unconscious reserve awarded an officer, Mason seemed suddenly much more amiable, and he quickly engaged the farmers in conversation. "So who is it lords these lands for Grantis these days?" he asked. "Who draws the levies?"

Geoffrey and Oliver exchanged a shrug. "No one as we know of," Oliver said. "Else, we might not have the troubles with the bandits."

"No one, you say?" Mason asked. "Then who do you pay your taxes to?"

Geoffrey slurped from his bowl. "No one," he said hesitantly.

"No one?"

Oliver shook his head. "Every few years, either Dwerin or Grantis retake the lands from the other," he said. "But the fighting's always so bad that neither one can ever spare the men to defend it afterward, nor do they want to keep paying hired mercenaries their due. As such, there's no lord, no castle, no taxes, but no protection either."

"That's the risk of the Spade," Geoffrey said. "We're not serfs but freemen. Without a Dwerin lord or a Grantisi governor, we keep all we grow, and we sell what we don't need ourselves in the markets we choose, Dwermouth or Granmouth, either one, though we try to take turns from harvest to harvest."

"The roads are always dangerous, though," Oliver added. "Since without pay, it don't take long before the mercenaries turn bandit, like the Red Boars as attacked our town."

"So it's great risks for great rewards then, eh?" Mason asked.

"Not great." Oliver shrugged. "But they're ours, and so is the land, at least for now."

"Until the bandits kill everyone," Geoffrey muttered bitterly.

Mason shook his head. "If the bandits are such a problem, why don't you form a militia and fight them yourselves?"

"We're not warriors," Geoffrey said.

Mason raised his eyebrows. "In Dwerin," he said, "if you've got a trade, you can sometimes make a decent living in a city or town as long as you can pay your taxes to the lord and your dues to the guild. Though, if you haven't got a trade, like most, you can either work the mines digging ore for the lords or become a soldier and fight the lords' battles." He paused. "Me, I figured I'd rather see the sky from time to time."

"However, were I a farmer," he added, "with my own lands, I don't think I'd just allow some thieving bastards to come in and have the run of the place without a fight."

Geoffrey stirred the contents of his bowl, ignoring Oliver's resentful gaze. Mason stood up from the fireside and returned to his horse. "All right, well, I should see to my girl here," he said. "Oi, Ernald! You'll keep an eye on our guests here, won't you, while I set Rosey here to rights, eh?"

The cook nodded. "Stew!"

"Too many hits to the head without a helmet," Mason muttered with a wink. "Welcome to the camp, men of Pyle."

When they were at last left alone, Oliver drained the last of his stew, leaned forward onto his knees, and took a deep breath. "How did you know about this whole Ashfort business?" he said quietly, though in a tone that demanded an answer.

"I don't know," Geoffrey said.

"Ah yes," Oliver said. "Right, well, that's not good enough this time."

"What does it matter what I know?" Geoffrey asked.

"Geoffrey," Oliver said, "we're in an army camp. For all we know, we could be held prisoner. How am I ever going to save my sons as a prisoner in an army camp?"

"I still wonder how you were planning to save them in the first place," Geoffrey said bitterly.

"Just because you've given up your boy for dead doesn't mean I have to give up mine!"

"Stop saying that!" Geoffrey hissed.

"Or what? You'll beat me with that club like you did those three men at Damon's?" Oliver said. "You know, you do that and bring this whole mess down on us, and still, you're too much of a coward to try to make amends, even when your own son's life is on the line."

"Shut up! This was not my fault!" Geoffrey shouted.

Suddenly, Ernald, the cook, turned around, and at one of the other campfires, another group of soldiers grew quiet and peered across the way at the two farmers to see what the commotion was all about. Geoffrey took a deep breath and tossed the dregs of his stew into the fire.

"You asked before how I knew of this Ashfort, and the answer is I do not know. Somehow, it simply came to me, like a memory, only not one of mine."

"And you only just then remembered this?"

"Yes!" he said, "Just as..." he hesitated, lowering his voice to a whisper, "just like at Damon's, if you must know. Only I didn't even have to think about it then. Somehow I just knew how to fight, like it was as natural as breathing. It was like I remembered it, but I couldn't have."

"How?" Oliver asked.

"I don't know," Geoffrey said. "Believe me. All I know is that it has something to do with the old man in the caravan, the one from who I got the club and the shield. I think they're his memories."

Oliver eyed Geoffrey skeptically. "If they're his, then why do you have them?"

"It was something he did," Geoffrey said, "or something he said." Suddenly, he recalled his dream from the previous evening: the bodies, the arrows, the words. "The words he said," he whispered, more to himself now than to Oliver. "The words, he needed to say the words..."

The first to walk into the fray,
the last to lay down arms,
from break of dawn 'til end of day,
shield all good folk from harm,
for when all life seems cold and hard,
and the weak flee before the strong,
Rise now, the Vanguard,
And right what evil wrongs.

"What was that?" Oliver asked. "Poetry?"

"I don't know," Geoffrey said. "I only remembered it just now." He sighed. "But it's strange. It's not just one memory, but *two*. I mean, it's like I have *two* memories, one of the old man speaking the words and the other of me hearing them."

"Madness," Oliver said.

Before they could discuss the matter any further, however, Mason returned alongside Captain Barrow and two other soldiers, one short, thin, and balding and the other tall and dark of hair and eye. Ernald, the cook, stood up straight and saluted at their approach, and taking his cue, Geoffrey and Oliver hurried to their feet.

Barrow dismissed Ernald with a nod, and the cook went back to his business. "I trust you've eaten," the captain observed.

"Yes, sir," Geoffrey and Oliver said together. "Many thanks." The sudden presence of the officers immediately invoked the farmers' automatic deference to authority and class.

"This is Sergeant Boyle," he said, "and Sergeant Dunn." Geoffrey and Oliver muttered greetings, but Barrow pressed on. "Now," he motioned to the men to sit down, "what can you tell us of this Ashfort and these bandits? The Red Boars, was it?"

"Aye, so they called themselves," Geoffrey said.

The soldiers remained silent, waiting for Geoffrey to speak. "Well," the farmer said, feeling rather ill at ease, "I'm afraid that there's not much I can tell you about Ashfort other than I already have." He sighed. "South of the forest road, the plain along the coast is dotted with old forts from the old wars, though most have fallen in disrepair. Ashfort's one of the better off ones."

"You've been there?" Barrow asked.

Geoffrey felt a stab of anxiety. How could he possibly explain? "No," he said, "but I saw it once," he said hesitantly. "It's a motte and bailey made in the old style, but during the last war, the little keep on the hilltop was reinforced with stone, so it's held up longer than those built only out of wood."

Barrow nodded.

"Below it, the bailey's surrounded by a palisade wall and connects to the keep by way of a narrow wooden stair." He paused. "My guess is that Lord Mathon, that's him who leads them, lives in the little keep with Karthan and the other leaders and all the goods they steal, while most of the rest of the men and all the horses live in the bailey below."

"That would make sense," the dark sergeant, Dunn, jeered. Barrow shot him a cold stare of rebuke before turning his attention back to the farmers. "You say *Lord* Mathon?"

"So he called himself...er, so they called him, I should say. He didn't speak so much as his man did, Karthan, the one who killed our cousin and burned the chapel." Geoffrey shook his head. Martin's murder was still too near for him to think about. "Have you heard of any Mathons who bear the Red Boar as their arms?"

Barrow's brow furrowed. "No," he said, "though that does not mean much. He could be a noble, though in all likelihood, he was simply some landless knight who found it easier to make a profit by plundering the poor folk than in the service of a true lord.

"Or," the other sergeant, Boyle, said, "he could be the descendent of some exiled lord out of Grantis. That could explain why he's taken up with common thieves and rogues." Boyle wagged a finger.

"In which case, he might be willing to fight the wolf pack, should he be properly compensated..."

Captain Barrow's eyes widened. "Yes, Boyle, you may have something there. However, I would have to speak to him first and report to Lord Reid."

"Aye, Captain," Dunn agreed. "The fort could be just the thing, and the thirty-odd men inside wouldn't hurt either if they agreed to fight for us."

"And begging your pardon, Captain," Mason interjected, "but we did find that dead wolf by the rocks where we met those two. If they killed one, they might kill more."

Suddenly, Oliver spoke, unable to contain himself. "Wait," he said, "you can't be thinking of working with them? They're bloody thieves! Bandits! Kidnappers and murderers!"

"If they fight the wolves for us, they can fuck my wife for all I care," Boyle said.

"Saves me from having too," Dunn added with a laugh. Mason grinned.

"Enough!" Barrow snapped.

The men of Dwerin fell silent at the captain's word. Geoffrey glanced at Oliver. His friend looked stricken with agitation. At length, Barrow sighed and nodded to his men, "Leave us."

"Aye, Captain," they said.

Barrow waited until they had gone and addressed the farmers. "I understand your pain," he said. "Believe me. I, too, have lost friends, a brother, and men of my command, too many. So believe me when I say that I understand your desire for vengeance."

"I can't believe this!" Oliver shouted. "They took our sons!"

Geoffrey sensed the heightening anxiety of the camp at Oliver's cry. Hurriedly, he reached out to grasp his friend's shoulder. "Oliver, please!" He turned back to Barrow. "Forgive us, Captain."

Barrow nodded. "I have a wife and a daughter in Oardale, in the lands governed by Lord Reid. Believe me, if either one of them was lost to me, I would hunt whoever took them to the ends of the world, and I would not rest until I'd split their insides on my blade." He sighed. "But I have my orders, and I must follow them."

"Do your orders include offering amnesty to bandits?" Geoffrey asked.

"There are many soldiers who take up arms as a means of making amends for earlier crimes," Barrow said. "Besides, if Mason and I had not come upon you, and the two of you had made it to Ashfort yourselves, it is certain that you would be as good as dead and perhaps your sons with you."

Geoffrey sighed heavily, and Oliver turned away to gaze into the fire. It was true, Geoffrey knew, and for all his optimism and resolve, Oliver must have too. Two men against the entire fort would have been suicide.

"However," Barrow continued, "though I may not be able to offer you vengeance, and it's highly unlikely that I will be able to return your stolen stores, if this Lord Mathon agrees to join us in the fight against Grantis and your sons yet live, I swear to you that you will have them back, and you will be free to return again to your homes when all is done."

Oliver's eyes went wide, and where so recently they had been marred by despair, they now shone with a glimmer of hope. Geoffrey, too, shared Oliver's relief, at least for a moment.

"You said this is all dependent upon whether or not the Red Boars accept your offer."

"Which is still dependent upon the will of my Lord Reid," Barrow said. "I will send a rider tonight with a dispatch to find out for certain if he will grant me the authority to offer the terms."

"Aye," Geoffrey said, "but what if he does not, or beyond that, what if Lord Mathon doesn't accept?"

"Well," Barrow sighed, "then I suppose I would have to grant you vengeance after all." He stood up from the fireside, "Regardless, I have messages to write. You are free to rest here within the perimeter of the camp. However, I ask that you keep to yourselves and that you do not attempt to flee."

"So we're prisoners then?" Oliver muttered.

"I would not say that," the captain said. "I would rather you consider yourselves guests, for you may keep your arms and take your meals with us. However, I simply cannot allow you to wander free, at least as of yet."

Geoffrey exchanged a glance with Oliver. "We understand," he said, "and thank you."

"Then I will leave you," Barrow said, but as he turned to go, he paused. "Believe me when I tell you," he added. "That I sincerely hope that the Kinship keeps your sons. Good night."

That night, Geoffrey and Oliver slept beneath the watchful eyes of the Ironmen of Dwerin, and though neither farmer slept too soundly, there was at least some comfort in knowing that the soldiers were on guard.

In the morning, when they awoke, the soldiers were already in the midst of their breakfast, and Ernald made sure to leave a bowl of soggy porridge for each of the farmers. It had already turned cold, but Geoffrey imagined that even had it been warm, it still would have tasted like mud (albeit warm mud). Even worse, however, were the images the terrible food conjured up in his mind of the Harvestide Feast that his fellow folk of Pyle had prepared and never got to enjoy. "Bloody bandits," he muttered, letting his spoon sink into the murky porridge with a loud splash.

Oliver looked up from his bowl. "I'm sorry. What was that?"

Geoffrey set his bowl aside and took up Oakheart, tracing the letters of its name on the leather wrist strap. "You know," he said, "you may call me a coward and all for worrying over the risks in following Mathon and that Red Boar lot, but you forget. I've already fought them. In fact, I killed three while you and the others just stood around gawking. I mean, Damon was already dead, his wife… taken, and the gods only know what could have befallen those children had I not done something. So shame on you, Oliver of Pyle, and shame on anyone else who blames me for this or questions my nerve. I don't see any other folk out here with us, searching for the boys or the winter stores! And you may think me weak for not running right out at the bandits like you would have done and attacked them head-on like a charging bull, but what good would that have done, eh? They'd have filled us both full of arrows before we came within an arm's reach and maybe killed the boys out of spite besides! So I've had enough of your mouth, and if you weren't my friend, I'd have knocked your block off a long time ago!"

Oliver's eyes widened. "Aiden's Flame, Geoffrey," he said. "I just couldn't hear what you said…"

"Oh," Geoffrey said bashfully.

A moment passed in silence, and suddenly, Oliver began to laugh, softly at first but increasingly louder. Before long, Geoffrey joined in. As they readied their horses for their morning patrols, a number of the Dwerin soldiers eyed the farmers quizzically and shook their heads. Folk were strange in the Spade, they muttered.

Oliver wiped the tears of laughter from his eyes and patted Geoffrey on the shoulder. "I'm sorry," he said.

Geoffrey shook his head. "No worries."

The day passed slowly in the Dwerin skirmisher camp. Riders in groups of two and four ventured out at regular intervals, returning hours later to give their reports to Captain Barrow. Geoffrey and Oliver were, of course, not privy to what it was the soldiers discovered in their ranging; however, their faces were often grave. According to the captain, a pair of riders departed a few hours before dawn carrying dispatches to Lord Reid, but until they returned, there was nothing more to be done with regard to Ashfort and the Red Boars, so they would just have to wait.

The soldier's life, Geoffrey soon surmised, seemed to be one often characterized by odd intervals of hurry and waiting, both times accompanied by a constant sense of imminent danger or even death, and he realized that such a life was not one for him. For though a farmer's life was hard and often full of misery, there was always something to be done, whether plowing or planting or harvesting or threshing, from spring to summer and summer to autumn. Even in the dead of winter when the cold hard ground could yield no crops, there was still plenty for a farmer to do to keep the mind busy enough to forget one's troubles. Still, both Geoffrey and Oliver were thankful for Captain Barrow and his men, for it was due to their concurrent interests in Ashfort that the two farmers now had some hope of reclaiming their lost sons.

It was well after nightfall when the messengers finally returned, though some time passed afterward before Captain Barrow sent word for Geoffrey and Oliver to meet him at his small pavilion. Inside, around a small table, Boyle and Dunn sat, sharing a small clay jug. The captain himself stood with his back to them and his arms folded across his chest. Atop a small wooden trunk beside his bedroll lay a few rolls of parchment and a lumpy leather sack.

"Here they are, sir," Mason said.

Barrow nodded silently, and Mason withdrew. Geoffrey and Oliver bowed their heads respectfully, and Boyle passed Dunn the jug. "The messengers have returned from Lord Reid," the captain said, turning toward them. "I'm to offer the Red Boars terms and take command of Ashfort until I am relieved. We will ride out together tomorrow at dawn. I imagine that you will, of course, accompany us?"

"Yes, sir," Geoffrey said.

"If all goes well," Barrow said, "you may take your sons and return to your village." He paused. "However, you must also know that any stores or provisions currently held at the fort will be seized in the name of Lord Reid and the armies of Dwerin."

Geoffrey and Oliver exchanged a glance.

"Everything?" Oliver asked, "But that food was to last us through the winter months."

Boyle and Dunn narrowed their eyes and regarded Oliver with a measure of scorn.

"I...am sorry," Captain Barrow said. "But that is the way of it, as I mentioned it might be. However, you should be happy that you will at least have your sons."

Oliver released a heavy sigh, but Geoffrey waved a hand to calm his friend. "Thank you, sir," he said. "We are. Thank you."

Barrow nodded. "You are dismissed," he said. "But as I said, we ride at dawn. You may follow with Ernald in the supply cart."

"Yes, sir."

Geoffrey and Oliver excused themselves from Barrow's tent and returned to their place by the cooking fires. Oliver was quiet, for although the return of their sons was paramount, without the winter stores, the village would still face starvation, and it was highly likely that many would not live to see the spring. "Well," Geoffrey said, "there's naught to be done about it now."

Oliver shook his head. "No, but one thing at a time."

Geoffrey shook his head bitterly. "We'd best get some sleep," he said. "Dawn comes soon enough."

A long time had passed since Geoffrey had last been to Alendis (or Commonwealth as it had been renamed under the Senate), though in the poor quarter, very little ever changed, which, he assumed, could probably be said in any city. The cobblestone streets were packed with filth left by passing pack animals, left to bake in the late summer sun alongside beggars who smelled nearly as bad. Their groping hands stretched out to seek handouts from the other poor folk who passed by, for a man who only had two coins to rub together still had more than a man who had none.

At the corner, where a man claiming to be a butcher sold bloody slabs of meat he claimed to be beef, Geoffrey turned left down the alleyway past a cadre of whores either too old or too ugly to find work in the flophouses around the canals, let alone the high-end brothels of the forum. They called out to him as he passed, offering a variety of sordid things, one of them waggling a saggy, pallid breast, and he hurried past, somewhat saddened that poverty and squalor would drive women so far as to offer themselves up for so little to such a gray-bearded old man as he. How Salasco could continue to live in such a place was beyond Geoffrey's comprehension; then again, it was hard to tend to the needs of the poor and the wretched without living among them, and so the men who bore the title of the Wall always had done.

The alley ended in another running perpendicular to the first, which ended on either side in high iron fencing, no doubt intended as an attempt to contain at least some of the vagrancy common to this quarter of the Grantisi capital. Geoffrey made his way among the dilapidated hovels to one whose door bore a crude charcoal drawing of a crenellated wall.

"Salasco!" Geoffrey called. "Open up, you old scab! Hurry up!"

When the door opened, there stood a man of Geoffrey's own height, though twice as stout, with arms as thick as tree trunks and a chest like a great wine barrel. Yet it was not the man's size that caused the eye to widen with amazement; it was the bandages. White strips of cloth dabbed with flecks of red covered great swaths of Salasco's body, sometimes over and sometimes under his ragged, rough-spun clothes. Even where the bandages did not cover, pink scars and red scratches showed through from his neck down all the way to his bare feet.

"Regnar," he said, peering at Geoffrey with one soft, brown eye—for the other (along with the entire crown of his head) was tightly wrapped in white bandaging), "When in all the years we have known each other, have you ever once found my door to be locked? Are you too feeble in your old age to try the knob?"

"Aye, I might be old," Geoffrey said. "But I'm still prettier than you!"

Salasco laughed and shook Geoffrey's proffered hand, "Come in, my friend. It has been some time."

Salasco's hovel was a single, dimly lit room sparsely furnished with a small wooden table, two stools, and a rough, burlap sack filled with hay that served as a mattress. "I'd offer you some wine," he said, "But I haven't got any."

Geoffrey shrugged and sat down on one of the stools. "I'm not thirsty," he said, "and I'm afraid I can't stay long."

"So I assumed, considering you come alone, Vanguard," Salasco said, taking the other stool, "tell me, where have the Blade and the Marshal got themselves, too?"

Geoffrey removed Oakheart from his belt and leaned it alongside Acorn against the table leg. "Well, Gareth has gone to Blackstone to cause trouble, as he's good at. This time to sow discord among the Beinn brothers," Geoffrey said, "and Crodane…" He paused. "Crodane's gone to Andoch to collect Galadin's grandson."

Salasco sat up straight in surprise. "So it's true, then?" he said. "It is as the Bard predicted?"

"You know Rastis," Geoffrey said. "He won't speak one way or the other about prophecies and premonitions. However, he fears what will happen once Kredor is crowned King. A year and more, the prince and this Keeper friend of his have been busy as bees plotting and sending out messages, and with King Valder nearing his end, Rastis believes Kredor will waste no time in seeking out the Protectorate."

Salasco shook his head. "The Senate would never accept it."

"But Dwerin will. The prince has already proposed an alliance, and the Beinns' accepted."

"Then the war for the Spade is to be renewed."

Geoffrey scoffed bitterly. "I'm not sure they'll be satisfied with just the Spade. The Senate's always made them nervous since they abolished the nobility, of course, and this new Sign of Four religion doesn't help."

"I wouldn't exactly call it a religion," Salasco said, "nor would it's believers, I should think. Alchemy, they call it, though some of it does seem to involve practices that one might consider bordering on the religious, or at least, the spiritual."

"I don't think the truth matters much here," Geoffrey said. "It's more a means to an end."

"Well, the Protectorate would explain why Crodane goes to fetch the boy then," Salasco mused. "What of Montevale?"

"Too caught up in the War of the Horses to care much about Kredor, though when King Marius requested help from Andoch after his son was killed, somehow or another, the council obliged. Still, Rastis appealed to the Warlord to send the Tower."

"So at least it's a man of honor. Good. There are few enough of them left in the Order anymore." Salasco sighed. "Has there been any word from the north? From the Bard?"

"Not as I know," Geoffrey said. "Not since the Ox returned to Rastis, but that was years ago. Still, I think Rastis planned on sending one of his lads north to inherit the title."

Salasco shook his head. "Strange to think that after all the Loremasters and their 'shades of gray,' Rastis may finally be the one to go completely Black."

"Aye," Geoffrey said, "though I can't say I like it. I fear for the old man. He's older than I am, and there are times I feel too old to be carrying this on."

"We all make sacrifices. It's part of the life."

"Aye, but Rastis sleeps in the dragon's den," he said. "If he wakes the beast, I fear he'll come to harm."

The sudden whinny of a horse woke Geoffrey from the dream, and he sat up with a start. Gone was the bandaged man in rags, gone the Grantisi city and its squalor. He shook his head and rubbed his eyes, wondering at the strange visions to which he had somehow just been privy. Oliver was already awake nearby and stood with his rusty sword resting against his shoulder. Ernald the cook threw the last sack of supplies in the rear of his cart and climbed up into the driver's seat behind the two hitched mules. Hurriedly, Geoffrey collected his things and got to his feet.

"You all right?" Oliver asked. "You were talking in your sleep."

"I'm fine," Geoffrey said. He rubbed his eyes again, took up Oakheart, and slipped Acorn onto his arm. "What did I say?" he asked.

"Just muttering," Oliver said. "I couldn't tell."

The two farmers climbed up into the back of the cart, and Ernald drove the mules forward to where the riders were forming their column on the plane. Captain Barrow rode up and spoke a few words to Ernald before turning to Geoffrey and Oliver.

"If all goes well," he said, "your sons will be returned to you before midday."

"Aye, by the Brethren," Geoffrey said, "thank you, Captain, for your kindness to us and your aid."

Barrow inclined his head. "Onward."

CHAPTER 29:
THE NIVANUS MOUNTAINS

The Nivanus Mountains marked the natural boundary separating the eastern Baronies of Nordren, Helmsted, and Edgeforth from the western Montevalen highlands. In centuries past, the Searoan Kings of a united Montevale built numerous fortified shell keeps to guard against invasion from the Brock; however, after the War of the Horses began, only the two nearest the Bloodline, Ironshod in Gasparn and Valeshade in Valendia, saw much use anymore, often as staging points for raiding the occasional caravan traveling by land to reach the markets of Baronbrock, for only a single mountain pass allowed for safe travel through the Nivanus, and whosoever controlled the pass controlled land trade. Any others would be forced to risk the dangerous mountain paths or else travel by sea to the port cities along the coasts of Nordren and Edgeforth, paying considerably higher tariffs on imported goods than in the landlocked barony of Helmsted.

After weeks of drilling with the other chosen men of the Tower's Guard, it was toward Ironshod that Bel and his fellows now rode. Accompanying them was a small force of one hundred men-at-arms on foot and four score archers, each company led not by noblemen or knights but rather by sergeants who were to report directly to the lord-general himself. This was highly unusual; however, much that the Tower did often seemed to break with common conventions. For in addition to the mounted cavalry formations and other horsemanship techniques, he also forced Bel and the other knights of the Tower's Guard to practice infantry formations, melee combat with a variety of weapons, and archery, both mounted and on foot. However, Bel found much wisdom in the Tower's leadership and soon understood why for generations, the title of the Tower had been so respected from one man to the next. For not only was Marcus Harding an experienced and highly skilled horseman and warrior, but extremely learned too, well-versed, not only in the tactical advantages of this or that formation or the great battle where such designs had been employed but also the historical context of such events and the cultures of the people who had first put them into use.

It was for this reason Bel believed the infantry had their sergeants, for to place another knight or noble in command would simply invite derision among the forces. On one hand, a noble commander could resent not being counted among the Tower's Guard and may therefore seek to prove himself their equal or better by acting not under orders but by his own accord. Yet, on the other hand, were a man found to lead the infantry who was not simply a glory-seeker, some of the Knights of the Guard might resent not being granted the command themselves and were instead forced to act like mere common soldiers following another man's lead. Sadly, it appeared that one of the constants in history was the competitive nature of the aristocratic ego, and more than one battle had been lost as a result of petty noble squabbling. Separating the common infantrymen entirely from the knights prevented internal strife that would otherwise threaten the unit's cohesion, a precarious notion among nobles at best.

In terms of cohesion, however, Bel had not yet found the opportunity to confront the other men of the Guard as the Tower had suggested, and although Sir Marcus had not spoken of it again since that first day, Bel—or "Sir Briden" rather—was finding himself increasingly stigmatized, and he wondered again at Dermont's appraisal of his charisma. The fact that a minor, landless knight like "Sir Briden" only continued to prove himself one of the most skilled among the Guard simply made things worse, particularly as Banshee slowly grew more accustomed to the life of a heavy horse—the feel and weight of barding armor, the heavier rider, and perhaps a greater degree of discipline and precision than she was used to from Lilia. Still, there was something about Banshee's change that made Bel sad, for the spirited horse reminded him of the spirited rider, and he feared how his Blood Blossom was fairing in the confinement of the castle. The dispatches that Canton's men gave to Jarvy made no mention of her, and Bel was reluctant to ask Dermont directly whenever he penned his response.

Bel sighed heavily just as nearby a shout marked the point on the horizon where Ironshod appeared in sight. Behind him, the men-at- arms and archers in their white cloaks and furs trudged ahead of the baggage train, and Bel could not help wondering how many of them might die as a result of his espionage. In the snowy highland cold, their breath hung on the air in little ghostly wisps, visible reminders of the lives that, in the coming days, weeks, or months could very well be snuffed out.

It was true that for a hundred years, these men had been his people's enemies; however, Bel found it increasingly difficult to see them as such, for when the civil war was over, old enemies would need to turn to each other as friends if the peace was ever to last. Unfortunately, Bel knew there were few on either side of the Bloodline that shared this sentiment.

As evening approached, the small force of soldiers reached Ironshod, where they were met at the small gatehouse by the shell keep's aging lord, Sir Hildan Cranat. Cranat, a stout old man with heavy jowls and a mustache like a walrus, greeted the Tower civilly and promised hospitality for both him and the knights of the Guard. The men-at-arms and the archers, however, were too numerous to take shelter within the walls of the keep and would need to camp along the slopes of the castle motte within the perimeter of the palisade. Sir Harding gave the sergeants their orders and followed Lord Cranat within.

Built in the same fashion as the other shell keeps along the Nivanus, Ironshod was a circular tower keep arranged around an open-air courtyard paved with cobblestones. Here, the knights dismounted and relinquished care of their horses to Lord Cranat's grooms. Anxiously, Bel glanced around for Jarvy, for he knew Banshee would not take well to a stranger's touch, but he knew the old skirmisher would have remained with Piper and their cart with the baggage train. Sure enough, when the stable hand drew near, the black mare stomped, shook her mane, and snorted in a warning. Bel tried to calm, but to no avail, and as the other knights were now filing into the interior of the keep, a few of them (the knights of lilies and rooster in particular) eyed him as one might a peasant woman failing to control her petulant child.

Tentatively, the groom took another step forward, reaching out a cautious hand toward Banshee's bridle, and this time, the black horse bucked. Again, Bel tried to calm her, whispering softly into her ear and patting her nose, and suddenly, much to his surprise, she stopped. However, it was not by his word or will that the mare calmed, but rather, when Bel turned, standing behind him in silence, stood Tempest, the Tower's great searoan, and through some unworldly instinct, Banshee appeared to grow docile and deferent at his approach, just as a man might a great king.

Bel nodded toward the groom, and Banshee allowed the man to be about his business with her while Tempest mutely watched. It had been years since Bel had last seen one of Galdorn's great horses, not since Prince Gislain still lived to ride into battle upon Squall, and even then, it had always been at a distance. They had become exceedingly rare over the last century, and though they could occasionally be found leading herds of wild horses across the plain, it was said that they had come to shun the sight of man out of disgust at Montevale's fratricidal war, and that they would suffer only worthy men of true heart and strong virtue to ride them. Now, to see one up so close, Bel felt nearly as stricken by the selfsame sense of reverence as Banshee had at the great stallion's approach.

In color, the searoan's coat, as its name implied, was the blue-gray color of the northern sea with flecks of white intermixed like foam upon the crest of a wave while its feet, nose, mane, and tail darkened to black. It was said that like the spirit hounds of Perindal, the searoans were as intelligent as men, and gazing into Tempest's eyes like two great onyxes, Bel believed that at least that legend must be true.

"Thank you," he whispered. However, the great horse merely swished his tail and sauntered off to his own stall, and Bel followed the rest of the Tower's guard up a short staircase and into the castle.

Inside, men of Sir Cranat's guard adorned with the knight's symbol, the white swallow, motioned Bel and the other men through a small antechamber into a long room that served as the Ironshod's great hall. Like the room itself, the lord's table was curved to fit with the circular shape of the keep while, on the far wall, one staircase led upward into the second floor of the castle while a second led downward into what Bel's stomach told him must be the kitchens, for the pungent odor of beef and onion soup made his mouth water after the long days of riding. However, it was obvious that the meal would have to wait, for Sir Cranat had apparently been preparing for their arrival, and rather than trenchers, basins, and other mealtime accoutrements, the tabletop was instead covered with large sheets of parchment displaying maps of the Nivanus Highlands from north to south. Beside them, a servant stood wiping the dust from a number of large figurines shaped like horses—some carved from alabaster and others from dark soapstone. When the knights had all assembled, the Tower addressed them.

"I know that you are weary after the long ride from Reginal, so I will be brief," the lord-general began. "As you may have surmised, we seek to take sole dominion over the Nivanus Pass so as to control the flow of trade into the Brock come spring. However, in truth, that is but the first of our objectives."

Sir Marcus paused and flipped through the maps strewn upon the table, finally choosing one that displayed the borders of a united Montevale and the various emplacements in both north and south. Bel wondered at the illuminated maps and their gilded patterns of horses and knotwork, for they were clearly the handiwork of a Guardian Scribe, though he could not recall any attached to either the Gasparn or Valendian courts since the War of the Horses began. This, of course, meant that the maps were at least a hundred years old. What a shame, Bel thought, that works of such beauty should also become casualties of war, and he could not help but imagine a horizontal bar of red dragged like a bleeding corpse across the center of the map.

"Now, for nearly a century, the White Horse and the Black have fought for over these lands, yet in all that time, the fighting has been concentrated along here," the Tower said, tracing the Bloodline. "True, a few attempts have been made, even a sea landing south when Sir Irwin Samant, the White Wave, sailed around Castone to assault Tremontane directly." He paused, and Bel watched a number of the other knights eye each other questioningly. Apparently, the Tower knew Montevalen history better than most natives did. "In each of those cases, however," Harding continued, "these attempts failed. Does anyone know why? What caused the White Wave's undoing or confounded the Highland Ghost who tried to cross the White Wood or the Shattered Shield who fell crossing the Tampant Ridge? Anyone?"

A few knights exchanged glances while most simply examined the floor, and Sir Cranat clicked his tongue with curmudgeonly disappointment. Though he knew the answer (for it was his father who had defeated the Shattered Shield and Sir Emory who personally slew the Gasparn knight in battle), Bel held his tongue; he did not want to be first to speak. Thankfully, Lord Talondaire saved him the trouble. "Supply lines," the young lord said. "Wagons cannot easily navigate the uneven paths of a forest, and sending ships around Castone not only takes time, but the Sorgund pirates haunt those coasts and find supply ships easy prey."

"True," the Tower said. "Supply lines are necessary for any prolonged conflict. However, there is a second reason. Sir Briden?"

Bel was hesitant. "Heavy cavalry cannot charge through trees, nor over a rocky upland, nor can they from the deck of a galley," he said. "They need an open field that is wide, solid, and relatively flat, which is why most of the fighting has been along the Bloodline."

"Correct as well," Harding said, "which is also why it is the most fortified region of Montevale, a strange thing that the strongest of a nation's defenses should occupy its heart rather than its borders, but such is the nature of civil war. Whitemane, Roanshead, and all the great fortresses lie within a day or two's ride from the line, which is why it is that area that I intend us to avoid entirely.

From the assorted figurines, he selected two large dark horses. "Now, as it stands, the Plague Prince has divided the Valendian forces into two large armies, and although we beat him soundly in the last battle, it was primarily his infantry that he lost, sacrificed to cover his own escape and that of his nobles. Still, the bulk of his heavy horse remains intact, and since then, his nobles have drawn further levies."

"Beardless boys and old men," one of the knights muttered.

"Don't forget the women," another said.

"At this point, they'll outnumber the men."

Bel remained silent.

"From what our scouts have reported," the Tower continued, placing the dark horses upon the map, "the Plague Prince currently leads the larger of the two armies and is encamped at Whitemane. With him are most of the cavalry and most of the great lords, but we also know that Prince Dermont employs many spies and assassins that allow him to remain quite dangerous in spite of his recent defeat and his current occupation of Whitemane. The fire that destroyed the keep at Jorgan's Den and the murders of Lord Malton and his family were yet the most recent examples. The second, much smaller army led by Lord Talvert, occupies the eastern lands here. However, it appears to act primarily in a defensive posture and, I believe, is no threat to us. He remains primarily around his castle at Ebon Keep, though he sends regular patrols out along the edge of the White Wood and along the Bloodline."

Bel sighed. Talvert was King Cedric's youngest brother, and though headstrong and reckless as a youth, he, too, had felt the sting of Larius's death, for scarcely ten years separated them in age, and they had been close. He would not cross into Gasparn unless Dermont ordered it.

"However, though still formidable, I believe we find ourselves suddenly at a distinct advantage, particularly considering the dire circumstances for the White Horse leading into our last encounter with the Black. It was believed then that a Valendian victory was assured, yet now the tables may have turned, and it seems the Plague Prince may be undone by his own overconfidence. He has refused the ransom of his uncle, Lord Leonis Tremont, who remains now a guest in his former home at Roanshead, and he has sent his brother, the Silent Prince, to Grantis seeking an alliance against both Gasparn and Andoch. However, given Grantis's current wars with both Andoch and Dwerin, I do not believe the senate will have much aid to offer. Thus, Dermont has denied himself the services of perhaps his greatest military leaders."

Bel might have blushed at the compliment, if he had heard it, but he stopped listening as soon as he heard Dermont's refusal of Leonis's ransom. His jaw clenched in anger, and his stomach tied in knots. He was tired of Dermont's lies and his excuses, and most of all, he was tired of turning a blind eye to the Plague Prince's sins. True, as Dermont had said, there were other men to be ransomed, good men who had been captive far longer than Leonis; however, Dermont had left them to rot too. Their ransoms could have been paid long ago, but instead, the men had simply been forgotten, and although he previously took his brother at his word, he knew the real reason. For when the lords of the castles were killed or captured, Dermont exercised his rights to assume custody of the lord's family and estate, gaining still greater power and influence by arranging matches for widows and daughters, elevating sons to take their fathers' places, or in some cases, promoting new lords entirely of his choosing while displacing the survivors of the old.

The Tower continued. From the assorted figurines, he now selected three alabaster horses.

"Now," he said, "since we find ourselves in a relatively secure position, King Marius and I have reorganized our forces into three separate armies. The eastern army, under the command of Lord Talevan, will occupy the castle at Pridel and there harass Talvert's skirmishers along the border. Lord Fabien will continue to occupy Roanshead but will now command the central army, the largest of the three, to check the progress of the Plague Prince should he attempt to advance." He paused to place two figurines on the map marking each location. "Meanwhile, the smallest army, the western army led by King Marius's cousin Lord Guillon, holds here"—he indicated a final point along the map—"at Castle Dunmorrow just to the east of here on the edge of the plane below the highlands. However, in truth, they simply lie in wait."

The men of the Tower's Guard eyed their commander questioningly; however, the Tower ignored their eyes and paced down the table to another map, this one marking the locations and the names of the various shell keeps and watchtowers along the Nivanus range. "Currently," he said, pointing to one of the towers, "we are here. In two days, I would like us to be *here*."

"Valeshade," someone whispered.

"Once we have done so," Sir Marcus went on, "Lord Guillon will quietly follow, occupying the keep while we move on to the next, and the next, and the next, and so forth until finally, we reach the last keep at Shoulderidge. There, Lord Guillon will join us in force, and we will drive east into the heart of Valendia. Fabien will attempt to attack the Plague Prince from Roanshead, joined by Talevan in the east while we assault Castle Tremontane and, by the will of the Brethren, force King Cedric to surrender and acknowledge King Marius's claims." At length, the Tower clasped his hands behind his back and stood up straight. "Are there questions?"

After a few moments of silence, the Knight of the Rooster spoke. "My lord-general," he said, "with respect, we are cavalry. What business do we have assaulting towers? A mounted charge will have little effect against a stone wall. Should we not be in the field?"

The Tower suppressed a smile. "True enough, Sir Gurney," he said, "though it was my understanding that your prowess in battle was not dependent upon your horse. I believed that you men were more than just horsemen but the finest warriors of your realm, and thus far, you have all proven yourselves capable of such accolades in our drilling. Do not belittle yourselves by thinking you are limited solely to the heavy charge. A wild boar is quite skilled in that regard, I assure you, but that does not make it a knight."

Sir Trenton, the Knight of Lilies, laughed at his friend; however, Lord Talondaire remained stoic. "My lord," he said, "I still believe that Sir Gurney raises a fine point, though. Even with the infantry and archer support, we are but two hundred men. How are we to possibly lay a siege?"

His inexperience begins to show, Bel thought.

"Lord Talondaire," the Tower said, "how many men-at-arms do you command at Taloncrest?"

"One hundred and sixty-five," he said, "plus the knights who manage our fiefs and their own retinues, though I believe since I have joined you, most follow my uncle under Lord Guillon."

The Tower nodded and turned to Sir Cranat. "My lord, Ironshod has the largest complement of soldiers among the Gasparn keeps along the Nivanus, correct?"

"Aye, sir," the old knight said.

"How many men make up the garrison here?"

"Twenty-four, sir, though there's a small village of goatherds to the northeast that I imagine we could always draw another score or so from should the need ever arise."

"I doubt that should be necessary, Sir Cranat," the Tower said. He turned back to the young Talon. "Yes, we are a small force, but as you can see, we significantly outnumber the defenses in any of the keeps. Furthermore, we have your uncle and the rest of Lord Guillon's army at our backs. No, I do not anticipate any true fighting save perhaps at Valeshade, nor do I seek to underestimate our opponents, for many a siege has been broken with but a handful of defenders. The archers will take care of any carrier birds the defenders might try to send, and you riders can ride down any messengers who attempt to flee on foot or horse. However, my hope is that the commanders of the keeps will show wisdom enough to simply stand down."

"And if they do not?"

"Then we will have no choice but to fight."

Bel considered the Tower's plans. A force of two hundred men presented a number that was sizable enough to allow the Valendian lord to surrender without disgrace while, at the same time, remained small enough to prevent accusations that the Gasparns were simply cowards for attacking such a small garrison with such overwhelming numbers. Thus, both sides kept their honor, though one was in victory and the other was in defeat.

Bel tried to remember who commanded the mountain keeps on the Valendian side, and he wondered how many he might know, or more importantly, how many might know him. Sir Lorgan Wilks had Valeshade, he knew that, with a command of at the very most fifty men, though even that number was unlikely considering Dermont's recent defeat and call for replacements. Bel knew Wilks by reputation as a skilled commander but had never met him personally. He did not doubt, however, that Sir Lorgan would require at least some nominal show of force before surrendering his command. From there, it would be Sir Jaren Freas at Widowridge, Sir Oran Bandry at Clearpoint, Sir Horton Codwin at Graymount, and finally, Sir Gregon Motts at Shoulderidge. Sir Jaren was a onetime political rival of Lord Harren who had apparently retired from politics amid scandal, and Bel did not know him nor the particulars of his fall either; but, Sir Oran and Sir Gregan, he did remember, though he had not seen either of them since he was small and he did not believe that they would recognize him now. Sir Horton, however, might be a problem; for the Thunder Mace (as he was once known) had been a loyal friend to King Cedric and once served as seneschal to Lord and Lady Coralina, father and mother of Larius's deceased wife. It was but a few years since Codwin had visited Bel's father at Castle Tremontane, and he at least might know the Silent Prince to see him.

A few days after the Tower's Guard began drilling, Bel and Jarvy had finally been able to gain residence in one of the local inns rather than face the deepening autumn chill in their pavilion. Soon after, they learned the reason for the inn's sudden vacancy: one of Canton's men served as a stable lad, and the hostler himself was accepting a tidy monthly stipend for turning a blind eye and keeping his mouth shut. Bel couldn't help but again wonder at the necessity of his own presence at the Tower's side when Dermont seemed quite capable of placing his spies wherever he pleased, even so far as the Gasparn capital. Still, thinking about it only conjured memories of Lilia's warnings, followed by memories of Lilia herself, and both were too painful for Bel to think on for too long.

Through Canton's man, Bel had been able to communicate on occasion with Dermont, though it was not something he relished. Thankfully, he had little enough to report anyway other than constant drilling until the last message when he informed Dermont that the Tower's Guard would be riding on the morrow westward toward the Nivanus. That alone was all he had said, for that was all he himself knew at the time. Had Dermont been able to learn anything further? Would Sir Horton be informed of the ruse? Or would the nominal forces believed to be guarding the western border keeps miraculously have swelled to their full complement? Bel knew none of the answers, and so he chose instead to remain Sir Briden, for there was nothing else that he could do.

When there were no further questions, the Tower released his men to find their quarters and remove their armor while Sir Cranat's staff prepared the great hall for the meal. The knights were to billet in the guardhouse in bunks that—should a war with the Brock ever come—would have served half a hundred soldiers. When Bel arrived with the others, he was pleased to find Jarvy installed already with Bel's things.

"There may be a battle two days hence," Bel said quietly after the old skirmisher had helped relieve him of his accursed plate. "We're to take Valeshade, though my hope is that we shall do so without bloodshed."

Jarvy nodded but said nothing; they both knew what it could mean: the opportunity—no, the obligation—to kill men who served the Black Horse. It filled Bel with both anxiety and disgust, for he would have to kill his father's men, men like Horn and Wendel, Jarvy and Sir Emory, and—he sighed with misery—perhaps women, women like Val or Lilia.

"What's the matter, Briden?" said a snide voice. "Are you afraid to fight?"

"Of course he is," said another. "For all he knows, there could be women manning the Valendian tower."

Bel looked toward the speakers and saw that, though the room was full of the knights of the Tower's Guard, the voices were undeniably those of Gurney and Trenton. Jarvy held his tongue, but Bel could sense the older man's anger.

"Show me a man who claims he's not afraid," Bel replied, tightening his baldric around his surcoat. "And I'll show you a liar."

The Cock and Lilies exchanged a grin and glanced around at the other knights. A few laughed quietly and shook their heads while others chose simply to ignore.

"Funny," Sir Trenton said, "I hope you do not intend to imply that Gurney and I are liars? Surely, you would not be suggesting that?"

"Aye," Sir Gurney snorted, "I'd find it a hard thing to be called a liar by a man who's done nothing but prove himself a coward since the tourney."

Bel stood still while, behind him to one side, Jarvy took a deep breath and forced himself to sit down atop the chest where they stored Bel's armor.

"I've seen battle," Bel said at last, his voice cold, "which is more than either of you can say."

"How dare you!" Sir Trenton spat.

"I mean a real battle, close-quarter fighting—not merely a mounted charge to scare off unarmored peasants wielding plowshares and pitchforks while you hide safe and sound atop your horses in your iron skin. Yet you talk to me of cowardice."

Sir Linton Traver, who shared the Young Talon's victory in the melee, paused, still half-clad in his armor, to intercede.

"Gentlemen, please," he said. "Sir Harding has forbid us dueling…"

Bel glanced at Sir Linton. He was a large man, tall and strong, and like Sir Gurney and Sir Trenton, appeared to be of an age somewhere in his middle twenties. In the last few weeks, he had been one of the other knights to show great skill under the Tower's tutelage, and though he and Bel had never before spoken, Bel had no cause to think ill of him. Beside him, however, the Talon stood watching in silence, and though the young noble did not intercede one way or the other, Bel sensed he was anxious to see the conflict through to its conclusion.

Sir Gurney strode in close to Bel and puffed out his chest as might the rooster on his crest. "We're not dueling," he said, "I'm just going to beat his fucking ass."

The room fell silent, and Bel felt his blood stir as it had not since the morning of the battle when he and Lilia defeated the Snow Bear. He met Gurney's gaze without flinching and stared back intently, his green eyes ablaze. Gurney's hot breath smelled foul, but Bel listened to it closely, waiting for the Knight of the Cock to make his move. When he finally did, Bel was ready and struck out first, hard and fast and, with one punch, knocked Sir Gurney to the floor, gasping for air, struggling in agony to reclaim his wind.

Seeing his friend fall, Sir Trenton lunged at Bel and pushed him backward into the frame of an empty bunk. His head struck the side of a wooden bedpost, but Bel ignored the pain, and when the Knight of Lilies attempted to punch him in the chest, he easily countered, knocking Trenton to the floor with blood streaming from his nose. The whole scuffle had lasted barely a minute; however, afterward, when Bel drew his sword, time stood still. A collective gasp traveled like wildfire through the remaining knights of the Tower's Guard, and Jarvy leaped to his feet.

Bel let the point of his sword fall to touch the floor beside where Sir Gurney still struggled to catch his breath, and Sir Trenton clutched at his broken nose, trying to stay the flow of blood. Both sets of eyes grew wide when they fell upon Bel's naked blade.

"If this were a real battle," Bel whispered coldly, "you would both be dead."

Sir Gurney wheezed in fright. Bel traced the tip of his sword along the floorboard with a scrape.

"Sir Briden, stop this," Sir Linton said, adding, "please."

For a moment, Bel ignored him, allowing the blade to linger, catching the light of the guardhouse fireplace. Then, finally, he returned the blade to its sheath.

"This is not a game," he said, loud enough for all men yet in the guardhouse to hear. "This is not a tourney. This is war, and it is brutal and bloody and hard. Some of you know this, but many more of you have yet to learn. The only way that any of us have a chance to live, the only thing that separates life and death in the coming days, is the trust we have in one another and our willingness to fight at each other's side." He paused, uncomfortable with the volume of his own voice. "Now I do not ask any of you to like me or to like each other, but I do ask that you fight beside me, for rest assured that I will fight with all my strength beside any of you." He gazed down at the two knights on the floor. "Even you two," he added and, without another word, left the guardhouse by way of the courtyard to take his meal in the great hall.

Thankfully, when Bel was seated at the long table, the servants wasted no time in pouring his wine, and he took a long, heavy drink to stay his shaking hands. A few of the other knights of the guard were already seated and at their meals, unaware of what had just transpired in the guardhouse. Neither the Tower himself nor Sir Cranat was in attendance.

Before long, the remainder of the knights began to file in. Without turning, Bel could feel their eyes upon him and tried to ignore the whispered gossip as the story of his fight spread throughout the hall. It would not be long then, he thought, until the Tower sent him away. At least now he could return to Valendia, and he was near enough to the Bloodline that he and Jarvy could pass undetected along the Nivanus—using the selfsame route the Tower intended. He would make his way back to Tremontane and Lilia before Dermont learned of his failure.

From there, though, he had no idea what they would do. They could try to flee Valendia, but that would mean leaving his men, his family, and his country behind, all of which was out of the question. He could try to appeal to his father; however, Dermont did not often condescend to acknowledge King Cedric's will anyway. For a fleeting moment, he considered appealing to Dermont for mercy. However, he knew well what his brother's mercy entailed. There were plenty of Gasparn soldiers who had gone to their graves without their heads for the price of accepting one of Dermont's offers of mercy in exchange for their surrender. A shadow fell upon Bel's musings, though it took a moment for him to look up and notice that it was cast not by his own dark thoughts but rather by Sir Linton's tall form.

Bel glanced up at the other knight's stern face with its sharp, angular features and light-brown hair cropped close to better fit beneath an arming cap. Sir Linton's brow furrowed as he regarded "Sir Briden," and he folded his arms across his chest, clad now in his surcoat, quartered red and blue.

"You're a madman," he said.

Bel sighed. "I suppose so."

To his surprise, however, Sir Linton sat down at the table across from him and raised a hand to call a servant for wine. "Gurney's up and about," Linton said once the wine had come, "And I think you broke Trenton's nose, but he'll live to fight another day."

"I had hoped this would be the end of it," Bel said.

Sir Linton paused while a servant returned with his food. "I think you misunderstand me," he said, tearing off a hunk of bread. "I mean that he will be fine for Valeshade. Neither one of them, I believe, will bother you any further."

"Oh."

"Frankly, I think some of the older men are a bit envious of you. I've heard both Sir Mathis and Sir Armel mention as much as least twice apiece."

Bel nodded and went back to his own meal.

"And you're not the only one who's seen battle, Sir Briden, though you may be the youngest. You're not yet twenty, are you?"

Bel paused and thought. What month was it? He vaguely remembered a celebration for the Feast of Tengale in Reginal. If that was true, then Oakentide must have passed, meaning it was now halfway through the Month of the Horse and very likely that his birthday had already come and gone. "I am twenty," he said, sounding perhaps a bit surprised. "Though I've been fighting since I was seventeen after my brother died."

"In Rosewood?"

Bel caught himself quickly and took a sip of wine to collect his thoughts. "Aye, in Rosewood," he said, "my father died there too with Lord Solidor. I received my knighthood during the battle."

"I, too, lost a brother," Sir Linton said, "and a sister, though she died in childbirth. Her husband was a sergeant under Sir Esborn Lenoy. I'm the first in my family to earn my spurs."

"You ride well," Bel said. "I'm sure your family would be proud."

"My father taught me. He probably could have been knighted first, but he lost half his leg against the Black Horse back when King Marius still took the field. He never tired of talking about it, though after riding with both the Tower and Prince Gislain, I may just about have him beat."

"You fought with Prince Gislain?"

"Aye, and half the men here, if they were old enough. Of course, there are some my age like Gurney and Trenton, tourney knights, whose fathers paid to avoid them having to serve, and thus, never had the pleasure. Since Gislain fell and King Marius annulled the scutage, though, the happiness of their company is ours once more."

Bel sighed. "I hear in Valendia, they still allow the scutage, though every Valendian king has at one time or another tried to annul it as well. In fact, the whole reason King Ignarius allowed women to fight was to shame the noblemen who hid behind the tax. It seems they were more willing to sacrifice their women than risk taking the field themselves."

"And if the gods are good," Sir Linton said, "that is precisely why our armies will defeat them."

Bel avoided a response by taking a drink of wine as another older knight of the Guard with a bald head and a neatly trimmed mustache sat down at Sir Linton's side. On his tabard, he bore an emblem of a tawny owl. "Sir Linton," he greeted them, "and, Sir Briden. So it begins, eh?"

"Sir Armel," Sir Linton said. Bel nodded.

"Quite a show you put on in the barracks, Sir Briden." The elder knight smirked. "Though perhaps not the type of melee those two are used to."

"I suppose not." Bel blushed, but Sir Armel gave a quiet chuckle and called for a servant to refill their cups.

The following morning, when the Tower and his forces departed from Ironshod, Bel (or rather, Sir Briden) felt at least somewhat more certain of his position, for without intending to do so, he appeared to have fulfilled Sir Marcus's orders and found his place among the rest of the Guard. Even Sir Gurney and Sir Trenton, rather than huddle together covertly plotting vengeance, appeared instead humbled, and though neither they nor the Young Talon said a single word to him, Bel did not sense the same measure of animosity with which they had regarded him with before.

Sir Cranat and a half dozen of his men accompanied the lord-general as far as the Nivanus Pass and the Bloodline and, while the knights, men-at-arms, and archers carried onward into enemy territory, the lord of Ironshod and his men saluted them in the formal fashion of Gasparn.

As he donned his steel skin that morning, Bel learned from Jarvy that the infantry had been rather busy the previous night, and as they marched, Bel discerned that two of the supply carts in the baggage train now carried large wooden frames, the disassembled components, no doubt, of a pair of ballistae.

By midday, the first of the Valendian keeps, Valeshade, was in sight. Like its fellows along mountainsides, it was in all ways an exact copy of Ironshod. The Tower issued orders to his men to set up camp and prepare for war. While the infantry assembled the siege weapons just outside of bowshot, patrols of men-at-arms and archers were sent out to guard against any messengers seeking to escape and warn Dermont in Whitemane, far to the east, or the other towers of the Nivanus Highlands further south. At length, when the base camp was established and the ballistae were ready, the Tower, Sir Linton, Lord Talondaire, and two other knights (Sir Welmsey Pitarn and Sir Cardalon Bloch) rode out before the gates of Valeshade to offer terms. Bel, the remaining knights of the Guard, the men-at-arms, and the archers stood waiting in their ranks while behind them to either side, the men at the ballistae loaded their war machines with heavy, iron-tipped bolts.

The west wind howled down the mountain, and in spite of the thick, quilted gambeson he wore beneath his plate and chain, Bel still felt the chill. When he sighed, his breath appeared on the air, and as he always did, he flexed the fingers of his swordhand against the cold.

Banshee, too, seemed restless, and two thin trails of steam rose like smoke from her nostrils in the frigid air. If it came to battle, they would both soon be warmed by the frenzied motion of war.

However, as he peered ahead at the gate, Bel suddenly had the feeling that something unusual was going on, and beside him, Sir Armel lifted the visor of his helm.

"I see no defenders upon the battlements," he observed.

Bel nodded, and a few of the other knights grunted in agreement. "What is it?" Sir Trenton's voice whispered hoarsely from behind his pot helm. "What's wrong?"

"Shut up," Sir Armel replied without turning.

Bel sighed and leaned toward where Gurney and Trenton waited side by side upon their palfreys. "Nothing," Bel whispered. "It's just…there seem to be no defenders on the walls."

"But wouldn't they have seen us setting up the camp?" the Knight of Lilies asked.

Bel wondered at Trenton's geniality in light of their former disagreement, and he wondered if it was truly meant out of peace or if it was simply the result of the anticipation (and subsequent fear) of battle. Regardless of the truth, Bel chose to view it as the former. "You're right," he said.

"There's no banner flying from the keep," Sir Gurney observed. "Do you think that means they've gone?"

Bel peered up at the castle. It was true. There was no banner. "I don't know," he said.

"Quiet, all of you," Sir Armel whispered. "Look. The gate opens."

And sure enough, it did. However, it was not a band of knights who passed through the open portal, nor men-at-arms nor any other type of warrior, but rather a pair of peasants bound tightly in furs against the cold, unarmed, and unarmored. A strange sensation settled in Bel's chest, and he wondered if the apparent absence of soldiers was his own doing, Dermont's, or simply the work of chance. In any event, it appeared there would be no battle today, for the Tower was already guiding Tempest through the gates, and shortly thereafter, Sir Welmsey returned and informed the rest of the forces that they might stand down and reform their camp around the palisade of the keep, for apparently there was to be no battle. Valeshade was empty, and its lord and garrison called away to reinforce the Plague Prince and his army at

404

Whitemane in the east, so it might well be for the rest of the keeps of the Nivanus Highlands.

Bel sighed. Something still did not seem right. Would Dermont really abandon the border, or did his spies allow him to piece together the Tower's plan? In which case, why did he not simply lie in wait and spring a trap? Even as a child, it was very rare that Dermont would part with anything so easily, at least anything he felt belonged to him. "Something is not right," Bel said aloud.

And suddenly, it dawned on him. Without a word, he spurred Banshee forward and rode hard for Valeshade's gate. Inside, the Tower, Sir Linton, Sir Cardalon, and Lord Talondaire had dismounted and were leading their horses to the stalls, though they turned and put their hands to their weapons at the thundering sound of Banshee's hooves. One of the two peasants drew water from the central well into a bucket while the other followed closely behind the four knights. When Bel noticed the shuffling gait with which the two men moved, his suspicions were all but confirmed.

"Sir Briden?" the Tower asked, relaxing his grip on Spire, "what is it?"

In a flash, Bel slipped from Banshee's saddle and drew his sword as the peasant with the bucket crept closer to where Sir Linton stood beside Lord Talondaire.

"Stop!" Bel shouted at the peasant and raised his sword at the man's throat.

The peasant held up a hand in alarm, though Bel knew the man's innocence was as feigned as his fear.

"Please, lord!" the peasant cried, muffled by his thick fur wrappings. "I only meant to offer the young knights a drink of water!"

"I'm sure of it," Bel said. He turned to the Tower. "My lord, these men are not servants. They're soldiers, or at least they were."

The Tower eyed the peasants carefully. "What say you to that?" he asked them.

In reply, the man with the bucket spewed its contents out over Sir Linton and ran to cower behind the stones of the well while the second man drew a dagger from his belt and lunged headlong at Bel. Bel sidestepped quickly and carefully brought his sword up into the man's belly, running him through, though he hesitated when he drew the blade out again so as not to splash himself with the dead man's blood.

Quickly, the other four knights advanced on the first man; however, when he saw that all was lost, rather than fight, he dived headfirst into the well. The abrupt end to his screaming told the men above that he was dead.

"So much for fresh water," Sir Cardolan observed.

"I feel I've had enough," Sir Linton said, shivering against the cold.

"We need a fire," Bel said, "and you need to get out of those clothes quickly and find clean water to wash yourself."

"Why?" Sir Cardolan asked, "What is it?"

Bel turned to the Tower. "My lord," he said, "those men were lepers. The rumors say that the Valendians use them to sow poison and spread disease. I'm certain that should we drink any water from this well, few, if any of us, would be left alive by week's end."

Sir Linton looked stricken.

"It seems the Prince of Plague did not leave his towers entirely undefended when he summoned his forces to him at Whitemane," the Tower observed, "Sir Cardolan, Lord Talon, help Sir Linton from his armor so that he might clean himself and one of you fetch his man at the baggage train with some new clothes."

"Yes, my lord."

The Tower stepped around the dead leper and nudged the fur scarf away from the corpse's face revealing the telltale signs of the horrid disease. "Well, Sir Briden," he said, placing his hand on Bel's shoulder, "it appears you may have saved many lives today and perhaps many more to come if it's true that the remaining keeps are garrisoned the same way."

"I had heard stories of tactics like this," Bel said softly, "with villages Valendia lost along the Bloodline, though I had hoped that they were not true."

"Often, men of honor can be blind to the wiles of those without any," the Tower said. "Thank the Brethren you were there to see the truth when I could not."

"Does that mean I have no honor?" Bel remarked.

Sir Marcus laughed quietly. "Of course not," he said. "But it means that I will have to put you to better use."

CHAPTER 30:
FERGUS

From the crossroads, Lughus followed Crodane northeast along the coastal road for another mile or so before abruptly turning into the woodlands. The swordsman moved swiftly, his long strides hurrying surefooted among the roots and uneven slopes of the undergrowth.

"If the Hammer does not catch up with us by nightfall, then it will mean that they have turned back."

"Then does that me we will be free?" Lughus asked.

Crodane shook his head. "No, merely that they have gone back to regroup, for they know where we are headed, and the Hammer does not give up easily. However, we can no longer walk the roads for fear of riders, nor can we walk the coasts as they will surely be on patrol by ship. Our only hope now is to take to the woodlands to elude their sight and pass the border into Baronbrock without their notice." He sighed. "I hope you are prepared. Galadin is many leagues away."

Lughus nodded but remained silent. He had made his choice to follow Crodane, but he was not yet certain that it was wise. Regardless, he could not go back on it now.

"How did you know that the Hammer was in that tavern?" he asked.

"He and I have met a number of times over the years under varying circumstances. As such, I have a certain understanding, call it a sense, if you will, of his ways."

"You have escaped him before?"

"Yes," Crodane said, "though he is never an easy one to elude, and more than once, we have come to blows. Harlow is particularly vicious, however. He and I first met shortly before the wedding of your mother and father."

Lughus stepped lightly over a large patch of moss and brambles while Crodane hurried on ahead. "What happened to them?" he asked, running to catch up. "Crodane, you said that you would tell me."

The swordsman paused. "True enough," he said. "But I will tell you as we walk. Do not fall behind."

"Fine."

"So be it," Crodane said. He paused for a moment to collect his thoughts and, when he was ready, began the tale.

"Twenty years ago, the baron of Brabant, who was a close friend of your grandfather, was killed—poisoned, some said—by men hired by the Baron of Denholm, long supporters of the Marthaines. Both often competed for control of the waters of the northern sea, and the Denholms claimed their ships were being raided by men of Brabant disguised as Wrathorn pirates. In any case, the new baron of Brabant sought backing from your grandfather, whilst the Marthaines were only too willing to back Denholm. Skirmishes broke out all over the borders, and before long, the Galadins and the Marthaines began rallying their soldiers as well, forcing many of the other baronies to choose sides. Soon, many feared a civil war was coming that would have made the War of the Horses look like little more than a family spat."

"Eventually, the Lord-Baron, Harlon Glendaro, elder brother of Loremaster Rastis, interceded. He summoned arbitrators from the Order, all Chancellor's men, and called an Assembly of the Barons in Highboard." Crodane paused. "I stayed in Galadin, of course, to safeguard your mother, but when Sir Wolfram and Baron Arcis returned, the mood was as grim as I'd ever seen, for it was decided at the assembly that to ensure an end to the fighting once and for all, the Galadins and the Marthaines would join their families and become one.

At that, the swordsman fell silent for a time, and Lughus did not press him to continue but rather simply followed along. After a short while, the woodlands gave way to farmers' fields where the common folk worked in groups bundling stalks of wheat or threshing grain in thick piles. Away on a hilltop stood a stout stone keep, its banners bearing the symbol of an argent wheel, and Lughus recognized it as the sigil of Lord and Lady Lunette, whom he recalled lived most of the year at court in the capital. It made him wonder that the common folk should toil such while their lord and lady made merry in Titanis alongside the King. No wonder the peasants of Lenard's Crossing had been so brutish and coarse, for in a world that treated them so unkindly, how could one expect them to be any different? Under such circumstances, it must be a rare type of virtue to be both a good man and poor.

When the keep and the farmers were well behind them, Crodane continued.

"Your mother," he said, "bore her sentence with dignity, as she always did any measure of difficulty. She joked that it was the Lady's way of humbling her for being so choosy since she was near twenty years old and not yet wed, for she had many suitors and was considered by many to be the finest of all women in Termain. However, she was so spirited and independent, and Baron Arcis doted upon her so, that in spite of the many offers from many great lords from Dwerin all the way to Montevale, your grandfather refused to force her to marry, and until the Lord-Baron's decree, promised that she would only do so of her own choosing."

Lughus listened, but again, the swordsman fell silent. The more Crodane spoke of his mother, the more he wanted to know. Yet he also wished to hear of his father—for what manner of man could kill such a woman as her of whom the swordsman so highly spoke.

"If she was as you say," Lughus asked, "then why would my father have killed her? Was he always such a bad man?"

Crodane's reply was simple and brief, "He was a Marthaine."

"What do you mean?"

"It means that he was my enemy and your mother's. It means that I am beyond trying to justify his ways."

Lughus sighed, and suddenly, something about his own skin made him feel sick. If his father had been a man willing to commit such evil, what did that say about him? Crodane claimed that as a Galadin, his blood was that of the Great Saint, but, as a Marthaine, did his blood now also bear the taint of a murderer?

"Still," Crodane added, "until the end, he did not treat your mother unkindly, and in truth, I, too, was surprised at what was to come, for had I sensed the slightest of indications, I would not have hesitated to kill him on the spot." He continued, "Beyond that, it is hard for me to say what your father was like, though I know he was as ambitious as your mother was kind, and though his children by her would one day inherit the baronies of both the Galadins and Marthaines, it seemed he was not content merely waiting. Your mother, now his wife, was your grandfather's only child, and your father knew that if Baron Arcis was to die, your mother's claims would pass the title on to him. He would no longer need to wait until his own father's death to become a Baron, and with the balance of power tipped in the Marthaine's favor, he might even be able to sway the vote to win the seat of the Lord-Baron away from Glendaro and claim dominion in Highboard. And so, he began to plot, and eventually, he set his plans into motion..."

At this, Crodane paused, "You should know Lughus that in spite of who your father was, your mother loved you dearly, and for your sake, she tried to love your father too. You were dearer to her than all the world."

Lughus nodded and looked off ahead at the horizon, for he knew not what to say. At last, he sighed and hurried on as Crodane continued walking. "Then what happened?" he asked. "What was... what was my father's plan? How did my mother die?"

Crodane was reticent. "Your...your grandfather was away—called away. He received word that there was a rebellion in the barony of Crofton and the lord there had a...tendency for putting his common folk to the sword. Your grandfather hoped to keep the peace. However, as it turned out, it was all a farce, a trap to lure baron Arcis to his death." He paused. "That night, after she retired, your mother happened to discover dispatches among your father's things, and when she confronted him, your father killed her and attempted to lay blame on me."

"Is that why you killed him and is that how you became a Blackguard?"

"In a sense. The two are not unrelated," Crodane said, "Baron Arcis and Wolfram of Parth, who remember was your grandfather's seneschal, fought through the trap, though when they returned, they found your mother murdered, myself in prison, and your father's lies. However, your grandfather knew that I would rather die a thousand deaths before I ever thought to hurt your mother, and he demanded a trial by combat, that I be allowed to challenge my accuser." The swordsman sighed. "So I did. I slew your father and won my freedom, but your father's guard sought vengeance of their own, and I was gravely wounded before Sir Wolfram cut them down."

"Since Aiden's sacrifice to defeat the Warlock, the Guardians have always sworn to protect his heirs, and so they have, even after the Siege of Three when those who refused fealty to the Drudish Kings were shamed with the label of Blackguard. Wolfram of Parth was no different, for he was secretly anointed the Marshal, and under that title, swore—like the Marshals before him—to defend the Galadins with his dying breath. But as was the case, Sir Wolfram knew that he was very old and that you—your mother's only son and the last of the Galadin heirs—were very young."

"Now, as Thom said, there are many stories of the Guardians, of St. Aiden, and of the miraculous things the Anointed can do. As you've seen, the Anointed heal quicker and find themselves more resilient to illness, injury, weariness, and disease—but there is a reason for this, an obligation and a cost. For like St. Aiden before them, the Guardians are not meant only to be warriors, but rather healers, defenders, to rebuild what the Darkness has broken, and to safeguard all people from the threat of evil and tyranny. The Anointed carry the burdens that might break other men, be it wound or injury or threat. However, if an anointed Guardian gives his life to save another, the man who lives must in return bear the title of the savior and take up arms in service of the Good."

Lughus shook his head. "I'm not certain I understand. But did you say the Marshal?"

"Aye, and when Wolfram the Marshal gave his life to save mine, he passed on his title, and his sword, Sentinel—as Thom so wisely guessed—to me."

"The Marshal!" Lughus exclaimed. "*The* Marshal?" He stopped short and suddenly his boot caught on a stone, and he nearly fell. "The Marshal is one of the Three!"

"The Marshals have served the House of Galadin since Aiden's death, and as one of the Three, we have sought to uphold the duties of the Guardians as they were in the beginning, before the Drudish Kings demanded the Oath of Fealty."

"Then the Three yet live?" Lughus asked. "And it's not just a story?"

"We live"—Crodane nodded—"though the reality rarely matches the legend." He paused. "So you see, Lughus Galadin, why as Black a Guardian as I might be, I would never harm you nor allow you to come to harm, for not only is it my duty as the Marshal to ensure that you stay safe, but the debt I owe your mother for having already failed her."

Lughus was silent for a time. "Then thank you," he said at last.

"You can thank me once we reach Galadin." Crodane smiled, gave a nod, and continued his trek. "Anything before that, I'm afraid, is premature with the Hammer on our tail."

"Why is he after us? Or rather, why is he after me? For he sought out Thom and me at the cathedral before he even heard that you were with us, saying Rastis made a mistake, but Rastis never makes mistakes."

"No, he does not, at least not often, and he would have taken great pains not to with the safety of his boys at stake. That old man has a great affection for you two and the third boy who stayed behind."

Lughus bit his lip, feeling a sudden longing to be back in the Tower lost among the books with his friends, the sound of the teakettle, and the odor of pipe smoke wafting about on the air. Those days were over now.

"The Loremasters have always questioned the Oath of Fealty," Crodane continued, waking Lughus from his forlorn reverie, "and Rastis is no exception. Think on Hobart. The Ox was a Blackguard for at least three generations. How often do any of the other councilors accept foundlings into their towers? The Chancellor's folk are more likely to execute them as traitors than accept an oath from a former Blackguard."

"But as for Rastis and the Hammer," he said, "after the deaths of your parents, the Galadins fell into despair. Your grandmother grew ill and died before the end of winter, though it might just as easily have been of a broken heart. Baron Arcis, after losing his wife now, his daughter, and Sir Wolfram, his friend, feared the Marthaines might try to steal you away. He appealed to the Lord-Baron, and out of guilt and shame for forcing the marriage to begin with, Harlon Glendaro called upon Rastis, and the Loremaster offered to conceal you and raise you until such time as you came of age."

"I spirited you away to Andoch myself," Crodane said, "with a young midwife and her husband, who Rastis promised to set up with a shop. I planned to take the Oath of Fealty so as to stay in Titanis and watch over you. However, Rastis discouraged it, believing the Marthaines would surely see through the ruse if I was around, and besides that, the Order would never accept an Oath of Fealty from one of the Three. Instead, Rastis wrote to the Vanguard and sent me off to rejoin him and the Blade."

"Rastis knew all three of you?" Lughus said. "This whole time?"

"And many more that others call Blackguards besides," Crodane said, "for whether he follows the King and council or keeps to the old ways of the knights errant, a Guardian is still just a man. There are good ones and bad ones in both camps, and while the Guardians raise up their heroes like your friend the Tower, there are others not so virtuous, like the Hammer."

"Harlow was there, you know, as part of the arbitration to prevent the war. He was newly anointed under the title of the Hammer, and right away, he knew who Sir Wolfram was, for the more a title knows another over the ages, so those who next bear the title might know each other. The Hammer has pursued the Three since the Siege, and when he knew the Marshal, he sought to bring him into custody. But Wolfram of Parth was no common criminal, and Young Harlow was a constable newly made. However, once I became the Marshal, Harlow went so far as to petition the council to grant him special dispensation to be relieved of his duties so that he might instead focus on hunting me. Rastis, King Valder, and Dandon Rood refused, for there was talk of hostilities again with Kord and the alchemists of the Sign of Four. Rather than send men out to hunt ghosts, the council ruled it more prudent to prepare in case of war." Crodane paused, and his lips twisted into a sardonic grin. "It's funny. It was said there was talk then of the Protectorate too."

"At any rate, it seems that now, however, the Hammer gets his wish, for Kredor tasked him with finding you, and as I accompany you, he finds even greater pleasure in the pursuit. Yet we will not make it easy for him!"

"What would the King possibly want with me?"

Crodane barked a laugh and hurried on through the tall grasses to where they gave way to the embankment of a small stream. "Kredor seeks to name himself High King, Emperor even, over all Termain, and he thinks he can do so by instituting the Protectorate, a difficult thing in a time of peace," he said, leaping lightly to the other side. "Convincing the other realms to recognize his superiority might require appeasing Dwerin with a gift of the Spade, or perhaps restoring the aristocracy of Grantis. Aiding the right horse in the war to the north might demand a show of gratitude from a united Montevale, and when he learned the heir of Arcis Galadin slept soundly beneath the roof of his very own castle, well..."

Lughus followed down to the stream's edge and paused to think before hopping to the other side. "So Rastis sent me away—"

"To spare Kredor using you as ransom to hold your grandfather under his boot."

For many miles more, Crodane led the way through the lands north of Galdoran, through countryside and farmer's field, through wilderness and wood, and Lughus followed behind. The swordsman's story gave the former apprentice much to think of (for "former" he must be, having chosen the side of the Blackguard), though without even Thom now to accompany him, Lughus felt suddenly very alone. As the hours passed and the shadows lengthened, his feelings of guilt mounted, and he wondered now how his friend was faring as Galdoran fell farther and farther behind. He tried to force these thoughts from his mind, however, and focused instead on the changing landscape. For the lands were far more pleasant than the river, particularly as the trees doffed their summer greens in exchange for the myriad colors of the fall, and the feel of solid ground beneath his feet was at least some reassurance from the currach's uneven roll. He let his mind wander among the old Bard's tales and fairy stories about the wilderness and the forests—of fabulous beasts and fairy mounds, when all of a sudden, he nearly laughed aloud, for he realized that the man who guided him onward to the north, was in and of himself a legend. So much had happened in such a short time—no more than half a day. At length, long after night had fallen and the paths through the undergrowth became more and more treacherous underfoot in the dark, Crodane halted beneath the cover of a large elm and set about kindling a fire.

"Sadly, this may be our last chance at such a luxury," he said once the small glowing embers had become a healthy blaze.

Lughus removed the sword and dagger from his belt and sat down upon the grass to lay out his bedroll. "Crodane," he asked, "are the Guardians now to be my enemies?"

The swordsman paused. "I would say that it depends upon the man," he said at last. "Rastis is your friend, of all things that you can be certain, and Hob for that matter, as am I, if a Blackguard counts as a Guardian." He turned away from the fire and began digging through his burlap sack. "But speaking of friends, I had best call Fergus."

"Fergus? Your friend?"

"Aye. We'll need his senses if we're to avoid the Hammer and any men he may have with him."

Lughus watched as, from within his sack, Crodane drew out a small leather pouch, inside of which was a crumbly brown substance wrapped in white cloth. The swordsman took a pinch of the substance and tossed it into the fire with a flash. Almost immediately, a sweet-smelling odor wafted about upon the breeze.

"What is that?" Lughus asked.

"Cloves mostly, and a few other spices from out of the Sorgund Isles or grown wild in Kord across the sea. Noblewomen often fancy them for their winter wines and teas," Crodane said. "Once Fergus catches the scent among the wilds he'll know to find us, though it may take some time. When we arrived in Galdoran, I assumed we would take ship so Fergus may have already headed north. He'll be a while turning back, but nevertheless, he will."

"He would not have come with us? On the ship?"

Crodane barked a laugh. "He's worse than your friend Thom when it comes to water." He tossed another pinch into the fire and returned the pouch to his sack. "At any rate," he said, rising to his feet, "care to continue your training? I hate to admit it, but you may have use for it soon."

Lughus breathed a sigh and took up his sword. "I suppose."

"You suppose? You train with the bloody Marshal, lad." Crodane smirked. "You should count yourself lucky."

Lughus smiled. "I'm sorry, but…this is all a great deal to take in…"

"I understand," the swordsman said. "Give it time. But for now, raise your sword."

That night and the next, Lughus slept uneasily, for between the threat of pursuit and the sounds of the woodlands, he found it difficult to rest, regardless of how weary the day's journeying left him. Most of all, however, he felt deeply the absence of his friends. He wondered if Royne had fared any better with his sudden solitude and thought about how simpler things had been back in the Tower when he was but an orphaned apprentice to the Loremaster. With any luck, the Hammer would return Thom to Titanis, and he and Royne could continue their studies together. A lanky cynic and a chubby ginger—what a pair! As for himself, the Brethren only knew where he would end up—old Goldimop! Crodane was at least some comfort, and Lughus was glad to know that the swordsman was truly his friend (or at least, so he had determined to believe), yet this still brought on other troubles in the form of sad stories about a family Lughus had never known and of a home of which he had no memory.

Two days more, and he found it difficult to differentiate between his waking hours and his restless sleep. Crodane appeared to notice this as well, for they appeared to pause for longer and longer periods of rest as they journeyed ever northward. Why was he so distressed, Lughus wondered, when he should have been overjoyed? He stumbled upon a real adventure, one where the worlds of rationality and fancy seemed to collide: the long-lost heir to a powerful lord, a swordsman right out of legend, a trek through un-trodden paths and forests—throw in a dragon or a damsel in distress and the Bard's song would be complete!

Perhaps this was what Rastis had meant when they parted, about the true task of the Loremasters being to seek out the truth. He had certainly done so in following Crodane, but why was he still uncertain? For that was truly it. He was uncertain. He was, quite literally, lost in the woods.

Perhaps that alone was it. For until now, his whole life had essentially been written. When his apprenticeship was completed, he would have become a scribe, then, with any luck, a scholar. If he showed true wisdom then, he might be elevated to the rank of sage, and after that, to seer—nearly all of which could have been done within the confines of the Loremaster's Tower. However, now—now the rest of his days were an open book filled with empty pages—be they but a few (should the worst occur as he fled from the Hammer) or a monstrously great tome as he became an old man. In either case, too much was left unwritten, which reminded him that in keeping up with his journal, he had been somewhat remiss. Perhaps the act of logging his adventure would help set his mind at ease…

And so he did that night after another evening of swordplay, or at least would have, were the moon bright enough for him to write. Still, simply holding the book in his hands and staring at the empty pages brought with it a certain calm, and when he lay down on his bedroll, he felt more at ease. His hand tightened around his mother's signet, hanging on its leather strand around his neck, and finally, at long last, perhaps due to simple exhaustion, he fell into a fitful sleep.

It was not long before he awoke from some illusory nightmare, that his blood suddenly turned to ice. For, beside him in the darkness, he felt the presence of something monstrously large and covered in hair. He cried out in alarm and defensively rolled away, reaching for his dagger or sword—only to find he had left them beside his bedroll.

In a flash, Crodane was on his feet—his blade, Sentinel, drawn and ready, glimmered in the light of the stars. "Lughus, what is it?" he called.

"A bear!" Lughus shouted. "Or some other...enormous creature. I don't know. I can still hear it breathing."

The woods around them fell very still until suddenly Crodane breathed a heavy sigh of relief and stifled a laugh. He sheathed his sword.

"Fergus, you turnip, you scared the boy half to death," the swordsman said.

"Fergus?" Lughus whispered.

"Just hold still and let me raise a light," Crodane said.

Lughus waited quietly while Crodane set himself to kindling a small fire. He could still hear the sound of the creature's breathing, and his eyes searched the darkness. Whatever Fergus was, Lughus realized, he was certainly not a man. Finally, after what seemed an eternity, the swordsman's fire sparked to life, and the monstrous shape reappeared.

At first glance, Lughus thought it an enormous wolf—yet, as his eyes adjusted to the light, the form became clearer. It was a hound, though one unlike any Lughus had ever set eyes on. He was large, long, and lanky, and from the tip of his tail to the end of his long snout, he was covered in thick, golden fur. Lazily, the great beast sauntered along the ring of firelight to lie down on the ground beside Lughus's bedroll and gazed up at him with luminous hazel eyes.

"A spirit hound?" Lughus gasped. "One of Perindal's great hunters?"

Crodane nodded. "He followed us along the riverside all the way to the city, though he kept out of sight. I'm sure you can imagine now why..." the swordsman sat back down upon his blanket. "About time you turned up," he told the hound.

Fergus sniffed and opened his wide jaws in a great yawn.

Lughus eyed the great hound curiously, though without fear. *A Spirit Hound of Perindal! Legends truly do walk amongst us!* Still, the sheer size of the dog gave him pause.

"Hello...Fergus..." he said at last, and turning to the swordsman asked, "Is it true he can understand us? That they're as smart as a man?"

Crodane nodded. "Smarter than most that I've met."

As if in answer, Fergus stood up and crossed the ground to where Lughus stood and lowered his head.

"See that. He means you can pat him if you like," Crodane told him, "It's only right that you two become better acquainted after all. You're of an age, you two. Brothers of a sort, you could say."

Carefully, Lughus touched the dog's head between the ears, and was surprised to find the thick fur rather soft. "What do you mean?" he asked.

"Your mother gave him to me shortly before you were born. She said that since she was to have a golden pup to look after, so should I." Crodane laughed. "When I told her I already had one, and I was more than busy keeping her out of trouble, she threatened that another word like that, and she'd let loose the bitch!" The swordsman shook his head at the memory. "She'd not be happy to hear me tell you that, but I told you she was funny. Clever. That was the true her, the one you would have known, free from the demands of the court and the politics, free to just be herself…"

Lughus smiled and allowed Fergus to sniff his hands. "Did you love her?" he asked suddenly, only to catch himself, "I'm sorry. I shouldn't have asked that."

Crodane waved the apology away. "It's all right," he said. "And yes, I did, with all of my heart, but…she was a lady, and…I was no lord. I served her, I protected her, but that was all it could ever be."

"I see…" Lughus said.

Crodane sighed and lay down on his back. "In any case, you've nothing to fear from Fergus," he said. "And with him here to guard us, we've little to fear from anything else that goes wandering in the night. We should sleep soundly."

Lughus nodded and gave the great hound another pat upon the head.

"Now try to sleep. We've a long road ahead of us."

"Yes, sir," Lughus said.

Before long, Crodane had fallen back to sleep, and Lughus returned to his bedroll by the dwindling fire. Fergus followed and sat down at his side. Strangely, in spite of his earlier fears and anxieties, something about the great hound's presence filled him with a sense of calm.

"Brothers of a sort," Lughus said aloud, as the hound's eyes watched him closely. He smiled, and offering Fergus one last scruff behind the ears, he closed his eyes and soon found that he too could finally sleep.

CHAPTER 31:
A MOTHER'S LOVE

Winter at Blackstone was a season that often arrived early and in force, for the cold mountain winds and the higher elevations often saw snow before the end of Horsetide, and by the Feast of Galdorn (the final day of the month), the castle lie coated in a permanent layer of white powder.

Still, in spite of the frigid temperatures and the damp, the sight of the snow-topped town below her window was always a vision Brigid found quaintly beautiful. The waddle and daub dwellings of the local burghers gave off a soft, warm light from their windows in the evening while, from every chimney, a thin serpent of smoke ascended into the ether to disappear among the low-hanging clouds. And although she knew of the difficulties the season brought with it for the common folk of the town, the snow at least gave the appearance of purity to mask whatever trouble might lie beneath.

Just like everything else in Blackstone, Brigid thought bitterly.

Unfortunately, the announcement of Josephine's impending betrothal (a ceremony in and of itself tantamount to a lesser lady's wedding), coupled with the renewal of the war with Grantis brought significantly more traffic to the castle than was common for this time of year, for with many of the lords away at war (and to ensure sufficient attendance for the Betrothal Feast come the Lady's Night on the fifteenth day of Moontide), the archduchess continued to invite the wives and daughters of the warring noblemen to join her for the winter at the capital, an invitation, which of course, could not be refused. So to add to Brigid's dismay, the Drove only increased in number, and as the temperature grew colder, she no longer even had the luxury of withdrawing to the sanctuary of her quarters, for she now—at her mother's behest and Livonia's enforcement—shared not only her privacy, but her very bed with no fewer than two other young ladies on a given night. How ironic, Brigid often thought, that whereas their presence was meant to keep her warm against the chill, it instead made her blood run cold.

Despite her unwanted guests, however, there was a solace to be found in the knowledge that her friend the Falcon yet roamed free around the castle, though he was most often to be seen following in her uncle's wake. Brigid saw him now daily at meals, and though they never spoke, on the rare occasion when her blue eyes met his gold, her heart warmed with resolve.

She had thought much about what he had said—the preposterous notion of a Mountain Queen—but she had no interest nor any designs of power, for often those she saw as powerful (her mother, her uncle, even Alan) solicited only her disgust. She remembered still the way that Alan had shamed the guardsman Hodges after his awful oration on the divinity of noble blood.

Yet there was nothing of the divine to staunch the flow of Young Reid's wounds, she shuddered to remember, nor had any gods seen fit to bring the young noble back to life, for if the gods were truly good, as folk were fond of saying and Brigid herself desperately wanted to believe, then they would have recognized that there was nothing noble in what Reid planned to do to her. As of now, the stories were circulating that the young knight had been lost upon the road en route to where his father's army camped along the Spade, for weeks had now passed since the morning he set out, and many feared some misadventure had resulted in the young man's tragic death.

In any case, Brigid thought, if the Brethren selected any among their mortal Kin, surely, they would not grant them the power to simply destroy—no, if anything, the gifts of the gods would be granted to those who chose not to attack, but to defend, who would not demand servitude, but serve others, and who sought not to harm, but to heal.

She could not forget the strange sensation that she felt when the Falcon touched her arm and took away the pain, for it was nothing short of miraculous. Since then, she discovered in herself a renewed interest in the Bard's tales and fairy stories of her childhood, for, if such miracles were truly possible, then what other mysteries relegated to the realm of fancy could exist out there in the larger world? And though she often felt foolish, Brigid could not prevent these fantastic elements from forcing their way into her daydreams, just as they had when she was a little girl.

However, her return to reading added but one more stone to the mountain of vexations that Brigid had apparently heaped upon her mother as of late—or so Livonia seemed quick to declare. A year—even six months ago—Brigid would have simply accepted the Archduchess's chiding; but now, though she had yet to defy her directly, Brigid refused to continue to play the part of a piece of jewelry or an ornamental poodle. To do so, to submit, was to resign herself to ruin—to the Reids of the world, or the Alans—and she would rather die than submit to their vile clutches.

But as the Falcon had warned her, she could not be reckless, and she knew well that it was unwise to go seeking a fight. Josephine was ruthless, and Brigid had plenty of memories to remind her of that, not the least of which was that of the poor drowned puppies, so she knew her rebellion must be subtle, else there was no telling the extent the archduchess's anger might reach. Slouching, sighing, rolling her eyes, thanking the servants, greeting the guards, refusing to laugh at Alan's jokes, refusing to feign interest in jewelry and clothes, reading, daydreaming—all these she could get away with if she was careful. Yet subtlety was becoming more and more difficult as Brigid's ill treatment at the hands of her mother became harder and harder to endure, and she wondered how long it would be before she could simply not suffer anymore.

For the rest of Horsetide, she had succeeded, and by succeeding, she had endured. But the first of the winter months, Moontide, though a celebration of the Lady, was also said to have a strange influence over women across Termain brought on by the shifting phases of the moon. It was in Moontide that women were thought most ripe to conceive and in Moontide when most young girls became maidens. It was said that babies born in Moontide were most often girls, though boys would be favored as lovers, bards, and poets—something Alan, one such birth, never tired of reminding everyone.

Yet it was also believed that Moontide brought with it certain madness that, in some woman, resulted in odd moods and temperaments. Wantonness was common, as were capriciousness, jealousy, and sudden bouts of hysteria or despair. If a woman took her own life, it was often done in Moontide. If a woman cuckolded her husband, it was often done in Moontide. In fact, it seemed that if a woman did anything out of the ordinary, it could somehow be linked back to Moontide. For her own part, Brigid refused to believe in such nonsense—regardless of her recent willingness to believe in miracles. Moontide, she believed, was simply an excuse for some women, an opportunity for drama and theatrics and a chance to act with impunity by simply blaming their behavior on the supernatural forces of the moon. It was, of course, no surprise then that the Month of the Moon was Josephine's favorite time of year.

By day, the archduchess and her entourage met within the quiet luxuries of Josephine's bower, and there, while dabbling politely in tea cakes and sweet hippocras, they would endeavor in the activities appropriate for women of rank and birth. Some practiced their needlework, elegantly embroidering shawls, veils, and gowns for the impending parties; others might be called upon to recite poetry or to sing, though many more would simply sit in idleness, engaging in polite conversation, which primarily consisted of base gossip.

Since Alan and the other young lads were now too busy practicing in the manly arts of war to engage in their former daylong flights of frivolity, the young ladies too had now become regular attendees of the archduchess's private court, as opposed to merely sometime-spectators reserved for special occasions. Josephine particularly reveled in the presence of the Drove, for their youth and puerile flippancy seemed to excite similar behaviors in the archduchess herself, as if by mere association, she might stay the sands of time to remain eternally youthful. They giggled over handsome men, spoke of melodramatic affairs and scandal, and through a blend of innuendo and double speech discussed certain matters reserved for the bedroom. Yet, although seated as always upon a pillow at her mother's side, Brigid felt a perpetual outsider, and though she knew that, in fairness, her exclusion was somewhat self-imposed, she could not help but feel a certain sadness knowing that she would never have her mother's approval.

"Tell me, my doves," Josephine would say. "Are you not excited for the Feast of the Betrothal?"

"Oh yes, my lady!"

"Oh certainly, Majesty."

"I fear I'll burst with excitement, Your Highness!"

"That's what I like to hear," Josephine beamed. "You'll make up for my poor daughter Brigid here. Oh, so frumpy!" The archduchess pursed her lips and reached out to run her finger down Brigid's cheek, "Worried sick, she is over Young Sir Reid, but you know what they say, girls, about the fisherman who lets his catch slip."

The Drove sighed in sympathy, and Brigid looked away only to see Livonia stifling a derisive chuckle. *Remember the Falcon*, she thought to herself. *Soon, he shall fly me away...*

"Perhaps at my betrothal, we shall find young men for all of you?" the archduchess continued. "Wouldn't that be grand? You know, Brigid's young Uncle Nealen lost his wife in childbirth last summer, and isn't he a handsome man?"

"Oh yes!"

"Oh my!"

Brigid sighed.

"All of Brigid's uncles shall be in attendance, mind you, ladies, and many other great lords besides," Josephine said. "Surely, there will be plenty of love to go around, as is appropriate in the case of a betrothal."

Caryn, who had over the past few weeks emerged as one of the archduchess's favorites, begged a question. "Lady Josephine," she mewed, "I was wondering..."

"Yes, darling?" the archduchess said.

"How does one know when she is in love?" she asked.

"Good question, my dear," the great lady said. "Let me think." She paused for a moment and pursed her lips. "I believe one is in love when the mere thought of your lover takes away your breath and turns your insides to jelly. How is that for an explanation?"

"Is that how you knew that you loved the Sheriff?" another girl asked. Brigid could not remember her name. There were far too many now to keep them all straight.

"What?" Josephine laughed, and the sound was like music. She turned to the lady sitting next to her, "Helena, do you hear these girls?"

The woman stifled a grin and shook her head. "Oh, youth," she said and went back to her embroidery.

"Darling," Josephine sighed, "I do not love the Lord Sheriff."

Brigid felt a flash of repugnance. "But you're to marry him."

Josephine shook her head sadly and touched her daughter's arm. "Pretty fool," she said. "I told you, Livonia, she's spending too much time reading those books. From now on, there's to be no more of it."

Brigid's gaze fell to the floor, and she folded her hands in her lap to hide her anger.

"My dears," Josephine said, "since you're young, let me tell you. Although the poets these days would have you believe otherwise, I assure you, love and marriage are not in any way the same things, believe me. In fact, where you have one, it is utterly impossible to have the other."

The young ladies nodded their heads at the epiphany and sat straighter in their seats to drink the honey of wisdom from Josephine's lips.

"Now listen here, when a knight is chosen by a lord, he is honor-bound to serve him. Whether he is fond of his lord or revolted by his lord, it makes no difference, for by sacred oath, he must do his duty. In return, he is granted lands, prestige, perhaps a castle, and all sorts of other wonderful things," the archduchess said. "Such is the case with marriage. For marriage is every woman's duty just as loyal service is to a knight. If she has lands or riches of her own, she gives them to her husband. When he is away, she manages his estates and minds his household affairs. When he seeks an heir, she lies with him and bears his children. These are a woman's duties. Love simply does not enter into it."

"What is love then, my lady?" Moira asked. "Tell us, please!" "Love"— Josephine grinned—"is different. For love is not about another, but about one's self."

As one, the Drove crooned with understanding, as if they had all removed their blindfolds after a game of blind man's bluff. Brigid allowed herself to slouch.

"If a woman takes a lover, she does so because it is her will to do so. If she gives him a gift, she does so for her own benefit, and if she invites him into her bed, it is for her own pleasure. There is no duty. There is simply a choice. That makes love different, and that makes love pure. Love and marriage are in no way the same, nor do they have any bearing on one another, and though I may be marrying the Lord Sheriff, and I admit to a certain fondness for him, I do not love him, nor does he love me. For, there is nothing in love that harms a marriage, and nothing about marriage to chasten love!"

Brigid could hold her tongue no longer. "If choice is what you value," she asked, "then why not simply *choose* to marry the one you love?"

"Oh, silly girl, there is much too much at stake to let one's heart decide a marriage," her mother said. "Tell her, ladies."

Lady Helena, the swollen middle-aged woman at Josephine's right agreed. "A marriage binds two families, two houses forever!" she simpered. "Even the common folk believe as such, though I must say, in a manner quite more vulgar. A man with a granary marries his daughter to the son of a brewer, and so both families prosper."

"When I married my husband," said Lady Marie, a thin, frail woman at the archduchess's left, "his holdings increased nearly threefold!"

"And think on how rich you've become, Marie," Josephine said. "Besides, Brigid, should your eyes find another, you can always take a lover so long as you are discreet." She smiled coquettishly at the others around her. "Lady knows that I have."

"Have you had many lovers, my lady?" Nora asked.

"Dozens, I should think," Josephine said, "though not all of them were lucky enough to receive the full benefit of my favors. Lesson learned, girls. Do not be too free, for modesty's sake. Save something for those you find particularly worthy or useful, no matter how lavish the gifts they may give you. String them along to get as much out of them as you can. Believe me, men will do anything in the name of love. Absolutely anything." The archduchess turned back to her daughter, smiling impishly at Brigid's blushing. "Now do you understand, my dear?"

"I understand what you say," Brigid said. "But I cannot accept it, for I've already sworn to myself and to the Brethren that if I marry, it will only be to a man that I love. A true partner. A true friend."

Josephine and the other elder ladies laughed, and after a respectful moment of hesitation, the young maidens joined them.

"Oh, darling," the archduchess sighed. "It is foolishness like this that drove Sir Reid away. No wonder men find you so disquieting. Just think, if it weren't for you, that poor gallant lad might still be with us and not lost in the lands along the Spade. I must admit that I would feel quite responsible if I were you, should he turn out to have been killed, gods forbid."

Brigid's blue eyes glowed hotly with anger, and when she spoke, her voice was cold. "Perhaps I am responsible," she said bitterly. "But forgive me, Mother, if I find your concepts of love and marriage to be rather stupid. I have come to think that a woman should respect herself and know that she is not a commodity to be bought or traded any more than she is an object of desire like a precious jewel or a fine horse. You do women a disservice, Mother, when you define our value only by our dowries and by what lies between our legs. Perhaps because you are incapable of seeing beyond the limitations of your own self-worth. Perhaps it is because you have never had a true partner, or a true friend? For all the talk of women's virtue and the Lady's grace, I seem to be having difficulty telling the difference between a fine noble lady and a painted whore."

All the air seemed drawn out of the room from the collective gasps of horror. From the noblewomen to the maidens to Livonia and the other servants, all eyes went wide as every jaw fell open, and though Brigid could not stave off a shudder of fear, her pulse quickened with a sudden rush of exhilaration.

"Pardon me," she added with a sardonic grimace, "Moontide must be upon me."

A long moment of silence passed as eyes wandered uncertainly from lady to lady and girl to girl. Only Brigid seemed able to move, and with a sigh, she drew a hidden book from beneath her pillow and began to read.

At long last, Josephine, frozen beneath the tide of her daughter's words, melted enough to smile and to speak.

"Leave me with my daughter," she said.

Together, the noblewomen, young and old, stood and offered the archduchess a curtsey of respect before filing out of the room. As they departed, voices whispered over and over in shock and awe.

"Did you hear what she said?"

"By the gods!"

"I can't believe what she said!"

When they were gone, only Josephine, Livonia, and Brigid remained in the room, and though she continued to read, Brigid made ready for the battle that she knew must come.

"Stand up," Josephine snapped.

Brigid breathed a heavy sigh and slipped a ribbon between the pages of her book to mark her place.

"You stand when your lady mother commands it!" Livonia snarled, snatching a gnarly handful of Brigid's hair and pulling her to her feet.

"Let go of me!" Brigid shouted. "You horrible troll!"

The old woman's grip slacked in shock, and Brigid leaped away, wheeling on her mother. "If you wish to speak to me, then do so," she said, "but not with that creature present!"

The archduchess and her handmaid exchanged a wide-eyed look of surprise. "Livonia," Josephine said softly, "perhaps you had better go…"

Livonia nodded and bowed low. "I will, my lady, but I will be right outside this door."

As the old woman hobbled away, Brigid breathed deeply, trying to master the inferno suddenly raging inside of her and prevent the great diatribe born from a lifetime of anger and resentment from pouring forth all at once. Yet, speak she must, for she knew somehow that a threshold had been crossed, and all the years of sorrow and pain she had buried beneath her mother's tyranny had finally shattered her nerves. *I must not cry!* she told herself. *For if I cry, she will have won…*

At length, the archduchess sat up straight upon her divan and fixed her daughter with a stern gaze. "Well now," she said, "for all your quiet, it seems that you have much to say."

"I do," Brigid said.

Josephine sighed impatiently. "Well, I'll not hear it," she observed dismissively. "It seems that all your words are poison and foolish and that in spite of all that I have done for you over these years, you remain an ungrateful wretch."

"Ungrateful?" Brigid nearly laughed.

"That's right," Josephine said, "and I will tell you this now too. Your uncle and I are to become happily betrothed come Lady's Day, but in truth, it was not for us that the celebration was originally intended, but rather for you and young Sir Reid." She sighed. "Though you can see now how you have managed to ruin that too. I swear, when I was your age, I was already a mother. Keep up behavior such as this, and you're likely to end up a wrinkled old prune with neither a home nor children to call your own. Say nothing of a husband! And Darren speaks now of trying to cart you off to Kredor! Ha! Preposterous!"

Brigid swallowed a heavy lump in her throat and bent her will to stay the flow of her tears. "I hate you," she muttered.

Josephine sighed and shook her head. "Well, if it's any consolation," she said blithely, "I hate you too. You've been nothing but a disappointment, from the very day you were born. Your father didn't want you because you were a girl, and, by the Brethren, my hips have just never been the same, so thank you for that as well. Of course, now there's this business with Sir Reid, Aiden's Flame! I admit I'm somewhat relieved for his sake that he had the good sense to flee. If you do indeed ever find that ridiculous love of yours, be sure to offer him my deepest sympathies! Lady's Mercy! What a horrible wife you would make!"

Do not cry! Brigid repeated. *Her power only grows if she sees you cry! You have proven your mettle once, and you are not without allies...*

The archduchess stretched wearily and turned to lounge upon the divan on her side. "You may leave now," she told her daughter, "for I tire of this. Remind me tonight to drink to Young Reid's happiness and his safe deliverance from you."

However, Brigid did not go. Rather than flee, she stood rooted to the spot and stood up straight in defiance of her mother's will. "I would remind you," she said, her voice a cold whisper, "if I thought that it would do any good."

Something about her tone must have piqued Josephine's interest, for the archduchess eyed her curiously and Brigid could sense her mother's uncertainty.

"I do not know what you mean," Josephine said. "Now go."

Brigid smiled grimly and stepped closer to where her mother lay. "I killed him," she whispered. "I killed Young Reid."

Josephine's face lost all expression, and for the first time in all her memory, Brigid sensed her mother's fear. For once, Josephine seemed to lack any sense of composure, and without expression, she seemed for a moment unable to speak. "Did you?" the archduchess said at last. "Well, now..."

"I did," Brigid said again, "for he was a scoundrel and, at my dear cousin's behest, sought to turn his desire for me into rape, but like you, he underestimated my courage and my resolve."

The archduchess fell silent, and Brigid let the moment linger, hanging ominously upon the air. At length, she leaned forward and spoke near her mother's ear, for her triumph had strengthened her, and the tears that once threatened her eyes sunk back from whence they had come. "Do not fear, Mother," Brigid said. "For it will not be long, I promise you, that I shall leave this place, and at long last, we will be free of each other. Perhaps tonight, you may drink to that instead."

"Perhaps I will," Josephine said.

"Then may our parting be soon," Brigid said, backing away to depart from the room, "for as much as you hope to be rid of me, believe that at least that much and more, I long to be away from you!"

CHAPTER 32:
THE TOWER OF THE JUDGE

The Tower of the Judge was one of the five lesser towers of Castle Testament arranged at the vertices of the fortress's outer curtain wall; however, unlike the four towers of the inner wall that surrounded the Keystone, the outer towers were, in a sense, monuments to the fallen. For, unlike in the case of the four who sat upon the Council of Five with the King, no men had borne the titles of the Watcher, the Merchant, the Soldier, the Purser, or the Judge for centuries.

Yet even without their namesakes, the towers continued to serve their functions under the auspices of others. So it was that under the oversight of the Chancellor, the Judge's Tower continued to serve as Titanis's courthouse and prison for housing those awaiting trial, execution, or transfer to Lockton-on-the-Breakers in Galdoran.

And it was here that Natharis Tainne led Royne now.

Nearly two days of feasting followed Kredor's hunt as the nobility of the castle made merry over the King's triumph in slaying the massive boar. In spite of his dislike for feasts and social events in general, Royne was forced to attend whenever Lord Tainne chose to do so. The fact that the creature being eaten had come so close to killing him also dampened his spirits and filled him with suppressed loathing. Of course, all could have turned out worse. For a while, he was forced to wait upon Lord Tainne. Revolting enough as that was, Kredor's remaining cherub, clearly disturbed from the sudden, violent loss of his brother, still bore the King's cup at the table, though Royne seldom noticed the sound of the boy's tambourine any longer.

It was at one of these visits to the feast that Kredor and Tainne first explained exactly how it was that Royne could show his gratitude for saving his life. For Rastis, they knew well, was a sentimental sort, and though they believed that he had willingly chosen Royne as a sacrifice to save the other two—an accusation alone that brought Royne's blood to boil—it was their hope that the old man might be willing to divulge the location of *The Book of Histories* to one who he himself had raised.

Though, of course, this was not how the King and his noble friend explained it when they addressed the young scribe. They were far more subtle, if much more patronizing, and though Royne hated humbling himself to feign naiveté, he did so, readily agreeing to the King's offer and veritably gushing with gratitude for his deliverance from the monstrous boar. Yet he needed to speak to Rastis, and if this was the only way, then so be it. If it allowed him to learn Rastis's plans, to gain the Loremaster's guidance, he would do it, and when he finished carrying out the old man's wishes, it was goodbye to the Order and good riddance.

And so, at the gates of the Judge's Tower, the red-cloaked sentries saluted Lord Tainne and allowed them to pass freely through the heavy ironbound doors guarding entry inside.

Never before had Royne been inside the Tower of the Judge. In fact, he had only once been inside of any of the lesser towers, that of the Watcher, the tallest tower, when as a boy, Rastis had taken the three apprentices up to the top so as to witness an eclipse of the sun. The Watcher's Tower often served as a residence for visiting dignitaries and other honored guests (though, of course, not honored enough to warrant an invitation to stay in the Keystone). Still, it was comfortable and rather cheerful, a stark contrast from the cold sobriety of the Judge's Tower.

Inside, the first floor opened to reveal a central, circular hall, marked in the rear by an elevated dais where at a high oaken bench, the judge (or, in contemporary times, counselors and commissioners of the Chancellor's Tower) would adjudicate legal matters unworthy of Rordan Baird himself, let alone the King. To the left of the entry, a pair of kingsmen guarded a staircase leading down to the foundations of the tower, and to the right, two more guarded a second stairway leading up. Royne had heard rumors of what happened below the basement stair, so it was with great relief that he followed Lord Tainne upwards.

Although it was midday, the tower was rather dark, for the windows of the prison cells were all high and narrow, and as such, many of the hooded sconces lining the walls crackled with flame. Up Tainne ascended, through the second floor, past the third and fourth, all the way up to the fifth and final floor of the tower. Above his head, Royne heard pigeons cooing in the rafters until suddenly, a large black raven silenced them with its call.

"Rastis is within," Natharis Tainne said, leading Royne to a door at the rear of the tower. "You may enter, but know that I will be right here."

"Yes, my lord," Royne said.

"Remember, it is imperative that we locate the book."

"Yes, sir."

Royne watched as Lord Tainne searched through the folds of his robe and withdrew an iron key, its handle fashioned from ivory into the likeness of a death's-head. Slowly, the nobleman fit the key into the lock and turned it with a heavy click. "Enter," he said.

Royne took a deep breath, nodded, and went inside as Lord Tainne shut the door behind him. "Rastis?" the scribe whispered into the dim light. He walked a few paces further, hearing the crunch of straw beneath the soles of his shoes. At the far end of the room, a small figure sat slumped upon a burlap mat beside a basin of water and a rough woolen blanket. "Rastis?" Royne whispered again louder.

"Hello, Royne," the old man said kindly from out of the gloom. "What a place we find ourselves, eh?"

Royne nodded and bit his lip. Rastis looked smaller and somehow older and thinner than when last he saw him, though he struggled now to remember how long that had been. In fact, he suddenly found it very hard to think clearly at the sight of the old Loremaster, reduced as he was now— almost like a skeleton in a tomb. Royne was torn between great anger and great despair, between weeping and flying at Lord Tainne in a frenzied rage. Instead, he put a hand to his brow and rubbed at his temples.

"How are you, my boy?" Rastis asked. "I hope you are keeping well?"

"Rastis…" Royne began miserably but caught himself as the old man lifted a bony finger to his lips and motioned to the ironbound door of the cell. Royne breathed a sigh and swallowed the lump in his throat. "I am well," he said. "King Kredor and Lord Tainne have both been…very kind."

"Good. I trust you have been keeping up with your studies?"

"Yes, sir."

"Then I am pleased," Rastis said. "Lord Tainne was educated at the Lighthouse, you know, and the Keepers know much about the days of Old Calendral, in the days before Dibhor's Fall."

"Yes, so I—" Royne paused, for there was something about the look in the old man's eye as he finished his last sentence. Royne cleared his throat loudly. "So I had heard, and so it seems, though we've mostly been studying the early days of the Order, from Aiden's death to when Halford Drude I was crowned Guardian-King."

"Indeed? Well, from what I recall, you've had many years of instruction in that regard," Rastis said. "Do not tell me that you have forgotten these things?"

"Of course not, sir."

"Then perhaps a test is in order," Rastis said, "for the sake of old times?"

Royne glanced anxiously back at the door to the cell. He knew that Tainne was expecting him to press Rastis about the location of *The Book of Histories*, but at the same time, he sensed that Rastis's proposed test was not merely idle banter. Suddenly, an idea came to him.

"I will submit to your test, Rastis," he said loudly, offering the old man an implicit glance, "However, if I pass, I would like a reward."

"And what might that be?" Rastis asked.

"In all my years as your apprentice," Royne said, "there is one book that I have desired to read more than any other, *The Book of Histories*. If I pass your test, will you allow me to look in it?"

Rastis's lips curled into a smirk, and he nodded with approval. "*The Book of Histories...*" he said. "I'm not certain that you are ready for that..."

"Please, Rastis," Royne said, "I only want a look."

The old man gave an exaggerated sigh, "I suppose you have earned that right, so long as you prove yourself."

"Thank you, sir."

"Let's not get ahead of ourselves, though. You still have to pass my test," Rastis said. "Now Royne, if you recall, it was said that the first Guardians led by St. Aiden were made up of men from all over Termain, save but a few who were born beyond the sea. There were Lavik and Radovan, two Kordishmen, and Osmund of Tulondis. Can you remember their titles?"

Royne folded his arms across his chest. "Lavik and Radovan," he said, "were Kordish smiths, and it's said that they crafted many of the Guardians' greatest weapons. As such, they were known as the Forge and the Furnace."

"Correct," Rastis nodded, "and Osmund?"

"Osmund was a dyer who was taken as a slave for trying to smuggle cloth back to Tulondis without paying the tariffs, which Emperor Veirne set higher than any foreign merchants could afford. They called him the Blue on account of the stains the woad left on his hands."

"Correct again, Royne," Rastis nodded, arching an eyebrow, "though mere facts do not offer wisdom. It is the application of those facts that matter most."

Royne thought carefully about the question Rastis had just asked him, and suddenly, his eyes went wide in understanding. The Forge and the Furnace crafted weapons to be true, but their great works of art were crafted in gold. There was a great gilded shield encrusted with star sapphires that marked the entryway to the room in the library where the romances were shelved. In fact, Royne remembered once when old Goldimop got in trouble trying to climb up and pull it down. Sage Vashon would have killed him when he caught him had Rastis not intervened, but Royne could remember the old sage shouting about the Forge and the Foundry.

"Yes, sir," Royne smiled.

"Next question, then." Rastis winked. "After Aiden's rebellion began, there were numerous cases of uprisings in the other provinces outside of Baronbrock, and though many of these failed, one of these was successful, and eventually its leaders joined Aiden and became members of the Order in their own right. Which case was this?"

Royne thought back to his studies, numbering through the uprisings inspired by St. Aiden. Most, sadly, ended in crushing defeat against the fear and fervor of Wrogan's devout. However, as the old man said, there was at least one that was successful. It began among the miners in Dwerin.

"It was the Fourth Rebellion," Royne said. "The first was Aiden's, the second, which began in Grantis was put down very quickly, the third ended before it began due to treachery, but the fourth succeeded, and it was led by"—he paused—"Hewen the Short!"

"Correct again," Rastis said. "The fourth case and the Short."

Royne nearly laughed aloud, for he understood now what the old man was onto. The fourth case meant the fourth bookcase in the room marked by the shield. As for the Short, Royne's lips drew back in a gleeful grin. Thom, forever the shortest among the three of them, had once decided that the shelves simply reached too high and, one afternoon, had set about reorganizing the books on beasts and birds so that not a single one was higher than the third shelf from the floor.

So, Royne thought, *where could* The Book of Histories *be found? Why, in the library, of course, where it always had been, lost among its thousands of fellows, hidden in plain sight in the room marked by the gilded shield on the fourth bookcase among the third shelf from the floor.*

"One last question," Rastis began again. "The final one for today, for I'm afraid that I grow very tired, and it is time that you must go."

Something about the look in the old man's eyes told Royne that those words carried greater meaning than on the surface, and he felt his spare chest tightening again, for there was something far too *final* about this final question.

"Yes, Rastis," he said. "I will answer your question, and you will tell me what you have done with the book."

"So I will," Rastis said. "After St. Aiden and the Lady of Light defeated the Warlock, they imprisoned Dibhor's Beast by binding it away with a key crafted from a fallen star. My question for you, Royne, is this. Where is the lock?"

"Where is the lock?" Royne repeated in confusion. "What do you mean?"

"The lock," the old man said, "for every key, there must be a lock, correct?"

Royne's eyes grew wide. "I'm afraid I never thought much about that," he said at last.

In reply, the old man motioned for him to come nearer and offered Royne a shaky hand.

"That," Rastis whispered, "is the question to which Lord Tainne hopes to find the answer, but he will not find it in *The Book of Histories*."

Royne shook his head. "What do you mean?"

"There's no time to explain, my boy," the Loremaster said, "for you must find the book and leave the city immediately."

"Leave the city?"

"All will make sense when you find the book."

"But, Rastis—"

Rastis cleared his throat and called aloud, "You had best think, Royne, for if you do not know the answer now, I begin to question whether you know anything at all."

"But I don't know the answer," Royne whispered. "Besides, the key, the lock, it's all just a legend anyway."

"Is it written somewhere that legends can never be true?"

"I…I don't know."

"Then you must find out," Rastis said hurriedly, "for listen to me. Dark times are ahead of us, and though even I do not understand what the future will bring, the Loremaster cannot help anyone as a prisoner."

"Then how can I help you escape?" Royne asked. They were too quiet, he thought. Tainne must know something was wrong.

"You can't," Rastis whispered, "which is why you must go. Hobart has arranged things. He waits at a boarding house in the Groundlings called The Crow & the Fox. You must go to him. You must. You must become the Loremaster and go."

"What?" Royne exclaimed. "Become the Loremaster? Rastis, you're mad!"

"Royne, listen," the old man pleaded. "I care for you, Lughus, and Thom like my own children, and if I could have spared you from any of what is to come, believe me, I would have. However, I believe in you three enough that come what may, you have the best chance of seeing it through, Kinship willing."

"Rastis, don't say those things."

"Royne, listen to me. Darkness surrounds us on all sides, my boy, for after many long years of waiting, the Dibhorites have returned!"

"The Dibhorites? Rastis, what are you talking about?"

"The Bard's Heresy! It is written in the Bard's Heresy."

"The Bard's Heresy?"

"There's no time to explain," Rastis said. "You will find all the answers in *The Book of Histories*. However, before you can read it, you must swear! You must swear by St. Aiden and the Lady to safeguard the Light."

"Rastis, I don't understand." Suddenly, Royne heard the sound of Tainne's key in the lock and shaking his head, he sighed. "Yes, Rastis," he said hurriedly, "I swear."

In the blink of an eye, Rastis's free hand lashed out and pricked Royne's fingertip with a bit of steel no larger than a pin. At once, a tiny bead of blood welled at the piercing.

"Swear it again," the old man said, "by blood."

Royne's heart pounded in his chest. "Yes," he said. "Yes, I swear it."

Rastis nodded, and quietly, Royne heard him intone the following verse:

Beyond the bounds of memory,
through all the ages past,
truth hides in history
until brought to light at last,
For when the present is uncertain,
and days ahead are filled with fright,
Rise now, Loremaster,
and bring the Dark to Light!

As soon as Rastis had finished, the door to the cell opened, and Rastis let go of Royne's hand as Lord Tainne strode in. Royne felt strange, muddled, as if he had just arisen from a nap—awake and weary at the same time. Lord Tainne gazed at him tersely.

"Do you have an answer to the old man's question, Royne?" the nobleman asked.

Royne was struck dumb, struggling still to process all that the old Loremaster had said. "My lord, I...I'm afraid I do not."

Rastis held up a hand, and his lips twisted into a wry grin. "Well, Natharis, care to try your luck?"

Lord Tainne's eyes flashed with hatred. "We Keepers are taught to rely on Truth over luck. Rest assured that as the new Loremaster, I will devote your former followers to proper study over foolish trivia."

"Strange to hear a Keeper speak of Truth," the old Loremaster smirked, "You and your fellows at the Lighthouse are so blinded by your own darkness that you fail to see that which lies in plain sight."

"I will fence with you no longer!" Tainne snapped. "Where is *The Book of Histories?*"

"You do not need the book to find the answer that you seek, Natharis," Rastis said mildly, "as I have told you time and again."

"You lie!"

At length, Rastis sighed, and as Royne looked at him, he noticed that the old man, in an instant, had seemed to age even more, and in the gloomy light of the tower, his skin seemed thinner than parchment and wrinkled like a crumbling egg shell.

"I will ask you one last time," the Keeper said, "one last time before the consequences of your silence come to bear," he said with a significant glance at Royne, "where is the book?"

"Very well," the Loremaster said. "I burned it."

CHAPTER 33:
ASHFORT

When the soldiers of Dwerin reached Ashfort, Geoffrey was gripped by an odd sense of anxiety, for as he peered across the plain at the fort, it was exactly as he had envisioned it in his mind: a stone stockade atop a motte, a bailey with a storehouse, a longhouse, and palisade surrounding it all. Beside him in the rear of the cart, Oliver breathed heavily, nervously fingering the pommel of his sword.

Before long, the men of the fort spotted the approaching column of horsemen, and a flurry of movement marked the palisade walls surrounding the bailey. Barrow sent a rider forth to hail the defenders, and as the skirmishers formed their lines, the captain and the two sergeants rode around them, inspecting the men for battle and preparing for the coming parley.

"Do you see the boys anywhere?" Oliver asked, his voice unsteady with apprehension.

"It's too far away," Geoffrey replied. "I can make out nothing." Ahead at the fort, the main gate slowly opened, and a small squad of riders emerged led by the man Geoffrey remembered as Karston, Cousin Martin's murderer. Captain Barrow nodded to Boyle and Dunn, Mason unfurled the standard bearing the Anvil of the Ironmen, and the four soldiers trotted out to meet the Red Boars. Lord Mathon was nowhere in sight. Oliver muttered something under his breath, and though Geoffrey could not make it out, he understood the meaning and found himself involuntarily tightening his grip on his club.

With bated breath, the farmers watched in silence, straining in vain to make out what was being said. Ernald, the cook driving the cart, dug out a piece of hard biscuit from a sack and took a bite before offering Geoffrey and Oliver a taste.

"No, thank you," Geoffrey said, for his stomach had already tied itself in knots.

Oliver shook his head. "Look there," he said suddenly, pointing across the field, "what are they at now?"

Geoffrey's eyes narrowed. "I don't know.

Across the field, Karston and his men returned to Ashfort's gate. Captain Barrow and his men lingered a moment longer before slowly turning to take their places back among the line of horsemen.

"Should one of us go ask him what's happening?" Oliver asked.

"I'm not so sure that would be wise," Geoffrey said.

Oliver breathed a heavy sigh. "I hate this waiting."

Time passed uneasily, but neither farmer could say how long. Still, Barrow remained among the line and, for now at least, seemed to have forgotten about Geoffrey and Oliver altogether. To escape the uneasiness of the moment, Geoffrey mulled over the content of his last dream, his last, strange memory of the old man's past. Who was the strange beggar, the bandaged man Regnar called Salasco? And what was this Vanguard business? It had to have something to do with those strange rhyming words he mentioned to Oliver, but what? Then there were all the other names—Gareth, Crodane, the Blade, the Marshal, and the man they called the Loremaster, the man called Rastis. Wasn't the Loremaster one of the council? The Council of Five, what led the Guardians far off in Andoch? Surely, they could not be the same? What would a lord of a far-off kingdom want with a beggar in rags and an old man-at-arms? Geoffrey expected to find no answers, though even if he had, the action at the fort afforded him no time. For the second time, the gates to Ashfort opened, and two men of the Red Boars passed through on foot, waving the Ironmen of Dwerin inside.

"It looks as if they've accepted Barrow's offer," Oliver said.

Geoffrey gave a nod and breathed a heavy sigh. Soon, they would have the boys returned to them, and their adventure would finally be over. They could return to Pyle with one crisis solved and begin work on solving the next: that of surviving the winter without the harvest's worth of stores. Geoffrey muttered a silent prayer to the Lords of the Kinship and asked that they continued to watch over them.

Ahead in the field, Captain Barrow reformed the column and led the remainder of his riders into the bailey, followed closely by Ernald, his cart, and the two farmers. As soon as the cart crossed the threshold, however, Geoffrey noticed something odd as the two Red Boars who opened the gates hurriedly shut them again as two more men dropped the heavy wooden beam in place, locking the riders inside. In an instant, Geoffrey felt the same unconscious instinct as the day of the attack on Damon's farm grab hold of him. He leaped to his feet in alarm.

"What's wrong?" Oliver asked.

Geoffrey did not stop to answer. "Captain!" he roared. Along the palisade, hidden among where their horses were hitched, the remaining Red Boars fit arrows to their bows. "It's a trap!"

Whether Barrow heard, Geoffrey did not know, for at the moment, he dropped down to the bottom of the cart and raised Acorn up over his head just as the bandits let fly. Men shouted, horses screamed, and from all directions, goose-feathered arrows fell like rain.

"Aiden's Flame!" Oliver cried as an arrow struck Ernald through the eye.

Two more followed, striking the dead cook in the shoulder and the chest before his lifeless body slumped forward and fell to the ground.

Geoffrey tightened his hold on Oakheart and Acorn, took a deep breath, and let the fury of battle set fire to his blood.

"For Pyle!" he shouted, rolling out from the back of the cart. "For Pyle and the Spade, for vengeance, and our sons!"

The first line of archers Geoffrey met were the same men who had barred the gates, kneeling now before it, firing off arrows at the column's rear. The nearest fell dead with a shattered skull as the second lay in agony, choking out his last breaths after a blow from the edge of the targe crushed his throat. The third man fell in the midst of drawing his sword when Oakheart smashed the bones of his wrist and caved in half of his face in a pulpy, red mess. The last man in the line fired his arrow at the ground in panic before attempting to flee, but he did not make it far.

In the center of the bailey, the scouts were in complete disarray as men and horses died, yet Geoffrey could still see Captain Barrow standing beside his fallen mount, shouting over the battle, trying to rally his remaining men.

Behind the cover of a stack of barrels, another group of bandits fired their bows, and one of the men at Barrow's side fell dead. Again, Geoffrey shouted his battle cry and charged them, a storm of violent retribution dealing out pain and death. His eyes were alight with wrath, and the blood of his enemies stained his clothes. The very sight of him set the Red Boars fleeing, for he was terrible to behold.

Mere moments later, another squad of bandits fell to his hand, allowing Barrow and his surviving soldiers a chance to gather together and mount a counterattack. The arrows rained now fewer and fewer, but the ground grew thicker with even more dead men, dead horses, and blood.

It was then that Geoffrey spied Karston and another squad defending the causeway leading up to the motte. From deep within the farmer's soul radiated tremors of righteous fury, and he roared like a mad beast advancing on Martin's killer. Eyes wide with horror, two more bandits fell before Geoffrey's advance, and Karston leaped back along the wooden stair gripping his sword in defense. Captain Barrow and his soldiers hurried to follow behind, dispatching the remainder of Karston's defenders as they fled from the farmer's might. Geoffrey raised Oakheart and readied Acorn before him as Karston swung his sword in frenzied terror. Geoffrey felt the sting as the blade bit into his shoulder, though it was but a scratch as the full force of the blow had been turned aside by the targe. Karston took another step back further up the stair to the stockade, and this time when he swung his sword, Geoffrey parried with Oakheart. The steel blade shattered against the sheer strength of the oaken club.

In the face of such power, the bandit's eyes grew wide. He fled to the top of the causeway and pounded upon the doors to the stockade, screaming for Lord Mathon to let him in. However, the captain of the Red Boars made no answer, and in desperation, Karston leaped from the causeway to escape, only to impale himself upon the sharpened spikes of the palisade wall surrounding the base of the motte below.

Geoffrey watched the bandit's corpse slide down the sharpened point of the wooden spike, his own chest heaving with exhaustion after the fight. Below, Barrow's men seemed to have secured the fort, and at the captain's orders, men with heavy-bearded axes broke through the stockade's doors. Captain Barrow offered Geoffrey a nod, and together, they entered.

Inside, the last Red Boars stood empty-handed, their weapons strewn idly before them upon the stone floor. The embers of a dying fire glowed weakly in the fireplace, and in the corner, two peasant women lay half-clad and beaten on a pile of burlap sacks. The bandits remained silent, eying the Dwerin soldiers, their captain, and the bloodstained farmer with the hollow eyes of children caught in the act of stealing from the larder.

Captain Barrow's mouth twisted with disgust. He offered a hand to the women in the corner, helping them to their feet, and nodded to two of his men to see to them. Then, without a word, Barrow paced across the room to the nearest of the bandits and stood within but a few inches, staring with his dark eyes into the man's face before striking him hard across the face.

"Take them outside and hang them," he said.

As the soldiers did their duty, Geoffrey glanced around. There was no sign of the boys anywhere. At the far end of the stockade, however, one final door remained, and it was to this that Barrow addressed his attention now.

"My name is Wilfred Barrow, Scout Captain to Lord Padraig Reid of the Sovereign Dukedom of Dwerin!" he shouted. "My men and I have taken command of this fort in spite of your efforts to betray us. If you seek any chance at mercy, you will surrender yourself at once!"

A moment passed, and the door opened. Lord Mathon, the Captain of the Red Boars, stood alone. "I surrender to your mercy, Captain," he stuttered, "though I expect fair treatment, for I have committed no crime!"

Geoffrey's chest shook with rage. "You stole all the stores from our village! You burned our chapel and murdered our poor preacher!" tears of anger filled his eyes, and his voice grew thick, "You stole our sons!"

"I did nothing but demand what was mine by right!" Mathon said. "These lands were left idle with no ruling lord. I laid claim. Therefore, I deserve tribute from those who farm my lands! Nothing more!"

Captain Barrow's face was impassive but stern. "Where are the boys?" he asked.

Mathon shook his head. "How would I know? Try looking among the dead, and if not there, then perhaps hiding in the longhouse. I am no nursemaid."

"No," Barrow said coldly. "But you expect children to fight your battles for you." He turned to his remaining men. "Hang him with the others like the coward and the thief that he is."

"What!" Mathon cried. "You promised mercy!"

"I promised nothing," Barrow said, turning his back on the bandit lord. "And this is more mercy than you deserve. Come, Geoffrey. Let us find Oliver and your sons. I pray they have come to no harm."

Together, the captain and the farmer left the stockade and descended the stairs of the causeway to the bailey below. "If I am ever to be knighted and placed in command of my own fief," Captain Barrow said, "may I never make enemies of my farmers, for if I had known that a farmer could fight as you did today, I might have to trade my commission for a few more field hands."

Geoffrey sighed bashfully and looked for a clean spot on his tunic to rub his eyes. "I don't know what to say, sir."

At the end of the stairs, Barrow paused. "I do not yet know the butcher's bill for today, Geoffrey, but I am certain that I have lost many of my men, and perhaps I would have lost many more—my own life as well—had you not fought alongside us or raised the call of alarm," he said. "As such, Geoffrey of Pyle, I offer you my hand in hopes that you might call me friend. You've earned that much and more."

Geoffrey shook the captain's proffered hand. "Thank you, sir." He nodded.

The bailey was as they left it, though now the remaining bandits from the stockade stood bound and waiting beside their onetime lord as the Ironmen prepared a makeshift gibbet upon which to offer them their just reward. Other soldiers attempted to gather up the Dwerin casualties and offered the gift of mercy to any of the horses that would not recover from their wounds.

Though wounded in the initial volley, Mason was still on his feet, although he appeared ready to collapse when he hurried toward Barrow to make his report.

"Boyle and Dunn are both dead," he said. "And another eight men with them. Six more were wounded after that, though there's probably two among them that won't live to see tomorrow's dawn. Beyond that, we lost eleven horses in the battle and another four as had to be put down, but there seems no short supply of horse flesh among what they have hitched up along the walls plus a few wagons and a half a dozen head of oxen."

Barrow nodded. "Have you checked the buildings?"

"Aye, sir," Mason said, "the storehouse is stocked to the gills, as it looks like there's more than one village these bastards put the squeeze on. There were two men left in the longhouse that surrendered without a fuss—we've got them helping us move the wounded—and about seven or eight young lads as might belong to the farmers here and some of the other villages."

Geoffrey's eyes lit up, and Barrow offered him half a forlorn smile. "Well, there's some good news at least," he said. "Thank you, Mason."

"Wait, sir." Mason paused. "There's more." He breathed a reluctant sigh. "Some of the lads in the longhouse…well, it seems when the fighting started, some of the stray arrows…well, there's three inside that fell, in addition to those still alive." He shook his head.

"And Geoffrey…" Mason gave another sigh. "Your friend, Oliver… I'm sorry…"

Geoffrey felt his stomach clench, and his fingers went cold and numb. "What do you mean?" he asked, though he already knew the answer.

Mason mutely turned his gaze to his captain, and Barrow put his hand on Geoffrey's shoulder.

"Oliver is dead."

CHAPTER 34:
THE WHITE HORSE

Following Bel's discovery of Dermont's "plague-bearers," or so they were known, the Tower's Guard hurried onward to Widowridge, the next of the Valendian keeps, leaving only a token force behind to await Lord Guillon's army. Morale was high, as was anticipation, for the men—both knights and infantry—came to suspect that the Plague Prince's decision to abandon Valeshade was a sign of his weakened strength following the Battle of the White Wood, for though he had plenty of noblemen at his back, noblemen alone would not agree to garrison a keep and a loss of nine thousand infantrymen was no easy vacancy for an army to refill. When Widowridge turned out to have been abandoned in the same manner as Valeshade, this suspicion came closer to a belief.

For Beledain, however, the revelation only served to increase his anxiety and frustration. For, like so many things, it confirmed, yet again, the rumors of Dermont's deplorable tactics and depravity in war. His willingness to act without scruples, and without even the slightest sense of honor. Yet, Bel knew that his brother was, perhaps above all else, exceedingly cunning, and he wondered, even now, if the Nivanus had truly been abandoned—or if all was yet another elaborate ruse. Perhaps Dermont was well aware of the Tower's intentions? Perhaps his plague-bearers were merely a counter-ruse while he took his time preparing to strike.

Sir Marcus Harding, too, seemed to find the lack of true Valendian resistance disquieting, as he confided in "Sir Briden" the morning after taking Widowridge. As with the first, it had been guarded by plague-bearers, and the well had been poisoned with rotting carcasses, carrion, and feces. Seated stoically atop Tempest, gazing out south along the ridge, the Tower sighed.

"This is not war."

"No," Bel agreed, "it is not."

"Prince Dermont is not the first to make use of such tactics, for many in the past have done the same. Tulondis did it in the last Great War when they lay siege to the Grantisi capital of Alendis, and it's said that Kalius Wrogan often used disease to thin the ranks of the Wrathorn, luring them into sacking settlements riddled with the Red Plague. Plague is often seen by cowards and knaves as a means to an easy victory. Yet pestilence is no soldier. It knows neither friend nor foe, soldier or citizen, man or woman...or child." The Tower shook his head bitterly. "It's craven and lacks all honor, not at all acceptable from a man who seeks to be a king."

"For my part," Bel said, "I only hope that a man who might order such a thing did so because he saw no other options."

"Even then," the Tower sniffed, "would you do the same? Whether it be a small mountain keep like this or a peasant village along the Bloodline?"

"I have no command."

"Not now, but someday, you might."

The lies and the deception had long since grown tiresome, but the more Bel saw of his brother's true form, the more he knew Dermont's threats concerning Lilia were more than idle words spoken in anger.

"What would you do, Sir Briden," the Tower asked again, "if you were in the position Prince Dermont finds himself?"

Bel was hesitant, and something about Sir Harding's line of questioning made him feel exposed. Clearly, the lord-general expected an answer, and at last, Bel shrugged.

"I never would have let it get this far," he said. "A hundred years of war is enough by my account. If there's no victor now, there very well never will be. Were I Prince Dermont, instead of taking the field at the Battle of the White Wood, I might have sued then for peace. A weakened enemy is like a wounded lion. It still has teeth, and the greater its fear, the more likely it is to use them."

The Tower sighed. "It's a shame you don't have the Plague Prince's command. Else, this whole bloody conflict might be over. King Marius, remember, has no male heir, and as I understand it, Cedric lost a son as well. Such a thing has a way of forcing men to set aside their differences."

"One can hope, though it can also fan the fires of vengeance."

"True, but did you know that before he sent for aid from Andoch, King Marius went so far as to offer a marriage between Prince Dermont and his daughter?"

"What?" Bel lurched up straighter in his saddle. At the sudden motion, Banshee stirred and Bel had to pull back on her reins to calm her down. "No," he said, "I did not know that."

"Few do," the Tower told him. "But the Plague Prince refused. He sent word back to Marius that if he wanted her, he would just take her once the war was over."

Bel cursed under his breath.

"What is to become of this land?" the Tower mused. "The Valendians hate the Gasparns, and the Gasparns hate the Valendians. Yet the whole reason they keep fighting is to reunite into one. It's madness."

"So it is," Bel said. "But it wasn't always so. Prince Gislain was a noble lord, and they say Prince Larius of Valendia was as well. Why those two could never come to terms, I never knew, for it always seemed like they at least respected one another as brother officers."

The Tower smiled. "Do you know the story of Sir Gavin Fenn, one of my predecessors, who fought the Blackguard Girard Volute, called the Spindle?"

"I do not," Bel said. "We hear few tales of the Guardians beyond those of the Bard."

The Tower clicked his tongue, and Tempest turned back toward Widowridge. "Then I will tell you as we head back," he began. "Nearly five hundred years ago, there was unrest among many of the lords tasked by the archduke of Dwerin to oversee the mines, for though their peasants mined the gold and ore, the lords felt that they saw little enough return. Eventually, they began withholding ore and selling it by sea on their own. This, of course, displeased the archduke, and he appealed to the Guardian King of Andoch for aid."

"Now, Girard Volute, the Spindle, was sent by the Warlord to aid the archduke in putting down the rebellion, and this he did. The lords agreed to return to paying the archduke his due with an additional fine levied for what they had sold on their own. However, afterward, Sir Girard happened to witness the conditions of the mines and the way in which the miners lived, and he was so reviled by what he saw that he refused to return to Andoch and, instead, set to raising the common folk in revolt."

"Who did they revolt against?" Bel asked. "The archduke or the lords?"

"Both," Sir Harding said simply, "for neither cared about the plight of the peasants, as is the case with most nobles across Termain, even today. At any rate, because he refused to return and had turned hostile to one of Andoch's allies, the Guardian-King had no choice but to declare the Spindle a Blackguard, and since Sir Girard appeared now to be leading an army of peasant miners, the Warlord sent Sir Gavin the Tower to face him in the field. Of course, Sir Gavin was not happy with this. He and Sir Girard had been close friends, but it was also his duty."

Bel sighed, for he knew one day that he could very well find the lord-general at the end of his lance, and if Dermont had his way, it was a certainty. "What happened?"

"Well, the armies eventually met—the Spindle leading his miners and the Tower leading the soldiers of the archduke and the lords, and it was very clear from the beginning who would win, for the miners were no soldiers, and their arms were mere hammers and picks. But rather than merely preside over the slaughter of a few thousand common folks, Sir Gavin invited Sir Girard to meet with him out between the armies in the center of the field. There, they shared a meal together and spoke for a while of old times, then, afterward, they agreed to fight one another in a Champion's Duel, as was sometimes done in Old Calendral, and whichever man won would claim the victory for all."

"And the archduke agreed to this?"

"He had to. When a nobleman, king or not, begs the aid of the Guardian King, he relinquishes his sovereign rights in such matters to the will of the Guardian sent to serve him. In return, the Guardian acts with honor in the best interests of the nobleman in mind. If the soldiers set to slaughtering the miners, the rebellions would never end. However, if the miners could somehow defeat the soldiers, the archduke would lose his sovereignty and his authority as well. Both cases, of course, were rife with dishonor. The duel was the only viable end, and once the Tower entered into the agreement (proposed it, in fact), the archduke had to honor it or else face the anger of the Guardian King."

Bel nodded. "I assume then that since you stand here now, Sir Gavin triumphed in the duel."

"He did, though not happily, for in doing so, he lost a friend."

"A hard choice."

"Yes," the Tower added after a moment. "However, before he returned to Andoch, Sir Gavin was able to convince the archduke to demand that his nobles' treatment of the common folk improve."

"I see."

The Tower sighed. "The point, though, is this. Even though men might find themselves enemies, they may still regard one another as friends. For war is a foolish, stupid thing, but it happens—often, and sometimes with no other choice. Yet, while two men might stand upon either side of the line of battle, there is no reason why they cannot at least meet one another with honor. I believe the Plague Prince has yet to learn this. Funny that his younger brother should have learned that lesson well before the elder. This...'Silent Prince' so he is called."

Bel felt a sudden shock of terror, as he did any time one of the Gasparns made mention of King Cedric's youngest son.

"So they say," he muttered uncomfortably.

"When his skirmishers attacked the Gasparn caravans, they said he never harmed a single one of the drovers who did not take up arms, and those that did were treated with mercy after they surrendered."

Bel remained silent and tried to mask his discomfort.

"And Sir Linton told me this 'Silent Prince' hanged two of his own men for trying to rape a girl after his brother sacked the village of Corandell."

"I had not heard that," Bel lied.

"So they say," the Tower said. "And at the White Wood, he cared for his brother's wounded while the Plague Prince simply ran away. Now that's a man that I could meet with beneath the flag of truce and perhaps put this whole War of the Horses to rest."

Bel's heart beat faster in his chest, and for a moment, he felt faint. *Did he know?* he wondered. *Has he finally seen through the ruse?* Thankfully, Sir Harding left the matter be, for something suddenly caught his eye. He brought Tempest to a full stop and, shielding his eyes with his gauntlet, peered up along the mountain path.

"Lady's Grace!" he said suddenly. "What madness is this?"

Bel scanned the highlands in the direction of the Tower's gaze. Far off in the distance, he made out a small caravan consisting of a pair of covered wagons and a cadre of heavily armored guards. Upon the tabards of every soldier and the banners unfurled at the wagons' four posts was the rampant emblem of the White Horse.

"Sir Briden," Harding commanded, "ride back to the keep and inform the other knights and sergeants that the king had decided to grace us with a visit. I will ride out to meet him and try to delay him long enough that we might treat him to a proper greeting."

"Yes, sir." Bel nodded, but his words were lost among the thunder of Tempest's hooves.

Within the hour, the king's caravan arrived at Widowridge. On either side of the shell keep's gatehouse, the men-at-arms and archers stood in ranks to greet him. The knights of the Tower's Guard, fully outfitted in plate and chain, stood before them at attention, their helmets doffed in respect.

"Welcome to Widowridge, Your Majesty," the Tower said as King Marius stepped forth from his armored wagon. The king waved away the proffered hand of one of his royal guardsmen and grinned with delight. The knights, soldiers, and servants assembled all dropped to one knee.

King Marius breathed in deeply and rested his hands on his hips with an air of satisfaction. His clothing, though simpler than when Bel had last seen him at the tourney and its feasts, was still appropriate to one of his status—soft ermine fur and white broadcloth embroidered with sable thread. "To think, Good Sir Marcus," he said, "to think that I stand now across the Bloodline! Never thought to do so again at my age! I feel younger by a good twenty years!"

"Then I am glad for it, my lord," Sir Harding said.

"Perhaps I shall ride out with you to the next tower. I did bring my armor to camp with my cousin Guillon, though we'd have to fetch it," the king mused. "Fetch my armor and a good, strong horse like Tempest there..."

"Father, you promised that you would not overdo it," said a voice, and Bel risked a furtive glance only to see two knights of the royal escort assisting the princess—Marina the Winter Rose—down to her feet.

"Aiden's Flame, he brought the girl too," Sir Armel whispered at Bel's side.

"Thank the Brethren he did," Sir Welmsey said. "The mountain air grows cold, and she brings the spring."

"Welmsey, you fool," Sir Armel muttered, "they put themselves at too much risk."

"Quiet," Lord Talondaire snapped.

The princess stepped lightly over to her father, and when the Tower bowed, she offered him her hand. "It is good to see you again, Sir Marcus."

"And you, Princess. The snow melts in your presence."

"Stole my line, he did," said Welmsey.

"Shut up, Welmsey," Sir Armel hushed.

"Father," the Winter Rose said, "do you plan to leave these men on their knees all day?"

King Marius raised his eyebrows. "Oh yes." He cleared his throat. "Thank you, men. You may rise!"

The Tower's forces stood, and though he was certain he was not the only one, Bel fought the inclination to stare at the princess. She was closer to him now than she had been ever before, and he could not resist finding her yet lovelier still—hair like fire and eyes like verdant emeralds, brighter even than his own. Her gown of white silk shone purer than the snow, and around her shoulders, she wore an embroidered shawl of soft, black fur. Truly, she looked the very part of a Montevalen queen; all she lacked was the crown. *What had Dermont been thinking, rejecting her so?* The thought gave him pause, for Dermont had no appreciation for beauty nor anything other than himself, and rather than feeling resentful for his brother's disregard, Bel heard himself sigh with relief. A flower like her would have either wilted from his brother's neglect or else been trod upon where it grew.

And again, Bel's mind filled with thoughts of another flower, and the aching chasm inside him groaned and grew wider. Memories that nearly every waking moment he bent his will to suppress came flooding into the focus of his mind's eye. He smelled the earthy scent of her hair and tasted the salty flavor of her sweat and the sweetness of her tongue. He remembered the weight of her body lying naked upon his and the sound of her breath afterward when she finally dozed off. But most of all, he remembered her brown eyes brimming with tears when finally, they parted.

Suddenly, the Tower's call of "Sir Briden" awoke him from his reverie, and he stepped forth to the lord-general's side and bowed his head respectfully. He forced all thoughts of Lilia back to the recesses of his mind and cleared his throat.

"Has all been made ready?" Sir Harding asked.

Bel was, of course, no stranger to the lengths that most knights and lords went to on the occasion of a royal visit, even a surprise one (though personally, he disliked all the clamoring). He would have to come up with a reasonable lie later for how Sir Briden Winfred might have knowledge of such things.

"The cooks are preparing a meal, and I had the servants convert the master's quarters." He paused. "I hope you do not mind…I had not anticipated the lady."

"Nor did I," Sir Harding whispered. "If you please, when the chance arises, excuse yourself discreetly and see to arranging something suitable."

"Yes, sir."

"You have my gratitude, Sir Briden."

Bel returned to his place among the knights, and the Tower returned to the princess and the king. Another moment passed while Sir Harding spoke of the keep and its defenses, warning all among the king's company not to drink from the poisoned well—they had men collecting barrels of snow to melt should they desire water, and quietly, Bel slipped away, aware that, somehow, he had assumed the role of the lord-general's steward.

That afternoon and into the evening, rather than make ready to assault the next keep, the Tower played the host and entertained the Gasparn king, which was somewhat difficult due to the limited nature of the soldiers' stores. As a result, a number of the archers were sent ranging in hopes of finding game worthy of a king, and although Marius made a great show of returning to "the soldier's life," the men—from the Tower down—seemed to feel that a point of pride was at stake. A number of the knights donated freely from their personal stores—wine, herbs, and other niceties that may improve the quality of the Tower's table. But real relief did not come until the archers returned from their hunt, and thankfully, in addition to the usual highland rabbits, the men had also been able to take a deer. By way of thanks, Sir Harding informed Bel that the sergeants among the common men were to join the knights in feasting the king and the princess in the great hall.

When the meal was finally ready to be served, Bel breathed a great sigh of relief. He thought again of Sir Emory, his father's seneschal, and of Clemant, his father's steward, and determined that when next he saw them, he would be certain to thank them. He had already decided long ago to appeal to King Cedric to have Jarvy knighted, but after the old skirmisher's help minding the kitchens, Bel would not be satisfied with anything less than a lordship.

At last, when all was completed, Bel returned to the hall just as the meal was served. In all, there were the two dozen knights of the Tower's Guard, the lord-general himself, the king, the princess, five sergeants from among the men-at-arms, and four sergeants from among the archers. Thirty-six in total, though as Bel accepted the seat reserved for him at Sir Harding's right hand (who in turn sat at the king's right, opposite the princess), he could only imagine how other men managed true banquets.

"Sir Briden, I owe you a debt," the Tower murmured at his side. "It's my duty, sir," Bel nodded.

"And that's your man yonder who drives your cart among the baggage train? The fellow over there serving as a sewer?"

"Aye, Jarvy's his name."

"I'll have a pouch of silver for him tomorrow morning."

Bel nodded, and a servant appeared to fill his cup. "The wine is the Talon's, I hear."

"He offered it freely, and that's one of his men acting as butler. In fact, all the men serving belong to one of the knights, except for those two there who are the archers that brought down the deer. They offered their aid at the table."

"Very generous."

"It is my shame for not employing a retinue of my own, though I am not used to such things. The Warlord offered me a partisan to serve as my attendant, but in my haste, I refused. I'll see that they are all rewarded—"

"Ah, Sir Marcus!" King Marius suddenly chimed in. "When do you intend to move along? Tomorrow?"

"Or the day after, Your Majesty," the Tower said, "although it's beginning to seem as if we've dressed for a banquet that's never to come. For with the exception of Prince Dermont's plague-bearers, we've met no other Valendian resistance."

"Outwitted them, have you?" Marius grinned.

"Perhaps, although I am reluctant to count my chickens before they've hatched, as the common folk say."

"That's probably wise."

Bel listened as King Marius spoke, and although they neither looked nor sounded much alike, something about him put Bel in mind of his own father—in the early days of his illness when his mind was just beginning to weaken, and though Marius and Cedric were removed from each other by four generations, the similarities he felt now in the Gasparn king's presence made him wonder if it was more than simply grief, but rather some poisoning of the blood visited upon the Tremonts as punishment from the Brethren for a century of fratricidal warfare.

"Tell me, Your Majesty, if I might be so bold as to ask," the Tower began again after a moment. "What is it that brought you this far south? I had thought you would stay in Reginal, for the winter fast approaches."

"Why! If this is to be the end of the war," King Marius said. "I want to be there! It would only be proper!"

"Father insisted he accompany cousin Guillon's army south," the princess added, "and unfortunately, Guillon accepted."

How could he not? Bel thought. Few were brave enough to refuse a king. Had Dermont not forced King Cedric into submission after Larius's death, who knows how much longer Bel's father would have taken the field, mad with despair, reckless enough to lead his men to ruin—or so Dermont had accused him.

"I would like to be there to accept this Prince of Plague's surrender," he said. "And I would like Marina there too if possible so he can see what his pride cost him."

The princess shook her head. "Father," she said, "I have told you before, I have no designs on meeting the Plague Prince, and I count myself lucky not to be his wife."

"That, my dear," the king said, "was *your* idea if you'll remember, not mine."

"My intention was to stop the war," she said, "and if you remember, Gislain had just died."

Beside the princess, the Young Talon cleared his throat, and Bel recalled they shared a family relation granting the lord a place at the lady's side. "If I might say so, Your Highness, were you taken to wife by Prince Dermont, I believe there's not a man in Gasparn who would not take arms again to rescue you from making such a sacrifice."

"That's kind of you to say, Lord Talon," the princess said. "But I have grown rather tired of this bloodshed. I've lost one brother, and I'm sure over these generations past, many have lost much more. If someone must sacrifice to staunch the flow, why should it not be one among the Tremonts? For it was our forbearers that began the war. Should we not be the ones to end it?" She pulled a face. "But I suppose I am just a woman. What do I know?"

King Marius sighed heavily, and he held up his hands as if swatting at flies. "Enough talk of martyrdom. I see no hierophant at this feast," he said. "Let us talk now only of the future. Did you know, Sir Marcus, that King Kredor has invited Marina to visit his court in the spring? Perhaps you might accompany her if all goes well."

"I would be honored, my lady." Sir Marcus smiled politely.

"Do you know King Kredor well?" Marius asked.

"I'm afraid not, Majesty. I am never in Titanis long, nor was the King, for that matter. He spent a great deal of time defending the northern borders of Andoch against the Wrathorn."

"Yes, we have heard of his victory even here," the king said.

"And now he fights Grantis alongside the archduke?" the princess asked.

"So I have been told, yes," the Tower said.

"You do not agree?" King Marius asked.

Sir Harding paused and seemed to think carefully before speaking. "I find it somewhat out of the ordinary that the King send more than simply officers such as myself, men of the Warlord's Tower. The kingsmen guard our cities and our borders; however, we have never truly had any overt conflict with the senate, nor were we ever strong allies of Dwerin. The Guardians always maintained a position of neutrality, for we safeguard and keep the peace, or at least try to. It is highly unusual that we should willingly engage in war."

"War after war…" Marina sighed, "will it ever end?"

"One can only hope," the Tower said, and raising his glass, he drank. A moment later, Bel did likewise, offering the general a nod, and suddenly felt the eyes of the princess on him.

"Sir Marcus," she said, "Who is the young knight who sits at your side? I nearly thought the seat was vacant for all of his silence. He's more quiet than the Talon here"—she offered the young nobleman at her side a smile—"though somewhat less dour."

The Tower turned to Bel and waved his hand. "Your Majesty, Princess, this is Sir Briden Winfred," he said as Bel rose from his seat and bowed his head. "His father was a knight in the service of Lord Solidar in Rosewood."

King Marius nodded his head in recognition. "I remember Rosewood," he said. "An unfortunate loss."

"So it was, Your Majesty," Bel said. The king waved a hand, and Bel resumed his seat, somewhat flustered to speak to the man who for so long had been his father's enemy, and even more so under the princess's continued gaze.

"Sir Briden..." she said, "I believe I remember you from the tourney."

"More likely from the melee, Your Highness," Lord Talondaire said politely.

Bel winced; he had hoped his relations with the Talon had finally reached a point of civility, or at least mutual respect.

"He's the one who lay down his arms," the young lord continued idly, then paused to take a drink. "But he's also the one who first spotted the plague-bearers in Valeshade. Had we drank the water, you might have found us there instead of here, all dying of the fever flux."

Bel glanced down the length of the table as the Talon offered him a short, curt nod.

"Sir Briden..." the princess said, "I remember you now. You fought finely in the lists, even my father said so, and now that Tally mentions it, you did give a fine speech before the melee, as I remember"—she grinned—"for one so quiet now."

Bel could feel himself suddenly blushing. "I apologize, Princess," he said. "But I have nothing of value to say."

"Oh, surely, that's not true," she said.

Bel shrugged. "I'm afraid it is, though again you have my apologies."

"Then..." the princess began, "tell us something of no value."

Bel blushed further. "My lady?"

"You said you have nothing of value to say?" She grinned, her red lips spread wide to reveal fine white teeth. "So tell us something of no value. Tell us whatever is on your mind."

Bel smiled bashfully and sat up straighter in his chair. He sighed, hoping to calm his nerves. "Well," he began, "is there any particular subject of nonsense about which you would like to know?

Princess Marina laughed, and Bel felt even more foolish. Beside him, the Tower and the King appeared not to notice, conversing in quieter tones. "Tell me…" the princess said. "Oh, tell me about horses. As one of the Tower's Guard, surely, you know something about that."

"All right." Bel gave a nod of resignation and paused to think. "When I was a boy," he said after a moment, "and I was first learning to ride, my father asked me to accompany him around the grounds so that I could show him how far I had come along. I took to riding rather quickly, as I imagine was the same with most of the men here, but because of this, I was so eager to impress my father that I began to…show off, or try to, for the horse would have none of it, and the more I tried to force it, the more the horse resisted. Eventually, it tried to throw me off and my father had to dismount and take the horse by the bridle to calm him down. I felt very foolish."

"However," Bel continued, "my father told me that to be a good rider, a man must not think in terms of himself but rather of his horse, for if a man seeks to control the creature by force, bending it to his will, it will naturally seek to resist him, as mine did, and rebel. Yet neither can a man simply let loose the reins and allow the beast to go where it will, for it will soon become lost or frightened and might easily get hurt. Thus, to be a great rider, one must be neither too forceful nor too lenient, but rather treat his horse with judicious moderation, and most importantly, with love. If I could strive to do that, my father said, I might not only make a great horseman, but perhaps a great knight. For if a knight's station is above his people like a rider sits above his horse, then it is his duty to treat them in the same manner, with just guidance, and with love."

"A fine sentiment," Lord Talondaire sighed, "though there are some who'd say the common folk react better to fear than they do to love, for we expect much and ever more from our lovers, sometimes more than it is possible for them to give. Such disappointments often then breed anger and even rage."

"True," Bel said, "though think on Prince Dermont and his plague-bearers. Much he does and more is meant to inspire fear."

"I, too, would choose love any day over fear," Princess Marina said. "There are enough vile things in this world for the common folk as it is. They should not have to live in fear that their noble lord is going to murder them in their beds."

"And thus, the people love their princess." The Young Talon raised his glass and took a drink.

"You knights and your horses, though. I swear you love them more than you love your wives!"

"You forget, Your Highness," Talondaire said. "I do not have one. Nor does the Tower, I believe, and Sir Briden?"

Bel was hesitant. "No," he finally said.

"Then perhaps we have just discovered the reason why"—the princess grinned—"though a sweetheart like Tempest would be hard for any woman to match. Sir Marcus, I've missed him most dreadfully since you stole him away."

"And I'm certain he has missed you," the Tower said, "as sure as I am that he would very much welcome a visit from you tomorrow should you desire it."

"I certainly will," Marina said, and again, Bel felt her eyes fall upon him. "Thank you for the story, Sir Briden, and though you might think your words have no value, whenever I think of them, I will give a gold piece to the poor."

Bel's cheeks turned as scarlet as the princess's hair, the sight of which seemed to widen her smile. "Thank you, Your Highness," he said. "You do me too much honor."

He was spared further embarrassment, however, when King Marius again began wondering about the Tower's plans. Sir Harding seemed somewhat reticent, subtly evasive even, and Bel noticed that it was at these times that Marina would often chime in to change the subject. He began to sense that Marius was rather serious about joining the Tower's Guard in their next advance—a risk neither the lord-general nor the princess was about to take.

The conversation continued with the meal, and thankfully, Bel was able to return to his silence. He gazed idly at the other men at the small, round tables filling the remainder of the long, curved hall. All seemed content. Bel breathed a sigh of relief, only to notice Jarvy eying implicitly him from nearby.

"There's a problem with the dessert…" he whispered to Bel, though at a volume just loud enough for the Tower to overhear. "And the cook has a question for you down in the kitchen…"

Sir Harding cleared his throat and nodded to Sir Briden dismissively. Bel hurried after Jarvy to the staircase that led down to the kitchen.

"A man appeared in the larder," Jarvy whispered. "Don't ask me how, but I know he wasn't among the servants of the baggage train, and there was fresh mud and the smell of the road about him. I think he might be one of that bastard Canton's bloody rats."

Bel's face fell. "Has anyone else seen him?"

"No one of consequence so far as I can tell."

Bel sighed. It was only a matter of time before one of them turned up. Dermont would be wanting a report.

The cook was putting the finishing touches on some manner of tart as Bel and Jarvy arrived in the kitchens. There was not nearly enough for all of the men; however, luxuries were limited and it would at least be enough to offer to the princess and the king.

At the sight of it, Jarvy gave a whistle. "Aiden's Flame, Rolf, that looks beautiful," he told the cook. "Why don't you present it to his majesty yourself?"

"Aye, thank you, Jarvy," the cook said, and noticing Bel added, "and thank you, my lord. First I serve the Tower, and now I serve the king!"

"You've more than earned the honor," Bel said.

"Thank you," the cook added, "I thank you, my lord!"

"I wonder sometimes at the things that you know, Jarvy," Bel said when the cook had gone. "How does an old skirmisher like yourself know how to manage a meal like this?"

"Not much of a mystery to that, I'm afraid," Jarvy grinned. "I was a potboy as a lad, way back in your grandfather's day. I kept my eyes open then too, as always. Speaking of which, my lord, if you'll just follow me, I left the rat in the larder."

Canton's man was dressed in the fashion of a mountain peasant, and in truth, he very well might have been one. He sat upon one of the empty barrels from the days long past when Widowridge was still occupied, and picked his nose thoughtfully. "On your feet, you bastard," Jarvy snapped. "Show some respect."

"Apologies, Silent Prince," the man said, grinning through blackened teeth. He stood and searched among his person for a folded piece of parchment. "You'll be wanting to burn that afterward when you're done."

Bel quickly scanned the note. "All it says is that my brother is gathering his forces, and he plans to leave Whitemane to engage the Tower in the east,"

Bel said. "But he knows the Tower headed west. Why would he send me this? It's meaningless."

"Well, I didn't read it," the man said.

"I doubt you can." Jarvy grunted under his breath. "But if I had to guess, sir, I'd say it was to confound anyone who captured this lout."

The man sneered and returned his attention to Bel. "Anyways," he said, "I'm to tell you that Canton and your brother know where you are and that they're coming."

"What do you mean?" Bel asked. "I haven't sent any word to Dermont since we left Reginal."

"He has plenty more eyes than just you. Hardly a moment goes by that someone's not watching the Tower, or the king and his princess for that matter." The man smiled. "She's a sweet one, eh?"

"Hold your tongue," Bel said coldly, "or I will kill you where you stand."

"Yes, sir." The man smirked. "Anyways, your brother plans to send a small force from Whitemane to attack the men in Roanshead. Then in secret, he plans to head out and attack the army as follows you from the north and cut off the Tower's path of escape. In fact, by my reckoning, he's on the path to do so right now."

"If that's the case, then why would Dermont send me on this fool's errand to begin with? Canton could have easily surmised that long ago," Bel said angrily. "And clearly, he has spies enough that he does not need me here, nor did he ever!"

The man shook his head. "Canton says he wants you to ensure that King Marius continues south with Marcus Harding. If he doesn't and he rejoins Lord Guillon's army, he could escape. Now, as it stands, when your brother finally sends the order, you'll not only slay the Tower, but take Ol' Marius prisoner. The princess as well, I should imagine."

"Why would I need to do that if he already has them trapped? This is absurd!" Bel scowled. "This whole ridiculous farce has been utterly meaningless from the beginning!"

"Settle down, lordling," Canton's man said. "I'm only passing word!"

Bel ground his teeth a moment longer and took a deep breath. "You tell my brother, or tell Canton, or whomever, that I want out of here! I want no further part in this charade!"

"I'm not that stupid," the man said. "You can tell him yourself when he arrives. Hard to imagine he'll be pleased."

Bel rubbed his eyes in frustration. "How soon will he be here?"

"How should I know?" the man shrugged, "I'm to remind you, though, that if you gave off like you was wavering, of the woman your brother has in his keeping and the promise he made before you left. Things might go a lot worse for her now it turns out she's with child."

All at once, the breath emptied from Bel's lungs, and he nearly doubled over as if gut-punched. "What did you say?"

The messenger's eyes narrowed. "What?"

"What did you say?" Bel demanded. "About the woman? What did you say about the woman?" He took a step forward, and the man attempted to take a step back and nearly tripped over the barrel.

"I...I don't know," he said, stammering in confusion. Despite his early swagger, something about the look in Bel's eyes seemed to evoke the man's fear.

"You said that she was with child," Bel said sternly, "Who told you that? Who sent you to me? Did Dermont send you directly, or was it Canton?" Bel ground his teeth again in anger and took yet another step closer, close enough that he could smell the man's awful breath. "Who told you this?"

"Who told me?"

"Who told you?"

The man took a deep breath. "Canton," he confessed at last, "though Canton only takes his orders from your brother directly."

"Is it true?"

"I don't know, I only—"

Bel grabbed the man by the collar of his tunic, pushed him back over the barrel, and held him pinned against the wall. "Is it true?"

"I don't know!" the messenger said. "I only know what they told me to tell you!"

A long moment passed. Finally, Bel released the man's tunic and stepped away, letting him slide down the wall. He covered his face in his hands and rubbed his eyes, forgetting all about Sir Briden and the Tower, King Marius and the princess. All he could think of was Lilia held captive by his own brother and his horrid promises of murder and rape. *If he harms her, St. Aiden, I will kill him—even should it curse me as a kinslayer! By all the gods of the Kinship, this I swear, damn him!*

462

The messenger regained his footing and his courage, now that he was free from Bel's grasp. "Now, I'll be going," he said, smoothing his tunic. "Is there anything else that you'd like me to tell him?"

Bel remained silent, unable to speak for inferno that raged within him, forcing the man to repeat the question.

"Canton and my brother did not ask for anything specific by way of reply then?"

"No," the man said.

"Nothing at all?"

"Canton only said to pass on your brother's commands."

"So he does not await an answer?"

"None as I can think of. Just a reminder that you keep to your place."

"Good."

In a flash, Bel drew the table dagger from his belt and thrust it between the messenger's ribs. The man's eyes widened in agony and surprise. His mouth stretched open as if to scream, but no sound came forth. Bel held him steady, watching the light fade from his eyes, until finally when the spy's body stopped twitching, Bel let him slump like a sack of grain to the cold stone floor. Blood ran red along the crenels between the flagstones, spreading into a crimson sea. At once, Jarvy hurried forward and turned the body over to try to control the direction of the flow of blood away from the larder door. Bel stood transfixed at the sight of the corpse, breathing heavily in a mixture of despair and remorse.

"My lord," Jarvy said hurriedly, "your hand. There's blood on it."

Bel bent down to wipe his hand upon the dead man's tunic and nearly vomited. His eyes burned, threatening to spill over with tears, and a great lump formed in his throat.

"By the gods" he asked aloud, though more to himself than anyone else, "What have I become?"

Jarvy slid the body behind the barrel and took the bloody knife from Bel's hand. "You are Prince Beledain of Valendia," the old skirmisher said, "who all men know as the Prince of Bells or the Silent Prince. You are a warrior and a knight of great worth, a leader of men, respected by the common folk, your soldiers, and your enemies alike. More than anything else, however, you are a good man who strives always to do what is right, even when all the world seems wrong."

Bel breathed a heavy sigh and rubbed his eyes. He was so weary.

"You had best get back to the Tower, my lord," Jarvy said. "I'll take care of things here. The well's already poisoned. This rat won't make it any worse."

Bel nodded and prepared to return to the role of Sir Briden. However, before he did, he turned back to Jarvy. "Do you think what he said is true?"

"You'd know better than I would, my lord," the old skirmisher said. "However, were she not held captive by your brother, would it bother you?"

"I don't know. I've never thought about it, or I have, but...I worry so much about her. I fear my mind will break if I worry anymore."

"Well," Jarvy said, "She's not one to go quietly."

"No."

"And I'm sure that Sir Emory will watch over her. He's a good sort."

"He is."

"But for now, my lord," Jarvy said, "I think it best you hurry back. And if this bastard can be believed, it seems this'll all be over soon enough."

"True enough," Bel said grimly, "One way, or the other."

CHAPTER 35:
MAGNUS

"Read to me what you have so far."

Thom sighed. It was very late, and he was both tired and hungry. His eyes stung from squinting as he tried in vain to write legibly in the dim firelight, and his head ached from trying to make sense of Magnus's stories, blathered as they were through half-drunken slurs and cursing. Thick clouds of acrid smoke wafted lazily through the air, burning his lungs, and from each of the hallways leading away from the common room, there echoed strange sounds.

Still, it was some small comfort to be back in his habit, and he was glad that he had decided to stow it in his pack after all, for with everything that had transpired at the Sandstone, his new clothes were far too soiled to be worth keeping (even his lovely cloak with its fur-lined hood). As for Magnus, the Wrathorn Blackguard had his pick of the gear belonging to the dead kingsmen (eleven in all, Thom counted), and although he was quite taller than most other watchmen Thom had seen, not a soul paid them any mind as they ventured from the guardhouse to find refuge in whatever house of ill repute this was along the Galdoran docks.

Since then, Thom had been forced to sit in abject fear while women of all ages, shapes, and sizes fritted about here and there, half-clad, steeped in perfume, giggling, prancing, and prattling on, while Magnus, rich from sacking the Sandstone, made merry among them like the Emperor of Calendral, pausing only occasionally to rest, refill his wine, or spin some horrible yarn.

"Come on," Magnus said. He waved a massive hand, and from the counter across the common room, a whore brought him yet another jug of wine.

"There's a good lass," the Wrathorn said, catching her hand and pulling her down to his lap. "Go on, Thom," he said. "Tell us a story!" Thom cleared his throat and fought to avert his eyes from the sagging neckline of the woman's dress. He took a deep breath and traced the scribbled lines of his journal with his finger. "Of all the clans of the Wrathorn," he began, "the greatest, by far, is that of Clan Bloodbeard. One of the oldest and most powerful, the Bloodbeards (or Blodbjorn in their native tongue, noting a slight mistranslation on the part of our scholars) are believed to carry in their veins the blood of the Great Bear, one of the ancient totemic gods of the Wrathorn tribes. Because of this, the Bloodbeards' strength in battle is unmatched, and they remain the only clan never to lay down arms against either the Calendral Empire or the Guardians of Andoch." The whore helped Magnus lift the heavy jug to his lips, and Thom wondered if the Wrathorn was even listening.

"The current chieftain of Clan Bloodbeard," Thom continued, "is Magnus, son of Grunor, king of all the lands north of the Firriny Mountains."

"At the age of five, Magnus killed his first man, a poacher of Clan Nordigar, captured in the act of dressing a deer taken on Bloodbeard lands. On his Spirit Hunt at the age of nine, he singlehandedly killed a bear and ate its heart, a feat not accomplished for more than a hundred summers. At the age of fourteen, he"—Thom paused—"he... wooed his first woman—"

"Wooed?" Magnus corrected. "Wooing is for nobles, bards, and men with shriveled cocks. Isn't that right, dear?" he asked the giggling prostitute. "See, she knows."

"He...lie with?"

"Did more than just lie there, I can tell you."

"He...coupled..." Thom muttered quickly, and when Magnus did not object, continued, "He coupled with his first woman, winning her favors in single combat against..."

"Einer, son of Geirr!" Magnus said.

"Einer, son of Geirr," Thom repeated, "a warrior four years his senior, during the Feast of the Salmon."

"If you kill a worthy man, remember his name. That way, if he haunts you, you know the right way to address him!"

"Finally, at the age of fifteen, which the Wrathorn call the Age of Death, Magnus became king."

"Go on."

"At that time, Clan Bloodbeard fought a great war against the Guardian-King of Andoch, carving the paths through the Firriny Mountains that Clan Thorwick would use many years later. The Bloodbeards raided a number of mines and herding villages north of Titanis, and again, young Magnus distinguished himself by taking several enemy heads." Thom sighed. "Finally, when the clan reached Titanis, the Bloodbeards wasted no time in attacking and set fire to the groundlings, the peasant town outside of the city walls, and nearly succeeded in breaking through the city gates into Weston. Unfortunately, due to the…failings of—"

"Weakness," Magnus said bitterly, "and stupidity."

"Due to the weakness and stupidity of the elder sons of Chieftain Grunor (whose names for shame are to be forgotten), the attack failed, and the Bloodbeards were forced to retreat northwards, raiding and pillaging the mountain villages as they withdrew. During this time, Chief Grunor's elder sons fell, the eldest by disease and the other two by kinslaying, leaving Magnus now the sole male heir."

"I had two elder sisters as well," Magnus told the whore. "But they were already married off to other clans, else they would have led."

Thom continued, "The Guardians, led by Longrine the Forester, pursued the Bloodbeards, with the aid of…the miserable, lapdog… cowards of Clan Brindlebairne who had betrayed their gods and their people by converting to the faith of the Kinship." Thom paused, for though he had written what Magnus told him, he did not quite understand (nor did he particularly enjoy) the next part.

"Chief Grunor, sensing that all was lost, led his people onward to their ancestral burial mounds along the Frozen Hills. There, strengthened by the souls of his ancestors, he planned to make his final stand. For six days, the battle raged on before Longrine and the Brindlebairnes forced Grunor and his remaining warriors back into the Heart of the Bear, the cave where the Great Bear gave birth to the first Bloordbeard chief…" Thom stopped. "Wait. I thought the Great Bear was a male. How did it give birth then if it's male?"

"It's a god," Magnus said. "It can be whatever it wants to be. Man or woman, spirit or flesh, anything it wants. Just shut up and keep reading."

Thom continued, "While Longrine and his men fought Grunor's remaining warriors, the chieftain himself called together the members of his family: his wife, his concubines, and his remaining son…"

"Go on."

Thom felt his stomach flutter, and he took a deep breath. "And one by one, he stabbed them in the heart."

"But…" Magnus said.

Thom took a deep breath. "But just before he was about to stab Magnus, the Forester and his men came in, and Grunor's blade slipped. Longrine, an archer, slew Grunor with an arrow to the eye…"

"I piss on archers! Cowards, all of them! Too afraid to stand toe to toe with a man and fight him for real!"

Thom kept reading. "Although Grunor missed his heart, Magnus lay bleeding and would most certainly have died. However, one of Longrine's fellow Guardians, Kedwin, called the Reaver, chose to save Magnus's life."

Magnus took another drink from the jug. "'You don't fell the last tree of a forest,' he told him, and he gave Longrine his axe and said when I was old enough, he was to give it to me."

Thom nodded, dipped his quill, and made a note. However, as he was about to begin reading again, he glanced up and noticed Magnus had suddenly fallen silent, and the laughter had gone out of his face. The whore ran her hand along his shoulder and loosened the laces of her bodice, but Magnus roughly waved her hand away. Thom stole a quick glance at her chest and then shamefacedly dropped his eyes to examine the floor.

"Well," the Wrathorn said, "you did a shit job with that."

"What?" Thom asked. "I wrote what you told me!"

"If that's all it took, I would have written it myself," Magnus said, "if I cared enough to know how to write, anyways."

Thom rubbed his eyes. "What was so wrong with it?"

"Well, for starters, it doesn't sound like any song I've ever heard." "It's not a song." Thom sighed. "It's a history."

"Then it's crap!" Magnus said. "You'll just have to do it again." He rose brusquely from the table, spilling the whore from his lap and catching her by the arm. "I'm to bed," he said. "How about it, darling? Coming with me?" By way of response, the woman giggled and took up the jug of wine in her free hand.

"But what am I to do?" Thom asked miserably. "And where am I to sleep?"

"Find a woman"—Magnus grinned—"or failing that…" He nodded across the room to where an old, drunken lecher had passed out face down on one of the tables. "Seems you can always sleep it off here."

Thom's stomach began to ache again, and his eyes welled with tears. "And what if the guards come looking for us?" he asked. "What are we to do then?"

"All these fucking questions!" Magnus said in disgust. "We figure it out as we go!"

Thom breathed a heavy sigh of despair and began to sob—or was about to when the Wrathorn struck him hard across the ear with the flat of his hand. The boy looked up in shock, his eyes wide with surprise.

"No more crying!" Magnus growled. "If I catch you crying, you'll get worse."

"I wasn't!"

"You were going to," he said. "Now if you're tired, there's plenty of room over there by the hearth. You can lie down with the rest of the dogs on the floor, or if you've half a backbone, you can find a room of your own. I will find you when I wake, and if I don't because you've run off, I'll find you eventually and split your skull."

Thom bit back his tears. They discovered Magnus's axe—the Reaver's axe—in the room with the strongboxes where the guardsmen kept the money they collected from taxes, fines, and tithes. It was an enormous thing and heavy—for even Magnus needed two hands to wield it. Thom had no head for the proper names of such things, but he knew Lughus would have known. All Thom could tell was that the blade hung longer on the bottom half than on the top— bearded, it may have been called, bearded like the Wrathorns themselves. No matter what, though, it was sharp and frightening, as Magnus was only too willing to demonstrate by cutting the head off of one of the kingsmen's corpses. Kedwin the Reaver called the axe by a different name, but Magnus had renamed the weapon "Death." There was no doubt in Thom's mind that, together, Magnus and Death could easily split his skull.

"Yes, sir," he finally said.

"'Til tomorrow then, boy," the barbarian called. "And none of that 'sir' nonsense. I'm Magnus, and you're Thom, yes?"

"As you say."

"Yes, it is. Now 'til tomorrow."

It was noon the next day before Magnus finally made himself known. Thom had already been awake for many hours after passing an uncomfortable night on his bedroll to the side of the hearth. The unconscious drunkard from the night before had been run off, and now the prostitutes had reclaimed the humid common room, fanning themselves after a long night of work, and Thom could not help but think on what a horrid existence they must lead. Still, they offered to share their breakfast with him, and since Magnus was nowhere to be seen, Thom readily agreed. They even tried to talk to him, though growing up surrounded only by men (and often very old ones at that), he found the wanton women extremely intimidating—terrifying even—and before long, they gave up.

When Magnus finally showed himself, he was dressed hastily in the stolen mail hauberk and red cloak of a kingsman, with Death strapped across his back. There were great, dark circles under his eyes, and he leaned heavily on yet another prostitute for support. Thom noticed a wave of disapproval pass between the eyes of the whores, and one or two of them clicked her tongue.

"Take care of this, would you, love?" Magnus said, passing one of the women his upturned helm. She refused, turning her nose up in disgust. It fell to the floor, spilling a great puddle of foul-smelling vomit.

"Dibhor's cock! You drunken fool!" came a shout. From down another hall, there appeared the middle-aged woman Thom remembered from their arrival the day before. It was her who Magnus paid his money, and from what Thom could tell, she seemed to be in charge. However, while she was only too friendly yesterday while Magnus was counting out his coins, whatever good graces the Wrathorn had bought now seemed to have all been spent.

"That does it!" she shouted, "Get your things and get out!"

"Hold on, dear." Magnus smiled apologetically. "No need to be cross."

"My right tit, there's no need to be cross!" she shouted. "You've been here one night, and it's like a whole pack of bloody mercenaries came through and spent the week!"

"Well, I fight like a whole pack of bloody mercenaries, so that very well might be true." Magnus grinned.

The madam pulled the whore from Magnus's side, and he only just righted himself to avoid falling in the puddle of sick on the floor. "You get out," she shouted, "before I call the guard!"

"Are you blind, woman?" Magnus laughed. "See this red cloak? I am the guard!"

"Yes, and I'm the Lady of Light! Get out!" She glanced at Thom. "And take your fat little eunuch with you! There's rumors abound of a slaughter at the Sandstone and a Wrathorn fugitive done killed them all!"

"He's not a eunuch," Magnus muttered, ignoring most of her words, "least, I don't think he is. Might account for the voice, though."

"Violet, call the guard!"

"Hold on, hold on," Magnus said, holding out his hands. "We're going. Just one moment." He took the purse from his belt and counted out a pile of coins. "For the trouble," he said, "and the gold ones are to still your tongue."

The madam heaved a sigh but accepted. "I'll say not a word for the week unless they come calling directly, but after that…"

"Fine." Magnus shrugged. "You're very kind, my lady." He turned to Thom. "Let's go, boy."

Thom hefted his rucksack onto his shoulders and trundled along after the Wrathorn warrior in silence.

"Farewell, darlings," Magus called. "You won't see me again."

Out in the streets, the docks were teeming with activity as men loaded and unloaded cargo from one place to another. Thankfully, most of the war galleys stood offshore, though here and there, Thom still saw the flash of a red cloak. Magnus, however, did not appear in the least concerned about drawing unwanted attention, and after they passed a particularly malodorous fish merchant, he paused along the pier to vomit over the side into the water. All eyes fell on him in disgust. At length, when he was ready, he moved on.

"Lovely places, brothels," he said. "You walk in, and the women fight to open their legs for you. You walk out, and they're never sorry to see you go."

Thom said nothing.

"I grew up in places like that, after I ran away from old Longrine, of course," Magnus continued. "Now, no matter where I am, city, town, or port, there's always something about a whorehouse that just feels like home, don't you think?"

"I wouldn't know," Thom said.

"*I* do. So I'm telling you. They *do*. Except, of course, for the cold," Magnus said, "though I'm not sure that's so bad. No one wants a freezing whorehouse. Imagine that, would you? If it were as cold and frigid as the north? Fingers and toes turnin' black and useless. Frostbite could crack your cock off like an icicle..." He paused. "By the way, you're not a eunuch, are you?"

"What?" Thom gasped. "No! Of course not!"

Magnus held up his hands. "All right, no need to get frosty. Just asking. Seeing you didn't seem to have a good time..."

"I was...simply not interested. That's all."

"Right." Magnus snorted. "Ah well, saves you coin, eh? Besides, these women here? They're fine, sure, but there's not a woman south of the Firrinies that can hold a candle to a true Wrathorn woman when it comes to coupling. Gods, how I wish more of them left the north!"

Thom remained silent, hoping Magnus would say no more. Yet he had learned early in their acquaintance that the Wrathorn was very fond of idle talk, particularly his own. He spoke loudly, and he spoke often, oblivious to the effects his vocabulary or his subject matter may have had on either his intended or unintended audience. Thom braced himself against the embarrassment that was sure to come as Magnus began again.

"First off," he said, with something of the air of a lecturer about him (it reminded Thom of the way Scholar Norris looked if you asked him about ale), "a Wrathorn woman will never fuck a man who can't beat her in a fight, so for someone like you, she'd just as soon cut your cock off before she let you put it to her."

Thom blushed and tried to avoid the stares of the passing dockside folk.

"Second, there's none of this bathing you folk do. You've not a single bathhouse in the north. Bloody water would freeze for one thing."

A passing woman eyed Magnus with terror, and he paused to stare at her maliciously, laughing to himself when she scurried off. "See that?"

Thom nodded, praying the woman would not run immediately to the guards.

"Where was I?"

"Bathing..." the boy muttered.

"Ah, yes. A woman, I say, should smell like a woman, not a flower or honey or whatever else. In the north, they do, every inch of them." Magnus eyed him sincerely, and Thom knew to nod as a reply.

"Next, there's none of this odd shaving business neither that's so fashionable with you southern folk, particularly among women, nor this concern with being so spindly thin and pale. I swear, a strong wind blows, and they're liable to fly away. There's even been times, mind you, that I've been with a woman, and she was so spare, I thought I might break her in two." He laughed. "Not that it didn't stop me from trying."

Thom sighed miserably and felt a cold stab of fear as he wondered if Magnus was expecting him to write this down. He nearly asked, but the Wrathorn had already continued.

"A real Wrathorn woman is strong and thick, and you'll never worry about breaking her because you're more concerned with her crushing you between her legs or biting you too hard on the neck or the arms! Oh, it's lovely!" He laughed. "And the hair! I tell you, if a woman were meant only to have hair on her head, she would have been born that way! Same with you southern men who shave your beards and cut the heads off your cocks!" Magnus stopped and fixed Thom with a questioning stare. "Why do you do that, eh? Tell me? I've always wondered."

Thom's face grew redder. "I don't know," he muttered. "The... hierophants say that the Kinship requires it, a sacrifice. They say it's cleaner, and they don't really...it's not like you think."

"Ha! Yet another thing wrong with your bloody gods!" Magnus laughed and spit on the ground. A passing sailor stopped short, wondering if the spit was meant for him, yet when he spied the big Wrathorn and his axe, he hurried on.

"If my gods told me something like that, I'd kill all the priests and find a new god."

Thom suppressed a flash of resentment. "Weren't you talking about women," he muttered.

"Aye, women!" Magnus sighed. "Up north, the women grow hair as thick as a bear, and they're proud of it—all of it. Everywhere. Under their arms, up their legs, between them! None of this plucking and scraping nonsense. Gods! I knew this one girl, thick as the forest! I swear, tupping her was like fucking the

Great Bear itself"—Magnus stopped suddenly and whirled on Thom—
"which can just as easily be a woman, mind you! As I said."

Thom nodded.

"But you people, hairless as fish! Why?"

The boy looked around him uncomfortably, "It's just a custom…"

"Come, tell me, oh wise boy of the Loremaster."

"It's supposed to…I don't know, be a mark of nobility," Thom said. "The
hairier a man is, the more like an…animal. The cleaner, the more…tidy his
hair, the more noble. A peasant can't afford a fine blade or the cost of the
bathhouse, so he grows a beard and cuts it with sheep sheers. A merchant,
maybe, can. Nobles have baths built right into their castles and shave their
faces smoothly. They say in Grantis, some noblemen even shave their chests,
their backs, and their arms to try and look like the statues from Old
Calendral, like they're carved from marble. It's the same with women, I
suppose, especially further south where the air is warmer, and they wear…less
clothes."

"So noble ladies and noblemen, fine, but more and more of the whores
too," Magnus said. "Why?"

"I don't know!" Thom shuddered in exacerbation. "I don't know them as
you! Maybe they do it because they want to appear fashionable too? That's
their…trade, isn't it?"

"All right, *you* then. Where's your beard? Or are you hoping to look like a
great boulder of marble, ha?"

"I don't have one. Not yet, at least." "How old are you?"

"Sixteen."

"Ha! I had a beard since the day I was born! Came out that way!"

"I highly doubt that," Thom said crossly and immediately regretted it.
Thankfully, the Wrathorn simply laughed and rubbed the stubble on his jaw.

"First time in my life I've been shaved. Bloody itchy."

"I wouldn't know."

"So if being smooth as a marble statue is noble, if I shave my ass and drown
in the bathhouse, how long before I become your king?"

"What?" Thom asked. "It doesn't work that way."

"What a load of shit." Magnus laughed and hurried on down the docks,
"The ways of the south are not for me! No way. Food's too spicy and always
cooked far too long! Can't even taste the blood. It's so burned!"

Thom sighed.

"And you can't do anything without treading on some sodding law or another! I tell you, a man cheats at dice, and you cut his hand off. End of discussion. But not here! 'Call the guards!' they say, 'Call the guards!' Cowards. A real man handles his disputes himself, one way or the other. In the north, we've no need for courts and laws and fucking red-cloaked bastards telling us what to do. All things are settled man to man, or if need be, man to god, should you do something to anger them. Even then, you talk right to them directly while the shaman only looks on, not by way of any of this praying crap or paying church fines of gold. What need has a god for gold anyhow, I ask you? It's blood they want, if anything. You anger the Great Bear or the Wolf Lord. You kill a deer or a moose or some such, something they can *use*."

"But..." Thom paused. "Not all your gods are animals, are they?"

In the calendar of Old Calendral, the months were named for the thirteen totems of the Wrathorn, though some had been adapted to fit with the Church of the Kinship. The Months of the Hound, Oak, and Horse, for instance, easily drew parallels to the three Brothers in honor of their three Gifts of Creation while the Moon that gives the light in the darkness easily became associated with Lady Callah. Even Harvestide, before the days of St. Aiden, was based on the old paganism of the Wrathorn, for where now it marked the celebration of the Harvest and the Father Alantir, in Old Calendral, it was also the time when folk made offerings to Dibhor that he might spare them through the long, harsh decline of autumn and winter. After St. Aiden, this practice stopped in the "civilized" lands, but to the Wrathorn, it still held its former significance as the month of appeasement for the thirteenth totem, Death.

"What happens if you anger the Stone or the Oak?" he asked. "Or even the Sun? What do you offer them? Surely, they don't eat."

He did not ask about mollifying Death, for he had already assumed an answer, and he had no wish to hear it confirmed.

"Of course, they don't eat." Magnus paused. "All right, so maybe they would like gold, or amber, or a fine blade or something. I don't know. Those gods handle...the weather or what have you...we leave dealings with them to the shaman. It's too complicated. They're always pissed off anyway. It's the reason for all the snow."

Thom's eyes narrowed. "I'm not sure that's right."

"Well, I'm not a priest, am I?"

"I suppose not."

"My point again. You folk of the south are just plain strange and wrong"—Magnus sighed—"although you do have wine, which we don't, but you also leave your villages so ripe for raiding that we could always just sail down and take it. Gods, I miss the north!"

"Then…" Thom said hesitantly, "why not…go back there?"

The Wrathorn shook his head. "Can't," he said matter-of-factly, "not now, at least. We're going to the Sorgund Isles if what the whores said was true."

"What? Why?" Thom's face went pale, and his palms instantly moistened with sweat.

"Never you mind that now," Magnus said. "I know some men headed out that way. We'll take ship with them."

"A ship?" Thom exclaimed. "No! No!"

His mind raced with a thousand possible horrors sure to come. The Sorgund Isles! They were full of nothing but pirates, smugglers, and—worst of all—slavers! Criminals all! The Wrathorn of the North were bad enough but the Sorgund Isles! Besides, the only way to get there was by ship, a ship that would have to cross the Sea of Calendral far out of sight of land!

"Shut up," Magnus said. "Pirates, slavers, any of them try to bother us, and they'll taste Death. Besides, you've lived through one battle already, though you did piss your pants, but either way, you've nothing to fear with me."

"I can't go to the Sorgund Isles!" Thom whined. "I just can't!"

"You can, and you are."

"No!" Thom cried, tearing at his ginger hair in agitation. "I can't go to the Pirate Isles! I can't! No! No!"

All around them, folk of the docks, sailors, merchants, fishermen, and fishwives stopped and starred. Thom felt his throat tighten and his hands quivering with fear. He collapsed in the center of the walkway like a great sea creature washed up on a beach.

Magnus eyed the boy with a glare of hostility. "Get up!"

"I won't go!" Thom said. "I can't."

Magnus glared around him maliciously at the crowd of onlookers hurrying them on their way. He leaned close to Thom's ear. "On your feet, you craven piece of shit," he whispered. "Or I will beat you here and now."

Thom breathed a great shuddering sigh and began to rise, his shoulders quivering with a heavy sob—only to be knocked flat on his stomach again as Magnus struck him hard on the back of the head.

"No crying!" he growled. "Get up!"

"People will call the guards!" Thom cried. "And they'll kill you!"

"Maybe," Magnus whispered, "but rest assured that I will kill you first!"

Thom sobbed miserably and remained still—until Magnus grabbed a great handful of Thom's hair and pulled him violently to his feet.

"Move!"

"Lady save me!" Thom wailed.

"Shut up!"

The Wrathorn dragged the big boy down the docks, ignoring the odd glances from the common folk. Thom was disgusted and astonished suddenly to realize that—in spite of his crying, his suffering, and his visible fear—not a single person seemed to have any inclination to help him. Some even laughed! It was like Lenard's Crossing all over again, only this time no Lughus or Crodane to save him. What wretched people! What a wretched world!

Magnus cursed continuously, swearing oaths of punishment and pain, and at length, realizing that he was only prolonging his eventual suffering, Thom stopped crying, stood on his own two feet, and resigned himself to following.

"I would crush your skull if you were worth it," the Wrathorn said, "though you act like that again, and I'll do it anyway."

Thom breathed a heavy sigh. "I'm sorry."

Magnus shook his head and took a deep breath, and when he spoke this time, his voice had softened, albeit slightly.

"What a creature you are!" he said. "As I said, you've nothing to fear from the Isles, nothing at all, for by the gods and the souls of my ancestors, they've much and more to fear from me."

CHAPTER 36:
THE LOREMASTER

The return from the Tower of the Judge was like a processional at the funeral of a king, utterly silent and grave, as if the world itself were covered in a burial shroud. Every step Royne took following behind Natharis Tainne seemed to reverberate with the hollow tolling of a bell. A death knell, for when Rastis lied about the book's destruction, Royne knew that the old man may well have authored his own execution, and with Rastis's passing, whatever it was the old man had planned now fell to him.

Find the book, find Hob, and flee the city…

As they crossed the threshold of the Loremaster's Tower, Royne fell to Lord Tainne's side. "Would you like me to fetch your dinner, my lord?" he asked.

"I will take my meal with the King," the nobleman replied without turning. "It appears that I have no further use for you."

Royne ignored the sudden flash of anxiety, wondering at the implications of such a statement. "Is there no way I can be of assistance?" he asked.

With a heavy sigh, Natharis Tainne turned and fixed his gaze upon the young steward, and at once, Royne knew what it was that he had found so unnerving about the nobleman's eyes. They were eyes of evil. Eyes that saw only darkness and shut themselves against any light. *Tainne is a Dibhorite, a servant of true evil, and through Kredor's brash arrogance, he has wormed his way into the very heart of the Order of the Guardians.* Royne felt his jaw set with quiet anger, and instead of turning away from the Keeper's gaze, he glared right back.

An eternity seemed to pass as their eyes held one another, locked in subtle combat until, at long last, Lord Tainne turned away and continued his ascent of the tower stairs.

"Do as you will," he said.

For a long moment, Royne stood in silence, listening to the sound of the nobleman's footfalls upon the stairs. His mind still felt clouded, like he had just awoken from a long sleep, ever since Rastis made him promise and spoke those words. The form of the poem stuck with him somehow as familiar. It had not come from the *Scrolls of the Hierophants* nor from any other famous work, though—strangely—something about its meter reminded him of the old songs Thom loved best, those said to have been devised by the Bard. It was hard to say, however, for the Bard refused to write anything down and left it to lesser bards and scribes to copy them. How odd.

And then there was this business of the Bard's Heresy. What was that about? Clearly, it was important, but why? What was it? Never before had he heard it spoken of—in text or conversation—yet of all things, it was that which Rastis desired him to know.

Find the book, find Hob, and flee the city... Royne remembered once more. *Oh, Rastis, Lady of Light protect you...*

He waited quietly until the sound of footsteps above fell silent and decided it was time to make his move.

Calmly, Royne made his way through the bookcases of the library, seeking the room marked by the gilded shield. The Tower was unusually empty for this time of day, and he wondered where the rest of the scribes and scholars were. It made him even more uneasy, and he felt strange to be skulking about like a thief in what for his entire life had been his home.

At last, he found the room, and he paused to examine the intricate craftsmanship of the Furnace and the Forge glimmering with its bright blue stones. For a moment, Royne considered stealing it, for as tall and lanky as he was, it was just within reach. He imagined the expression on Lughus's face when he presented it to him as a gift in Baronbrock. However, there was no way he could hide such a thing long enough to escape the castle town. It would have to remain behind.

Hurriedly, Royne entered the room and counted the bookcases and the shelves. His finger traced the spines of the leather-bound volumes leaving a thin, clear runner in dust that could very well be centuries old. Finally, standing between *The Ballad of Sir Reginald* and *The Hunt for the Cinnabar Bird*, he found it: the Loremaster's ancient tome, *The Book of Histories*.

Without further pause, he grabbed the great book, held it tightly under his arm, and, with steadfast resolve, made for the door. Outside, the yard was relatively empty but for the usual kingsmen on guard. Royne's heart thundered like a drum, but he fought to control his demeanor, adopting the impassive façade of Lord Tainne. He soon realized, however, that even to the castle sentries, the men of the Loremaster's Tower, with their ankle-length burgundy habits and tendency toward myopia, were hardly a cause for alarm—least of all the gangly, awkward steward who always seemed to frown.

Quickly, Royne passed through the castle's outer gates and into the Nobleton district. Aristocrats in their fine clothes walked about idly with their house guards in tow or rode by in carriages drawn by teams of horses. Aster, sedum, monkshood, and other fall flowers blossomed in the gardens and in small beds among the green commons, and the trees lit the cobbled streets in an array of colors as the sunlight shone through their changing autumn leaves. Small fountains bubbled merrily from the lips of sculpted fish or the phalluses of marble statues, and spoiled noble children played games with their tutors and nursemaids who were always careful enough to let their patrons' young heirs and heiresses win.

Royne tried to exude an aura of great purpose and prestige as if his "master" had sent him on an errand of utmost importance. He tromped along steadily with his head held slightly forward as if his willpower was somehow so resolute that it veritably dragged his body behind. In truth, this was not hard, for he was dead set upon achieving his purpose; it just so happened that that purpose was one of complete and utter defiance.

Yet when he reached the gate through to Easton, he spied something that, strangely, gave him pause. Beside the basin of a fountain, half-hidden by a low hedge, was Kredor's remaining page boy sitting alone with his tambourine. Why the boy hindered his progress, Royne was unsure, for he never cared for either of the twins and, in fact, found them the height of annoyance. They bickered, they giggled, they waggled their tambourines at one another, and were just altogether irritating. However, since the hunt when the boar cut the terrible pair by half, Royne could not help but feel a certain reluctant sympathy for the solo twin.

"Aiden's Flame!" Royne cursed aloud, and with a heavy sigh, he halted his charge and made his way over to the cherubim boy.

"Hey, you!"

The motley page leaped to his feet in fright. His eyes went wide in horror, and his apple cheeks turned as red as his motley. For a moment, Royne thought he would run off, but something held him still. "What are you doing here?" he asked, but the boy gave no answer.

"Look, I'm not going to hurt you," he tried again. "I'm sorry about your brother."

The boy turned back to the water and splashed his fingertips along the surface. "Is that what my insides look like too?" he asked softly.

Royne's brow furrowed, and suddenly, his stomach felt sick at the memory. "I don't know," he said at last, "probably. Probably mine do too."

If the boy found his answer as disquieting as Royne did himself, he did not show it. "The King is practicing swordplay with the master-at-arms, so I sneaked away," he said, "I should probably go back soon. Gerry and I could get away with sneaking off before so long as one of us stayed behind. Not now, though."

Royne sighed. "What's your name?" he asked.

"Conor. My father was Lord Vendik, but he's dead too."

"I don't have a father either," Royne hesitated, "and my brothers are gone too."

"Oh."

"How old are you, Conor?"

"Seven, but I'll be eight next year. My birthday's the fourteenth of Falcontide, like my brother's."

Royne chewed his lip in thought for a moment. If he was to be the Loremaster as Rastis said, he deserved a steward of his own, and what better way to spite the King?

"I'll tell you what, Conor," he said, his lips twisting into a wry grin. "I'm sneaking off myself, and if you promise to keep your mouth shut and throw away that bloody tambourine, I'll let you come too."

"You will?" the boy's eyes lit up.

Royne was torn between a warm feeling of self-satisfaction and a cold chill of self-loathing. "But we need to go now. There's no time for packing."

"Yes, sir."

"And remember what I said. The tambourine stays behind," Royne said sternly, "throw it in the fountain."

The boy did as instructed, and as Royne watched it teeter upon the surface halfway between sinking and floating, he patted his new steward on the shoulder and decided he felt rather good. "Well done, Conor," he said. "Well done. Now let's be off—"

"There you are, you little shit!"

Conor went rigid with fear, and Royne whirled around in alarm to see a soldier in a chain mail hauberk and the red tabard of Andoch striding toward them. For a moment, he thought it was a kingsman and readied himself to turn tail and flee, yet when the man grew closer, Royne recognized the steel helm of a Warlord's partisan and the brooch fashioned in the shape of two crossed swords, the Warlord's steward's pin. He tightened his grip around *The Book of Histories*.

"Pryce."

"Oh, look here," Pryce said. "I went looking for a little shit, and I found a great big one."

Royne ignored the insult. Connor made to run, but Royne held him still. "I thought you only wiped the Warlord's ass," he said. "But I guess you're more than willing to go hunting shit for the King."

Pryce snickered. "So you *are* a piece of shit then?"

Royne sighed with impatience. "Yes, Pryce," he observed drolly. "I suppose I am."

"So what are you two up to here back behind the bushes?"

"I don't know. What does shit do?"

"What?"

Royne shook his head. "Just forget it. Go back to the King and tell him Conor'll be along in a minute."

"Who's Conor?"

Royne gave a heavy sigh. "Just go." He was impatient to be going and cursed himself for his strange, uncharacteristic show of compassion. *Why did I stop?* he wondered. *Why do I give half a damn about this bloody imp?*

Pryce remained unmoved. His lips twisted naturally in an arrogant sneer. Apparently, the King's orders could wait a little while longer. *Kredor's a bully too*, Royne thought. *Surely, he'll understand.*

"So how do you think old Rastis is holding up atop the Judge's Tower? Any better than Goldimop and Thom Fatty lost out in the wilds?"

Royne's heart beat faster, and his blood began to burn.

"Tell me," Pryce continued blithely, "who do you think will die first?"

From the depths of Royne's soul came suddenly a great cry of despair, and without warning, the floodgates broke, and all his fears and anxieties over the welfare of his friends burst forth in a torrent of rage. He dropped *The Book of Histories* at his feet and, pushing Conor aside, flew headlong at his childhood nemesis.

However, Royne had never been a fighter, and Pryce easily halted his charge by tripping him to the ground. He felt the air rush out of him, and he feared his lungs collapsed, for his breath came only in short, agonizing gasps.

"You have no idea how long I've waited for this." Pryce laughed and kicked him in the side—again, and again, and again.

Conor scurried for cover behind the edge of the fountain and, at the sight of such violence, erupted into crying.

"Shut up!" Pryce shouted and kicked Royne again for emphasis. "Shut! Up!"

Royne shuddered at the impact of every blow, struggling desperately to shield himself by curling into a ball. He knew he was crying, but he no longer cared for shame.

Then all at once, he felt very strange, as if he could sense the presence of something powerful—something familiar—drawing near, and he heard a panicked voice cry. "Rastis!" He opened his eyes just in time to see something large barrel into Pryce, grab hold of him, and throw him down to the green. For a moment, he had visions of the wild boar.

"Blood and Fire! What are you doing?!"

A hand gripped Royne's shoulder and rolled him over onto his back. To his astonishment, he found himself staring up into the startled face of Dandon Rood, the Warlord.

The old warrior's face looked strange, caught between concern and confusion. "The scribe?" he said at last.

Royne took a deep breath, struggling against the pain in his ribs, and slowly got to his feet. Pryce's face went white, and behind the fountain, Conor had crouched into a ball, covered his ears with his hands, and shut his eyes.

The Warlord glanced from Royne to Pryce to Conor and back, his expression finally settling into utter bewilderment. At length, Rood's heavy jaw clenched in anger, and his eyes narrowed on his steward.

"My lord," Pryce said, "he attacked me! I was only defending myself!"

"Silence!" the Warlord shouted.

Pryce bowed his head, and Royne wiped his face upon the sleeve of his habit. It was over now. He would never get away. He would never reach Hob. Whatever it was Rastis had planned no longer mattered. He was caught. It was all doomed.

Dandon Rood leaned forward and glowered into Pryce's face. His skin grew as red as the sun, and the veins on his forehead looked fit to burst. "I elevated you to partisan and steward against all inclination because your father is a friend of the King and because you're brute enough to be halfway decent with a sword." The Warlord grimaced. "But I'll be damned if I'll permit any man of my tower to behave with such gross dishonor! How dare you? How *dare* you? You are not fit to carry my blade!"

Pryce had sense enough to remain silent, but his lip curled in resentment at his forced humility.

The Warlord sighed with frustration, and suddenly, to Royne's horror, the big man walked slowly over to the fountain and stooped to pick up *The Book of Histories* from the ground. For a moment, he glanced at its cover and, with a sad smile, held it out in front of him.

He knows! Royne thought. *He knows!*

"Here, boy," the Warlord said, leveling his gaze to hold Royne's eye. "I take it your master sent you on some errand or another. Best you take *your* book here and *go.*"

"Thank you, Warlord Rood," he said, hugging the book tightly under his arm. "Come, Conor. We still have things to do."

From behind the fountain, the page got to his feet and hurried to Royne's side. "Goodbye, Warlord," Royne said.

"Goodbye."

Without further hesitation, Royne ran—beaten, bruised, and bloody— through the inner gate to Easton, across the Highbridge to Weston, and through the closest outer gate to the peasant quarter, the Groundlings, propped up outside of the city walls. In one arm, he clutched *The Book of Histories*, and in the other, he practically dragged the pageboy Conor behind.

The only other time Royne had seen the Groundlings was on the day of the hunt when the King's company passed through on their way to the woodlands outside the city. It seemed little more than a slum then and even more of one now, and as he searched for the sign of "The Crow & the Fox," he was glad he was doing so under the light of day.

When at last he found the place (by way of a sign that bore two shapes sharing little resemblance to either animal), he ran inside expecting to find Old Hob merrily drinking himself silly, frothy ale staining his beard and mustache. However, the Wrathorn Scribe was nowhere in sight.

"Aiden's Flaming Sword!" Royne cursed aloud.

"Is there something you be needing?" called the barkeep.

Royne sighed heavily. "I'm to meet a man here," he said and suddenly stopped in shock. "Hob?"

The barkeep smiled and rubbed his hand along his clean-shaven chin. His head, too, was shaved, and he wore a long-sleeved tunic to hide his tattoos. "Royne."

"Brethren! Look at you!" Royne laughed. "Rastis said I'd find you here, but…wow!"

"Keep your voice down," the Wrathorn whispered. "Wait a moment, and we can talk. Once I get someone to mind the bar."

A few minutes later, Hob led Royne and Conor down a hallway to a small room lit by a fireplace. A pot of stew boiled over the hearth, and Hob filled three bowls. He nodded toward the page. "That's one of the King's pets, eh? What's he doing here?"

"Kredor took one of ours, so I took one of his." Royne grinned. "Plus, if Rastis wants me to be the Loremaster, I figured he could be my steward, unless, of course, you want your old job back?"

Hob sighed. "So it's done then?"

"What?" Royne asked.

"Rastis spoke the words?"

Royne paused. The wounds he bore from seeing Rastis in the Tower were still too fresh, and he did not like to think on them. "He said something." Royne sighed. "Some poem or other and poked me in the finger with a needle or the like, but I don't know what it was."

"You will in time," Hob said, offering the boys their bowls. "Anyway, I'm glad you're here. I don't know how much longer the Wayfolk are willing to stay. I'll let them know, and you can leave tonight."

"Wayfolk? The wanderers? I thought they were all vagrants and thieves?"

Hob sighed. "Maybe some, not all though, and they don't take from folks in need or folks who got little to begin with. Still, if you're going to escape the city and travel the roads in secret, there's no better folk to be with."

"Aren't you coming too?"

Hob shook his head. "I'm staying here in case the Hammer returns with Thom."

"What about Lughus?"

"The Hammer is a mean bastard, but he's no match for Crodane. He'll see Lughus to Baronbrock or die in the attempt," Hob said. "It's Thom I'm more worried for, even more than I am for you. He would have been safe with my people up north, but now that he's been taken by the kingsmen, I don't know. So until I find out, I'm here."

"Thom Fatty opened his big mouth, you know. It's his fault Rastis got locked up," Royne said bitterly. "It might do to let him share a cell in the Judge's Tower next to Rastis to let him feel the sting of what his fear has bought."

"Don't say that," Hob scolded. "Thom's just not made of the same stuff as you, and neither is Lughus. Each of you has your strengths, and as sure as I know Rastis, he took all that into account before setting each one of you on your separate paths."

"And so I'm to join the Wayfolk?" Royne smirked. "I didn't know Rastis figured me for a thief."

"The Wayfolk are clever," Hob said, "as are you when you hold off being so snarky. They'll take care of you, and you'll have no reason whatsoever to fear them. Besides, there's no safer way to secret you south across the border into Grantis."

"Grantis?" Royne's heart sank. "Rastis said I was to leave the city, but Grantis? Why not Baronbrock with Lughus? With King Kredor's men making war on the republic, I hardly see sense in sending me there. Would Rastis have me flee the frying pan for the fire?"

"Baronbrock is far too obvious," Hob said. "The first place an enemy will look for you is among friends. No, Rastis would have you go to Grantis to meet a man named Salasco, called 'the Wall.'"

"'The Wall?' Is that a Guardian title?"

"It is, or at least, it once was."

Royne's eyes widened. "You mean he's a Blackguard."

"My boy"—Hob laughed—"we're all bloody Blackguards now."

"Not me," Royne said. "I'm not Anointed."

"Oh, you're not, are you?" Hob smirked. "Well, then, do me a favor, Royne. Open the book."

"What?"

"*The Book of Histories*," he said. "Read it."

Carefully, Royne unfastened the latch and, with utmost care, opened the book to a random page. Yet when he looked down to read, his face went white, and he began flipping through the pages in a frenzy, for every single one was blank.

"What is this!" he cried. "It's all empty!"

"Wait," Hob said calmly. "Just wait. Calm yourself, look at the pages, and think."

Royne took a deep breath and tried to do as Hob said. He shut his eyes and thought of Rastis, thought of Lughus and Thom and the times they had in the tower as children. When at last, he felt relaxed, he opened his eyes and looked down at an open page. It remained blank. However, in his mind's eye, he saw a hand and a quill scribbling busily, and somehow, he knew the text that had never actually been written on the page.

...in the days of Old Calendral. Still, it begs the question as to how? How is it possible that after so long, they could still exist?

Today, I appealed to the council to send the Archer and the Shield east in search of answers, for we must know. Else we shall continue to wander about in the Dark. If it is true that the Dibhorites reside yet upon our shores, we must know...

Royne looked up from the page and turned toward Hob, "I can read it."

"Of course you can," the Wrathorn scribe said, a smile playing at the corner of his lips. "You're the new bloody Loremaster."

CHAPTER 37:
THE BORDER CROSSING

It was said that the Hounds of Perindal could track a man's scent across the continent a full ten years after his death, and with Fergus's nose to guide them and Crodane's knowledge of the terrain, the trio moved swiftly northward toward the Brock. Yet in spite of the threat of danger, the deepening cold, and the long hours of tromping through the undergrowth, the knowledge that he walked alongside a mythical hound and a legendary swordsman filled Lughus's heart with renewed vigor and his eyes once again shone with the light of adventure.

For a fortnight and a half of another, they continued onward, through the fields and farmlands of at least a dozen lords, and across forested woodlands and boggy moors where days might pass without encountering another soul. The stores in Crodane's sack had dwindled; however, Fergus was a fine hunter and could easily supply them with wildfowl and rabbits and, on one occasion, had even brought down a deer. At dusk, before the light grew too dim or sometimes while they rested during the day, Crodane would continue instructing Lughus in his swordsmanship, reviewing guards, parries, footwork, and various thrusts. Before long, the Marshal was pleased enough with the progress of his young pupil that the routine forms and legwork gave way more and more to simple sparring.

"The first thing we'll do when we reach your grandfather"—Crodane grinned—"is find you a better sword. That old blade's far too dull and far too crude for a burgeoning swordsman such as you. You've come a long way."

"Thank you," Lughus said. "It helps to have a good teacher."

"I suppose, but that won't save you if your blade breaks."

He drew his sword, Sentinel, and held it out for Lughus to peruse. "The strongest swords are made of folded steel, though on a blade like this, it's hard to tell. If you look closely, you can see the pattern of waves made by each fold. Others are more pronounced. When you meet Gareth, ask him to show you Whisper and Shade. They're beautiful but far too audacious for my taste."

"Gareth? You said he's the Blade?"

"Aye," Crodane said, "and Regnar is the Vanguard, but rather than steel, he carries a cudgel and a targe made of holy oak."

"Holy oak!"

"You'll see them soon enough." Crodane smirked. "They took ship to Dwerin when I left to meet you, but come spring, they'll return to Galadin if all goes well. Regnar went to see an old friend of ours in Commonwealth, and Gareth had business in Blackstone. They considered heading north afterwards to visit Old Sigmund, but decided to wait so as to have a chance to meet you."

"Who's Sigmund?"

Crodane suddenly seemed reticent. "Another friend. It was he Thom was to go to."

Lughus's enthusiasm faded at the mention of his fellow apprentice. "North among the Wrathorn?" he asked. "With Hob's people?"

"Aye. Clan Brindlebairne." Crodane sighed. "At any rate, we should continue on."

By the afternoon of the following day, the terrain became steadily rockier, and in the distance far to the northwest, Lughus could make out snow-topped mountain peaks. He recalled the time spent planning the journey, pouring over old maps with Royne during that last week. Once again, Lughus wondered how his lanky friend was faring and if he had adapted to life yet as Rastis's sole apprentice, or if the Hammer had returned Thom yet to their tower home. When he felt his wonder turning to grief, however, he turned to Crodane.

"Is that the eastern horn of the Firrinies?"

"So it is," the swordsman said. "Stretching all the way west from here back to Titanis, but it also marks the boundary with the Brock and the southernmost barony of Nordren. It was there we were to reach, taking a ship from Galdoran by sea."

Lughus nodded and watched Fergus run off ahead to scout the path, a golden flash beneath a graying sky. "I thought the borderlands were rife with bandits."

"Oh, they are," Crodane said. "And we must be cautious, but with Fergus to guide us, we'll be able to pass right by them without their ever knowing we were here." He paused and gazed northward. "Still, keep a sharp eye, and remember, you can be certain that the Hammer is out there somewhere too. He'll seek to waylay us before we cross too far into Nordren. He's had nearly a month to get ahead of us and prepare, regardless of whether he went by ship or by horse along the coastal road."

"I almost forgot him." Lughus sighed.

Crodane sniffed the air. "We're not far now. Two or three days more, and we'll be safely in the Brock. The baron of Nordren is an ally of the Galadins. Should we meet any of his men along the road, they will be certain to see us to their master, and from his court, ensure you make it safely to the Houndstooth."

"Baron Arcis does not seem to lack friends," Lughus said, "nor enemies."

"Such is the way of politics in the Brock, I'm afraid," Crodane said.

According to Crodane, the fifteen Baronies of the Brock were comprised of fourteen independent city-states, each with their own ruling family, lands, and minor fiefs. The fifteenth and smallest (little more than a large castle town itself) was Highboard, and it was there that every five years, the other fourteen barons men to elect the Lord-Baron, who became, in addition to governing his own barony, the master of the capital city and the arbitrator of all disputes. The office of Lord-Baron had changed many times over the centuries from baron to baron; however, of all the nobles of the Brock, none held the position longer or more often than the House of Glendaro, particularly when hostilities between the Galadins, the Marthaines, and their respective allies ran high. Traditionally, the Galadins, backed by Brabant, Nordren, and Derindale, were opposed in all things by the Marthaines and their allies in Denholm, Edgeforth, and Caradon, which left Crofton, Helmsted, Waldron, Agathis, and Igrainne seeking balance under the leadership of neutral Glendaro. However, now that it appeared the bloodlines of both the Galadins and the Marthaines were ending, a few of the younger barons seemed willing to vie for more prestige.

"To be honest, Lughus"—Crodane grinned—"I do not envy you, for much and more will be expected of the young man who is the son of both Galadin and Marthaine and educated under the wise uncle of Baron Glendaro. You may find yourself regretting your decision to follow me, not for the danger we find ourselves in, but rather for the endless bickering of noblemen and the hours and hours of talk. I'd take the life of a scribe any day over that of a politician."

"Now you tell me." Lughus smirked.

"You can always go back with the Hammer when we meet him."

"I've dug my grave," the young man said. "It's mine to lie in."

"Indeed."

They continued their journey on into the evening, warily keeping watch for any bandits or kingsmen wandering the mountain lowlands. That night, they made camp beneath the shelter of an old standing stone concealed behind a small patch of wild holly bushes. Again, they lit no fire but rather made a spare meal of dried biscuit—the last of Crodane's stores, and when Lughus rolled out his bedroll to sleep, he was warmed again by the great hound lying curled up at his side. Crodane, Lughus noticed, had once again remained awake but for a few short naps while Fergus took a turn on watch; however, for the most part, just as he had during the passage down the river, the swordsman merely sat awake with his naked blade across his lap. It was not long after they began their journey again in the morning that the Marshal's preternatural call for caution was confirmed.

It was Fergus who made the discovery, for it was the first time in their journey together that Lughus had heard the hound bark. Crodane leaped at the sound, and Lughus had to run to keep up, hurrying after him down a shallow gully to a small clearing behind a ridge. There, around the smoldering remains of a campfire, were the bodies of nearly a dozen mountain men. Some bore the slashes of sword wounds, others the great punctures of spears, though most had their heads bashed open and their skulls caved in.

"Aiden's Flame," Lughus said, covering his face against the smell of rotting carrion. A large black crow stood upon the chest of one dead man pecking grotesquely at his vacant eye socket.

Crodane hurriedly searched among the corpses, striding about the grass and the overturned crates of goods. Fergus barked again from beneath the shadow of an ash tree about a dozen yards away where the bodies of another group of men lay. These ones had their hands bound behind their backs with rope, and each one had been killed by a single blow to the back of the skull."

"Bandits," Crodane said, "executed for their crimes by the Hammer."

Lughus's stomach churned, and he worried he might vomit. "How do you know?" he asked.

"Look at the mark on the skull here. It's circular, just like the head of a war hammer. The others by the camp must have been caught unawares while these men here must have surrendered to the Hammer's mercy."

Lughus followed the swordsman back to the ruined campsite. "This was done last night," he said. "Embers still burn in the fire."

"Yes," Crodane said quietly. "No more than a few hours ago. They are close."

Lughus felt his heart quicken, and his hand went for the hilt of his sword. Crodane took another brief walk around to scour the campsite and discovered from among the wreckage an old leather arming cap and a wooden shield.

"Here," he said, "Hide your hair. If the sunlight catches it, they'll know you from a long way off. In any event, if they come upon us, I'd rather you not risk fighting them. Just stay close to Fergus and cover yourself with the shield. From the look of things here, the Hammer has a dozen men with him, maybe more, scouting the woodlands."

Lughus donned the cap, though it smelled of must and rain, and took up the shield. "I can help you fight them," he said.

"No, not unless you have no other choice," Crodane told him, gathering what food was still edible from among the bandits' stores. "I will engage them, and Fergus will get you safely away. The Hammer will be more focused on me than on you, should there be a battle. We must use that to our advantage. Regardless, if I should fall, Fergus will see you to your grandfather. He knows the rest of the way."

Lughus gave a heavy sigh, and his brow creased with concern. "Don't look so stricken." Crodane smirked. "The Marshal survived the Siege of Three and many other battles besides. Surely he can survive the Hammer!"

"True." Lughus smiled weakly.

"Come," the swordsman said, patting him on the shoulder, "we near the end of our journey. Let's be off!"

From the ruined campsite, Fergus led the way through the steepening uplands east of the mountains. Steadily, the fall foliage of the deciduous trees gave way to the rugged evergreens of the higher elevations. The air smelled of pine, and underfoot, grass gave way to patches of lichen, gravel, and blankets of soft needles. High up on the edge of a precipice, a ram stood, raised its great horns, and grunted. The spirit hound eyed the creature, his green eyes alight at the challenge; however, at a word from Crodane, Fergus gave a snort and trotted onward, using his nose to guide their way.

At midday, they rested again near a thicket of holly. Low white clouds rolled in across the sky from the southwest, and down below them, along the route they had climbed, a flock of sparrows alighted all as one upon the branches of a yew. Lughus sat upon a small gray stone jutting out from the hillside and leaned forward onto his knees, the wooden shield slung across his back. In all his years at the Loremaster's Tower, he had imagined what it would be like to adventure out in the world, and thinking back to Lenard's Crossing, his first experience had nearly been his last. So much had happened in the span of only a few months, and now he stood upon the brink of a new nation, the remnants of a new family, and an elevation from a mere apprentice to the heir of a great lord. It was frightening, for as Crodane had said, there was much expected of him.

In spite of his residency in Titanis, his interactions with real members of the nobility had been rather limited—a fact that, in truth, he actually preferred, for the only true nobles he had the chance to know were Rastis (who, of course, seemed to have thrown off the mantle of aristocracy long, long ago), and the young men among the cadets, particularly Pryce. He supposed Marcus Harding may also have been a lord, for he was at least a knight. However, the Tower had no lands to speak of, and his aristocracy seemed more honorary than by birth, awarded to him by merit on account of his rank as a cavalier in the Warlord's Tower. Otherwise, to Lughus, the nobility was altogether foreign—people in fine clothes who fritted about in carriages, young men his age with gold enough to carry swords and receive martial training, and pretty girls he saw only from the tower window that he was sure would never condescend to talk to him.

Yet now, he was expected to walk among them! And not merely as a knight or a landed lord but a bloody baron! What madness to go from donning the rough woolen habit of an apprentice to the fine embroidered doublet of a nobleman! He breathed a heavy sigh and once again mourned the separation from his friends—his brothers—and, of course, Rastis. With Thom and Royne at his side, he might know what to do, for in spite of Thom's Foolery, his naiveté often tempered Royne's misanthropic brooding. The three of them together might have at least some idea how to manage a fiefdom, but a whole barony alone was simply beyond reason.

"Crodane…" He sighed. "I don't know if I can do this—"

"Silence!"

Lughus glanced over and, for the first time, noticed the swordsman crouched low to the ground, sword drawn, tense, and alert. Fergus was nowhere in sight.

Lughus sat rigidly upon his stone for fear any movement might cause further alarm. His fingers tingled, and his knees began to ache as if, in the sudden intensity of the moment, they had decided to simply go to sleep. His gray eyes scanned the woodlands, but he could discern nothing overtly wrong.

"The Hammer is near," Crodane whispered, "and he can sense that we are too."

"What do we do?" Lughus murmured under his breath.

"When I tell you, drop to the ground. Fergus and I will carve a path, and then you must follow him away. I will follow as I can."

"Where are they?"

Rather than answer, Crodane smiled kindly and held a finger to his lips.

"Now!"

Lughus rolled forward onto the ground just as the swordsman issued a whistle. Scarcely a few feet behind where Lughus sat, he heard a man cry, "Holy shite!" and with a low growl, Fergus leaped out from somewhere unseen.

From where he lay, Lughus watched Crodane spring forth from hiding to surprise a pikeman dressed in the bloody red cloak of a kingsman. With one swipe of his blade, he knocked the man's spear aside and, with a second, brought the blade down through his shoulder. Over Fergus's snarls, the first man screamed until abruptly, his cries fell silent.

"Run!"

Together, the trio burst forth from the cover of the holly as another group of men rushed after them. Lughus glanced quickly over his shoulder and saw two men charging forth with their pikes. Another stopped long enough to kneel and take aim, sending a quarrel from his crossbow into the dirt at Lughus's feet. Crodane stood his ground to meet the oncoming pikemen, while Fergus loped back in a wide arc toward the crossbowman, lunged through the air, and brought the man down by the throat.

Crodane sidestepped one spear thrust and parried the second wide, then whirled Sentinel around, singing through the air to sever the first kingsman's leg at the knee. The second man dropped his spear at such close quarters and made to draw his blade, but before it was even halfway free from its sheath, he fell, run through upon the Marshal's sword.

Lughus's lungs burned from the uphill flight, and while he paused to catch his breath, he readied the shield upon his arm and drew his sword. Fergus caught up to him and dashed around in a circle, barking to urge him on. A moment later, Crodane appeared again, engaged with another man wielding a sword. The kingsman gave a mighty swing, which Crodane knocked aside with a grimace, then countered, bashing his pommel into the guardsman's face before finishing him off with another quick thrust.

"Keep going! Run!" the swordsman shouted, his chest heaving for air. "Do not stop!"

Another pair of quarrels whistled by Lughus's ear, and he ran, raising the shield in front of him as he fled. He did not get far, however, before he was forced to stop short as something heavy struck the shield's boss and knocked it aside. From behind him, Crodane grabbed his shoulder and pushed him to the ground just as a kingsman with a heavy mace turned his wrist to make a second blow. The swordsman thrust forth as the soldier attempted to follow through, and another of the Hammer's men fell to Sentinel's deadly song.

Seven men so far had met their end in pursuit of the Marshal, the Galadin boy, and the hound, yet when the trio reached the crest of the hill, another four kingsmen charged forth to stand against them. Crodane halted the advance of the first two, and with a quick parry and thrust, another lay dying. He squared his feet to engage the second, and the light of battle glowed grimly in his eyes. Fergus crouched low on his haunches, and if his sheer size alone did not give the kingsman pause, then it was the glistening sheen of the hound's red maw. Regardless, his hesitation proved his undoing as the great dog swiftly tore out the man's throat.

Lughus met the final man, his heart beating like a blacksmith's hammer against the walls of his chest. For as long as he could remember, the red-cloaked kingsman had been the symbol of authority, law, and order, and he had seen men dressed in identical garb outside the doors of the Loremaster's Tower each and every day. Yet now, this man stood as his enemy—threatening him with his sword, ready to spill his blood—but he knew that he could not falter, for he was long past the point of no return.

The man's first blow turned against the shield, sending a shockwave of pain down Lughus's arm while the man's second strike knocked it from his grasp entirely. The kingsman grinned and muttered a curse, but Lughus could not hear it for his focus. He readied himself as Crodane had taught him, gripping his sword in both hands, and narrowed his gaze. When the soldier renewed his attack, Lughus easily parried it to the side, thrust, and the man fell backward in pain. A strange shiver ran through his arm as he saw his opponent fall in defeat. His shoulders quivered, and his blood ran cold, yet before he could again submit to his guilt, more kingsmen ran up to engage.

Bodies lie strewn upon the ground, their insides gleaming in the sun. Those still wracked in the final throes of their fates cried out in agony. Another man fell to Lughus's blade and another to Fergus's teeth. The Brethren alone could keep count of those to die upon the Marshal's sword.

Then, abruptly, the kingsmen drew back. They held their blades ready before them but did not renew their assault, for in between them, his namesake held tightly in his hand, Willum Harlow, the Hammer strode forth to meet them.

"Go, Lughus! Go with Fergus!" Crodane said quickly, his body splattered with the red paint of his art. "Go now! Run!"

"He will not get far, Blackguard," Harlow said, "though if it's any consolation, the King wants him alive. Still, I shall have to devise a fitting punishment so he might properly pay for the blood he's spilled. Your influence, no doubt."

"Turn back now, Harlow," Crodane said, "before any more of your men have to die. I've had more than my fill for today."

"You know very well that's not going to happen, Crodane. I have a duty to perform."

"As do I."

Harlow leered menacingly, and Lughus wondered that Thom should ever have been anything but frightened of such a man. "What do you know of duty, Blackguard?" the constable asked, and, without warning, shouted, "Now!"

A quarrel shot from the hillside whipped through the air at Crodane; however, the crossbowman misjudged the angle of his aim, and instead, the bolt struck Lughus squarely in the chest.

Lughus dropped to his knees, and at once, tasted the metallic tang of blood. He let his sword fall from his hand, and clutched at his side as the very air he breathed seemed transformed into fire.

The Hammer's sneer twisted in anger at the kingsman's blunder and Crodane's eyes blazed with wrath. He leaped from the hilltop, his sword held high in a strike that would have cleaved the constable's head in twain. Yet at the very last moment, the Hammer lurched backward, and rather than kill him outright, the blade sheared off his arm at the elbow.

The constable shrieked in horror at the sight of the bloody stump, as the severed hand still gripping the hammer rolled awkwardly down the hill. Harlow roared at his men to renew the attack; however, faced with the fury of the legendary Marshal, they instead took up their wounded captain and fled.

At once, Crodane hurriedly sheathed his sword and ran to Lughus's side. The quarrel had penetrated deeply, for the crossbow had been fired from no great range, and the force of such a weapon was often capable of piercing through armor.

"I'm sorry..." Lughus whispered against the pain. His legs already felt like dead weight, and his breath came in short, shuddering spasms, "You said to run...and I...hesitated..."

The swordsman shook his head in bitter grief, and he tore the boy's tunic to inspect the wound. Quickly, he rubbed his eyes upon the back of his arm. "You did well," he said after a moment. "If anyone is to blame, it's me."

Lughus twisted suddenly, wracked with pain, and the swordsman lifted the edge of his cloak to soak up the blood.

Fergus finished barking his threats after the fleeing kingsmen, and when they were well away, he trotted back to the boy's side and gently licked the palm of his hand. Lughus watched it happen, but he could not feel it. "Am I dying?" He gasped, for he could see tears in the swordsman's eyes, despite the man's efforts to hide it.

Crodane breathed a heavy sigh. "No," he said, "you're not."

Lughus smiled weakly. "You said you would never lie to me."

The Marshal removed his baldric, sword, and scabbard. "I'm not," he said, "for you will not die today."

Lughus shut his eyes. "It's all right," he said. "At least I got to have one great adventure."

"You'll have many more besides," Crodane said gently. "I promise—just as I did after I became the Marshal."

The boy's gray eyes flashed open, lightning in the storm. "What?!"

"I swore I would protect your mother," he said. "And when I failed, I swore that I would protect you, even if it meant my death." He smiled. "You're Elen's pup."

"No..." Lughus said weakly. He had feeling enough yet that the tears still burned in his eyes, "You can't..."

"Hush..." Crodane said, taking hold of the boy's hand. "There has not been a Galadin among the Guardians for a thousand years. However, I want you to swear to me that as Baron and as Marshal, you will do your mother proud and become the good man that I know it is in you to become. Be kind, be loyal, be just to your people, safeguard those who are weaker, and strive always to do what is right, for yours is the blood of the Blessed Saint."

"Crodane, please..."

"Swear it, Lughus. There's not much time..."

Lughus took a deep breath, "I swear to do as you said."

"Good," the swordsman said. "Sentinel is yours now, and look after Fergus."

"But...why...?"

"Hush, all will be well shortly. I just need to pull the quarrel. It pierced your lung, and when I remove it, it's going to hurt a great deal. But even still, I want you to remember this pain. I told you once that a sword may take life or give it. When you take life, what you feel now is the pain you cause; however, when you use your sword to give it, you prevent another from suffering this harm."

Lughus shut his eyes to prepare himself and suddenly felt the shock of the lethal spike being ripped from his chest. Blood burst forth in a great torrent, and every muscle in his body writhed in agony at the trauma of the wound. His breathing grew shallower and shallower, and beneath his eyelids, he saw the sky turning black, but before he finally gave himself over to oblivion, he heard the swordsman whispering:

> *Many men swear to take up arms,*
> *and uphold the cause of right,*
> *to safeguard cities, roads, and farms,*
> *from those who haunt the night,*
> *and though many flee and many falter,*
> *this one will never stray.*
> *Rise now, the Marshal,*
> *And drive the Dark away!*

CHAPTER 38:
THE BROTHERS BEINN

In exchange for Brigid's harsh words of defiance against her mother, the next two weeks passed painfully slow and riddled with the constant fear of maternal retribution. Josephine seemed to regard the incident as never having occurred in the first place, and though that in a sense was its own kind of insult, Brigid was cautiously relieved. For, in her anger, she realized that not only had she exposed herself as the agent of Young Reid's death but had also perhaps threatened both her own life and, as her accomplice in escape, the Falcon's as well. Where had this temper suddenly come from, she wondered, or was it merely that the Falcon's landing in Blackstone had helped her to realize the truth she had always felt inside? Regardless, she feared she may have placed him in danger.

Desperately, she sought to warn him; however, as the day of the betrothal ceremony drew nearer and the guests—in particular her uncles—began to arrive, she saw less and less of him around the castle, and when she did, he was dressed in the guise of a household guard standing at the Lord Sheriff's side.

As was only proper, the three other Beinns, Waylon, Master of the Mines; Graham, the Admiral of the Fleet; and Nealen, the Grand Castellan, returned to the castle of their birth to see their elder brother vow to take their eldest brother's widow to wife. Not one of them spoke much to Brigid beyond a few polite words of greeting, though it was clear upon their arrival that they were by no means pleased with the prospect of the betrothal.

Waylon, who was responsible for the traffic of gold and ore from the rich mines of Dwerin (and who had, in fact, brokered the alliance with the Guardians in Andoch), brought with him a small cadre of clerks to ensure that trade continued as uninterrupted as usual. By day, they sat together in the parlor of one of the guest towers drafting and redrafting notices and contracts, leaving their single Andochan Scribe laboring by candlelight late into the night, copying the documents in their final version. Waylon had been married once, though his wife, Lady Rita, died not long after and without bearing any children. However, the considerable lands her dowry included were more than enough to stay Waylon's mourning.

Graham, the Admiral of the Fleet, spent his time pacing the great hall when it was empty, or wandering around the snowy wards with his squire in toe. He wasted no time upon his arrival, losing himself in a fog of drink, and often, he seemed unable to notice when the profane comments he thought confined to the privacy of his mind issued forth from his mouth. Clearly, he hated Blackstone almost as much as he hated his brothers. Yet, this hatred carried with it a type of fragile resentment that seemed born from grief over Brigid's long-dead grandmother. One night, Brigid was awakened by shouting from the yard, and when she slipped free from her sleeping bed-warmers to glance out her window, there was Graham weeping bitterly against the awkward embrace of his poor squire's outstretched arms with wailing cries of 'Mother!' She wondered how a man could command a fleet when he lacked any command over himself. Perhaps the roll of the waves beneath a keel made his drunkenness feel natural.

Nealen, the youngest, arrived last among the brothers in the company of six heavily armored guards. As Castellan, he was busy leading the soldiers of Dwerin against Grantis in the place Brigid's father died, called the Spade. Some months ago, not long after Harvestide, his men had captured an old stone fort, and since then, Duke Nealen and Reid's father had been turning it into a proper castle. It was to be the first of its type in the area and would help to secure Dwerin's lasting presence. As such, from the moment of his arrival, he made it clear that though propriety demanded his attendance, he was eager to return to Lord Reid, whose noted absence was explained away by his continued search attempts for his missing son.

And so for the first time since the death of Brigid's father, the archduke, a death that, according to the Falcon, they themselves had engineered, the four remaining Beinn brothers shared one roof.

It was strange seeing Blackstone so full of people and so teeming with simmering resentment. Nightly meals in the great hall took on an added level of reserve as the nobles, long since used to kowtowing to the indulgences of the archduchess, the Sheriff, and his son, now found themselves caught between fawning over one Beinn only to incur the disfavor of another. Neither did the brothers make it easy, as they were only too ready to needle one another through subtle slights and droll remarks at one another's expense masked beneath filial camaraderie. Yet one thing, at least, the brothers had in common was their willingness to dote upon Brigid's mother, and to her surprise, Brigid noticed that when tempers flared too hot, Josephine was somehow able to smooth things over.

Conversation at court, at meals, the Sheriff's solar, and the archduchess's bower (a place Brigid was now happily forbidden), primarily buzzed with details of the betrothal. From time to time a few rumors might circulate regarding the eventual wedding, rumors no doubt conceived of by Josephine herself. However, there was also talk of other things that stretched beyond Dwerin's borders. King Kredor, it was said, extended an invitation to the archduchess and her daughter to visit Titanis in the spring. Other gossip spoke of a Montevalen princess who some believed could make a fine match for Young Sheriff Alan—if she was not already spoken for. There were stories now that after a hundred years, the War of the Horses was finally over.

"Such is the price of kinslaying," some of the nobles intoned, shaking the dust from their piety of convenience in preparation for the impending ceremony.

Regrettably, the aged Provincial Hierophant Tooms could not make the journey from Orandel, despite Duke Waylon's offer that he accompany him, for the weather alone was much too harsh, and it was feared that were he to travel, it would be the end of him. In his place, however, the betrothal would instead be presided over by Dauphin Lemb, a prelate and next in the hierarchy of the Kinship who resided in the town of Silverlyn. When he was admitted to the Blackstone court upon his arrival, he was announced by the herald as also having been anointed with the title of "the Thrush." Brigid, however, quickly decided that he would more appropriately known as "the

Toad." Flesh hung in great pallid folds from his jowls, and his thick lips seemed to spread wide with an expression suggesting that he had just swallowed a bug. When he walked, he leaned on a cane, though not due to any injury or wound, but rather to act as a third leg to support his tremendous girth. He opened the meal the night of his arrival with a homily about holiness and the purity of the poor, but Brigid found it difficult to believe the sincerity of a man wrapped in such fine white silks and who took such care when daintily dipping his bejeweled fingers into his dish at the table. Worst of all, though, was the look he gave her upon their introduction and the way he tried to touch her cheek to offer her his blessing. Had she not tilted her head just out of reach, she might have spit in his face with disgust. If a man like that could bear a Guardian title, she thought, no wonder there were Blackguards.

At long last, the fifteenth of Moontide, the Feast of the Lady, had finally arrived, and with it, the archduchess's betrothal. Livonia woke Brigid two hours before the sun to return her young roommates to the quarters they shared with the rest of the girls so as they might make ready. Then by the light of her fireplace, the old woman set to work selecting raiment appropriate for the occasion. Since the day in the bower, Livonia had barely spoken to Brigid, other than the occasional grunted command when helping her to dress or arranging her hair—a concession Brigid agreed to in the interest of avoiding all-out war. However, was it fear that curbed the crone's abuse or some foreknowledge of a punishment yet to be actualized?

Either way, Brigid kept her peace as Livonia readied her for the ceremony, for as the archduchess's daughter, she was expected to be, once again, on display. Her long dark hair was again plaited, swept up, and bound into two large buns behind her ears while upon her brow she wore a silver circlet set with sapphires. Her gown of blazing blue was selected to match the depth of the color in her eyes, embellished with fine embroidery and pearls along its hems and bodice. To guard against the cold of the winter weather, a mantle of soft black fur rested upon her shoulders, bound by a brooch fashioned of silver and enameled with her lozenge. For a fleeting moment, as she gazed, uncharacteristically, at herself in the mirror, she considered donning the Falcon's baldric, imagining Whisper and Shade glittering at her narrow hips on either side. Yet she forgot all about it a moment later when Livonia swooped in with a brush wet with crimson to begin making up her face.

"No," Brigid said simply, but in a voice of cold command.

For a moment, the old woman's eyebrows creased in vexation, but she relented. "You're lucky enough at least to have been born fair," she muttered, "though you're not your lady mother, I can tell you that."

"I don't want to be."

"No, and you never will be," Livonia grunted and, without another word, hobbled off to begin the grand ordeal of preparing the archduchess for her momentous day.

At dawn the cavalcade of nobles set forth from the castle processing down from Blackstone to the large cathedral in the town, and Brigid tried to remember if she had ever set foot inside the strange pentagonal building before. As she noticed the city burghers and the peasants gawking from the windows of their daub and wattle houses, their vacant stares of mild confusion led her to wonder just how momentous an occasion as their sovereign's betrothal truly meant to their lives. *Little enough more than the wedding itself*, she thought, keeping her eyes fixed upon the ground, for the finery of the nobility in contrast to the peasants' squalor made her sick to her stomach with embarrassment, even shame, and when the hired minstrels passed, she noticed not a single townsman clapping.

At the front of the noble column, the archduchess and the Sheriff led the way to where the Toad awaited their arrival upon the front steps of the cathedral. Brigid was forced to follow, walking side by side with Alan, though thankfully he had not offered—nor had anyone forced her—to take his arm. Behind them walked the remaining Brothers Beinn, clad in the full regalia of their offices—gilded armor for the Castellan, fine leather lamellar for the Admiral, and thick robes of broadcloth for the master of the mines. Each man's face was a mask of grave frustration, which could easily have accounted for the Young Sheriff's heightened sense of self-control.

Both the Sheriff and his son were clad in sable velvet adorned with stitching, buttons, and embroidery all of gold. Their mantles too were made of black fox fur stitched together with cloth of gold, and around their waists each wore a thick belt of plates bound by a large buckle fashioned in the shape of a gilded anvil. Fine, gem-encrusted blades rested at their hips and around their necks each wore a heavy medallion set with a single red ruby that glittered in the morning sun.

As dark as the Sheriff's and his son's raiment, so much and more did Josephine strive to embody an almost hubristic representation of the Lady of Light. Her gown of silk and lace was whiter than the new fallen snow. Her bodice glittered with strands of pearls on thread of gold. Her skin was clear as fresh cream and smelled of honey. Her neck was a pillar of marble upon which rested the benevolent face of a goddess ensconced in flaxen tresses that, bound within its diamond encrusted netting, shone like a second sun. Yet for all the symbolic suggestion of purity, traipsing like a maiden to the altar, Brigid wondered how many others saw the irony of such behavior in a woman so recognized for her vast experience in the lovers' arts.

Indeed, Brigid felt sick, not only from watching her mother, but also at the pretentious opulence of the noble cohort as they marched to the cathedral, and although she had no idea what might be the rate of exchange, she was fairly certain that a single pearl from her dress could allow a family of peasants to eat for a month or more.

The ceremony itself, once it began after the required pageantry of the couple's arrival, only seemed to further the catalogue of absurdity. What was the point, she wondered, of taking time to announce plans everyone already knew? To announce the betrothal was to announce plans to wed, which, by announcing the impending betrothal, they had already done weeks ago. It was like telling a person that tomorrow you would visit them only to inform them that you were visiting them the next day. Yet as it went on, in spite of the nobles' clear ignorance of their own religion—muttering incomprehensibly along with the sonorous invocations of the Toad—there was something about the concept of the ceremony that Brigid still found on its own to be rather nice, even beautiful. She even wondered, watching her mother's practiced weeping as her uncle made his pledge, if she might one day find herself in a cathedral doing the same (without the false tears, of course). However, soon, she recalled her mother's words decrying her as a horrible future wife.

When the ceremony was at last over, the Toad himself led the assembly of nobles back to where the feast awaited them at Blackstone. The prelate attempted another hymn; however, very few lords and ladies knew the words, and in the face of such a comical sight as the aristocrats muttering gibberish under the auspices of piety, Brigid found she had to struggle to keep from laughing. She remembered once when she was a girl when she stood with her father atop the walls of the castle, watching a parade of fools and jugglers dancing through the streets below during the summer fair. It was one of the few times she could ever remember there being a fair in Blackstone and one of even fewer memories she had of spending any time with her father.

That thought alone was enough to curb her laughter as she again remembered another one of her mother's remarks. She had little doubt that the archduchess hated her and probably always had. However, even though she never truly knew him, had her father really, truly hated her too? She did not necessarily believe him to be a good man or a bad one, but as his daughter, she could not help but hope that he held some small affection for her.

When the congregation returned to the great hall of the castle, the minstrels took their place in the gallery, and the nobles found their seats in accordance with their well-established ranks and honors. The Toad stood up to offer a prayer of blessing, and for a few moments longer, he mused aloud, and just when it seemed the irreverent nobles could stand no more, the wine was poured, and the steward announced the first course.

Brigid took a small sip from her glass to calm her nerves; however, she was wary of the effects of wine. With the return of her uncles, her seat had been moved further down to the far end of the high table. To her left only did she suffer a neighbor, the besotted Admiral, Duke Graham, who, like the others, disregarded her presence. She was contentedly alone with her own thoughts until suddenly, for the first time that day, she spied the Falcon pass her in the guise now of a servant.

"Tonight," he whispered to her while refilling the admiral's goblet.

"Tonight?" she nearly gasped. Her cheeks flushed suddenly with excitement, and her lips tugged at a smile. *At long last!* she thought, *I am to leave! My gift to you, Mother! I will be gone!* Her fingers tingled with excitement, and her blue eyes shone with new light.

"After the *sotelte* is served, the Sheriff will withdraw to his solar with his brothers. Once they are gone, feign sickness and excuse yourself. Then wait for me in the entryway. Can you do that?"

Brigid glanced over at the Admiral, and her back went rigid, fearing he might have heard.

The Falcon smiled, and his golden eyes shone bright with mischief. "He is so drunk right now, my dear Mouse, that I could bash him over the head with his goblet, and he would not notice."

"Are you certain?"

In answer, he winked. "You'll remember our friends, won't you?"

"I will," she said furtively. "What...what else should I prepare?"

"Nothing," he said before disappearing. "All will be taken care of."

For the remainder of the day, she did not see him, dressed either as the servant, the guard, or the courtier. However, the thought of her escape at once kindled in her both great hope and fear. In recent weeks, she had begun to escape into daydream less and less, for the prospect that one day soon she would venture forth beyond Dwerin's captive walls was enough to sustain her, but now that the moment had finally come, she wondered what she might find there. Where would he take her? What might she need? She had no money, but she had her jewelry—what she wore and what she had in her room. She could even cut the tiny pearls from her gown after she retrieved the Falcon's blades. Oh, to finally be going! To be gone!

Course after course, the meal continued, interrupted every so often for a particular poem or song. At one point, Alan insisted he be allowed to sing a ballad. Later on, two men performed a play with obscene puppets, and afterward, the jugglers and tumblers performed their arts. When at long last, the cooks brought forth the *sotelte*, an enormous sculpture of a dove carved from hardened sugar, Brigid knew it would soon be time for her to go. The Sheriff gave orders for the minstrels to lead the assembly in the formal dances appropriate for the feast and, after a few whispered words with the master and castellan, roused the admiral, and the four of them quietly withdrew. There was no need for Brigid to feign sickness, for she had learned long ago that her presence or absence made little difference. Livonia was picking at the bones of one of the feast's courses—some manner of songbird baked inside a chicken baked inside a goose—while Josephine made her way luxuriantly to the center of the floor to lead the young women of the Drove in the dance.

Hurriedly, Brigid scurried up the stairway at the rear of the hall, noting on her way the conspicuous absence of any guards, and she wondered if this, too, was the Falcon's doing. Once to her quarters, she tore out her tresses and exchanged her fine clothes in favor of her favorite dress—the one her mother said made her look a peasant girl—and retrieved the Falcon's baldric and blades from beneath her mattress. She did not want to risk the time it would take tearing the pearls from her gown; however, she gathered up any other jewelry she could find among her things and bound it all together in a cloth with a piece of ribbon. Then, at long last, donning her mantle against the cold, she returned to the stairway, ready to begin her final flight. Her fingers quivered, and her breath came in shallow gasps of excitement. Once again, she felt the exhilaration of defiance at the prospect of freedom and, in the frenzy of the moment, tied Whisper and Shade around her slender waist. It was time!

But when she reached the hallway on the first floor, a strange sound gave her pause. For a moment, she thought it revelers spilling over from the feast in the hall, yet then she heard it again—a great crash, this time followed by a cry. It was near, around the corner at the end of the hallway. Her blood ran cold, and her heart fluttered suddenly with fear. What if it was the Falcon? What if, in readying for their departure, he had finally been caught?

For a moment, she fought with herself, whether to continue to flee, hoping he would be there, awaiting her, or to take a quick look. If it was the Falcon, she thought, he could be in danger, he could need his blades, he could need her help! However, if it was not, she ran the risk of her own discovery. With a deep breath, she steeled herself for what might come and then ever so silently, scurried to the corner and peered out.

A man lay face down on the flagstones, red blood spilling forth from some unseen wound. Yet it was not the Falcon thusly dead, but rather her uncle, the admiral, while above him stood the Lord Sheriff and one of the absent castle guards.

"Get rid of them," her uncle said sternly, "and clean this up."

The guardsman nodded and lifted the body of Duke Graham from the floor. To Brigid's horror, she watched three more guardsmen appear from within the Sheriff's solar, dragging the bodies of Duke Waylon and Duke Nealen after them. The Sheriff, meanwhile, checked his hands for the stain of any blood and, with a weary sigh, went off to rejoin the festivities in the great hall. Brigid ducked back into the stairway to hide, and as he passed, she noticed a certain self-satisfied spring in his step. Now more than ever, it was time to leave Blackstone.

From the stairwell, it was but a short run through another passage that ran parallel to the great hall. Night had fallen outside, and the small flames burning in the sconces painted the walls with flickering shadows, a strange contrast to the sounds of festive music and merrymaking echoing from the feast. In the wake of the bloody scene she had just witnessed, Brigid's eyes grew wide, and in her agitation, she marveled at her foolishness in daring to escape from her mountain prison. The Sheriff was a cold man, obviously a killer, a true murderer, and if he had even the least bit of suspicion that Brigid had seen what she saw, she knew that she was next. Perhaps it was better to remain the mouse, to scurry about frightened and ignored? What was she doing? She could be killed?

Still, there was only one way forward now; she had come too far. To return now was to live forever in an eternity of terror, wondering forever if her uncle would discover what she knew. She ran, darting from shadow to shadow, around the edge of the great hall all the way to the entryway and its tapestries.

And then, at long last, it was over, for in the dim light of the two great braziers, she could see him now shrouded in the darkened corner.

"Falcon," she whispered, "Falcon, I am here. Hurry! We must go!"

"What are you on about?" cried an angry voice, "Go away!"

To her great horror, Brigid watched the figure draw back into the light of the flame to reveal not the sardonic smile of her friend, but the sneering leer of her greatest enemy.

Behind Alan, one of the nameless maidens of the castle drew her bodice up over her bare breast and, at the sight of Brigid's stricken face, fled in mortified fear.

"Wait! Damn you!" Alan called, but the girl disappeared among the crowded feast hall. Made bold by debauchery and drink, he whirled on his cousin. "Beast take you! You fucking—" He stopped, and his voice softened in surprise. "Brigid?"

Brigid froze. As brave as she so recently thought herself, between the magnitude of her departure, the sight of her uncle's kinslaying, and now the absence of the Falcon, she lost all her nerve.

"What are you doing here?" Alan snapped. "Other than ruining things for me…"

Her blue eyes melted in fright, and she could feel the tears beginning to form.

"What's the matter?" Alan laughed. "Cat got your tongue?"

"No, I…"

"Do you remember the last time we ran into each other like this?" he said. "And you told me that story about the hawk and raven? You were so rude, Lady

Frigid, so, so rude to me, and all I wanted to do was to tell you a little secret..."

His eyes narrowed as his leer grew wider, and all at once, he sprang. She tried to leap away, but he caught hold of her cloak and pulled it from her shoulders. In the light of the braziers, the gilded hilts of Whisper and Shade glittered.

Alan's jaw dropped open and he trembled with abject fury. "You!" he growled. "You!"

In a flash, Brigid drew one of the daggers, but before she could stab him, Alan was upon her. His hand tightened upon her wrist, twisting it around behind her back as she tried to flee. The golden hilt was torn free from her hand, and she tried once again to slip away, but Alan held her fast long enough to stab her just above the baldric in the lower back. Her body went rigid with the intensity of the pain, and when he drew back the blade, she fell to the floor.

"You frigid bitch," he spat, rolling her onto her back with his boot, "You killed my friend. Now I get to watch *you* die."

"I killed him, yes, and I would do so again," Brigid whispered. "And if I had the chance, I would kill you too." She turned her head and gazed up from the floor; she could barely feel her legs, and she wondered if this was what Reid had felt as he lay dying. Worse, one could only hope. She began to lose consciousness, and shutting her eyes, she envisioned, for one last time, a pair of golden orbs.

"That was unwise" came a whisper, seething with anger. "Most unwise."

Brigid's eyes flashed open, and from where she lay, she saw another figure, black as the night, grab hold of Alan, and throw him across the flagstones. He collapsed on the floor in a heap, quivering with fear.

The Falcon knelt at Brigid's side, and she felt his gentle touch on her cheek. "My dear Mouse," he said, his voice thick with emotion, "I'm so, so sorry."

"Do not worry," she said as her tears began to flow freely. "Perhaps if I smile..."

The golden eyes of the Falcon shone with rage. "Hush, now, and do not fear," he said, "for if Death comes for you, he will have to face us both...after he has your cousin." He drew the second blade from Brigid's baldric and, returning to his feet, whirled on Alan.

"Get up."

Tentatively, Alan tried to rise. He had hit his head against the wall after the Falcon threw him, and a small trickle of blood settled on his brow. He took one look at the Falcon and turned back toward the feast, where the music had grown louder with sounds of merriment and manic laughter. The young noblemen and women held hands in concentric circles and raced around each other faster and faster as the minstrels increased the tempo of their song.

"They will not hear us," the Falcon said, "and even if they should, they cannot save you." He motioned toward the blade, glimmering in the torchlight where Alan dropped it. "Pick it up!"

Alan's voice trembled with terror. "I don't want to fight you," he said.

"You were brave enough when I was chained."

Alan shook his head and glanced at Brigid, "I was only avenging my friend! She killed him!"

"Justly. Now come."

"No!"

"Come!"

"No!" Alan wailed. He threw himself on the floor and tossed the dagger away. "I'll not fight you!"

From her place on the floor, Brigid's voice was strained, barely a whisper. "Let him go..." she said, "He is nothing...less than nothing..."

At length, the Falcon shook his head, collected his other dagger, and returned them to the baldric. Then, gently, he lifted Brigid into his arms, and she wondered, perhaps absurdly, if ever her father had held her this way when she was a baby, long before his brothers arranged to have him murdered.

Alan still crouched, cowering in fear.

"Should we ever meet again," the Falcon swore, "you will pray that I had killed you here and now, for it will not be pleasant, and it will not be swift."

And without another word, he kicked open the heavy doors of the entryway wide enough to slip through, and, cradling the wounded Mouse, flew out into the darkness.

CHAPTER 39:
THE SILENT PRINCE

With the king and the princess in company, the Tower's Guard lingered another two days at Widowridge before departing to attack the next Valendian keep—Clearpoint, and Beledain Tremont, disguised as Sir Briden Winfred, was consumed with bitter self-loathing. King Marius, fortunately or unfortunately, needed no convincing to continue the ride ahead south, for without a single word of urging from Bel or any other man, and in spite of the polite protests from the Tower and the (sometimes) impolite protests from the princess, the king rode forth. However, Sir Harding had at least been able to appeal to him not to send back for a horse and his armor, which meant that thankfully, whether there be a battle or not, the king would remain with the princess safely protected in his armored wagon.

The snow had begun to fall steadily since the morning the men departed Widowridge, and great clouds of steam rose from the flanks of the knights' horses. The Tower atop Tempest led the column of men along the mountain path. Beside him rode Sir Linton and Sir Armel and half a dozen other knights followed by the men-at-arms. After them came Sir Briden, the Young Talon, and four others leading the king's wagon and his royal guards, behind which marched the archers, the remaining knights, and the baggage train carts and wagoners.

From a small, wooden hatch, King Marius, warm beneath the blankets and furs of his wagon, enjoyed the robust mountain scenery and the brisk morning air. Opposite him, Princess Marina sat wrapped in soft white furs, looking the very image of her title as her face flushed with the cold. On occasion, she, too, opened her window and gazed thoughtfully in silence out over the valley to the east far below.

"One might be trapped in ice and still feel warm for the sight of her." Sir Welmsey sighed.

Bel might have agreed had the quiet storm raging in his mind these last months not suddenly grown into a blizzard. The words of Canton's messenger echoed through the hollows of his breast. It was all too much to come to terms with at once—Dermont's plan to trap the Tower, Bel's obligation to slay him and subdue the king, and most of all, the intimation that Lilia was with child. His hands shook now as he adjusted his helm, and he felt a sudden hostility for his heavy armor. In anger, he tore the thing from his head and dropped it; one of the archers, having recovered it, ran up along the column to return it.

"Thank you," Bel muttered and set the great helm before him upon the pommel of Banshee's saddle. The archer offered him a quick salute and hurried back to his place.

Bel breathed a heavy sigh, coughed against the cold, and readjusted his grip on his lance and shield before rechecking the rest of his equipment. After killing the leper, his sword had been scoured with Sir Linton's armor, but unfortunately, the leather wrapping the handle started to crack, so he exchanged it with Jarvy for a battle axe until it could be repaired. The axe hung now with his dagger upon the studded baldric cinching his tabard.

"How now, Sir Briden?"

Bel glanced over to see the princess gazing at him from her hatch in the royal wagon. Her red hair and lips seemed all the more vibrant against skin made even fairer by the cold. Her green eyes regarded him warmly.

"Is all well? You seem"—she paused—"out of sorts."

Bel smiled bashfully and looked away. He had come to find it hard to look at her for too long. "I have not slept well these past two nights, my lady," he said. "Nothing more. I will rest easier after the battle."

She sighed. "Do you really think there will be one this time?"

Bel felt the widening of the great chasm inside of him. "It is difficult to say," he said.

"Well," the princess said, lowering her voice, "for my father's sake, I hope not. He promised we would return to cousin Guillon after Clearpoint, but"—

she paused—"he wanted to taste battle once more. He sleeps now to rest for the occasion."

"As I understand it," Bel said, surprised at the princess's candor, "His Majesty was a great warrior."

"What a sentiment that is," Marina said, "a 'great warrior.' My brother was a great warrior too, yet all it warranted him was an early grave."

"I grieve with you, your highness," Bel said. "I, too, lost a brother."

"Was he a knight as well?"

Bel nodded. "However, he did not die in battle, though that was what my father wanted to be known. In truth, he took his own life in despair, for his wife died in childbirth, and his son was…stillborn. A death in battle is much more honorable than the shame men attribute to suicide."

"Yet it is still a death in either case and one born out of great suffering and sorrow."

"So it is, your highness."

The princess regarded him thoughtfully for a moment and suddenly smiled. "Sir Briden, give me your arm."

"My arm?" Bel repeated.

She beckoned him closer, and he slowly rode Banshee up alongside the wagon. "Raise your arm," she said again.

Resignedly, he did so, racked with guilt as he anticipated her intentions.

"I was going to give this to Sir Marcus out of friendship," she said, taking hold of Bel's arm. "But I enjoy our talks together, and for all your silence, when you do speak, your words are fair and wise." From within the wagon, she produced a white, silken handkerchief embroidered with red roses and fastened it to his shoulder.

Bel bowed his head. "My lady," he said, "you do me much more honor than I deserve."

"Oh, nonsense." She smiled. "I have many of those and more just like it."

Dermont, you bloody fool! Bel thought.

"Now off with you." The princess laughed. "The air grows colder, and I want to close the window!"

Clearpoint, unlike Valeshade and Widowridge, appeared upon first sight to have been abandoned for some time, and when the Tower and his men first approached the shell keep the following day, they found the doors of its main gate hanging slightly ajar. The plague-bearers tasked with holding the place were, at first, nowhere in sight. Only after exploring the interior of the keep were their bodies discovered—three of them dead six months at least all having succumbed to their disease. Quickly, the men set to burning them and anything else that might possibly pose a risk while the men-at-arms gathered barrels of snow from the mountain, and the archers attempted once again to hunt down game fit for a king's feast.

The token of the Winter Rose pinned to Bel's arm quickly made him the envy of every knight in the guard, and for the entire time they were set to work righting the stables and the living quarters of the keep, Sir Welmsey begged Sir Briden for the chance just to smell it. Bel declined. For him, the mark of the princess's favor had become a mark of great dishonor instead. It marked him as her champion when, soon enough, he was to become her captor and, even worse, the Tower's murderer.

But what other alternative was there? For to refuse Dermont was to forsake Lilia, but to carry out his orders would be the worst of betrayals and the height of dishonor.

Four months had passed since the Battle of the White Wood and just over two since the tourney on the Feast of Perindal that selected the men of the Tower's Guard. Before that, it was two years that Bel commanded the light cavalry, raiding caravans, disrupting supply lines, and scouting the Gasparn border towns. Now at twenty years of age, Bel felt old, and he recalled what the Tower had said to him at the tourney feast under the guise of Sir Darren Helm.

Standing by Jarvy in the stables of Clearpoint, patting Banshee down, Bel's eyes scanned the faces of the other knights, men he professed in the barracks of Ironshod to consider his brothers-in-arms. Sir Linton, Sir Armel, Sir Welmsey, Sir Cardolan, many more he barely knew—even Sir Gurney, Sir Trenton, and the Young Talon—he swore to fight beside them, not stab them in the back.

And, of course, there was the Tower. From the very beginning, Sir Marcus Harding had treated Bel with nothing but the utmost courtesy and respect. Since his visit as Sir Darren Helm following Bel's first victory in the tourney, through the drilling, the journey from Reginal, and the campaign across the Bloodline through the Nivanus highlands, Bel had come to regard the Guardian cavalier as not only a man of honor who he respected but also a friend. He could not kill him.

"Jarvy," Bel said softly, "if something should happen that I should be discovered, I will not expose you. However, if you can, get word to Sir Emory and my father. Tell them the truth and ask them to take Lilia under their protection. I'm not sure it will mean anything to Dermont, but…"

"Now I don't like hearing that sort of talk, my lord," Jarvy said. "I do not like hearing that sort of talk at all."

Bel sighed. "Goodbye, Jarvy," he crossed the courtyard and ascended the stairs into the great hall. Inside, the Tower stood alone, leaning over his maps, biting his lip in consternation.

"Have the king and the princess been properly installed?" he asked Sir Briden.

"I believe so."

The Tower looked up and smiled. "It seems she favors you."

Bel blushed at the princess's token on his arm. "I do not deserve it."

Sir Harding laughed. "If she says you do, then you do. There is little room for argument with royalty."

Again, Bel sighed. "My lord," he said, "I must speak with you on a matter of…grave importance."

The Tower looked away from his maps and stood up straight to offer Bel his full attention. "What is it?"

Bel bowed his head. "As we speak," he began, "Prince Dermont and his forces from Whitemane are on their way to attack Lord Guillon unawares. A token force covered their departure by attacking Lord Fabien in Roanshead." *All sent to slaughter, most like,* Bel thought. *Another sacrifice to serve Dermont's victory.* "Should he succeed in defeating Lord Guillon," Bel continued, "we will all be trapped in Clearpoint far below the Bloodline…the king and the princess included."

The Tower's face remained calm, though his knuckles went white. "How is it that you know this?"

"A man arrived in secret at Widowridge during the feast, a spy in the service of Prince Dermont, a man whose corpse now poisons the keep's well." Bel took a deep breath and raised his eyes to meet the Tower's gaze. "You see, my lord"—he paused—"though it shames me to admit that I have deceived you, my name is not Sir Briden Wilfred, nor do I know if such a man ever existed. My name is Beledain Tremont, Son of King Cedric of Valendia, known as the Silent Prince or the Prince of Bells."

The Tower sighed. "I know who you are."

Bel's eyes grew wide. "You know?"

"I have known who you are since the tourney," Sir Harding said, "though it took until the melee before I finally remembered your face, for I was among those men to meet you with Giles Pronet, though I wore another man's helm. I wanted to see this Silent Prince in person, to know the truth rather than simply the idle chatter of rumor and hearsay. As I told you, the true measure of a man can only be taken when he believes that no one is watching."

"And you simply let me be?" Bel asked. "Why did you not imprison me or put me to death as a spy?"

"What cause had I to do either? You did not do anything to warrant as such beyond offering a false name and being born south across the Bloodline. On the contrary, you simply acted as any knight should—with dignity, courtesy, and honor—more so than most, in fact."

"I did not," Bel said, shaking his head in anguish. "I spoke to men. I sent messages to my brother—"

"And we saw them," the Tower said, "or their content was known to us in any case. Your words were so vague and uninformative that in many cases, we simply allowed many of your brother's men to go, for anything you told him could be learned just as easily by a man dressed as a farmer watching us from a field, many of which I'm certain Prince Dermont already has in his pocket."

"You saw the dispatches I wrote?"

"Your brother may pay this man Canton enough to keep him loyal. However, Canton is not so openhanded on his own, and some of his men were unhappy," the Tower said. "If a man can be bought once, sure enough, he can easily be bought again, and he wastes no time in seeking new employ if he thinks it profitable."

Bel remained silent.

"So, know, Prince Beledain," Marcus Harding said, "that I do not hold any malice toward you, though I shall miss Sir Briden, for I had grown rather fond of the young knight."

"And he of you," Bel said miserably. A long moment passed before he asked, "What are we to do?"

The Tower breathed a heavy sigh. "I do not know," he said. "I admit that your news regarding your brother's attack on Lord Guillon is distressing. I suppose, for my part, that the king's cousin will not be the victor and that those of us here must prepare Clearpoint to endure a siege." He paused and sat down at the table. "What I do not understand in all of this, however, is why your brother would send you on this errand in the first place. It makes no sense to me."

"He told me I was to gain your confidence and then kill you," Bel told him. "He holds someone very dear to me hostage to force me to fulfill his commands. Even still, while he plans to trap you here below the Bloodline, he orders me to kill you and take the king and the princess into custody…"

"But that still makes no sense," the Tower said. "For clearly, you are no assassin, and he holds many and more in his employ. Why send you?"

Again, Bel heard Lilia's voice whispering in his head. *He sends you to your death!* And suddenly, he knew.

"Dermont believes that if I was to kill you, the other men would waste no time in killing me. Such a thing would give him cause then to attack as he wishes, claiming vengeance," Bel scowled bitterly. "And the Brethren only know the depths of the Plague Prince's depravity. However, in the eyes of the common folk of Valendia, he would be known as the prince who won the war. As of now, they have no love for him—and he knows it, but were I gone, there would be no other heir on either side of the Bloodline to carry the Tremont name. They would accept him as their rightful king by default."

"But Gasparn would never bow to him," the Tower said.

"That depends on the fates of the king and the princess."

Sir Harding thought a moment and sighed. "He has already rejected her once."

"Until you told me, I did not know about that," Bel said. "And if he meant it, I believe he would have made a show of it to all the world that he might heap shame upon his rival king, and I mean *king*, for though my father still lives, he is infirm, and Dermont has already secured for himself all aspects of his power…"

"No," the Silent Prince continued. "He rejected her out of spite and cruelty and because it was an *offer* meant to achieve peace. Dermont does not accept other men's offers. He requires that they submit to his demands. However, he would not publicly reject an offer he may later claim."

For a long moment, the Tower sat brooding. Bel, though in some sense relieved of the burden of the constant deception, felt still the sting of shame and the bitter ache of anguish. At length, Sir Marcus Harding returned to his feet and regarded the Silent Prince with grave resolve.

"If all that you say is true, then I have not a moment more to lose," he said. "I must send scouts north to seek the truth regarding Lord Guillon and your brother, and I must speak with the king." He paused. "I was sent north at the behest of King Marius under orders from the Warlord to end this war, and I intend to do so at whatever cost. You, Prince Beledain, whether in the guise of Sir Briden or the Silent Prince, I believe to be a man of honor and a man who shares a desire for peace. So I ask you to tell me, one man to another, in truth and fidelity, am I to regard you as enemy or an ally?"

Bel breathed in deeply and, as he removed his gauntlet, fought to keep his hand from shaking.

"I am your ally," he said.

"Then I am yours," the Tower said, accepting the prince's hand. "And whatever your brother holds over your head, I will do what I can in return to spare it."

"Thank you, my lord," Bel said. "Thank you dearly."

"Say not a word of this or anything else to anyone. We will discuss this further once I know more for certain."

Within the hour, the Tower sent two riders north to return to Widowridge, where a small contingent of men-at-arms and archers awaited Lord Guillon. Bel did not know under what pretense the men were sent; however, they were men among the infantry riding horses from the baggage train, and the Tower spoke to them alone before they departed. For a moment, Bel considered sending Jarvy and Piper but decided, in the end, to keep the old skirmisher by his side. The meal that night in the great hall was meager, for the snow continued to fall heavily all day. There was very little in the way of merrymaking as well. The king and the princess did not stay long at the table before returning to the privacy of their quarters, claiming the day's journey had left them weary and cold. As they withdrew, Princess Marina offered Bel a forlorn smile that left him wondering how much she knew.

Rather than sleep in the garrison, many of the knights chose to sleep instead in the great hall. Since the fireplace had long been lit and the kitchen hearth blazed just below it, the lofty room was still warmer than the barracks, and in the center of the courtyard, a bonfire was kept near enough to the stables to provide the horses with something akin to heat. The absence of any true inhabitants had left Clearpoint drafty and in disrepair, and Bel wondered when it was exactly that Dermont recalled Sir Oran Bandry and his garrison. It set his mind wondering what the Tower's Guard might have found should they have pressed on all the way to Shoulderidge. A ruin? Perhaps an entire colony of plague-bearers? Yet more so than that, he wondered how the old keep would stand up to Dermont's siege.

By mid-afternoon on the following day, the Tower's scouts returned, bringing with them not only the occupying force from Widowridge but also a motley crew of other soldiers numbering no more than two score. Neither Bel nor Sir Harding needed to speak with the men to know who they were and where they came from, but before long, word spread among the other men of the Plague Prince's army and his surprise assault on Lord Guillon while en route between Widowridge and Valeshade. The lord and the bulk of his remaining forces were driven north toward the Bloodline while the Plague Prince sent horsemen under the command of Wilmar Danelis, the Sundering Hand to hunt down any other stragglers.

With him, Dermont had at least six hundred heavy cavalry, two hundred light cavalry, two hundred Wrathorn mercenaries, three thousand infantry consisting of men-at-arms, pikemen, and archers, and an additional fifteen hundred ragged commoners wielding farming tools and armored in nothing more than furs. It was this last group who, to no one's surprise, suffered the heaviest losses.

The Tower gave orders for the refugees to be rested and fed, and ordered the ballistas built atop the gatehouse. Men were sent to forage and gather as much water as possible, while others were tasked with securing the defenses of the shell keep. No longer would the infantry camp outside, but would be stationed inside the keep, filling every room and every larder, camping in the courtyard and upon the walls. Soon, the confidence and high morale that had accompanied the journey south began to give way to feelings of resentment and fear at what now appeared a gross miscalculation on the part of the lord-general, one that seemed also to place the king and the princess in harm.

By nightfall, Clearpoint had made itself as ready as it would be to withstand a siege, and after another spare meal in the great hall, the Tower called Sir Briden to join him in council with the king.

The fireplace crackled with warmth in the corner of the room, in contrast to the stone-cold gravity that lined the countenances of Sir Marcus Harding and King Marius. Princess Marina, too, was in attendance, though her expression was one of resignation, and a melancholy light lingered in the depths of her green eyes.

"Welcome, Sir Briden," King Marius said, "or shall I say, Prince Beledain."

Bel accepted a seat at the table between the Tower and the princess, but all he could think to say was an awkward "Hello."

"You know," the king observed, "I wonder now as we three sit here, which of us is the greatest fool, a senile old man who drags himself and his daughter into harm out of nostalgia for his lost youth, a famous general who allows himself to be trapped like a rabbit in a snare because he's blinded by his own ruse, or a treacherous young man who willingly exposes his attempt to destroy the other two?"

"Father…" Marina said softly.

"Your Majesty," the Tower added, "the prince has declared himself our ally."

"It seems neither here nor there now, considering he has been the artisan of our demise."

"Father…"

Bel breathed a heavy sigh. "Your Majesty, your hostility toward me is entirely warranted, and I will not insult you by attempting to apologize," he said. "Yet in spite of all, I pledge myself to aid you and your daughter in this, though in doing so have placed someone important to me at grave risk. However, I believe, as does Sir Marcus, and as your daughter has also spoken, that this war *must* end, for the good of Valendia and Gasparn separately, or together as one united Montevale."

King Marius folded his hands upon the table and allowed a moment to pass in silence. "What then shall we do?" he asked. "Your brother is a wicked, hateful creature, and though you and I may share a common purpose, what assurances do we have that he will honor any agreement we two should make?"

"None," Bel said. "For your assessment of my brother's character is regrettably true. I cannot deny that anymore, and I, too, have long suffered as a result of his defects." He paused. "I still do. However, though he holds me hostage, if you will it, I will become yours."

"If all is as you said," the Tower observed, "I do not believe such a thing would stay his hand any more than were we to execute you."

Bel shook his head bitterly. "I feel there are very few scenarios that do not result in Dermont slaughtering everyone in this castle, or else, letting us starve to death in siege."

"Are we truly that ill-prepared for such a thing?" the king asked.

The Tower considered it. "We have plenty of water, what with the snow and all. However, our greatest concern will be food. We have soldiers' stores and what little the men I sent out could forage, but the weather has not been of any help. Still, we have these walls and enough fuel to keep our fires, though we will have to burn economically." He paused. "And should it become a matter of life or death, we have…horseflesh."

"The weather will be no help to Dermont either," Bel said. "His men will have to face the full brunt of the winter should he intend to dig in. However, this might also speed up his attempts to take the keep as soon as possible by force. At least his cavalry will not be of much help to him unless we should ride out to meet him."

"And we will most certainly not," said the king.

"Of course not," said the Tower.

King Marius scowled. "What are the chances of Guillon rallying our other armies and bringing the full force here to relieve us?"

"It might take weeks," the Tower said.

At last, Princess Marina, who had so far remained silent, spoke, "You said you wished to find a way to end the war, yet everything any of you have suggested thus far will only prolong it. Whether a siege or a battle or the winter's cold, the war only continues."

The men bowed their heads in humility. "True," the Tower said.

The Princess sighed and turned to King Marius. "Father," she said, "I would like to speak with Prince Beledain for a moment in private."

"What?" the king's eyes went wide. "Of course not!" Bel felt just as surprised.

"Father, please," she continued, her green eyes alight with conviction. "I understand your distrust, and to a degree, I also feel it, yet, in spite of his deception, he has done nothing to compromise his honor."

"He betrayed us! He played us false from the beginning!" Marius rose from his chair and turned his anger upon the Tower. "And you too, I might add,

Lord-General! You claim to have known who he was since the tourney, yet still, you accepted him into your ranks! And all the while, you told us nothing!"

"Prince Beledain has done nothing but fulfill his duty to me and to you," the Tower said sternly. "I saw no reason to begrudge him that."

"No reason!" King Marius paused and caught himself. His face had grown as red as the princess's hair, and beads of sweat appeared upon his forehead. He slumped back into his seat and wiped his brow. "Seeing as I am clearly outnumbered," he said at last, "I will allow you the chance to speak. But know this, Silent Prince, I will be standing with Sir Marcus just outside that door. If I hear one word of discourtesy, I will inform every man downstairs of your identity, and though your brother may raze this keep to the ground, I will first see you dead."

"Really, Father..." the princess said tersely.

The king threw up his hands. "Come, Sir Marcus," he said and hurried from the room.

Left alone with Princess Marina, Bel felt his breath suddenly shorten. Upon his arm, her handkerchief remained pinned. "I should return this to you," he said.

Her green eyes flashed as they caught his. "Did I ask for it?"

Bel said nothing, turning from the force of her eye and the frightful beauty of her face, choosing instead to stare within the flickering depths of the fire.

"Now I understand your silence," she said after a moment. "The more one speaks, the easier it is to betray one's web of deceit."

"I am sorry," Bel said miserably. "But though it means nothing, beyond the falseness of my name, every word I spoke to you was the truth."

"The story about learning to ride with your father?" she asked. "And...what you said about your brother?"

"Larius," he muttered, "yes. It's all true."

The princess sighed. "I have heard it said that the Plague Prince reigns because King Cedric has...gone mad."

He nodded. "Not quite mad, but...he is losing his mind."

"I fear..." she hesitated. "I fear the same may be true for my father. He forgets things. He speaks to others, sometimes addressing them as people long dead. Once he...once he began calling for Gislain and grew cross when my brother did not answer. It took some minutes before he believed me when I reminded him that Gislain was dead."

The prince sighed. "I wondered as such at Widowridge. Something about his way was...familiar."

Princess Marina shook her head and breathed a heavy sigh. A single tear escaped her eye and traced its way down her fair cheek. "Lady's Grace, I hate this war," she cursed.

Bel stared into the flames, and in his mind, he saw Lilia lying beside him in his quarters back in Castle Tremontane. "So do I," he said, "and though this war began in such a way, I find myself now wishing my brother dead."

"Is he truly that wicked?"

"Yes. I refused to believe it for a long, long time, but I cannot ignore it. Yes, he is. He is governed only by pride and greed, and I often wonder these days if there has ever been any good in him."

"Perhaps the good that might have been born into him, instead carried over into you?"

Bel shook his head. "I am not as good as all that. I have done wrong. I have killed men."

"In war."

"Is there any difference?" He smiled sadly. "As you said, a death is still a death, and my hands bear the stains of many other men's blood."

"Then let us end this war," Princess Marina said, "for if both our fathers have fallen to infirmity, and our brothers are either wicked or dead, then it *must* fall to us," she paused, "We two must marry."

Bel's gaze turned quickly from the fire and fell upon the beauty of the princess. Her face bore an expression of anxious anticipation, and her green eyes were wide, waiting for him to speak. Bel felt within his chest the pain of a hundred daggers as he thought of Lilia and her myriad refusals to either accept or return his words. *Until the end*, he thought. *Until Dermont sent me across the Bloodline to die in the north...*

"This is the second time you offer me something of which I am far too unworthy," he said at last, his voice thick with the misery of uncertainty.

"Yet still I offer," Marina said, "and unlike in the case of your brother, to you, I do so without despair, but rather...hope."

Bel's head fell to his hands, and he rubbed his eyes bitterly in anguish, "My lady..." he began, and stopped, "My brother...there is..."

The princess bit her lip and appeared to swallow a lump in her throat. "What your brother holds hostage," she said. "It's a woman."

"Yes."

She offered him a forlorn smile. "I had heard stories of the Silent Prince and his Wild Woman. Is it she?"

"Yes. There's a chance she may carry my child," he told her, "And…I love her dearly besides."

The princess remained silent for a long moment. "She is very lucky then to have earned a prince's love," she said, "for I seem to have failed to do so twice."

"It is not that," Bel said vehemently. "It is not that at all, for since I first saw you at the tourney, I felt great sympathy for you, and these last days I have found myself looking forward to our talks, however brief, for you are kind and good and beautiful, and like me, you want nothing more than peace. You were even willing to sacrifice yourself to see it done, and now you do so again."

"This time, it is no sacrifice." She smiled. "And I find it something I desire more and more with every word you speak. But still, you refuse?"

"I…don't know," Bel said. "To marry you is to end a hundred years of war and suffering for both our lands, yet to do so would mean forsaking her whom I love and the child we might have made."

"What if…" Marina said, "What if…you kept your woman, but—at least in name and for raising heirs—you married me?"

"No," he said vehemently, "Absolutely not. To do so would be to paint all of us in shame."

"Then what are we to do?" she asked.

"I don't know," Bel said, returning his gaze to the fire.

"Think on it, then," she said. "But we have been over long, and I will call my father and the Tower to return."

"Well," said King Marius, "is the king permitted to return now to his own room?" He returned to his seat at the table. "I hope you intend to inform us of what it was you were discussing for so long a time."

"Father, I—"

"I was apologizing," Bel interrupted, casting the princess a glance. "I was apologizing for having deceived your daughter and begged her forgiveness."

Marina smiled wanly. "And you have it."

Sir Marcus Harding returned to the table, eyeing the prince and the princess pensively, and Bel wondered how much the Tower had been able to surmise. At length, the lord-general breathed a heavy sigh, and when he spoke, his voice was grave.

"There is only one other way that this can end that does not result in all of our deaths."

CHAPTER 40:
OF FARMERS & SAINTS

It was with great sorrow that Geoffrey set out from Ashfort the day after the battle. To speed him along the way, Captain Barrow had offered Ernald's cart and two of the bandits' horses to more easily carry Oliver's body and that of Geoffrey's son Karl. To the farmer's utter despair, he was one of the three lads felled by stray arrows in the bandits' treacherous volleys. Axel and Nicholas, Oliver's sons, though shaken by the ordeal and the death of their father, were—at least physically—unharmed.

If Oliver's death was not severe enough, the discovery of Karl's body, pierced by an arrow through the chest, plunged Geoffrey into a dark desolation from which he could not imagine ever recovering. At twelve years old, Karl had been on the brink of manhood; he already helped with the farm, and one day, Geoffrey hoped to set the boy up with a cottage and homestead of his own. Perhaps even taking Oliver's daughter to wife, when she was old enough. Now, he was dead, and Geoffrey could only interpret it as punishment from the gods for his cowardice and his reluctance to follow Oliver in search of their children. Nothing Geoffrey had ever experienced could compare to the gut-wrenching anguish and horror that now consumed him, and once more he could not help but weep for the futility that seemed so often to characterize the lives of peasants and common folk like him. In part, he cursed himself for following Oliver, believing that had he remained in Pyle, Karl at least might still live; however, at the same time, he knew that to have stayed home was to have resigned the lad to a life of banditry and perhaps ensured that the rest of his family would starve. In the end, either choice seemed just as likely to have ended in tragedy and suffering, and he bemoaned the fact that the world could be so cruel and unfair.

Axel and Nicholas said very little over the course of the journey home to Pyle, and Geoffrey sensed that somehow they resented him for their father's fate. Yet such were the ways of grief and anger, and he hoped that in time they would find peace. Their silence, however, offered Geoffrey a chance to think on the bandits, the Spade, the war, and what was to come of Pyle. In spite of his orders, Barrow had given them two barrels of stores from among the stolen goods at Ashfort, but it was in no way enough for an entire village to eat, let alone the Grantisi legion they discovered encamped around Pyle on their return.

"What is this?" Axel asked.

"Soldiers?" Nicholas whispered. "Wolves?"

Hurriedly, they drove the cart along the main path of the village to where the burned out remains of the chapel stood as a ruin in the center square.

"What do you have in the cart there, farmer?" a soldier stopped them.

"Dead," Geoffrey said sadly. "Killed by bandits." He motioned to Axel and Nicholas. "Their father...and my son..."

"All right then." The soldier sighed without emotion. "Carry on."

From the square, they turned the cart along the path toward their cottages, and soon, word spread of their return. The other folk of Pyle, their friends and neighbors, came forth from their houses to follow behind the cart at a respectable distance. At last, they came upon Annabel and Agnes with the rest of the children, and Old Amos leaned forward mournfully upon his cane. Even without sight, the old man knew the news was grave. Geoffrey brought the cart to a stop and prepared for the moment he had been dreading.

The farmers of Pyle wasted no time in preparing the bodies for burial, returning to the soil what the Spade's bounty had for so many harvests raised. However, without Cousin Martin, there was no one to preside over the service, so in the end, Old Amos simply stood up, took a handful of soil from the ground, and muttering a prayer silently to himself, sprinkled the dirt over the graves. Soon, the other villagers joined him while, far off, a handful of Grantisi soldiers on patrol stood by to watch, marveling at the strange piety of the superstitious farmers.

After the bodies were buried, the families of the deceased stood by in vigil late into the afternoon, until finally, at sundown, they, too, returned to their homes.

"We cannot stay here any longer," Geoffrey declared. "I am tired of this. I am tired of this injustice. I am tired of all this death." He sat outside his cottage on an old stump across from his father while Old Amos paced back and forth, his pipe hanging thoughtfully from his mouth. Annabel, Frederick, and Greta had already gone to bed—the children, confused and frightened at the loss of their brother, their mother silently crying herself to sleep.

"What do you intend to do?" the old man asked.

"I don't know." Geoffrey sighed miserably as his tears began to flow. "I will not bury another child."

Amos puffed at his pipe and rested a spindly hand upon his son's shoulder. "St. Aiden was a farmer," he said. "And he, too, fought for his child."

Geoffrey buried his face in his hands and gave himself over to his grief. Great shuddering sobs shook him, and his eyes burned with weeping, and then, he remembered.

He lay near the hilltop that night long ago when the bandits attacked the caravan. An arrow jutted forth from his side in the same place where he now bore the strange scar. He tried to prop himself up to a sitting position; however, breathing did not come easy, and his lips were moist with the metallic taste of blood. Above him in the night sky, the stars shone brightly, fading in and out with his vision as he wept for what might become of his family now without him.

"You're alive."

It was a voice that Geoffrey now knew well, yet, at the time, was altogether unfamiliar. He glanced over, and the old man-at-arms appeared, staggering beneath the weight of his wounds. Countless arrows pierced his flesh, and Geoffrey wondered how a man, let alone an aged one such as he, could stand such pain.

"I'm dying," Geoffrey said.

The old man leaned upon his club, breathing heavily. "Perhaps," he said, "though, for me, it is a certainty."

"I don't want to die!" Geoffrey sobbed. "I can't."

The old man clambered up beside Geoffrey and collapsed as he tried to sit with his back resting against the trunk of a nearby tree. "All men die," he said. "What matters is what they do while they live."

Geoffrey winced as pain surged through his abdomen, and he gripped the arrow, steeling himself to pull it out.

"No, don't do that!" the old man said. "If you do, the blood will flow, and you'll die quicker."

Geoffrey wiped his eyes and lay back on the ground in despair. "I have a family," he whispered. "What will come of them if I die?"

"You're not the first to ask that, though rarely do any of us get to know the answer," the man said. He set his club and shield down beside him on the grass. "What if I told you…" He gasped. "What if I told you that I could save you, but at great cost? Would you accept it?"

"You can't save me," Geoffrey cried. "I'm going to die."

The old man laughed bitterly before erupting into a fit of coughs. "Forgive me," he said. "But saving you is about the only thing left that I *can* do." He cleared his throat and spit a great wad of blood. "However, if I do," he added, "there is something you must swear to do in return…"

"If you can save me, and I can go back to my family," Geoffrey said hurriedly, "then I will swear to it, whatever it is!"

"Do not be so hasty." The old man grinned, his teeth stained crimson. "Hear it first." He paused again to breathe. "My name is Regnar, called the Vanguard, and I am one of the Three. That may mean nothing to you, yet in other parts of Termain that means much and more, for the Vanguards have a long history reaching back to the days of St. Aiden who the first of my name followed into battle against the Darkness of Dibhor and the Warlock. Now what is your name?"

"Geoffrey of Pyle."

"A farmer?"

"So I am," Geoffrey sobbed.

"Well, Geoffrey of Pyle, if I save you, you must swear to do as I have done, as the Vanguards *all* have done."

"What does that mean?"

"The Vanguard follows the old ways, hunting the Darkness wherever it dwells. He fights against injustice and villainy. He protects the weak and cares for the poor, and most importantly, he acts as a guardian for all good folk who have none. If I save you, Geoffrey of Pyle, do you swear to do this?"

"Yes…yes, I do."

"Seek out Gareth the Blade in Dwermouth. He will know you when he sees you. However, just in case, take my club and my shield. If Gareth is not there, make your way to Baronbrock, and in the barony of Galadin, look for a man named Crodane, called the Marshal. You should find him at the Houndstooth." Regnar's breath came in a great wheeze, he winced again in pain, and his body lurched in agony. "A man who bears a title must do so until his death, his sacrifice, or to aid another in greatest peril. There is no going back. Say again, do you swear?"

"I swear!"

"Then pull the arrow from your side and give me your hand…" Again, Geoffrey heard Regnar's voice intone the strange, poetic verse as he lost consciousness from the sight of his unstoppered blood.

As the scene faded into memory, Geoffrey wiped his eyes again and glanced up at not Regnar, but his father standing at his side.

"I must go."

Slowly, Old Amos nodded. "Go where?"

"To Dwermouth," he said. "There is a man that I must see, and then to a place called Baronbrock."

"Baronbrock?" Amos said. "It's a country far to the north and east."

"I believe I'm supposed to go there. To a place called Galadin."

"The birthplace of the Saint!"

"St. Aiden?" Geoffrey said, "Aiden Galadin?"

"Of course, you turnip." Amos smiled and took a long pull from his pipe. "And you must take Annabel and the children with you. The Spade is no longer safe."

"And you will come too, Da."

Old Amos smiled and patted his son on the back. "No," he said.

"Of course, you will," Geoffrey exclaimed. "You must!"

"I am not leaving Pyle," he said. "I'm old. I have not much time left. In fact, I feel long overdue."

"Nonsense! You must come."

"No, son." Amos sighed. "I will stay here and keep Karl and your mother company. You, however, *you* must take your family and go."

Geoffrey was silent for a long time, "We'll leave tomorrow by midday. Everything I have I leave to you and to Oliver's boys. Do you think the soldiers will allow us to go?"

"I believe that there is nothing in this world that will stop you, my boy"—Amos laughed—"for I believe you answer the call of the blessed saint himself!"

Geoffrey sighed and hugged his father close. "St. Aiden *was* a farmer"—he wept—"as you said."

"That he was, son," Old Amos whispered as tears fell from his blind eyes. "That he was."

CHAPTER 41:
THE MOUSE TAKES FLIGHT

For a long time, Brigid sensed only darkness and the bite of the wind against her face. The searing pain in her back had stopped hurting long ago, but the cold was growing worse. At times, she could hear the sound of men shouting, though what they were saying, she could not make out, for the only words she could discern were those of the Falcon as he whispered.

"Hold on, Mouse. Hold on."

Time passed, and vaguely, she discerned the smell of horse. The shouts had all died away now, and with them, the Falcon's words, or at least, if he spoke them, she no longer heard. Then, at last, something changed. She no longer sensed movement, and once again, she lay still.

"I did not want this for you, Mouse," she heard the Falcon say. "But I cannot let you die. Just promise me this, if you can hear me. Promise that you will retain your goodness though at times you, too, may walk in shadow. Do not let anger poison you, as wicked and evil as might be those you hope to defy. Seek only justice, not vengeance, and to heal rather than harm. But, more than anything else, Mouse, remember what it is like to feel very small."

"I promise."

Beneath the veil of nightfall,
dark and dire deeds are done.
To stand upon the shadow's edge,
is a task for only one.
When evil lurks behind the light
and all seems lost and cruel,
Rise now, the Blade,
so the Darkness knows fear too!

Brigid opened her eyes to see the flickering flame of a single wax candle illuminating a thatched roof storehouse. She lay upon a pile of lumpy burlap sacks stuffed with grain, but otherwise, she was without pain. For a fleeting moment, she tasted the joy of victory—they had escaped Blackstone! She lurched upright hoping to find her savior when, suddenly, she remembered the cost.

"No!"

He was reclining against a barrel surrounded by a widening pool of blood. Brigid hurried to his side. "No!"

The Falcon smiled weakly. "It must have worked, though I wonder that Death should find your smile so frightening. I, for one, have always found it rather beautiful."

Brigid wept, great burning tears streaming down her cheeks, "No, no, no..."

"Hush, Mouse," he said. "I would rather it be this way. It was my fault anyway for the delay. That's twice I failed you. First with Reid, then Alan. I told you I would protect you. Let this make amends."

"I'm sorry," she whispered. "I'm so sorry."

The Falcon waved her apology away. "Listen, I rode as far and fast as I could away from Blackstone. You need to continue south until you reach Dwermouth. It's a market town on the edge of the Spade, but it also has a port. A friend of mine will meet you there, though he'll be expecting me. He bears a red acorn on his shield. His name is Regnar. You'll know him when you see him, and he will certainly know Whisper and Shade, for they are yours now too. He will help you, but..." He stopped short and wiped the blood away from the corner of his mouth. "But in any case, with or without him, you must get to Baronbrock and to Baron Galadin at Houndstooth."

"I don't want to leave you here," she wept.

The Falcon sighed. "Mouse"—he paused—"Brigid, the world is changing, and you will be needed. I told you I had a purpose in Blackstone. The first was to sow treachery among your uncles, to turn their evil on each other. Yet you—*you*—became my second purpose, for I believe that you will accomplish great things and bring good to many people, many more than I might have."

"You think too much of me…"

"I did not say…you would be alone," he stammered. "There are many mice in the woodpiles of the world. You must teach them to grow wings…and fly…"

CHAPTER 42:
THE TOWER RISES

A light snow was falling when the Valendian army under the command of Prince Dermont arrived out of Widowridge in the north to surround the shell keep at Clearpoint. As the infantry marched and the horsemen approached the gates, a lone horseman appeared bearing the Montevalen banner of truce. The soldiers of the Black Horse formed ranks of archers, pikemen, and men-at-arms while, behind them, the knights and lords in their heavy armor stood in one long line as if preparing for a mounted charge. To their right, the horsemen of the light cavalry formed their own blocks, packed closely together in furs and boiled leather, and in front of all, the peasant conscripts gathered, ready to be sacrificed as fodder. At length, the lone horseman trotted out and raised his banner, and before long, the Valendian commanders rode out to meet him.

"Little brother"—Dermont smirked—"I'm a bit surprised to find you are the one chosen to meet us here. I take it you've succeeded in gaining the Tower's trust?"

Beneath his furrowed brow, Bel's eyes regarded his brother in full regalia of war, in armor that had not once been made to serve its function in real battle. Beside him, stern and sneering, stood Dermont's trusted men, the bullies of Bel's childhood grown in size and wealth but in little else.

"So I have," the Silent Prince said.

"I'm glad to see you safe, my prince," said another voice, and Bel's face softened suddenly at the sight of his cousin Valerie's sincerity.

"You too, Val," Bel said. "I hope our men are well."

"They are, though they look forward to your return from Grantis." She smiled. "Doubt they'd recognize you now in all that armor."

Dermont sighed. "So we've got the rats trapped within, eh? The Tower, the White Horse, and the Winter Rose too?"

"Marius and Marina are here too, yes," Bel said.

"How many other men?"

"A hundred men-at-arms, four score archers, a handful of others that escaped your battle with Lord Guillon up north"—Bel sighed— "and the twenty-four finest horsemen in all Gasparn."

"Ah yes." Dermont laughed. "The Tower's Guard! Funny that they should all die in their very first battle. Tell me, any fall ill from drinking the water?"

"No. Your lepers were discovered in the northern keeps. The ones stationed here were already long dead."

"Pity, it might have thinned their ranks all the further," the Plague Prince said. "At any rate, we should get on with it, as I suppose they're expecting to hear back from you. Tell them we offer no terms. Once we begin our assault, take care of the Tower, and see if you can open the gates. We'll take it from there." Dermont's lips spread into a wide leer and Bel tried to calm his inward fires of hatred. "Today, we win the war, little brother."

"I'm afraid I'm not permitted to pass back through the gates," Bel said.

"What?" Dermont sneered.

"The Tower discovered me," he lied. "He caught Canton's spy."

"Dibhor's cock!" the Plague Prince swore. "No matter, we'll simply raze the fortress or let them starve."

Bel shook his head. "You won't need to."

"Why? Has Marius already surrendered?"

"No, but Marcus Harding and I have made an accord."

Prince Dermont's eyes narrowed and Bel could sense his brother's anger simmering just beneath his frown. "And what, pray tell, have you decided?"

Bel spoke slowly, for he knew that he must choose his words with care if he was to convince Dermont to agree. "The Tower sought to challenge you personally in a Champion's Duel. However, as father's heir, you are too valuable to risk." *And too cowardly to accept*, Bel thought. "As such, I convinced the Tower to face me instead."

The Plague Prince paused and itched his brow with a narrow finger in thought. "Interesting," he said. "And what are to be the results of this duel?"

"If I win, Marius surrenders without a fight, and the war is over," Bel said. "If the Tower wins, Marius and the princess are released into his custody. The Tower is, after all, sworn to the Order of the Guardians. He serves simply as a soldier in Marius's employ. If he returns to Andoch and his charges accompany him, you are left the sole Tremont heir and undisputed King of Montevale."

"What's to stop Marius from returning to fight again?"

Bel sighed. "He and father share much in common. Though Marius is younger, the effects progress the same…"

"And the princess? What of her?"

"The Tower will most likely take her to Andoch. As a woman, she has no right to claim. Perhaps she will marry some minor lord or even Sir Marcus himself? Either way, you will be free of her."

Dermont's eyes widened, and his smirking leer returned. "It sounds like in either case, I win," he said, "though, of course, I lose a brother. How can I accept that?"

"If it is my duty to fight for you," Bel said, "I must do it. I have already agreed."

"Yes, which you should not have done without first consulting me," Dermont said. "However, if this is something you have chosen to do, then I will not stand in the way of your duty."

"One final concession," Bel said, "regardless of who wins, the men in the keep are to be allowed to go free. I agreed since it would show mercy to men—good knights and lords—who will have to show you fealty as their king. To put them all to death would only incite discontent. Mercy may also convince them to persuade their brother soldiers under Guillon or in Roanshead or far off in the east that they would be wise to accept you as well."

"Ha! Very good," the Plague Prince grinned. "I pray you find victory, for little did I know how clever you could be, little brother!"

"So you agree?"

Dermont nodded and raised his right hand. "You may tell Marcus Harding that I agree to those terms."

"Good."

"Farewell, then, brother," Dermont said, turning his horse to go. His men followed alongside him. "Good luck!"

Val lingered a moment longer, and Bel sensed the concern in her eyes. "I hope you know what you are doing," she said.

"Val…" Bel whispered, "Tell me. Is Lilia with child?"

She sighed. "Your mind should be focused on the battle."

"Val, please! I must know."

Valerie Tremont, the Iron Fist, gazed out across the snow at the gates of Clearpoint Keep. "She is," she said, "all the more reason why you must survive. Good luck, cousin."

Bel remained a moment longer after she departed, steeling himself for the coming fight. However, he found it almost impossible to do so in light of what Valerie had just confirmed. In an instant, the weight of his armor increased tenfold. Gently, he spurred Banshee onward and rode back to Clearpoint's gates.

From atop the gatehouse, Marcus Harding looked down, "What says your brother?"

Bel struggled to keep his voice steady. "He agrees."

Harding sighed. "Will he honor it?"

"I do not know."

Soon, the gates opened, and from inside, the Tower upon Tempest rode forth, followed on foot by Jarvy, who exchanged Bel's banner for a lance.

"May the Brothers keep you, my lord," the old skirmisher said, tears welling in his eyes. "And should the worst happen, serving beside you these months has been the greatest honor of my life."

"You are my good friend," Bel said softly.

"I promise to do whatever it takes to look after herself should… you know…"

"Thank you."

When Jarvy had returned to the gatehouse, the heavy wooden doors were shut. Sir Marcus Harding urged Tempest forward, and he removed his helm. "So it comes to it," he said.

Bel nodded.

"Then, Silent Prince," the Tower said, "before we begin, come take my hand."

Bel removed his gauntlet, and he and the Guardian shook. "It has been an honor to serve you," Bel said.

"And you, my friend," the lord-general smiled suddenly and nodded toward the princess's token attached still to Beledain's arm, "I'd say you have a distinct advantage."

Bel glanced up at the gatehouse and, through a portal, spied the princess and the king.

"Promise you'll protect them," the Tower said, "should I fall."

"I swear it," the prince said.

The Tower breathed a heavy sigh and offered one last nod. Then donning his helmet, he raised his lance, the Spire, and saluted his opponent. Beledain returned the gesture, replaced his own helm, and the two men maneuvered their horses to position across from one another on either side of the gates.

In the sudden silence, the sound of the wind was like a great wave crashing in from the sea. Bel watched the snowflakes fall and alight upon the steel of his vambrace, just as he had on the morning of the tourney. The chill air caught in his lungs, and his eyes burned, wondering how long it took until his waiting tears froze.

"All right, Ban," he whispered gently. "It's time."

Ahead, the Tower raised his lance in a signal. Bel offered his own wave, and the two knights dug their spurs.

With a great crash, the horses came together, and both knights landed blows upon the boss of the other's shield. After the pass, Bel still felt the sting of the impact throughout his arm, yet miraculously, in spite of such a tilt, the Tower's lance was not broken. His own blow had been weak, betrayed at the last moment by his troubled mind. His lance barely scratched the Tower's shield yet it too remained intact.

A second time, the knights spurred their mounts, and this time, Bel's lance shattered beneath the force of his blow; however, the sheer might of the Tower's charge reduced the prince's shield to splinters. Bel's arm burned as if suddenly set aflame, and it hung limp, almost certainly broken. Slowly, he let himself slip softly from his saddle and curled his arm into his side. He winced against the pain but rose unsteadily to his feet and sent Banshee out of harm's way with a soft slap. Across the gate, the Tower drew back on Tempest's reins and dismounted. He tossed his shield to the snowy ground and, with both hands, gripped his Spire. Bel drew the axe from his baldric and stepped forth to meet him.

The ancient lance sang through winter air, cutting through snowflakes with the force of a mountain gale, and though Bel was able to turn aside each of the blows, his broken shield arm throbbed with great pain, and he knew that he was weakening. Yet still, the Tower fought on, and if anything, his strokes came faster. At last, the Silent Prince fell to one knee, swinging ineffectually at the Guardian and his lance. Suddenly, he felt the sting of the Tower's Spire like the strike of a viper, around the edge of his breastplate, deep into his chest.

Beledain Tremont fell back upon the snow, feeling the warm blood flow out of him. His hands and feet were losing feeling, and his mouth was wet and red with the taste of blood. His breath came quick and shallow, and his broken arm felt cold. From above him in Clearpoint's gatehouse a woman's voice cried out in despair, and he could not tell if it was that of the Blood Blossom or the Winter Rose.

"I'm sorry," Bel whispered. "I'm so sorry."

"Steady, lad," a gentle voice hushed him, and Bel opened his eyes to see Marcus Harding kneeling beside him, tears welling in his eyes. "Hear me now, Prince Beledain," he said as he removed Bel's helm. "I was sent to end the War of the Horses, but I cannot do it, nor do I believe I ever could, for that task must fall to you. Swear to me that you will do so."

"I'm dying," the prince said without rancor. "I've failed."

"No," the Tower said. "You will not die, so long as you swear."

Bel closed his eyes. "I swear it."

"So be it."

> *Upon the bloodstained battlefield*
> *where wars are waged and won,*
> *let not virtue fade nor honor yield*
> *no matter what the enemy has done,*
> *for one must keep the beacon alight,*
> *to guide all through shadow and fear.*
> *Rise now, the Tower,*
> *For the Darkness now draws near!*

A strange sensation washed over the prince's body like cool water. He felt his lungs inhale deeply, and a quiet calm settled upon him. The numbness disappeared from his limbs, and his shield arm no longer seethed with pain, nor was the taste of blood upon his tongue.

"Is this death?" he whispered.

"No," came an answer, "it is life."

Bel opened his eyes, and he felt suddenly as if he had woken from a dream. He rose to his feet and gazed across the field at his brother's army lying in wait. In confusion, he turned, and beside him upon the ground, Sir Marcus Harding knelt, cradling his shield arm, the side of his armor and his lips wet with blood. Bel hurried to his aid as the gates of Clearpoint opened, and men of the Tower's Guard ran forth to their fallen commander.

"What happened?" Bel asked. "You—" He shook his head. "*You* defeated *me*!"

"So I did," Sir Marcus said. "But you cannot die."

Bel shook his head and bit back his tears. "No, this is not right!"

"No, this is how it must be," the lord-general said. "*You* must be the Tower now. *You* must end this war. *You* must stand for what is right. That is why *you* will live and *I* shall die."

"It's the general!" a knight shouted.

"Aye, and the traitor!" shouted another.

Sir Harding stirred and, leaning on Bel, rose unsteadily to his feet. "Hear this now!" he shouted. "You men of Gasparn have sworn to follow the Tower to end this war! Henceforth, this man, Beledain Tremont, Prince of Valendia, called the Silent Prince, shall be anointed with the title of the Tower!" he motioned toward his spear and, as it was handed to him, passed it on to Bel. "Where is the king?"

"Here!" Marius called.

"Will you accept this man, the Tower, as your lord-general to end this war and finish what I have started?"

Marius's breathing was shallow and full of uncertainty, but in the end, he answered. "Yes!" he said. "Yes, I will!"

"And you men?" Harding cried. "Will you continue to follow the Tower? With you stand by your oaths?"

"We will!"

"Very good!" he shouted. "Go now!"

Suddenly, the great knight went limp in Bel's arms, and the weight of the man and his armor nearly toppled the prince over onto the ground. Men of the guard rushed to his aid, and together, they lifted the body of their lord-general between them just as heavy horsemen of Valendia rode up to surround them.

"Well done, little brother!" Dermont said from among his armored friends, "Truth be told, I fully expected to find you dead and to have to either cut these men down myself or else leave them locked in Clearpoint to starve and to die in the cold."

"That was not the agreement," Bel said.

"I had no part in the agreement." Dermont snapped, and suddenly, he laughed. "Is that old fool over there King Marius or should I say, the White Horse and False King?"

Bel's anger surged within him. "Marius is under *my* protection!" he shouted. "And these men are under *my* command. You will *not* mistreat them!"

Dermont's eyes flashed. "Quite a voice, for one supposed to be silent."

"The Tower chose Prince Beledain as his successor, and so my father agreed!"

Bel turned and, to his horror, saw Princess Marina standing defiantly beside the king.

"You must be Marina," Dermont said, "my, my. It seems you are rather pretty."

Bel hurried to stand before her, the ancient lance, Spire, held firmly in his hand. "They are *both* under my protection and are to be released to me!" he shouted, "They are *not* to be harmed!"

"Marius made the deal, brother," Dermont said. "If you win, Marius surrenders *to me!*"

"And if the Tower won, they are released into his custody," Bel said. "And as I am now the Tower, they are released to me!"

"It would be far easier to simply kill you all right now," Dermont shrugged in mockery.

"If you seek to keep all of Gasparn against you and turn half of Valendia who despise you and love me," Bel said, "how many men of your infantry right now would rally at my call? Or the light cavalry? Say nothing of the

Guardians in Andoch, nor any others who might curse you as a kinslayer for spilling my blood. I'm certain Father would also be most displeased."

"Father can hardly remember to dress himself in the morning." Dermont laughed. "You should come visit King Cedric, Marius. It will show you what you have to look forward to, if the rumors are to be trusted."

"The Beast take you!" the princess cried in rage.

Dermont grinned. "Such fire!"

Sir Armel's hand went to the handle of his mace. "We are with you, Lord Tower."

"Aye," Sir Linton said, "all of us."

The Young Talon unsheathed his sword. "To a man."

"Stand down, men," Bel called, though his eyes never left Dermont's. "I will honor the conditions set forth by the Tower's agreement. Marcus Harding bested me."

"Yet, I assume that corpse is his," Dermont snapped, "And somehow you live!"

"And I am also the Tower," Bel said, "I choose to end the bloodshed and hold to the terms of the accord. You can either accept this peace, brother, or continue the war."

Dermont stood silent for a long, long time. Bel watched his every move, afraid even to blink. His mind felt strangely clear for one who so recently lay upon the brink of death, and though he had no understanding of just what Sir Harding had done, the events of the moment did not allow him time to sit and reflect.

At last, Dermont spoke, "I want you and Marius both to lead my army north to Reginal, where I will take possession. I also demand that the nobles of Gasparn present themselves to me to offer their fealty. Those that do so in good faith will be granted favor. I will allow them to keep their lands and arm their soldiers. Those that do not will be considered hostile. You and Marius will issue a proclamation in support of this."

Bel looked to Marius.

"We have no choice," Marius said.

"Fine," Bel said to Dermont.

"Wait," Dermont added. "Next, I want Princess Marina there to join me in Reginal as my wife."

"No," the Silent Prince said without hesitation. "You passed on that opportunity, and I would not have her suffer beside you."

"Not beside." Dermont smirked. "Beneath."

"Bastard," Sir Armel grunted.

"Mind your men," the Plague Prince warned.

"I don't forbid my men from speaking their minds," he said, "And you can't have the princess. She has already sworn to marry me."

"Is that so?" Dermont laughed. "You honestly surprise me, brother! For all your talk of honor, you would forsake your common girl and the bastard child you put in her belly?"

Bel gnashed his teeth in anguish, and his knuckles went white as they gripped the Tower's spear—until a light touch upon his arm restrained him.

"No," the princess whispered, "I will not make you do this. I will go with him."

"No," Bel said, "Never."

"Your brother is gallant," Marina called out. "But what he says is not true. I am not promised to him. However, neither will I go with you if he does not wish it. My father and I are under his charge, and for any marriage to take place, the hierophants demand consent. Add that to the list of things you do to call forth the Guardians' ire!"

"You are a princess," Dermont said in disbelief, "and your father yet lives. My brother is not your keeper."

"By the Tower's agreement, I gave my proxy!" Marius shouted. "And I stand by my word to your brother!"

"Very well then," the Plague Prince told Bel. "Keep all your whores! Pack them up with your senile old men, your peasant lackeys, and penniless lords! For after we reach Reginal, you will return to Tremontane Castle with all your fine followers in toe—the princess, the wild woman, the false king, and any others who wish to go! Consider it my gift and your prison, for if I catch but one of your people wandering outside of the castle walls, they will be mine to do with them what I will!" His lips twisted in repugnant glee. "But, fine! Why should I care anyhow? I am the king of a united Montevale! I am the victor of a hundred years of war! Yes, brother, I will keep this peace, and I will swear to it, but in return, you must also keep mine!"

Beledain Tremont, the Silent Prince of Bells, lord-general of Gasparn, anointed the Tower, breathed a sigh, and bowed his head before the Plague

Prince, his brother, and although for the moment it seemed that after a century, the War of the Horses was over, something told him that the real conflict had only just begun.

"So be it," Bel said.

CHAPTER 43:
DWERMOUTH

Through the rest of the autumn months and into the winter, Geoffrey struggled to provide enough food for his family to eat. Since arriving in Dwermouth, he had attempted countless jobs; however, town life was not well suited for a farmer. Annabel was able to make some money, at times working as a seamstress or laundering clothes; however, for Geoffrey, months of idleness and what seemed now to be uselessness were taking its toll. Funny enough, much of the real work was back out in the Spade as they said the soldiers were hiring workers to repair an old stone fort; however, that was one job Geoffrey most assuredly did not want. Even months later, the memories of Ashfort and all its tragedies still cut him right to the bone.

Whoever this Gareth was that Regnar spoke of surely was taking his time! Every day, Geoffrey made his way to the docks at Dwermouth, eyeing any ships bound for the Brock. However, without enough money to feed his family, Galadin seemed a forlorn hope. What a fool he had been to leave Pyle, even in the face of starvation. For in Pyle, at least he had his neighbors and friends, not like these townsfolk. Bitter, resentful, always looking to find a way to take advantage—even the celebrants presiding over the churches! What shame!

However, there was no time to dwell on his past mistakes or the failings of other folk; he needed work! Without work, his family would have no food, and without food, they would be in the same state as they would have been had they never left the village.

The weather had grown cold, and as he walked along the wharf eyeing the merchant flutes and galleys, Geoffrey glanced up into the gray winter sky just as snow began to fall. A gull mocked him with its laughter, drowning out the gurgling suck of the surf below the dock. The wind howled through the canvas sails of a ship bearing the mark of a stout round tower, and the blue pennants trailing from its mastheads swam like eels on the breeze. It was only the second ship to arrive out of Baronbrock since Geoffrey's arrival, and soon, it too would depart. What was he to do?

Somewhere a ship's bell sounded, answered somewhere in the distance by another. A group of sailors passed him by on their way to a tavern, having been relieved after a long, cold night on watch. For a moment, Geoffrey watched them, wondering how long it would take him to learn to be a sailor or failing that, a fisherman. Those jobs at least always seemed to need filling, and a fisherman at least had a better chance of keeping his family fed than a farmer with no land.

Or, at worst, he could always hock Oakheart or Acorn. Holy Oak was rare, as Cousin Martin said so long ago. Surely, there was someone willing to pay? If not the lord at the keep, then perhaps the Church?

No, Geoffrey thought, he couldn't do that. He had to keep true to the old man. Plus, there was protection in walking around armed as such, and in the slum where he and his family lived, protection was a good thing. Simply setting his hand to Oakheart's grip had been enough to silence that scum trying to chat up Annabel, and a stern gaze sent him off almost at a run. No, he could not sell his arms. Besides, how would this Gareth fellow know him without the mark of the Acorn?

Suddenly, a strange feeling took him, and from somewhere close by, he sensed something…familiar. His eyes scanned the length of the wharf, searching for anything out of sorts. Snow-topped barrels, crates of goods covered with oiled tarps, an old salt smoking his pipe—

And there it was, a slight figure cloaked and cowled beneath a black hood tentatively walking toward him. Geoffrey eyed it curiously, for somehow, he felt as if he knew whoever it was. Could it finally, finally be Gareth, the one Old Regnar had called the Blade? In any case, it was good to be cautious. He patted Oakheart for reassurance and slid the Acorn into place down his arm.

"Are you Regnar?"

Geoffrey's mouth fell open in surprise, for it was not the voice of a man but a mere wisp of a girl, and a pretty one at that. This was not Gareth, not at all, yet somehow, he had a distinct feeling that whoever she was or had been, she was now the Blade.

The girl raised her head slightly, awaiting his answer, watching him with eyes that shone with an almost unnaturally deep blue. He could sense a heavy weariness about her, and behind her cautious glare, there was the shadow of grief. However, her shoulders, tense and ready, suggested that she would not be taken lightly, and beneath the draping of her cloak, Geoffrey knew that she, too, was armed.

"I'm not Regnar," Geoffrey said. "He…he died."

The girl sighed. "You now bear his shield?"

Slowly, Geoffrey nodded. She was certainly no common girl, for her speech and bearing were far too noble. Just who was she? "I bear the Acorn shield," he said at last, "and Oakheart the cudgel. My name is Geoffrey. I was a farmer in the village of Pyle in the Spade, though now, I'm supposed to be something called the Vanguard."

"My name is"—she fixed him with her gaze again, still uncertain—"my name is Brigid…the Blade."

"You know Gareth then? I've been waiting here for him since the Month of the Hound."

She bit her lip and nodded. "I knew…Gareth," she whispered, "though by a different name. He…fell."

Geoffrey sighed. "I'm sorry."

She shook her head and took a deep breath. "I need to get to Baronbrock," she said. "He said that Regnar would help me…"

"Aye," Geoffrey said, "to Galadin."

"Yes."

"It hasn't been easy. For months, I've been trying to scrape together the coin, but with the winter and all, I can barely earn enough to keep my family fed."

"You have a family?" she asked.

"Aye, I do," Geoffrey smiled, "A wife, a son, a daughter…" He paused. "I had another son, a bit younger than you maybe, but…he died."

Brigid was hesitant. "I have no one," she said at last. "But…I have this." She paused and, from beneath her cloak, held out a linen sack.

Inside, Geoffrey was amazed to see a pile of silver bangles, rings, necklaces, brooches, and all sorts of other jewelry encrusted with pearls and blue gemstones. His eyes darted quickly around the wharf, and he pressed the bag of riches back to her. "Lady's Grace!" he whispered. "Put that away!"

Brigid concealed the sack beneath her cloak. "Is it enough to get us all to Baronbrock?" she asked. "You, your family, and myself?"

Geoffrey met her eye curiously, "You would…take us with you?"

"Why not? You need to get there as well, and…I'd prefer not to go alone."

Geoffrey sighed. Months of struggling to get a foothold, and suddenly a strange girl appears with a sack of treasure out of nowhere? It did not seem right. It was all so odd. "Listen," he said at last, "I can't take your money…"

"I didn't steal it if that's what you're worried about." Brigid smirked. "It was all mine. I'm not afraid to part with it either, believe me."

"It's not that. It's just…I expected Gareth to have a job for me. I'd rather work my way. I've never taken charity to date. I'll not start now."

Brigid raised an eyebrow and flashed a crafty smile. "Fine then," she said. "You want work? Then I shall hire you, Geoffrey of Pyle."

Geoffrey shook his head. "Now, young lady, that's very kind, but…"

"No," she said, "I shall hire you, for I cannot get there alone. I…I know very little about life outside of"—she paused—"away from my home. I'm amazed frankly that I made it this far. I walked two days along the road, not even sure I was headed in the right direction. The night in between, I slept in an old sheepfold, though it did very little against the cold. Thank the Lady, I met a pair of handmaids on their way here from the priory. If not for them, I probably would have died in a ditch along the road." She sighed, and as she did so, she seemed to wilt. "Please, Geoffrey? Help me get to Galadin, and anything left in the bag belongs to you and your family."

For a long moment, Geoffrey was silent. It was work, that was certain, and a means to Baronbrock. They could leave on the very ship they now stood beside. Yet, who was this girl, and if he chose to help her, would he only be inviting more trouble? If she'd run away from a castle somewhere, surely her people would be looking for her, and he didn't want to get mixed up with that. However, he also couldn't just leave her. The world was dangerous and getting worse, it seemed. A pretty girl all alone in an unfamiliar place with a bag full of riches—it was a recipe for a horrible end.

"Please, Geoffrey," she pleaded, "I need help."

At long last, Geoffrey sighed. "Alright. Let's go."

CHAPTER 44:
VISIONS OF THE PAST

When Lughus awoke, Crodane was already dead, the side of his chest red and wet beneath his hauberk. The great hound, Fergus, lay mournfully in silence beside his former master's feet, his great hazel eyes heavy with sorrow. Beneath the stars that night, the new Marshal buried the old one atop the hill where he gave his life. No sign remained of the kingsmen or their leader but for an iron war hammer lost among the holly. It was this that served as a headstone to mark the fallen swordsman's final victory.

Not long after dawn, Lughus awoke from where he had fallen, his body sore from the battle, from digging, and from the memory of the wound. A pink scar now marked where the quarrel had struck him, tearing through his ribcage on the right side, and much of his clothing was ruined with blood. From among the kingsmen's corpses, he found a light chain hauberk that fit him, and beneath this, he tore one of the red cloaks and draped it over his shoulders like a tunic. Thusly garbed, he fastened the Marshal's baldric around his waist, slipped Pryce's dagger into his belt on his right hip, and replaced Stokes's rusty blade with Sentinel, the heirloom sword. Fergus sat regally beside him, and the new day sun shone like fire on his golden fur.

"Goodbye, Crodane."

Three days later, the young Marshal and the golden hound reached the walls of the Baronial port city of Nordren, and there, the baron received him like a man entertaining a ghost. Much of this time, Lughus's mind felt muddled, for between the ordeal of the battle, the long hours of travel, and the weight of his grief, he was very weary, and often waking life seemed shrouded by a heavy fog. He saw strange visions of battles, yet what upset him most was the recurring image of a pair of soft green eyes.

Still, in Nordren, his hair, his sword, and his mother's ring opened many doors, to say nothing of the Spirit Hound, Galadin's symbol, standing larger than life at Lughus's side. The baron, Leoric Nordren, had received word long before of the journey of Arcis Galadin's heir by way of the port; however, with the tardiness of his arrival, the few with knowledge of the matter began to fear the worst. For two days more, Lughus was a guest of Baron Nordren, though still in secret for fear of the clamor his sudden reappearance might create. As Crodane had mentioned, Arcis had spread rumors among the Brock for fifteen years that his grandson was dead; any resurrection was certain to cause a stir. So it was without any feasting or great pomp that the baron wished him farewell. However, he replaced Lughus's tattered clothing with new raiment of baronial blue and set him on the road with a small detachment of his household guard led by the Baron's own son, Theobold.

From Nordren, it was but a few days' ride northwest to Galadin and the journey's end at last. Lughus had never ridden a horse before, yet somehow, he took to it like a fish to water. Theo, Leoric's son, was a thin, spare man in his early twenties with a ready laugh. His hair, cropped short beneath his helm, matched the color of the twin salmon of his surcoat set, as was true across the Brock, upon a field of blue. Along the way, he pointed out the fiefdoms of his father's knights and other points of interest until, finally, late one morning, he reined his horse beneath the shadow of a ruined stone tower and, with a grin, turned to Lughus.

"Welcome home."

"This is Galadin?" Lughus asked.

"Aye, the border," Theo said, "come."

Lughus followed Theobold up the stairs of the ruin, with Fergus at his heels, to the very edge of the stone where the crenulations were cracked and broken. The young Nordren pointed far off into the distance. "If you look closely, you can see it, the Houndstooth, where your grandfather resides." He laughed. "Wish our castle had such a name, though with a salmon for an emblem, what would we call it? The Fish Pond? The Spawn...ing...Pool? No, that's not right."

Lughus eyed the horizon with wonder, just able to discern the outline of the castle in the sunlight, and suddenly, he felt very strange. His vision seemed to grow cloudy, and in his mind's eye, something like a memory appeared, though not one that he could have ever known. He saw a young woman with hair like waves of gold hastening up the stairs of the ruined tower to the place where he now stood. She was thin as a willow and spry as a blade of grass, dressed in a light velvet dress of baronial blue and hemmed with a pattern of golden thread. She leaned against the crumbling stones, out of breath from running, and suddenly, Lughus felt her gaze turn upon him— the same bright green eyes he saw in his dreams.

"Hurry up, Old Crow!" She laughed, and at the sound, the sun seemed to grow brighter.

"You're far too close to the edge, my lady," Lughus heard himself say, though with a voice he thought never to hear again. "Please, these stones are old."

"What do you mean?" She grinned and backed another step away. "Afraid I'll fall?"

Lughus felt his nerves turn prickly. "Yes," he said, "I am. Very much so."

"And what if I did fall?" she teased. "What would you do then?"

He breathed a heavy sigh. "I suppose I would have to throw myself over the side after you."

"And why in the world would you do something like that?"

"Because it would mean that I failed in my duty."

"You mean," she said, her eyes alight with merriment. "You wouldn't be able to go on living without me?"

Lughus felt a great pain in his chest, though one that he had somehow grown used to. "No," he said, "I could not."

The girl sighed and suppressed her smile. "Then I suppose I should take a step back."

She offered him her hand, and when he took it, Lughus marveled at its softness. "We should return to Sir Wolfram and your father," he said. "They only went to inspect the new mill, and it won't take them long."

"What's the matter?" she said. "Tell me you're not afraid to wander about the countryside a bit?"

Lughus sighed uneasily; she had not yet let go of his hand. "There could be...bears or...perhaps bandits," he muttered. "There are many dangers on the road."

"Bears!" she laughed with disbelief and gave his hand a gentle squeeze, "I have no doubt that whatever appeared, you would always protect me."

"So I would."

"Even if it were a bear"—she smiled again—"or some bloody bandit lord leading a great horde of brigands."

"It would be my duty."

"But what if they were to capture me?"

"I would save you or at least die trying."

"So grim." She nodded pensively. "But what if they gave you another choice?"

The pain in Lughus's chest grew more acute. He could sense where this was leading. "There is no other choice than the one that would result in your freedom."

"What if," she said, "in order to secure my release, the bandit lord ordered you to kiss me?"

Lughus's arms felt weak, and he breathed another great sigh. "Elen..." he said softly and reluctantly slipped his hand free from hers, "you know very well, even were I to be knighted, you are..."

The young woman glanced once more out from the tower, and the light in her eyes seemed to dim. "Fine," she lamented after another moment, "Then, for fear of your bears and bandits, we will go."

"The Net? The Fishery?"

Lughus shook his head and returned to his senses, "I'm sorry, what?"

"No matter." Theo shrugged. "Anyhow, we should reach the castle by nightfall." He paused and eyed the young Galadin curiously. "Something wrong?

Lughus bit his lip and swallowed the thick lump in his throat. The young woman in his dream—he had called her *Elen*... Crodane had said it when he lay dying, *Elen's pup...Luinelen...*

"Lughus, you all right?"

At last, Lughus sighed and shook his head. "I'm fine," he said. "Just weary."

Theobold nodded and patted Lughus on the shoulder with a hearty slap. "It'll all be over soon, and then your grandfather can feast us for bringing you safely home." He grinned. "Come. To Houndstooth!"

The story continues in Part II of
The Bard's Heresy:

THE
BLACKGUARD'S
BOND

THE TERMAINIAN CALENDAR

The Termainian calendar contains thirteen months, each month consisting of four weeks of seven days each for a total of 364 days a year. However, the thirteenth month, Harvestide, contains one extra day (Harvestide 29), known as the Feast of the Father, and is traditionally celebrated as a holiday. People across Termain either refer to the months with the suffix "tide" or by simply saying "the Month of the Bear" or "the Month of the Sun."

Seasons and Months:
Spring: Beartide, Stonetide, Salmontide
Summer: Suntide, Stagtide, Falcontide
Harvest Month: Harvestide
Autumn: Houndtide, Oakentide, Horsetide
Winter: Moontide, Wolftide, Owltide

Days of the Week:
Alanday
Perinday
Tengday
Galday
Kalladay
Aidenday
Kinday

Some Holidays of Note:
Beartide 1—Awakening (the first day of spring)
Salmontide 12—Lover's Night
Suntide 15—The Feast of St. Aiden
Harvestide 29—Harvest Day
Houndtide 15—The Feast of Perindal
Oakentide 20—The Feast of Tengale
Horsetide 28—The Feast of Galdorn
Moontide 15—The Feast of the Lady

DRAMATIS PERSONAE

The Nation of Andoch and the Order of the Guardians

- High King Kredor Drude, Lord of Titanis, Protector of Andoch
- Rordan Baird, the Chancellor
  - His followers in order of rank: commissioners, constables, counselors, courtiers, pages
  - William Harlow, chief constable, anointed "The Hammer"
- Hagan Shawn, the Grand Hierophant
  - His followers in order of rank: hierophants (provincial), prelates, ministers, celebrants, acolytes
- Dandon Rood, the Warlord
  - His followers in order of rank: justiciars, cavaliers, gallants, partisans, cadets
  - Sir Marcus Harding, cavalier, anointed "The Tower"
  - Marcel Pryce the Younger, "first" cadet
- Rastis Glendaro, the Loremaster
  - His followers in order of rank: sage, seer, scholar, scribe, apprentice
  - Hobart Brindlebairne, scribe, steward to the Loremaster, anointed "The Ox"
  - Lughus of the Order, apprentice
  - Royne of the Order, apprentice
  - Thom of the Order, apprentice

- Nobles of Andoch
  - Lord Natharis Tainne, boyhood companion to King Kredor, Keeper of the Lighthouse of Castone, first degree
  - Lord Marcel Pryce, the elder
- Other assorted nobles Other folk
  - Walter, Proprietor of The Book & The Barrel Public House
  - Crodane, a wandering swordsman and guide
  - Stokes, a mercenary

The Nation of Dwerin and the Castle Blackstone
- Archduke Danford Beinn (deceased)
  - His wife, Archduchess Josephine Beinn
  - Her maid, Livonia
  - His daughter, Brigid Beinn
- Duke Darren Beinn, the Sheriff
  - His son, Alan Beinn, called the Young Sheriff
- Duke Waylon Beinn, the master of the mines
- Duke Graham Beinn, the admiral of the fleet
- Duke Nealen Beinn, the grand castellan
- Lord Padraig Reid
  - His son, Young Reid, a friend of Alan, suitor to Brigid
- Wilfred Barrow, captain of Lord Reid's scouts
- Assorted members of the Court in Blackstone
- The Prisoner

The Common Folk of the Village Pyle in the Spade
- Geoffrey of Pyle
  - His wife, Annabel
  - His eldest son, Karl
  - His youngest son, Frederick
  - His daughter, Greta
  - His father, Amos

- Oliver of Pyle
  - His wife, Agnes
  - His eldest son, Axel
  - His son, Nickolas
  - His daughter, Bethany
  - His daughter, Laura
  - His youngest son, Erik
- Cousin Martin, a lay preacher of the Church of the Kinship
  - Assorted Farmers
- The Old Man-At-Arms (deceased)

The Nation of Montevale, currently divided in the War of the Horses

The Southern Kingdom of Valendia
- King Cedric Tremont, called the Laughing King
  - His wife, Queen Eloise (deceased)
  - Prince Larius Tremont (deceased)
  - Prince Dermont Tremont, lord-general of the Armies of Valendia
  - Prince Beledain Tremont called the Silent Prince or the Prince of Bells, captain of Prince Dermont's light cavalry
  - His Seneschal, Sir Emory
- Lord Leon Tremont, Cedric's younger brother, called the Black Lion
  - His daughter, Lady Valerie Tremont, called the Iron Fist, second-in-command of Prince Dermont's light cavalry
- Lord Talvert Tremont, Cedric's youngest brother called the Summer Storm
- Men and Women of the Light Cavalry under the command of Beledain Tremont
  - Lilia, Jarvy, Horn, Wendell, Rallo
  - Briden, Beledain's standard-bearer
- Other assorted nobles of Valendia
- Canton, Prince Dermont's chief spy in Gasparn

The Northern Kingdom of Gasparn
- King Marius Tremont
  - His wife, Queen Annalisa (deceased)
  - Prince Gislain Tremont called the Snow Prince (deceased)
  - Princess Marina Tremont called the Winter Rose
- Other assorted nobles of Gasparn
  - Lord Giles Pronet
  - Sir Raylon Jace called the Snow Bear
  - Lord Talondaire called the Young Talon
  - Sir Linton Traver
  - Sir Gurney called the Knight of the Rooster
  - Sir Trenton called the Knight of Lilies
  - Sir Welmsey
  - Sir Armel
  - Sir Cardolan
  - Sir Galen Helm

The Baronies of Baronbrock
- Lord-Baron Perin Glendaro, son of Harlon Glendaro and nephew to Loremaster Rastis Glendaro
- Baron Arcis Galadin
  - Sir Wolfram of Parth, Seneschal to Arcis Galadin
- Baron Roland Marthaine
- Baron Leoric Nordren
  - Sir Theobold Nordren, his son

Other Folk of Note
- Magnus Bloodbeard, a Wrathorn Blackguard
- Lord Mathon, captain of the Red Boar Brigade
  - Karston, Lord Mathon's second-in-command

ACKNOWLEDGMENTS

I first came up with the idea for many of these characters sometime between high school and college. I know that somewhere floating around my house is my original red spiral-bound notebook containing lists of names, plot points, and the first map of Termain. Over the years, however, this world and its still unformed characters often got lost among other projects as I struggled internally to write something that I thought would have more potential for critical acclaim or objective appeal.

Fast-forward about ten years. By this time, I was a high school English teacher, teaching courses on science fiction and classics, focusing particularly on medieval literature and Campbell's *Hero's Journey*. For years, I had also been running an extracurricular RPG Club (we'd have called it the D&D Club, but you never know when the remnants of the old "Satanic Panic" of the '80s will emerge to rear their ugly heads). In any case, the year that the RPG club seniors were graduating, we held a final session to serve as a send-off. We'd already finished our epic three-year campaign, and this was merely a fun, final one-shot with plenty of overpowered magic items and an epic final showdown with an ancient red dragon.

Afterward, reminiscing like old adventurers in the stereotypical D&D tavern, the kids asked me if I'd ever thought about writing a fantasy novel. "Well, I've always had this idea…" I remember saying. "Do it," they told me. "You need to do it."

A week later, sitting at my computer, struggling to work my way through the vague, pretentious draft I had been playing around with, I remembered the kids in the club, and I decided to take their advice. By the following June, the first draft was complete.

So with the origin story out of the way, I want to acknowledge and thank a number of people who are important in my life.

First and foremost, always and forever, is my wife and fellow writer, Dominique. When we ran into each other in the coffee shop all those years ago, I was sitting there editing this, and when you mentioned trading and discussing our writing, it was this that I wanted to send you. In spite of the 212,000 words in this manuscript, none of them could ever adequately capture how much I love you.

For my children, George, Heidi, and Sebastian, I hope that one day you read this and you find something in it that speaks to you. I love you all so, so much, and I hope that the adventure I wrote makes you even a fraction of how proud I am to watch the three of you on your great adventures.

To Mike and Cassie Frank, Shayne and Rachel Evans, and your families, I can't express how much your friendship and support mean to me. There are no other people I'd rather roll with and no better party members for life's great campaign.

To Craig Mysliwczyk, my colleague, guitarist, fellow writer, and, most importantly, friend, your thorough review of my first draft is something for which I will always be grateful.

To Ray French, for your constant support and encouragement and for your mentorship and friendship when I was just beginning my adventures.

To my parents, aunts and uncles, and the rest of my extended family and friends, thank you all for the support.

Finally, to my late hound dog, Percy, you sat at my feet for uncounted hours as I wrote, forced me to take breaks to eat or go for a run (albeit selfishly), and served as the most patient (if judgmental) sounding board as I worked through the plot and characters. I miss you, Buddy.

ABOUT THE AUTHOR

For as long as he can remember, Justin Bello has been a lover of adventure stories. As a writer, he likes to create morally ambiguous worlds full of characters who struggle to fight for good even when faced with seemingly insurmountable evil. He enjoys reading, writing, drawing, tabletop role-playing games, and more hobbies than he realistically has time for. A full-time English teacher, he lives in Pittsburgh with his wife, Dominique, and three children. Visit his official website at justindbello.com or follow him on Instagram @justindbello_author

www.ingramcontent.com/pod-product-compliance
Lightning Source LLC
Chambersburg PA
CBHW060239030726
47493CB00024B/1381